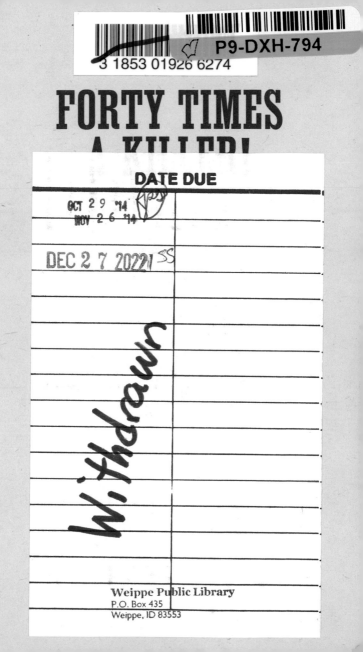

P9-DXH-794

3 1853 01926 6274

FORTY TIMES
A KILLER

FORTY TIMES A KILLER!

WILLIAM W. JOHNSTONE
with J. A. Johnstone

PINNACLE BOOKS
Kensington Publishing Corp.
www.kensingtonbooks.com

PINNACLE BOOKS are published by

Kensington Publishing Corp.
119 West 40th Street
New York, NY 10018

PUBLISHER'S NOTE
Following the death of William W. Johnstone, the Johnstone family is working with a carefully selected writer to organize and complete Mr. Johnstone's outlines and many unfinished manuscripts to create additional novels in all of his series like The Last Gunfighter, Mountain Man, and Eagles, among others. This novel was inspired by Mr. Johnstone's superb storytelling.

All Kensington titles, imprints, and distributed lines are available at special quantity discounts for bulk purchases for sales promotions, premiums, fund-raising, educational, or institutional use. Special book excerpts or customized printings can also be created to fit specific needs. For details, write or phone the office of the Kensington special sales manager: Kensington Publishing Corp., 119 West 40th Street, New York, NY 10018, attn: Special Sales Department; phone 1-800-221-2647.

ISBN-13: 978-0-7860-3344-7
ISBN-10: 0-7860-3344-4

First printing: June 2014

10 9 8 7 6 5 4 3 2

Printed in the United States of America

First electronic edition: June 2014

ISBN-13: 978-0-7860-3345-4
ISBN-10: 0-7860-3345-2

CHAPTER ONE
Death in the Street

"John Wesley Hardin! I'm calling you out, John Wesley!"

My friend turned to me and his left eyebrow arched the way it always did when his face asked a question.

"All right. I'll take a look," I said, laying aside my copy of Mr. Dickens' *The Life and Adventures of Martin Chuzzlewit*, partially set, as you know, on our very own western frontier.

I rose from the table and limped to the saloon's batwing doors, more a tangle of broken and missing slats than door. I guess so many heads were rammed through those batwings that nobody took the trouble to repair them any longer.

Three men wearing slickers and big Texas mustaches stood in the dusty street. All were armed with heavy Colt revolvers carried high on the waist, horseman-style. They glanced at me, dismissed me as something beneath their notice, and continued their wait.

I told John Wesley what I saw and he said, "Ask them what the hell they want."

"They're calling you out, Wes. That's what they want."

"I know it, Little Bit. But ask them anyhow." Wes stood at the bar, playing with a little calico kitten, the warm schooner of beer at his elbow growing warmer in the east Texas heat.

The railroad clock on the wall ticked slow seconds into the quiet and the bartender cleared his throat and whispered to the saloon's only other customer, "James, this won't do."

The gray-haired man nodded. "A bad business." He stared through the window. "Those men are pistol fighters."

He was not ragged, as most of us Texans were that late summer of 1870. His clothes were well worn, but clean, and spoke of a good wife at home. He might have been a one-loop rancher or a farmer, but he could have been anything.

I stepped outside into the street, if you could call it that.

The settlement of Honest Deal was a collection of a few raw timber buildings sprawled hit or miss along the bank of the west fork of the San Jacinto River, a sun-scorched, wind-blown scrub town waiting desperately for a railroad spur or even a stage line to give it purpose and a future.

I blinked in the sudden bright light, then took the measure of the three men. They were big, hard-eyed fellows. The oldest of them had an arrogant look to him, as though he hailed from a place where he was the cock o' the walk.

That one would take a heap of killing, I figured. They all would.

I swallowed hard. "Mr. Hardin's compliments, and he wishes to know what business you have with him."

"Unfinished business," the oldest man said.

Another, tall and blond and close enough in looks and arrogance to be his son, said, "Gimp, get back in there and tell Hardin to come out. If he ain't in the street in one minute, we'll come in after him."

The man's use of the word *gimp* surprised me. I thought the steel brace on my left leg covered by my wool pants was unnoticeable. Unless I walked, of course. I'd only taken a step into the street, so I could only assume that the tall man was very observant.

Wes was like that, observant. All revolver fighters were back in those days. They had to be.

Measuring him, it seemed to me that the younger man was also one to step around, unless you were mighty gun slick.

"I'll tell Mr. Hardin what you said." I smiled at the three men. I had good teeth when I was younger, the only part of my crooked, stunted body that was good, so I smiled a lot. Showing them off, you understand.

I figured I knew why those three men didn't want to come into the saloon after Wes unless they had to. The place was small, little bigger than a railroad boxcar, and gloomy, lit by smoking, smelly, kerosene lamps. Only Yankee carpetbaggers could afford the whale oil that burned brighter without smoke or stink. If shooting started inside, the concussion of the guns would extinguish the lamps and four men would have to get to their work in semidarkness and at point-blank range.

Against a deadly pistol fighter like Wes, those three fellows were well aware that no one would walk out of the saloon alive. They wanted badly to kill Wes, but outside where they would have room to maneuver and take cover if necessary.

I can't say as I blamed them. A demon with ol' Sammy's revolver was Wes, fast and accurate on the draw and shoot.

That's one of the reasons I idolized him. I'd never met his like before . . . or since.

Well, I turned to go back into the saloon and tell him what the three gentlemen outside wanted, but I'd taken only one clumping step when Wes stepped around the corner of the saloon, a smile on his face and a .44 1860 Army model Colt in each hand.

All his life, Wes favored those old cap-and-ball pistols, and he would often say that they were both wife and child to him.

He wore black pants held up by suspenders and a vest of the same color over a collarless white shirt. Shoulder holsters bookended his manly chest and he sported a silver signet ring on the little finger of his left hand, the hallmark of the frontier gambler.

"You fellows wish to speak with me?" he said, making the slight bow that he considered the stamp of a well-bred Southern gentleman.

Well, the three men had been caught flatfooted and they knew it.

The oldest of them was the first to recover. He pushed his slicker away from his gun and said, "You know why we're here, Hardin."

"Damn right you do," the blond man said.

They were on the prod, those two, and right then I knew there would be no stepping back from this, not for Wes, not for anybody.

"I'm afraid you have the advantage over me," Wes said. "I've never seen you gentlemen before in my life."

"You know us, damn you," the older man said.

"We're here for my brother Sonny," the blond man said.

Wes smiled again, showing his teeth.

Lord-a-mercy, but that was a bad sign. John Wesley was never a smiling man . . . unless he planned to kill somebody.

"I've never heard the name Sonny, nor can I attach it to a remembered face," he said. "How do you spell it, with an *O* or a *U*?"

"You're pleased to make a joke." This from the man who hadn't spoken before, a lean, hawk-faced man whose careful eyes had never left Wes, reading him and coming to a decision about him.

He was a gun, that one, He'd be mighty sudden and would know some fancy moves.

"I made a good joke?" Wes asked. "Then how come I don't hear you gentlemen laughing?" His Colts were hanging loose at his sides as though he had all the time in the world.

"You go to hell." The hawk-faced man went for his gun.

Years later, I was told that the lean man was probably a ranny by the name of Hugh Byrd who had a vague reputation in Texas as a draw-fighter.

Word was that he'd killed Mason Lark up El Paso way. You recall Lark, the Denver bounty hunter with the Ute wife? Back then nobody considered Lark a bargain and even John Wesley once remarked that the man was fast on the draw and a proven man killer.

Well, for reasons best known only to himself,

Byrd—if that really was his name—decided to commit suicide the day he drew down on Wes.

His gun hadn't cleared leather when two .44 bullets clipped half-moons from the tobacco tag that hung over the pocket of his shirt and tore great wounds in his chest.

I didn't watch him fall. My eyes were on the other two.

The blond man got off a shot at Wes, but he'd hurried the draw and the slug kicked up a startled exclamation point of dirt an inch in front of the toe of Wes's right boot.

The towhead knew he'd made a bad mistake. His face horrified, he took a step back and raised his revolver to correct his aim.

But the young man's hurried shot had been the kind of blunder you can't make in a gunfight . . . and Wes made him pay for it. His bucking Colts hammering with tremendous speed and accuracy, he slammed three or four bullets into the man's upper chest and belly.

Gagging on his own blood, the yellow-haired fellow dropped to his knees.

Wes ignored him. He swung on the older man who hadn't made a move for his gun. His reactions slower than the others, the fight had gone too fast for him and there was no way he was going to play catch-up.

He tossed his Colt away and raised his hands to waist level. "I'm out of it, John Wesley. Now you've killed both my sons and I want to live long enough to grieve for them."

The man was not scared or afraid to die, but I knew living would be hard for him, each passing day another little death. Blood had drained from his features and I looked into the gray, blue-shadowed face of a corpse.

"No, mister, you're in it," Wes said, smiling. "There ain't a way out. You brought it, and now you pay the piper." He raised his Colt, took careful aim and shot the old man between the eyes.

The blond man was clinging to life, coughing up black blood. He turned his head as the older man fell into the dirt beside him. "Pa!" He reached out and put his hand on his father's chest. His mouth was a shocked, scarlet O. "Are you kilt dead, Pa?"

"Yeah, he's kilt dead," Wes said. "Now go join him in hell."

The Colt roared again . . . and then only the desert wind made a sound.

I reckon the whole population of the town, maybe a dozen men and a couple women, young'uns clutching at their skirts, stood in the street and stared at the three sprawled bodies. The faces of the men and women were expressionless. They looked like so many painted dolls as they tried to come to grips with the violence and sudden death that had come into their midst.

"This won't do," the bartender said. "This is a job for the law." He glanced hopefully around the crowd, but nobody had listened to him.

Fat blowflies had already formed a black, crawling crust on the gory faces of the dead and I fancied I already got a whiff of the stench of decay.

The bartender, who seemed to have appointed himself spokesman for the whole town, looked at Wes. "Who were they, mister?"

"Damned if I know."

The bartender made it official. He reached into his vest pocket and took out a lawman's star that he pinned to his chest. The star looked as though it had been cut from the bottom of a bean can. "I heard one of them say they were here for Sonny," the bartender-sheriff said. "You ever hear of him?"

Wes shook his head. "No, I don't reckon I have. Unless his name was spelled with a *U*."

"You ever hear of a man named Sunny, with a *U*?"

"No. I don't reckon I have." With every eye on him, Wes made one of those grandstand plays that helped make him famous. He spun those big Colts and they were still spinning when he dropped them into their holsters. "Sheriff, a man in my line of business makes a lot of enemies. Hell, I can't keep track of all the men who want to kill me."

"And what is your business?" the sheriff said.

"I'm a shootist," Wes said.

Me, I looked into John Wesley's eyes then. There was no meanness, no blue, luminous light I've seen in a man's eyes when he takes pleasure in a killing . . . but there was something else.

Wes looked around the crowd, his gaze moving from face to stunned face, and his eyes were bright, questioning. *Look at me! Look at me everybody. Have you ever seen my like before?*

Right then, John Wesley was Narcissus at the pool, the man who fell madly in love with his own reflection.

And the people around him, as soon as the gun-shots stopped ringing in their ears, fed his vanity.

All of a sudden, men were slapping him on the

back, shaking his hand, telling him he'd done good. The women looked at him from under lowered eyelashes and wondered what it would be like to take a gladiator to bed.

Even the sheriff stepped off the distance between Wes and the dead men and grinned at the crowd. "Ten paces, by God. And three men hurled into eternity in the space of a moment!"

This drew a cheer, and Wes bowed and grinned and basked in the adulation.

He was but seventeen years old and he'd killed eleven white men.

The newspapers had made him a named gunfighter, up there with the likes of Longley and Hickok, and he'd have to live with it.

And me, I thought, *But in the end they'll kill you, Wes. One day the folks will forget all about you and that will be your death.*

CHAPTER TWO
The Dark Star

"I got an idea, Little Bit," John Wesley said. "Hell, it's a notion that can make us both rich."

"Wes," I said, laying Mr. Dickens on my lap, my thumb marking the page I'd been reading by firelight, "does your brain ever stop?"

Wes grinned, glanced at the full moon riding high above the pines, and pointed. "No, I'm like him up there, always shining. And when I get an idea, I shine even brighter."

We'd left Honest Deal at first light that morning, heading west for the town of Longview over to Harrison County where Wes had kin. I was all used up. The dog days of summer were on us and the day had been blistering hot and as humid as one of those steam baths that some city folks seem to enjoy.

The night was no better, just darker.

My leg in its iron cage hurt like hell and all I wanted was to read a couple chapters of Martin Chuzzlewit and then find my blankets.

But Wes, who had a bee in his bonnet, wouldn't let

it go. His shirt was dark with arcs of sweat under his arms, and his teeth glinted white in the moonlight. "Well, don't you want to hear it?"

"Hear what?" I asked.

"Don't mess with me, Little Bit. I told you I have a great idea."

I sighed, found a pine needle that I used to mark my page, and closed the book. "I'm all ears," I said, looking at Wes through the gloom.

"All right, but first answer me this. Do you agree that I'm a man destined for great things?"

I nodded. "I'd say that. You're a fine shootist, Wes. The best that ever was."

"I know, but I'm much more than that."

"So, tell me your idea."

"Listen up. My idea is to star in a show. My own show."

"You mean like a medicine show?" I smiled at him. "Dr. Hardin's Healing Balm."

"Hell no. Bigger than that and better." Wes raised his hands and made a long banner shape in the air. "John Wesley Hardin's Wild West Show."

His face aglow, he said, "Well, what do you think? Isn't it great, huh?"

"I don't know what to think. I've never heard of such a thing."

"A . . . what's the word? . . . *spectacular* show, Little Bit. With me as the hero and you as . . . as . . . well, I'll think of something."

"On stage in a theater, Wes? Is what you think?"

"Maybe. But probably outside in an arena. We'll have drovers and cavalry and Indians and outlaws and cattle herds and stagecoaches and . . . hell, the possibilities are endless." Wes leaned closer to me and the shifting firelight stained the right side of his eager, handsome face. "I'll be the fearless frontiersman who saves the fair maiden from the savages or captures the rustlers singlehanded, stuff like that."

"Sounds expensive, Wes. I mean, paying all those hands and—"

"Damn it, Little Bit, that kind of thinking is the reason you're not destined for greatness. I'll get rich backers, see? They'll bankroll the show for a cut of the profits."

Wes smiled at me. "Hell, we got three hundred dollars for the horses and traps of them dead men back at Honest Deal, so we already got seed money." He read the doubt in my face and said, "It can't fail. Nobody's ever had an idea like mine and nobody else is going to think of it. Man, I'll make a killing and a fortune."

He again made a banner of his hands and grinned. "John Wesley Hardin's Wild West Show! Damn, I like the sound o' that." He let out a rebel yell that echoed like the howl of a wolf in the silence. "Little Bit, it's gonna be great!"

Around me, the pines were black, and they leaned into one another as though they were exchanging ominous secrets. I felt uneasy, like a flock of geese had just flown over my grave. "What do I do, Wes?"

"Do? Do where?"

"In the show, Wes. What do I do in your Wild West Show?"

Wes's eyes roamed over me and I was well aware of what he saw . . . a tiny, stunted runt with a thin, white face, boot-button brown eyes, and a steel brace on his twisted twig of a left leg.

I wasn't formed by nature to play any kind of western hero.

John Wesley was never one to get stumped by a question, but he scowled, his thick black brows drawn together in thought. Then his face cleared and he smiled. "You read books, Little Bit, don't you?"

I nodded and held up my copy of Mr. Dickens.

"Then there's your answer." Wes clapped his hands. "You'll be my bookkeeper! And"—he beamed as he delivered what he obviously believed was the snapper— "a full partner in the business!"

I said nothing.

"What's wrong? I thought you'd be happy with that proposition."

"I am, I really am."

"Then why do you look so down in the mouth you could eat oats out of a churn?"

"Because the thought just came to me that before you can do anything, Wes, you'll have to square yourself with the law."

John Wesley sighed, a dramatic intake of breath coupled with a frustrated yelp that he did often. "Little Bit, are you talking about Mage again?"

"Well, Mage for starters, but there are others."

"Mage was your friend, wasn't he?"

"Not really. We were together a lot because he wanted to learn how to read and do his ciphers."

"Negroes are too stupid to learn to read," Wes said. "Hell, everybody knows that."

"He was doing all right. He liked Sir Walter Scott."

"He wasn't doing all right in my book," Wes said, his face tight. "Mage was an uppity black man who needed killing."

I smiled to take the sting out of a conversation that was veering into dangerous territory. When Wes got angry bad things happened.

"Ah, you were just sore because he beat you at rasslin'," I said.

"Yeah, but I bloodied his nose, didn't I?"

I nodded. "You done good, Wes. Mage was twice as big as you."

"And ugly with it."

Wes was silent for a while. A breeze spoke in the pines and a lace of mist frosted by moonlight drifted between their slender trunks. I fancied that the ghosts of dead Comanches were wandering the woods.

"You know what he said, don't you?" Wes asked.

"Let's drop it. It isn't that important."

"You know what he said?"

I shook my head. I didn't feel good that night. My leg hurt and the salt pork and cornpone we'd eaten for dinner wasn't sitting right with me.

"He said that no white boy could draw his blood and live. Then he said that no bird ever flew so high that could not be brought to the ground. He was talking about a shooting, Little Bit. He planned to put a ball in my back."

"Mage shouldn't have said that."

"Damn right he shouldn't. And he shouldn't have tried to pull me off my horse, either."

I made no comment on that last and Wes said, "All I did was shoot him the hell off'n me."

I felt his angry blue eyes burn into my face.

"You would've done the same."

"I guess so. If I could shoot a revolver, I might have done the same."

"Everybody in Texas knew it was a justified killing. Everybody except the damned Yankees."

"That's why you should make it right with them, Wes," I said.

"Damned if I will. Since when did the killing of an uppity black man become a crime?"

"Since the Yankees won the war."

Wes spat into the fire. "Damn Yankees. I hate their guts."

"A lot of Texas folks think like you, Wes."

"And how do you feel, Little Bit? Until real recent, I never pegged you as a Yankee-lover."

"Wes, my pa died at Gettysburg, remember. How do you think I feel?"

"Yeah, you're right. I forgot about that. You got no reason to cotton to Yankees, either." Wes grinned at me, his good humor restored. "I'll pour us some coffee, and before we turn in, we'll get back to talking about my Wild West Show for a spell." He frowned. "Damn it. We'll have no Yankees in it, unless we need folks to shovel hoss shit. Agreed?"

"Anything you say, Wes. Anything you say."

CHAPTER THREE
"I Don't Enjoy Killing"

I saw John Wesley Hardin being born, I was with him when he died, and in between I was proud to call him my friend. He was everything I wanted to be and couldn't.

Wes was tall and slim and straight and moved with the elegance of a panther. He'd a fine singing voice and the very sight of him when he stepped into a room set the ladies' hearts aflutter. Many men admired him, others hated him, but all feared him and the wondrous things he could do with revolvers.

Like England's hunchbacked king, I was delivered misshapen from my mother's womb. My frail body did not grow as a man's should, and even in the full bloom of my youth, if you'd be pleased to call it that, I never weighed more than eighty pounds or reached a height of five feet.

Do you wonder then that I admired Wes so, and badly wanted to be like him? He was my noble knight errant who sallied forth to right wrongs, and I his lowly squire.

I think I know the answer to that question.

And why I pledged to stay at his side to the death.

As I told you earlier, we were headed for Longview to visit with Wes's kin for a spell, but he wanted to linger where we were for a day longer.

"This is a pleasant spot and we can talk about my idea some more. Sometimes it's good to just set back and relax."

I had no objections. I felt ill and my leg continued to give me trouble.

The day passed pleasantly enough. I sat under a tree and read my book and Wes caught a bright yellow butterfly at the base of a live oak. He said it meant good luck.

But when he opened his hands to let the butterfly go, it could no longer fly and fluttered to earth, a broken thing.

Wes said not to worry, that it was still good luck. But he seemed upset about the crippled butterfly and didn't try to catch another one.

The long day finally lifted its ragged skirts and tip-toed away, leaving us to darkness and the Texas stars.

Wes built up the fire and put the coffee on to boil. Using his Barlow knife, he shaved slices of salt pork into the pan and said there would be enough corn-pone for supper with some leftover for tomorrow's breakfast.

I was pleased about that. It was good cornpone,

made with buttermilk and eggs, and I was right partial to it back in those days.

After supper we talked about the Wild West Show, then, as young men do, about women. After a while, I said I was tired and it was about time I sought my blankets.

I stretched out and tried to ignore the pain gnawing at my leg.

Night birds fluttered in and out of the pines making a rustling noise and a puzzled owl asked its question of the night. A pair of hunting coyotes yipped back and forth in the distance and then fell silent.

I closed my eyes and entered that gray, misty realm between wakefulness and sleep . . . then jolted back to consciousness when a shout rang through the hallowed quiet.

"Hello the camp!"

I sat upright and saw that Wes was already on his feet. He wasn't wearing his guns, but stood tense and alert, his eyes reaching into the darkness.

Even as a teenager, John Wesley's voice was a soft baritone, but to my surprise he pitched it near an octave higher and broke it a little as he called out, "Come on in. There's coffee on the bile."

I wondered at that, but didn't dwell on it because the darkness parted and two men rode into the clearing.

Men made a living any way they could in Texas when Wes and I were young, and those two strangers looked as though they were no exception. They were hard-faced men, lean as wolves. I'd seen enough of their kind to figure that they were on the scout.

Astride mouse-colored mustangs that couldn't have gone more than eight hundred pounds, they wore belted revolvers and carried Springfield rifles across their saddle horns. As for clothing, their duds were any kind of rags they could patch together. The effect, coupled with their dirty, bare feet, was neither pleasant nor reassuring.

But the Springfields were clean and gleamed with a sheen of oil.

Whoever those men were, they were not pilgrims.

One of the riders, bearded and grim, was a man who'd long since lost the habit of smiling. "You got grub?"

"No, sir," Wes said, using that strange, boy's voice. "Sorry, but we're all out."

The man's eyes moved to our horses. "Where did you get them mounts?"

Wes didn't hesitate. "We stole them, sir. But we're taking them back to Longview to square ourselves with the law."

The man turned to his companion, "Lem, how much you figure the paint is worth?"

"Two hundred in any man's money," the man called Lem said. He looked at Wes. "You stole a lot of horse there, boy."

Wes nodded. "I know, sir. And that's why we're taking him back to his rightful owner."

"Who is his rightful owner?" Lem asked.

"We don't rightly know," I said. "But we aim to find out, like."

"Well, you don't have to worry about that, sonny," Lem said. "We'll take the paint off your hands, and the buckskin as well. Ain't that so, Dave?"

The bearded man nodded. "Sure thing. Pleased to

do it. And, being decent folks, we'll set things right with the law for you."

"We'll do it ourselves," Wes said . . . in his normal voice.

And those two white trash idiots didn't notice the change! They sat their ponies and heard what they wanted to hear, saw what they wanted to see.

What they heard was the scared voice of a half-grown boy, and what they saw was a pair of raw kids, one of them a crippled, sickly-looking runt.

Beyond that they saw nothing . . . an oversight that would prove their downfall.

It was a lethal mistake, and they made it.

They'd underestimated John Wesley Hardin, and as I said earlier, you couldn't make mistakes around Wes. Not if you wanted to go on living, you couldn't.

"Lem, go git them horses and saddles," Dave said. "Now, you boys just set and take it easy while Uncle Lem does what I told him."

"Leave the horses the hell alone," Wes said.

Lem was halfway out of the saddle, but something in Wes's tone froze him in place. He looked at Dave.

"Go do what I told you, Lem," the bearded man said. Then to Wes, "Boy, I had it in my head to let you live, since you're a good-looking kid and could come with us, make yourself useful, like. But my mind's pretty close to a-changing, so don't push me."

Lem dismounted and then, rifle in hand, he grinned at Wes and walked toward the horses.

"I told you, leave the horses be." Wes stood very still, his face like stone.

I swallowed hard, my brain racing. *Wes, where the hell are your guns?*

"Boy, step aside," Dave said. "Or I'll drop you right where you stand."

"And you go to hell," Wes said.

Dave nodded as though he'd expected that kind of reaction. "You lose, boy." He smiled. "Sorry and all that."

He brought up his rifle and John Wesley shot him.

Drawing from the waistband behind his back, Wes's ball hit the Springfield's trigger guard, clipped off Dave's shooting finger, then ranged upward and crashed into the bearded man's chin.

His eyes wide and frantic, Dave reeled in the saddle, spitting blood, bone and teeth.

Wes ignored him. The man was done.

Wes and Lem fired at the same instant.

Unnerved by the unexpected turn of events, Lem, shooting from the hip, was too slow, too wide and too low. Wes's bullet hit him between the eyes and he fell all in a heap like a puppet that just had its strings cut.

Never one to waste powder and ball, Wes didn't fire again.

But something happened that shocked me to the core.

Despite his horrific wound, his face a nightmare of blood and bone, the man called Dave swung his horse around and kicked it into the darkness.

Wes let out a triumphant yell and ran after him, holding his Colt high.

They vanished into the murk and I was left alone in silence.

In the moonlight, gun smoke laced around the clearing like a woman's wispy dress wafting in a breeze. The man on the ground lay still in death and made no sound.

A slow minute passed . . . then another. . . .

A shot! Somewhere out there in the dark.

Uneasy, I picked up a heavy stick that lay by the fire and hefted it in my hand. Small and weak as I was, there was little enough I could do to defend myself, but the gesture made me feel better.

"Hello the camp!" It was John Wesley's voice, followed by a shout of triumphant glee.

The black shades of the night parted and he walked into the clearing, leading the dead man's mustang.

I say dead man, because even without asking I knew that must have been Dave's fate.

"You should've seen it, Little Bit," Wes said, his face alight. "Twenty yards in darkness through trees! One shot! I blew the man's brains out." He laughed and clapped his hands. "If he had any."

Without waiting for my response, he said, "Now we got a couple more ponies to sell and two Springfield rifles. Their Colts are shot out and one has a loose cylinder, so I'll hold on to those." His face split in a wide grin. "What do you reckon, Little Bit, am I destined for great things or ain't I?"

I didn't answer that, at least not directly. "John Wesley, the killing has to stop."

He was genuinely puzzled and toed the dead man with his boot. "You talking about these two?"

"No, I guess not. I mean, the killing in general. You have to think about the Wild West show."

"These men needed killing, right?"

I nodded. "Yeah, I guess it was them or us." I was still holding onto the stick and tossed it away. "Maybe you could've let the other one die in his own time and at a place of his choosing. I say *maybe* you could. I'm not pointing fingers, Wes."

"Name one man I killed who didn't need killing, Little Bit. Damn it, name just one. And don't say Mage. He was a black man and don't count."

He waited maybe a full second then said, "See, you can't name a one."

"Wes, there are some who say you pushed the fight with Ben Bradley."

"He cheated me at cards and then called me a coward. A man who deals from the bottom of the deck and calls another man yellow needs killing. At least in Texas he does."

"I was there, Wes. You kept right on pumping balls into him after he said, 'Oh Lordy, don't shoot me anymore.' I remember that. Why did you do it?"

"Because in a gunfight you keep shooting till the other man falls. And because only a man who's lowdown asks for mercy in the middle of a shooting scrape, especially after he's gotten his work in."

I was silent.

Wes said, "Well, did Ben Bradley need killing?"

I sighed. "Yeah, Wes. I guess he did at that."

"Then what's your problem?" Wes's face was dark with anger. "Come on, cripple boy, spit it out."

"Don't enjoy it, Wes. That's all. Just . . . just don't enjoy it."

Wes was taken aback and it was a while before he spoke again. "You really think I like killing men?" he finally asked.

"I don't know, Wes."

"Come on, answer me. Do you?"

"Maybe you do."

"And maybe I was born under a dark star. You ever think of that?"

Above the tree canopy the stars looked like diamonds strewn across black velvet. I pointed to the sky. "Which star?"

"It doesn't matter, Little Bit. Whichever one you choose will be dark. There ain't no shining star up there for John Wesley Hardin."

Depression was a black dog that stalked Wes all his life and I recognized the signs. The flat, toneless voice and the way his head hung as though it had suddenly become too heavy for his neck.

In later years, depression, coming on sudden, would drive him to alcohol and sometimes to kill.

It was late and I was exhausted, but I tried to lift his mood. "Your Wild West show is a bright star, Wes."

I thought his silence meant that he was considering that, but this was not the case.

"I don't kill men because I enjoy it. I kill other men because they want to kill me." He stared at me with lusterless eyes. "I just happen to be real good at it."

"Get some sleep, Wes," I said.

He nodded to the body. "I'll drag that away first."

"Somewhere far. You ever hear wild hogs eating a man? It isn't pleasant."

Wes was startled. "How would you know that?"

Tired as I was, I didn't feel like telling a story, but I figured it might haul the black dog off Wes, so I bit the bullet, as they say. "Remember back to Trinity County when we were younkers?"

"Yeah?" Wes said it slow, making the word a question.

"Remember Miles Simpson, lived out by McCurry's sawmill?"

"Half-scalped Simpson? Had a wife that would have

dressed out at around four hundred pounds and the three simple sons?"

"Yes, that's him. He always claimed that the Kiowa half-scalped him, but it was a band saw that done it."

"And he got et by a hog?"

"Let me tell the story. Well one summer, I was about eight years old, going on nine, and you had just learned to toddle around—"

"I was a baby," Wes said.

"Right. That's what you were, just a baby." I hoped he wouldn't interrupt again otherwise the story would take all night to tell.

"Well, anyhoo, Ma sent me over to the Simpson place for the summer. She figured roughhousing with the boys might strengthen me and help my leg. Mrs. Simpson was a good cook and Ma said her grub would put weight on me."

"What did she cook?" With the resilience of youth, Wes was climbing out from under the black dog, and that pleased me.

"Oh pies and beef stew, stuff like that. And sausage. She made that herself and fried it in hog fat."

"I like peach pie," Wes said. "And apple, if it's got raisins in it."

"Yeah, me too."

"And plenty of cinnamon."

"She made pies like that." Then quickly, before he could interrupt again, I went on. "I was there the whole month of June, then on the second of July, the day after my ninth birthday, the cabin got hit by a band of Lipan Apaches that had crossed the Rio Grande and come up from Mexico."

"Damned murdering savages," Wes said.

"The youngest of the Simpson boys fell dead in the first volley. His name was Reuben or maybe Rufus, I can't recollect which. The others, myself included, made it back into the cabin, though Mrs. Simpson's butt got burned by a musket ball as she was coming through the door."

"Big target."

"Yeah, I guess it was."

"Hold on just a minute." Wes grabbed the dead man by the ankles and dragged him into the brush. When he came back he said, "Then what happened?"

"Well, Mr. Simpson and his surviving sons held off the Apaches until dark when all went quiet. But they were afraid to go out for the dead boy's body on account of how the savages might be lying in ambush."

"Damned Apaches. I hate them."

"Well, just as the moon came up, we heard this snorting and snuffling sound, then a strange ripping noise, like calico cloth being torn into little pieces."

"What was it?" Wes asked.

"It was Reuben or maybe Rufus being torn into little pieces."

"The big boars have sharp tusks on them. They can rip into a man."

"They ripped into the dead boy all right. Come first light all that was left was a bloody skeleton. But the head was still intact. The hogs hadn't touched it." I stared at Wes. "Why would they do that?"

"I don't know, Little Bit. There ain't no accounting for what a hog will do."

Wes stepped to the brush, then turned and said, "I'm taking this feller well away from camp. Your damned story about them hogs has me boogered."

CHAPTER FOUR
Wes Has Big Plans

We rode into Longview at the noon hour under a sky that had been burned out by the scorching sun. There was no breeze and the air hung heavy as a damp blanket.

Few people were on the street, probably because the sporting crowd was still abed and wouldn't appear until the dark of night.

Casting no shadow, Wes and I rode to the livery stable, the two mustangs in tow.

Longview was a rough railroad town and the smart moneymen reckoned that the arrival of the iron rails would soon bring prosperity on a massive scale to all concerned. Half the buildings that lined the street were saloons. Gunfights were common and most days the town could be depended on to serve a dead man for breakfast.

No doubt about it, the booming town had snap.

The business district, a cluster of hastily built timber-frame buildings, surrounded the train depot.

Wes said there was enough money in the district to bankroll his Wild West show with plenty to spare.

A painted sign hung above the door of the livery.

JAS. GLEE, *prop.*
HORSES FOR SALE AND RENT
Carriage Repairs a Specialty

In person, Jas. Glee, prop. was a tall, loose-geared man somewhere in early middle age. A red beard, shot through with white, hung to his waistband. His eyes were large and expressionless, popping out of a cadaverous face like a pair of black plums.

He wore a threadbare shell jacket of Confederate gray with a corporal's chevrons on the sleeves and thus immediately jumped up several places in our esteem.

"A stall and hay is two-bits per day per hoss," Glee said. "I'll throw in a scoop of oats for two-bits extry."

Wes said that we'd spring for the oats.

Glee gave him a sidelong glance. "You boys staying in town long?"

"I'm visiting kin," Wes said. "Depending on the welcome, it could be one day or ten."

"Don't make it any more than one, John Wesley," Glee said.

Wes was surprised. "How do you know my name?"

"Seen you a few years back when I was visiting with your ma and pa."

Glee turned to me as though he thought there was something I ought to know. "The Rev. James Hardin is a fine man. And his wife Mary Elizabeth is a most singular woman and mighty purty."

"Well, thankee kindly," Wes said, answering for me. "When next I see them, I'll tell them what you said."

"Yes, do that, and add my kind regards," Glee said.

Was propped the Springfields against the side of a stall. "I'm open to offers for the mustangs and those two rifles."

Glee cast his eyes over the horses, then the rifles. "A hundred is the best I can do. That's giving you thirty dollars apiece for the scrubs when they ain't worth any more'n ten. As for the Springfields, seems that everybody these days wants repeaters, so they'll be a hard sell."

Wes scowled. "Hard sell, hard bargain."

"Hard times," Glee said.

"Done and done," I said. The last thing I wanted was for Wes to fly off the handle and put a bullet into Jas. Glee, prop. Not in the man's own town.

"All right, a hundred it is, payable in gold coin." Then, still smarting a little, Wes said, "Now what's all this about us staying only one day in Longview?"

"The law is after you, John Wesley," Glee said.

Wes grinned. "The Yankee law is always after me."

"Stay here. Let me put up your mounts." Glee led the horses into stalls, forked them hay and then returned, his face grim. "John Wesley, this time it's serious. There's a state police lieutenant in town by the name of E.T. Stakes, known as Ned to them he considers friends. He's been asking about you, talking to your kin and the like."

"Did he mention charges?" I asked.

Glee stared hard into Wes's eyes. "You want to hear this?"

Wes grinned. "Lay it on me, like I give a damn."

"One count of hoss theft and three counts of

murder. All four of them charges are hanging offenses in Texas."

"Wes, maybe we should light a shuck," I said.

"Hell, no we won't," Wes said. "I'll find this Stakes feller and talk to him. If he's interested in polite conversation, then fine. If he isn't, well, Texas will be rid of another Yankee lawman."

"Wes, if you kill a state constable, the law will never leave you alone," I said. "They'll come after you until they catch you, or worse."

"The young feller's right, John Wesley," Glee said. "You can bed down here tonight and ride out at first light. I got a nice pot of beef stew on the simmer, if you'd care to make a trial of it, and I can find some whiskey if you're an imbibing man."

Wes seemed to be thinking over that proposition, but he wasn't. "Who's the richest man in town?" he said after a while.

Glee's head jerked back in surprise. "Why, I guess that would be Sam Luck. He owns the bank, a couple saloons, a sawmill outside of town, and maybe a dozen other properties he's foreclosed on in the past twelve-month."

"Where can I find him?" Wes said.

Glee consulted the nickel railroad watch he took from his pants pocket. "At this time of day, he'll be taking lunch at the Excelsior Hotel."

"Is this Luck feller a carpetbagger?" I asked.

"He's a black man and a close, personal friend of President Grant," Glee said. "What does that tell you?"

"Yeah, well I can stand it," Wes said. "I don't mind doing business with the devil if I can spend his money."

"Sam Luck is a grinder, a real hard-ass," Glee said. "He ain't likely to give a loan to a ranny he don't know."

"I don't want to borry money," Wes said. "I'm looking for business partners."

I read the question on Glee's face and said, "John Wesley plans to start up a Wild West show."

A second question overlaid the first on Glee's face, but then he articulated his puzzlement. "What the hell is a Wild West show?"

Wes said, "We'll tour the country and bring the frontier to the folks—drovers, Indians, cavalry rough riders, settlers, pretty saloon gals, shootin', scalpin'— you name it. Folks will sit in grandstands and watch."

"And the folks will pay good money for this?" Glee said.

"Sure they will," Wes said. "I'll get rich and so will my partners."

"Hell, boy, all folks have to do is walk into the street to see a Wild West show the likes of what you're talking about. There's one in Longview every damn night of the week."

Wes could look pompous at times.

He puffed up and said, "This is why you'll never be great, Mr. Glee. You don't see the big picture. My show will tour the east where folks walk into the street and all they see is high buildings and trolley cars. They'll pay through the nose to see the Wild West right in their hometown of Boston or New York or wherever."

"You're serious about this, ain't you?" Glee said.

"Damn right I am," Wes said.

"Damn right he is," I said.

"Damn stupid if you ask me," Glee said.

"Well, I'm not asking you," Wes said. "Now I'm gonna see that black man and hope he's got a heap more business savvy than you."

Glee shook his head and walked away. Then he stopped and said over his shoulder, "Think about the stew, huh?"

CHAPTER FIVE
The Mark of Cain

The Excelsior Hotel was a two story building with a generous porch supplied with bamboo and rattan rockers and wooden side tables. Swallows had built their nests in the corners and ollas, beaded with condensation, hung from the rafters to cool the sitters.

"Nice place," I said as we stepped onto the porch. "It looks expensive."

"Where else would a damned carpetbagger lunch?" Wes asked.

We stepped out of the day's intolerable heat into the shaded coolness of the hotel lobby.

A clerk stood behind the front desk talking with a plumed, beautiful officer resplendent in the blue, silver, and gold dress uniform of the U.S. Cavalry. The fussy, bespectacled man shifted his attention from the officer to us, as dusty, shabby and trail-worn a pair as ever was. "What can I do for you"—he gave a moment's pause—"gentlemen?"

"I'm here to see Sam Luck." Wes would not put *Mister* in front of a black man's name.

The uppity clerk did. "Mr. Luck is lunching." He had a funny left eye that turned inward toward the bridge of his nose.

"I know." Wes could see that the dining room opened onto the lobby and he stepped toward the door.

"Wait. You can't go in there," the clerk said.

The beautiful officer stroked the blond, dragoon mustache that fell in waves to the corners of his mouth and his nose wrinkled as he regarded us.

Perhaps he believed that we'd spent the night in a pigsty somewhere.

Wes ignored the clerk and strode quickly into the dining room, me limping after him.

The place was full of big-bellied men in broadcloth, their women in silk, and cigar smoke hung in the air like a blue fog. I identified the fragrances of steak, lamb chops, and sizzling bacon and my hollow stomach rumbled.

Wes stood still for a moment, looked around, then yelled, "Sam'l Luck! Show yourself, Sam'l!"

I cringed with embarrassment as every face in the room turned to us. A few seemed mildly amused, but the majority were openly hostile and stared at us with a mix of disapproval and disdain.

"I'm here to see Sam'l Luck," Wes called out again.

After that, things got rapidly out of hand.

The beautiful officer marched into the dining room, a riding crop in his hand. He grabbed Wes by the shoulder and yelled, "Out you go, my buck."

"You tell him, Custer!" a man yelled. And people laughed.

"Who the hell are you?" Wes said, his eyebrows drawing together.

Custer knew he had a captive, adoring audience and made a grandstand play. "General George Armstrong Custer," he grandly announced. "And I'm the equal of an 'undred, nay, a thousand, of you."

As he knew it would, this bold statement drew a round of applause and cheers, and, amid the loud huzzahs, I heard yells of, "Give him hell, General!" and "Remember the Washita!"

Wes hated Yankee soldiers, was widely believed to have shot several, and he took a set against Custer. His hands blurred and an instant later the muzzles of two blue Colts pushed into the blue belly of Custer's frock-coat. "Back off, soldier boy." His voice was as cold as death.

Looking back, I have to give Custer credit. The man had sand. He wasn't too smart, but he had bark on him and he didn't even blink.

"Pull those triggers and you'll hang like the damned Rebel dog you are," he said.

"Might just be worth it," Wes said, smiling.

Oh sweet Jesu!

John Wesley's knuckles were white on the triggers and America was about to lose a hero.

"General Custer!" A small, frail black man stood up at his corner table. In the sudden hush that followed, he said, "Please allow the gentlemen to draw closer to me without harm or hindrance."

He'd phrased that request so that Custer could extricate himself without losing face.

But I still don't know how things would have ended had a pale young waitress, *in extremis*, not dropped a tray of dirty dishes that clattered and crashed onto the wood floor.

The sudden clamor broke the spell that had plunged the room into silence.

Custer took advantage of it. He lowered his riding crop and said to Wes, "I'll deal with you later, sir." Then he swung on his heel and stomped away, his spurred boots chiming.

Wes grinned, spun his Colts, and let them thud into their shoulder holsters. "There goes a lucky man."

Custer wasn't the only one who loved to make a grandstand play.

Sam Luck, for indeed that was the identity of the delicate little black man, waved us over to his table.

Wes sashayed across the room like a new rooster in the hen house and basked in the crowd's attention.

He didn't deign to hear, or chose to ignore, the hear-hears after one fat Yankee with broken veins all over his nose and cheeks called out, "We should hang the rascal."

But when Luck ushered us into chairs, the diners settled down and the normal buzz of conversation and the clink of cutlery resumed.

I'd formed a picture in my mind of what Sam Luck would look like, a big-bellied, shiny-faced black man in a loud checkered suit smoking a fat cigar the better to show off the diamond ring on his little finger.

He was none of those things.

Luck was tiny, spare, dusty and worn, like a leather-bound book on a disused library shelf. His skin was coffee-colored, his eyes small and dark as raisins, and his mouth was a thin gash, tight, hard, and mean.

The black broadcloth he wore, once expensive, was

much frayed and stained and his linen was yellow with age.

Withal, he was a very unimpressive figure . . . but for the most singular scar that marred his forehead. The letter *R* had been burned into his skin with a hot iron. The brand was fairly small—I could have covered it with a silver dollar—but it was sharp and deep.

I recognized it for what it was, of course.

The *R* marked Luck as a runaway slave who'd once tried to flee his lawful master and was thus never to be trusted again. It was a Mark of Cain that he'd once richly deserved.

Luck made no effort to offer us coffee, but did listen intently to what John Wesley was saying to him about the Wild West show. All the time, the black man's thin fingers crumbled the bread roll on his plate.

When Wes finished speaking, Luck said, "The officer you threatened with death is General George Armstrong Custer. He's leaving for Kansas today to take command of the Seventh Cavalry." Luck's brief smile was the flash of a knife blade. "I rather fancy that the gallant Custer will soon provide enough action against the savages for a dozen Wild West shows."

"My point exactly," Wes said. "I want to bring that kind of frontier excitement to audiences back east and even beyond, to Europe."

When he put his mind to it, Wes could talk like a lawyer, even to a Negro.

Luck brushed bread crumbs off his lap and without looking up said, "No one has come up with an idea like yours before, Mr. Hardin, and it just might work."

"It can't fail," Wes said.

Luck raised his eyes. "Any business can fail. I just

lost money on a Mississippi plantation that I was sure I could resell at a profit. Somebody burned down the big house and I was left with six hundred acres of land, half of it swamp."

Wes wouldn't say it, but I did. "Sorry to hear that." My face was empty.

Again Luck's smile was slight and fleeting. "Yes, I'm sure you are."

"Well," John Wesley said, "what do you think of my proposition?"

"It interests me, young man," Luck said. "I believe your Wild West show idea has potential."

"Good," Wes said, beaming. "How much do you want to invest?"

"Not so fast. First I want to see a business proposal from you."

"What's that?" Wes asked.

Luck steepled his fingers and cocked his small head to one side. "You will draw up a cover letter, executive summary, business and market feasibility analyses and studies, financial data, and supply me with the *curriculum vitae* for all the members of your management team."

"Hell, is that all?" Wes blinked like an owl.

"For the time being, yes," Luck said. "Have it on my desk by the end of next week."

Wes nodded, then turned to me. "You heard the man, Little Bit. Have all that stuff on his desk by the end of next week."

My face said, "Huh?" but I heard the croak of my voice say, "Sure thing, Wes."

"Very well, our business is concluded," Luck said.

"Now, if you gentlemen will withdraw and allow me to finish my lunch?"

Wes rose to his feet and I did the same.

"Don't worry, we'll get you all that . . . stuff," Wes said.

Luck nodded. "Good. In the meantime stay clear of Custer. He can be a dangerous enemy."

CHAPTER SIX
The Wrath of Custer

"Well, what do you think?" John Wesley asked me.

"Hell, I don't know anything about that business stuff."

"You read books."

"Not about being a tycoon and the like."

Wes thought about that for a spell. "Well, just do what you can."

"I'll need a pencil and paper," I said.

"There's a general store across the way. It'll have what you want."

We stopped in the middle of the street to let a heavily loaded dray drawn by an ox team trundle past.

The wagon kicked up a cloud of yellow dust and when it cleared three men stood staring at us. One of them was Custer and he had his plumed hat set at a fighting angle. He jabbed a finger at Wes. "That's the scoundrel who threatened my life, Constable."

One of the men with the general, a tall, rangy

fellow with a magnificent, black cavalry mustache that rivaled Custer's, had a shotgun leveled at Wes's belly, both hammers eared back.

Beside him, a smaller, slighter man, was similarly armed. He had the eyes of a snake and his fingers were crooked on the Greener's triggers. "You are under arrest."

John Wesley tensed, a thing I'd seen before when he was determined to draw down on a man.

But he was bucking a stacked deck and I think he knew it.

It's a hard thing to die in the street when you're but seventeen years old with a great business idea.

"Let it go, Wes," I said. "They'll cut you in half."

"Truer words was never spoke," the rangy man said. "We have reason to believe you are John Wesley Hardin, the man killer. Give us any kind of excuse to gun you right where you stand and we'd sure appreciate it."

A dust devil spun between us and Custer and them, then collapsed. People had gathered in the street and judging by the eager expressions on their faces, they hoped Wes would make a play.

"We're in a hell of a fix, Wes," I whispered.

John Wesley knew that as well as I did.

As I said, a man who hopes to have a Wild West show one day doesn't brace a couple hardcases with scatterguns. Not at a range of three or four feet, he doesn't.

Wes tried to brazen it out. "The soldier boy I've already met. Who the hell are you two?"

"I'm not in the habit of giving out my name to low persons," the rangy man said. "But since I'm arresting you and expect to watch you hang, I'm Lieutenant E.T. Stakes of the state police and this here is Constable Jim Smalley."

"What's the charge?" Wes asked.

Stakes' grin was unpleasant. "Don't worry about that, Hardin. You're facing enough murder charges to send you to the gallows."

"My name is Wesley Clements," Wes said. "You got the wrong man."

"Let's go ask Sam Luck about that," Custer said.

I guess that's when Wes knew he was running out of room on the dance floor.

"Go to hell," he said.

"Constable Smalley, the ruffian has two murderous revolvers under his armpits," Custer said. "Do your duty and relieve him of those."

Stakes raised the muzzle of his shotgun. "Be careful, Jim. He can make fancy moves."

Smalley slapped the butt of the Greener. "I got the cure for fancy moves right here, Lieutenant."

Later, John Wesley told me that he'd had a passing fancy to go for his guns and that Custer would get the first ball. But when the muzzles of Smalley's scattergun pressed into his belly and he looked into the man's cold, reptilian eyes, Wes decided it was not the time to make a play.

After Smalley removed the Colts from their holsters, Stakes slapped a pair of massy, iron handcuffs on John Wesley's wrists.

General Custer then stepped forward, his face like thunder. "You damned Texas cur." His lips curled into a snarl as his riding crop slashed across Wes's left cheek, leaving an angry red welt and drawing blood from the corner of Wes's mouth.

Wes took the blow without a sound, then leaned forward and spat a mix of blood and saliva onto the chest of Custer's beautiful coat, right between the parallel rows of gilt buttons.

Enraged and foaming at the mouth, Custer wielded his riding crop and rained cut after cut back and forth across Wes's unprotected face.

I heard Smalley as though he yelled at the far end of a tunnel.

"Hell, General, leave enough of him for us to hang!"

By then I was already moving. I limped as fast as I could to Custer and threw my fist into his face.

Small and stingily built as I was, my punch did little damage, but it made the general back off a step. I followed him, my puny arms windmilling as I tried to land another blow.

Something hard slammed into the back of my head and I saw the ground cartwheel up to meet me.

Then I saw nothing at all.

CHAPTER SEVEN
A Pathetic Creature

I woke facedown in the street, my mouth full of dirt and clots of blood in my nose. How long I'd lain there I had no way of telling.

The business of Longview proceeded around me. People stepped past me on the street and wagons and horses detoured around my prostrate body.

I felt something wet at the back of my head and explored it with my fingers. They came away bloody and stained with manure. At one point, a horse must have crapped on my head as I lay unconscious. No doubt it had occasioned considerable mirth in the passersby.

I attempted to rise but my head spun and I sank slowly back into the dust and dry manure of the street. To add to my misery, a cur dog, as mangy a brute as ever cocked a leg, decided to bark at me and tug at my clothes . . . as though they weren't ragged enough already.

"Git the hell off'n him!" The man's voice came from above me.

I turned my head and beheld Jas. Glee, prop. aim a

kick at the dog's ribs. The wily canine dodged expertly and lit a shuck.

"Let's get you on your feet, young feller," Glee said.

"John Wesley has been taken," I said.

"Yeah, I know. There's nothing you can do for him now, boy."

The man helped me to rise and his nose wrinkled. "Lordy, but you smell bad. You got hoss crap in your hair."

"And blood," I said.

"Yeah, that too. I'll take you back to the livery and get you cleaned up."

"They got Wes," I said again.

Glee nodded. "You told me that already."

"They plan to hang him."

Glee nodded. "Seems like. Pick up your hat."

I did as he said and he half-carried, half-dragged me to the stable.

A rain barrel stood at one corner. Glee took off my hat, grabbed me by the scruff of the neck, and plunged my head into the green, scummy water. He dunked me again and again until I thought I must surely drown.

Then he raised my head for the last time and, my hair dripping, guided me into the livery where he tossed me a scrap of towel. "Dry yourself good, boy, then let me take a look at your head. I think you've got a bad cut back there."

"Somebody hit me with something, maybe a shotgun butt," I said, rubbing my thin hair with the towel.

"Seems like." Glee shook his head. "You're a pathetic-looking creature for sure."

* * *

The cobwebbed clock in Glee's office claimed it was two in the afternoon as I sat eating his stew, my head wrapped in a fat, fairly clean, white and blue striped bandage torn from one of his old shirts. Around a mouthful of beef and onions I said, "I reckon I'll go visit with Wes."

"If they'll let you," Glee said. "Them state lawmen are hard characters."

The wind had picked up and outside sand was blowing. The sky was the color of mustard and the sun a hazy, orange ball. In their stalls, the two mustangs we'd brought in were restless.

Glee walked to the door of the livery and stared down the street. "Custer is leaving, getting into the stage, him and his wife. I reckon she's a right pretty gal, at least from this distance."

"I hope the savages do for him," I said. "Scalp them yellow ringlets from right off'n his head."

Glee turned to me and smiled. "No use in hoping fer something that ain't got a chance of happening, boy. Custer is an Injun-killer from way back. The Sioux, Cheyenne, all them raggedy-assed tribes are terrified of him. One look at the general on his white hoss and they'll cut and run."

"Before the Indians, he was a Reb-killer."

Glee nodded. "Yup, he was real good at it, an' no mistake. That's why they made him a general and him just a lad."

I scraped up the last of my stew, set the bowl aside, and got to my feet. "I'm going to see Wes." I balanced my hat on top of my bandaged head.

"Seems like there's a sandstorm blowing up," Glee

said, looking at the sky and not at me. "If'n I was you, I'd step real careful."

Longview seemed a dark, joyless place as I walked along the boardwalk to the town lockup, my steel-caged leg clumping on timber with every step. Maybe it was because of the wind-driven sand that lifted off the street in tattered yellow veils, found every rip and hole in my clothing, and rasped like sandpaper against my skin that the town seemed so bleak.

But more likely it was the melancholy fact that the Yankee law had John Wesley in its talons and would drag him all the way to the gallows.

In those days, the Longview jail was a low, log structure with a single timber door with three massive wrought iron hinges, each hammered into the shape of what the French call a fleur de lis.

Above the door was a rectangular painted sign. *FIAT JUSTITIA RUAT CAELUM*

In keeping with the door, I figured the motto must be written in French, and I had no idea what it meant.

It was only many years later when Wes became a lawyer that he told me it was Latin for Let justice be done though the heavens fall.

Like me, he never forgot that sign.

To the left of the door was the window of the jailer's office. On the other side was a barred window, one of the panes spider-webbed by a stray bullet.

To this day, jailhouses make me uneasy, but I swallowed hard and pushed on the door. It swung open on oiled hinges and I stepped inside.

A tall man rose from the desk opposite from where I stood and his ice blue eyes warned *Stay right where you are and don't make any fancy moves.*

The jailer had a close-cropped square head, like a Prussian soldier's, and a waxed mustache that curled up at the ends in magnificent arcs. But his forehead was disappointing, low and brutish with massive brow ridges that gave him the appearance of the lowest form of Negro.

Nonetheless, his voice was pleasant enough. "What can I do for you?"

He was a good four inches over six feet and I felt intimidated, like a puny David getting his first glimpse of Goliath.

"I'm here," I said, my voice breaking, "to see John Wesley Hardin."

"State the manner of your business," the lawman said.

"No business. John Wesley is my friend and I'm here to visit."

"Comfort him like."

I nodded. "If he needs comforting."

"He does. Any man facing the gallows needs comforting." The jailer ran his eyes over me from the crown of my battered hat to the fat bandage around my head and then to my down-at-heel shoes. His gaze lingered for a moment on the outline of the steel brace that showed through my pants.

"You can see him," he said. "God knows you've got enough to contend with without me giving you another problem. What's your name, son?"

"Most folks call me Little Bit, but my given name is William, William Bates. Bates by name, Bates by nature, my ma always told me."

"Uh-huh." The jailer lifted the keys from a hook on the wall behind his desk and said, "Ten minutes."

"Thank you kindly," I said.

Perhaps lest I thought him too friendly, the man then said, "Name's Alan Henry Dillard and I'm a hundred different kinds of hell in a fight."

"I imagine you are."

Dillard nodded. "Just so you know . . . you and John Wesley Hardin."

CHAPTER EIGHT
A Daring Plan

"Did Dillard search you?" Wes asked.

I shook my head.

"Good, then he trusts you."

"What's your plan, Wes?"

There was only one cell, furnished with an iron cot and a straw mattress, a bucket that stank and a framed, embroidered motto on the wall that read HAVE YOU WRITTEN TO MOTHER?

It seemed that the town fathers of Longview were big on instructing the criminal classes.

Wes wrapped his long, fine fingers around the black iron bars of his cell and pushed his face closer to mine. "Little Bit, bring me a pistol. I can break out of here real easy."

I felt like pinching myself to make sure I was awake. "Wes, that's nigh on impossible, This here jail is built like the First National Bank of Texas."

"Listen, and listen good," Wes said. "Dillard said a Negro woman will bring me grub twice a day. Once I have the gun, I'll squeeze out tears, pretend I'm broke up about hanging an all, and set them at ease, figuring I'm just a scared kid. But when the woman brings in the tray I'll"—he made a gun of his thumb and forefinger—"Pow! Pow!—kill her and then Dillard."

"It's way too thin, Wes." In fact, I was horrified. John Wesley's words were emotionless, as though murdering two people meant nothing to him.

"The hell it is thin. Just bring me the Colt and I'll do the rest."

I had to unload the thought churning in my head. "Wes, you're talking about killing a lawman . . . and a woman."

"So what?"

"It ain't right, Wes. It can't be right."

"Would you rather see me hang?" Wes asked.

"No, I—"

"Then it isn't my fault. Dillard and the black woman are just two more damned traitors shoving me toward the gallows. They both need killing."

The jailhouse was a solid building, but I heard the relentless rush of the wind, the hiss of driving sand, and the curses of a muleskinner in the street, his team balking at the storm.

I looked into Wes's eyes, so cold to be almost colorless, like ice in winter.

"Well, Little Bit, will you help me or will you help drag me to the gallows with all the rest?"

My guilty conscience was the joker in the deck, but nonetheless I decided to play the hand Wes dealt me. "I'll bring the pistol,"

The ice in John Wesley's eyes melted away in the sun of his smile. "I knew I could depend on you, Little

Bit. Come back tomorrow morning and bring the gun." Wes thought for a spell, then said, "And a bag of sour drops."

"Sour drops?"

"Sure. Dillard won't suspect that a kid with a bad leg and a bag of sour drops in his hand is hiding a pistol, now will he?"

The key rattled in the door that led to the cell, and Wes said urgently, "Make sure all six of the Colt's chambers are charged. I'll have some fast shooting to do."

I nodded and turned away from Wes as Dillard said, "Time's up, son."

"I'll see you tomorrow, Wes," I said. "I'll bring you some sour drops."

Dillard didn't even blink. He had no way of knowing that the words I'd just uttered sounded his death sentence.

I slept that night at the livery and next morning bought candy at the general store. They had no sour drops so I substituted molasses taffy, long a favorite of mine.

When I returned to the stable, I ate some more of Jas. Glee, prop.'s stew, cold and congealed with fat though it was, then searched through Wes's saddlebags for the old Colt revolvers.

To my considerable distress, only the gun with the loose cylinder was fully charged. The other had three empty chambers.

Wes was adamant that he wanted a fully loaded pistol, and since I had no money for caps, powder and shot, I decided that the defective revolver would have to do.

I had a deal of confidence in John Wesley's shooting skills with any kind of firearm, including a Colt that was falling apart.

As I'd seen Wes do, I shoved the revolver into the waistband behind my back and covered it with my coat.

Glee walked into the livery carrying a fine English sidesaddle and caught me in the act. He placed the saddle on a rack, then stared at me for a long time before he spoke.

"I hope you're not thinking of doing anything foolish, young feller. If you're planning to brace Al Dillard, forget it." A fly landed on his cheek and he brushed it away with an irritable hand. "Draw down on Dillard and he'll kill your fer sure, like he's done to seven or more afore ye, all of them bigger and meaner men than you."

My belly churned and I racked my brain for the right . . . no, *any* words.

Finally I managed to say, "Wes and me have a lot of enemies. I figured I should go armed."

Glee looked at me, through me, then said, "Can you shoot?"

"Some."

"*Some* don't cut it, young feller. But *real good* does. Can you shoot real good?"

"No, I guess not."

"Then best you leave the pistol here."

"Jas. Glee, prop., that's probably sound advice, but I won't take it."

Glee shook his head. "Then suit yourself, boy. But

mind what I said about Dillard. He don't take kindly to sass."

Glee took up the sidesaddle again, studied a small tear in the leather of the cantle, then his eyes shifted to me again. "What I said about Dillard taking no sass, tell that to John Wesley as well."

I nodded. "I surely will."

"Makes no difference, really," Glee said. "He won't listen."

I'd slept late, so by the time I headed for the jail-house the sun was high in the sky. All traces of yesterday's sandstorm had fled but for grit on the boardwalks and in the corners of windowpanes. A few innocent white clouds drifted in the indigo sky like lilies on a pond and the air smelled fresh with the promise of the new day.

Despite the beckoning morning, I felt ill at ease and the breakfast I'd eaten was a red-hot cannonball in my belly.

I never carried a gun in those days. My wrists were too thin and weak to absorb the recoil, and on those occasions when John Wesley bade me try, I never once managed to hit a mark, be it at ten paces or two.

Thus I was very conscious of the three-pound Colt that dragged down the back of my pants and I was sure that everyone I passed in the street could see it.

In truth, several men gave me slit-eyed looks as they walked by, but that was probably because a ragged little runt who looked like he'd missed too many meals in his childhood, limping along with his left leg in a steel cage, was a sight to see.

When I stepped into the jailer's office, Alan Dillard glanced up at me from a leather-bound ledger and said, "What you got in your poke?"

My heart jumped in my chest. Had he tumbled to the revolver?

I hesitated, and Dillard prompted, "In your hand, boy."·

I was so relieved, I felt like I'd been touched by an angel. "Oh this?" I held up the candy sack. "It's molasses candy. Wes is right partial to it and I thought it might cheer him up."

"Never cared for it myself," Dillard said, making a face. He pointed at the door to the cell with the steel pen he'd been using. "It's unlocked. Ten minutes, mind. No longer."

I nodded my thanks and stepped through the door into the wretched half-light of the cell area.

Wes was lying on his cot. When he saw me he jumped up and a quick stride took him to the bars.

"Did you get it?" He looked like an excited kid asking about a birthday present.

I nodded, moved close to the bars, and turned my back. "Hurry." My anxious eyes were fixed on the door.

It took only a moment. Wes grabbed the revolver and in a trice, fourteen inches of Colt disappeared into his waistband.

It always surprised me that a man with such a narrow, sharply defined face and thin lips could pout. But Wes did.

Sounding petulant, he said, "You brought me the bust-up Colt."

"I know. It was the one with all the cylinders charged."

"Damn it. I thought I taught you how to load a gun," Wes said, a hint of anger in his voice.

"I didn't have the price of powder and shot. All the money we have is in your pocket." I was a little angry myself, getting little thanks for walking past a named man killer like Alan Dillard with a contraband revolver stuck down my pants.

Wes's smile was a little forced, I thought.

"Well, at least you brought the sour drops," he said, glancing at the paper sack in my hand.

"They didn't have any at the general store, so I bought you molasses taffy."

"I don't like molasses taffy," Wes said, pouting again. "I declare, Little Bit, can't you do anything the hell right?"

I stifled the sharp retort on my tongue as he reached through the bars and pulled me closer to him.

"Listen, earlier the black woman brought me coffee and said she'd be back around one with my lunch. Dillard came in with her and he opened the cell to let her inside."

This time John Wesley's smile was genuine. "I'll kill them both, then make a run for the livery. Have the horses saddled, ready to go."

He scowled. "Think I can trust you to do that right?"

I didn't answer his question. "Wes, Jas. Glee, prop.

says Dillard is a real good gun. I think he'll be hard to kill."

I saw it again, as I'd seen it so often before. Wes puffed up and his handsome young face took on that everybody-look-at-me expression that was so difficult for me to stomach.

"Hard to kill for you, maybe, but not for me. Dillard may be good with a gun, but on his best day he can't shade John Wesley Hardin."

I was Wes's only audience, and not much of a one at that, so all he wanted to hear were his own boasts . . . and he believed every single word of them.

In the event, his plan came to naught.

The door slammed open so violently it banged against the partition wall and two men stepped inside, their spurs ringing.

One of then carried manacles, the other a rope.

CHAPTER NINE
Yankee Assassins

The man with the manacles was E.T. Stakes, the other, holding a rope that I thankfully noted didn't end in a noose, was Constable Jim Smalley. Alan Dillard, the cell key in his hand, stood behind them.

"We're taking a ride, John Wesley," Stakes said, "so gather up what's your'n."

For a moment, Wes's eyes were calculating, figuring his chances against three guns. He obviously decided against making a play. "Where are you taking me, and why?"

"Waco," Stakes said. "Where you'll get a fair trial before you're hung."

Stakes had pouched black eyes and the small, tight, intolerant mouth you sometimes see in elderly nuns. When he smiled, the effect was most unpleasant. "I'll hang bunting on the scaffold myself, John Wesley. Make it look festive for your send-off, like."

"Waco is two hundred miles away," Wes said.

"A hundred and seventy-five to be exact," Stakes

said. "But never fear, Mr. Hardin, I'll do everything I can to make your trip an enjoyable one."

"You're a damned liar," Wes said.

Stakes smiled with his lips shut, like a closed steel purse. "Ain't I, though?"

He turned to Alan Dillard. "You took his guns?"

The jailer nodded. "Yeah, they're locked in my desk."

"Who is he?" Jim Smalley looked at me the same way a man does the sole of his boot after he's stepped in dog doo-doo.

"He's nobody." Dillard turned to Stakes. "I'll release the prisoner."

Before the jailer stepped to the cell, I said, "I want to tag along with John Wesley."

It was Stakes' turn to gut me with a withering stare. "What the hell for, boy?"

"Sir, Wes is a friend of mine and I've got nothing else to do." Then I quickly added, "I'm a good trail cook." That was only partially true, but indeed, I could boil coffee and dredge salt pork in flour and fry it with the best of them.

It seemed that I amused Stakes. "You got a hoss, boy?"

I nodded. "Sure do."

He said to Smalley, "What do you say, Jim?"

The man's answer was to step in front of me and pat me down. "What's in the poke?"

"Molasses taffy. I like it, but Wes doesn't."

Smalley turned to Stakes. "He's an idiot."

"I know, but he's an idiot who can cook," Stakes said. "It will take five, maybe six days to reach Waco. Do you want to rustle up the coffee and grub?"

"Hell, no." Smalley thought for a moment, then said, "All right, let the idiot do it."

"What's your name, boy?" Stakes asked.

"Folks call me Little Bit," I said.

"All right, Little Bit, listen up," Stakes said. "I'm a plain man, bacon and pan bread is what I want, and coffee strong enough to float a silver dollar. You got that?"

"Yes, sir."

"Good, then we'll get along." Stakes nodded to Dillard. "Let Hardin out, jailer."

Before the cell door swung open, Wes smiled at me and winked.

I knew what that meant.

He had killing on his mind.

I returned to the livery and saddled my horse, then started in on Wes's mount.

As I looked around for the blanket, Jas. Glee, prop. stopped me.

"Them lawmen already got a hoss fer John Wesley," he said. "They requisitioned one of the mustangs you and him brung in."

"What does that mean?" I said, never having tussled with the word *requisitioned* before.

"It means they took it in the name of the law, boy."

"Wes's saddle is still here."

"No matter," Glee said. "He ain't going fur."

"It's nigh on two hundred miles to Waco," I said.

"He won't get there."

"They mean to kill him?"

"That's my guess."

"But Stakes promised him a fair trial."

"What E.T. Stakes promises and what E.T. Stakes delivers are seldom one and the same thing, boy." Glee put his hand on my shoulder, a fatherly gesture no man had ever done to me before. It felt strange.

"Listen, boy," he said. "The Yankees who currently rule the great state of Texas have had enough of John Wesley and his kind—unreconstructed Johnny Rebs that claim the war didn't end at Appomattox. As far as the government is concerned, a trial would be a waste of time. Better to gun Hardin on the trail and, for the price of a few cents' worth of powder and ball, tie up everything nicely in a big blue bow."

"What can I do?" I felt scared, lost, like a blind man trying to feel his way out of a burning building.

"How badly do you want to keep on living?" Glee said.

I shook my head, bewildered. "What kind of question is that to ask a man?"

"I'll answer it for you, boy. You ain't a man, not yet you aren't. As to the question I asked, if you want to remain above ground, stay here in Longview. If you want to take your chances on getting a bullet in the back, go with John Wesley."

"I'll go. He's my friend."

Glee smiled. "You're learning, boy. That was a man's answer."

CHAPTER TEN
A Murderous Plot

I led my horse back to the jail where John Wesley was already mounted on the mustang; his only saddle a ragged blanket, his legs lashed under the pony's belly with a rope.

"Dillard, sell me a saddle or let me get my own from the livery," Wes said. "This hoss has a backbone like the thin end of a timber wedge."

"Sorry," Dillard said. "You'll be less likely to make a dash for it, John Wesley."

"At least give him another damned blanket," I said.

Nobody paid me the least mind.

Stakes gathered up the mustang's lead rope then swung into the saddle.

Jim Smalley followed suit, slid the Henry rifle from under his knee and laid it across the saddle horn. "Let's ride. We're burning daylight and we need to put two hundred miles of git between us and Longview."

I mounted, and then Alan Dillard did something that surprised me.

He stepped off the boardwalk and slipped a jar into my coat pocket. "Pickles. For the trail."

I was dumfounded, but managed to nod and mumble my thanks before I kicked my horse into motion and followed the others.

Since Alan Dillard drops out of my narrative here, let me mention that he didn't live to scratch a gray head. He died of jungle fever on Samoa in 1889 while working as a civilian contractor for the U.S. Navy. It is interesting to note that Dillard passed away in the parlor of the novelist Robert Louis Stevenson, author of *Treasure Island*, who was living in the island nation at that time.

We camped that evening under a disused railroad trestle, the temperature surprisingly cool after the heat of the day. Around us lay a world of broken ground, treeless hills and patches of thorny cactus. The moon rose fat and fair, its pale light banished by the crimson glow of our campfire.

After a hearty supper of strong coffee, salt pork, and sourdough bread, we sat around the fire and I wondered where Wes had hidden the Colt I'd given him.

Only later did I discover that he'd tied it under his arm and then covered the big revolver with his shirt and coat.

Stakes had untied Wes's legs, and it caused considerable merriment in Jim Smalley. "Here now, Hardin," he said, staring at Wes over the rim of his coffee cup. "How far do you think you'd get if you stood up and made a break for it?"

Before Wes could make any kind of answer, Stakes grinned and said, "One step, Jim. I'd gun him for sure."

"Well, E.T., I think I'd let him run for a spell and then go after him. Make it a chase, like."

Stakes nodded. "It would be good sport."

"I won't run," Wes said. "All I ever did was try to obey the law. I'm in great fear that the kin of the men I killed in fair fights will lay for us on the trail and try to do for me."

"Don't worry about that," Smalley said. "We'll protect you, young feller. I mean, we want to watch you hang in Waco, hear that *snap!* when your neck gets broke."

Stakes cackled. "Hell, Jim, it won't be like that." He made a pantomime of a hanging man, his tongue lolling out of his mouth as he made horrible strangling sounds.

Then he smiled. "They don't break necks in Waco. It's too quick and robs the folks of a show."

"I say, Hardin," Smalley said, "when you're standing there on the gallows, piss and crap running down your legs, and the hangman asks if you've got any last words, here's what you say. 'Fancy whores and strong drink led me to this pass, but I had a good mother.'"

Stakes grinned. "You're right, Jim. The women love that."

"I don't want to hang," Wes said, his voice a scared whine. Then, I swear, he squeezed out a single tear that trickled down his cheek like a raindrop. "This will break my poor mother's heart."

"Aw, that's a shame, ain't it, E.T.?" Smalley said. "Even this piece of garbage, the lowest of the low, has a mother."

"Please don't let them hang me," Wes pleaded, his red-eyes fixed on Stakes. "I'm so afraid, Mr. Stakes."

"Sure, sure, kid," the lawman said. "I'll see what I can do."

Smalley almost choked as he suppressed a giggle.

I remember sitting there in the chill of the night, the steel brace cold against the skin of my wasted leg, thinking that even the most naïve circuit preacher would have more sense than the two fools mocking John Wesley Hardin. The preacher would know all too well that it's dangerous to tease the devil.

As most of you will recall, winter came early that year of 1871, and by the time we reached the Sabine River we all shivered with cold.

The lawmen, taking no chances, lashed Wes's feet under his pony again and placed him in the middle of the procession as we prepared to cross the swollen waters.

Wes, playing his role of terrified youngster to the hilt, rambled on about death and life everlasting, and when we were midway across he even launched loudly and tunelessly into a grand old hymn.

> "Shall we gather at the river,
> Where bright angel feet have trod,
> With its crystal tide forever
> Flowing by the throne of God?"

"Shut the hell up," Smalley yelled. His horse had stumbled and plunged him underwater and he was soaked to the skin and mad as a rained-on rooster.

"Sorry, Mr. Smalley," Wes said. "As I get nearer to

judgment and death, I feel a need for the comfort of religion."

"Wail that damn song again, and you'll be a sight closer to death than you think," Smalley said.

Wes grinned but said nothing. Taking my cue from him, I also kept my mouth shut.

By the time we reached the far bank of the Sabine we were all frozen and wet, but we rode for two more miles before Stakes called a halt and told us to dismount and prepare a camp.

There was a ramshackle ranch house in the distance, but Stakes said he wouldn't ask for shelter, since the rancher was likely to be kin of his prisoner. "Go ask him if we can borry an axe, and then chop up some kindling," he told me. "Be quick. It's damn cold and we need a fire."

I did as I was told, but when I reached the gate to the property I quickly drew rein.

A sign on the gate, badly printed with a brush and tar, warned:

SHARPS .50 RANGED ON GATE.

And under that, in a neater hand was *There's a hell of a lot of shooting going on around here.*

Stakes' fears were justified. I figured the rancher must be kin of Wes's, right enough.

I opened the gate, made sure to close it, and then rode at a walk toward the ranch house, expecting a bullet at any time.

The wind was cold and bladed through my soggy rags like a razor. The sky was grim, gray as slate, and under that gloomy tyrant the surrounding pines rustled and bowed, as though paying quaking homage.

I was yet ten yards from the house when the door threw open on its rawhide hinges and a one-legged man with a crutch under his armpit and a Sharps in his hands stepped outside.

"Stay right where you are." He was a large, heavy man, his face a brown triangle almost hidden behind a beard and unkempt mane of black hair. His eyes were blue and hostile. "I got a possum in the pot, coffee on the bile, but none o' that's fer you, on account of how I only got enough for my ownself. So ride on. There's no grub here."

Then, to make sure I got the point, he said, "This here rifle gun is both wife and child to me. Just so you know."

I was scared, but I told him that a party of well-armed and determined state police and likely a town constable were camped to the west of his spread and needed to borrow an axe to cut kindling. Then I dropped John Wesley's name, but the rancher seemed unimpressed.

After a moment's thought, he said, "There's an axe in the woodshed over yonder. When you bring it back, leave it at the gate."

He turned, stepped inside, and slammed the door shut on me.

Now, I'm sure the man had lost his leg in the war fighting for the Noble Cause, so I didn't fault him for his lack of hospitality then or now.

But he was a mean old cuss and no mistake. And not a one for sharing.

* * *

After I cooked supper, we huddled around the fire and gradually our clothes dried.

Smalley continued to tease Wes, describing the marks on a man's neck after he'd been hung with a hemp rope, and how long it took for the condemned to strangle to death . . . vicious, cruel stuff like that.

For his part, John Wesley stayed silent, although every now and then he forced out a tear and muttered the prayers he'd learned at his mother's knee.

But often I saw him glance sidelong at the lawmen. Then his eyes glittered in the firelight and his teeth gleamed, like a cougar anticipating a killing spree.

And they didn't see it! Idiots!

Those two fools Stakes and Smalley saw only what they wanted to see, and that was a boy demented by terror over the thought of a cruel death on the gallows.

Indeed, the fool does not see the same peril as the wise man, and there's truth.

The next day, we ferried across the muddy, sluggish Trinity then rode north into swamp country that was foreign and forbidding.

Gradually the pines, post oak, and black hickory of our own soil gave way to bald cypress, water tupelo, and shrubs like swamp privet and water elm.

The going across the wet country was exhausting and I felt sick. My face and hands were covered in insect bites. To my surprise Wes made no move, even when we were within a few miles of Waco.

Overtaken by darkness and used up, Stakes halted and we made camp.

He left to obtain fodder for the horses and cornmeal

from one of the surrounding farmers, if such could be found in the wilderness. "Keep a close eye on Hardin, Jim," he said from the saddle. "He's scared and he might bolt."

"If he does, he's a dead man," Smalley said. "Depend on it."

Then Stakes said something strange that really upset me. "Hold up on the shooting until I get back. We've got to be in it together, mind."

Smalley smiled and nodded. "He'll keep, E.T."

Stakes' eyes and mine met, tangled, and what I saw in his cold, penetrating gaze chilled me to the bone.

He meant to murder Wes.

Soon.

That very night.

CHAPTER ELEVEN
Gut Shot

With no moon the sky was dark as printer's ink. Such breeze as there was came chill from the north and carried with it the musty smell of muck and of the swamp pools where lime green frogs jumped.

Jim Smalley sat on the sawn trunk of a tree, his grin malicious. "Not long now, huh, Hardin? I mean the noose a snotty-nosed killer like you so richly deserves."

"Please don't chide me, Mr. Smalley," Wes said, his voice breaking.

I added a few sticks to the fire, then said, "Leave him be. The man is scared enough."

With deliberate slowness, the lawman turned his head to me. "Another word out of you, gimp, and I'll put a bullet in you." His lip twisted. "Who's gonna miss a damned raggedy-assed pauper like you. Me?" He nodded is Wes's direction. "Him? Anybody?"

I said nothing, and Smalley stared at me for a few moments, and then said, "From now until we reach Waco, keep your ignorant trap shut."

He again directed his attention to Wes. "Hey,

Hardin, we haven't even talked about your burying yet." He smiled. "How remiss of me. I mean, a famous shootist like you doesn't want to go under the ground in any old pine box. How about a mahogany casket with a nice glass window so you can see the worms come for you?"

Wes had been squatting by the fire. He rose to his feet and sobbed, "I can't stand this anymore." He stumbled to the mustang and buried his face in the animal's neck, his shoulders heaving as he sobbed.

Smalley's derisive laughter followed him. "Hell, boy, leave the caterwauling for the gallows," he yelled as he slapped his leg, enjoying himself.

John Wesley turned, a gun in his hand and a grin on his face.

And in that awful moment, Constable Jim Smalley knew he was a dead man.

He spiked a terrified, "No!" Then jumped to his feet as his hand dropped to his gun.

He never made it. Didn't even make it halfway.

John Wesley's ball hit the lawman in the belly.

Shock, pain, and the realization that he'd suffered a death wound, slowed Smalley. He took a step back, tried to complete the draw, but suddenly found the Colt was too heavy to drag from the leather.

The revolver tumbled out of his hand and Smalley went to his knees, his eyes on Wes. "Kill me, damn you. I'm gut shot."

Wes grinned. "Hell, I know that, Jim. I aimed for your belly."

Smalley had seen gut shot men before. He knew he had only a few words left in him before the worst waves of pain hit and then all he'd be able to do was scream.

"How did you hide the damn—"

"I've been there before, Jim." Wes smiled. "I'm too old a cat to be played with by a kitten."

"Then get it over, damn you," Smalley said.

"We've got time." Wes's hard mouth stretched in a grin. "I know, I'll sing you a song, help you on your way, like. Hey, Jim boy, do you know this one?"

> *"As I walked out in the streets of Laredo,*
> *As I walked out in Laredo one day,*
> *I spied a young cowboy wrapped up in white linen,*
> *Wrapped in white linen and cold as the clay."*

Wes took a knee beside Smalley, who was lying on his back, groaning in pain, his teeth bared in a grotesque grimace.

"Here's the darlin' part, Jim," Wes said.

> *"Oh beat the drum slowly and play the fife lowly,*
> *Play the Dead March as you carry me along.*
> *Take me to the green valley and lay the sod o'er me,*
> *For I am a young cowboy and I know I've done*
>   *wrong."*

Wes scowled as he rose to his feet, his eyes savage. "Damn you, Jim. You don't like my song. I can see it in your face. Well, you don't know dung from honey, so be damned to ye for an ungrateful wretch."

He raised his boot and brought it down fast and hard onto Smalley's bloody belly.

The lawman shrieked, horribly, loudly, like a

damned soul that's just been thrown into the lowest pit of Hell.

Wes had to raise his voice to make himself heard. "It ain't my fault, Little Bit. He would've done the same to me."

I grabbed a burning stick from beside the fire and advanced on John Wesley. "Damn it all, Wes. End his suffering and do it now."

Wes looked at me and smiled. "Oh, all right. On account of how you look right scary holding that there twig. Well, good night, Jimmy boy." And without seeming to even glance at Smalley, Wes casually shot him between the eyes.

The screams stopped. But the racketing echoes of the gunshot seemed to go on and on forever.

"There," Wes said. "Happy now?"

"Yes," I said, my voice flat. "Happy now."

Wes was silent for a while, then he said, "The gun has a bad cylinder. It shoots low. That's why I gut shot him."

"Is that what it was?"

"Yeah, that's what it was. Smalley sassed me all the time, made me feel bad. He was borrowing trouble."

"He surely was. Borrowing trouble, all right." I didn't mention the brutal kick to the dying man's belly and neither did Wes.

But I was sick inside and disappointed, though that's an inadequate word to describe how I felt. *Betrayed*. Yes, that's a better way to put it.

Wes had betrayed my trust in him. I'd always known he was reckless, vengeful sometimes, and too quick to shoot.

But I'd never known him to be purposely cruel.

Until then.

Kicking Smalley had been a wanton, barbarous act and it instilled fear in me. I dreaded that John Wesley might become a monster.

If he wasn't one already.

Wes saddled Smalley's sorrel horse then turned to me. "Should we wait for Stakes to get back?"

"No. Best we get the hell out of here."

Was gave me his petulant look. "He sassed me, Little Bit. Just like Jimmy boy did."

"I know. But Stakes is a state policeman, Wes. Chances are you'll run into him again."

John Wesley brightened at that. "Yeah, you're right. Hell, he might come back here with a bunch of sodbusters."

"Maybe so." To flatter him, I added, "Sodbusters are a real probability. A lot of folks want to shake the hand of John Wesley Hardin."

Wes took the compliment with a smile. "And I ain't near done with my shootist career or started in on my Wild West show yet."

He swung into the saddle, gave Smalley's body an indifferent glance, then grinned. "Damn it all. I'm gonna charge through life at a gallop and be a great man." His blue eyes glowed in the gloom as I kneed my horse beside his. "Ain't that right, Little Bit?"

And me, weak, craven creature that I was, once again hitched my wagon to my friend's malevolent star. "The greatest."

CHAPTER TWELVE
A Strange Encounter

A wise man once said that fate is the friend of the good and the enemy of the bad. Looking back, I can only conclude that he was right.

We were destined to make a clean escape, and we did.

Wes was determined to head south through friendly country and visit with his mother and father who were residing in Mount Calm, a tiny hamlet struggling for life at the ragged edge of nowhere.

We rode through the dark of night, constantly checking our back trail for any sign of pursuit. There was none and that pleased Wes enormously.

"Ned Stakes' hoss was tuckered. He won't come after us until first light, if he comes at all." Wes drew rein, then kneed his horse close to mine. "Here's what we'll do. We'll lie low for a spell, eat Ma's good home cooking and grow fat and sassy. Maybe even spark a girl, if there's any to be found in Mount Calm. Once everything blows over, I'll get back to organizing my Wild West show."

Of course, Wes hadn't organized anything so far, but I wasn't about to pop his bubble.

"I can get started on the business proposal for Sam Luck," I said. "Seems to me all we'll have at Mount Calm is time."

Wes was far away, staring through the tree canopy at the black sky with nary a star in sight. He turned his head to me. "What did you say, Little Bit?"

"I said I should draw up the business proposal for Sam Luck."

Wes nodded. "Yeah, you do that. Good idea."

I hesitated before I spoke my mind, but asked finally, "Wes, you sure your folks will make us welcome?"

"Of course they'll make us welcome." He reached into his coat pocket and produced a crumpled scrap of paper. "This is the last letter I got from Ma. Well, a piece of it. I tore off and kept the good part."

He passed the paper to me and I glanced at the small, crabbed handwriting. "It's too dark for me to read it, Wes."

"No matter. I know it off by heart, memorized it, like." He turned his face to the sky again. "Come quickly, Johnny. If you are in Pisgah, come. If you are in Groveton, come. Return home to Ma. I want to tell you so many things and see your sweet face, ere long. Come home, my own John. Come home, Johnny."

Wes dashed away a tear with the back of his hand. "Damn, but that's purty. Ain't it, Little Bit?"

"Sure is. I reckon your ma wants you to settle down."

Wes nodded. "She does, but it's way too early for that. I'll walk a wide path before I'm done."

We let the horses pick their way, and they led us

onto a narrow lane between the pines. It was still dark, but ahead of us we saw the glow of lanterns.

I thought it might be a cow outfit rounding up mavericks in the brush and said so to Wes.

"Could be. But it also might be lawmen or the army."

I pulled up my tired horse. "Do we ride around them?"

"We'll dismount and get closer. See what we can see," Wes said.

We swung out of the saddle and walked our horses, always a chore for me on uneven ground. After a couple minutes, I heard a woman's laugh, followed by the bellowing roar of a man.

"Doesn't sound like lawmen or the army, either," I said.

Wes had close-seeing eyes and after he peered into the darkness, he said, "Damn it all. I can't see a thing."

"Let's get closer," I said.

Wes had Smalley's Colt butt forward in his waistband and he adjusted the big revolver for a fast draw. "Little Bit, you see anything that suggests lawmen, holler out I'll cut loose and then we'll ride back the way we came."

I said that sounded just fine with me and we walked on.

The path, no more than a sliver of game trail, led though a pine and brush thicket, then into an open area dominated by the skeleton of a lighting-struck tree that lifted skinny white arms to the dark sky.

After maybe fifty paces, I made out a large wall tent in the distance and next to that a canvas lean-to. The silhouettes of men and a couple women moved back and forth in front of the fire. Beyond the camp, barely visible in the gloom, a parked covered wagon had its tongue raised. Nearby, a tethered mule team stood in a hipshot row.

"Well, what do you see?" Wes sounded on edge.

"Men and women. Travellers more than likely."

"I could use a cup of coffee and some grub," Wes said.

"Then we'll go visiting. It seems safe enough to me."

"We're a pair of drifting farm boys looking for work. Got that?"

"I got it." I led my horse forward and when I was within hailing distance, I yelled, "Hello the camp!"

The answer came immediately. A man yelled, "Good-bye your ownself. Come on out."

"Welcoming folks," I said. "Ain't they?"

Wes said nothing, but I could tell from the stiff, alert set of his head and shoulders that he was wound up tight as a clock spring.

As we drew closer, a man who looked big in the darkness stepped forward and said, "Are ye frontwards or are ye backwards?"

I'd no idea what the man was talking about, but I took a shot in the dark. "We have good mothers."

It took a while for the big man to understand the implications of my answer, but when he did, he said, "Then advance and be recognized, friend." Another pause, then, "If ye'd said ye were frontward there would have been no welcome for you at our fire."

Beside me I heard Wes groan or growl. To this day, I still can't figure the right of it.

The big man walked out to meet us and made a great show of waving us into camp, like St. Peter ushering the righteous through the Pearly Gates.

He was dressed in black broadcloth. Under that he wore a white collarless shirt, mighty yellow and stained. His hat was low-crowned and flat-brimmed, his face wide, fair, and handsome.

The two men with him were clothed in the same fashion and all three were close enough in looks to be brothers.

I guessed that the two women were wives, thin, severe, and modestly attired in black dresses with white at the collars and cuffs.

One of the women smiled at me and said, "Goodbye."

"Indeed," the big man said. "Sleep, put your horses up, and then have coffee."

The other men stepped forward, smiled, and shook hands with us. "Good-bye," they said. "Come again some time."

Wes gave me a sidelong look and I noticed that his thumb was hooked into his waistband, close to the Colt.

"My name is Isaac," the big man said. "And these are my brothers Charley and Milton." He bowed as he introduced the women. "My dear wives Goldie and Estelle."

"Right pleased to meet you, an' no mistake." I figured these folks were tetched in the head.

More so when the man called Isaac said, "After you sleep, we'll teach the word to you about the Contrarians and our faith."

"I could use a cup of coffee," Wes said.

"Yes, yes, of course," Isaac said. "But that comes sooner."

Now, I don't know why I thought I could engage in

polite conversation with a man with loco camped out in his eyeballs, but so help me I tried.

"Where are you folks from?" I said.

"Ah, we're headed south for the Oklahoma Territory," Isaac said.

"That's north," Wes said.

Isaac's kin giggled as he said, "Why, of course it is. Very well said, young man. You see, because Oklahoma is north, we're going south." He smiled like a benign favorite uncle. "That is the Contrarian way."

"But you'll never get there," I said.

"But we will," Isaac said. "The good Lord will show us a road."

The woman called Estelle, a pretty young blonde with smoke gray eyes and a small, prim mouth, decided to do some preachifying. "Although it can be very difficult at times—or should that be easy?— we Contrarians live backward."

"Oh, yes, very, very difficult," Isaac said, shaking his head. "And there I state the case dishonestly."

"We sleep during the day and go about our business at night," Estelle said. "We eat dinner as our first meal, and breakfast for our last. But that is just some of the simpler, back-to-front things we do."

"We even tried walking backward," one of the brothers said. "But Charley stepped into a gopher hole and broke his ankle, and Isaac said that such means of locomotion was too dangerous, so now we desist from that."

Wes had been listening with the utmost interest as he studied Estelle's small, high breasts. "Why the hell do you live backward?"

This occasioned another burst of laughter, then

Isaac said, "Well, you see, by living backward we won't be a day older tomorrow, we'll be a day younger."

"And eventually," Estelle said, "we'll become children again."

"Why do you want that?" I asked.

"To enter the kingdom of heaven, of course," Isaac said.

Estelle warmed to her subject. "In the Gospel of Matthew, chapter eighteen, verse three, Jesus says, 'I tell you the truth, unless you change and become like little children, you will never enter the kingdom of heaven.'"

"And that in a nutshell, boiled down, in brief, is the very basis of our Contrarian faith," Isaac said. "To enter Heaven, we must retrace our steps through life, go backward and become little children again."

The woman named Goldie, who had remained silent, tilted back her head and yelled, "Backward is forward, forward is backward! Hallelujah!"

"Amen, sister, amen!" Isaac said, his arms spread wide.

He turned to me. "Years ago, in my wild youth, I was smitten with a dread disease, given to me by one of the fallen women of the town. One night, after even the mercury cure failed, I prayed that God would cure me, and I heard his voice in my head say, 'Live backward, Isaac. Become a child again.'"

"Hallelujah!" Goldie yelled.

"When I woke up the next morning, I was free of the disease," Isaac said. "And that was when I became the first Contrarian."

"Hallelujah!" Goldie yelled again.

"We don't want you to join us to share in Isaac's miracle," Estelle said.

"That's fine, we won't," Wes said.

"Hallelujah!" Goldie exclaimed. "That means you will."

"No, it means we won't," Wes said.

Now, I don't know how this unreal conversation would have ended, probably with Wes shooting somebody, but the flat report of a rifle shot shattered the shadowed night . . . and we were again in a heap of trouble.

CHAPTER THIRTEEN
A Terrible Fright

A V of dirt spurted between John Wesley's legs, then, over the rack of a Henry rifle, a man's voice said. "Don't make a move, Hardin. I can drop you from here real easy."

Without turning his head, Wes said. "How many, Little Bit?"

I glanced briefly behind me. "Three that I can see. Two shotguns."

"They got the drop on me."

"Seems like."

Feet pounded behind me and a man pushed me aside, so roughly that I stumbled and fell.

Wes cursed and rounded on the man, his hand reaching for his gun.

Too late!

The walnut stock of the Henry swung and crashed into the side of Wes's jaw. He went down in a heap and lay still.

The man who'd pushed me and hit Wes raised his

rifle, covering the people around the fire. "You folks kin of his?"

"Yes we are," Isaac said.

"Then I'm arresting you all on the charge of harboring a fugitive from justice," the man said. "There's an eleven hundred dollar reward on this man's head."

From the ground, I said, "They're Contrarians."

The man glanced at me. He had a huge, hooked nose and under it his gray mustache looked like the bow wave of a steamer. "What the hell does that mean?"

"They live backward and say the opposite of what they mean. They're no kin of Wes's."

The man looked confused.

I explained. "We rode into their camp looking for coffee."

"You wouldn't lie to me, boy, would you?" the man said.

I shook my head. "Not about them, I wouldn't. They're all crazy."

Wes groaned and the man leaned over and relieved him of his revolver. "I'm Constable Chance Smith." He nodded to the bearded men with him. "Constables Davis and Jones."

I struggled to my feet.

Smith stared at me, measuring me. "Ned Stakes told me you're harmless, youngster. Looking at you, I'd say he was right." He turned to one of the other lawmen. "Search him. I'd still like to know where Hardin got the gun he shot Jim Smalley with." The constable shook his head as he stepped toward me. "He was mean as a snake in your drink."

After patting me down, the lawman said, "He's clean."

"Good, now you and Davis get Hardin on his feet," Smith said. Then, as though he thought he owed Isaac and his crazy kin an explanation, he said, "We're taking this man to Austin where he'll get a fair trial and then be hung."

Isaac shook his head, and the two women looked distressed.

"No, that is not right," Estelle said. "You're doing that all wrong."

"You got something agin hanging, lady?" Smith asked.

"She means it's not the Contrarian way," Isaac said. "A man should be hung and then tried."

Smith pulled a long-suffering face then nodded. "Whatever you say, mister."

He pushed Wes toward his horse. "Mount up. We're riding." He gave me a hard look. "You too, runt. Hell, I never hung a dwarf with a tin leg afore, but there's a first time for everything, I guess."

As we rode through the darkness, the three lawmen passed a bottle back and forth. They seemed to be in good spirits, maybe because of the eleven hundred dollars reward posted by Hill County for John Wesley's apprehension.

After an hour, more than slightly drunk, Chance Smith declared that he could go no farther and needed some shut-eye. After some coffee, he'd take the first watch, Davis the second, and Jones the third.

Wes was ordered to sit across the fire from Smith with his back against a pine.

"I see you even bat an eyelid, I'll blow a hole in you with this here scattergun," he said. "You understand that, huh?"

Wes, perhaps tired of playing the scared youngster, said nothing. He leaned the back of his head against the tree trunk and pretended to sleep.

Smith motioned with his shotgun and indicated that I should sit next to Wes. "One barrel of buck each if you and your friend suddenly feel ambitious. You catching my drift, runt?"

"I ain't planning to do nothing but sleep," I said.

Smith nodded. "Sleeping your life away, boy. If I was fixin' to get hung, I'd try to stay awake as much as I could." He smiled. "Savor the moment, you might say."

The lawman took another swig from the bottle then lifted his head. "You smell it, boy?"

"Smell what?" I said.

"There's death in the wind."

"I don't smell it."

Smith ignored that because, half drunk, he was talking to himself, not me.

"Smelled it once before, on the night afore the Battle of Champion Hill. Death walked through our camp and then ol' General John C. Pemberton ran around the tents asking everybody he met, 'What's that smell, boys? What's that accursed smell?'"

Smith drank from the bottle and wiped off his mustache with the back of his hand. "The next day Grant and his Army of the Tennessee kicked our asses and piled our Confederate dead in heaps as high as a man." His eyes sought mine in the darkness. "It was a great battle and the field of honor stank like a charnel house. It was the smell I'd smelled the night afore, the smell I smell now. Death just took a stroll through our camp, boy. But whose death?" He smiled. "Not mine, so maybe yours, huh? Or Hardin's."

Beside me, I became aware that Wes's eyes were half open, studying Jones and Davis who, overcome by alcohol, were sound asleep. His eyes slanted under his lids, fixing the location of the lawmen's weapons.

Behind the glow of the crackling fire, Smith laid his shotgun across his knees and sang softly to himself.

> *"O, I'm a good ol' Rebel,*
> *Now that's just what I am.*
> *For this 'Fair Land of Freedom',*
> *I do not care at all."*

Wes watched the lawman with wolf eyes.

> *"I'm glad I fit against it,*
> *I only wish we'd won,*
> *And I don't want no pardon*
> *For anything I done."*

Smith's head dropped on his chest and he jerked awake.

Wes tensed . . . a young man-eater getting ready to spring.

The lawman took another swig and sang again.

> *"I hates the glorious Union,*
> *'Tis dripping with our blood—"*

Smith's voice faded. His head bobbed, lower . . . lower. . . .

> *"I hates their stripèd banner,*
> *I fit . . . it . . . all . . . I . . . could. . . ."*

The lawman's voice ebbed . . . died away . . . grew silent. . . .

He snored softly.

And John Wesley Hardin descended upon him like the wrath of God.

Wes carefully lifted the shotgun from Smith's lap, then stepped to the sleeping constables and grabbed Davis's Colt.

He returned to Smith and let the snoring man have both barrels in the face.

Smith, his head practically blown off his shoulders, died without making a sound.

Davis and Jones woke and sat up. Davis yelled, "What the hell is happening?"

Expertly working the Colt, Wes thumbed two shots into him.

Davis screamed and fell back, sudden blood staining his mouth.

Jones, the youngest of the three, threw off his blankets and scrambled to his feet.

"For pity's sake, don't shoot me," he called out. "I have a pregnant wife and a three young'uns at home."

Wes hesitated, and I thought for a moment he felt inclined to show the young lawman mercy.

How foolish I was. How unspeakably stupid.

The concept of mercy was as alien to John Wesley as sin is to a cloistered monk. He smiled, then shot the crying, sobbing Jones between the eyes. Standing in the red glow of the firelight, gun smoke drifting around him, Wes looked like the devil incarnate.

At the time I said nothing. Nothing at all.

He turned to me then, his face like stone, his eyes lost in pools of darkness . . . and he pointed his *murderous revolver* at my head.

Sweet Christ save me! I stood transfixed, terrified to move.

John Wesley smiled. "Did you think I'd shoot you, Little Bit?"

"I don't know."

"I don't know either. Maybe I would. Maybe if you did me wrong I'd gut shoot you."

"I would never wrong you. I'm your friend."

Wes waved the Colt around the clearing. "Was this my fault?"

Fearing for my life I didn't hesitate. "No, Wes, not your fault. Smith said he smelled death. He said death walked through our camp."

"He was right."

"Wes, quit smiling like that and put the gun away," I said. "You're scaring the hell out of me."

He did neither.

"I smelled it too, Little Bit. Death walked close to

me and it looked like a column of black mist and stank like a rotting thing. I've seen it before, you know. Sometimes it watches me and says nothing. It just stares and stares with its cold eyes."

Now I was really boogered. I stood there and pissed myself. Warm urine streamed down my legs and trickled onto the toes of my shoes.

"It wasn't my fault. They should never have arrested me." Then, like a man suddenly waking from a trance, Wes grinned and let the Colt drop to his side.

"Little Bit, how come you just pissed all over yourself?"

CHAPTER FOURTEEN
A Grieving Father

John Wesley armed himself with a brace of revolvers he took from the dead men, but he decided to leave their horses behind, as they'd attract too much attention to us.

We stuck to our original plan to stay with his folks in Mount Calm where we'd be safe and welcome and took to the trail at first light.

I must admit that I rode with a heavy heart, the deaths of the three constables, especially Jones, weighing on me. And consider this—the death of Smith put paid to the lie that Wes would not pull the trigger on a man who'd worn the gray. He knew Smith had been at Champion Hill, heard him say so, yet he blew off his head with a shotgun.

Need I say more?

And one more thing . . . I'm often asked how many men Wes had killed after he dispatched the three constables. I've heard it suggested that he'd killed one man for every year of his life; like that Billy Bonney kid did later, up New Mexico way.

Wes was seventeen when he gunned Smith, Davis and Jones, and by then I reckoned he was creepin' up on Bonney's twenty-one.

Some folks will tell you different.

But, hell, I know better because I was there.

Mount Calm lay in the middle of the east Texas hill country. A store, a school, and a handful of whitewashed houses were splattered across flat, sandy ground like spilled milk.

Wes said there was talk of the railroad laying a spur to the place, but nobody, including his pa, put any stock in that.

James Gibson Hardin was a tall, slender man, a Methodist minister by profession, who bore, I fancied, a resemblance to the great Jefferson Davis of blessed memory. The Reverend Hardin didn't exactly welcome his prodigal son with open arms, but neither did he send him away.

In contrast, Wes's mother, Mary Elizabeth, an attractive, stiff-backed woman, showered kisses on her son and called him, "My golden boy," and "My dearest Johnny."

After remarking how thin Wes had become, she hurried into the kitchen and left her husband with Wes and me in the parlor.

"Three state constables, you say, John?" Rev. Hardin's face was pale as death, his high, intelligent forehead wrinkled with emotion.

"It wasn't my fault, Pa," Wes said.

"It never is, John."

"They were damned Yankees and they arrested me

only because I was a Texas boy. Said they were going to torture me and then see me hang." Wes looked at me, his eyes pleading. "Ain't that right, Little Bit? Weren't they taking me to the gallows?"

I remembered Smith, who'd fought for the Cause, and I didn't answer right away.

The Rev. Hardin noted my hesitation and said, "Don't bring Little Bit into your lies, John. The Bible says, 'Thou shalt not kill.' If I am to believe what I hear, you've already broken that dictate a score of times."

"I was defending myself, Pa. The Yankees hate me and want to see me dead. It's not my fault."

"Son, you're a liar and a killer," the elder Hardin said. "I fear that there is no place for you in God's heart." He paused for just a moment. "Or in mine."

Mary Elizabeth opened the door and stuck her head into the parlor. "Johnny dear, roast beef and taters on the table, and plenty of it."

She glanced at me and I saw that she was trying to be cheerful, even charming, I guess, but the strain in her blue eyes and the deepening lines on her face betrayed her true feelings. "You too, Little Bit. You need some weight on those skinny bones."

Mary Elizabeth had been listening at the door. That much was obvious, and she'd been wounded by what she'd heard.

The meal was awkward to say the least—silent, like a wake for dead kin. But I ate heartily, by no means sure where my next grub might come from.

Mary Elizabeth tried, God bless her. She and the reverend had ten children together, though two had died young, and she chatted about the family and what they were doing.

But her husband's silence and John Wesley's slow-simmering anger was not conducive to polite conversation. Even when Wes mentioned his plan for a Wild West show, though his mother clapped loudly and declared, "How wonderful!" it was greeted by a stony silence from his father.

When the tense meal was over, the Rev. Hardin lit a cigar. "John, I've been thinking things over and have asked the Good Lord for guidance. I want you to go to Old Mexico and remain there for—"

"How long?" Wes interrupted, astonished.

"I don't know. Years maybe."

"The Yankees never forget, Pa, They're mighty long on hatreds and short on forgiveness."

"As we Texans are ourselves," the reverend said.

"What the hell will I do in Mexico?" Wes asked.

"No profanity, John, please," the reverend said, speaking behind a cloud of curling blue smoke. "Find honest work, I suppose."

"As a laborer?" Wes said.

"If that's all you can do, then yes, that's the kind of work you must find."

Wes sprang to his feet, his eyes blazing. "I'd die before I'd blister my hands on a damned shovel."

"The boy is right, James," Mary Elizabeth said. "Johnny's delicate constitution is not suited to the laborer's trade."

"Then what is he suited for, my dear?" the reverend asked carefully.

It was a loaded question, mildly asked, and I awaited Mrs. Hardin's answer with some unease.

She rose to the challenge, exclaiming, "The stage! You heard Johnny say that he wants to put on a show. He has the looks, the poise, and the erudition to become a fine actor. Why, he might even perform in Shakespeare like the noble Booth brothers."

She dragged me into the talk. "Is that not so, Little Bit?"

I hedged. "It's a Wild West show, ma'am."

"Yes, and a most singular idea it is," Mrs. Hardin said. She raised her pretty eyes to her son. "You'll be very good at it, Johnny, and, I declare, become rich and famous quicker than . . . well, quicker 'n scat!"

Before Wes could speak, his father rubbed his forehead and said, "I grow weary, Mary Elizabeth. I will retire to my study, reacquaint myself with Holy Scripture then seek my bed early."

He rose to his feet. "John, Little Bit, there's a zinc bathtub out back. I strongly suggest you both use it."

"And I have a fresh bar of Pears soap all the way from England," Mrs. Hardin said. "I know how delicate your skin is, Johnny, dear."

CHAPTER FIFTEEN
Unwelcome News

The next morning at breakfast, the Reverend Hardin said that John Wesley and I could stay with him for a couple days before leaving for Mexico. Wes said nothing, but I saw by the expression on his face that he was unhappy with this arrangement.

Everything changed early the next day when a man named Crow Duplin knocked at the door and was admitted by the Hardin maidservant, then ushered into the parlor where we all were.

I figured that Duplin got his name from the black crow feathers he wore in the band of his gray kepi. He had a long, sad face and eyes so saggy his bottom eyelids showed red rims.

The Rev. Hardin said, "Well, Crow, what errand brings you to my home so early in the morning?" Belatedly, he introduced us. "My son John you know, and this is his friend Little Bit."

"Pleased to make your acquaintance, I'm sure," Crow said.

I'd thought him a Texan, but he spoke with a strong English accent. He grinned, revealing few teeth and those black, and pumped my hand with the greatest show of affection.

"In answer to your question, Reverend," Crow said, "I'm on a mission of the greatest moment, and it concerns young Master Hardin, here present, and those who would do him great bodily harm."

Crow grabbed my hand again and pumped that already punished extremity even harder. "Howdy do?" He grinned wider than before. "This is indeed a plumbed and squared pleasure."

"Likewise, I'm sure," I said, withdrawing my crumpled fingers.

"Before we hear what you have to say, can I offer you coffee, Mr. Duplin?" Mary Elizabeth said.

Crow bowed with all the flair of an Elizabethan courtier. "Now, as to that question, dear lady, if I say no, you may think me an ungrateful wretch. But if I answer yes, then I fear I may put you to the greatest inconvenience."

"It's no trouble at all," Mary Elizabeth said. "I'll bring you a cup directly." Her gray morning dress rustled as she turned and headed for the kitchen.

"Let's hear your news, Crow." Wes seemed quite unconcerned, nibbling on a corner of toast left over from breakfast.

"And there it is in a nutshell," Crow said. "A forthright question from a forthright youth. And I will answer it honestly and in full. Duplin by name, Duplin by nature, I always say."

"Proceed, Crow," the Rev. Hardin said, a tinge of impatience in his voice.

"And proceed I will, with the greatest dispatch." Crow bowed low, then accepted a cup from Mary Elizabeth "I was a-sitting in my cabin with the missus, discussin' our hard times like, and me sayin' that I was much afeerd of more coming down—"

As though she felt the need to explain Crow's straitened circumstances, Mrs. Hardin interrupted. "Mr. Duplin has twelve children, Little Bit, and, unfortunately, most of them are simple."

"All of them, dear lady, except for little Nancy," Crow said after a sip of coffee. "She's as smart as a whip, that young 'un."

Wes and his father exchanged irritated glances, and the reverend said, "So, Crow, you were sitting in your cabin, and . . ."

"And Mrs. Duplin, bless 'er heart, happened to glance out the window, and what does she see?" Crow waited expectantly.

Wes snapped, "Tell us."

"Sojers! Blue coat sojers!"

The Rev. Hardin was much taken aback by this intelligence and displayed the utmost agitation as he exclaimed, "Soldiers? Here in Mount Calm?"

"Yankee sojers as ever was." Crow bowed as Mrs. Hardin took his cup. "A score of black cavalry and a white officer."

In her sudden anguish, Mary Elizabeth dropped the cup and it smashed on the wood floor. She ran to Wes and threw her arms around his neck. "My poor Johnny, the God's cursed Yankees are after you."

"Indeed they are, ma'am," Crow said. "Upon my inquiring as to their presence in our little town, the officer said, 'We're hunting a damned scoundrel, traitor, and murderer by the name of John Wesley Hardin. Have you seen him?'" Crow wrung his hands in agitation. "When I said that I hadn't, the officer said, 'Then we'll tear apart every house in Mount Calm until we find the rogue.'"

The Rev. Hardin immediately grasped the seriousness of the situation and cried out, "John, into the root cellar without delay. You too, Little Bit." He quickly reached into his pocket and pressed some money into Crow's hand. "You have done my family a great service."

I thought so too, but Wes seemed to have a different opinion. Despite the considerable amount of money in his pocket, he brushed past Crow without a thank-you.

Not for the first time, I realized that gratitude and generousness were not two of Wes's virtues.

For his part, Crow reached out to take my hand again. But I placed that tormented appendage behind my back, smiled, and tipped him a little bow.

Much pleased by this, Crow himself bowed. "It's been a real treat meeting you, Mr. Little Bit."

"And for me too," I said.

"Quickly now," Rev. Hardin said, grabbing my arm. "There's no time to be lost."

From outside, I heard the thud of hooves and the jingle of cavalry bits. The Yankees were at the door!

CHAPTER SIXTEEN
Across the Rio Grande

To my dying day, I will never understand why the soldiers ransacked the Hardin home, but didn't search the root cellar. Perhaps it was because the underground cellar was small and had not been used in some time, thus its single door was partially overgrown with brush and was difficult to see. Whatever the reason, our hiding place went undiscovered, and Wes and I remained there until dark.

Coyotes yipped in the hills when we heard footfalls approach the cellar.

Wes had retrieved his pistols before we fled from the house and he pointed them at the timber door. He grinned and whispered in my ear, "If a Yankee opens that damned door you're going to see a hell of a fight."

"John Wesley, it's me. Don't shoot." It was the Rev. Hardin's voice. He knew better than to walk up on Wes without being announced.

"Are the Yankees gone?" Wes asked.

"Yes, about an hour ago," his father said. "They did

some damage in the house and your mother got a black eye trying to stop them."

"Open the damned door," Wes said. "I'm going after the one that did it."

"Too late for that, son," Mr. Hardin said. "The Yankees are long gone, and the soldier that struck your mother told his officer that it was an accident."

After the door creaked open on rusty hinges, Wes clambered outside. "Describe him, Pa." His voice was shaking with fury.

"He was a Negro, John, and they all look alike," the reverend said. "How can I describe him, that he was a man with a black skin?"

"Then I'll kill them all," Wes said. "That way I'll be sure of getting the right one."

"Revenge is a dish best served cold, John. It will wait. Your mother wasn't badly hurt and I have other plans for you." The reverend wore a wide-brimmed hat and an oilskin. He carried a new Henry rifle, an odd thing for a man of the cloth.

Drizzling rain slanted in a shivering wind and everywhere around us the lost, lonely land was hidden in darkness.

"Your horses are saddled and I'll escort you as far as the Rio Grande," Mr. Hardin said.

"We don't need an escort," Wes said, his face stiff as a board.

"I know you don't, son. But I want to make sure you do as I told you." The reverend turned his attention to me. "Little Bit, I know you're much attached to novels of the more sensational kind, so I brought you this." He handed me a cloth-bound volume with gilt lettering on the cover.

"It is the historical work, *Quentin Durward*, by the late Sir Walter Scott. I hope you'll find time to enjoy it."

Indeed, I had read the story of dashing young Quentin before.

You will recall that Sir Walter's tale is about a young Scots cavalier in search of honorable adventure. By his senses, firmness, and gallantry, he becomes the fortunate possessor of wealth and rank and then gains the hand of a beautiful lady whose family tree is as noble as his own.

I'd read the work years before (and, oh, how I wanted to be Quentin!) and was eager to reacquaint myself with its entrancing prose. I thanked the Rev. Hardin profusely and put the book under my coat out of the rain, where Quentin Durward's pure heart could beat against mine.

A few minutes later we took the trail to Mexico. Wes was silent and sullen, but his father sat tall and alert in the saddle, his eyes constantly reaching out into the darkness around him.

He needn't have worried.

The rain grew heavier, the wind colder, and no hostile traveller would venture forth on such a night.

We reached the north bank of the Rio Grande at daybreak, under a sky that stretched formless gray as far as the eye could see. The rain had lessened, but the drizzle fell steadily. Having no oilskin, I was thoroughly soaked.

The Reverend Hardin shook my hand and then his son's. "You will be safe in Mexico, John. Lay your guns aside and find good, honest work. Son, take the word of God in Psalms to heart, 'He shall be like a tree planted by the rivers of water that bringeth forth his fruit in his season; its leaf shall not wither; and whatever he doeth shall prosper.'"

The reverend pointed to the Rio Grande where stately wading birds hunted frogs and minnows in the shallows. "There is your river of water, John. All you have to do is cross it and whatever you do will prosper."

Wes took this advice with ill grace. Without another word, he swung his horse away and rode into the river.

The Rev. Hardin said to me, "Little Bit, when you get settled, see that John writes his mother. She does worry about him so."

I nodded. "I will make sure he writes at least once a week."

We shook hands and parted. The Reverend Hardin rode away and did not look back at his son.

My soul was weighed down by a burden I couldn't fathom. Maybe it was the leaden sky, or maybe it was because of the mysteries and dangers of Mexico, then an unknown land to me.

Or maybe, in my heart of hearts, I knew that James Hardin's dreams for his son would never come true.

He was a fine man, the Reverend Hardin, but born to parlous times.

CHAPTER SEVENTEEN
Killings and the Joy of Mescal

The ride south of the border took close to three weeks. We rode hard during the day and camped at night, arriving in October.

The Mexican village lay about three miles south of the river and it wasn't much—modest adobe buildings clustered around a central plaza. A fountain stood in the middle of the square, but it was dry as dust and didn't look like it had run water since the time of the old Spaniards.

But there was a cantina with a blue coyote painted on the outside wall. The smoke that rose from its chimney smelled of mesquite and the tang of fried beef.

Until then, John Wesley had been silent since we crossed the border. "I could sure use some breakfast."

"I'm feeling sharp set my ownself," I said.

"Then let's eat."

Four other horses already stood at the cantina's

hitching post when we dismounted. That surprised me because their saddles were double-rigged Mother Hubbards, popular in Texas at that time. Only white men sat such a rig.

Hungry and cold as I was, I didn't give the presence of white Texans another thought, but I should have, the way things turned out.

The owner of the place was a small, plump man, with a round, pleasant face that bore a worried, almost fearful expression.

The reason was not hard to find.

Four white men sat at a table, sharing a bottle of what I later learned was mescal, the strong, smoky and potent liquor of Old Mexico. They were a wolfish, un-curried bunch, who looked like they'd just come in off the trail. All of them wore dusters, good boots, and fancy spurs, and each carried a brace of revolvers in tooled holsters.

Such men bring trouble with them, and I sensed it, but Wes seemed totally indifferent.

After the worried little Mexican sat us at a table and took our order for tortillas, beef and frijoles, Wes got up from his chair and stood with his back to the blazing log fire.

He looked over at the four men and smiled. "Ahh, it does a man good to warm his butt at the fire after a long ride."

It was at this point that the proprietor put a bottle of mescal and two earthenware cups on the pine table in front of me. I draw this detail to your attention only because I have always believed that bottle of mescal was the first step on my long road to the hopeless drunk I later became.

As I said, Wes stood in front of the fire and made a remark that the four men seemed to take with considerable good humor. But appearances can be deceptive when it comes to hard cases of that kind. Even rabid wolves can smile.

One of the four, a redhead big in the chest and shoulders, sporting a magnificent, sweeping handlebar mustache I'd have given my eye teeth to own, grinned. "You quit blocking the fire, sonny, or I'll warm your ass for you over my knee."

The others laughed and Wes laughed with them.

"Hey, that's funny. A real thigh-slapper." Then the laughter drained from Wes's face, his eyes a bright, piercing blue. "Now come here and let me see you put me over your knee." Suddenly he was on the prod.

Wes was touchy, and I knew he felt that being called *sonny* was an insult to his manhood.

The four men at the table wanted trouble and they were not shy about bringing it. The big redhead looked around at the others and grinned. Then he slowly rose to his feet, with a considerable, easy elegance I must add.

"You gonna lower your britches, youngster, or am I going to do it for you?"

"Studying on it," Wes said, "I reckon I'll leave that up to you."

Lacking gun leather, John Wesley's Colts were shoved into each side of his waistband, butt-forward, in what some now call the cavalry draw position. They were hidden by his coat.

This mode of carry was much favored by another famous shootist, but more of him later. First things first, as I always say.

The big man, his spurs ringing, stepped across the cantina floor. Then he stopped, his eyes locked on Wes's face.

The Mexican proprietor, steaming plates in hand, stepped between them and said to Wes, his voice tremoring, "Senor, your food is served."

In recent years I've heard men say that the redhead's name was Archie Keller or Kenner and by the time he clashed with Wes, he'd killed seven men. They say he was mean enough to pour water over a widow woman's kindling, and so profane, he used the Holy Bible for cigarette papers.

Maybe these things are true enough, but what isn't true is that he saw his own death in Wes's eyes and backed down real quick. Hell, he wasn't scared of Wes any more than he was scared of me. I'm convinced he knew that killing what he thought to be an unarmed, beardless boy would do little to enhance his gun reputation.

As it was, let's call him Archie Keller. He just grinned, willing to let it go "Yeah, you go eat your breakfast like a good boy."

And there it might have ended.

But it sure didn't.

One of the others at the table, a young towhead with the eyes of a carrion eater, said, "Aw hell. I'll take down the pup's britches an' whup him good, Arch."

The towhead got up in a hurry and advanced on Wes. But I had my good foot resting in a chair and I pushed it into him.

The man got all tangle-footed with the chair and fell.

Keller turned his head to see what had happened.

And that was all the break John Wesley needed. In an instant, his guns were in his hands.

The big Colts bucked as he slammed two shots into Keller and then another hit the towhead in the throat as he struggled to free himself from the chair and get to his feet.

Keller, hit twice in the chest, lay dying on the floor as Wes covered the other two men at the table with his revolvers.

"You brought it," he said. "You want I should finish it?"

But the two survivors wanted no part of Wes on that day, and by the horrified look on their faces, on any other.

"We're leavin'," the older of the two said, so fast there was no space between his words.

"Then leave," Wes said.

Death rattled in Keller's throat and all the life that was in him left.

The towhead lay gagging on his own blood for a spell, then, after making a horrible, gurgling sound, he too gave up the ghost.

Wes glanced at the two bodies. He stood slender and significant like some kind of avenging angel. "Take these two and bury them across the border. I will not have Texans lie in foreign soil."

The older man got up to do as he was told, but the younger man, hard-faced and defiant, his eyes reckless, said to Wes, "I'll remember you. There will be another place and another time."

That was not a wise thing to say to John Wesley Hardin when his blood was up and his eyes were cold as a killing frost.

Wes raised his Colt and shot the man just where his hat met his forehead. His suspenders cut, the youngster hit the floor with a thud and lay still.

"For God's sake, Wes!" I yelled. "For God's sake!"

"This was not my fault." Wes's eyes flicked from me to the older man, who was ashen and looked like he might puke at any second. "He threatened me and I will not leave a sworn enemy on my back trail." He glared at the fellow Texan. "Now you have three men to bury."

The man had bark on. He dug deep and rediscovered his courage. "I hope I'm around when they bury you."

Wes smiled. "You figure on living another fifty years, huh?"

"You won't live that long," the man said. "One day you'll run into a man who's just as hard as you, and he'll kill you. You'll get it in the back and die on a saloon floor with your face in a spittoon."

Wes shook with anger, or maybe a goose flew over his grave. "All right, I'll turn my back on you right now. Then shuck the iron, old man, and we'll see who bites the ground."

"Kid, you go to hell." The man turned away, his talking done.

Then, with the help of the Mexican, he dragged the dead men out of the saloon and into the dusky gloom of the dank, drizzling day.

Our food lay cold on the table, but I'd lost my appetite anyway. I picked up the dark blue bottle. "What the hell is this stuff?"

"Mescal. It's made from some kind of cactus." Wes absently studied the three blood trails that smeared across the floor like the tracks of snails. His eyes held nothing. No regret. No interest.

"Is it good?" I asked.

"How should I know?" Wes said. "Try it."

The mescal poured into my cup like a glittering river of gold and smelled like the smoke from a campfire in Paradise. Saliva jetted from the back of my tongue as I put the cup to my lips and drank.

Oh, heavenly elixir! My lover! My new companion!

Thus was born my love affair with alcohol that burns just as passionately today as it did then. Although I no longer drink (The Sisters of Charity frown on alcohol) I remain in constant mourning for the loss of my dearest, but most treacherous friend.

I drank and drank again.

Wes said, "Go easy on the busthead, Little Bit. We got riding to do." He looked at me with a puzzled expression. "I never known you to indulge in liquor before."

"I never knew how good liquor was before," I said.

Indeed, the booze was working its magic quickly on my tiny body. My leg no longer hurt and I felt that I was drifting on a pink cloud three feet above the floor. For the first time in my life, I realized that the world was a wonderful, shining place and that I'd at last found my niche in it.

I'd let the genie out of the bottle and I vowed never to cork him up again.

CHAPTER EIGHTEEN
A Terrible Wound

"Give me that!" John Wesley snapped. He grabbed the bottle from the table and threw it into a corner where it smashed into pieces, the golden liquid spilling like angel's blood over the floor. "Now, listen up. We're heading back across the border and heading for Gonzales County. I got huggin' kin there, the Clements brothers. Fine, upstanding folk."

My brain was fuzzy and I'm sure I had a silly grin on my face. "But your pa—"

"I know what's best for John Wesley, not my pa," Wes said.

"But, Wes, you promised—"

"Damn you, I promised nothing." He stared hard at me, then waved a hand around the cantina. "I crossed the border to get away from trouble, but all it did was follow me, like, like some kind of plague. Lookee, three men dead through no fault of my own. Hell, we've only been in Mexico an hour and we've already worn out our welcome."

Before I could say anything, Wes waved the Mexican

over. He'd been jabbering away to a couple peons who'd just walked in. All three regarded us with fearful eyes.

"Hey you, get over here," Wes yelled.

The little man shuffled over to our table.

Wes said, "You want to invest in my Wild West show?"

The Mexican was confused. "I-I don't understand, senor."

"Hear that," Wes said, directing his attention to me. "How are we going to raise money for my show in greaser towns?" He turned to the Mexican. "Get lost."

The little man scurried away, no doubt thanking his lucky stars that he was still alive.

"On your feet, Little Bit. We're heading back to civilization."

I rose and staggered a little.

With that casual cruelty that came so easily to him, Wes said, "Hell, just what I need, a drunken cripple."

"I'll be all right," I said.

"Sure you will, once the bug juice wears off. You'd better be. The Clements boys don't suffer fools gladly."

"I'm not a fool, Wes," I said with all the dignity I could muster.

I saw the flipside of the John Wesley Hardin coin.

"Of course you're not, Little Bit." He smiled, his hand on my shoulder. "I was just joshing you. Hell, you're going to be my business manager one day, aren't you?"

"Sure thing, Wes." The alcohol had made me mellow.

* * *

We recrossed the Rio Grande and camped that night in a stand of post oak and bois d'arc, a stone's throw from a willow-lined stream where blue and silver fish jumped.

It was way down in the fall. The rain, though intermittent, seemed widespread. Every now and then a shower rattled through the trees. Urged on by a north wind, it soaked everything.

For the first time in my life, alcohol, my beautiful new mistress, showed what hell she could cause. The mescal hangover she inflicted on me was the ninth circle of Dante's Hell.

Wes, of course, was highly amused, and teased me constantly. He made a masterful show of bolting down the cold tortillas and beef he'd brought from the cantina and expressed the wish that he had a bottle of mescal to wash it down.

In addition to a churning belly and my other miseries, my bad leg ached. Once when I moved it closer to the fire, I cried out from the sudden pain.

"What the hell was that?" Wes said.

"My leg hurts real bad," I said.

"Which one?"

"Which one do you think?"

"Let me have a look at it."

"I got to take off my pants," I said.

"Lord a mercy, can I bear the shock?" Wes grinned.

Raindrops ticked from the oak branches and I heard the rumble of distant thunder as I pulled down my pants. The leather and steel contraption around my wasted limb gleamed in the firelight.

"That leg is thin, by God," Wes said. "Like a stick."

"Don't you think I already know that?"

"How the hell does it hold you upright?"

"It doesn't. The steel does."

"Where does it hurt?" Wes asked.

"Up here, right at the top of my thigh."

Wes's strong, nimble fingers undid the buckles that strapped the cage to my leg, then he set it aside. He looked at my leg again and his eyes flew wide open. "Damn. Take a look at that."

I looked down and saw what Wes saw. A huge sore—raw, red, deep, and streaked with yellow pus—had formed under the leather strap, caused by its constant rubbing against my skin. The ulcer was about twice the size of a silver dollar and it smelled bad, like rotten fish.

"How long have you had this?" Wes looked queasy.

"It started just after we left Longview. And it's been getting worse since."

Wes said nothing.

I said, "What can we do about it?"

"I don't know. I'm not a doctor." Wes picked up the steel brace, rusty in spots. "You can't wear this. The leather will rub on the sore again and make it worse."

"I can't walk without it." I felt sweat bead on my forehead.

"Then I'll carry you to your horse. The Clements brothers have womenfolk up in Gonzales County and they're known to be good at patching up wounds."

"This isn't a bullet hole."

"I know, Little Bit. It's a sight worse."

But the worst was still to come. That night the fever struck.

CHAPTER NINETEEN
Talk of the Chisholm Trail

I was burning up, out of my mind with fever as we made our way to the cousins. Time meant nothing to me, but I learned later it took almost two weeks. Wes wasn't happy about it, but he never left me by the side of the trail. The concerned triangle of John Wesley's face drifted in and out of my consciousness.

He held wet leaves to my forehead, and from the far end of a scarlet tunnel I heard him say over and over, "You'll be fine, Little Bit, just fine."

I remember (or did I imagine?) grabbing him by the front of his coat, babbling to him about the pale men who stood in the shadows, watching us.

And Mage was there. But, unlike the rest, his face was black as mortal sin and his eyes glowed with a sable fire.

They were all there . . . all the men Wes had killed. They stood still as graven statues.

Watching.

Silent as the grave.

"Look! Look, Wes!" I yelled.

A white mule stepped among the trees, a gambler's ghost. On him sat a man who held a walking cane across the saddle horn. The man smiled and made a gun of his fingers and thumb and he fired at the back of Wes's head.

I heard the bang of the pistol as the man's thumb fell, and blood, bone, and brain haloed around Wes's shattered skull.

I cried out in my terrible fear. "Oh merciful Jesu!"

"It's thunder, Little Bit," Wes said. His face ran scarlet with thin streams of blood and rain. "It's only thunder."

I clutched at Wes again. "Don't leave me. Wes, I'm sore afeerd."

"It's the fever. The fever makes a man see things." He held a cup to my mouth. "It's water. It will help cool you down."

I drank greedily and noisily. "Did you see Mage? Over there by the post oak. He's come back from hell, Wes."

Wes smiled. "Hell, you can't see a black man in the dark."

"And I saw a white mule."

"A gambler's ghost . . . just passing through."

I grabbed for him again. "Beware of the man with the cane, Wes."

"I surely will, Little Bit."

I lifted my face to the cool rain and opened my mouth to catch the drops. Then I lapsed into a troubled sleep again, my dreams filled with dead gamblers and pretty, laughing saloon girls in rainbow-colored dresses and the man with the cane who pushed me aside with a terrible curse.

Him I feared most of all.

"You cut it close, Little Bit," the man's voice said. "For a spell there, I figured you were gonna cash in fer sure."

The face of a young man I didn't know swam into focus.

"Where am I?" My voice was thin as a wafer.

The young man answered. "At my brothers' ranch in Gonzales County. We're south of a town called Smiley if'n you feel inclined to go on a tear with the whiskey and gals."

"Not hardly," I said.

"Figured that." The man smiled. "The name is Gip Clements. My brothers James, Mannen, and Joe own this ranch, including the bed you're lying in."

"How long?"

"A week since Wes brought you here more dead than alive."

"For sure it's winter then. Where is Wes?"

"Talking with my brothers. He plans to help them drive a herd up Kansas way."

I felt a spike of panic and tried to sit up in the bed. "My leg—"

"Is doing just fine," Gip said. "Brother Joe's lady says you'll be up and about in no time. Another month, maybe so."

I pushed down the sheet, terrified of what I might see, and pulled up the borrowed nightshirt. The sore on my leg had shrunk in size and was no longer red and angry. When I touched the puckered skin around the wound there was only a little pain.

"You got Mae Ellen to thank fer that," Gip said. "She says looking after you was like caring for a little, hurt dickie bird."

"Thank her from me. Thank her most kindly."

"You can thank her your ownself. She'll bring you some rabbit and onion soup right soon."

"When does the herd leave?" I asked. My heart thumped in my chest. If Wes was going, I didn't want to be left behind.

"The gather isn't finished, but I reckon Wes and my brothers will head 'em north by the middle of next week."

"I've got to be on the drive. Tell Wes I need to talk to him. Better still, bring me my leg brace and I'll go tell him my ownself."

Gip smiled at me. "Hell, Little Bit, your leg ain't fully healed yet. Strap on all that damned steel and it will open right up again." He gave me a sympathetic look, or tried to. "Besides, a scrawny little feller that keeps as poorly as you ain't gonna be much help on a two month cattle drive up the Chisholm. That's rough country, to say nothing of fire, flood, an' wild Indians."

Well, that was a boot in the teeth. But I managed to keep a brave face.

"I'm a good cook," I said.

"We got plenty of them, good and bad. And assistant cooks."

"Then I could be the assistant cook to an assistant cook," I said.

"You'd better talk with John Wesley. He's the one

doing the firing and hiring." Gip shook his head. "Don't get your hopes up."

The door opened and he said, "Ah, here's Mae Ellen with the grub. Put meat on them scrawny bones o' your'n."

Gip left and Mae Ellen said, "How are you feeling, Little Bit?"

"Good enough to go on the trail drive," I said.

Mae Ellen, a pretty, worn girl who probably looked older than her years, smiled. "Not this time, Little Bit. You've got to rest up and get your strength back."

As she put the tray on my lap, I said, "I want to thank you for taking care of me."

"You were no trouble. Just like a little sick animal." She straightened up and worked a kink out of her slim back.

I tried the soup, but it was still too hot. I didn't want Mae Ellen to leave, so I said a stupid thing. "You saw me naked, huh?"

She smiled. "I've seen worse." She stepped to the door. "I'll be back to look at your leg. Old Ma Atsa is a Navajo witch woman and she gave me a new salve to try."

"Will it work fast?" I asked.

Mae Ellen laughed. "We'll see."

Then she was gone and all that remained was a lingering scent of lavender and a lonely, empty space where once a woman stood.

CHAPTER TWENTY
I Join the Cattle Drive

"Damn it all, Little Bit, I had to kill another man. After I shot him, he lingered for a couple days and I just heard he died an hour before sunup this morning." John Wesley sat on the edge of the bed. "And you can't pin this one on me. It wasn't my fault."

"What happened?" I said, not really wanting to know.

I mean, Wes was Wes. When a man did or said something he didn't like, Wes killed him.

Simple as that.

"Well, me and a couple Clements boys fell in with some vaqueros, as Joe Clements called them, and one of them suggested a card game."

"Poker?"

"Nah. Some greaser game called Spanish Monte," Wes said. "I'd never heard of it before."

"I saw it played years ago by a couple Rangers," I said. "Now that I study on it, one of those boys said he was quarter Mexican, something like that."

Wes looked irritated. "Hell, Little Bit, is this your story or mine?"

"Yours, Wes. Proceed."

"Well, we played a couple hands and I started to get the hang of it." Wes held up his left hand and showed the silver ring on his little finger. "I don't wear this ring for nothing, you know."

But he did.

Wes had no claim to the professional gambler's ring, since he didn't play cards for a living. The few times he tried, he invariably lost and for a while would become sullen and dangerous.

"So we played another hand. All the while them Mexicans are jabbering away in that heathen language of theirs that nobody understands but them—"

"We never had any dealings with Mexicans before," I said.

"That's because they're all flannel-mouths," Wes said. "I don't like them."

"So you played another hand . . ." I prompted.

"Yeah, and I had a queen. I tapped my card and said, 'Pay the queen.'"

"The queen loses in Spanish Monte, as I recall."

"Damn it, Little Bit. That's the position the Mex dealer took," Wes said.

I cut to the chase. "So you shot him." The rabbit and onion soup lay sour in my belly.

"Hell no, not the dealer. Two other fellers," Wes said. "Him, I just chunked over the head with my gun and cleaned his plow real good."

I opened my mouth to speak, but Wes held up a silencing hand.

"The two fellers with him rose up and started in to shuck iron. Well, I shot one of them in the gun arm, near took the damned thing off, and t'other through the lungs."

"And what happened after that?"

"I told you. The Mex I shot through the lungs died this morning. They cut the arm off the other one, but he ain't expected to live either. Lost too much blood, like."

"What about the law?"

"Hell, there ain't no law in this part of Gonzalez County, except for what a man makes for himself. But the white folks around had a good laugh with me afterward and told me I did a fine thing shooting them two. They got no liking for Mexicans, especially the kind that cheat at cards." Wes rose to his feet and stretched. "Wasn't my fault, Little Bit," he said through a yawn. "They should have paid the queen."

I changed the subject. "Wes, I want to go on the cattle drive."

He stared at me, the imp of amusement in his eyes. "Little Bit, how the hell would you make Abilene? If things go bad, it could take three mighty hard months to get there."

"I'll take my chances." It was boastful talk coming from a skinny pipsqueak with a bad leg and eyes too big for his little pale face.

And John Wesley knew it. "You figure to ride herd, Little Bit? Maybe bring up the drag on a half-broke pony with the wherewithal of a cougar that would like nothing better than to break your damned fool neck?"

Desperate, I lied in my teeth. "Gip said I could be the assistant cook's assistant."

"Gip said that?"

"Sure did," I said, blinking.

"You'd carry water and firewood on a gimpy leg?"

"I'd surely like to give it a try." Then I told another lie. "I'm stronger than I look."

Wes considered that for a while, then said, "Little Bit, we can't nurse a man who doesn't pull his weight, not when we're driving sixteen hundred head of wild steers up the Chisholm. If you fall behind, we'll leave you."

"I won't fall behind."

"Apaches, bears, thirst, hunger . . . that's what you'll face if you can't keep up with the herd," Wes said. "Best you stay here and make plans for the Wild West show and draw up them business documents that Sam Luck needs."

"Wes, you're my friend, and you're ramrodding the drive. I want to go with the herd. Don't let me down."

Wes sighed. "All right, Little Bit, you can help the cook. But don't expect any special favors from me. You drop out, you'll be on your own."

"Thank you, Wes. I won't let you down."

John Wesley crossed the floor, picked up my leg brace and tossed it on the bed. "Then get the hell up," he said, unsmiling. "You've laid there too long."

CHAPTER TWENTY-ONE
Murder on the Canadian

We didn't own the cows we were to drive north. John Wesley and the Clements boys made the gather for three fellers by the names of Jake Johnson, Columbus Carroll, and Crawford "Doc" Burnett. They weren't cattlemen either, but were contracted by ranchers to supply the drovers needed to drive their herds to Kansas and the railheads.

Back in those days, none of the Texas cattlemen could afford to hire their own cowboys, so they left it to the contactors to sign up out of work punchers, men on the scout looking to get away from the law, and any dancehall lounger, porch percher, or footpad willing to fork a bronc for eighty cents a day.

Being a lowly assistant of the cook's assistant, I got twenty-five cents, but was allowed to ride in the Studebaker chuck wagon that was invented by good ol' Charlie Goodnight.

The cook was an irritable, abrasive man, as they all were, but since a ten-pound cannonball had run away with his right leg at Gettysburg he took a liking to me, probably because we were both gimps.

His assistant was a stove-up cowboy named Lou. He was a few years past middle age, had a long, sad face and an alarming habit of, at the drop of a hat, shedding sudden tears for the woman he'd loved and lost years before. Her name was Sarah, but he imparted no further information, though I often pumped him for more.

John Wesley took a dislike to him, declaring that shedding tears for a woman wasn't manly. It was unbecoming of a Texan.

As for me, Lou never asked me to do too much by way of hauling water and firewood, so I liked him just fine.

At the end of February 1871, Columbus Carroll and Jake Johnson pushed north for Abilene with sixteen hundred beeves. Wes was in charge of a second herd of the same size that left a week later.

Wes and Jim Clements were paid handsomely, each receiving a hundred and fifty a month, but getting the herd to Abilene intact was a heavy responsibility. Just keeping order among a dozen hands, most of them hardcases, was no easy task.

That's why, for the first time in his life, John Wesley drew gun wages. It indicated how his reputation as a named shootist was growing.

Needless to say I was immensely proud of him as we left Texas at Red River Bluff and crossed into the Oklahoma Territory. We pushed north without incident and followed the Chisholm into the Nations.

Fifteen herds crossed the Red on the same day and

the trail became a great winding river of Texas beef headed for the railheads and Yankee bellies.

Then John Wesley killed an Indian on the south bank of the Canadian that even now, many years later as I enter my dotage, I can only call cold-blooded murder.

One early evening as the herd rested, Wes took me on the back of his horse to show me the river we'd have to cross the next morning. The Canadian was a slow moving waterway at that time, bounded by red mud flats and treacherous quicksand and was swollen by the recent rains.

"Once we cross, we're halfway there, Little Bit." Wes drew rein on a brushy rise overlooking the river. "Ain't it a sight to see?"

And indeed it was. The setting sun tinged the sky scarlet and jade and the Canadian looked like a river of molten brass. The night birds squawked at the sentinel stars and far off coyotes talked.

"Want to ride closer, Little Bit?" Wes said. "If your leg will stand it."

My steel cage stuck straight out from the side of the horse, but the sore had healed pretty well and I had little pain. "Sure. I'd like to be the first of the outfit to drink water from the Canadian."

Was turned his head and grinned at me. "I'll join you and we'll both boast of it in our old age."

As we rode down from the rise toward the river past a stand of salt bush, the horse shied. Wes grabbed for the horn and yelled, "What the hell?"

Mind you, I heard that from the ground where I'd landed in a heap, scared to move, worried that I'd discover a brand new misery. A moment later, as I rubbed dirt out of my eyes, I heard a shot.

Then a terrible scream.

I was in time to see a young Indian boy topple forward into the brush, a scarlet rose blossoming on his chest.

Wes swung out of the saddle, and then stepped warily toward the body, Colt in hand.

The young Indian, a Kiowa as we later learned, was dead, his black eyes dully staring into nothingness.

"He had a bow and arrow," Wes said. "I saw it plain."

I rose slowly to my feet and stepped to the body. Half-hidden in the brush lay three dead cottontails and the boy, for that's what he was, still clutched a small bow.

"He was rabbit hunting," I said.

"The hell he was. He was trying to bushwhack us."

"Wes, he's only a boy. No more than twelve or thirteen years old, I reckon."

"Older than that," Wes said. "Look at him. He's a warrior."

"He was just a boy hunting rabbits," I said.

But John Wesley wasn't listening. A hint of a triumphant smile tugged at the corners of his mouth. "Since I started this drive, the only talk I've heard is Indians, Indians, Indians, and that they'd recently killed two white men in the Nations. Everybody is scared of them—except me."

He prodded the slim, brown body with his toe. "Hell, I'm no more afraid of a damned Redskin savage than I am a raccoon in a tree. I was anxious to meet one of them on the warpath and now I did." His smile grew wider. "And I done for him."

Wes reached into his pocket, produced his Barlow, and opened the blade "I think I should scalp him. That's what you do with an Indian you've killed, isn't it? Or should I cut off his ball sack for a tobacco pouch?"

"Wes, leave him be," I said. "Damn it, you killed him. Isn't that enough?" My face was blazing.

Wes looked at me. He smiled and closed the knife. "Well, I don't know how to scalp a man anyway. Mount up, Little Bit, and we'll go down to the river and have a drink like we planned."

I shook my head. "It's getting late. We should head back to the herd."

"Suit yourself," Wes said.

But suddenly he wasn't smiling any longer. "I sure never took you for a damned Indian-lover, Little Bit."

The next morning, Wes took Jim Clements and some of the drovers to see the dead Indian and they all agreed that he'd been a fearsome warrior. A puncher named Gray scalped the boy and gave the scalp to Wes who kept it for a couple days before he threw it away. He said it was a filthy thing.

CHAPTER TWENTY-TWO
Strong Drink and Wild Women

The Osage Nation was the last Indian reservation we had to cross before entering Kansas and the tribal elders demanded a tax of ten cents a head to let us through.

John Wesley told them to go to hell and pushed the herd north.

That led to another killing and a second dead Indian.

The morning after Wes's meeting with the Osage, he and most of the hands were out scouting the trail ahead of us.

I helped the cook prepare breakfast—cornbread and fried salt pork. The meal is stuck in my memory because of what happened later that day.

Wes had not yet returned when half a dozen Osage rode into camp, demanded their tribute, and started to cut out cattle.

The cook and me, with only two good legs between

us, could only stand and watch. He hurled cusses at the Osage now and again that the savages pretended to not understand.

One of the two hands left in camp, a young fellow by the name of Tin Cup Sam, looked at me, his eyes scared. "Are they gonna massacree us?"

"I sure hope not," I said. "I'm not up for a massacree this morning."

"Well," Tin Cup said, "I'm going to fetch my pistol."

The cook agreed. "Me too. I will not be murdered by thieving savages."

How this would have ended I don't know. The cook was only halfway to the wagon when Wes and the rest of the hands rode into camp.

He drew rein and said to me, "What the hell's happening, Little Bit?"

"The Indians are taking some of our cattle," I said.

"The hell they are." Wes swung his horse around and rode to the chuck wagon where an Osage with a bright red scalp lock had dismounted. He demanded food from the cook, all the while brandishing a *bloodthirsty tomahawk* of the largest size.

As I watched Wes swing out of the saddle and approach the savage with a determined stride, I very much feared for my friend's safety. But he ignored the Indian and stopped beside the warrior's horse, which bore an ornate silver bridle cunningly inlaid with a beautiful blue stone the Navajo call lapis lazuli.

After examining the bridle closely, Wes advanced on the savage, his hand on his pistol. "That bridle was stolen from our camp. I'm taking it back."

A huge, brindle steer that had wandered into camp was grazing close to the smoky fire built to keep the flies away. The Osage walked his horse to the steer, pulled a pistol from his belt and pushed the muzzle into the animal's forehead. "If I cannot keep the bridle, I will kill this cow."

"Harm that animal and I'll kill you," Wes said.

To my surprise, *shock* I should say, the stupid savage pulled the trigger!

The brindle steer bellowed in pain and then it staggered a few steps before its legs buckled and it fell.

Wes raised his Colt and slammed a shot into the Osage's head. The Indian's dead body joined the steer on the bloody ground.

Turning to the hands, Wes grinned. "Well, he killed the beef and I killed him. I guess now we're all even."

This drew a cheer from the punchers as the remaining warriors fled.

The cook, with the single mindedness of the truly dedicated, glanced at the Indian, then at the dead steer. "Looks like we're having beefsteaks for dinner tonight, boys."

The cook had made a good joke, and we all laughed.

A couple days later, we crossed into Kansas and drove the herd toward Cowskin Creek, about twenty miles south of Wichita.

At this juncture I would like to ask all ladies of gentle breeding to forbear reading from here to the end of this chapter of my narrative, for I will talk of whiskey and loose women and wish to spare your maidenly blushes.

I was up on the wagon seat with the cook and his assistant, when a delegation of well-dressed gentlemen met us on the trail and hailed John Wesley in a most friendly manner. After what seemed like a congenial conversation, the men left after a deal of smiles, handshakes, and back slaps.

Wes then explained to the assembled hands that the businessmen had extended everyone an invitation to visit their new town, Park City by name, and be prepared to whoop it up.

Privately Wes told me that he'd mentioned to one of the men, a Mr. Millard, that Park City, soon to rival Wichita as a cattle town, might be the ideal spot to debut his Wild West show. "I told him I'd act out how I killed the Kiowa warrior to save a fair maiden from a fate worse than death and how, though badly wounded, I bested the murderous Osage. And he was very interested." Wes slapped me on the back. "Park City could make us rich, Little Bit."

And so it was that Wes veered the herd a few miles west of the Chisholm and followed a wagon road into the town, a raw, rough settlement that smelled of newly sawn lumber and boasted three saloons, a hotel and bath house, a dancehall, and cattle pens large enough to accommodate up to five thousand cattle.

There was no church and no school, but the place was booming.

The saloon whiskey passed muster and, to punchers fresh off the trail, all the girls were pretty and wild as cougars.

Wes and I raised a few pints to celebrate his eighteenth birthday a couple weeks away and his obvious success as a shootist. Half drunk and loving it, we staggered from saloon to saloon, bottle to bottle, woman to woman.

Despite my unprepossessing looks—for was I not a pale, twisted, little goblin?—the girls took a liking to me and treated me like a sick puppy, cooing as they stroked me and kissed the top of my head.

As you no doubt have already guessed, I lost my virginity that very day . . . and have never regretted it.

Suffering from massive hangovers we headed back to the Chisholm the next morning. All agreed wholeheartedly with John Wesley when he said, "Boys, I reckon a good time was had by all."

Wes never again mentioned Park City and his Wild West show in the same breath. That was just as well. After the railroad bypassed the town, it died a quick death.

Finally its dust was blown away by the prairie winds and today there is no sign that Park City ever existed.

CHAPTER TWENTY-THREE
Dead Man's Trail

After fording the Little Arkansas River, Wes pushed the herd into Newton Prairie where the Chisholm widened from a mile to nearly three. There was plenty of good graze, and room for following herds to pass us if they needed to.

One Mexican trail boss didn't cotton to swinging wide around our herd. He wanted to push us aside and go straight on through.

Well, when that idea didn't set too well with John Wesley, I knew bad things were bound to happen.

The stage was set for a killing.

Things went from bad to worse when the point of the boss vaquero's herd collided with our drag and cowboy cusses were exchanged in English and Mexican.

The cook, his assistant, and I went back to see the fun in time to hear Wes yell to the Mex trail boss, "Go the hell around!"

The air was thick with yellow dust as our hands started to turn the Mexican herd. Fistfights broke out all over the place, but since the scrapping was done from horseback, no great damage was done to either side.

But the boss vaquero was on the prod and mad enough to bite the head off a hammer. He swung back to the rear of his herd, grabbed a Henry from a wagon, and galloped back to the point again, a chaotic scene of tussling, cussing punchers and vaqueros, bawling steers, and dust so thick I could hardly see a hand in front of my face.

Beside me, the cook shook his head. "Son, this ain't gonna end well, mark my words."

The old-timer was right. The herds were all tangled up and the whole sorry affair was turning into a regular donnybrook. Above the din, I heard Wes yelling orders, but nobody seemed to be paying him any heed.

A paint pony bucked out of the melee, the puncher's chaps flapping as he white-knuckled the horn. He nearly cannoned into the boss vaquero who swung out of the saddle and stepped into the cartwheeling dust, his rifle up and ready.

I didn't see what happened next because of the lack of visibility, but one of the hands later told me how it all shook out.

The Mexican trail boss, his name was Jose, or so I was told, spotted Wes through the murk and took a pot at him. He missed then stepped forward and fired again.

Another miss.

His Henry jammed, probably from grit and dust, and he shifted the rifle to his left hand and drew a Colt with his right. He advanced, shooting every few steps, but did no execution.

For some reason John Wesley was carrying a revolver so old and abused it had shot loose and the cylinder wobbled.

It happened time after time to those old cap and ball Army Colts. I blame roosters who loaded so much powder into the chambers they had to shave the balls to allow the cylinder to turn.

I don't think Wes figured he'd get into a gunfight that day, and he paid for his lack of oversight.

Still mounted, he fired several times at the advancing Mexican, and only God knows where the balls went.

"Git off the damned hoss, Wes, and hold the cylinder!" Jim Clements yelled. He was unarmed and could not join in the shooting scrape.

The hand I spoke to afterward told me, "Well, ol' Wes jumps off'n the pony, holds onto the iron with both hands, an' cuts loose. His ball burns the Mex across the thigh and then his piece locks up solid and he can't shoot no more."

It seems the vaquero then charged Wes and the two fell into the dust and began to grapple, bite, and eye-gouge.

When guns were drawn on both sides and it looked like the shooting was about to become general, Jim Clements stepped into the fray and separated the warring parties, including the principal combatants who were rolling around on the ground.

"Here," Clements yelled, "this won't do! All hostilities must end. We were all drunk and didn't know what we were doing."

It wasn't much by way of a peace talk, but Wes, always canny, agreed to a truce, knowing he couldn't open the ball again with a useless gun. But back at camp, nursing a shiny, black bruise under his right eye and a chawed ear, he was a powder keg, vowing revenge on the Mexican who had so roughly handled him.

The fuse was lit when a hand rode in and said, "Boss, the Mexicans are pushing their herd up again, comin' on fast."

Enraged, Wes threw away the beefsteak that he'd been holding to his black eye and armed himself with his own Colts, stuck into shoulder holsters. He and Jim Clements then rode out of camp, two men well skilled in the use of arms and on fire with a blazing rage and the urge to kill.

Once again my narrative must resort to hearsay, but since Jim Clements himself relayed the details of the gunfight that followed, you can depend on my accuracy.

"When the Mexicans saw us coming, six vaqueros, including the one they called Jose, circled around toward us, their weapons drawn," Clements said. "After a merry quip, Wes put the reins in his teeth, drew both Colts and charged. Never, since the late war ended, had a Southern cavalier advanced on a superior enemy so gallantly.

"Firing at the gallop, Wes shot Jose through the heart and the wretch tumbled off his horse with a terrible cry and died. Then a vaquero, cursing in the vilest fashion, rode directly at John Wesley, his gun blazing. Cool as ever, Wes would not be stampeded. He turned in the saddle and, working his Colts with great rapidity, shot the Mexican cur in the head. The man was dead when he hit the ground, and good riddance."

Clements said that he and Wes then captured four of the Mexicans.

"Two of the vaqueros, both very young, said they'd had nothing to do with the affray, and, out of the goodness of his heart, Wes let them go. But the other two, after agreeing to surrender, were filled with typical Mexican deceit and treachery. They pulled their murderous pistols and fired point-blank at John Wesley."

Clements said that both vaqueros missed, but Wes didn't.

As Wes told it to me later, "The first I shot through the heart and he dropped dead in a moment. The second I shot through the lungs and Jim shot him, too. The man begged me not to shoot him again, and put up my guns. Hell, I knew the greaser was a goner anyway."

The shooting of the traitorous Mexican assassins made John Wesley a hero, and I, as his best friend, bathed in his reflected glory.

Cowboys from other herds dropped into camp just to catch sight of the famous kid shootist. Cowmen—I'm talking of great cattle barons, not one-loop nesters—shook his hand and told him what a fine fellow he was.

Wes took the opportunity to speak to these powerful and wealthy men about his Wild West show and introduced me as his, "partner and business manager." My narrow little chest swelled with pride.

A few expressed interest, but again, due to circumstances, in the end it all came to nothing.

CHAPTER TWENTY-FOUR
Abilene, Queen of the West

Our herd reached the bedding grounds of the Chisholm in late May 1871 and joined another hundred thousand Texas cows waiting to be sold and shipped. Just thirty miles south of Abilene, the resting cattle spread out along the North Fork of the Cottonwood River.

On June 1, Columbus Carroll sent word that John Wesley and his drovers should join him in town to be paid off. Of course, I went along with them. My jaw dropped when I first beheld Abilene. Its teeming populace and majestic buildings overwhelmed my reeling senses.

Why, the Drovers Cottage hotel where we went to draw our wages had a hundred rooms! And the Alamo Saloon, a shining palace dedicated to gambling and the god Bacchus, had a forty-foot frontage on Cedar Street, two engraved glass doors, and a full orchestra that performed morning, noon, and night!

Abilene was a booming, bustling, bespangled city to rival ancient Athens, Rome, and Babylon and even the modern capitols of London, Paris, and Berlin.

I'd never seen the like before.

As Wes and I rode along Texas Street I turned in the saddle and said, "I never knew there was this many folks in the whole country."

"In the whole world." Wes was trying his best to avoid looking like a rube, but his eyes were big as silver dollars, as were mine, and his head was on a swivel as it turned this way and that.

The street was a sea of people in town for the summer season, speculators, commission men, cowboys, gamblers, outlaws on the scout from mysterious places, and careful-eyed gunmen who looked at nothing but saw everything.

Solid, red-faced businessmen in broadcloth planted themselves in the middle of the street and made deals with cattle buyers wearing uncomfortable celluloid collars and cattlemen in high-heeled boots and wide-brimmed hats. The crowd broke around them like a sea around rocks.

Here and there ladies, many of them pretty, passed by.

Staid matrons, in collar-and-cuffed brown cotton, rubbed shoulders with saloon girls whose scarlet mouths, bold eyes, and candy cane dresses marked their calling.

I even saw a parson who walked among the throng, brandished a Bible like the sword of Gideon and railed against the evils of strong drink, fallen women, gambling, and mortal sin in general. Nobody listened to him of course, but the old boy had sand. His stovepipe hat was punctured with holes where inebriated punchers had taken pots at it.

It was mighty dangerous to wear a top hat in Abilene in those days.

Wes and I looped our horses to the hitching rail then stepped onto the broad veranda in front of the Drovers Cottage. An old timer sat in a rocker smoking a pipe. He smiled and nodded as we walked to the door. Wes's jingle-bob spurs rang with every step.

"You boys just get in?" the old man said.

"Seems like," Wes said.

"Well, don't fergit Wild Bill's bath at four sharp. It's a sight to see. I tell that to all the young fellers come up the trail."

I would've questioned the old timer further, but Wes said, "Yeah, we'll be sure to do that, pops," and opened the door.

Away from the burning heat of the day, the hotel lobby was a cool, dark oasis of polished wood, red velvet, and shining brass. Dirty and trail worn, the smell of horses on us, we stood for a moment, a bit awed and uncertain of what to do next.

The desk clerk solved that problem. "What can I do for you gentlemen?" Better dressed than anyone I knew in Texas at that time, he didn't raise an eyebrow at our dusty, sweat-stained trail clothes and three-months-without-a-bath odor.

Too many rich cowmen, who I bet sometimes

looked and smelled worse than we did, walked through the door of the Drovers Cottage.

"Mr. Hardin to see Mr. Columbus Carroll," Wes said with stiff formality.

"Ah yes, gentlemen, he's expecting you," the clerk beamed, as though we were the most honorable of honorable guests. "Mr. Carroll is in the salon, first door to your left."

Note that he said *salon*, not *saloon*. The Drovers Cottage was a classy place and catered only to the best.

The *salon* was a large room shaded by leafy potted plants and beautifully appointed with heavy leather chairs, mahogany side tables, and Persian rugs on the floor. A discreet bar with three barkeeps stood against the far wall and a massive stone fireplace promised plentiful heat when the winter blizzards struck. A three-piece orchestra played "Oh Wed Me Not to Grandpa" as we walked inside.

The room was crowded with cigar-smoking men and a few sleek women, but Carroll spotted us through the blue fog as soon as we entered. "John Wesley! Over here!"

Every head turned in Wes's direction and I realized that his fame had already spread far and wide, even to the hallowed halls of Abilene. And he was only eighteen years old.

He wore his Colts and basked in the admiration of the awed crowd as he walked tall and vital to Carroll's table . . . the deadly young shootist come to collect his gun wages.

And I, like a moth following a flame, stepped after him, doing my best to reflect just a gleam of his vibrant light.

Columbus Carroll sat alone at a table that bore a decanter of whiskey and crystal glasses on a silver tray, a cedar humidor of cigars, and a large tin box.

With every eye on John Wesley, the conversation died away to a murmur as Carroll complimented him on bringing the herd in on time with minimal losses. He then announced, louder than was necessary, I thought, that he was paying Wes a hundred dollar bonus for a job well done.

Such largess was greeted with gasps from the assembled patrons and not a few shouts of, "Hear, hear!" and "Stout fellow!"

Wes had the good grace to blush, and this endeared him even more to the crowd, especially the ladies. I felt a thrill that I was friend to such a great and famous man.

CHAPTER TWENTY-FIVE
Wild Bill's Bath

My wages amounted to twenty-three dollars, but Columbus Carroll deducted a dollar for four cups I'd broken on the drive. Still, twenty-two dollars was more money than I'd ever had in my life.

John Wesley bought a bottle of Old Crow and shared it as we sat in tubs in a Chinese bathhouse on Texas Street. A couple young Oriental girls with soap and washcloths helped us bathe after pointing to a sign on the wall that read LOOKEE NO FEELEE.

Wes thought this a good joke. Helped along by the bourbon, we were in high spirits when the owner, a small, slender man wearing some kind of heathen robes, approached us and gave a low bow.

"Gentlemens, you leave pretty damn soon. Wild Bill come for bath four o'clock, very prompt. He like bathhouse to himself."

It was only a little after noon, so Wes said, "Hell, we got plenty of time."

The Chinaman bowed again. "Maybe so, but Wild Bill always on time and get angry if anyone else in tub." He shook his head. "Bill a bad man when angry. Go bang! Bang!"

"How come he likes to bathe alone?" I asked.

The two girls giggled behind cupped hands and the owner said something sharp in the Chinese tongue that hushed them instantly.

Then to us, he said, "Bill bathe every day. Very strange thing. That why many peoples come to watch."

There may have been some twisted, Oriental logic there, but I failed to grasp it.

"But you told us he likes to bathe alone," I said, accepting the bottle from Wes's soapy hand.

Again the girls giggled and the owner, I later heard that his name was Willie Chang, silenced them with a glance.

"Peoples arrive after Bill in tub. Peoples leave before Bill get out of tub. This always the way."

"So he's shy," Wes said, grinning.

"No shy," Chang said. "Bill never shy."

"Then what is he?" Wes asked.

Chang looked over his shoulder then leaned closer to us and his voice dropped to a conspiratorial whisper. "Wild Bill have *xiao niao.*"

"What the hell does that mean?" I said.

The girls giggled again, but Chang, his wrinkled face solemn, didn't stop them.

"In Chinese, *xiao niao* has very bad meaning. It mean, *little birdie.*"

Wes looked at me, then exploded into raucous laughter. "You mean Wild Bill Hickok has a tiny dick?" he yelled.

Chang was alarmed. He waved his hands at us and

made a hushing sound. "No! No say! Wild Bill kill you for sure, by God!"

Wes laughed so hard he slipped backward into the tub and bubbles rose to the surface from his open mouth. He surfaced, choking from soapy water and laughter. It was a good two or three minutes, the girls slapping his naked back, before he could talk again.

Finally he could. "Well, don't that beat all. Wild Bill keeps a little birdie in his pants." Thinking about Wild Bill's shortcomings sent Wes into convulsions again, to the wretched Willie Chang's babbling distress.

He flapped around us like a beheaded chicken and yelled, "You go now. Now nice and clean mens. Two-bits each. Go, go, go!"

Well, I reckon Wes had gotten his money's worth because he made no objection and was still laughing as we left the bathhouse and crossed the street. He headed directly for a store with a sign in the window that proclaimed

SOLOMON LEVY, MEN'S CLOTHIER
BESPOKE TAILORING A SPECIALTY
All Boots and Shoes Sold At Cost

Wes bought a dark suit off the rack and a new shirt and hat. He tried the celluloid collar that came with the shirt but tossed it aside, telling Levy that it could choke a man.

At first I couldn't understand why he removed his guns and spurs and didn't put his flashy silver hatband on the new John B. Then it dawned on me that he didn't want to look like a lowly, working cowboy but a businessman of some standing.

You've all seen the tintype likeness he had made after we left the tailor's store. I'm sure you'll agree with me that, standing tall, Texan and handsome, he succeeded very well . . . but for those cold, Hardin eyes that not even a new hat and fancy suit could soften.

As for me, I tried a broad-brimmed Stetson myself, but Solomon Levy, a man of some perception, told me I looked like a "damned toadstool." I finally settled on a brown bowler, and Levy, much impressed, said folks would take me for a visiting English duke, or at least a lord.

I didn't believe him.

The hat was dusty, as though it had lain on a shelf for a long time, there being no great demand for bowlers in Abilene until I came along.

In the west at that time, people who took regular baths were as rare as tears at a Boot Hill burying, but a man who partook of the tub every single day, rain or shine, was agreed by all to be one of the frontier's most extraordinary sights.

Wes and I, tanked up on Old Crow and feeling no pain, got in line outside the bathhouse with two dozen other people of both sexes (Bill's long hair and fine mustachios made feminine hearts flutter) and waited with growing impatience for the witching hour of four when the doors opened.

"Wes, when we get inside, if you value our friendship, to say nothing of our lives, don't mention"—I glanced around me then dropped my voice to a whisper—"you-know-what."

"Not a word," Wes grinned.

"Wes, listen to me. Wild Bill is quick to take offense and mighty sudden on the draw and shoot."

"So am I."

"Well, just don't slight his manhood, is all."

"You know all about that, huh, Little Bit?"

I don't think he was going out of his way to be cruel, but surely he knew it hurt me. "Yeah. I know all about that."

"The door is opening," Wes said, smiling in anticipation.

Wild Bill Hickok was already relaxing in the tub when we spectators filed in to share a moment with the great man. Like his friend Custer, he was indeed a beautiful sight. His golden hair spilled over broad shoulders and his eyes were a clear, gun smoke gray.

A result of his nocturnal lifestyle, his skin was pale and pink as a woman's. Bill's cheekbones were high and downy, and he had a habit of looking down at them under his long lashes, as though inspecting a speck of dust. The mannerism made him appear shy.

Beside me a woman sighed and bobbed a little as her knees turned to jelly.

Behind him, on either side of the tub, stood two hard-eyed women of the lowest sort, each cradling a shotgun across their breasts.

When he spoke, Bill's voice was pleasant to hear, somewhere between a tenor and a baritone, well modulated, with just a trace of the nasal Yankee accent I despised so much.

"Good evening to all of you and welcome," Bill

said, steam rising from his tub. "Some of you already know the ladies behind me. On my right is High Timber, currently a hostess at the Bull's Head Saloon, and on my right, the one and only Little Nell, proprietor of the Naughty Kitty cathouse."

That last drew a cheer from the men and frowns from the ladies, especially when Nell dropped a little curtsy and batted her eyelashes.

To my wondering gaze, the women were a sight to see. High Timber stood at least six-foot tall and was as skinny as a bed slat. On the other hand, I reckoned Little Nell would probably dress out at around three hundred pounds. Both had eyes that were as warm and friendly as tenpenny nail heads.

Wild Bill shrugged apologetically, "If any ranny draws a gun in my presence this evening, High Timber and Nell will immediately fill him full of buckshot. They've both killed their man in the past, so be warned." He smiled. "Now, enough unpleasantness. After my ablutions are complete, a hat will be passed among you. Please give generously."

High Timber cradled her scattergun under one arm, then leaned over and passed Bill a brown bottle with a white label.

"One more word, ladies and gentlemen," Wild Bill said. "As my bath progresses, you will see me partake of liberal doses from this here bottle. It's . . . what the hell is it?"

Bill turned the label to him. "Ah yes, Dr. Simms Trophy-Winning Tonic for Genteel Folk. It's guaranteed to cure the rheumatisms, ague, toothache, cancer, consumption, running sores, and female miseries. It will also fill you with new pep and energy, improve sight and appetite, and soothe fussy babies."

Bill held the bottle high, revealing a muscular, if soapy arm. "Dr. Simms tonic can be purchased at Will Gardener's general store for the cost of just one dollar a bottle. But if you say, 'William sent me,' you will receive a ten cent discount."

Before he returned the bottle to High Timber, he added, "Buy Dr. Simms Tonic for Genteel Folk today. Accept no substitute."

The two young Chinese girls approached Bill's tub with all the reverence of Vestal Virgins and poured liquids from pink, blue, and white bottles into the water. Immediately the scent of wildflowers filled the room with an underpinning of sandalwood, pine, and exotic Oriental spices.

As Wild Bill sniffed, then nodded approval to his acolytes, Wes whispered in my ear, "I can't see his dick. Can you see it?"

I shook my head, terrified that Bill, who was reputed to have the ears of a bat, might hear.

"Damn it all," Wes whispered. "He's got so much parfume in there, the water turned blue." He was silent for a moment, then added, "He did that on purpose."

I said nothing, enthralled as the rest of the crowd, as the bathing ritual continued.

One of the Chinese girls held up a bar of amber soap. Pears, I noticed, the kind John Wesley's ma used.

"I," Wild Bill said, "use a fresh soap for every bath. What's left, I donate to the poor."

This drew a ripple of applause, but Wes said, "The hell with the soap. I want to see his damned manhood."

The girls used sponges the size of soup dishes to

wash Bill all over, and even plunged their hands into the water to get at his private parts . . . much to the wide-eyed interest of Wes.

Bill then began to regale us with tales of his derring-do on the wild frontier.

I vividly recall him telling us how he galloped through the entire Comanche nation, killing two score of savages en route, ere he reached a cavalry fort to warn of an impending Indian attack.

In later years, when I became a writer of dime novels, I used a fictionalized account of this true adventure in my book *Wild Bill Saves the Day or The Warlike Wrath of William.* I should add here that this volume is still available for purchase wherever fine books are sold.

Alas, we must come to an end. After the girls poured a couple buckets of water over Bill's golden head and then produced huge towels of snowy whiteness, his shotgun guards announced that the proceedings were concluded.

After Bill shook himself off and lit a cigar, his announcement that the hat would be passed around precipitated a stampede for the exits, and Wes and I found ourselves back out in the street.

"I would have put a dollar in the hat if I'd seen his pecker," Wes said.

"Disappointing," I said.

"Damn right it was. And I plan to tell him so."

CHAPTER TWENTY-SIX
John Wesley Backs Down

Early that evening, Columbus Carroll offered John Wesley a hundred and forty dollars a month to look after his herd until the buyers shipped them out. "But first tell me how are you with Wild Bill. I want no trouble on that score."

"I stand square with Bill," Wes said. "We have no problems."

"Then the job is yours," Carroll said.

Wes readily agreed to stay on since two of his gambler friends, Ben Thompson and Phil Coe, were in town. Both men were good with a gun, but neither had the status, nor the shooting skills, of Wes and Wild Bill.

That brings me to the undercurrent of gossip that had swept Abilene since Wes arrived—if there was a showdown between Hardin and Hickok who would prevail?

To my certain knowledge, bets were already being placed. Even Wes's erstwhile friends, Coe and Thompson, had a wager going.

Ben bet a thousand dollars on Wes and Coe put the same amount on Bill. Both confidently expected to be the winner.

That evening as Wes and I left the Alamo, matters almost came to a head. As was my rapidly growing habit, I was half drunk, Wes less so, when Wild Bill met us on the boardwalk.

He carried two ivory-handled Navy Colts at his waist, butt forward in black leather holsters and was dressed in his gambler's finery, a massive silver ring on the little finger of his left hand. He smelled like . . . well, you know when a man opens the door of a bawdyhouse and gets his first whiff of that wonderful odor of perfume, soap, bonded bourbon, and just a hint of sweat? That's what Bill smelled like.

No wonder I thought him a truly magnificent specimen. I'd always longed to be Wes, now Wild Bill was also a source of my adoration.

Ha! Pale, puny, prattling pygmy that I was, I still dreamed big in those days.

As we approached Wild Bill, Wes smiled and touched his hat.

Maybe there was something in that smile that Bill didn't like. A touch of, "I-know-what-you-ain't-got" perhaps.

Bill's shaggy eyebrows drew together and he growled at Wes, "Here, why are you wearing those guns in town? Take them off and give them to me or face arrest and a seventy-five dollar fine."

A huge moon hung over Abilene that night and its light turned Wes and Bill into silvered statues. Neither man moved a muscle, for just the twitch of an eye could open the ball.

"My friend and I are just enjoying a promenade before bed, Marshal," Wes said. "We're taking in the sights, like."

"I don't give a damn what you're taking in, get those guns off." Bill didn't seem to be in much of a mood for compromise. However, he did seem to be in the mood for a killing.

Wes smiled. "I always comply with the law."

Whiskey made me speak out of turn. "Man is the noblest of all animals, but separated from law and justice, he is the worst." I smiled at Bill. "Aristotle said that."

Without looking at me, Wild Bill said, "Did he though? Tell me where he is and I'll put a bullet in him. He's lying ." Then to Wes, "Give me those guns, boy. I won't tell you again."

You all remember what came next. God knows, it's been repeated a thousand times in print.

Wes drew his guns and offered them to Bill butt-forward, then spun them in his hands so the muzzles were pointed at the marshal's head.

In my novels, I christened this, "the road agent's spin," and the name seems to have stuck.

The story goes that Bill looked at the Colts, hammer-back and ready, and said, "John Wesley, you're the gamest and quickest boy I ever saw. Let us go and have a drink and I'll be your friend."

Except it didn't happen like that.

Wes did the trick with his revolvers all right and then said, "Still want to take my guns, Marshal?"

"I reckon," Bill said. "Try to use them Colts, boy, and I'll gut you like a hog."

Only then did I see moonlight gleam on the blade of

the wicked knife in Wild Bill's hand, the point sticking into Wes's belly. Where it came from I'll never know.

Bill was that fast.

Wes was a revolver fighter. Knives were an anathema to him, a barbaric weapon used only by Mexicans and red savages. The pig sticker pricking the skin of his belly gave him pause. He swallowed hard. "I was joshing, Marshal."

"I wasn't," Bill said.

Man, he was pushing on that blade pretty good.

Wes had sand, but he wasn't up for a cutting. He let go of the Colts and let them hang from his trigger fingers.

Bill turned to me. "You with the plug hat, come take his guns. And do it slow."

I did as I was told, then Bill stepped back and the blade disappeared again. "You can pick up your guns when you leave town."

Wes knew Wild Bill had put the crawl on him, but he put a brave face on things.

"Would you really have used that blade on me?" He smiled, or at least tried to. "Answer me that."

"Would your guts be all over the boardwalk if you hadn't surrendered your guns? Answer me that." Bill didn't smile. He grabbed the Colts from my hands and said to Wes, "Next time I see you carrying guns in Abilene, I'll kill you."

"There won't be a next time, Marshal," I said. "This was all just a misunderstanding."

"I don't like misunderstandings. Bad things happen when I misunderstand people." Bill turned away and his boots clumped along the boardwalk until he melted into the darkness.

Wes stood where he was for a long time, then he said, "Next time, I'll make sure there's six feet of ground between us."

"Wes, let's go back to the herd and then blow this town."

John Wesley didn't answer right away. Then he said, "What do you think? Can I beat him, Little Bit?"

"I think it would be a draw. And that means two men dead on the ground."

"Unless I shoot him in the back."

"They'd hang you for sure."

Wes nodded. "All right, let's go get a drink, and we'll talk about plans for my Wild West show." He spat. "Hickok isn't going to be in it."

CHAPTER TWENTY-SEVEN
Death of a Carpetbagger

Looking back, I consider that Saturday evening when John Wesley and Wild Bill almost got into a shooting scrape as the night that never ended. We drank some more . . . well, a lot more . . . at the Alamo bar and then repaired to the dining room to get a bite to eat.

Wes was quiet, almost sullen. Every time I mentioned his show, he cut me off with a curt, "Not now. We'll talk about it later."

He brightened up a little when Eddie Pain, the one-armed Mississippi gambler, joined us at our table and ordered the waiter to burn him a steak.

As Wes and Pain ate, they discussed the gambling scene on the riverboats and in Denver, and how pretty the ladies were in New Orleans. Wes talked about his Wild West show. Pain declared it a capital idea then sang a few verses of "Goodbye, Eliza Jane," a popular song that was sweeping the nation, and told Wes that he should put it in his show.

Pain showed Wes a beautiful Alsop .36 caliber revolver that he kept in a shoulder holster, away from the prying eyes of Wild Bill.

"A fine weapon indeed," Wes said, turning the Alsop over in his hands.

Thus the final hours before the clocks tolled midnight might have passed pleasantly enough due to Pain's convivial company, had not the Yankees spoiled it as they do everything.

Two big-bellied bullies, with the look of carpetbaggers about them, barged into the room and loudly demanded the best table, the prettiest waitress, and the oldest bourbon in the house. Both wore broadcloth, and the watch chains across their bellies, cunningly wrought from gold coins, must have weighed two pounds apiece.

Florid, forceful and, in the event, foolish, the older and bigger of the two pounded his fist on the table and yelled, "If there are any damned Texans in here, I advise them to leave now." He drew a Colt and placed it on the table in front of him. "I'll shoot any Texas scum who doesn't leave because I can't abide their rebel stink. The Texan hasn't been born yet that can corral me."

The two carpetbaggers thought this a good joke and laughed so uproariously they didn't notice Wes slowly rise from his chair.

But the other diners did.

A dead silence fell over the room as Wes said, "Eddie, let me have your pistol."

The gambler slipped the Alsop into Wes's hands.

Talking softly across a quiet drawn as tight as a bowstring, John Wesley said, "I'm a Texan."

Standing there in his new suit, I thought Wes a brave sight. He was not as flamboyantly picaresque as Wild Bill, but he still cut a dashing figure.

How could I have been so stupid as to think there would be no gunplay? Why did I believe that both parties would call it all a misunderstanding and settle their differences over a drink?

I should have known better.

The big man, used to lesser mortals stepping out of his way, picked up his Colt. "Why, you insolent young pup. I'll teach you some civilized manners."

The fool, for that's what he was, adopted the traditional duelist's stance. The right side of his body turned to Wes, the arch of his left foot behind his right heel, revolver straight out in front of him at eye level.

He and Wes fired.

And missed.

The carpetbagger's ball hit Pain's good arm, shattering bone.

The big man, sobering quickly, decided he wanted out before Wild Bill heard the shots and got there. He ran for the door to the street and Wes fired again.

The .36 ball hit the fool just as he cleared the doorway. Struck behind the left ear, the ball exited the carpetbagger's mouth and scattered teeth, bone, and brain matter all over the street.

Wes spared a quick glance at Pain, who groaned pitifully in his chair, and ran for the door.

I went after him and saw him jump over the dead Yankee then crash into a man toting a deputy's star. He pushed the deputy away and then slugged him over the head with his revolver.

Before the lawman dropped, Wes vaulted onto the unconscious man's horse and headed at a gallop for the bedding grounds on the Cottonwood.

Abandoned, all I could do was step back inside and check on Eddie Pain.

"Murder! Murder!" The Yankee's companion ran through the dining room, hands fluttering in the air, his eyes wild.

"Get the marshal!" somebody yelled.

"Get me a damned doctor." Pain groaned. "Damn, getting shot in my only good arm is hard to take."

The carpetbagger, his large nose covered in warts, stopped and pointed an accusing finger at Pain. "He and the assassin were in cahoots," he yelled. His stabbing finger jabbed for my heart. "And so was he!"

"You go to hell," I said.

"Damn you. Now I'll do for you!" The Yankee reached into his coat, but ere he could draw, Wild Bill strode into the room and quickly disarmed him.

"Do we have a dead 'un?" Bill looked around.

The warty man cursed and attempted to wrench his revolver from Wild Bill's hand.

In one swift, elegant movement, Bill skinned one of his Navy Colts and slammed the barrel over the carpetbagger's head.

The man groaned horribly, dropped to his knees then stretched his length on the floor.

Bill was as drunk as a hoedown fiddler and all the more dangerous for that.

"Over there, Marshal," a respectable-looking citizen said. "By the side door."

Bill crossed the floor in a couple long strides and got down on one knee beside the dead man.

After a while he rose to his feet, staggered a little, then told everyone what we already knew. "He's as dead as mutton." Wild Bill burped then politely excused himself. "The ball entered the back of his head and came out his mouth. Took most of his teeth with it." His eyebrows knitted together and asked if anyone knew the dead man.

"He came into the dining room with the gentleman who's currently unconscious on the floor," the respectable gent said.

"Who done for him?" Bill asked.

"It was that young Hardin boy," a pretty woman said. She wore green eye shadow and had pink rouge on her cheeks.

"Damn," Bill said. "That boy is causing me no end of trouble. And he buffaloed Mike Williams, my deputy."

"Bill," Pain said, "I'm bleeding to death here."

"I see you, Eddie. You'll keep. You've been shot before."

Pain grimaced. "The dead man, whoever he is, shot first. Wes was defending himself."

"Defending himself? Even when the victim was making a run for it?"

"He could have come back, Marshal," I said.

"Maybe so." Bill looked at me for a moment, then said, "You know where Hardin is?"

I shook my head.

"No matter. By now, he's probably with Columbus Carroll's herd down on the Cottonwood and it's out of my jurisdiction."

Bill's deputy staggered into the room. He held his hat in one hand and rubbed a bump on his head with the other.

"How are you, Mike?" Bill asked.

"I got a headache."

Bill kicked the unconscious man who was drooling from the mouth and didn't look good at all. "Take this down to the jail and lock him up, Mike."

"What's the charge?" the deputy asked.

"Carrying a firearm contrary to the town ordinance. If he pays his seventy-five dollar fine, I'll let him go later."

"Bill, for God's sake, he put a bullet in me," Pain said.

Wild Bill nodded. "I know, Eddie, but you can't charge a man for shooting somebody by mistake. I've studied on the law books and there's nothing that says it's a crime."

Since Bill later killed Mike Williams, his deputy, by mistake, maybe it's just as well that the law took a lenient attitude toward the odd, accidental shooting in those days.

As Williams hauled the eye-rolling, weak-kneed Yankee to his feet, Bill said, "Somebody go get the undertaker."

"Bill," Pain cried, "for God's sake!"

"Oh yeah, and bring Doc Henderson. We have a wounded man here." Bill laid a hand on Pain's shoulder. "Eddie, a man with only one wing should stay away from the likes of John Wesley Hardin. You lose t'other one, hoss, you might as well blow your brains out." He smiled. "Though how you'd hold the gun, I do not know."

Through clenched teeth as his wound throbbed, Pain said, "Bill, you're all heart."

Wild Bill smiled. "That's what folks say about me." He turned his attention to me, his gray eyes searching into mine. "Come here, little mouse," he said, curling his finger.

When I stood in front of him, my eyes were level with the middle button of his frockcoat.

The crowd in the dining room grew noisy again as they talked about the killing, but Wild Bill leaned over and whispered into my ear. "Tell your friend to stay out of Abilene. I'm writing off this killing as self-defense, but if John Wesley kills another man in my town, I'll gun him." He straightened. "Tell him that."

"I sure will. I reckon once the buyers pick up the herd, we'll head for Texas."

Bill nodded. "Live longer that way."

CHAPTER TWENTY-EIGHT
The Vengeance Posse

John Wesley had booked us accommodations at the Alamo, but since he'd skedaddled, I couldn't afford two rooms, or even one, so I bedded down in the livery stable.

That night, aided by a lantern and moonlight, I remade the acquaintances of Quentin Durward in the novel the Reverend Hardin had given me and a pint of cheap bourbon. By the time I rolled into my blankets, I'd started one and finished the other.

Come the cold dawn, I woke with a splitting headache. It was a miserable chore to saddle my horse and ride out under a sky ominous with thunderheads.

I didn't linger in Abilene, but rode directly to the Cottonwood, arriving in a pouring rain and soaked to the skin. Wes immediately pumped me for information.

I told him what had transpired after he ran out of the Alamo dining room. "Wild Bill gave me a message for you, Wes. He told me to tell you to stay out of Abilene."

Wes smiled. "Well, that ain't going to happen, is it?

I'll buckle on my guns and head for the Alamo any time I want. I don't back off from any man, except my pa."

"Bill's taken a set against you, Wes. He's made that clear."

"Like I give a damn."

Wrapped up in my own cold, wet misery I said nothing.

We sheltered under a canvas tarp rigged from the chuck wagon and a small, smoky fire burned between us and gave no warmth.

I sat hunched over, a damp blanket across my shoulders. My leg was playing hob and the ulcerous sore had opened again. In pain, dog-tired from the ride from Abilene, I was in need of hot coffee and dry clothes.

I had neither.

Wes, wrapped up in his ownself as usual, didn't notice or care.

He finally drifted away to join the other punchers who kept boredom at bay by drinking, gambling, and arguing about everything and anything. He and four other cowboys gathered under a larger tarp, held in place by tree limbs. Their fire was bigger and a blackened coffeepot smoked on the coals.

Between me and the others lay fifty yards of open, muddy ground—a vast distance for a sick, weak, and shivering gimp like myself.

Driven by a north wind as cold as a stepmother's breath, rain peppered the mud and birds rose out of the trees against a sky that looked like broken coal. I watched a coyote approach the horse line, think better of it and slink away, raindrops silvering his shaggy coat.

I fancied I could smell the coffee, distant though it was, and determined to make the effort. Rising to my feet, I stood for a few moments to let my reeling head settle, then stepped from under the tarp.

Unfortunately, as I bent my head, the brim of my bowler hat hit the edge of the canvas and about a gallon of water poured down my neck, so icy I thought my heart would stop. Thus it was that by the time I reached Wes's tarp, I was wetter and even more miserable than before.

No one greeted me—the assistant to the assistant cook didn't stand very high in the cowboy hierarchy, well below the drag rider in fact—but I heard no objections as I poured myself a cup of coffee and found an out of the way corner to seat myself.

Then John Wesley, that unpredictable chameleon, stepped to my side with a bottle in his hand. He smiled, poured a stiff shot of Old Crow into my cup, and said, "This will warm you up, Little Bit."

What to make of such a man?

One minute disinterested and uncaring, the next kind and concerned. Was John Wesley a knight in shining armor or an unmitigated knave?

I never did find the answer to that question. With Wes gone and me in my old age, I guess I never will.

Later that day, a rider on a blown horse galloped into camp with news of a killing. His slicker dripping water, he swung out of the saddle and stepped directly to Wes. "Billy Cohron is dead. Shot in the back."

Wes knew and liked Cohron and the news staggered him. "Who did it?"

That was typical of Wes. His first thought was of revenge.

"Greaser by the name of Bideno," the cowboy said. "Him and Billy quarreled about something and then a couple minutes later Bideno snuck up behind him and triggered a shot into him." The drover's voice broke as he added, "Billy lingered long and he suffered something terrible the whole time."

Billy Cohron was a likeable fellow and a steady hand who'd come up the trail as boss herder for Colonel O. W. Wheeler. As I recall, he'd been married just a six-month before his death.

The Wheeler herd was bedded down close to our own.

"Where is Bideno?" Wes asked.

"He rode south on a stolen hoss," the cowboy said. "I guess he's headed for the Nations."

"When did this happen?" Wes let his breath out in a rush, then his mouth tightened into a hard line.

"Day afore yesstidy," the drover said.

"Hell, and you're only telling me now?"

The drover, his name was McKenzie, thought about that a moment then said, "Wes, like I told you, poor Billy lingered. Nobody knew right then if he'd live or die, so we loaded him into a wagon and took him to Abilene. That's where he breathed his last, and then everything was confused."

"Nothing confusing about who shot him though, is there?" Wes asked.

"No, I guess not." McKenzie reached inside his slicker and brought out a folded paper. "Brung you a letter from Colonel Wheeler. It says it all, or so he told me."

Wes read the letter silently, then read it aloud for the benefit of the hands who crowded around him.

"To John Wesley Hardin, Esq.

"By now you have heard the news of William Cohron's death at the hands of a foul and treacherous murderer, whose name is not fit to mention here. Given your skill at arms, it is my request, seconded by fellow cattlemen, that you pursue this vile killer and bring him to justice.

"I have sent out riders on swift horses to square you with the herds now coming up the trail, in the matters of fresh horses and provisions. If you are willing to undertake this task, which will be to your credit if you do, please inform this courier.

"May God ride with you and may you seek out and destroy the fiend who robbed us of a fine man, loving husband, and Southern patriot.

"Yours Respectfully.

"Colonel Oliver Walcott Wheeler.

"There it is, boys. This letter touches my heart and stirs my blood," Wes turned to the courier. "Please inform the colonel that I accept this commission and, as God is my witness, I'll bring this vile assassin to justice."

It was a pretty speech, and, pursuant to what we were talking about earlier, perhaps indicated how John Wesley saw himself . . . as an avenging knight of the plains.

Not a black knight, mind, but a Sir Galahad in shining armor, pure of body and spirit, and always ready to take up a noble cause . . . so long as there was killing involved.

For breakfast the next morning I drank coffee laced with whiskey. It was not in me to stand aside and not play Sancho Panza to my delusional Don Quixote. Sick, tired, and used up as I was, I saddled my pony under a vast, scarlet and jade sky alongside Wes and a surly puncher named Jim Rogers then joined the others as they rode out of camp.

"We must catch that murderer before he reaches the Nations," Wes told us. He looked at me. "Little Bit, we got some long-riding across hard country ahead of us. Can you stand the pace?"

Made brave by the whiskey, I said, "Wes, my horse's nose will be up your sorrel's behind the whole way."

Brave talk from a cripple, and a sickly one at that, but we were all young in those days, and more than slightly crazy.

The rain had passed and by the time we reached the village of Newton the hot sun had dried my clothes and I felt better.

Johnny Cohron, Billy's brother, was waiting for us outside the Wells Fargo office with another cowboy named Hugh Anderson. The two men joined our avenging posse and we reached Wichita, seventy-five miles south of Abilene, that evening.

I got drunk that night and felt like death when we headed south again at first light.

Colonel Wheeler had arranged horse changes with the herds coming up the Chisholm and we switched mounts every few miles.

Riding those half-broke mustangs was an ordeal for me, but I gritted my teeth and kept at it. I would have no man accuse me of being a quitter.

Wes was jumpy as a frog in a frying pan, worried that we'd lose Bideno. He was still somewhere ahead of us.

But when we rode into the cow town of Sumner City, our luck changed.

Wes asked a passerby if a vaquero wearing a big sombrero, riding a good horse, had blown into town recently.

The man said, "He sure did. Right now he's over to the Silver Spur saloon." Because westerners are a naturally curious breed, he asked, "He a friend of your'n?"

"No," Wes said. "No, he sure ain't."

Our little posse rode up to the Silver Spur and dismounted. Wes sent Cohron and Rogers around the back of the saloon to cut off that avenue of escape. Wes and Anderson stepped into the saloon.

Me, I was left to my own devices since I didn't carry a gun. I followed Wes.

The saloon wasn't busy at that time of day and when Wes and Anderson entered with guns drawn, the bartender quickly realized that something was afoot. He stared at John Wesley, a question on his face.

Wes said quietly, "Mexican. Big hat."

The bartender nodded and used the glass he was polishing to point to the door that led into the restaurant.

Wes stepped through the door and recognized his man.

Now, in Wes's memoirs, he claims he said to Bideno, "I am after you to surrender. I do not wish to hurt you, and you will not be hurt while you are in my hands."

Well, I was there and what he really said was, "Get up, Bideno. Take it in the belly like a man."

The Mexican had a cup off coffee halfway to his lips, but he dropped the cup, cursed, and clawed for his holstered Colt.

Wes fired. Shot Bideno smack in the middle of the forehead.

I heard a *Ping!* as Wes's ball hit a potbellied stove against the far wall after crashing clean through the Mexican's head.

Johnny Cohron took Bideno's bloody sombrero for a souvenir.

And that's all there was to it. Just another routine kill for John Wesley.

Bang! You're dead.

CHAPTER TWENTY-NINE
Wes Strikes It Rich

Shortly after we rode back to the Cottonwood, a deputation from Abilene arrived in camp with a purse made up by some wealthy cattlemen. It contained a thousand dollars and a flowery letter that thanked Wes for killing Bideno.

Now, let me tell you something about that. It was the worst thing that could have happened to John Wesley.

Years later, in the harsh Wyoming winter of 1903, I interviewed Tom Horn for a dime novel before he was wrongly hung for murdering a boy by the name of Willie Nickell. I recall Tom saying to me, "The worst lesson I ever learned in life was that wealthy citizens would pay me for killing people they considered undesirables. It was a hard lesson and it led to my downfall and death."

Well, Wes had learned that same lesson . . . and it would kill him just as surely as it killed poor Tom.

By my count, John Wesley had killed around thirty-one men and he could justify every single one of them. To his mind, all of them were men who needed killing.

I never heard Wes say that his conscience troubled him or that dead men haunted his dreams at night. He believed that thirty human beings lay in dank graves because they were bad, wicked, criminal, or just plain wrong.

It was entirely their fault, not John Wesley Hardin's.

In his own eyes, Wes was not a killer but a lawful executioner dispensing his own brand of justice to evildoers of every stripe.

I pen this now as an old man, but at the time I didn't think on all this so deeply. All I knew was that Wes would lead and I would follow.

That was the nature of things in those days.

"Little Bit," Wes said to me a couple days after our return. "Do you not agree that I'm a man of substance, respected by rich and poor alike?"

"I'd say that."

Since he'd not given any of the posse members, myself included, a red cent out of his reward, he still had a thousand dollars in his pocket, plus most of his trail wages. To me, that was wealth beyond imagining.

"Then there's no reason why I shouldn't visit Abilene is there?" Wes asked.

I smiled. "Just one."

"You mean Wild Bill?"

"As ever was."

"I have nothing to fear from him. Since I killed Bideno, I'm bull of the woods in Abilene."

"Reason enough for Wild Bill to gun you, Wes."

"I'm a respectable businessman in the cattle industry and I'll soon own a Wild West show. Hickok is drunken trash. He wouldn't dare draw down on me." Wes used a stick from the fire to light his cigar. "If I kill him, who would blame me? Any future trouble between us will be his doing, not mine."

I drank from the pint of whiskey I'd bought in Sumner City and set aside for when my leg got to aching real bad and listened to the night. We were so close to the river I heard fish jump. A cool breeze carried the odor of longhorns and trampled mud, the only reminder of the great cattle herd that had been there for a little while.

"Tomorrow," Wes said, his cigar glowing red in the dark, "we'll ride into town, get noisy, get a woman, get drunk, and be somebody."

I laughed out loud. "Sounds good to me, Wes, so long as Bill doesn't spoil the party."

"He won't. He knows better than that."

I leaned my head to the side. "Think you can take him?"

Wes nodded once. "Damn right I can. Any day of the week."

My leg brace lay beside me and I picked it up. I slept with it on in those days. With Wes around, there was no telling when we might have to light a shuck in a hurry.

"How is the sore?" Wes asked.

"It's all right."

"You're lying to me, Little Bit. You look like you got one foot in the pine box."

"What foot? The good one or the bad one?" I smiled, feeling the drink.

"Hell, maybe both." Wes lit the lantern close by and held it high. "Let me take a look at that damned thing."

Orange light splashed over me like wet paint as I dropped my pants and revealed the open, weeping wound at the top of my thigh. It was as big as a man's palm.

Wes stared at the sore for a long while, then said, "That settles it. We're riding into Abilene tomorrow and you're seeing a doctor."

John Wesley was rich and famous, and oh how I basked in his attention.

He shook his head. "Little Bit, I've asked you this before. Even with the steel brace, how do you stand on that leg? It's as skinny as a carpetbagging Negro's walking cane."

"It isn't easy. Pains me some." I reached for the brace, but Wes pushed it out of reach.

"Leave that off until you see the doc." He saw the doubt on my face and added, "I'll help you into the saddle." He laid the lantern aside and poured coffee. "Want some?"

I shook my head. "Still got whiskey in the bottle."

"Well drink it down. We'll pull out of here at first light." He studied me for a spell, then said, "Damn it, Little Bit, how do you live?"

"Well enough, I guess."

"No, I mean how do you *survive*? You look like, I don't know, one of them little white-faced goblins in the fairy stories my ma used to read to me when I was a younker."

"Goblins survive, Wes, and so do trolls and imps and dwarves and gnomes," I said. "Somehow or other, they manage to live. For me, all survival takes is will and the ability to delude myself."

Wes grinned. "You want to be six foot tall, don't you?"

"No, just as tall as you."

"It ain't going to happen."

"I know that."

"When I have my Wild West show I'll put you in a tent and show you off as a freak. I could charge folks two-bits to see you and shake your hand."

"Like Wild Bill taking his bath," I said.

"No, not like Wild Bill. He's six feet if he's an inch. You're just a nubbin'."

I corked the whiskey bottle. "Whatever you think is best, Wes."

"Ah hell, I was only joshing. I won't put you in a tent."

"Then where will you put me?"

"Why, behind a desk where you belong. Even a crippled goblin can count our profits, huh?"

"That sounds better," I said.

"Damn right it does," Wes said.

Before I drifted into an alcohol-troubled sleep, I remember thinking that come tomorrow, maybe the doctor could fix my leg . . . but some of the wounds Wes so casually and thoughtlessly inflicted on me would never heal.

CHAPTER THIRTY
Doctor's Orders

We rode into Abilene through a blue dawn and the town was sound asleep. All the dust and drama of the night before had been laid to rest with the rising of the sun. Like Mr. Stoker's vampires, Wild Bill and the rest of the sporting crowd were abed behind shades and would not rise again until the sun began its scarlet descent to the horizon.

When we reached the doctor's house, Wes lifted me from the saddle and carried me inside without effort, as though his arms cradled a child.

Doctor John Henderson, a young man with black hair and earnest brown eyes, directed Wes to sit me on the edge of the examination table.

Wes handed the physician my leg brace. "This is his. It gave him a sore"—he pointed to the top of his thigh—"right there."

Doc Henderson's nurse was middle-aged and not pretty. She had one of those tight, prim mouths you see on women who exist on a diet of prune juice and scripture. Her eyes were small, blue, and intolerant.

She snatched the brace out of Wes's hand. "Please be seated in the waiting room."

Then it was lecture time. "The carrying of firearms is not permitted in Abilene."

"So I've been told," Wes said. "Doc, holler when you need me."

After Wes stepped out of the room, the doctor examined me. "How long have you had this?"

I nodded at the brace. "Off and on, as long as I've been wearing that."

"For the time being, we'll keep the wound wet and make sure it doesn't get infected," Henderson said. "Don't wear the brace until I get this healed." He smiled at me. "Can you do that? Will your friends find you a place to stay and help you get around?"

"Oh sure, Doc." Of course, that was a boldfaced lie.

Without the brace, I'd have to lie in bed. Where? And who would look after me? Wes might push me around in a wheelchair for a while, but then he'd get bored, ride out of town, and leave me to my own devices.

Abilene was not a place for an impoverished, helpless cripple. Without the brace, all I'd be able to do was die of neglect and starvation.

"Just do what you can, Doc," I said.

Doctor Henderson put various salves on the wound, one of them that smelled suspiciously of honey, and then he bandaged the wound.

Wes was called back to the surgery and the doc said, "Your friend will need plenty of bed rest and help getting around."

"What about his brace?" Wes asked.

"He can't wear it until his wound heals," Henderson said.

"Can he ride?"

"No. I'm afraid not."

"Just as far as Texas," Wes said.

The doctor smiled. "Not as far as the edge of town."

To say that Wes looked unhappy is an understatement. It was obvious that taking care of an invalid didn't enter into his thinking.

"He's not even kin," he said.

That comment raked across my heart like a knife blade. It hurt a sight worse than my leg.

"I'm sure you will help," the doctor said.

"It's Christian charity after all," the nurse said.

"Then you take care of him, lady," Wes said.

"Wes, I'll be no trouble," I said. "I promise." God help me, I even winked at him, trying to allay his fears.

It didn't work.

"How long will it take his leg to heal, Doc?" Wes asked.

Henderson shrugged. "It's too early to tell. Weeks, maybe a couple months."

Wes looked at me with an odd mix of pity and irritation.

"The patient is not strong. He's suffering from malnutrition and, I suspect, alcohol abuse. The prognosis is far from good."

"But with God's grace and abstinence, he can recover," the nurse said.

"Yes. Yes indeed," the doc said. "But he'll need first rate care."

That was not what John Wesley wanted to hear. "Hell, we could be snowed in here come winter."

Henderson smiled. "Come fall, you mean." He glanced at the door. "Well, I have other patients waiting." To me he said, "Keep the dressing clean and come back and see me at the end of the week. Nurse Meadows will let you out."

"Your bill for today will be two dollars." The woman gave me a hard look that said *And don't even think of telling me you can't pay it.*

Desperate, Wes clutched at a straw. "Doc, can he stay here with you? That way you can treat him real good. He's quiet and doesn't eat much." Then, as an afterthought, "And he has some money."

Henderson shook his head. "I'm afraid that's impossible. I don't run a hospital here." He smiled. "Now, if you'll excuse me?"

It was obvious from Wes's hangdog expression that he knew he'd run out of space on the dance floor. He picked me up and stepped to the door.

Nurse Meadows let us out and handed Wes my brace. "Two dollars, please," she said when the door of the surgery closed behind us.

"Pay the lady, Little Bit."

Outside, Wes lifted me into the saddle, then led my horse and his in the direction of the Alamo. The day had brightened and a few women in morning dresses were out and about, shopping baskets over their arms, faces set and determined as they hunted only the best bargains.

A brewer's dray trundled past, the barrels creaking against their retaining ropes. The team of four magnificent Percherons in the traces had hooves as big as soup plates, and I fancied one of those would be the ideal knightly mount for Quentin Durward.

Wes had been fuming silently since we left the doctor's office, but as we passed an alley on our left, I intruded into his quiet. "Wes, lead my horse into the alley there."

"Hell, piss at the Alamo," Wes said.

"I want to put my brace back on."

"The doc told you not to do that."

"Yeah, well I'm doing it. The doctor told me not to drink, and I'm doing that, too."

"Your funeral," Wes said, frowning.

Secretly, I think he was relieved.

Once in the alley I sat down, dropped my pants, and buckled on the steel cage. The doc had wrapped a fat bandage around the top of my thigh and when I stood I discovered that it padded the wound pretty good.

"How does it feel?" Wes asked.

"All right."

He stared at me and wrinkled his nose. "You sat in dog crap."

CHAPTER THIRTY-ONE
The Snoring Man

John Wesley decided against the Alamo where we'd be likely to run into Wild Bill and instead we headed for the American Hotel, less grand but safer.

Not that Wes was afraid of Bill, but he knew he'd get used up in a gunfight, even if he proved the victor. Wild Bill was no bargain. He had sand. He'd take his hits and put lead into a man as long as he'd strength to pull the trigger.

As Wes told me, "Let sleeping dogs lie."

Gip Clements was in town and he joined us at the bar of the hotel saloon where we proceeded to get pretty drunk.

Wes had taken the wise precaution of keeping our horses close and under saddle. I believe his carefulness saved his life later that night.

A friend of Gip's, a man named Charlie Cougar, joined us at the bar. I didn't know the fellow, but he seemed a good sort and stood his round. So I have nothing bad to say about him . . .

Except that he snored with a racket like a freight train in a tunnel.

Now, people often ask me, "Is it true that John Wesley Hardin killed a man for snoring?"

And my answer is, "Well, he did, but it was an accident."

As Wes said later, "Hell, it was all Cougar's fault. How was I to know he'd sit up in bed the very moment I fired a warning shot across his bow?"

Some of you may have a different opinion on that killing, but in my heart of hearts, I can't blame Wes. By one in the morning all four of us were roaring drunk, talking nonsense and seeing double.

Wes said, "I don't want to meet Wild Bill in this state so we should go to bed and sleep off the whiskey."

Gip and Charlie agreed that it sounded like an excellent plan and so did I, though nobody much cared about my opinion.

Wes booked a room for all of us, but Charlie insisted on sleeping alone, so he got the one adjoining.

Staggering, Wes and Gip threw off their clothes and, wearing only their long johns, threw themselves on the bed and were asleep within seconds.

Me, I found myself a corner and tried to make myself as comfortable as I could. My hurting leg was numbed by whiskey, but the rough pine floor was hard and I couldn't drop off.

Ten, fifteen minutes passed . . . and then the snoring erupted.

Remember, the partition walls in frontier hotels were paper-thin and the noise of Cougar's snoring was horrific, a racketing ripsaw roar that reverberated around the room and rattled the portrait of Robert E. Lee on the wall.

Gip shot up in bed like a man waking from a nightmare. "What the hell is that?"

"Charlie Cougar is snoring," I said. "Seems like."

"Hey, Charlie!" Gip yelled. "Turn over for God's sake. You're waking up the whole damned town."

Cougar's bed creaked, the snoring stopped and Gip's head, that seemed to be as heavy as an anvil, hit the pillow again.

A slow count to ten . . . and the stentorian serenade of the ear-shattering slumberer started again.

Wes sat up and groped for the Colt on his bedside table. "I'll scare them snores the hell out of him." He thumbed three fast shots through the partition wall . . . and the snoring abruptly stopped, followed by the sound of a body hitting the wood floor.

For a few moments, Wes listened into the cold, echoing silence, then he whispered, "Hell, Gip, I think I shot too low."

Gip nodded. "I think you did. I reckon you done for ol' Charlie an' no mistake."

This verdict was confirmed when voices were raised in the hallway and on the stairwell.

"Get the marshal!" a man yelled.

I heard the door to Cougar's room open and then a woman shrieked, "Murder! Murder!"

Gip Clements jumped out of bed, put on his hat, and pulled on his boots. "Wes, I'm heading back to Texas. Wild Bill will gun us fer sure."

"I'm with you," Wes said.

I crossed to the window and looked out, just as a

hack pulled up and disgorged four deputies. "The law!" I yelled.

Gip ran to the window, saw that the lawmen were already inside the hotel, and jumped.

Like Gip, wearing only his underwear, boots, gun belt, and hat, Wes was ready to follow when I yelled, "What about me?"

Without a word, he picked me up and threw me through the open window. I fell two floors and hit the sandy ground with a thump.

A moment later, Wes landed feet first beside me. "Let's go!" he hollered.

I thanked my lucky stars that I fell on my butt. If I'd landed on the steel brace it would have split me open like a ripe watermelon.

Wes hauled me to my feet and we made a dash for the horses, still saddled in the hotel corral. Well, I didn't dash, but Gip and Wes did.

The moon was up and Texas Street was bathed in a soft, mother-of-pearl light that was soon streaked by gunfire. Balls thudded around me as Wes and Gip rode out of the corral, Gip leading my horse.

Fear helped me climb into the saddle and we rode out of Abilene at a gallop, followed by searching gunfire and a cloud of yellow dust.

Wes pulled his horse beside mine, laughing, and yelled, "Damn, Little Bit, I never shot a man for snoring before." He shook his head. "I guess there's a first time for everything."

That reminds me to hammer home the point I made before. I'm sick and tired of some rooster coming up to me and asking, "Is it true that Hardin shot three men for snoring?"

Sometimes it's three men, sometimes four, and even five.

Let me put the record straight yet again. Wes shot only one man for snoring and it was an accidental killing. Nobody can pin a murder charge on him. Hell, if you want to blame somebody, blame Charlie Cougar for sitting up in bed at the wrong time.

CHAPTER THIRTY-TWO
The Dark Star

We rode into Texas in August.

To my surprise, Wes talked about hanging up his guns and going straight. "It's time to get the Wild West show organized, Little Bit. I reckon we could be up and running in a year, maybe less."

"Gip, you reckon the Clements boys will help us?" I asked.

"Sure they will. And Wes has kinfolk all over Texas who'll pitch in money. You can lay to that."

I was pleased that John Wesley was finally considering a settled, peaceful way of life. "We have cowboys aplenty, Wes. Now all we need is some tame Indians."

"A lot of them around," he said.

"Where?"

"Oh, up Montana way and places. Blanket Indians they call them, since they got whipped by the army and depend on government beef. They're a raggedy-assed bunch, but with some paint and feathers, they'll work just fine."

I smiled. "Wes, you know, I think we can do it."

"Damn right we can. And we can round up buffalo by the hundreds. The Plains are covered with them." He drew rein then stood in the stirrups, a young man, eyes alight dreaming his dream. "Think of it, boys"— he made a sweeping, circular motion with his hand, building a stadium in the air—"an Injun buffalo hunt right there in the arena . . . the buffalo stampeding around and around, the savages whooping and hollering and shooting arrows, the dust, the noise . . . the crowd cheering."

"Hell, Wes, folks will pay big money to see that," Gip said, catching Wes's enthusiasm.

"Damn right they will,"

"But don't you go shooting them Redskins," Gip said. "You'll need them alive."

"Nah, I'm done with all that. From now on, John Wesley Hardin is a respectable businessman, an entre . . . ontre . . ."

"Entrepreneur," I supplied.

"Yeah, that's what I am," Wes said.

You'd be right in saying that Wes was really happy . . . and so was I.

As usual, I should have known better.

John Wesley was born under a dark star. Its light was black . . . black as midnight. Sometimes a man can't get out from under that somber glow, no matter how hard he tries.

I didn't know it then, but I know it now. Wes was doomed from the moment he was born . . . and, God help me, I hastened his inevitable end.

A month later, we rode up on the Clements homestead in Gonzales County. It was more fortress than home, a frame cabin with a shingle roof, the windows backed by heavy oak shutters. The walls were covered with gun ports and pockmarked by bullets.

At that time the saying was, "If you're a fugitive from Yankee justice and on the scout, there's a welcome waiting for you at the Clements' house." Wes and I relaxed for a time, enjoying the peace and quiet. Indeed, his guns hung on a nail in the wall the whole time we were there.

He had once been sweet on a girl whose pa owned a general store in Nopal, a small town up in DeWitt County close to the Gonzales County line. Along about October, he decided to ride up there and get reacquainted.

Of course, I decided to go with him.

"To keep me out of trouble, Little Bit?" he asked.

"To keep that Bowen girl out of trouble."

Wes laughed.

Neill Bowen welcomed us to his store with a smile, and then told us to help ourselves to cheese and crackers while he dealt with another customer.

Nopal was a dusty, ramshackle little burg, scorched by sun and scourged by wind. It didn't have a single redeeming feature, no place to go where you shouldn't be, not even a saloon. I think a hundred people existed there, maybe less.

John Wesley would soon put that miserable, humble little hamlet on the map.

The trouble began a few minutes after we arrived when a black state policeman, wearing brown canvas pants and a faded blue shirt stepped into the store.

He was a tall, lean, muscular man who wore a Colt cavalry style on his right hip. His name was Green Paramore and he'd killed his man in the past, but I didn't learn that until later.

The Negro and Wes saw each other at the same time, but Wes was trying to live up to his peaceful ways. "There's crackers and cheese, but eat them outside."

The lawman wasn't much of a one for conversation. He skinned his Colt and said, "Hardin, throw up your hands or I'll drop you right where you stand. You're under arrest for murder."

Wes, always a consummate actor, pretended to be nervous. "Look out, old fellow. That iron is likely to go off, and I don't want to be shot by accident."

"Then unlimber those pistols and hand them over," Paramore said. "I see a fancy move and I'll kill you."

"Very well then. You've got the drop on me fair and square." Wes slowly and carefully drew his Colts from the holsters and extended them to the lawman, butts forward.

I knew what was about to happen next and the breath bunched in my throat.

Suddenly those pistols cartwheeled and flamed lead.

Paramore, his eyes bugging out in his black face like boiled eggs, took two balls in the forehead and dropped as though his legs had been swept from under him, dead before he hit the floor.

"John Wesley," Neill Bowen yelled. "Outside!"

Wes stepped over the body of the dead man and hurried to the door.

John Lackey, a mulatto policeman from Tennessee,

sat astride a fractious mule, but he snapped off a shot at Wes and missed.

Wes fired and the man toppled out of the saddle. Squealing like a strangled piglet, he quickly climbed on board again and lit a shuck, flapping his chaps.

Wes thought this so comical he didn't fire again, contenting himself to double up with laughter.

I didn't laugh. I knew that after this shooting, hard times would come down fast.

And they did.

CHAPTER THIRTY-THREE
The Reluctant Husband

Just a week after the Paramore killing, a posse of Negro policemen came down from Austin, vowing to collect John Wesley's scalp and tack it onto the door of the nearest outhouse.

Wes was told by kinfolk that the lawmen were camped near the DeWitt County farm of a man called Monroe and that they were constantly drunk and had abused the fellow's wife and teenaged daughter.

This last enraged Wes and he strapped on his guns determined to uphold the honor of white, Southern womanhood.

My knight rode forth, but I was again sick in bed at the Clements home and couldn't follow him.

Since I wasn't there, I'll pass over what followed quickly.

As I heard it from Wes, he rode into the drunken Negro camp and cut loose with his *avenging six-guns*. He killed three of the vile riffraff and put the rest to flight.

Needless to say, he returned to a hero's welcome.

"Wes, surely that makes two score," Gip Clements said as the whiskey ran freely.

It seemed that the whole of Gonzalez County had turned out to honor Wes.

Despite being ill, my pride in him swelled. I recall that a hush fell over the house as the merrymakers strained to hear the answer to Gip's question.

And Wes, as usual, rose to the occasion. He struck an orator's pose. "I do not count blacks, Mexicans, or Indians in my score. So the number of white miscreants, carpetbaggers, low persons, traitors, and trouble-makers I have put in the grave must stand at twenty-two."

This brought a chorus of delighted huzzahs and the fiddler struck up "Home with the Girls in the Morning." I cheered louder than anyone else.

Again I must beg my reader's indulgence, as I pass lightly over Wes's marriage that took place around that time . . . for no other reason than he took it so lightly himself.

His bride was a dark-haired lass named Jane Bowen who was fourteen at the time. Wes four years older.

"I'm not a family man, Little Bit, preferring the company of rough men," he told me after the wedding. "Jane's duty is to have children and I will support them the best I can."

I've heard some people say that they were a devoted couple.

They were not.

Wes was a negligent husband. He and Jane seldom

slept together under the same roof, even after she gave birth to their first child when she was fifteen.

Oh, how I wish, for the sake of the ladies, that I could pen a romance worthy of Miss Charlotte Bronte or Miss Jane Austen and cast John Wesley and his bride aglow in the light of love as they embarked on their path to marital bliss.

Alas, I cannot.

Thus, we must leave poor Mrs. Hardin—of the unkempt hair and the *Oh my God, what have I done?* look in her eyes—alone and lonely in her small home above her father's general store, and go on to more manly pursuits.

On June 8, 1872, Wes told me that he was driving a herd of grade horses to Louisiana for sale to the army.

Though still thin and wasted, I had recovered from my illness and asked if I could follow along.

As always, Wes was reluctant. "Little Bit, I'm riding with Jess and John Harper, rough men who are quick on the trigger and take no sass."

"I can keep my mouth shut and pull my weight," I said.

That made Wes smile. "How much weight, Little Bit? I swear you don't go seventy pounds."

"I can cook. You know that."

"Yeah, you're pretty good at rustling up grub."

"Well?" I said.

I guess I caught Wes in a good mood because after three months of marriage he was eager to take to the trail again.

"All right, you can ride with us, but don't ask me for

wages, or the Harper brothers either. After the drive, if I think you've been worth it, I'll pay you something."

"Sets fine with me," I said.

"How's the leg?"

"It will hold up."

"How's the leg?"

I hesitated a moment, then said, "It's been better . . . and worse."

"Same thing applies as I told you the last time. You fall behind and we're leaving you."

"I'll stick."

"You'd better." Wes smiled. "Them Apache bucks would love to get ahold of you, Little Bit."

CHAPTER THIRTY-FOUR
Downed by Buckshot

We never did reach Louisiana.

Wes got bored with the drive and gave up when we reached the Sabine River. He sold the herd to the Harper brothers for what they would pay, then we headed back for Texas.

Oh, I almost forgot, at a burg called Hemphill in Sabine County, Wes put a hole in a lawman's shoulder for giving him backtalk. It wasn't a fatal wound, so it's hardly worth mentioning here. But that officer surely scampered after Wes plugged him.

My leg was troubling me, so Wes decided we should stop off at Trinity Station and rest up for a spell. The town was a shabby, dusty little settlement without snap or character, but it was close to the Trinity River and was a stop on the Houston and Great Northern Railroad. For the life of me I couldn't figure out why.

Most of the houses and stores clustered around the station, but the pride of the metropolis was the John Gates Saloon at the corner of Caroline and Parke streets. A banner slung across the building's false front proclaimed 5¢ BEER & 10-PIN BOWLING

"Hell, that's the place for us, huh, Little Bit?" Wes said. "I like to bowl."

As I climbed off my horse at the hitching rail, the breath caught in my throat and I was filled with a sense of foreboding . . . dread you might say. I wanted to tell Wes how I felt, but I knew he'd laugh at me and call me an old woman, so I bit my tongue.

Hell, the panels on the saloon's timber door were shaped like a cross. I took that as a bad omen.

And it was.

That day, poor, timorous, craven creature that I was, I almost caused the death of John Wesley Hardin, the greatest man of his era.

The John Gates was a saloon like any other, its raw whiskey and warm beer like any other. The only thing that set it apart was a space at the rear set aside for bowling.

I prevailed on Wes to leave his pistols behind the bar, since the risk of running into the law in Trinity Station was remote.

He readily agreed and handed his Colts to the bartender. With a whiskey at his elbow, he looked around the saloon . . . and saw someone he knew. "You see that fellow over at the table with the shotgun at his side?"

I looked at the man in the French mirror behind the bar. "I see him."

"His name is Phil Sublett and he killed a carpetbagging black man by the name of George Stubblefield with that there scattergun."

"Then he's a patriot," I said.

"Damn right he is. And a farmer."

Sublett glanced over at us and Wes raised his glass. "Howdy, Phil."

Sublett, a tall, thin man with a goatee and roughly cut brown hair, joined us at the bar. He had hard, blue eyes that never looked at you directly, as though he constantly found items of interest in the corners of the room. "Howdy, Wes. It's been a while."

"Seems like." Wes introduced me. "This here is Little Bit."

Sublett gave me a quick, disinterested glance, and dismissed me. "Been hearing things about you, Wes."

"People talk."

"They say you put the crawl on Wild Bill Hickok."

Wes puffed up a little. "He tried to corral me, but now me and William are on the square."

"Glad to hear it," Sublett said.

"You're farming, I heard."

"Not for much longer. I'm tired of pushing a plow, staring at a mule's butt all the damned day."

"You should go into the cattle business, Phil," Wes said. "A man on a hoss can see forever if his eyes are good."

"Something to keep in mind. Let me buy you a drink and maybe we'll bowl later, huh?"

"Sounds good to me," Wes said, fingering his gambler's ring. "What are the stakes?"

"Two-bits a game too much for you?"

"Hell, that's for maiden aunts playing Old Maid," Wes said. "Lets make it fifty cents."

"I'm your daisy." Sublett's unsmiling face was stiff.

I realized then that this man was no friend of Wes.

I thought maybe he was jealous of Wes's reputation and fame and was glad my friend's guns were behind the bar.

After Wes and Sublett left for the bowling pins, I took a bottle to the table, stretched out my bad leg and concentrated on the whiskey.

As Wes and Sublett yelled and argued the rules, I got slowly drunk . . . then faster drunk . . . then I-don't-give-a-damn drunk. I even lowered my pants and poured whiskey over the open wound on my thigh . . . and passed out from the sudden shriek of pain.

I don't know how long I was unconscious, but when I raised my head I heard John Wesley yell, "Damn you for a cheat, Sublett! Keep it up and I'm gonna put a bullet in your damn belly!"

They had switched from bowling to cards.

Wes was a bad gambler and a sore loser. I'd feared something like that could happen. I didn't know that he'd stashed away a sneaky gun or I'd have felt a sight worse.

"And damn you for a scoundrel, Hardin!" Sublett roared. "Come outside and give me six feet of ground."

Wes held a small revolver of the bulldog type with its muzzle jammed into Sublett's belly.

I figured that a killing was only seconds away, but during the time I was out, other men had come into the saloon. I heard shouts of, "No, that won't do!" and, "Put away your weapon!"

Well, to my surprise, Wes calmed down and shoved the bulldog into his pocket, saying that his temper had gotten the better of him.

Urged by the crowd to shake hands, he and Sublett

did just that and everyone repaired to the bar where some rooster ordered rum punches all round.

But Phil Sublett didn't stay. Shotgun in hand, he walked out of the saloon and into the darkening street, his face thunderous with anger.

Wes had lived by the gun for so long that he had the instincts of a hunted wolf.

I watched bleary-eyed from my table as he got his guns from the bartender and shoved them into the shoulder holsters.

As lamps were lit in the saloon against the crowding darkness, Wes drank little, his gaze fixed on the door.

Then came the moment of hell that I dreaded.

Sublett's voice echoed from outside, harsh and challenging. "Hardin, get out here and meet me like a man!" he yelled. "You'll eat supper in hell tonight, by God."

A silence fell on the saloon . . . except for my drunken sobs, the consequence of my fevered thoughts. *Phil Sublett, the failed farmer who envied John Wesley enough to kill him, was outside with a murderous shotgun . . . he planned to slaughter a man of virtue . . . a man much finer than himself . . . my Quentin Durward . . . my knight without compare . . . my hero . . . my friend . . .*

Wes stepped to the door.

I stumbled to my feet. "No, wait," I said, slurring my words. "I'm coming . . . I'm going . . . I mean, I . . ."

Wes threw me a look, ignored me, and stepped outside.

A moment later, I heard the blast of a shotgun and the sharper bark of Wes's Colts.

"Wes!" I screamed, foolish drunkard that I was. "I'm coming!" I staggered to the door, fell, and scrambled to my feet again.

"You, get back here!" a man yelled.

But I ignored him and lurched outside.

Wes stood in the shadows to the right of the saloon door. A lantern at the corner of the building cast a shifting circle of light onto the street and entrance to an adjoining alley.

I stumbled to Wes, tears in my eyes, and grabbed him by the lapels of his coat. "John Wesley," I yelled, "I'm with you! Together we can whip this whole damn town!"

Wes cursed and pushed me away. I stumbled back and pulled him with me . . . into the lantern light.

Sublett's shotgun roared and Wes staggered, hit hard.

The damned, yellow-bellied assassin then turned tail and ran. Wes, leaving behind a trail of blood, went after him.

Rapidly sobering, I stumped after him.

How well I remember that night.

There was no wind. It was as though the town held its breath, waiting for what was to happen. A yellow dog with amber eyes snarled at me as I thudded past and its gleaming fangs were white as ivory. Ahead of me, I saw Sublett turn into an unfinished timber building.

Wes, bent over and reeling, went after him.

Then a shot.

Followed by silence.

Wes staggered out of the building and stood with a

supporting hand on the doorjamb. He saw me and said, "I put a hole in him, but he's gone."

"Are you hit, Wes?" I asked, knowing full well he was.

"I'm done for. He got me in the belly." He dropped to a sitting position, scarlet blood leaking through the fingers of the hand that clutched his stomach.

A crowd gathered around him. I kneeled beside him, but Wes threw my arm off his shoulder and yelled, "Get the hell away from me. You've killed me."

As you might guess, that was a wound, but then Wes was hurting and thought he was at death's door, so I forgave him.

He looked around at the concerned faces of the people. "My time is short."

"No!" a woman screamed.

"You good people are witnesses to my last will and testament," Wes said.

"I'll get Dr. Carrington," the screaming woman said.

"No, not yet. Listen to me, all of you."

The crowd of maybe two-dozen quieted down.

Wes said, "My money belt holds two thousand dollars in gold and there's another five hundred in silver in my saddlebags. Give the money to my wife in Gonzales County, along with whatever my horse, saddle, and guns will bring." He grimaced as a wave of pain hit him. His voice got weaker. "Tell my dear Jane that I honestly tried to avoid this trouble. But my foeman done for me with a scattergun. Such is the way of cowards."

Then, before unconsciousness took him, he said, "Bury me in Gonzales County. Don't let my body lie in foreign soil."

Willing hands carried Wes to the doctor's office,

bloody, like a gallant matador gored in the arena. I followed, heavy of heart.

Dr. Carrington, an intelligent man of middle age, said that the big silver buckle Wes wore on his money belt had taken most of the shotgun blast and saved his life. However, two buckshot had succeeded in doing their deadly work. They had ripped into his belly and were lodged between his backbone and ribs.

"They have to come out," the doctor said. "I can give you something to dull the pain."

John Wesley, that fearless stalwart, said, "I'll have no truck with opiates. Cut away, Doc, and be damned to ye for a butcher."

Well, that's not really what Wes said, on account of how he fainted when he heard the diagnosis. But had he been conscious, he would have said something of that ilk, I'm sure.

Thus I may be accused of putting words in my hero's mouth that he did not utter. But then, how else am I to express his noble, gallant and generous nature?

CHAPTER THIRTY-FIVE
Thirty-six Dead Men

The town of Trinity Station harbored a nest of traitors.

John Wesley was still recovering from his terrible wounds when a grand jury convened and indicted him for the attempted murder of that vile hound Phil Sublett!

There was no appeal against this grave injustice and Wes, wounded though he was, had to flee the town by dark of night, like a common criminal.

He became a hunted animal, relentlessly pursued by posses. I'm proud to say that, weak and sick as I was, I rode with him through those trying times. On the scout, we slipped from one hideout to another, and finally found refuge in Angelina County at the home of Dave Harrel, a Hardin family friend.

But the state police would not leave us alone. Three or four times packs of hunters rode close to the house.

Sitting in the Harrel parlor, Wes said to me, "Little

Bit, the wound in my belly is festering and I need medical help. I think I've no option but to surrender."

I was not in good shape myself. The wound on my thigh had grown to twice its size and it smelled. We'd had little to eat since leaving Trinity Station and I'd lost weight. The calf muscle of my bad leg was about as big around as a walnut.

"A jury will clear you of all charges, Wes," I said. "Sublett shot at you first."

"Damn right he did." After some thought, Wes said, "Yeah . . . maybe I should take my chances with the law."

"You're a respectable businessman, Wes. And you'll soon have your own Wild West show. There isn't a jury in Texas that will convict you."

But Wes suddenly seemed a little hesitant. "Dave Harrel's wife is making up a salve for my wound. She says her ma used it on her pa after he came back from the war all shot up and it worked wonders." He began to reassemble the Colt he'd been cleaning "Now I study on it, I guess I'll wait a spell, see how the salve works."

All at once, I was exasperated. "Wes, you must see a doctor. A gut shot man needs more than hog fat and aloe."

"That means surrendering," Wes said.

"Yes, that's what it means."

"Well, I—"

A fist pounded on the front door of the house and a man's voice yelled, "Open up in the name of the law!"

A few moments later Dave Harrel stepped into the parlor, his face pale. He held a shotgun in his hand.

"State police," he said, dropping his voice to a whisper. "At first I thought it was road agents."

"How many?" Wes asked.

"Two. That I can see anyway."

Wes rose, wincing, from his chair, the unhealed belly wound punishing him. "Dave, keep them talking. And give me the scattergun."

"I don't want no trouble." Harrel's thin, brown hair was plastered to his head in damp strands.

A fist pounded on the door again. Louder.

"That's up to them, isn't it?" Wes grabbed the shotgun from Harrel's unresisting hand and slipped through the back door.

"Let's go talk to them, Dave," I said.

Two men stood outside, one with a revolver in his fist.

"What can I do for you worthy gentlemen?" Harrel said, his face beaming with pretended good humor.

So far, so good, I thought.

"We have reason to believe that a murderer by the name of John Wesley Hardin is hiding in this residence," the lawman with the Colt said.

Unfortunately, Harrel froze. His throat bobbed, but no words came out.

"He's not here," I said.

The lawman was a big fellow with hair as a black as a Sioux Indian's and a dragoon mustache of the some shade. He was huge, like a force of nature is huge, as though he could lower his head and butt his way through the house from front to back. "We were told Hardin is riding with a lame little runt, Is that you?"

"It sure is," I said. "And it's a great honor."

Well, that was honest enough.

The roar of a shotgun immediately followed my declaration and the big lawman took a barrelful of double-aught buck right in the face.

No matter how big he is, how tough and mean he is, a man can't suffer a blow like that and live.

As he fell, the officer's face reminded me of a smashed raspberry pie I once saw on a baker's floor. It was a sight I'll never forget.

Yet as he went down, the lawman's dead finger twitched convulsively on the trigger and his ball slammed into Wes's thigh.

The other policeman, much younger, wide-eyed and nervous, glanced down at his brother officer and promptly bent over and threw up so violently I could tell what he'd had for his last three meals.

After the man straightened, saliva trailing from his mouth, Wes pushed the muzzle of the shotgun into his belly. "I can make it two real easy. You want to go for a deuce?"

The youngster tried to speak, but couldn't. He retched a couple of times, then said, "I've never seen anything like that before. His . . . his face . . ."

"Lead in the face can make a mess of a man," Wes said. "Now state your intentions and be quick."

The lawman shook his head. He had brown eyes as pretty as a woman's. "I'm out of it."

"Only if I say you're out of it," Wes said.

The youngster made no answer. I doubt if he could.

"All right, you're out of it. I'm in a good mood today." Wes nodded in the direction of the dead man.

"Load what's left of that onto his horse and get the hell away from here."

Harrel, leaning against the wall of his house, looked sick to his stomach, as though a yellow, porcelain mask covered his blunt features, but he helped get the dead lawman across his saddle. He stepped back and stared at his hands, holding them up in front of him, a horrified light in his eyes. His hands and forearms were streaked with scarlet runnels of blood, mixed with gray fragments of bone and brain. "Ahhhh . . . ahhhh . . ." he hollered, somewhere between a groan and a shriek.

"Damn you, wash them off!" Wes yelled. "Wash your damned hands!" Harrel's wails had unnerved him and he turned on the young lawman. "Get him the hell out of here!" he roared. "Now!"

The officer mounted, gathered the reins of the other horse and led it away, the pulped head of the dead man swaying with every motion.

Harrel, stripped to the waist, frantically worked the handle of the pump. The water cascaded over his hands and turned red.

Mrs. Harrel, a handsome woman with heavy breasts and hips, rushed outside with a bar of yellow lye soap and a towel, and helped her husband wash.

"Martha, did you see?" Saliva gathered at the corners of Harrel's mouth. "Did you see his head?"

"I saw it." She turned to Wes. "Go away. Leave us alone and never come back."

"Bang, Martha," Harrel said, wonder in his voice. "Bang, and he'd no face left."

"I know, Dave. I know how it was."

Wes stepped beside me, the shotgun still in his

hand. Blood oozed from his wounded thigh. "Little Bit, I've killed 37, but now they're starting to get lead into me. I think my luck is changing for the worse and hard times are coming down fast."

"Wes, we should head back to Gonzalez County where you have kin," I said. "They'll find a doctor to take care of you."

"The Yankee law will hunt me down no matter where I go," Wes said. "They'll never forgive me for taking a stand against tyranny."

Harrel was drying his hands on his towel. He'd calmed some, but looked at Wes as though he was some kind of dangerous, uncaged beast.

"Where is the nearest law?" Wes said to him.

"That would be Richard Reagan, the sheriff of Cherokee County," Harrel said.

"Where's he live?" Wes asked.

"He has a farm a couple of miles south of here," Harrel said.

"Bring him. Tell him I want to surrender."

"Canada, Wes," I said. "We could go to Canada."

John Wesley looked at me as though I'd just crawled out from under a rock. He looked back at Harrel. "Bring him, Dave. Tell him I'm shot through and through and damned tired of running."

CHAPTER THIRTY-SIX
Hell on Earth

Sheriff Richard Reagan was a tall, slender man with a kindly face. He was a careless dresser, but everything he wore was much washed and clean. Men of such appearance have dutiful wives and that is to their credit. He carried a holstered Colt that looked ill at ease on him, as though he considered it more badge of office than weapon.

Reagan arrived with four, hard-eyed deputies, but they remained outside while he and Wes repaired to the Harrel parlor.

Since nobody objected, or even seemed to notice me, I joined them.

Reagan got right to the point. "Dave Harrel led me to believe that you wish to surrender."

"He led you along the right path," Wes said. Covered by a cloth, his holstered guns were on the parlor table, as was the bulldog revolver.

In his memoirs, Wes says Reagan agreed to all kinds of conditions before he surrendered. He said the sheriff treated him like a superior kind of person, a God-fearing patriot who'd been persecuted by greedy carpetbaggers and vindictive Yankee lawmen.

The first part of that is not true, of course.

Wes made only one condition. Seriously wounded and fearing that he was dying, he begged Reagan to take him to a doctor who could save his life. "I don't want to leave my wife a grieving widow at so tender an age."

Reagan took Wes at face value. The face in question looked as contrite as a sinner's at a tent revival and was strained from pain.

"I will see what I can do," Reagan said. "But first you must surrender your firearms."

"Willingly. They have caused me nothing but trouble." Wes stepped to the table, pulled aside the cloth and picked up his guns.

Then tragedy struck.

An overzealous deputy who stood near the window saw what Wes was doing and opened fire. The ball hit Wes in the knee and he cried out in pain and dropped to the ground.

"Murder!" I yelled, angry that my friend now had four bullet holes in his body, two of them inflicted by so-called peace officers.

Reagan crossed the floor to the window and severely reprimanded the sullen deputy who made no attempt to apologize. He then kneeled beside Wes. "I'm sorry, old fellow. That was an honest mistake."

A mistake, yes, but not an honest one. The law had it in for John Wesley and seemed determined to kill him one way or the other.

I know they preferred a rope, but a bullet would do.

* * *

Wes was taken to the nearby town of Rusk to be held in a hotel owned by Sheriff Reagan where his wounds were treated and he was allowed to greet the many admirers who called on him.

I saw an immediate improvement in his attitude.

Wes liked people and they in turn liked him. He treated each visitor as though he or she was the most important, interesting person in the world. In those days, before prison ground him to dust, Wes was outgoing and charming. His love of life and inner glow cast a flattering light on all who came in contact with him.

But these were just a few of the attributes that made him a great man. Had the vengeful law left him alone, Wes would have found fame and fortune and a statue of him would stand in every town square in Texas.

On September 22, 1872, John Wesley was taken to Austin to stand trial. I did not join him right away because I felt too sick to travel.

Wes didn't appear to be troubled by my desertion, saying only that I should take care, say my prayers, and stay away from strong drink and fancy women.

I was sleeping rough and took a job as a saloon swamper to pay for my whiskey and the doctor who treated my leg.

The doc managed to help the recurring wound on my thigh, but warned that my bad leg should be amputated as soon as possible since it was withering away, possibly cancerous, and undermining my health.

I told him I never had any health to undermine, and he agreed that seemed to be the case.

"But," the doc said, "that doesn't alter the fact that the leg must be amputated, sooner rather than later."

The swamper job soon proved to be too much for me, but I felt well enough to take the trail to Austin, then a boomtown thanks to the arrival of the Houston and Central Texas Railroad.

The saloon owner, who'd either taken a liking to me or pitied me, gave me an old army greatcoat, cut to fit a much bigger man than me, and a paper sack with salt pork, a chunk of smelly cheese with blue stuff in it, and half a loaf of sourdough bread.

I was grateful for the coat. The early morning I reached the city it was pouring rain and a cold fall wind blew from the north.

After making some enquiries from a prim matron in the street, I discovered that Wes had been incarcerated in a broken down jail on the Colorado River.

The place was a hell on earth, the woman told me, and she warned that I should stay well clear because the jailors would think I looked like a desperate character, inclined to all sorts of mischief.

I didn't need further instruction on how to find the jail. Its stench could be detected from a mile away. The hellhole was jammed with such a reeking, heaving, mass of humanity that in the summer the prisoners stripped naked to survive the intolerable, humid heat.

I was allowed to speak to Wes through a grill in an iron-studded door that wafted a stink like bad morning breath.

After an exchange of pleasantries, Wes whispered,

"Little Bit, bring me a hacksaw blade. I'm going to cut my way out of here."

I felt a jolt of alarm. "Wes, if you're caught, they'll gun you for sure."

Wes's teeth flashed white in the gloom of that place. "The guards are all kin, or friends of kin. They'll turn the other way."

"Are you sure about that?"

"Hell, this is Gonzales County, my home range. Of course I'm sure." He crooked his finger and I put my face closer to the grill. "Manny Clements is in town. Tell him to have a horse ready for me on the south side of the jail."

I never liked Manny Clements much, a big, over-bearing bully of a man, but I had to bite the bullet, as they say. "When?"

"Bring the saw later today and I'll be ready by midnight tomorrow."

"I'll be with Clements when you break out."

"Yeah, you do that, Little Bit. Now go get me the saw blade."

I had no money to buy the hacksaw blade and when I stepped into a dry goods store with the intention of stealing one, the suspicious owner kept his eyes on me the whole time I was there. Finally I was forced to leave empty handed.

My only option was to find Manny Clements.

Since Clements usually hung with a town's sporting crowd, I doubted he'd be up and about much before noon, and it was still not yet ten.

My horse stood hipshot in the rattling rain outside

the dry goods store. He needed a place to shelter and so did I. The Houston and Central Texas train station lay close by, so I gathered up the reins and walked my mount up the slanted loading ramp to the platform. We found shelter under the wooden awning. I sat on a bench then pulled the paper food sack from under my coat. I ate the piece of cheese and crust of bread that was left. It didn't satisfy my hunger, but it was better than nothing.

About two inches of whiskey were left in my bottle, so I drank that and began to feel a little better, though I was still cold, damp, and shivering. I coughed incessantly.

The sky was gray to the horizon, but black thunderheads piled one on top of the other to the north and promised more rain, more misery, and the perplexing problem as to where I'd sleep that night.

It seemed that I'd have to depend on the generosity of Manny Clements, a man not noted for his giving nature.

I was so lost in a tangle of thoughts, none of them pleasant, I didn't notice the ticket agent step onto the platform.

He spotted me, then turned his head and said, "Shamus, come out here."

A tall, heavy man wearing a railroad hat with a shield-shaped badge on the front and an oilskin cape came from inside, a tin cup of coffee in his hand and a scowl on his face.

It was the first time I'd ever seen a railroad bull, those private, strong-arm thugs the rail companies were hiring to stop tramps, vagrants, and other riffraff riding free in the freight cars.

I later learned that the bulls had orders to shoot to kill. Some say they gunned at least a thousand white men in Texas alone. Add Negroes and Chinese and that number triples.

The bull laid his cup on a bench and slowly stepped toward me. The *thud, thud* of his boots on the wooden platform sounded like the drums of doom. He loomed over me. "Git that damn hoss off the platform." He had a round, red, Irish face and small eyes that looked like hard blue marbles.

"I certainly will, sir," I said, getting to my feet.

The bull toed the crumpled, greasy paper sack I'd dropped. "That yours?"

I nodded.

"Pick it up."

I did as he said, then gathered the reins of my horse. "It was nice to meet you."

But the bull wasn't done with me, not yet anyway. "Do you have a ticket?"

"No," I said.

"Why are you here?"

I decided to tell the truth. "Just sheltering from the rain. I meant no harm."

"Sheltering on railroad property?"

"I guess so." I pointed upward. "It has a cover."

Some things I remember vividly about that morning . . . the drip at the end of the bull's nose . . . the whiskey on his breath . . . the rumble of distant thunder and the snare drum rattle of the rain on the roof. I remember all that, but after the bull accused me of trespassing and followed up with a punch to the middle of my face, I recall very little.

I had an instant glance of a fist as big as a ham

coming at me, and then my lights went out. I'd never been punched before and wasn't prepared for it.

As far as I can tell, since I was unaware, worse was to happen.

My horse spooked as I dropped, but my left hand was tangled in his reins and he swung around and dragged me down the ramp. At a frenzied gallop, he hauled me into the muddy street and finally shook me loose after I slammed into a boardwalk, then a hitching rail, and came to rest in a dung-covered puddle.

I mean, I guess all that happened. When I woke with a broken nose and bruised, swollen eyes, the puddle was where I found myself.

Hurting all over, I tried to get to my feet, but my bad leg slipped out from under me and I landed on my back, the furious rain lashing at me.

Two respectable ladies holding umbrellas looked down at me, then one whispered into the other's ear. That lady nodded, reached into her purse and held out her hand. She was holding something I thought was money and reached out to take it.

"Read it and take it to heart, young man," she said.

Then she and the other woman walked away, their noses high and backs stiff.

I looked at the paper in my hand. It was some kind of leaflet. On the front was written DRINK IS A MOCKER. BE NOT DECEIVED. And under that, *Verily, there's a serpent in every bottle and he biteth like the viper!*

Suddenly I was angry . . . angry at myself for being a cripple, angry at myself for being poor, and angry at the world for not giving a damn. I struggled to my feet and saw the two respectable ladies gesturing to one another as they stared into a store window.

"Hey!" I yelled. "Go to hell!" I held up the pamphlet and began to tear it into little pieces. "You hear me? Go to hell!"

The women turned their heads, stared at me for a moment, then hurried away, lifting their skirts so their white petticoats and button-up boots showed.

"Go to hell," I said in a whisper, my hurting head bent. "Everybody go to hell."

CHAPTER THIRTY-SEVEN
The Good Irishman

After a search, I found my horse standing outside a livery stable and led him away. He must have had visions of a dry stall and oats in the bucket, because he was reluctant to leave. But I dragged him after me.

If I was going to rough it, so was he.

I glanced through a bank window and to my surprise the clock on the wall said it was thirty minutes after noon. I'd been unconscious longer than I thought.

It was time to find Manny Clements.

He wasn't hard to track down. He was a well-known character in Austin and a passerby told me he could usually be found at that hour taking lunch at the Scholz Beer Garden on San Jacinto Street.

I led my horse through the rain and somber grayness that drifted like smoke from the north and looped him to the hitching rail outside the restaurant.

The beer garden was a splendid place with windows on all four walls and a fine gable roof, but I was in little mood to enjoy it. I could barely see anyway. My left eye was completely swollen shut and the right was headed that way.

Fortunately, the rain had washed away the blood from my flattened nose, but before I went inside I scrubbed my hand over my top lip and chin just to make sure.

Can you imagine what I looked like when I stepped inside Mr. Scholz's pride and joy?

I was soaked to the skin and my huge, sodden coat dragged on the floor. I'd found my hat in the street, but it had been run over by a wagon wheel and I'd had to punch it back into shape. It didn't look too good.

Imagine then, my pinched, pale little face, a nose blue and broken, eyes black and swollen shut, and me smelling of mud, and manure, and you'll get some idea why I wasn't exactly welcomed into the beer garden with open arms.

To his credit, the waiter who met me at the door was polite and kept his eyes empty. "Do you wish to be seated, sir?"

"No." I said.

The waiter looked relieved.

"I'm here to see Manny Clements."

"Would that be Mr. Mannen Clements?"

"Yes. That's him."

"Please wait here and I'll see if he's inside," the waiter said. "Whom shall I say wishes to speak with him?"

"Just tell him it's Little Bit."

"Very well, Mr. Bit. I'll find out if Mr. Clements is available."

The waiter left and I stood, hat in hand, dripping onto the polished wood floor. I smelled steak sizzling, possibly corned beef and cabbage bubbling in the pot, definitely frying bacon, and perhaps just a soup-con of grilled German sausage. My stomach rumbled and I fervently hoped that Manny, a great trencher-man in his own right, would feed me.

He didn't.

With the waiter leading the way, Manny left the dining room and met me at the door. I smelled sausage and mustard on his breath.

"What the hell happened to you?" Manny asked.

"I ran afoul of a railroad bull," I said.

"Were you trespassing on railroad property?"

"A platform."

Manny nodded. "You're lucky he didn't shoot you."

"Yeah, real lucky, I guess. John Wesley sent me."

"He's in the *juzgado*."

"I know."

"What does he want?"

I told him.

Blood is thicker than water in Texas, and Manny didn't hesitate. "Tell Wes I'll be there. He'll come out of that hellhole naked, so tell him I'll bring him clothes and a gun." He stared at me, obviously not im-pressed by what he saw. "Can you remember that?"

"Yeah, I can. But I've no money to buy a hacksaw blade."

Manny reached into his jingling pocket and gave me half a dollar. "A blade doesn't cost more than that." He took a step back, looking me up and down. "Little Bit, I'd say you're a sight for sore eyes, but I'd be telling a big windy. You look like crap."

"I feel like crap. And I'm hungry."

"Be outside the jail at midnight tomorrow," Manny said. "You can hold the horses."

He stepped away, back to his lunch, and left me to sadly contemplate my empty, sunken belly.

The hardware store owner sold me a hacksaw blade, slightly rusty, for twenty-five cents. I was overjoyed. That gave me enough change for five beers and allowed me to partake of the free lunch advertised on a chalkboard outside the Star of Erin saloon.

It was good to get out of the rain. I bought a beer and then nonchalantly strolled to the free lunch bar like a well-fed man in the mood for a snack. The menu was fish oriented—pickled herring, sardines in oil, and slabs of yellow, dried cod. But they also had hardboiled eggs in the shell, a massive crock of butter, and a basket of rye bread.

Since crockery tended to walk out the door with the customers, thick brown paper shaped into cones served as plates.

An ominous, chalked sign above the bar read No Scum Allowed.

Since I was a paying customer, I ignored that. I filled my cone with herring, cod, a couple chunks of bread and butter and sat at a table to enjoy my feast.

Alas, my happiness was short-lived.

The saloon was busy, but one of the four bartenders left his post and stepped over to my table. He was as big as the railroad bull, but not quite as mean. "Take your lunch outside, son," he said, in a strong Irish accent.

I was chewing a mouthful of bread and butter. When I finally swallowed, I said, "Why?"

"Because the patrons say you smell bad." The bartender smiled, showing teeth like little white pegs.

I always liked white teeth, my own being of that particular shade.

"Son, they're right. You stink like the pigs o' Docherty, so out the door with you. There's a bench outside where you can sit. It's sheltered from the rain."

I'd learned a lesson from my run-in with the bull, and I didn't want to antagonize an Irishman with massive forearms and a head as big as a nail keg. Without a word, I rose and carried my paper poke and beer outside.

"Good lad," the bartender said after he saw me seated on a bench covered by the porch roof. He was a good man, that Irishman.

No sooner was I seated than he returned with a schooner of beer. "This one is on the house. For the inconvenience, like." He stared at me for a long time as though sorting out some sentences in his mind. "You look sick, son, and you've been beaten."

I nodded. I had no sentences of my own, sorted or otherwise.

"Then you take care," he said.

"Thanks for the beer."

I ate my food—the cod and pickled herring were as salty as the sea—and stepped into the rain again.

I knew Wes would be worried about me.

CHAPTER THIRTY-EIGHT
A Troubled Evening

"Did you bring it?" John Wesley asked me.

"It's down my pants leg."

"Slip it through the grill."

"What about the guards?"

"They're looking in every other direction but this one."

I did as he told me, and Wes said, "You spoke to Manny?"

"He'll have a horse and clothes and a revolver."

"Good. I've got scores to settle." He looked at me, as though seeing me for the first time. "What the hell happened to you?"

"Railroad bull," I said.

"You were trespassing?"

"On the station platform. Me and my horse."

"You're lucky you're still alive."

"I guess."

"Stay out of trouble."

"I will. What about the railroad bull?"

"What about him?"

"Look at my face, Wes."

"Yeah, that's too bad. Don't go near the station again."

"If I could shoot, I'd gun that bull."

"I'm sure you would."

Wes glanced over his shoulder. "I got to go. See you tomorrow night."

"I'll be here."

Wes's face vanished from the door grill and a guard ushered me out of the jail.

That evening I spent my last twenty cents on beer in a saloon with a three-piece orchestra and bummed a whiskey off a puncher who said he'd stand treat if'n I stayed at least ten feet away from him.

Finally, my beer ran out and the bartender's patience wore thin. I was tossed into the rainy street again.

I staked my horse on a patch of bunchgrass behind a Chinese laundry and spent the night in their outhouse.

But come first light, the Chinese chased me away and, damn it all, it was still raining.

I'd taken the precaution of stashing some of the dried cod and bread in my pocket, so I sat on a hotel porch and made a good breakfast.

The outhouse had been uncomfortable, just a narrow, single-holer. I had not rested well. By comparison, the hotel rocker felt like a king's throne. I tipped my hat over my eyes and waited for sleep to take me.

I vaguely remember the sound of a train whistle in the distance . . . the rumble of a freight wagon in the street . . . the *slam-slam-slam* of a screen door opening and closing in the wind . . . the bark of a dog . . .

Then I heard nothing at all.

Something hard poking into my shoulder awakened me. I opened my eyes, tipped back my hat, and saw to my surprise that it was full dark. Reflector lamps had been lit up and down the street.

The beating I'd taken and the bad night in the outhouse had tired me more than I thought. I hurt all over.

"It's time you went home now, young fellow." It was a man's voice, the Deep South accent smooth and unhurried as molasses dripping from a barrel. A tall, slender man with white hair and a trimmed imperial regarded me with mild blue eyes. He held a cane in his hand, but had a soldier's bearing.

"I must have fallen asleep . . . Gen'ral," I said.

The old man smiled. "You've promoted me, sir." He gave a little bow. "Lieutenant Colonel Miles Hannah, late of the Sixty-first Regiment Alabama Infantry."

"Pleased to make your acquaintance, Colonel."

"You must go home now, son," the old soldier said. "The cause is lost, the regiment is disbanded, and I see that you are sorely wounded in the leg as I am."

The rocker creaked as I sat up. "Colonel, do you own this place? I could sure use a glass of whiskey, on the slate, like."

The old man smiled again. "No, I don't own this hotel, but I live here. I'm disabled from battle wounds, you understand. Many battles, many wounds."

"Sorry to hear that, Colonel. But what can you do about the whiskey?"

The old man thought for a few moments, then said, "My daughter and her husband own this hotel. I'll ask them to fill a convivial glass for an old soldier."

I saluted. "That's me, Colonel, an old soldier as ever was."

"We had times, boy, did we not? Fighting for freedom, shoulder to shoulder against the Northern aggressors."

"Sure thing. Good times with Bobby Lee and Longstreet and them."

"But the great cause was lost and now the Bonnie Blue Flag lies trampled in the dust."

"Yeah, that's sad," I said. "Colonel, about the whiskey . . ."

"Ah yes, the whiskey. Stay there. I'll see what I can do directly." Using his cane, the colonel limped to the door. Then he turned to me and said, "What was your rank, son?"

"Sergeant." I hated to deceive this kind and brave old man, but my entire being cried out for whiskey and I'd no other source but him.

He smiled at me. "The most important rank in any army is sergeant." Then he stepped through the open door.

Rain ticked from the porch roof and, illuminated by the lanterns that glowed outside the stores and saloons, fell on the street like a cascade of steel needles. Thunder rolled like dim drums in the distance of the night and lightning flashed gold within the storm clouds.

I sat and waited and worried that the old colonel

had fallen down somewhere and couldn't get up again.

After about ten minutes, a woman stepped onto the porch. She was pretty, looked to be in her mid-thirties, but she was much too thin and her eyes were tired. "You're awake."

"Yes," I said. "I hope you don't mind me using your porch."

"People need shelter from the rain. But I think you should move on now."

"Is your father Colonel Hannah?"

"Why do you ask?" She seemed surprised.

"He told me he'd bring me a glass of whiskey," I said, then quickly, "On the slate."

The woman gave me a long look, but I couldn't read her face.

Finally she said, "The colonel has done this before."

I hoped my smile was ingratiating. "He's a fine old soldier."

Without another word, the woman turned on her heel and stepped into the hotel.

But she returned within a couple of minutes with a glass of bourbon. "Drink this. Then please leave."

I said my thankee and took the glass.

The woman stepped away, then stopped and turned to me. The right side of her face was lit by the oil lamp beside the door, the other half in shadow. "My father, Colonel Hannah, died of his wounds two years ago." Then she left me and I heard the quick thud of her boot heels on the timber floor inside.

My hands shook and I held the glass in both as I drank the whiskey like a man dying of thirst.

Whether my tremors were from a lack of booze or

my brush with the supernatural I don't know, but I can tell you this. Like most Texans, especially those who'd been around cow camps, I was deathly afraid of ghosts and ha'nts and such. As soon as I downed my whiskey, I got off that porch double quick, collected my horse, and didn't look back.

Some things that are not meant for mortal eyes leave indelible memories, and the specter of the dead old colonel visits me still on thundery midnights, troubling my restless sleep.

CHAPTER THIRTY-NINE
War Clouds Gather

I arrived at the jail well before midnight, but stayed back out of sight. Hidden by darkness, I awaited the arrival of Manny Clements. The November night was cold and the thunder that had warned of continuing rain had made good on its promise. It was not a heavy downpour, just a steady drizzle that soaked me to the skin and made it difficult to see anything around me.

After about fifteen minutes, Manny showed up. He was mounted on a rawboned buckskin and led two other animals, a paint mustang and a pack mule. He drew rein beside me and said, "Seen anything yet?"

I shook my head. Realizing it was very dark, I said, "Not a thing. I haven't heard anything, either."

Manny swung out of the saddle and bade me do the same. "Hold onto the horses. I'll go see what's happening." He reached under his slicker, adjusted the lie of his holstered revolver, and walked away from me.

Soon Manny was swallowed by the gloom and I

heard nothing but the hiss of the rain and the beat of my own racing heart.

Dreary minutes passed with agonizing slowness . . . then footsteps, squelching in mud, came toward me. The darkness parted and two men appeared, Manny's supporting arm around Wes's waist.

His teeth gritted against pain, Wes wore only ragged long johns and there were bloodstains on the front of the shirt.

Alarmed, I said, "What happened?"

"I had to pull him through the window. The stumps of the iron bars dragged across his wounded belly." Manny helped Wes sit with his back against a tree, then stepped to the pack mule.

I kneeled beside Wes. "Are you all right?"

He looked through me rather than at me. "What do you think?"

I didn't have to answer that because Manny came back, holding a slicker and a bottle of Old Crow. "Here, Wes, before you get some of this whiskey in you we'll put the slicker on you. We'll dress you properly after we light a shuck out of here."

We helped Wes to his feet and got the slicker on him.

Manny passed him the bottle. "Now get the whiskey down you. It will do you good."

Wes drank from the bottle. "I needed that." He passed it back to Manny who also drank deeply.

He wiped his mustache with the back of his hand and corked the bottle. "Now we'll get you mounted."

"Manny, I could sure use a drink of that whiskey," I said.

The man stared at me for the briefest of moments, then said, "Help get Wes up on his horse."

There would be no whiskey for Little Bit that night.

You may think that Manny Clements was harsh, ignoring me like that, and indeed he was, but he was a product of his time and place, a hard man bred to a hard land where fighting men were esteemed above all others. In Texas in those days such men drank whiskey but in Manny's eyes I was far from being any kind of a man. He would not waste Old Crow on such as me.

No, he was not being cruel.

If you'd asked Manny why there was no whiskey for Little Bit, he would be surprised by your question, just as he was surprised that I'd even made such request in the first place.

I was not worthy. Simple as that.

A crippled little nonentity learns to live with hurts of all kinds, so now I'll drop the matter and say no more about it.

After the jailbreak, Wes decided to remain in Gonzales County among friends, and I rode with him to a tiny burg named Coon Hollow where he met up with his wife again.

Jane, who was heavy with Wes's child at the time, took me aside. "Little Bit, John will be a man with a family soon, and I want you to talk to him."

"About what, Jane?" I was surprised at the request. Mrs. Hardin had always made it clear by word, thought, and deed that she didn't have much time for me.

"About settling down." Her pretty little face creased with worry. "I don't want my husband to get shot again.

The next time could be his last." She lightly touched her fingertips to my wrist. "I know he'll listen to you."

I wanted to say, *When did Wes ever listen to me?* but I didn't. Instead I said, "Jane, Wes is talking about splitting his time between Karnes and Gonzales Counties."

"He didn't tell me that," Jane said, her quick temper flaring.

"Wes didn't tell you because he says you've got enough to deal with right now, what with the baby coming and all."

It was a barefaced lie. Wes had said no such thing. But it worked.

Jane's face relaxed and she smiled. "He's a good husband, isn't he?"

"The best," I said. Another lie then a kernel of truth to support my claim to his worth as a husband. "Now that he has responsibilities, Wes plans to buy and sell cattle and rope and brand mavericks. He's even talking about making another drive to Kansas."

Jane just stared into my eyes and said nothing, so I threw in a kicker. "And, of course, he wants to get his Wild West show off the ground and moving. He says it will make us millionaires."

"He's talked to me about that before. Do you think it's possible?"

"More than possible, Jane, probable."

"What about the law? All those men they say John killed?"

"Jane, Wes never killed a man except in defense of himself or others. Of course, the law can make him stand trial, but a Texas jury will never convict him."

"Can I believe you, Little Bit? You're offering me hope."

"Yes, you can believe me," I said, assuming my sincere face. "You and Wes will grow old together and spoil your grandchildren."

So I spun a fairytale that lit up Jane's eyes and if the circumstances had been different it might even have come true. Who knows?

But that very night a grim Manny Clements walked into the house . . . and called in favors. He made war talk with John Wesley . . . and the stage was set for Wes's long, tortuous descent into madness and death.

CHAPTER FORTY
The Sutton-Taylor Feud

John Wesley had tried to stay aloof from the vicious Sutton-Taylor feud that was tearing Texas apart. But with the coming of Manny Clements he could no longer stand aside. Family honor was at stake.

The Suttons were murderous, carpetbagging trash who had already shot down many members of the Taylor clan in cold blood.

William E. Sutton, a former Confederate soldier and turncoat, got himself appointed as a state police force sergeant under Captain Jack Helm. This unholy duo was given command of a detachment of Union troops, and they received but one order from Washington. CRUSH THE REBEL SCUM AND ENFORCE RECONSTRUCTION AT BAYONET POINT.

Pitkin Taylor, a brave man and patriot, brother of a renowned Texas Ranger, could not let this stand. He vowed to resist with fire and sword the Suttons, their Yankee allies, and all their evil schemes . . . and thus the feud that in the end would claim two hundred lives was born.

Wes, that gallant Southern cavalier, rode forth with the Clements brothers to stamp out William Sutton, his works, and all his vile brood.

And I tagged along.

Despite the war raging around him, Wes continued to seek additional markets for his cattle and on April 9, 1873, his search put us on the trail to the town of Cuero in DeWitt County. The settlement was prospering, three new hotels were under construction, and Wes assumed there would be a demand for beef.

We were still almost a score of miles south of Cuero when a heavily armed rider appeared on our back trail. Behind him trailed three others, but those looked like respectable cattlemen and I saw no arms on them.

I made the decision right there and then that their leader was either a lawman or a desperado. Because of the feud, he could well be both.

When the man got close and touched his hat, Wes drew rein. "Good morning. A fine day is it not?"

The rider, a tall, thin man with a long, joyless face and bleak blue eyes did not return the greeting. He wore two Colts at his waist and the stock of a new Henry rifle poked out from under his knee. "Do you live around here?"

"No," Wes said. "I'm heading for Cuero on a business trip."

"Me too," the stranger said. "To find a blacksmith shop. My horse threw a shoe back a ways." The man had the eyes of a buzzard.

I didn't trust him.

I trusted him even less when he said, "Name's Jack Helm. I'm the sheriff of DeWitt County. These men are traveling under my protection."

"You're the sheriff . . . among other things." When he spoke like that, low and flat and unfriendly, John Wesley was the most dangerous man on earth.

Maybe Helm, damn him for a black-hearted Suttonite, sensed this because he managed a slight smile when he said, "And you are?"

Wes gave his name.

"Pleased to meet you after all this time, Mr. Hardin." Helm extended his hand for a howdy-do, which Wes ignored.

"You're not facing a frightened woman or child now, Helm, but a Southern gentleman, face-to-face," Wes said. "I heard you've called me a murderer and a coward and have ordered your deputies to shoot me on sight." Wes opened his coat and revealed his revolvers. "Well, now you've got your chance. Shuck the iron and open the ball."

Helm's face paled and his voice was unsteady. "John Wesley, I'm not your enemy. I'm your friend."

Suddenly Wes's guns were in his hands. "You're no friend of mine. You belong to a band of murdering scum who have killed better men than yourself."

I swear that Wes's eyes glowed like candles in blue ice.

"Your killing days are over, Helm, so shuck the iron and defend yourself or I'll shoot you down like a dog."

The sky was dark blue, the breeze cool and birds sang in the trees. It was not a good day to die.

And Helm knew it. "John Wesley, you're too brave a man to shoot me down in cold blood. I want you to join my vigilante group in ridding our land of rustlers, killers, and all manner of low persons."

"Hear-hear," one of the respectable cattlemen said. "Let us shed our differences and continue·to Cuero in peace and good fellowship."

To my surprise, Wes holstered his guns. "Helm, when we reach Cuero, we'll talk of this again."

Now there are them who say that the whole affair was a setup, arranged by Helm and Wes. They say that Wes's dark personality had long since abandoned every shred of honor and loyalty and that he wanted to change sides for his personal gain.

That Helm brought along three witnesses to attest to John Wesley's change of heart meant that they would also be present when the sheriff outlined to Wes what he would gain, legally and financially.

Obviously the supposed bait was a full pardon for past crimes and large donations of money from the Sutton faction, many of them quite wealthy.

But I don't believe a word of it.

Wes wanted to kill Jack Helm, an evil scoundrel, real bad, but at the last moment he decided it shouldn't be done in front of three respectable witnesses whose testimony could hang him.

That is the simple explanation of why Wes lowered his lance and backed down.

And it is the right one . . . as future events would reveal.

Wes and Jack Helm did talk again in Cuero, at the corner of Hunt Street and Morgan Avenue, but few words passed between them.

All Wes said to me later was, "Helm would have to do a whole lot of work to get me clear of trouble. And I would have to do a whole lot of work for him in return."

I didn't pursue the matter because another dramatic event overtook us in the form of an Irishman bent on suicide, who chose John Wesley as the instrument of his self-destruction.

It was such a pathetic, useless death that it passed largely unnoticed at a time when belted, feuding men were dying violently all over Texas.

CHAPTER FORTY-ONE
"Pimm's All Round!"

The suicide death come up after John Wesley spoke to Helm. We stepped into a saloon in Cuero Square where a noisy poker game was in progress. Wes sat at the table, asked for cards, and I stood at the bar and bought whiskey with the dollar he'd given me.

We'd done some long riding recently and my leg was playing hob. My wound had gathered into a head then burst and I felt blood and pus seep down my leg. I felt most unwell and the only medicine that helped was whiskey, the stronger and rawer the better.

I had never been a big eater and the notion that food might boost my strength never entered into my thinking.

It had gone noon but the sun merely smoldered sullenly in the spring sky and the day was cool, fanned by an east wind. It was one of those strange, Texas days when a man could step from winter to summer just by crossing the street from shade into light.

I have always been of the opinion that an east wind drives men mad. I believe Gettysburg was fought in such a wind, and was not that the greatest madness of all?

It seemed that the wind had worked its dark sorcery on the unfortunate Irishman.

Wes had just won a five-dollar pot when the suicidal son of Erin jumped up from the table, did a little jig, and declared that the winner must buy, "Pimm's all round!"

Wes merely smiled. "Perhaps, if I win a few more hands."

The Irishman's ruddy face was covered with broken veins that looked like tributaries of blood. "Now!" he yelled. "Pimm's for everybody or, by Christ, I'll take a stick to ye."

The bartender hammered a glass on the counter. "Here, Morgan, the man doesn't want to buy drinks. Remember that you're a deputy sheriff of this county and act the gentleman."

When Wes heard this, he threw down his cards and stepped outside.

Only later did I learn that J.B. Morgan, a stonemason by trade, was a Suttonite thug who'd been hired by Jack Helm to terrorize the Taylor patriots of DeWitt County.

Wes had entered the poker game under the alias of Mr. Johnson, but did Morgan know his true identity?

Of course he did.

Everybody in Cuero knew the famous shootist John Wesley Hardin was in town.

Then why did Morgan brace a known mankiller?

Bear this in mind. The hatreds engendered by the Sutton-Taylor feud ran deep and I believe to this day that Morgan threw away his own life to bring down Wes.

In fact, he succeeded all too well.

After a few minutes quiet contemplation, John Wesley stepped into the saloon again.

Morgan, still belligerent, immediately confronted him. "Here you. Are you going heeled?"

"I'm armed, yes." Wes was so polite and quiet you'd have thought he was accepting an invite to tea by old Queen Vic herself.

"Well, then it's time you thought about defending yourself," said Morgan, that willful blackguard. He brushed aside his high-button coat and made a show of reaching into the back pocket of his pants.

"Get your hand away from there," Wes ordered.

"I never carry a gun in my pocket," Morgan said.

Wes drew and fired. A bullet crashed into Morgan's face, just below his left eye.

The man had time to throw up his hands and scream, "Oh God, he's murdered me!" Then he fell to the sawdust-covered floor, dead as a rotten stump.

Through a gray drift of smoke, Wes looked around the saloon, then said to the bartender, "Pimm's all round."

But no one took him up on his generous offer.

CHAPTER FORTY-TWO
Wes Plans a Murder

The killing of Morgan placed John Wesley firmly in the Taylor camp, and me too, of course, not that anybody much cared. Their need was for fighting men, and on that score I didn't qualify.

I did however acquire a notebook and pencil and began to write what would become my first published dime novel, a saga of how Wes stopped a train robbery, saved a virgin in peril of being undone, and tracked down and killed the outlaws.

As I will do throughout this narrative, I'm pleased to give you the title of the novel, so you can pick it up wherever fine books are sold and read it at your leisure. *Captain Hardin to the Rescue*, or *The Maiden On The Train Of Doom*. Wes was newly incarcerated in federal prison when the novel was published, but he read it and liked it so much he declared it, "Crackerjack!"

I've written many more books since, but that's the one that will always remain in my memory, mostly because of its enthusiastic reception by John Wesley.

As I've said, Wes had thrown in with the Taylors

body and soul, but this fact was unknown to Jack Helm who invited him to a parley in the town of Albuquerque, a bustling settlement in western Gonzales County.

In part, the letter Helm sent declared that, "Albuquerque is my town, John, and I am cock o' the walk. Come quickly that we may discuss our urgent business at hand."

Wes had just met members of the Taylor clan, including Jim Taylor, a man with an abiding hatred for Jack Helm and the oppression he stood for. We sat in the front room of his ranch house.

"I say you accept the invite, Wes," Taylor said. "We can get rid of that damned Yankee turncoat once and for all."

For once in his life, Wes was wary. "You read what he said, Jim, that Albuquerque is his town. Helm is an important man and we could face a lynch mob."

Taylor wasn't intimidated in the least. "I'll do the killing, Wes. Just be there to back me up if need be." He jutted his chin in my direction. "And him."

"Little Bit doesn't carry a gun," Wes said.

Taylor nodded, his face empty. "No, I don't suppose he does."

"Helm needs killing," Wes said. "Am I right in saying that?"

"Damn right you're right," Taylor said. "Kill him and we'll tear the guts right out of the Suttons." He picked up his whiskey glass, put it to his lips, and said over the rim, "Are you game, Wes?"

John Wesley hesitated for only a moment. "I'm always game. We'll ride up that way at first light tomorrow."

Taylor looked at me. "You?"

I was flattered that a member of the fighting Taylor clan even noticed me. "I'll ride with you."

"Then it's all set," Taylor said. "We'll gun Jack Helm tomorrow."

I was horrified and couldn't just sit there and keep my mouth shut. The whiskey I'd drank helped. "Wes, kill Helm and there can be no going back from it."

"What the hell do you mean?" Taylor asked.

"Helm is a big man in Texas and he has powerful friends, including the army," I said. "I don't think they'd take his death lightly."

"Hell, you can stay behind." Taylor cut me a slit-eyed look. "You wouldn't be much help anyway."

"Helm can die like any other man and no one will mourn him." Wes perched on the edge of his chair like a bird of prey, all his arrogance on show. He shook his head, a slight smile on his lips. "Little Bit, why do I keep you around? You're the gloomiest cuss I ever knew."

Taylor said, "You don't keep him around for the laughs, that's fer sure."

"Wes, I beg you. Don't kill Jack Helm. It will be an ill-done thing." As one last yelp of despair, I said, "Think of your wife and child. Think of the Wild West show."

"The show can wait until the Suttons are all dead," Wes said. "Anyway, I'm thinking of selling the idea, like I'd sell a cow or a horse, except for a sight more money."

"Wes, I heard talk about your Wild West show idea," Taylor said. "I'd surely admire to be in it."

"Well, if I don't sell it, I'll make sure there's a place for you, Jim." Wes turned his attention to me. "Little Bit, you look peaked. I'm leaving you behind tomorrow."

Our eyes locked and I opened my mouth to speak.

Wes shut it for me. "Don't argue. Just do as you're told."

Taylor grinned. "Hell, Wes, pop a cap on him and put the little feller out of his misery."

"The whiskey will do that soon enough," Wes said.

It was not a thing a friend should say.

CHAPTER FORTY-THREE
The Death of Jack Helm

"One day, in a playful mood, John Wesley Hardin gave Sheriff Jack Helm a broadside . . . and sunk him."

That's how a Texas Ranger summed up the killing of Helm to his superiors.

He was only half right.

The way John Wesley told it later, him and Jim Taylor rode into Albuquerque and found Helm in the blacksmith's shop, toiling at the anvil. He was part owner of the forge and enjoyed working with iron. He was hammering a glowing knife blade into shape when Wes and Taylor saw him.

Wes said, "Then suddenly I heard Helm scream at Jim, 'Hold up there because I mean to arrest you!'"

Now, since Helm had never met Jim Taylor I don't see how that was possible.

But John Wesley may have misspoken himself. In reality, the vile threat was hurled at him since he'd so steadfastly refused to join the traitorous Suttonite faction.

I do know this. Helm plunged the red hot knife

into a barrel of water, and no sooner had it stopped steaming and sizzling than he advanced on Taylor, the *brutish blade* held low for a gutting.

Alarmed, Wes said he watched Helm close on Taylor. "I carried a shotgun because Jack Helm was known to be a dangerous man with a gun and had put many lively Taylor lads into the grave."

To save Taylor's life, Wes cut loose with one barrel of the shotgun. Helm, hit hard, staggered, and Jim Taylor opened up with his revolver.

"Helm fell with twelve buckshot in his chest and several six-shooter balls in his head," Wes recalled in his autobiography. "Thus did the leader of the vigilante committee, the terror of the county whose name was a horror to all law-abiding citizens, meet his death."

So you see why I say the Ranger was only half right.

Wes and Taylor shared the kill, though Wes would later claim it as his thirty-ninth.

Jack Helm was bleeding all over the ground, gasping his last when Wes and Taylor rode out of town.

Nobody tried to stop them.

When Wes returned to Gonzales County the word quickly spread that he'd killed the hated Jack Helm. Letters of thanks poured into Wes's ranch from the wives, widows, and mothers of Helm's many victims, and men patted him on the back and said, "John, killing Helm was the finest thing you ever did in your life."

And me, miserable little weasel that I was, once again bathed in the reflected light of John Wesley's glory and convinced myself that I was indeed a man and counted myself lucky to have such a friend.

CHAPTER FORTY-FOUR
Terror by Night

I believe that John Wesley wanted to separate himself from the Sutton-Taylor feud and he'd even talked of trying to broker a peace treaty between the two factions. Despite his best intentions, the fighting still raged, and *hooded nightriders* spread terror across south and central Texas, killing, maiming, and burning by the light of the moon.

Others took advantage of the chaos and rode moonlit trails for their own personal gain. The worst of them were the murderous Roche brothers, a trio of killers so fiendish that Wes refused to take any credit for his part in their ultimate destruction.

Now, for all the doubters who say John Wesley was a common killer, the story I'm about to narrate reveals Wes at his best. As I saw him, he was a noble knight in sable armor who sallied forth to right wrong wherever he found it.

My dire predictions about the consequences of Jack Helm's murder had not yet come true, but Wes, wary of the Suttons and their nightriders, had sent his wife and baby daughter to Comanche in Central Texas to live with his younger brother Joe, a successful young lawyer.

It was the midnight hour, a couple days before the eve of Christ's birth. Outside the night was cool and the bright moonlight covered the ground like a frost.

Wes and I sat before a blazing log in his parlor, sharing a bottle of fine port wine. Despite suffering from a severe attack of bronchitis, I felt happy and privileged.

Jane would never allow me to remain long in the house. She said she could smell me and my diseased leg from two rooms away.

Wes, who was drowsing in his chair, woke with a start as hoof beats sounded outside, then a horse whinnied as it was reined to a violent stop. "Nightriders."

He leapt from his chair, grabbed his pistols and stepped to the window. As he pushed the curtain aside to take a look into the darkness, fists pounded on the front door.

"John Wesley!" a man yelled. "It's me, Andy Conlan."

Wes threw me a quick glance. "He's one of ours."

"Or somebody impersonating his voice," I said.

Made wary by my warning, Wes left the parlor and a moment later I heard the door open.

This was followed by a man's squeal of fright. "Wes, don't shoot for God's sake! It's me, old Andy Conlan as ever was."

Wes said something I couldn't hear. The door closed and Conlan stepped into the parlor.

He was a man of late middle years, short and stocky, and he sported a beard that spread over the chest of his wool mackinaw like a gray fan and at some time or other a bullet had clipped an arc out of the top of his left ear. He looked like a man who'd just seen the devil himself and he shivered, from cold or fear I did not know.

Wes put his guns back on the table, then poured whiskey for Conlan. "Drink this. Then tell me why you're disturbing a man's peace in the middle of the night."

Conlan gulped the whiskey. "Wes, a terrible thing has happened. A horrible thing."

Wes waited for a moment, then said, "So horrible you're not going to tell me about it?"

As though he was indeed reluctant to relive the frightening memories that lingered in his mind's eye, Conlan said, "Wes, you know me. I was a mountain man, then an army scout. I fit Injuns and I seen what the Comanche and the Apache can do to a man." He drained his glass. "This was worse, a sight worse than anything I seen."

"Tell it, Andy." Wes glanced at the china clock on the mantle. "It's gone midnight."

Conlan held out his glass. "Fill this first, Wes. Me pipe is dry as a stick, like, and I'm nervous as a whore in church."

Wes poured more whiskey, waited until Conlan drank, then said again, "Tell it, Andy."

"Late this afternoon I rode to the Goodson place—"

"On Dead Deer Creek?" Wes said.

"The very same, though now it's more dry wash than creek."

Wes waited and Conlan said, "When I got there it was already dark, but I figured I could stay the night, the Goodsons being such nice folks."

"What was your business there?" Wes asked.

"Sam Goodson had a Mulefoot sow for sale, and I figured I would buy it if'n the price was right."

"So what happened?"

"You know Sam is ages with me, and he wed that pretty young Walker gal from the Trinity River country," Conlan said. "How old was she . . . fourteen . . . fifteen?" The old mountain man laid down his glass and rubbed the back of his hand across his eyes, banishing images.

Once more, I must implore the ladies, especially those of a nervous disposition, to pass over the next few paragraphs with closed eyes.

"The girl was heavy with child." Conlan hesitated a heartbeat, then said, "Ask me how I know that."

Wes didn't ask, nor did I.

But Conlan told it anyway. "Because the living child was torn out of her belly and thrown in the fire. That's how come I know."

The crackle of the log in the fireplace and the timid tick of the china clock were the only sounds in the room.

"The girl?" It was a silly question, but I needed to break the deafening silence.

"Dead," Conlan said. "Strung by her long hair from a crossbeam. Sam was hanging by his heels since both his hands had been burned to the bone. He was tortured because the three killers wanted something. I would guess his money and the few valuables he possessed."

Ladies, my compliments. You may reenter the story from here.

Wes frowned. "How do you know there were three of them?"

"I was a scout, remember?"

"Damned Suttons. They'll pay for this, by God."

Conlan shook his head, almost sadly. "It wasn't the Suttons, Wes. Trash they may be, but they wouldn't treat a white woman like that. No man with even a shred of decency would."

"Then who?" I said.

"Wolves in the guise of men," Conlan said. "That's my guess."

"I'm going after them," Wes said. "I'll kill them all for Sam, who was a Taylor man through and through."

"Be careful, Wes, and remember what they say," Conlan said. "Never trust a wolf until it's skun."

"You can remind me of that on the trail, Andy," Wes said. "On account of you're going with me."

Conlan was horrified. "Wes, it will be close work in darkness. I'm not a revolver fighter like you."

"I know, and I'm not a scout like you," Wes said. "Find me those three men, Andy. That's all I ask. I'll do the rest."

"Maybe we should round up a few more men and pick up their trail in the morning," Conlan said.

"How far ahead of us are they?" Wes said.

"Three, maybe four hours."

"Then we go now. It's cold, and they'll probably hole up somewhere for the night."

Conlan thought that through then said, "I'll find them, Wes. But I'll leave the gun fighting to you."

"Of course you will," Wes said, smiling. "That's my game."

CHAPTER FORTY-FIVE
Death in the Meadow

"Damn it, Little Bit, quit that coughing," John Wesley snapped at me. "I don't know why the hell you insisted on coming along."

I stifled a cough. "Sorry."

"Sorry don't cut it," Andy Conlan said, his voice stressed. "You'll get us all killed."

The three of us rode under a full moon through shallow hills and among pines. The light was cold and white, as though we travelled through an ice cave. The old scout led us to the dry wash that had ceased to be a creek maybe a score of years before, and there were pale skeletons of dead trees on both banks.

Conlan followed the wash's looping course that took us to within twenty yards of the Goodson cabin. The place was dark, ghostly, and achingly lonely now that the people who'd lived there were gone.

"You want to see in there, Wes?" Conlan asked, his face shadowed by his hat.

"No, we'll come back and bury them."

Conlan spoke to himself. "Ground's like iron."

"Pick up their trail, Andy," Wes said.

This time Conlan said it aloud. "Ground's like iron."

"You've tracked men across iron before," Wes said.

The old man nodded. "I'd say I have. Let's go."

For the next two hours, across dark country, we rode in silence, except for my strangled, gurgling coughs.

Andy Conlan broke the quiet twice to tell us he'd seen bad omens. Once a crow that shouldn't have been there flapped over his head and his horse shied at a dead coyote.

He turned to me in the saddle. "The crow is death's scout and the dead coyote means that the grim reaper passed this way and touched the animal."

Wes grinned and his teeth gleamed. "Stand behind me when the shooting starts, Andy. I'll gun ol' death before he lays a bony finger on you."

"Death can't be stilled and he can't be killed." Conlan held a red, coral rosary in his fingers.

Wes laughed. "Hell, man. There ain't nothin' a Colt can't kill."

The sinking moon had spiked itself on a nearby pine when Conlan drew rein, tilted back his head, and tested the wind. "Smoke," he whispered.

"How close?" Wes said, his own voice quiet.

"Close."

The old mountain man made a motion with his hand. "Climb down. We go the rest of the way on foot."

Wes was the greatest pistol fighter who ever lived, but he'd taken the precaution of jamming a shotgun into the rifle boot. He slid the gun free then said, "Let's get it done."

Conlan shook his head. "This is as far as I go, Wes." He indicated with his bladed right hand. "They're camped in that direction, maybe a hundred yards, maybe less."

"Three. You're sure?" Wes asked again.

"Three men riding shod ponies," Conlan said. "Yeah, I'm sure."

Wes pointed a finger at me. "Little Bit, you stay here with Andy. This will be hot work and dangerous."

Without another word, Wes turned and silently vanished into the darkness.

Of course, I girded up my old army greatcoat and followed.

I kept my distance from Wes, knowing that if he saw me he'd send me back. My iron leg ensured that I was no Dan'l Boone in the woods, but I stepped as quietly as I could.

The smell of smoke grew stronger and somewhere ahead of me in the gloom I heard men yell and laugh, the whiskey-fueled, false merriment I knew so well from the saloons.

Around me the pines thinned and I walked into a clearing about as big as a hotel room. Moonlight dappled the grass and silvered a boulder to my left. A wind whispered in the trees and a thin mist hovered at the limit of my vision.

I walked on, stepped around the boulder, and froze as a gun muzzle shoved into my left temple, just under my bowler hat.

A muffled curse came as Wes holstered his Colt. He

grabbed me by the front of my coat and his fierce, stiff face got close to mine. He didn't speak, but his eyes were burning. Finally, he pushed me violently away from him with so much force I stumbled back and fell on my butt.

Then Wes was gone, moving like a ghost through the pines.

Like a whipped puppy, I picked myself up and humbly followed . . . my master.

It was my ill luck on that star-crossed night that I should stumble over a tree root and lose my footing. I staggered forward and crashed into Wcs who was standing at the edge of a small, wildflower meadow.

Off balance, he stumbled forward . . . into a gunfight . . . at a time not of his choosing.

My feeble, sputtering pen cannot do justice to what happened next.

It all came down too fast, one flickering image following rapidly after another, like a demented magic lantern show.

I saw two men sitting by the campfire, tussling over a plain gold ring, yelling and laughing as they pulled each other back and forth.

The third man, standing by the horses saw Wes, cried out and charged at a run, a gun in his hand.

Wes let him have both barrels of the scattergun. Screaming, exploding, blood haloing around him, the man fell.

Wes threw down the shotgun and drew his Colts. The man on his left, a towhead wearing a fur coat, got to his feet and scrabbled for his gun. Wes killed him.

The third man rolled, jumped to his feet, his gun

in his hand. He emptied his Colt at Wes. Missed with all five.

Wes fired. The ball slammed into the corner of the man's left eye. He went down hard, then chewed up the ground with his kicking, booted feet. Another shot from Wes and the scoundrel lay still.

Three men dead . . . in the time it takes a grand-father clock to chime five.

Smoke drifted across the meadow as though the gray souls of the dead men were rising from their corpses.

As I stepped into the meadow, Wes glanced at the three bodies, then said, "White trash." He turned his head slowly in my direction. "They didn't know how to fight."

"Do you recognize any of them, Wes?" I asked.

He shook his head and walked over to one of the dead men.

I went after him.

"Look at that face," he said.

Indeed the man looked strange, small piggy eyes, slack mouth, and lopsided forehead, the temples hollow.

"Know what that is?" Wes didn't wait for my answer. "That's inbreeding. His mother couldn't run fast enough to get away from her brothers." He looked around him. "The other two are just as bad. Andy was right, they're not Suttons, just murdering scum."

Given my stunted body and deformed leg, I figured my own ancestry was nothing to boast of, so I kept my mouth shut.

"Little Bit, keep this between us. I won't take credit for shooting down . . . shooting down—"

"Cretins," I said.

Wes nodded. "Yeah, cretins." He smiled. "I don't know what the hell it means, but it's a top shelf word."

"I'll be silent, but will Andy Conlan keep his mouth shut?"

"If he knows what's good for him he will," Wes said.

As it turned out I needn't have worried about it . . . Conlan's mouth was shut forever. Struck in the head by a stray bullet, we found him dead beside his grazing horse.

Death is a black dog that barks at every man's door and Conlan read the signs and knew it was coming. He could not have avoided the bullet that passed through ten acres of trees and killed him because death had his name marked down in his book.

And there's my explanation for it.

Conlan had a wife and kids, so Wes collected the ponies of the dead men, their guns, and the twenty-seven dollars he found in their pockets and later gave it all to the widow. He told her that Andy had been murdered by Sutton nightriders.

Before I close this chapter of my narrative and move on to other adventures in Wes's life, let me just say that I broke my word to him and told about the three cretins he killed only because John Wesley is dead and it doesn't matter any longer.

We didn't bury the bodies in the Goodson cabin.

Wes said, "Let somebody else do it. The ground is too hard to dig graves and they'll need dynamite."

But he did keep Mrs. Goodson's wedding band, the ring the trash had been squabbling over, and gave it to his wife as a gift.

My hero knight deserved a trophy, did he not?

CHAPTER FORTY-SIX
The Killing of Charlie Webb

In late January 1874, John Wesley joined his wife in Comanche and I was reacquainted with his brother Joe, a man I'd always liked. He was a slim young lawyer with a lovely wife and a thriving legal practice. He was well respected in Comanche and owned a large amount of property in the town. Jane was not happy to see me.

Much later, she didn't object when I celebrated the last weekend in May with the Hardin family.

The town fathers had declared the date a festival, and Comanche was going full blast. The saloons, splitting at the seams, roared and throngs of people patronized the racetrack.

Wes entered his American stud, Rondo, in several races and the big horse won easily, earning him three thousand dollars, fifty head of cattle, fifteen saddle horses and a Studebaker wagon. Naturally, a celebration followed and the rum punches flowed freely.

The day shaded into night and the lamps were lit around the town square. Jane and most of the other friends and family called it a day, but Wes, Jim Taylor, and myself decided to celebrate further. Drunk, we staggered into Jack Wright's saloon where Wes tossed a double eagle onto the counter and ordered drinks all round. We were noisy and boisterous certainly, but not belligerent.

Wes was friendly to everyone and even pressed a second gold coin into the hand of a saloon girl who had a birthday that night.

But trouble soon appeared in the form of Comanche deputy sheriff Frank Wilson, a decent sort, who'd also been drinking. He stepped beside Wes and put his hand on his arm "John, the people of this town have treated you well, have they not?"

Wes, grinning, admitted that they had and said he had his racetrack winnings to prove it.

"Then don't drink anymore. Go home to your wife and avoid trouble," Wilson said. His eyes narrowing a little, he added, "You know it is a violation of the law to carry a pistol."

For some reason, in my drunken state, I took exception to this statement and pushed between Wilson and Wes. "Leave us the hell alone. We're not bothering anyone."

Wilson stared at me for a moment as though trying to figure out what species I was, then his balled fist came down like a sledgehammer on the top of my bowler, ramming it down over my eyes.

I staggered around, trying to push the damned thing off my head.

This brought cheers, jeers, and laughter from the crowd and more than a few empty bottles were thrown in my direction.

Finally, I grabbed the brim in both hands and shoved upward with all my strength. My head popped free of the bowler like a cork out of a bottle and I could see again. I caught Wes's look of utter disdain.

He focused on the deputy again. "Frank, my pistols are behind the bar. Out of sight, out of mind, as my ma says." Wes didn't mention that hideout gun he carried under his vest.

"Leave the weapons right here, John," Wilson said. "Pick them up in the morning and stay for breakfast."

Jim Taylor, drunk as a skunk himself, pleaded with Wes to go home. In the end, he agreed, saying that the evening had lost its snap anyhow.

"Remember to let the guns stay behind the bar, John," Wilson said. "Pick them up in the morning and then have breakfast. You haven't lived until you've tasted Jack's biscuits and gravy."

Things might have ended amicably . . . but outside a predator stalked the night, a man with an overinflated ego and a yearning to be known as a *pistola rapida*.

Brown County Deputy Sheriff Charlie Webb was a two-gun man. He carried his newfangled Single Action Army Colts in crossed gun belts, the holsters finely carved in a flowered pattern. He was said to have killed four white men and a Negro, and his fine mustache and dashing good looks impressed the ladies when he cut a dash.

I believe that Webb was looking for trouble that night and had selected John Wesley as his target. Killing Wes was a way to enhance his reputation and establish himself as a dangerous man with a gun.

How it come up, Webb had been pacing up and down outside the saloon and walked within a few feet of Wes who stood on the boardwalk with me, Jim Taylor, and Bud Dixon, Wes's cousin.

For some reason the sight of Webb irritated Wes. "Have you any papers for my arrest?"

"Easy, Wes," Dixon said. Then to Webb, "That man has friends in this town and won't be arrested."

"Hell, man, I don't know you," Webb said to Wes.

"My name is John Wesley Hardin and I come from good Texas stock."

"Well, now we've been introduced, I remember the name," Webb said. "But I still don't have an arrest warrant."

"You're holding something behind your back." Wes was on edge and sobering rapidly.

"Only a ten-cent stogie." Webb produced the cigar, its tip glowing red in the gloom.

I saw Wes relax. Now he was prepared to be friendly. "Come, join us for a drink, Deputy Webb. A hot gin punch is warming on such a chilly evening."

"By all means," Webb said, smiling.

Wes turned to reenter the saloon—and I saw Webb's hands drop for his guns.

"Look out, Wes!" I shrieked.

John Wesley turned as Webb fired. The lawman's

bullet burned across Wes's ribs on his left side, ripping a gash in his coat and his skin.

Wes instantly returned fire and his ball hit Webb in the face, just below his left eye.

Cursing, his mouth running blood, Webb took a step back and fired again.

His bullet splintered wood from the sidewalk between Wes's feet.

Jim Taylor and Bud Dixon cut loose. Their .44 balls tore great holes through Webb's body and he fell dead.

Thus perished an arrogant man whose gun skills fell far short of his ambitions. I shed no tears for him.

Within a couple minutes of Webb's death, all hell broke loose. The news of Webb's death was carried through the town like a fiery cross. Comanche spawned a ravening pack of vigilantes yelling, "Hang the killers!" The bloodthirsty mob rushed Wes and his stalwarts, myself included, only to be driven off by a rattle of pistol fire.

Recently appointed Comanche sheriff John Carnes rushed to the scene, just as the vigilantes launched another attack.

Believing, I'm sure, that a fine man like John Wesley didn't deserve to be the guest of honor at a hemp party, Carnes held off the mob with a scattergun.

Fearlessly, Wes handed his gun to Carnes. "It was not my fault, John. Webb tried to murder me, but I didn't think things would come to such a pass."

"Get the hell into the saloon and stay there. This situation could get out of hand real fast." Carnes turned to me. "You too, Peckerwood, go with them.

And if you've got any prayers, this would be a good time to say them."

Scared, my weak bladder betrayed me as I scrambled into the saloon after Wes and the others. I was almost knocked over as the crowd inside stampeded for the door and a saloon girl with yellow hair and big blue eyes pushed me aside and yelled, "Get the hell out of my way, gimp!"

From somewhere inside I heard Wes shout, "The side door!"

The noise in the street had risen to a roar as men demanded Wes's head. I heard Carnes plead with them to calm down and he vowed that he would see *justice done.*

Throwing tables and chairs aside, I limped to the side door in time to see Wes and Jim Taylor in the alley outside, swinging into the saddles of horses they didn't own.

"Wes!" I screamed. "Wait for me!" I was terrified of hanging, and my despairing wail sounded frantic, even to my own ears.

Wes saw me, heard me, ignored me. He galloped out of the alley into the street, but Jim Taylor, a big and strong man, leaned from the saddle, grabbed me by the back of my coat and threw me on a horse. Then he too was gone.

The paint I straddled didn't like the feel of my steel leg and he bucked a few times. But I managed to grab the reins and leave the alley at a dead run.

Bullets split the air around me as I followed Wes's dust, a billowing cloud tinted orange by the street's reflector lamps. I glanced behind and saw John Wesley's wife in the street, a handkerchief to her eyes. Beside her stood his father with his brother Joe, both holding shotguns.

Then I was beyond the town, galloping into the night.

I allowed the paint to pick his way since I don't see real well in darkness. After half an hour I caught up to the others who sat their blown horses outside a burned out cabin.

Wes grinned at me. "You made it, Little Bit."

"No thanks to you," I said, feeling mean and petty as I uttered the words.

"In a situation like that, it's every man for himself," Wes said. "If you didn't know that before, you sure as hell know it now."

"Truer words was never spoke," Jim Taylor said.

A strange thought popped into my head as I sat silent in the saddle after listening to Wes and Dixon. *How many of his precious cattle would Wes give to save my life?*

No matter how I studied on it, up, down, sideways, I came to the same conclusion.

The answer, that liked to break my heart, was *none*.

CHAPTER FORTY-SEVEN
Wes Plans Revenge

Anger over the killing of Charlie Webb was out of all proportion to the worth of the man himself.

Wes had shot Webb in self-defense. Everybody knew that except the town fathers of Comanche and their damn, foaming-at-the-mouth citizens. The imbeciles even sent a letter of complaint to Governor Coke demanding a strong force of Texas Rangers to rid their county "of murderers and thieves led by the notorious John Wesley Hardin."

Wes was no murderer and although he lifted stray cattle and horses now and then, he was not a thief. However, he had managed to rope in a couple cousins who supported him in this matter.

The authorities, aided and abetted by vengeful Yankees, thrust Wes into the same category as the Mexican bandits who came up from the Rio Grande to kill and plunder.

It was an outrage.

But worse was to follow.

A force of fifty Rangers arrived in Comanche with

orders to hunt down "the John Wesley Hardin gang of murderers who are preying on the citizens of this county."

Wes was enraged. "Call those Rangers what they are. A vigilante band leading a mob composed of the enemies of law and order."

We were living rough in the brush, every man's hand turned against us, when Wes got news that his wife and many of his relatives and friends had been taken into "protective custody" and were locked up in a two story rock house in Comanche.

That was the straw that broke the camel's back.

Wes huddled with Jim Taylor and they made war plans.

After a while, they called the rest of us over and we sat around a spitting fire in a cold, drizzling rain, surrounded by a tangle of scrub oak, thorn briar, and thickets of poison ivy.

"We follow the lead of the great Bloody Bill Anderson and raid into Comanche," Wes said. "We'll free my wife and my father, then teach those turncoats and Yankees a lesson they'll never forget."

"He was a rum one, was Bill," Wes's cousin Ham Anderson said. "He'd kill them all, like he done in Lawrence, Kansas that time."

"And so will we," Wes said. "Except the women and children. We're Southern patriots fighting Yankee tyranny, not the murderers of innocents."

"Hear, hear," Jim Taylor said.

And me, caught up in the moment, exclaimed, "Huzzah!"

Anderson glared at me, the skin of his young face

tight to the bone. He didn't like me. "You only get to say that when you bear arms like a man."

Wes smiled. "Let him be, Ham. Little Bit is one of us."

"To the death," I said.

But nobody listened to me or cared.

"When do we hit them, Wes?" Taylor asked.

"In a couple days. We need a few more men."

"Once the word gets around, they'll come in," Taylor said. "I guarantee we'll have two score fighting men soon. When our boys open the ball, they'll play Comanche such a tune they'll remember it forever."

Days passed, but the volunteers never materialized.

Men stayed close to their homes and loved ones as lynch mobs roamed the countryside, hanging or shooting any man they deemed an outlaw or just a damned nuisance.

The Rangers, in their eagerness to root out anyone connected with John Wesley Hardin, seed, breed, and generation, turned a blind eye to the mayhem and the murder of patriots.

Then came the day that Ham Anderson, and Alec Barekman, another young Hardin cousin, weighed the odds against them and decided to cut and run. Their intention was to surrender to the authorities in Comanche, but within twenty-four hours they were both in shallow graves . . . gunned down by the Rangers.

Dead men tell no tales, and when the Ranger fusil-lade was over, both Anderson and Barekman weighed about five pounds heavier deceased than they did when they were alive. Those poor boys took a lot of

Ranger lead, and their deaths plunged Wes into a deep depression.

All talk of a raid on Comanche ceased and Wes took to compulsively reading a Bible that someone had brought to camp.

"Wes," I said to him, "we have to ride north and live among the savage Canadians for a spell. With no Yankee law chasing us, we can sit back and make plans for the Wild West show, big plans."

Wes looked up from the Good Book and regarded me with lusterless eyes.

"And there's gold up there," I said, talking into his silence. "Nuggets big as a man's fist just lying on the ground for the taking." I smiled. "Within a few months, maybe just weeks, we'll have enough gold to fund the show and have plenty to spare. Hell, you could ride back into Comanche in a carriage and pair. A rich man can thumb his nose at everybody, including the Yankee law."

"Who told you there's gold for the taking?" Wes asked.

"I read it in a book."

"There's only one book a man should read—the holy book I'm holding in my hand."

"At least let's get out of Texas," I said. "We'll head to the New Mexico Territory. No one will find us there."

Wes stared at me with quizzical eyes. "What's this 'we' and 'us' business? There's only me and you. There's no 'we' and 'us.' If I decide to leave Texas, I'll go by myself. A cripple would only slow me down."

Wes dropped his eyes to the Bible again and read, his lips moving. Without looking up, he said, "Get away from me, Little Bit. Leave me the hell alone." After a pause, he added, "And take a bath sometime, huh?"

Wes was worried about his wife and kinfolk, and I forgave his harsh words. Besides, later that day he gave me whiskey and a cigar and said I was "a stout fellow."

CHAPTER FORTY-EIGHT
Men Without Mercy

Since I talked about John Wesley's new interest in the Bible, it's somehow appropriate that terrible news reached our camp carried by a rider on a pale horse . . . *and his name was death and hell followed close behind him.*

The rancher Long Tom Lee swung off his lathered gray and walked directly to Wes. "John Wesley"—he breathed hard like a man in pain—"I don't have the words."

Wes's face took on a stricken, blotched look. "Jane? Is it Jane?"

Long Tom held his battered Stetson in his hands. "Jane is fine and so is your daughter."

"Then find the words, Tom," Wes said. "And find them damn quick."

"They're harsh, John."

"Damn it, say them," Wes said.

Long Tom, a veteran of Stonewall's brigade, was a tall beanpole of a man with a bloodhound's face and the tired, seen-it-all eyes of an Inquisition executioner.

"Your brother Joe is dead, John Wesley, and with him Bud Dixon and his brother Tom."

"How?"

"Hung."

That was a punch in the guts.

Wes rose to his feet, his face drained of color. He loved his brother Joe, the quiet one of the family, and the news of his death devastated him. "Tell it, Long Tom. Every last word of it."

"Hung is hung, John," the rancher said. "There ain't no more to tell. Let it go. Pick at it, and you make the wound worse."

Wes's jaw muscles bunched and his teeth gritted. "Tell it all, Long Tom."

"All right, I'll say what I know." His hat crushing in his twisting hands, Long Tom told how it had been. "Twenty nightriders, all of them masked, rode into Comanche about the one o'clock hour. There was a full moon and the town looked like it was lit by silver lanterns." Long Tom flushed. "I mean, that's how I saw it."

"Go on," Wes said.

"The vigilantes rode to the rock building where your wife and family were held, and overcame the guards."

"Name them," Wes said.

"Does it matter?"

"Name them."

"John James and the county clerk, a man called Bonner," Long Tom said. "They're not lawmen, John."

"Names to remember," Wes said. "But I know Bonner. He and Joe were brother Masons."

"Well, the way it was told to me, Bonner did nothing

to save Joe," Long Tom said. "And he should've. Joe was a mighty shady lawyer all right, everybody knew that, but he did nothing that deserved getting hung."

"Joe did nothing that other lawyers don't do," I said. "He was hung only because he was John Wesley's brother."

"That's a natural fact," Long Tom said. "I can't argue with that."

"The vigilantes overcame the guards, or so they say. Then what happened?" Wes said.

"John . . ."

"What happened?"

"Joe and the Dixons were drug to a tree and hung," Long Tom said.

Wes lifted his head and for long moments stared at the clear blue bowl of the sky where a few crows wheeled like charred pieces of paper. Finally, without looking at Long Tom, he said, "Did . . . did Joe . . . was it quick?"

The rancher's face was grim. "I'm not a lie-telling man, John."

"Then say it."

"Joe died hard. He pleaded for his life as he strangled to death and he kicked for a long time. An awful long time."

At first Wes showed no reaction and stood as still as a statue. Then he drove his fists into his belly and doubled over, screaming. His mouth agape, he fell to his knees, but the screaming did not stop.

I feared it never would.

Long Tom replaced his hat then looked at me. "Is there anything I can do?"

I shook my head.

"Then I'll leave." He cast a final look at Wes in a paroxysm of grief, swung into the saddle, and galloped away.

Jim Taylor stepped beside Wes, put his hand on his shoulder, and whispered, "Wes, don't go to that dark place. Come back, now."

The screaming stopped, and Wes kneeled with his head on his knees and made no sound, no movement. He stayed in that position until night fell.

None of the vigilantes were ever identified or brought to trial.

The Texas Rangers wrote the murders off as a necessary evil, unworthy of their notice.

As their captain said, "Why all the fuss? Often violence is the only way to get rid of undesirables."

CHAPTER FORTY-NINE
Revenge of the White Knights

Now begins what I call the "wandering time," when John Wesley was cast out and forced to flee Texas, his ancestral home.

"And he will be a wild man; and his hand will be against every man and every man's hand against him; he shall live to the east of all his brethren." Thus the Bible speaks of Ishmael the Wanderer, and I use those same words to speak of John Wesley, since he too was an outcast condemned to wander the earth.

Jim Taylor was dead, murdered by Suttonite vigilantes, and I was the only one to join Wes in his bitter exile.

After a brief reunion with his wife and daughter in New Orleans in the late summer of 1874, Wes fled to Gainesville in Florida, a rough and tumble settlement in the middle of the state.

Wes was appalled at the number of blacks in the town, brought in to harvest the cotton crop. He soon joined the local branch of the Young Men's Democratic Club, a Ku Klux Klan organization, and pledged to uphold white supremacy and the American way.

Wes bought a saloon that just about wiped out all of his money, and he lived in a room at the back. I worked as swamper and slept on the billiard table at night.

He'd become John H. Swain by then, adopting the last name of Jane's kin. His intention was to earn enough money from the saloon to establish his Wild West show in Great Britain where he could live in peace, unmolested by Yankee law.

"I bet old Queen Vic will come and watch," I said one night as we sat at a table sharing a bottle after closing. "She's real interested in wild Injuns and such."

"How do you know that?" Wes asked.

"Read it in a book. This one," I said, pulling the book out of my pocket. "It's called *The Visitors Guide to Great Britain*, and tells us everything we need to know about living over there."

"We'll need a special box for the queen and her court," Wes said. "She can sit beside Jane."

"And me," I said.

Wes shook his head. "Queen Vic won't want to sit beside you, Little Bit. You're low class and you smell."

I took exception to that. "I'll have a bath before I sit with Jane and the queen."

"You'll still be low class."

"Maybe she'll surprise you and make me a knight like Quentin Durward," I said.

Wes nodded. "Maybe, if she likes the show enough."

I was about to say more, but Wes raised a silencing hand.

"An argument going on out there. It sounds like them uppity blacks from around here." He rose to his feet and got a long-barreled revolver from behind the bar, one of those new cartridge Colts that were becoming all the rage.

The saloon door slammed open and a young man wearing a star on his vest stepped inside. "Mr. Swain, I need help. Luke Wilson, remember me?"

Wes recognized the sheriff as a fellow member of the Democratic Club. "The blacks rioting?"

"Arguing with me," Wilson said. "They want to come inside and drink more alcohol and I said no."

"Don't they know better than to give a white man sass and backtalk?"

"Not the blacks around here," Wilson said. "The Yankees got them uppity, telling them that they rule the roost."

"Not in my saloon, they don't," Wes said. "And not in my town."

"Good," Wilson said. "I now appoint you as my deputy."

I followed Wes and the sheriff outside into the humid, tropical heat of the Florida night. Cicadas and frogs carried on an endless, chattering, croaking argument and out in the swamps alligators bellowed their opinion.

Five black men stood outside the saloon, illuminated by the lanterns that hung on each side of the saloon door. They looked angry and one of them wore an old Union army blue jacket with a sergeant's chevrons on the sleeves.

"You men go about your business," Wes said. "The saloon is closed."

"The hell it is," the man in the coat said. "The door is open and we're going inside."

"Eli, go home," Sheriff Wilson said. "You're drunk enough already."

"I'll tell you when I'm drunk enough." The black strode straight at Wes who stood still and let him come.

At the last second, Wes sidestepped and swung the Colt. The barrel crashed into the side of the Negro's head and the man dropped like a felled ox.

Another tall, thin man uttered a vile curse, born of the savage heart of darkest Africa, and drew a wicked knife of the largest size. He charged and then fell stone dead a moment after Wes's bullet tore his heart apart.

The three remaining Negros decided that they wanted no part of Mr. Swain that night. In the most abject fashion, they threw themselves on their knees, raised their hands in prayerful supplication, and begged for mercy.

"Lock them up, Sheriff." Wes glanced at the dead man. "Then throw that to the alligators."

Wilson, young and impressionable, raised an eyebrow. "Quick to shoot, aren't you, Mr. Swain?"

"And so should you be, Sheriff, if you hope to live long."

But we were not yet finished with the Negro who wore the blue coat. His name was Eli Brown and he had dreams of one day standing for public office. The blow to his head from Wes's gun enraged him and inflamed his already ferocious hatred of the white race.

What better way to express his loathing than to rape a white woman, a Southern belle of good breeding and fine family who resided in Gainesville town?

Thankfully, the girl's cries were heard before she was cruelly undone, and the cursing, struggling Brown was thrust into jail.

That night there was a gathering of brave and resolute men in John Wesley's saloon, Sheriff Wilson among them. Each man, including Wes, wore a dazzling white robe like a holy Crusader knight ready to do battle with the Infidel.

I was not one of them, but my heart swelled with pride as I beheld such a glorious scene and I felt honored that I was of their race.

"I've got a rope," one stalwart said. "I say we string him up from the nearest telegraph pole."

But Wes would have none of it. "The jail is old and the wood is as dry as tinder. Set fire to the place and we can watch the black demon roast in hell."

This brought a round of applause and cheers for Mr. Swain.

"Drink up, boys," Sheriff Wilson said. "It's almost midnight and time to get it done. I don't want that damn black breathing the same air as us for a moment longer."

This brought another round of huzzahs, then the white knights drained their glasses, donned snowy hoods, and sallied forth into the darkness.

* * *

Eli Brown died horribly. He burned to death even as he stood at a window, his sizzling arms reaching through the bars, pathetically begging for his life.

It was a fate the Negro richly deserved.

Later, we all repaired to the saloon and enjoyed champagne cocktails. Mr. Swain, who had a fine voice, sang "When This Cruel War Is Over," to much applause and many a manly tear.

It was a happy time.

CHAPTER FIFTY
A Chilling Warning

Four thousand dollars. That was the sum the vindictive Texas legislature placed on John Wesley's noble head . . . *dead or alive.*

The happy times had been short and they were about to end.

Wes had long since sold his saloon, kept one step ahead of the law and trusted no one.

The reward was enough to interest the Texas Rangers, especially that redheaded scoundrel J. Lee Hall and his able lieutenant John Barclay Armstrong.

You remember Armstrong. As a Ranger sergeant he arrested, shot, and hung a score of the survivors of the Sutton-Taylor war, and he's the man who took King Fisher into custody.

According to the Yankee authorities, Fisher, a friend of Wes's, was the second worst man in Texas.

We all know who was first.

What worried Wes most was Governor Hubbard's appointment of Jack Duncan, the famous detective, to help in the hunt. "Look at that," Wes said, tossing a newspaper on the table in front of me. "This time they mean business."

The front-page headlines said it all.

JOHN WESLEY HARDIN SCOOTS
FAMOUS SLEUTH ON HIS TRAIL
Ordered to Capture—or Kill!
'Hardin will hang,' vow Texas Rangers

We were residing in Pollard, Alabama, with the Bowen family, relatives of John Wesley's wife, but the news about Duncan had Wes on edge. "Damn it, I've heard of the man. He's a bloodhound and once he's got the scent, he never gives up the trail."

Wes had taken to wearing his guns in the house, something he'd never done before, and his eyes had a hollow, hunted look, as though he felt the very walls were closing in on him. He sat at the breakfast table and crumbled a piece of dry toast in his fingers, lost in thought.

Then his nose wrinkled. "Little Bit, hell, you're stinking up the place."

"My leg is bad, Wes. It's so rotten it hardly supports me any longer." I managed a weak smile. "And the brace is rusting."

"Seen you walking with a limp recent." Wes nodded to himself. "I sure enough have."

"It has to be amputated," I said.

"Pensacola," Wes said, sitting up straight as he snapped his fingers.

"Huh?"

"That's the place for me." Wes lifted his eyes to

mine. He had cold eyes and I swear they'd gotten colder with every killing.

"Hell, it's just across the Alabama border and Chance Rawlins—you know him?"

"The gambler."

"Yeah, him. Chance says Pensacola is a gambling town because of the fortunes being made in cotton and lumber. Hell, I could make a big score there."

"Seems like."

"If the Florida law gets too close, all I have to do is skip back across the border into Alabama again."

"Seems like," I said again.

"Then it's done. I'll see Jane settled, and head east."

"Maybe you'll win enough to stake the Wild West show."

Wes nodded. "Yeah, maybe so. Head for England like I planned."

"I'd need to get a wooden leg first. I mean, before I met the queen."

"Sure, a wooden leg would do the trick." Wes grinned at me. "Then them royal folks won't call you the gimp with the limp, huh?"

"No, I guess not."

My leg was indeed odorous and nobody knew that better than me.

The Bowens would not allow me to sleep in the house and I was banished to the barn, where I shared my quarters with the horses and mules, the occasional pig, and a nightly horde of mosquitoes.

I was not then very familiar with women of the respectable sort, though a few had treated me well, as they would a bird with a broken wing or a wounded puppy. Alice Flood, a distant Bowen cousin, fell into that category.

An orphan, Alice depended on Bowen charity. They provided her with food and board and in exchange, they demanded she act as a skivvy, cleaning out the fireplaces, scrubbing floors, washing clothes with the harsh lye soap that chafed her hands red, and whatever else they needed.

The Bowens called Alice a housemaid, but it was slavery under a different name.

I guess it was inevitable that we should be drawn together, two pathetic, miserable creatures who found solace in each other's company.

Alice was neither pretty nor smart, neither joyful nor sad. She had no past, no present and no future. She just existed from day to day . . . like me.

Ah, my self-pity is showing, is it not?

Alice lifted me out of that pit of despair. As fate would have it, I had her for only a few short years, but those were the best years of my life.

The evening after Wes made his decision about Pensacola, Alice visited me in the barn as she did every evening. As always, she brought me little treats from the kitchen, usually a piece of cake or some cookies.

As I recall, it was cookies with shredded coconut in them that evening, though I was fairly drunk and set them aside for breakfast.

Alice removed the brace and bathed my leg. She frowned. "It's getting much worse, William." She refused to call me Little Bit, saying it was a disrespectful name for a man.

"Not much of it left, is there?"

"You're limping terribly."

I smiled. "I can still ride a horse."

"But not for much longer, I fear." She had unremarkable brown eyes, brown hair and a brown skin, but I thought her beautiful that night.

"It has to come off," I said. "Then I can get a wooden one."

"I think modern artificial limbs are made of metal, and some can bend at the knee."

"How do you know that?"

"I met Dr. Dinwiddie in town and asked him. He says great strides—"

"Ha-ha." I laughed. "Great strides. I like that."

Alice smiled. "Anyway, artificial limbs improved very quickly because of the war. So many boys lost arms or legs."

"Well, that gives me hope." Then as romantic as Quentin Durward, I said, "You give me hope, Alice."

She took my hand and kissed it. "You and me are fated to be together."

A moment later our bodies joined.

Shall I draw you a word picture of two singularly unattractive people making love on straw in a barn among farm animals to the music of yipping coyotes?

I think not.

But after it was over and I lay back exhausted, Alice seemed troubled.

"I'm sorry," I said.

"For what?"

"I disappointed you."

Alice smiled. "You didn't disappoint me, William. Nothing about you disappoints me."

A silence stretched between us, then she said, "About your friend, John Wesley."

"What about him?"

"He talks too much and too loudly."

"I don't understand."

"In front of Brown Bowen."

I felt a stab of alarm. Bowen was Jane's brother, a truly vile creature without a trace of loyalty or manhood. He was a rapist, murderer, and robber.

Ultimately, he dangled from a noose. When he was cut down, no one shed a tear for him or claimed his carcass.

"Do you think Brown might betray Wes?" I asked.

"He's betrayed everyone else." Alice smiled and picked a piece of straw out of my hair. "Maybe I worry unnecessarily."

"You like Wes, don't you?"

"He's a fine man and a true patriot."

"He's both of those things, and much more," I said.

"Will you talk to him? About Brown Bowen, I mean?"

"Yes I will. First thing in the morning." I took Alice in my arms. "But in the meantime . . ."

CHAPTER FIFTY-ONE
The Mighty Are Fallen

John Wesley would not hear a bad word about Brown Bowen. "He's kin. And in Texas, kin don't betray each other."

"Wes, he's vermin and the only reason you put up with him is because he's your brother-in-law," I said.

Wes's temper was always an uncertain thing, and it flared. "And you? What about you? Why the hell do I put up with you?"

"I don't know."

"Neither do I. All you're good for is stinking up the place and sticking it to that Flood gal whose face would scare a cur off a gut wagon."

"Wes, don't say things like that about Alice," I said, my own anger rising.

"Then take back what you said about Brown. I won't have the likes of you ragging on my kinfolk."

I shook my head. "Wes, he's a yellow-belly and sly as a fox. He'll sell you down the river to save his own worthless neck."

"The hell with you, Little Bit." Wes's lip curled. "Go back to your two-dollar whore."

I hit him then.

I mean, I hit him on the chin with all the power of my eighty pounds and little bony fist.

Wes wore his guns and he'd killed men for less. But for a moment he looked shocked, and then mildly amused, the red welt on his chin no bigger than a mosquito bite.

"Don't ever talk about Alice like that again." I was breathing hard, angry as hell, and more than a little scared.

To my surprise—and considerable relief—Wes didn't utter another word. He just turned on his heel and walked away.

He never again mentioned Alice's name in my presence, even when we got married while he was in jail.

He could have killed me that day, but didn't.

That says something about him that's all to the good, doesn't it?

For the next few days, the relationship between Wes and me was frosty and we exchanged few words.

But he made no objection when I asked if I could join him on his gambling trip to Pensacola, saying only, "You're on your own, so just don't ask me for money."

Later, I branded the date of our trip into my memory. August 24, 1877.

The day that John Wesley Hardin's long martyrdom began.

In addition to myself, Wes travelled with fellow gamblers Shep Hardy, Neal Campbell, and Jim Mann, a nice young fellow who'd just celebrated his twenty-first birthday. Notably absent was Brown Bowen who was supposed to make the journey with us.

When the train pulled into the Pensacola depot, Wes decided to linger in the smoking car to finish his pipe and sprawled on a seat alongside the aisle. Mann and I stayed with him, while Hardy and Campbell got off to stretch their legs.

We'd shared a bottle on the trip from Alabama and I was tipsy. I'd say Wes was relaxed and young Mann, who wasn't a drinker, coughed around the black cheroot between his teeth.

No sooner had the locomotive clanked and steamed to a halt, than a man who walked with a limp sat in the aisle seat opposite Wes.

I later learned this was the famous John B. Armstrong, who'd accidentally shot himself in the crotch a few weeks earlier. Unfortunately, he'd missed his balls.

Something about the man made me uneasy, especially when he moved in his seat and I saw the handle of a Colt sticking out of his waistband.

A few moments later, two big, muscular men barged down the aisle, throwing off drunks and laggards, and I knew that the law was about to open the ball.

"Wes! Look out!" I yelled.

John Wesley moved with the reaction of a panther.

"Texas, by God!" he yelled as he rose halfway out of his seat.

You're too late, Wes!

The pair of lawmen jumped on top of him, even as Wes tried to draw his Colt from his waistband. But the hammer stuck in his suspenders and one of the lawmen wrenched it from his hand.

Then it became a free for all.

Wes punched and bit, but the big lawmen pounded him into his seat. His face was soon covered with blood and saliva.

Armstrong sprang to his feet, a long-barreled Colt in his hand.

Young Jim Mann didn't recognize Wes's assailants as lawmen. "Assassins!" he yelled, drawing his gun.

Armstrong fired and Mann slammed back into his seat, his chest pumping blood from a dead-center bullet wound. He died within seconds.

I rushed at Armstrong, my puny fists flying, but he pushed me away and I fell on my back on the carriage floor.

The Ranger ignored me and joined his fellow lawmen. He didn't take part in the struggle, but waited his opportunity with his clubbed pistol raised.

He didn't have to tarry long.

As soon as he got a clear shot at Wes, he crashed the barrel of his Colt into Wes's skull.

Wes didn't cry out. He just went limp. Within seconds, they shackled him hand and foot. His hair was matted with blood, his face a vivid, scarlet mask. His head lolled on his shoulders when they dragged him to his feet, no fight left in him.

My God, my knight had fallen!

Enraged, I scrambled to a standing position and was greeted by the muzzle of Armstrong's revolver ramming into my forehead.

"Call it." The Ranger thumbed back the hammer of the Colt and its triple click sounded like my death knell.

"Call it." he said again. His eyes were bloodshot and wild. Flecks of saliva foamed on his lips.

I am not cut from heroic cloth. "I'm out of it."

"Then get the hell away of here," Armstrong said.

After one last glimpse at the unconscious John Wesley, blinded by salt tears, I stampeded from the car.

Behind me I heard Armstrong yell, "And take a bath!"

Men laughed as I stumbled onto the platform and into . . . I knew not what.

CHAPTER FIFTY-TWO
"He'll Dance at Our Wedding"

That evening I got drunk on somebody else's money. I had to since I had no funds of my own. I rolled a drunk in an alley. I'm not proud of what I did, but desperate times required desperate measures.

The man was taking a piss against the wall of the Penitent Pelican saloon and I crept up behind him and hit him over the head with a bottle. After he dropped, I went through his pockets and found twenty-three dollars, a nickel railroad watch, and a small Roman Catholic medal with an image of the Virgin Mary that, never being inclined to popery, I stuffed back into his vest.

The man started to groan and attempted to rise, and I scampered.

I bought a bottle of Old Crow, and, since the stores were still open, a necklace for Alice—a small, enameled bluebird on a silver chain.

I thought the necklace was pretty, but before I could give it to my sweetheart, I lost it.

I drank myself into oblivion and spent the night on a park bench. No one troubled me because in those days Pensacola was full of homeless vagrants like me.

Come first light, I breakfasted on the last inch of whiskey in the bottle, then went in search of Wes.

I didn't get far. After but a few steps, I collapsed in the street, overtaken by the stress of my friend's capture and the liquor I'd drunk.

I recall the disgusted faces of women looking down at me, then, after I returned from unconsciousness again, the jolting misery of a wagon and a clear blue sky passing above me.

After that, I knew nothing until I woke in darkness. For a few minutes, I lay still and listened to the chatter of insects and the rustles and gibbering cries of forest animals.

Where the hell was I?

I rose to a sitting position and my head reeled. It took a while before the darkness ceased to cartwheel around me. Then came the slow, terrible dawning that I was alone in a vast wilderness. Dusky moonlight revealed a forest of scrub pine, live oak, and tangles of bushes with wide, leathery leaves. It also shone on the sheet of white paper pinned to the front of my coat.

I tore the paper free, then, after much squinting, read

STAY OUT OF PENSACOLA. RETURN
AND I'LL HANG YOU FOR VAGRANCY.
—Wm. H. Hutchinson, Sheriff

It was easy to put together what had happened. I'd been loaded into a wagon and dumped outside the city limits—well outside, if the backcountry where I found myself was any indication.

Had they gotten rid of me because of vagrancy, or was it that I'd been identified as a friend of John Wesley?

I decided on the former. I wasn't significant enough to be taken seriously as a Hardin associate. I'd just been dumped like so much garbage littering the street.

A goblin gets used to that.

I still had fifteen dollars and change in my pocket—enough, I hoped, to see me across the border into Alabama and my darling Alice. She would have news of Wes.

I'd ridden the cushions to Pensacola, but I'd have to walk at least part of the way. I figured some long miles across rough country on a bad leg until I found another town with a railroad depot. I may have well thought about walking to the moon.

I had no option but to try.

Come morning, I padded my leg with the big green leaves of the plant that grew everywhere, then set out, pointing my nose to the east.

I was a hundred and fifty miles from Alice . . . and my long journey had begun.

The fine readers of this narrative are interested in the life and times of my friend and hero John Wesley Hardin, not Little Bit. So let me just say that my odyssey was a long and painful one, but after two weeks (Yes, that long. Such was my hobbling gait and occasional drunks until my money wore out) I arrived at the Bowen farm.

Alice welcomed me with a glad smile and open arms, but the Bowens did not. Brown had been arrested and was facing the hangman's noose. That cast a pall over the family.

I was once again relegated to the barn, told I could stay only a few days, and would have to work for my keep, helping Alice with her chores mostly. Again, this is all beside the point, because I did learn that Wes had been taken to Austin to stand trial for the murder of Charlie Webb.

My worst fear had finally caught up to me.

The night I arrived, Alice joined me in the barn, and she was worried. "You'll go to Austin, won't you?"

"I reckon Wes needs me more than ever now."

"He won't be imprisoned, the public would never stand for it."

I shook my head. "Alice, Wes has friends, but he's got some mighty powerful enemies who'd like to see him hang."

Her eyes took on a dazed look, as though trying to understand the implications of what I'd just told her. Finally she said, "If you go to Austin, I'm going with you."

"I'll have to walk, unless I can hitch the freight cars." I remembered the railroad bull. "It's dangerous and I don't think you'd like that."

"I have a little money. Enough to get us to Austin."

"I don't want to take your money, Alice."

"You said that John needs you. I don't think you

can refuse my offer. How could you live with yourself if you desert him now because of masculine pride?"

I smiled. "I don't have any pride, masculine or otherwise."

"Then we'll go to Austin together. I'll take pride in you."

"You're a wonderful girl, Alice." Then, because I had nothing to offer her, I said, "I bought you a present in Pensacola, but I lost it somewhere. It was a necklace, a bluebird on a chain."

Women are full of surprises . . . and Alice surprised me then.

She reached into the pocket of her dress and brought out a little paper package. She opened it carefully, almost lovingly, and held up what it contained . . . a plain gold wedding band. She smiled. "This was my mother's wedding ring." She laid her hand on mine. "William, the only present I want from you is the right to wear this ring on my left hand."

"You mean—"

"Marry me in Austin."

My words got tangled up in my throat and the only sound I could make was a strangled croak, like a bullfrog with a hernia.

Alice took her hand from mine and wrapped up the ring before returning it to her pocket. "You don't want to marry me," she said, her eyes bruised.

"Of course I do," I said, my voice coming back.

"Then why are you so hesitant?"

"After I check on Wes, we'll get hitched, I promise."

"Do you really mean that? Can I trust you?"

"Yes I mean it, and yes you can." I held out my open hand. "Give me the ring." I placed the slim band on her wedding finger. "We'll make it official in Austin. Right after I see Wes." I smiled. "I'm dying to tell him about us."

Alice kissed me. "He was very good to you, wasn't he?"

"The only friend I ever had."

"Then he'll dance at our wedding, William. I just know he will."

CHAPTER FIFTY-THREE
Twenty-five Years at Hard Labor

The Travis County Courthouse in Austin was a brand new, three-story limestone building of breathtaking size, built in what was then called the Second Empire style.

Alice and I stood outside for a while, at the corner of Eleventh Street and Congress Avenue, and stared up at its ornate ironwork, palatial dormers, and lofty Mansard roof. We looked exactly what we were, a pair of open-mouthed rubes fresh in from the country with dung on our shoes.

The monumental, elegant courthouse dwarfed us into puny insignificance. For the first time in my life, I realized just how colossal was the edifice of the law and how effortlessly it could crush even a giant of a man like John Wesley Hardin.

In a small, nervous voice, Alice asked, "William, are you sure we can we go in there?"

"Of course we can," I said with more confidence than

I felt. "It's a big place, but remember that it belongs to the people of Texas."

"People like me and you?"

"Yup, just like us."

The *us* that morning was a less than imposing sight.

Lacking a portmanteau, Alice had tied up her few belongings in a sheet that she slung over her back. I still wore the huge army greatcoat and battered bowler hat. Underneath were pants, shirt, and shoes much the worse for wear.

When we walked into the echoing, marble magnificence of the building and asked for the clerk of court, the uniformed doorman looked as though someone was holding a dead fish under his nose. "What do you people want? Court is not in session today."

"We're here to see a friend." I dropped the name. "Mr. John Wesley Hardin."

"All sorts of scoundrels"—the man looked hard at me—"are dragged through those doors. I can't be expected to remember their names. Come back tomorrow and talk to the clerk of court."

Alice said in a tremulous whisper, "William, we can come back tomorrow."

"Indeed," the doorman said, "when court is in session."

A tall young man in a dark gray suit, some sort of lawman's shield on his vest, walked past with a sheaf of papers in his hand. He stopped when he saw Alice and me.

"Everything all right, Mr. Murdoch?" he said to the doorman.

Before the man could answer, I said, "Sir, we're here to visit with our friend John Wesley Hardin."

"I told you court is not in session today," Murdoch said. "Now be off with you."

"It's all right, Mr. Murdoch." Then the young man spoke directly to Alice, perhaps because she was so nervous. "Mr. Hardin has already been tried and convicted of murder in the second degree. I'm afraid he was sentenced to twenty-five years at hard labor."

I felt as though I'd been stabbed in the heart and Alice's face was as pale as an oyster.

"I'm sorry I have no better news for you." The young man gave a little bow. "Good day to you both."

"All right you two, out you go." The doorman surprised me. "Hardin has appealed his sentence. Try the county jail behind us at 11th and Brazos."

He slammed the door on our heels and for a few minutes we stood, struck dumb, at the corner.

The young man's words kept spearing through my mind . . . twenty-five years at hard labor . . . twenty-five years at hard labor. . . .

For a freedom-loving knight errant like Wes, it was a death sentence.

CHAPTER FIFTY-FOUR
Jailbird

John Wesley was to spend a year in the Travis County Jail as his appeal progressed, so I will describe at some little length, that grim bastion as it was the first day I ever set eyes on it.

Imagine if you will, a massive building fifty feet wide by sixty long with walls of solid stone two feet thick. It contained twenty-four dank, dark cells only eight feet by ten, their ceilings two stories high. A lever arrangement meant that all the doors could be opened and closed at the same time, without the jailors coming in contact with the prisoners.

There could be no escape from such a bastille and Wes was well aware of that fact.

After we left the courthouse, Alice and I walked down Eleventh Street to the jail. Gas lamps lined the shady avenue. We drew many stares, some highly amused, others openly hostile. A couple of ragged country bumpkins were a rare sight—one to see and talk of later.

The coming of the Houston and Central Texas

Railway had attracted many wealthy, sophisticated residents to the city. The beautiful Austin belles in watered silk fascinated Alice, their huge bustles and tiny hats perched atop masses of glossy, piled up hair in stark contrast to her own threadbare, homespun dress and shabby leather shoes.

As we walked, I vowed there and then that Alice would one day wear silk.

Foolish Little Bit, again building his rickety castles in the air.

We were ushered into a tiny visiting room partitioned by an iron grill. The prisoner stood on one side, the visitors on the other. There were no chairs or benches and no window, the gloomy interior lit by an oil lamp hanging from the ceiling.

When Wes was ushered inside, a prison guard cradling a shotgun stood against the door. He made it perfectly clear when he stared at Alice and me, he didn't like what he saw.

The feeling was mutual.

Wes looked really good. His hair was neatly combed and brushed straight back from his forehead and his mustache was trimmed. He seemed to be in good spirits. "So what brings you here to Austin?"

I smiled. "You, of course. How are you getting along?"

"Real good. My lawyers say I'll be out of this hell-hole within the week."

"I'm glad to hear that, Wes. Have you made plans?"

"Of course I've made plans. And the most important of them is to get even with them as put me here. Beginning with that damned traitorous dog Brown Bowen."

I wanted to say *I told you so*, but I didn't.

"Take it easy, John," the jailor said. "Keep it light."

"Sorry," Wes said. "But Bowen tried to pin all his foul and disgraceful crimes on me."

"I know that, John," the jailor said. "But you'll be a free man when you see him hang."

For some reason I've never been able to fathom, law enforcement officers of every stripe liked John Wesley. The big jailor was no exception. Maybe they saw something of themselves in him—Wes's regard for law and order and his grit, determination, and coolness under fire. Whatever it was, he received respect and admiration from lawmen all his life.

In fact, Wes also liked peace officers. He proved that to me when he said, "Little Bit, if you see Ranger John Armstrong, tell him I've got no hard feelings. He treated me fair and square and he's a credit to Texas."

"I sure will, Wes," I said, although I'd no intention of ever talking to Armstrong again. My one brush with him on the train was enough. To bolster Wes's spirits, I told him a little lie. "I've been working on the business proposal for the Wild West show."

Wes smiled. "How much funding do we need?"

I picked a number out of the air. "I'd say twenty thousand." To soften the blow, I added, "But maybe a lot less."

"Hell, twenty thousand is nothing," Wes said, grinning. "I can make that at the gambling tables in a good year." He thought for a moment, then said, "Or I can talk to Sam Luck again."

"Either way, we can raise it, Wes."

"Good. Then bring the proposal to me and I'll read it." He slammed his right fist into the open palm of his left. "Damn it, Little Bit, we're off and running."

"I'll let you read it in a few days, once I add a few finishing touches."

"Yeah, take some time and get it right. I might even be out of here the day after tomorrow."

"I sure hope so." I believed him, every word. I really believed Wes's lawyers could work a miracle.

Out of the blue, Wes asked, "Where is my gun, Little Bit?"

I shook my head. "Wes, I have no idea."

"Then talk to the Rangers, get it back for me. It's my property, not theirs, and I'll need it when I'm freed."

Rather than suggest that asking for his gun might not be such a good idea, I said, "Hell, Wes, you can buy a new one."

"No. I want my own Colt back. I've never used a revolver that balanced as well as that one."

"I'll see what I can do."

"I'll see what I can do," Wes repeated in a high, sarcastic tone. "Don't see. Do it!"

"Of course, Wes. I'll get it for you."

"Time's up, John," the prison bull said.

I talked fast. "Wes, say howdy to Alice. You remember her."

Wes gave my intended a stiff little bow, his face empty.

"We're getting hitched," I said. "Right here in Austin."

"Don't forget the gun." Wes turned on his heel and the iron door clanged shut behind him.

Alice spoke into the ringing echoes of the door. "He doesn't like me."

I smiled at her. "You're Bowen kin and he's upset about Brown telling all those lies on him."

"It's not that."

"Then what is it?"

"You're showing some independence, William, and John doesn't like that. He has nothing but contempt for you, but he enjoys the idea that you count on him for everything, even your self-esteem."

I laughed then. "Alice, I don't have any self-esteem."

"I know, because John Wesley Hardin took it away from you. But I'm going to give it back to you, William."

"Well, Wes told me that he wanted his gun is all."

"Damn him and his gun!" Alice yelled. She stomped out of the room, her back stiff.

I stood openmouthed with shock. I'd never heard sweet little Alice cuss like that before.

CHAPTER FIFTY-FIVE
A Grim Reality

John Wesley's appeal dragged on for a year and kept him behind bars.

During that time, his family—he now had three children—descended into poverty. Jane, already dying from cancer, moved them in with Wes's mother. The Reverend Hardin had passed away in 1876 while his son was on the scout in Florida.

I can't say that Wes's spirits were high.

I believed that in his heart of hearts he knew his appeal would founder and that twenty-five years in state prison was close to becoming a grim reality.

Alice and I were married by then. She restricted my visits to the jail, but one day after he'd spent five months in his cell, I found Wes elated, beside himself with joy.

"Good news! Hot dang, Little Bit, I'll be out of here soon."

Happiness is contagious, and I eagerly awaited the good tidings.

"Read this!" Wes yelled. His face fell. "You can read, can't you?"

"Wes, you know I can read."

His face brightened. "Oh, yeah, that's right. You can."

The jail rules dictated that nothing could be passed from prisoner to visitor, so Wes held a letter up to the iron grill. "Read it!" he shouted, or I should say *roared*.

The prison guard stirred uneasily and gripped his scattergun tighter, his eyes never leaving Wes for a moment.

I moved closer to the grill, and saw that the letter was from Elizabeth, Wes's ma. After telling her son to praise the Lord and look to Heaven for guidance, she wrote:

> *I am willing to speak with the lawyers about your case, dearest boy. Your pa wrote a true statement of the killing of Charlie Webb, but died before he could publish it. I am willing to do so now.*
>
> *Your father said that there was a plot to murder you on the day Webb was killed and that you only defended yourself from a hired assassin.*
>
> *My loving, dutiful son, your pa's deathbed testament will set you free!*

After I indicated that I'd read the letter, Wes said, "Well, what do you think? Don't Ma milk a good cow?"

Since his attorneys had used this same argument before the jury that found Wes guilty, I figured his ma was milking a dry cow.

As it happened, indeed she was. The reverend's statement never saw the light of day.

But I withheld my gloomy misgivings. "Wes, that's wonderful. Just wonderful."

"Damn right it is. Everybody believes a reverend, don't they?" Wes carefully folded up the letter and put it in his pocket. "You get my Colt back?"

I lied my way out of that question. "I sure did. Ranger Armstrong gave it to me and it looks as good as new."

"They hung Brown Bowen," Wes said. "They say he died pretty well."

I nodded. "Heard that."

"There will be others like him when the reckoning comes."

I didn't know the guard and he looked mean. I changed the subject. "I'm still working on the business proposal for the show."

"Yeah, good," Wes said, with little enthusiasm. He looked me over. "You look like hell, even skinnier. That woman not taking care of you?"

"She takes care of me just fine."

"How's the leg?"

"Bad as ever."

"All right, that's enough. Move it, Hardin." This from the guard.

Then this from Wes, "Sure thing, boss."

After he was gone, I felt oddly depressed about two things. The first was that Wes didn't remember that I was a reader, the second that he was losing the respect of his jailors.

Later, I read in the newspaper that Wes had beaten an old trusty to within an inch of his life for being late with his dinner. This might explain the change in attitude of the guards.

But his memory slip troubled me. It was the first indication I had that Wes's mind was going. It would be a long, destructive process, spanning decades, but in the end it would contribute to his death.

CHAPTER FIFTY-SIX
I Turn a New Page

Alice found work as a kitchen maid while I stayed at home to write what I knew best—dime novel tales of the West, its heroes, bad men, and beautiful maidens in every stage of distress.

After a few tries, I got the hang of the thing, and was soon selling on a regular basis.

From this happy time in my life, I'm sure you recall that my best sale was for a book I wrote in less than a week. *Hands Up!* Or *John Wesley Rides The Vengeance Trail.*

Sadly, the day the novel came out, Wes's appeal being denied, he was transferred to the Huntsville Penitentiary in June of 1879 to east Texas to begin his quarter-century of confinement.

I wrote him and gave him my address, *Mr. & Mrs. William Bates, 27 Sunnycourt Crescent, Austin, Texas,* and asked how he was faring in that dreadful prison.

Several months later, Wes replied. He addressed the envelope to *Little Bit, Esq.* He said he'd already made two attempts at escape, and both were foiled. After the second one . . .

They threw me into a cell and spread-eagled me on a concrete floor, then gave me forty lashes, less one, with a bullwhip. Little Bit, my back and sides were torn up something awful, but I was taken from there and thrown into a solitary cell. I was there for three days without food or water. After a week, I was tossed into yet another cell and now I have a high fever and I'm too weak to walk.

My health is not good, but I'll beat them in the end, Little Bit. They may kick me, flog me, and starve me, but I won't let the scum win. I'll keep on trying to escape until I am successful. In the meantime, I will bear my persecution with Christian fortitude.

Wes's letter depressed me and may have been the cause of my bad leg finally giving out on me two days after Christmas. Cancerous, it was amputated in my own bedroom. The surgeon used chloroform so I felt little at the time, but the stump pained me considerably and my drinking worsened.

I experienced even greater pain when Alice, who'd been failing for some time, died of what a doctor said was, "consumption and a mighty hard life." She passed away in the spring of 1881, not yet twenty years of age.

I was lost. The happiness I'd known had been abruptly snatched away from me, and I turned more and more to the whiskey bottle for solace. Yet through it all I continued to write, thanks to the urging of my editor, Frank Starr, a fine man who never gave up on me. I was, I believe, the first drunken writer in Texas, though others have since followed my path.

My novels sold very well, and, despite myself, I began to prosper.

I was fitted with a fine artificial leg that helped me walk better than I ever had before, and I gradually reduced the amount of whiskey I drank. By 1884, the Little Bit of old was gone forever. My old leg brace, bowler hat and filthy army greatcoat I burned . . . and with them the name, Little Bit.

I was a fairly rich man and I dressed the part, favoring three-piece ditto suits of somber shade and winged collars with an ascot tie and diamond stickpin.

"Bill, you owe that man nothing," Frank Starr said. "What did he ever do for you but turn you into a drunk and a fugitive?"

We sat in my parlor while Cassie, my housemaid, served us afternoon tea, Frank being a temperate man.

"I owe him a great deal. Wes helped me survive. What chance did a crippled little runt like me have in Texas after the war? Wes was my protector and my inspiration. I wanted to be like him."

"If you'd turned out like him, you'd be serving time in Huntsville right now."

"Maybe, but without John Wesley, I'd probably be dead."

Cassie poured the tea and I said, "Earl Grey. I hope you like it. I understand it's a favorite of old Queen Vic. And please make a trial of the sponge cake."

After Frank declared the tea good and the cake better, I reached into my inside coat pocket and produced a letter and a newspaper clipping. I passed the clip to Frank, but he declined.

"I left my spectacles on the train from New York," he said. "I'm afraid you'll have to read it to me."

"It's short. The newspaper is dated September 12, 1884, and it says, 'The health of the notorious John Wesley Hardin is very bad and has taken a turn for the worse. He is not expected to survive much longer. He has served out five of his twenty-five year sentence.'"

"Well, I guess I'm sorry to hear that," Frank said. "But what has it got to do with you?"

I opened Wes's letter. "This may explain why."

I read aloud, "'The shotgun wounds I got from Phil Sublett and the pistol ball injury that Charlie Webb inflicted on me became first inflamed and then abscessed. Little Bit, they did not allow me in the prison hospital but confined me to my cell where I lay in great pain for eight months. When they thought I was recovered, they told me I must work in the rock quarry, but I spit in their eye. I was lashed and after two weeks on a bread and water diet, was sent to make quilts in the tailor shop.'"

I looked at Frank and said, "And then this. 'No one comes to visit anymore. Manny came a few times but not for the past couple years. Has the world forgotten me, Little Bit?'"

Frank flicked the letter with his forefinger and smiled. "No, Mr. Hardin. The world's moved on and you've been left behind."

"I've not left Wes behind," I said. "I'm going to visit him."

"Bill, you just signed a contract for four more novels."

"And I'll meet my deadlines. I'll only be gone for a week at most."

Frank drew a deep breath. "I hope you know what you're doing. Hardin has always been a baleful influence on you and I'd hate to see you go back to what you were."

"What was I?"

"I can tell you what you were *not.* You were not a successful, respected author who makes enough money to live comfortably for the rest of his life."

I smiled at that. "Trust me, Frank, I won't stumble and fall."

"Then I'll take you at your word," Frank Starr said. "I don't want to bury you in a pauper's grave like I did Edgar Allan Poe."

CHAPTER FIFTY-SEVEN
That Scoundrel Buffalo Bill

A penitentiary is a wheel within a wheel and together they grind slowly . . . inexorably . . . a motion that's unrelenting, unalterable and pitiless. The purpose of a penal institution is to crush a man between the turning wheels, pulverize his soul, his mind, his being, while keeping his useless carcass alive so that he can remain only healthy enough to suffer his just punishment in full measure.

The man I met in Huntsville was no longer the John Wesley Hardin I knew.

A man can't be whipped, beaten, and starved into submission without it leaving a mark on him. Wes had served less than six years of his sentence, but already, he was broken by the wheels.

We met in a Huntsville Penitentiary visiting room during a thunderstorm, my affluent appearance and the hired carriage at the gates allowing me immediate access. The room was furnished with a table and two wooden chairs. A barred window high in one rock wall glimmered with lightning and allowed inside the sullen roar of the thunder.

Clanking iron shackles bound Wes hand and foot.

The prison guard pushed him into a chair. "Ten minutes," he said to me. "And make no physical contact with the prisoner."

The guard carried only a billy club. Judging by Wes's bruises, he had made its acquaintance recently.

I smiled at him, prepared for the usual polite *how-are-you?* exchange.

But Wes grabbed my wrist. "Did you hear?"

"Hear what?" I asked.

"A damned scoundrel by the name of Buffalo Bill Cody has started a Wild West show on the North Platte, up Nebraska way."

"I'm sorry to hear that, Wes."

"He stole my idea, and, by God, he'll pay for it." Wes leaned closer to me and dropped his voice to a conspiratorial whisper. "As soon as I get out of here, and it could be any day now, you and me will ride up to the North Platte and shoot that thief." He leaned back in his chair, his shackle chains chiming. "And then we'll take over his show and get rich, just like we planned."

I didn't like Wes's eyes, the odd way he stared at me. In the flickering light of the thunderstorm, he seemed much older. The bright, inner glow of his golden youth was gone. He was a man old before his time.

Every time I looked at him I died a little death.

Out of nowhere, he said, "Did you hear about Jane?"

"Yes I did. She was a fine woman and you have my deepest sympathy. Alice also passed away."

Wes ignored what I said. "Why are you all dressed up like a dude?" It was as though he saw me for the first time.

I smiled. "Why, to meet you of course."

"Are you a spy?"

"I don't understand."

"You ain't Little Bit."

"I was Little Bit."

"He wasn't much."

"He was your friend."

"I don't have any friends. Nobody comes to visit me."

"I've come," I said.

"Have you brought tobacco?"

"No. But I'll bring some next time."

"Get Passing Clouds Navy Cut. Accept no substitute."

"I'll remember that."

Then, as he'd so often done in the past, Wes surprised me. "Little Bit, I can't take another twenty years of this hell."

He'd finally remembered who I was and I took that as a good sign.

"Wes, I'll do everything in my power to get you out of here," I said.

"Make it soon."

"It may take a little while. In the meantime, just don't kick against the system any more or it will destroy you. Play their game, Wes. Toe the line."

"I don't want to be whipped again."

"Then don't try to escape again or refuse to work. I'll see you're freed. Trust me on that."

"Bear it with Christian fortitude," Wes said.

"Yeah, that's the ticket." I almost said *And the years will fly by*, but I bit my tongue.

After my visit, Wes took my advice and became a model prisoner. He managed the library and led Sunday devotions for his fellow cons and, as far as I am aware, was never punished again. In addition, he studied law and by all accounts became very learned in all its twists and turns.

Thank God, I didn't know then that, despite all my efforts on his behalf, John Wesley would spend a total of fifteen years, eight months, and twelve days in Huntsville.

Finally, at my urging and that of other prominent citizens, his lawyer W.S. Fly met with newly appointed Texas governor James B. Hogg. He was said to be, "All for the underdog when the underdog has a grievance."

I ask you, who was more sinned against than John Wesley?

Fly met with Hogg and declared, "I can get a thousand men in Gonzales County who will sign an application demanding that John Wesley Hardin get a full pardon. I have faith in his integrity and manhood and believe it is not misplaced."

Petitions soon poured into the governor's office from all over Texas, signed by judges, businessmen, politicians, and twenty-six sheriffs. In addition, a flood, nay, a deluge, a torrent, a cascade of letters came from private citizens.

"Parole granted!" a delighted Hogg declared on February 7, 1894.

John Wesley walked out of Huntsville, a free man, ten days later. He was forty years old.

I had a carriage and pair waiting for him at the gates.

When Wes was released, the frontier he had known no longer existed . . . except in isolated communities like the wild border town of El Paso. Even so close to the beginning of the twentieth century it still had more than its share of resident gunmen.

Of course, the town would eventually attract Wes like a moth to a flame.

CHAPTER FIFTY-EIGHT
Beginning of the End

"Gentlemen, I now declare to you that my future life will be one of peace and goodwill toward all men."

Thus, on July 21, 1894, did Wes address the District Court of Gonzales County after it allowed him to practice law in any of the state's district and lower courts.

W.S. Fly was so moved, he jumped up and in a loud, stentorian voice, addressed the court. "You have all read Victor Hugo's masterpiece, *Les Miserables*. It paints in graphic terms the life of a man so like Mr. John Wesley Hardin, a man who tasted the bitterest dregs of life's cup, but whose Christian manhood rose, godlike, above it all and left behind a path luminous with good deeds."

The audience cheered and no huzzahs were louder than my own.

I didn't realize it then, but it was the last time I'd ever feel proud of Wes and bask in the dazzling radiance of his glory.

* * *

Restless as ever, Wes ran for sheriff of Gonzales County, lost by a mere eight votes, then closed up his law practice and relocated to Kerrville in the hill country around the Guadalupe River. Before he left, he sent me a letter explaining the move. He said that one of his kin, Jim Miller, needed help with a legal wrangle.

But what really drew him west was a woman.

Callie Lewis was a flighty fifteen-year-old who'd fallen in love with the Hardin legend. She apparently admired desperadoes and their deeds of derring-do and thought it would be a hoot to wed and bed one.

What she didn't realize was Wes was a man old beyond his years, his bullet-scarred body stiff and not easy to get going in the morning.

But he wanted her. She was a flashing, vibrant, beautiful girl who reminded him of his own reckless youth, He hoped he could recapture all those lost Huntsville years if he made Callie his wife.

And so vivacious Callie played Catherine Howard to John Wesley's stooping, stumbling, aging Henry Vlll and the end result was just as tragic.

The happy couple wed in London, Texas, on January 9, 1895, and parted forever early the next morning, a few hours after they'd exchanged their vows.

Callie never said what caused the split, but to me it was obvious—the sickly, middle-aged man she married fell far short of the legend.

To me later in the day, he tried to make light of what had happened. "She took one look at me, standing nekkid as a jaybird by the bed, and promptly fainted. Hell, every time I tried to wake her up, she took one look at me and fainted again. Come morning, she threw on her duds and skedaddled out of there."

"Sorry to hear that, Wes," I said, though I had no liking for Callie. She was air-headed as they come and not very intelligent.

We were seated at a table in the Black Bull saloon. My artificial leg became intolerable if I stood at the bar for too long. I poured us both whiskey from the bottle we shared and glanced around me. The saloon was busy since evening was coming down, but no one paid us any heed.

Once well-wishers would have crowded around Wes and slapped his back, told him what a fine fellow he was, and the saloon girls would have vied for his attention.

But that night . . . nothing.

I felt a pang of sadness, almost painful in its intensity, and a deep sense of loss. *John Wesley you are a man of your time and that time is over.*

"Maybe it's just as well," Wes said.

I was shocked. Had he read my mind? "What's just as well?"

"When I go after Bill Cody, Cassie would just slow me down." Wes leaned across the table, his face within inches of mine. "I think she was in on it. That's why she left me. She was scared I'd find out."

I frowned. "Wes, I don't think that's the case. I don't think Cassie even knew about the Wild West show."

"How the hell do you know that, Little Bit? You know nothing and you never did."

"Buffalo Bill is an important man," I said, refusing to take offense. "You can't gun him."

"Yeah I can, because I'm an important man myself. Watch this."

Wes turned in his chair and yelled, "Which one of you rubes will buy John Wesley Hardin a drink?"

He got blank stares and no takers.

I watched anger flare in him. "Take it easy, Wes."

He ignored me and rose to his feet, staggering a little. He yanked a blue Colt from his waistband and yelled, "Do I have to leave men dead on the floor to get a drink?"

Standing there, half drunk, he did not look the heroic figure of old.

He was what he was—a sickly, rapidly aging man whose day was past. The owlhoot trails he once rode were scarred by the slender shadows of telephone wires and the tracks of horseless carriages.

Then I witnessed the start of John Wesley's terrible downfall.

The bartender, a massive brute with a bullet head and hairy forearms the size of rum kegs, stepped from behind the bar, strode up to Wes, and wrenched his revolver from him so roughly I heard Wes's trigger finger break.

Yes, it was that swift and that easy.

The brute tossed the gun to me. "Get him the hell out of here before he gets hurt."

Twenty years before, the bartender would have been dead on the floor and Wes would have ordered a round of rum punches for the house. Now, he clutched his broken finger to his chest and meekly allowed me to guide him into the pale blue light of the gas-lit street.

I had discovered two truths that night. The first was that my knight in shining armor was no more. The second was that I was finally free of him.

CHAPTER FIFTY-NINE
This Was Once a Man

I returned to Austin and resumed my writing career. I'd always been an admirer of Poe, and in later years I kept up a lively correspondence with Bram Stoker of *Dracula* fame. With Frank Starr's blessing I wrote my first horror novel in June 1895.

I'm sure you've read the work. *The Phantom of Yellow Fork, A tale of Western terror.* If you haven't, I believe it's still available . . . after thirteen printings.

In July I got a letter from John Wesley. He stated that he'd hung his shingle in El Paso and was walking out with a married lady and sometimes prostitute named Beulah M'Rose.

Two weeks later, I received a second missive. Wes said that his lady's husband, Martin M'Rose, had just been murdered under mysterious circumstances and that he was the prime suspect. He wrote:

But I didn't shoot the dirty dog. Though God knows he deserved killing. By holding true to my Christian

*faith and by dint of much prayer, I know I will
triumph in the end.*

Then a postscript that deeply troubled me:

*Little Bit, send me $5. I am in dire financial straits
right now.*

There is no witness so dreadful, no accuser so terrible, as the conscience that dwells in the heart of every man. I had abandoned John Wesley to his fate and turned my back on him when he needed me most. Our years of friendship were *gone for nothing*.

I could not live with that.

Whatever slender claim to manhood I possessed would be forever crushed under the jackboot of treachery and I would never be the same again.

This I knew, even as I lied to myself that a trip to El Paso would be an excellent opportunity to do some research for my next book. Almost without thinking about it, I found myself hurriedly throwing my things into a valise, including the Colt revolver that the London bartender had taken from Wes.

Why I packed the weapon I'll never know. Its blue, oily sheen and cold black eye told me nothing.

But I did, and there's an end . . . and a beginning . . . to it.

I arrived in El Paso on the morning of August 19, 1895. It was a hot, dusty town surrounded by the Chihuahuan Desert with a distant view of purple mountains against a sky that stayed blue almost the entire year. The place was booming. Ten thousand people crowded its streets.

During my short walk from the train station to my hotel, I rubbed shoulders with priests and prostitutes, gamblers and gunmen, businessmen and beggars, and more Mexicans than I'd ever seen in one place in my life.

The throngs made the town noisy. Rumbling drays and spindly carriages vied for road space. Their drivers cursed each other and street vendors hawked their wares in loud, raucous roars from the boardwalks.

The town smelled of dust, beer, smoke, Mexican spices, and sweaty people.

But, by God, it had snap.

After I checked into my room, I came back downstairs and asked the desk clerk to direct me to the law office of Mr. J.W. Hardin.

The man looked at me as if I was an insane person. "What law office? Hardin hasn't set foot in the place for months."

"Then where can I find him?"

The clerk smiled. "Mister, there are a dozen saloons in El Paso and the same number across the border in Juarez. He could be in any one of them."

"This early?" I said, more from shock than curiosity.

"Hell, man. He's the town drunk. Where else would he be this early?" The voice came from my right side.

I turned and saw a stocky man of medium height with hard gray eyes glaring at me. He wore a holstered revolver, supported himself on a cane, and had a lawman's shield pinned to the front of his vest. "You a friend of his? Kin of his maybe?"

"I'm John Wesley's friend," I said.

The man nodded. "When you find him, give him a message from me. Tell him the only curly wolf in El Paso is me. Nobody else. You got that?"

I felt a spike of anger. "And who are you?"

"Constable John Selman. Your friend Hardin has been messing with me and mine for too long."

I said nothing.

Selman said, "Watched you walk here. You some kind of gimp or something?"

"Or something," I said.

"Don't forget what I told you." Selman limped to the door, then turned to me and said, "If Hardin doesn't leave El Paso, I'll kill him."

After Selman left, the clerk gave me a worried look. "If Hardin is your friend, I'd get him out of El Paso. Selman is a hardcase and he's put more in the grave than I can count on one hand."

"He'd like to be known as the man who killed John Wesley Hardin. That's what I think."

"Mister, you need to catch up with the times. Hardin might have been somebody once, but that was a long while back. Now he's a drunk and a laughing-stock. To prove how good he is with a gun, he shoots holes in playing cards at five paces and sells them to folks for whiskey money. He misses a lot more than he hits." The clerk shook his head. "Get him out of El Paso or take the next train to anywhere yourself."

"I'll find him." I stepped toward the door.

The clerk said to my back, "Try the Wigwam first. He's usually there this early. And another thing—"

"You sure are a talking man," I said.

"Maybe so, but listen to this—Selman has you marked.

If I was you, I'd be looking over my shoulder"—he spun the register and glanced at the last entry—"Mr. Bates."

As the desk clerk had predicted, Wes was at the Wigwam saloon. He wasn't mean drunk, or silly drunk . . . just drunk.

Unnoticed, I stood inside the doorway and studied him for a few moments.

He sat at a table with his back to the wall. His face was red-veined and bloated and he looked every day of his hard, forty-two years. I'd seen his like many times before, men who were used up, had a past, but no present and less future.

All that's left for men like that is to die with as little fuss, bother, and inconvenience as possible.

When Wes looked up and saw me step toward him, his hand dropped from inside his coat. "Little Bit, you again. You keep showing up like a bad penny."

"Just passing through, Wes. I thought I'd stop and see my old friend."

"I don't have any friends, old or new," Wes said.

"That's a hell of a thing to say to me, Wes."

He motioned to a chair. "Sit down."

After I did, Wes said, "I didn't mean that. I guess I've got old friends, just no new ones." His voice dropped. "A lot of men want to kill me."

"You're square with the law. Those killing days are over."

"Maybe. But wouldn't you like to be the man who killed John Wesley Hardin?"

I shook my head. "No, I wouldn't like that one bit."

"Well, there are them who'd revel in it."

"Are you talking about John Selman?"

Wes stiffened. "You heard about him?"

"He talked to me at the hotel. He said you've got to leave El Paso."

Wes rubbed a trembling hand across his mouth. "I'm scared, Little Bit. I'm real scared."

His words hit me like a shotgun blast to the belly. "No! John Wesley, you're afraid of no man."

"I'm afraid of John Selman. I think he can shade me." Wes grabbed my hand. "Little Bit, I want out of this town. Take me with you."

"Sure, Wes, you can come with me. But you'll have to leave the bottle behind."

"I will, Little Bit. We'll leave tomorrow."

"No, Wes. We'll leave on the next train out of El Paso."

That should have ended it, but it seemed there was no end to Wes's humiliation. He called for more whiskey.

Instead the bartender brought a ledger bound with black leather. "Hardin, I'm getting mighty sick and tired of this." He pointed a thick finger to an underlined entry. "Pay the thirty-eight dollars and ten cents bar bill you owe or you'll get no more whiskey in this house."

"Damn you, Matt," Wes said. "I'm part owner of this establishment."

"The hell you are. You drank away your share a long time ago."

A second man stepped up to the table. He looked big enough and mean enough to be a bouncer. "Got some trouble here, Matt?" He rested a huge, clenched fist on the table in front of Wes.

It was an aggressive play, but Wes didn't seem to recognize it as such.

"No trouble. I'll pay Mr. Hardin's bill," I said.

The bartender had huge side-whiskers that curled around his cheeks like billy goat horns. I was dressed well, looked prosperous, but it seemed that being in the presence of John Wesley did not engender trust.

"Show me your shilling, mister," the bartender said.

I reached into my coat for my wallet and gave him two twenty-dollar bills. "Now, coffee for two."

"The hell with that," Wes said. "Bring me whiskey. We're in the money!"

CHAPTER SIXTY
Four Sixes to Beat

I returned to my hotel room sick at heart. The man I'd known and adored as John Wesley Hardin was gone forever, in his place a scared, drunken imposter.

And only I could help him.

El Paso was a rickety skip in the middle of a vast, desert sea. By late afternoon, a strong east wind drove sand along the street outside and drove people to the boardwalks where the sting was less severe.

As he had for most of the day, John Selman was at his post under the awning of the New York Hat Shop, his eyes fixed on the window of my room.

Well, I thought, let him stand there all he wants. In a few hours, Wes will be clear of this burg forever.

We'd agreed to meet that evening at the Southern Pacific Railroad Station to board a sleeper train leaving at seven-thirty for San Antonio with a connection to Austin. In the meantime, I sat in an easy chair, a box of good cigars and a bottle of brandy at my elbow, rising occasionally to check on Selman.

Despite the windblown sand, he stood at his post like a good soldier, ever watchful.

That puzzled me. Why this interest in me? Did he suspect something and didn't want Wes to escape his clutches?

Only time would answer that question.

I rose and retrieved the Colt revolver from my valise.

During all my western adventures I'd never carried a gun, never fired at another human being. That was about to change. I prayed for one good shot, just one straight aim . . . one unerring bullet.

Yes, I said I prayed, but not to God. I prayed to the devil.

I arrived at the station fifteen minutes before the appointed time.

The train arrived twenty minutes late. I watched it pull in, load up with passengers, and depart. I did not see John Wesley.

A Southern Pacific slumber car was to be the start of my redemption plan for Wes, but it had failed. I knew there could be no other unless I made it happen.

I returned to my room, dropped off my bag, and shoved the Colt into my waistband as I'd so often seen Wes do.

Though the town lights were lit and the wind had grown stronger, John Selman had returned to his post on the boardwalk. I suspected that he'd followed me to the station and back.

That was all to the good. He was where I wanted him.

I walked . . . I should say *hobbled*, since my stump

was paining me . . . down the stairs. The same desk clerk was on duty.

He saw me and smiled slightly. "The Acme. This time of night." He told me where the saloon was.

"Do you have a back entrance?"

"Of course," the clerk said. "Just turn right and follow the hallway. Good luck, Mr. Bates."

Surprised, I looked at the clerk, but he'd turned his back to me and I couldn't see his face.

The back entrance took me out onto Overland Street. Despite the driving sand, it was busy with people and wheeled traffic.

My head bent against the wind. Constantly checking the position of the revolver, I turned left and walked along a street lined on both sides with boarding houses and commercial buildings. I can't remember its name.

Then I turned right onto San Antonio Street. The desk clerk had told me the Alamo would be on my left, opposite the Clifford Brothers grocery store.

I hadn't caught a glimpse of Selman, but I was sure if he intended to follow me he'd have picked up my trail by now. My legs dragged as I drew closer to the Alamo and faced the harsh reality of what I planned.

People passed, heads bowed, without sparing me a glance.

A windblown leaf hit my face, then fluttered away, and I found myself listening to the *thump-thump-thump* of my artificial leg on the walk, like a bass drum at a funeral.

The Alamo was lit by electric lights and glowed in the darkness. I walked closer and heard the voices of men inside the saloon. I was sure I recognized John Wesley's drunken laugh.

Despite the wind, the night was warm. The door of the saloon was ajar. I heard footsteps behind me and looked around, but they'd suddenly stopped and I saw nothing.

I pulled the Colt and stepped closer to the door. My heart thumped in my chest and my mouth was dry, the brandy I'd drunk sour in my stomach.

I stopped at the door and looked inside. Wes stood at the bar, his back to me, playing dice with a man I didn't know.

I swallowed hard. Dear God, was I doing the right thing?

Then the thought, like a whisper in my ear. *Take the shot, Little Bit. It's an act of mercy, the first and only noble thing you've ever done for your friend.*

I pushed the Colt through the doorway and took aim.

"Brown, you've got four sixes to beat," Wes said.

I pulled the trigger.

Before you ask, yes, I saw the bullet hit.

I saw it crash into the back of Wes's head, saw the sudden eruption of blood and skull—and then John Selman was on me like a rabid wolf.

He shoved me aside and I fell on my back in a heap.

Selman rushed inside and I heard two shots, then a yell of triumph. "I killed him, by God," he shrieked. "I'm the man who killed John Wesley Hardin."

You know, after that yell, I heard a few scattered cheers.

I didn't wait to hear more.

Sick to my stomach, I got to my feet and lurched into the night. My long torment of grief and guilt had begun.

CHAPTER SIXTY-ONE
Afterward

John Selman, his hand on his gun, saw me off at the train station.

I remember his words to me plainly. "I knew you would kill him the first time I ever saw you. You had to do it, didn't you?"

"Yes, I had to do it. Once, John Wesley was a great man and my friend. I could not let him suffer any longer."

"Well, you keep your damn trap shut about what really happened, understand?" Selman said.

"I will never boast of it."

"See you don't, or I'll come looking for you." Selman's eyes were ugly.

"No you won't, Mr. Selman." I smiled at him. "You are the man who killed John Wesley Hardin, remember? You will be killed very soon."

And he was.

* * *

Without John Wesley, the end of my story is of no importance.

I resumed my writing career, but was stricken with a virulent blood cancer and given months to live.

Fearing to die alone and unmourned, in the spring of 1914 I bestowed my fortune on the Sisters of Charity on the condition that I be allowed to spend my last days in one of their hospices.

The good sisters readily agreed, and now, as it snows outside, my last hours are at hand and the sisters stand around my bed.

Putting pen to paper is very difficult for me, but I am at peace with God. I know he's forgiven my most grievous sin.

~~I will meet~~

~~I will see~~

I know Wes has forgiven me and will meet me at the gates of Paradise.

Oh wondrous sight!

Golden revolvers will be strapped to his chest and he'll hold the reins of two milk-white horses. And he'll be as he was in his shining youth.

He'll grin at me as he did so often of old and say, "Mount up, Little Bit. We've got riding to do."

I'll run to him then, wearing my old army greatcoat and bowler hat, but on two sturdy legs.

And we'll

William Bates died before he could quite finish this account of the famous outlaw John Wesley Hardin. Mr. Bates had converted to Catholicism before his death and was fortified by the Last Rites of Holy

Mother Church. He asked that this narrative not be published until a hundred years after his death. We will honor his wishes.

> —*Sister Mary Frances Walters.*
> *Written this day, November 8, 1914.*

J. A. Johnstone on William W. Johnstone
"When the Truth Becomes Legend"

William W. Johnstone was born in southern Missouri, the youngest of four children. He was raised with strong moral and family values by his minister father, and tutored by his schoolteacher mother. Despite this, he quit school at age fifteen.

"I have the highest respect for education," he says, "but such is the folly of youth, and wanting to see the world beyond the four walls and the blackboard."

True to this vow, Bill attempted to enlist in the French Foreign Legion ("I saw Gary Cooper in *Beau Geste* when I was a kid and I thought the French Foreign Legion would be fun") but was rejected, thankfully, for being underage. Instead, he joined a traveling carnival and did all kinds of odd jobs. It was listening to the veteran carny folk, some of whom had been on the circuit since the late 1800s, telling amazing tales about their experiences, that planted the storytelling seed in Bill's imagination.

"They were mostly honest people, despite the bad reputation traveling carny shows had back then," Bill remembers. "Of course, there were exceptions. There was one guy named Picky, who got that name because he was a master pickpocket. He could steal a man's socks right off his feet without him knowing. Believe me, Picky got us chased out of more than a few towns."

After a few months of this grueling existence, Bill returned home and finished high school. Next came stints as a deputy sheriff in the Tallulah, Louisiana, Sheriff's Department, followed by a hitch in the U.S. Army. Then he began a career in radio broadcasting at KTLD in Tallulah, which would last sixteen years. It was there that he fine-tuned his storytelling skills. He turned to writing in 1970, but it wouldn't be until 1979 that his first novel, *The Devil's Kiss,* was published. Thus began the full-time writing career of William W. Johnstone. He wrote horror (*The Uninvited*), thrillers (*The Last of the Dog Team*), even a romance novel or two. Then, in February 1983, *Out of the Ashes* was published. Searching for his missing family in a post-apocalyptic America, rebel mercenary and patriot Ben Raines is united with the civilians of the Resistance forces and moves to the forefront of a revolution for the nation's future.

Out of the Ashes was a smash. The series would continue for the next twenty years, winning Bill three generations of fans all over the world. The series was often imitated but never duplicated. "We all tried to copy the Ashes series," said one publishing executive, "but Bill's uncanny ability, both then and now, to predict in which direction the political winds were blowing brought a certain immediacy to the table no one else could capture." The Ashes series would end its run with more than thirty-four books and twenty million copies in print, making it one of the most successful men's action series in American book publishing. (The Ashes series also, Bill notes with a touch of pride, got him on the FBI's Watch List for its less than flattering portrayal of spineless politicians and the growing power of big government over our lives, among other things. In that respect, I often find myself saying, "Bill was years ahead of his time.")

Always steps ahead of the political curve, Bill's recent thrillers, written with myself, include *Vengeance Is Mine, Invasion USA, Border War, Jackknife, Remember the Alamo, Home Invasion, Phoenix Rising, The Blood of Patriots, The Bleeding Edge,* and the upcoming *Suicide Mission.*

It is with the western, though, that Bill found his greatest success. His westerns propelled him onto both the *USA Today* and the *New York Times* bestseller lists.

Bill's western series include *The Mountain Man, Matt Jensen, the Last Mountain Man, Preacher, The Family Jensen, Luke Jensen, Bounty Hunter, Eagles, MacCallister* (an Eagles spin-off), *Sidewinders, The Brothers O'Brien, Sixkiller, Blood Bond, The Last Gunfighter,* and the upcoming new series *Flintlock* and *The Trail West.* May 2013 saw the hardcover western *Butch Cassidy, The Lost Years.*

"The Western," Bill says, "is one of the few true art forms that is one hundred percent American. I liken the Western as America's version of England's Arthurian legends, like the Knights of the Round Table, or Robin Hood and his Merry Men. Starting with the 1902 publication of *The Virginian* by Owen Wister, and followed by the greats like Zane Grey, Max Brand, Ernest Haycox, and of course Louis L'Amour, the Western has helped to shape the cultural landscape of America.

"I'm no goggle-eyed college academic, so when my fans ask me why the Western is as popular now as it was a century ago, I don't offer a 200-page thesis. Instead, I can only offer this: The Western is honest. In this great country, which is suffering under the yoke of political correctness, the Western harks back to an era when justice was sure and swift. Steal a man's horse, rustle his cattle, rob a bank, a stagecoach, or a train, you were hunted down and fitted with a hangman's noose. One size fit all.

"Sure, we westerners are prone to a little embellishment and exaggeration and, I admit it, occasionally play a little fast and loose with the facts. But we do so for a very good reason—to enhance the enjoyment of readers.

"It was Owen Wister, in *The Virginian* who first coined the phrase *'When you call me that, smile.'* Legend has it that Wister actually heard those words spoken by a deputy sheriff in Medicine Bow, Wyoming, when another poker player called him a son of a bitch.

"Did it really happen, or is it one of those myths that have passed down from one generation to the next? I honestly don't know. But there's a line in one of my favorite Westerns of all time, *The Man Who Shot Liberty Valance,* where the newspaper editor tells the young reporter, 'When the truth becomes legend, print the legend.'

"These are the words I live by."

Turn the page for an exciting preview!

THE GREATEST WESTERN WRITER
OF THE 21ST CENTURY

*William Johnstone is acclaimed for his
American frontier chronicles. A national bestseller,
the legendary storyteller, along with J. A. Johnstone,
has written a powerful new novel set in Texas—
one century after the Revolutionary War.*

LIBERTY—OR DIE FOR IT

One hundred years ago, American patriots
picked up rifles and fought against British tyranny.
That was Boston. The enemy was King George III
and his British troops. Now, in Last Chance, Texas,
in the Big Bend River country, it's Abraham Hacker,
a ruthless cattle baron who will slaughter anyone
who tries to lay claim to the fertile land and anything
on it. For Last Chance, freedom is under siege one
violent act at a time . . . until wounded Texas Ranger
Hank Cannan arrives in town. Seeing the terrorized
townsfolk, Cannan is ready to start a second
revolution. It's going to take a lot of guts. But one
way or the other, Cannan is out to set Last Chance
free . . . with bullets, blood, and a willingness to
kill—or die—for the American right of freedom . . .

DAY OF INDEPENDENCE

by William W. Johnstone
with J. A. Johnstone

On sale now, wherever Pinnacle Books are sold.

CHAPTER ONE

Texas Ranger Hank Cannan was in one hell of a fix.

In fact, he told himself that very thing.

"Hank," he said, "you're in one hell of a fix."

He uttered that statement aloud, as is the way of men who often ride long and lonely trails.

About ten minutes earlier—Cannan couldn't pin down the exact time—a bullet had slammed into him just above his gun belt on his left side, and another had hit his right thigh.

In addition, after his horse threw him, he'd slammed his head into a wagon wheel and now, for at least part of the time, he was seeing double.

With so many miseries, Cannan reckoned that his future career prospects had taken a distinct downhill turn, especially since the bushwhacker somewhere out there in the hills was seeing single and was a pretty good marksman to boot.

The rifleman had earlier stated his intentions clearly enough, but Cannan could not bring himself to agree to his terms.

Yelling across a hundred yards of open ground, the man had demanded Cannan's horse, saddle, guns, boots and spurs, his wallet, watch and wedding ring, and whatever miscellaneous items of value he may have about his person.

"And if I don't?" Cannan called back.

"Then I'll kill you as dead as a rotten stump."

"You go to hell!" Cannan said.

"Ladies first," the bushwhacker yelled.

Then he laughed.

That exchange had happened a good five minutes ago, and since then . . . nothing.

Between Cannan and the hidden rifleman lay flat, sandy ground, thick with cactus and mesquite, but here and there desert shrubs like tarbrush and ocotillo prospered mightily.

The Texas sun—scorched hot and drowsy insects made their small music in the bunchgrass. There was no other sound, just a vast silence that had been scarred by rifle shots.

Cannan, long past his first flush of youth, gingerly explored the wound on his side with the flat of his hand. It came away bloody.

One glimpse at his gory thigh convinced him that he had to end this standoff real quick or bleed to death.

But the drawbacks to that plan were twofold: His rifle was in the saddle boot and the horse under that saddle could be anywhere by now, as was his pack mule.

The second, and much more pressing given his present circumstances, was that the only weapon he had available to him was his old Colt .45.

Now there were many Rangers who were skilled

with the revolver, fast and accurate on the draw and shoot.

Cannan wasn't one of them.

His colleagues rated his prowess with a Colt as fair to middling, but only on a good day, a nekkid-on-the-back-porch kind of good day.

Hank Cannan could never recall having one of those.

But most gun-savvy men allowed that he had at least the potential to be a widow-maker with a rifle—except now he had no rifle.

After his horse tossed him, he'd landed in a creosote bush and his forehead had crashed into an ancient wagon wheel half buried in sand. It had been the wheel's iron rim, still intact, that had done the damage and made Cannan see stars and, later, two of everything.

He'd hunkered down in the creosote bush and had propped up the wheel in front of him, where it provided at least an illusion of cover. But he knew he had to move soon before he grew any weaker.

His only hope was to outflank the bushwhacker and Injun close enough to get his work in with the Colt at spitting distance.

Cannan stared out at the brush flat, sweat running through the crusted, scarlet stain on his forehead.

He didn't like what he saw.

The ground was too open. Even crouched, he would present a big target. Two or three steps, and he'd be a dead duck.

Cannan sighed. Jane a widow after just six months

of marriage, imagine that. It just didn't seem right somehow. He'd—

"Hey you over there!" the bushwhacker yelled. "You dead yet?"

"Yeah, I'm dead," Cannan called out. "Damn you, I'm shot through and through. What do you think?"

"I'm a man gets bored real easy, and this here standoff is getting mighty tiresome. When do you reckon you'll pass away, if it's not asking an impertinent question?"

"By nightfall, I reckon. Depending on how I bleed, maybe a little sooner."

"Hell, that's way too long. I got places to go, things to do."

"Sorry for the inconvenience," Cannan said.

"Tell you what," the rifleman said.

Cannan said nothing.

"I'll take your hoss and leave you to die at your leisure. I can't say fairer than that. What do you reckon, huh? State your intentions."

"All I can say is that you're a good Christian," Cannan said. "Straight up an' true blue and a credit to your profession."

"Well me, I learned that Christian stuff from a real nice feller I shared a cabin with one winter over to Black Mesa way in the Arizona Territory. He'd been a preacher until he took up the bank-robbing vocation. We were both on the scout at the time, you understand."

"Yeah, I can see that," Cannan said. "Being on the scout an' all."

"Well, anyhoo, come spring I split his skull open

with a wood axe, on account of he had a gold watch chain I wanted. I'm wearing it right now in fact."

"Well, wear it in good health," Cannan said.

There was a moment's pause, then the bushwhacker said, "You're a right personable feller, a white man through and through, and it's been a pleasure doing business with you."

"You too," Cannan said.

He wiped away sweat and blood from his forehead with the back of his gun hand then gripped the blue Colt tighter.

He needed a break. He needed the drop. And right then neither of those things seemed likely.

But there was one option open to Hank Cannan, stark though it was.

He could die like a Texas Ranger.

Better one moment of hellfire glory, bucking Colt in hand, than to slowly bleed to death in the brush like a wounded rabbit.

But first . . .

Cannan reached into his shirt pocket and found the tally book and a stub of pencil that every Ranger carried.

He held the little notebook against his bent left knee and wrote laboriously in large print:

DEAR JANE, I THOUGHT OF YOU TO THE
LAST. I DIED GAME, AS A RANGER SHOULD.
      YOUR LOVING HUSBAND,
      Henry Cannan, Esq.

Cannan read the letter, read it again, and smiled, deciding it was crackerjack.

He tore the page out of the tally book, folded it carefully, and shoved it into his pocket where an undertaker was sure to find it.

Then he rose painfully to his feet, and, his bloody face set and determined, staggered toward the hidden gunman.

He planned to keep on shooting until the sheer weight of the bushwhacker's lead finally put him down.

They say fortune favors the brave, and if that is so, Cannan caught his first lucky break.

His ambusher, a big, bearded man wearing a black coat and pants, was in the act of mounting his horse and didn't see Cannan coming at him.

He'd also slid his rifle into his boot. A fatal mistake.

The Ranger tottered forward, then the bearded man turned his head and saw him.

He grabbed for the Winchester under his knee as Cannan two-handed his Colt to eye level and fired.

It was a nekkid-on-the back-porch kind of day for Ranger Hank Cannan.

He scored a hit, then as the big man tried to bring the rifle to bear, scored another.

The bushwhacker's horse did not behave well.

A tall, rangy, American stud, it got up on its toes and white, fearful arcs showed in its eyes. The horse attempted to shy away from Cannan's fire, and its rider cursed and battled to get his mount under control.

It was now or never for the Ranger.

A plunging, moving target is difficult to hit and he missed with his third shot, scored again with his fourth.

Cannan had no time to shoot a fifth because the

bearded man toppled out of the saddle and thudded onto the ground, puffs of dust rising around him.

Aware that he'd only one round left, Cannan, bent over from the pain in his side, advanced on the downed man. But the bushwhacker, whoever he was, was out of it.

Blood stained the front of the white shirt he wore under his coat, and the left side of his neck looked as though it had been splashed with red paint.

The man stared at Cannan with rapidly fading blue eyes that held no anger or accusation.

Cannan understood that, because he recognized his assailant as Black John Merritt, bank robber, some-time cow town lawman, and lately, hired gun.

Professional gunmen like Merritt held no grudges.

"I recollect you from your wanted dodger," Cannan said. "The likeness didn't do you justice."

"You've killed me," Merritt said.

"Seems like."

"My luck had to run out sometime, I guess."

"Happens to us all."

"I got lead into you."

"You surely did."

"I hope your luck doesn't run out."

Merritt licked his lips.

"Hell, got blood all over my damned mouth."

"You're lung shot," Cannan said. "Saw that right off."

"Figured I was."

Merritt had been leaning on one elbow, now he lay flat and stared at the sky, scorched almost white by the merciless sun. He gritted his teeth against pain, but made no sound.

Then he said, gasping a little, "Who are you, mister?"

"Name's Hank Cannan. I'm a Texas Ranger."

Merritt smiled, his scarlet teeth glistening. "I should have suspicioned that. You boys don't know when you're beat."

"Goes with the job, I reckon."

Cannan lowered the hammer of his Colt and shoved it into the holster.

He felt lightheaded and the pain in his side was a living thing with fangs.

"Why did you decide to bushwhack me, Merritt?" he said.

"I was bored. It gave me something to do."

"You tried to kill me because you were bored?"

"Why not? I'm a man-killer by profession. Another killing more or less don't make much of a difference. I've already gunned more than my share."

"Merritt, I don't much like talking harsh words to a dying man, but you're a real son-of-a-bitch and low down."

"Truer words were never spoke, Ranger."

The gunman was barely hanging on and gray death shadows gathered in his cheeks and temples. His gaze was still fixed on the sun-scorched sky, as though he wished to carry that sight with him into hell.

Merritt's words came slow, labored, like a man biting pieces off a tough steak. "Where you headed?" he said.

"I'm hunting a man. I go where he goes."

"What manner of man?"

"A man like you."

"Then he'll head for Last Chance."

"Where's that?"

"A town on the Big Bend, down by the Rio Grande."

"There are no towns in this part of Texas. Nothing for miles around but sand, cactus, and rock."

"Last Chance is there . . . due south . . . ten, twelve miles . . . hiring guns . . . gold . . ."

Cannan tensed as Merritt reached into his coat, but the man brought out only a gold double eagle.

"Ranger, take this," he said. "Make sure they bury me decent."

The coin slipped from Merritt's fingers and dropped into the sand.

"Promise me . . ." he whispered.

"I'll send you to your reward in a good Christian manner, Merritt," Cannan said.

But he was talking to a dead man.

CHAPTER TWO

Black John Merritt was a big man, and heavy, and Hank Cannan had a hard time getting the gunman draped across his horse.

Cannon's own bay wandered back with the pack mule, but the Ranger was all used up and it was a while before he mustered strength enough to climb into the saddle.

After the gnawing pain in his side subsided a little, Cannan sat his horse and thought things through.

He'd lost Dave Randall's trail two days before in the deep ravine country up by Dagger Mountain. Figuring the outlaw might head for Mexico, Cannan had scouted as far south as the Chisos Mountains when Merritt decided to take a pot at him.

Now, at least one bullet in him, he was in need of urgent medical care. But around him stretched miles of hostile brush desert and raw, limestone mountain peaks that held themselves aloof and didn't give a damn.

As Cannan had told himself before, he was in a hell of a fix.

Unless . . .

Cannan stared at a sky slowly fading into turquoise blue at the end of the burned-out day, as if to seek the answer to the question he hadn't yet asked.

Could there really be a settlement due south of here on the big bend of the Rio Grande?

Cannan told himself that it was a ridiculous notion.

All this land would grow was a fair crop of rocks and cactus, and starving cattle would soon leave their bones on the desert sands, as would those who owned them.

If there really was a Last Chance, by now it was a ghost town inhabited by owls, pack rats and the quick shadows of people long gone.

Cannan decided to take the gamble.

Last Chance was the only card he had left to play.

At best, he'd find a town. At the worst, a ruined roof to sleep under.

Or die under.

Hank Cannan would remember little of his ride south.

He'd later recall that the mule and the dead man's sorrel stud ponied well and didn't try to pull his arm out of its socket.

The yipping coyotes challenging the rising moon— he remembered that, and the far-off howls of a hunting wolf pack.

Cannan didn't remember trying to build a cigarette and cursing as both tobacco sack and papers fell from his weakening hands.

Nor would he recall staring at Black John's face in

the moonlight, bone-white, the wide-open eyes glinting behind slate shadows.

And perhaps it's best that he'd never bring to mind Merritt's ghostly, hollow voice whispering to him that hell is not hot, but cold . . . colder than mortal man can imagine.

"You're a damned liar!" Cannan yelled. "You're burning in fire. I can feel your heat! You're making me burn with you."

Black John whispered that hell is a gray, soulless place, covered in ice, and it has a constant north wind that cuts and slashes like a knife edge, and leaves deep, scarlet scars all over a man's naked body.

Then Black John said, his voice like a death knell, "Feel them, Ranger . . . feel the winds of Hades . . ."

And Cannan did.

He was hot before, but now he shivered as an icy blast hit him, and it cut like a saber and stank of sulfur from the lowest pits of hell.

"Hell is a wind!" Black John screamed. "A wind that blows bitter from Satan's mouth!"

"Liar!" Cannan yelled. "Liar, liar, your pants are on fire . . . in hell!"

Then suddenly he felt burning hot again.

Then cold.

Then hot.

And when he rode into the moon-splashed town of Last Chance, windows stared at him with blank, emotionless eyes . . . and all at once the ground cartwheeled up to meet him . . .

And then Hank Cannan felt nothing . . . nothing at all.

CHAPTER THREE

"Ah, the sleeping beauty awakes."

Hank Cannan thought he recognized the man's voice, but he lay still amid the soft comfort that surrounded him, unwilling to move.

"This may come as news to you, huh? But you're alive, Ranger Cannan. I saw your eyelids flutter."

Cannan opened his eyes and groaned.

"Baptiste Dupoix," he said. "Then I must be in hell."

"Close," the Creole gambler said. "You've been raving about Black John Merritt and a ghost town. But to set your mind at ease, you're in a burg called Last Chance, and you're a current resident of the Big Bend Hotel."

"What are you doing here, Dupoix?" Cannan said. "I thought I hung you years ago."

"No, you haven't yet had that pleasure," Dupoix said. "Though God knows you tried."

Cannan lifted his head off the blue-and-white-striped pillow and tried to rise to a sitting position.

"Here, let me fluff that for you," Dupoix said.

The gambler reached behind Cannan, pounded

the pillow into shape then propped it against the brass headboard.

He helped Cannan sit up and smiled, his teeth very white against his dark skin. "There now. Comfy?"

Two oil lamps, lit against the darkness outside, cast shadows in the room, especially in the corners where the spinning spiders lived.

"What the hell time is it?" Cannan said.

"Early. It's just gone six."

"Morning or night?"

"Dawn soon. When a sporting gent like me should already be in bed."

"But you postponed slumber to visit me, huh?" Cannan said. "Out of the goodness of your heart."

"Bad enemies are like good friends, Cannan. They're to be cherished."

"I've got a dozen questions," Cannan said, ignoring that last.

He lifted the sheets and saw that he was naked, but for the bandages around his waist and thigh.

"How I got here will be one of them," the Ranger said. "But first tell me what happened to the dead man I brought in."

"You mean Black John?"

"How many dead men did I have?"

"Only him, and he'll be sorely missed."

"I promised him I'd bury him decent."

"The nice folks of this fair town buried him, with all due pomp and ceremony, I assure you."

"When?"

"Why, two weeks ago."

Cannan was shocked.

"I've been lying in this bed for two weeks?"

"Uh-huh, that's what I said. The doctor told me you were at death's door." Dupoix grinned. "It was a mighty uncertain thing. Touch and go, you might say."

Cannan waved a hand around the hotel room. "Who did all this?"

"Not me, I assure you. My hypocrisy goes only so far. No, the town fathers put you up here. There are some really nice people in Last Chance."

Dupoix, a tall, elegant man who moved like a cougar, thumped a bottle of Old Crow and a couple of glasses onto the table beside Cannan's bed.

"I did do something for you, though," he said. "A couple young ladies of my acquaintance took care of you. You were out of it, but you did take nourishment now and again. Chicken gumbo mostly, made to a recipe handed down by my swamp witch grandmother back in Louisiana."

Dupoix poured whiskey into the glasses.

"It's a bit early, isn't it?" Cannan said.

"Early or late. It doesn't make any difference to a man confined to his bed. Oh, and remind me to tell you about my grandmother sometime. She's a very interesting woman."

"How did you know that I was the Ranger who brought in Black John?" Cannan said.

"From the description I got from the men who picked you up off the street. Big man, they said, maybe four inches over six feet with shoulders an axe handle wide and the face of a dyspeptic walrus. Who else fits that description?"

Cannan accepted a whiskey, then said, "Do you have the makings?"

"No, I've never succumbed to the Texas habit, but I can offer you a cigar."

"That will do just fine," Cannan said.

"I thought it might."

After Dupoix lit Cannan's cheroot, the Ranger said from behind a cloud of blue smoke, "Now tell me why you and I are breathing the same air in a town a hundred miles from anywhere."

"You first, Ranger Cannan, since you're feeling so poorly."

"I was tracking a feller—"

"Dave Randall. Yes, I know." Dupoix read the question on Cannan's face and said, "He's here in Last Chance." The gambler smiled. "And so is Mickey Pauleen."

That hit Cannan like a fist to the belly. "What's a killer like Pauleen doing here?" he said.

"Him, and Dave Randall. And Shotgun Hugh Gray. And a half-a-dozen other Texas draw fighters. But Mickey is the worst of them, or the best of them, depending on your point of view. The day after he arrived he shot the town marshal."

"And where do you come in, Dupoix?" Cannan said.

"I'm here for the same reason Mickey and them are here. For gun wages. Two hundred dollars a day until the job is done."

"What job? And who's paying you?"

Dupoix, elegant in a black frockcoat, boiled white shirt, and string tie, stepped to the window then turned and said, "You've never forgiven me for that time in . . . what the hell was the name of the place?"

"Horse Neck," Cannan said.

"Yeah, Horse Neck. A benighted burg at the end of a railroad spur, as I recall."

"It was a hell-on-wheels tent town and I was sent there to keep the peace, Dupoix," Cannan said. "You ruined it for me and nearly got me kicked out of the Rangers."

"Cannan, those three gentlemen playing poker with a marked deck were asking for trouble. They took me for a rube."

"That's why you shot them, Dupoix, because your pride was hurt."

"They were notified."

"You left three dead men in the saloon, then lit a shuck on a stolen horse."

"The buckskin I left at the livery was a superior animal in every way to the one I . . . borrowed. Its owner got the best of that bargain."

Cannan held up his cigar, showing an inch of gray ash at the tip.

Dupoix picked up an ashtray from the table and laid it on the bed.

"You did take a pot at me, you know," he said. "My right ear felt the wind of your bullet. Now why did you do that?"

"I was aiming for the hoss," Cannan said. "My shooting was off that day."

"Ah, yes, as I recall you're no great shakes with a revolver."

"I wish I'd brought my rifle along. Then I would have hung you for sure."

"Suppose I tell you that those three Irish gents drew down on me first?"

"Wouldn't have made any difference, Dupoix. You took me for a rube and my pride was hurt."

The gambler smiled. "Touché, Ranger Cannan."

Dupoix refilled Cannan's glass then his own. He stepped to the window again and lit a cigar.

"You never answered my questions, Dupoix," Cannan said. "Why—"

"Am I here and who's paying my wages?" Dupoix said.

"Well?" Cannan said.

The gambler pulled back the lace curtain. "Look out there," he said. "A fair town with a schoolhouse and a church with a bell in its tower. It's got a city hall where the flag flies every single day of the year and the people dress in their best of a Sunday and go to worship."

Dupoix turned his head to Cannan and spoke over his shoulder.

"Last Chance was started by tin pans," he said. "They came here looking for gold, found none, and most of them left. But a few decided to stay and set down roots. In the early years they went through hell, but in the end they built something worthwhile."

"You still haven't answered my questions," Cannan said.

"Patience, Ranger, I'm answering them. Unless you're planning on going somewhere?"

"Funny, Dupoix. Go ahead."

"All right. Now, where was I?"

"You were talking about folks trying to build a town in a wilderness where there shouldn't be any town," Cannan said.

He suddenly felt irritable, from the whiskey or the pain of his still-healing wounds, he didn't know.

"The people of Last Chance worked together to irrigate the fertile bottomland with canals that carry water from the river. Despite droughts and floods and all the other things that plague farmers, they grew wheat, corn, oats, and now there's talk of planting cotton."

"They built their prosperity on farming?" Cannan said.

"Not entirely. They act as middlemen for Mexican trappers who supply them with fox, beaver, wolf, and bobcat fur. Last Chance also trades hogs, turkeys, and bees with Mexico for hard cash, and a few raise cattle on the floodplain farther along the river." Dupoix smiled. "You could say the hardy folks out there have turned this part of the desert into a Garden of Eden."

"Then why are you and the other gun hands here, Dupoix?" Cannan said.

"Because, Ranger Cannan, we're going to take it all away from them," Dupoix said.

Praise for *Attending*

"At a time when physicians are being replaced by algorithms and AI, *Attending* reveals the true roots of healing. One of the best and most relevant books on mindfulness I've ever read."

—Dean Ornish, M.D., founder and president of Preventive Medicine
Research Institute and author of *The Spectrum* and
Dr. Dean Ornish's Program for Reversing Heart Disease

"Ronald Epstein cuts through the cacophony and illuminates the heart of the medical enterprise—the attentive and compassionate connection between doctor and patient. In a world awash with medical error, patient dissatisfaction, and burned-out doctors, this attention to mindfulness is much-needed balm. *Attending* is at once penetrating, counterintuitive, and profoundly humbling."

—Danielle Ofri, M.D., Ph.D.,
author of *What Patients Say, What Doctors Hear*

"This book is phenomenal, and will be phenomenally useful to physicians and to all of us who are desperately in need of true health care and caring. It is hard for me to imagine a doctor reading it and not immediately recognizing, taking to heart, and implementing its messages in any number of different ways, being so commonsensical, clear, innately transformative, and healing. And it is equally hard for me to imagine that it will not energize all of us, when we find ourself in the role of 'the patient,' to demand greater mindfulness from our caregivers across the board, and know what we mean by that."

—Jon Kabat-Zinn, Ph.D., author of *Full Catastrophe Living* and
Mindfulness for Beginners and founder of MBSR
(Mindfulness-Based Stress Reduction)

"The life of a physician is a journey that explores mind and heart and soul. Here, Ronald Epstein, a consummate clinician, illuminates those domains of life, finding truths for his patients and for himself. This book will educate and inspire professionals and laymen alike."

—Jerome Groopman, M.D., author of *How Doctors Think*

"*Attending* got my attention from the opening paragraphs. Beautiful, compelling, and wise stories of how medicine and care-taking can be (and should be) when approached with common sense, a fierce sense of what is best for both the doctor and patient, and a compassionate heart. A timely and important book!"

—Marc Lesser, cofounder and former CEO of Search Inside Yourself Leadership Institute (SIYLI), and author of *Know Yourself, Forget Yourself* and *LESS: Accomplishing More by Doing Less*

"As a student admissions committee member reviewing Ron Epstein's application to medical school, I knew he was special, a view surpassed by his visionary achievements illuminating the important nature of how physicians care for their patients, and how they can best care for themselves. *Attending* is the book every medical caregiver needs to strengthen their mind and harness their resilience to care for others— and every patient needs to understand how doctors think. This is a work of heart and head, a beautiful synthesis of inner wisdom and hard-earned scientific empirical findings that point the way to proven methods for improving the lives of both giver and receiver of medical care. With clear explanations, captivating stories, and well-described challenges and approaches to their solutions, this book is exactly what the field of medicine needs."

—Daniel J. Siegel, M.D., author of *Mind* and *The Mindful Brain* and executive director of Mindsight Institute and founding codirector of UCLA Mindful Awareness Research Center

"Ronald Epstein truthfully and powerfully describes the challenging and changing worlds of both the physician and the patient. *Attending* will encourage the recognition that mindfulness and compassion training contribute to effective medicine. The book clearly demonstrates how these contemplative practices can help enrich the lives of everyone involved in health care."

—Sharon Salzberg, author of *Lovingkindness* and *Real Happiness*

"I recommend *Attending* for anyone interested in health. In a most accessible way, Epstein makes a very convincing case for how doctors and patients would prosper from doctors becoming more mindful."

—Ellen Langer, Ph.D., professor of psychology, Harvard University, and author of *Mindfulness* and *Counterclockwise: Mindful Health and the Power of Possibility*

"In *Attending*, Ron Epstein takes us on an inspirational journey from his early days as a student at Harvard Medical School to a lifetime of mindful practice as a consummate physician-humanist. Medical students, residents, and other health professional trainees who read this wonderfully written book will gain tremendous insights into the power of mindfulness in healing—both for their patients and for themselves."

—Edward M. Hundert, M.D.,
Dean for Medical Education, Harvard Medical School

"This powerful and inspiring book opens the pathway to bringing care, wisdom, and mindfulness into the practice of medicine. A must-read for all clinicians and for lay readers as well."

—Joan Halifax, Ph.D., author of *Being with Dying*

"Epstein presents for general readers a concise guide to his view of what mindfulness is, its value, and how it is a skill that anyone can work to acquire."

—*Library Journal*

"A deeply informed and compassionate book . . . [Dr. Epstein] tells us that it is a 'moral imperative' to do right by our patients. And he shows why and how."

—Lloyd Sederer, M.D., *New York Journal of Books*

"Worthy reading for medical students and practitioners but also applicable to other fields: artists, writers, musicians, teachers, et al., can also fall into formulaic ruts and autopilot behavior and need literally to change their minds."

—*Kirkus Reviews*

"Vivid . . . Epstein's candor and courage . . . make the book so compelling."

—*The Pharos*

"Among the best books about how to teach the humanistic aspects of doctoring. Epstein weaves together an insightful collection of experiences that examine the clinician's situation, starting from inside her own mind and ending at the system in which she practices."

—*Arnold P. Gold Foundation*

"Thoughtful company in times when we've never needed thoughtful company more."

—*Harvard Medicine Magazine*

Attending

MEDICINE,
MINDFULNESS,
and HUMANITY

Ronald Epstein, M.D.

SCRIBNER

New York   London   Toronto   Sydney   New Delhi

Scribner
An Imprint of Simon & Schuster, Inc.
1230 Avenue of the Americas
New York, NY 10020

First Scribner trade paperback edition January 2018

SCRIBNER and design are registered trademarks of The Gale Group, Inc., used under
license by Simon & Schuster, Inc., the publisher of this work.

For information about special discounts for bulk purchases,
please contact Simon & Schuster Special Sales at 1-866-506-1949
or business@simonandschuster.com.

The Simon & Schuster Speakers Bureau can bring authors to your live event.
For more information or to book an event, contact the Simon & Schuster Speakers
Bureau at 1-866-248-3049 or visit our website at www.simonspeakers.com.

Manufactured in the United States of America

5   7   9   10   8   6

Library of Congress Cataloging-in-Publication Data
Names: Epstein, Ronald, author.
Title: Attending : medicine, mindfulness, and humanity / Ronald Epstein.
Description: New York : Scribner, [2017] | Includes bibliographical
references and index.
Identifiers: LCCN 2016024695| ISBN 9781501121715 (hardcover : alk. paper) |
ISBN 9781501121722 (trade pbk. : alk. paper) | ISBN 9781501121739 (ebook)
Subjects: | MESH: Physician-Patient Relations | Mindfulness |
Physicians—psychology
Classification: LCC R690 | NLM W 62 | DDC 610.69/5—dc23 LC record available at
https://lccn.loc.gov/2016024695

ISBN 978-1-5011-2171-5
ISBN 978-1-5011-2172-2 (pbk)
ISBN 978-1-5011-2173-9 (ebook)

Two poems of Jellaludin Rumi translated by Coleman Barks used with the
permission of Coleman Barks.
CT scan image appearing on page 18 reproduced with the author's permission.

To Deborah, Eli, and Malka,
my inspiration

Contents

Author's Note

I believe that the practice of medicine depends on a deep understanding between clinicians and patients, and that human understanding starts with understanding oneself. This book is the product of a career in medicine seeking opportunities to know myself better as a clinician and to help others do the same—ultimately to make health care more mindful, attentive, and humane. Writing this book, I've explored realms that I had not previously imagined: the cutting edge of social and cognitive neuroscience, the psychological and philosophical underpinnings of contemplative practices, and the writings of Zen masters, baseball heroes, and ecstatic poets. At each juncture, innumerable friends, colleagues, and total strangers whom I contacted out of the blue offered guidance, correctives, consolations, and camaraderie that helped me find my voice as a writer: from the heart, personal, rooted in stories.

For privacy and confidentiality, I cannot name all of my teachers. Many of them are my patients, and it would be too much to ask them to make public the most intimate moments of their lives. I have altered details of each patient's story and in some cases created a composite of two or more similar stories. Thus, any resemblance of those mentioned in this book to actual living patients and their families is coincidental and not intentional. I have taken similar precautions with the health professionals mentioned in the book, as it is difficult to know if I might unwittingly reveal something that they would rather not have made public. For convenience and readability, when referring to health professionals and patients I have used the singular pronouns *he* and *she* rather than use the more awkward *he or she* and *his or hers*. This is not to suggest any generalizations based on gender.

In medicine, the senior physician responsible for a patient's care is called the attending physician, or just "the attending." The attending's responsibility is to direct the clinical team's attention to the most important things, take charge, make the patient feel attended to, and provide attentive care. Attending means showing up, being present, listening, and accompanying patients when it matters most. Attending is also a moral imperative: by being attentive, doctors not only provide the best care, they also honor each patient's humanity.

1

Being Mindful

Even as a third-year medical student, I knew that pink was good, blue was bad.

I was assisting Mark Gunderson, a senior urologist at a university teaching hospital during my first clinical rotation in surgery. Being in the operating room was engrossing and revelatory, but I felt some trepidation about how I'd fit into the rigid hierarchy of surgical culture. Gunderson was performing a retroperitoneal lymph node dissection, painstakingly removing the lymph nodes surrounding both kidneys and the aorta. The patient, eighteen-year-old Jake Willits, had testicular cancer and the stakes were high; one false move could result in sexual dysfunction or the loss of a kidney.

After Gunderson finished operating on Jake's left kidney, we traded sides of the operating table so that he could work on the right, keeping the left kidney within his peripheral vision. I had a straight-on view of the left kidney. After a few minutes, I noticed that the kidney was turning blue. Gunderson didn't seem to have noticed.

I agonized about what to do. As a lowly medical student, I knew it wasn't my place to offer an opinion to a senior surgeon, but I felt compelled to speak up: "I'm not sure you've got a good view, but the left kidney is looking bluish to me." I spoke loudly enough to be heard, but tentatively enough so as not to appear arrogant. No response. Gunderson asked the scrub nurse for a scalpel. His gaze didn't move. I became increasingly anxious and broke into a sweat.

After a few more minutes, the kidney had turned an ominous dusky purple. I quietly mentioned this to the scrub nurse at my side, who talked to the resident, who then talked to the surgeon.

Gunderson looked and didn't like what he saw. The left kidney had become twisted, blocking blood flow through the renal artery. He tried to untwist the kidney, first one way, then the other. No success. The room became tense and quiet. Now Gunderson was sweating too, knowing that with each passing minute a few more kidney cells would die. After what seemed like an eternity but was probably only a few minutes, Gunderson called in a vascular surgeon to do an urgent repair of the renal artery. Apparently, when the kidney twisted, the intima—the inner lining of the renal artery—had been torn, blocking blood flow. The vascular surgeon had to clamp the artery, make a longitudinal slice, open up the injured area, and excise the torn fragment—delicately, while leaving the outer layers of the artery intact—then sew up the artery. This mishap extended the operation by more than an hour, and while the operation was successful, blood tests just afterward showed that Jake's kidney function was not quite normal. While the surgery likely cured Jake of his cancer, no one knew when—or if—his kidney would fully recover. The next morning, on rounds, Gunderson informed Jake and his parents that an "unavoidable" complication had occurred.[1]

Today when I tell this story to an audience of doctors, I always see nods of understanding. I know that this situation does not mean that Gunderson is a "bad doctor"; so do they. Surgery is difficult and intense, and errors are easy to make. Even the most experienced clinicians—surgeons and otherwise—can suffer lapses of attention and ignore that which in retrospect seems obvious.[2]

The kidney getting twisted might have been unavoidable. But Gunderson's failure to notice and act was not. He was focused, for sure. But his inattention to that which was in plain sight—even after it was pointed out to him—was stunning, especially given that he was an accomplished surgeon at a major teaching hospital. Certainly, the light reflected by the blue kidney was picked up by his retina, and no doubt his ears could detect what I had said. Nevertheless, something happened in that crucial moment to prevent that visual and auditory data from being fully transmitted to his conscious awareness. In essence, Gunderson hadn't engaged his whole mind.

This event had a powerful impact on me. I realized how easily I could put my patients' lives at risk in a similar way. I was distraught. I lost sleep wondering if I had done something wrong; perhaps, I thought, if I had spoken up more assertively, Jake wouldn't have suffered as much damage to his kidney. And I felt uncomfortable allowing the family to believe that the surgeon was blameless.

I made an appointment to speak with the chief of surgery the next week. I asked if I could talk confidentially. He was a good listener and assured me that I had done the right thing by talking to him and that the mishap was in no way my fault. He was visibly concerned and assured me that he would talk with the surgeon and check in with Jake and his family. We discharged Jake a few days later, in good spirits.

I never saw Gunderson again, and unfortunately I could never know what he truly believed. While I was upset that an error had occurred, it wasn't a surprise to me that even the most expert surgeons could be fallible. The most important lessons, though, were that mindless inattention could result in disaster and that competence is fragile and takes mindful vigilance to maintain. This experience planted the seed of an idea in me—that I'd need not only skill and expertise, but something else to be the doctor I wanted to be, something no one had spent much time teaching me in medical school: the ability to be self-aware, attentive, and present, especially when the stakes were high. I'd need to be a guardian of my patients' health and *also* of my own "inner operating system" in each moment.[3] Awareness of my own mind might be one of the most important tools I could have in addressing patients' needs.

I thought of this event again later that month, while working with Ashwin Mehta, a vascular surgeon at the same hospital. When I arrived at the operating room, Mehta had already made a large incision in Lena Hagopian's abdomen. Mehta was moving quickly, tying and cutting sutures faster than I could count. I couldn't help but notice his focus and intensity, his large hands moving rapidly and decisively as he got ready to repair a cholesterol-clogged aorta to open up blood flow to the patient's oxygen-starved legs. Soft rock music played in the background as he worked and bantered with the operating room staff. Then, suddenly, the bantering stopped. The operating room grew quiet, a silence different from Gunderson's. The time had come to sew a large blood vessel back together, a procedure that required delicacy and precision. But, the anastomosis—the connection between the two parts of the blood vessel—was leaking. Unlike Gunderson, Mehta noticed that something was awry before anyone else did. By the time *we* realized it, Mehta had already shifted seamlessly from autopilot to more deliberately choreographed action—first tango, then ballet, then a few minutes later back to tango—all without missing a beat. No panic, only calm focus, surgical mindfulness in action. His shifting of gears was so smooth that I wondered if he was even aware of it.[4]

Only decades later did I understand. A surgeon colleague, Carol-Anne Moulton, made the connection for me. She was researching what made great surgeons great and had observed dozens of surgeons performing complex operations. She had documented in detail how during difficult moments masterful surgeons would shift gears. Those who "slowed down when they should" when encountering speed bumps were the true masters; those who kept going full speed ahead tended to make errors.[5] Mehta had slowed down when he should.

Yet when Moulton interviewed surgeons about these slowing down moments, many of the masters didn't realize that they had shifted gears until it was pointed out to them, and only upon reflection could they put into words exactly what triggered them to make the shift. Mehta was not any more technically skilled or knowledgeable than Gunderson; that's not what made him a master. His expertise resided in his exquisite moment-to-moment awareness: he was able to be present and to bring what was needed to each moment. While operating on Mrs. Hagopian, he could also monitor his own inner operating system so that he would realize when he might need to slow down or get help. He accepted and anticipated the possibility that something could go wrong. Whether he thought about it this way or not, Mehta was being mindful.

I discovered that mindfulness is also essential outside the operating room. Later in my third year, I worked with a senior psychiatrist, Dr. Peter Reich. Reich eventually became a mentor—from the first time I met him, I felt drawn to him by his thoughtfulness, insight, and curiosity about the human condition. At that time, he was responsible for the care of medically ill patients in the hospital who also presented mental health problems. Halfway through the one-month rotation, he and I were called to the neurology unit to see Douglas McCallum, a man in his thirties who had sustained a head injury in a motorcycle accident. Doug was not cooperating with the specialists handling his rehabilitation program; he was moody and irritable and had angry outbursts that frightened the staff. Part of his brain was damaged, the part that had made him the Doug that he and others had known. You could see Doug trying to make sense of his situation, yet his thoughts would leap from one topic to the next and he was unable to retrieve what he had just been saying. His thinking was fragmented. He was frightened because he knew that something was very wrong. He had become a stranger to himself.

The medical team wanted Dr. Reich to help manage Doug's erratic behavior. Reich had a long list of patients to see; given that this one had apparently irreversible brain damage, I expected Reich to assign a diagnosis quickly and prescribe medications to control Doug's behavior—something I had witnessed other psychiatrists doing under similar circumstances. To my surprise, Reich did something radical: he temporarily set aside the imperative to diagnose and treat so that he could get to know Doug as a person. He asked, "What does that feel like?" and "Help me understand." Reich nodded and smiled kindly, indicating that he was not in a rush and was fully engaged. He sought to discover what *was* working in Doug's mind, as well as what wasn't.

While surgeons' tools are scalpels and forceps, Reich's tools were words and gestures. His interview with Doug would flow smoothly for a while, with Doug appearing almost coherent, remembering details and the order in which things occurred. Then Doug would freeze, unable to complete a thought. The circuits were jammed. These uncomfortable pauses reminded us how seriously his mind had gone awry.

Reich was mindful in the same ways as Mehta—he was attending and present—but I could see that there was more to mindfulness than attention and presence. Reich was curious about Doug's experience.[6] He set aside preconceptions so he could see Doug in a new way. As impressed as I was by Reich's ability to help Doug construct a coherent narrative from a set of disorganized thoughts, I also noticed that Reich was gently persistent during those awkward moments. When Doug abruptly transitioned from one story to another with no logical connector—talking about riding his motorcycle the previous week and then about a camping trip with his brother twenty years prior—Reich encouraged him, saying, "What happened next?" If Doug's reply still didn't make sense, Reich would add, "Are you feeling sometimes that things aren't making sense?" That helped Doug achieve enough clarity to say, "Yep, my thoughts just come and go."

Reich was shifting back and forth between an expert's perspective—making a diagnosis—and a "beginner's mind," stepping into Doug's chaos rather than merely diagnosing it. Reich's openness allowed him to achieve an understanding of the patient as a person without imposing interpretations or judgments. How easy it would have been to reduce Doug to a category, a diagnosis, a problem to be solved. As Doug's attending physician, Reich understood that Doug needed to feel understood, and the more Doug felt understood, the less he'd need to express his distress through disruptive behavior. Reich's resolve to share his patient's experience, rather than ignoring it, distracting himself, or turning away, was courageous and compassionate. He responded to Doug's need—as a suffering human being—to feel understood and cared for, and in that way reaffirmed Doug's humanity.

TURNING INWARD

Mehta and Reich demonstrated to me what was possible. Their habits of mind and presence seemed instinctive. I'm not even sure Mehta and Reich could fully explain what made them mindful during those critical moments. I saw how awareness, flexibility, and attention are crucial for all clinicians, regardless of specialty or profession.

The question was how to get there. Because of the paucity of attention to self-awareness during medical education, I had to rely on other experiences. In my teens, I studied piano, then harpsichord, hoping to be a performing musician—self-awareness of my breathing, tension, heartbeat, and emotions made the difference between a performance that was technically adept and one that sparkled. When I was sixteen, I learned how to meditate. I spent an evening with a friend's older brother who was a serious student of Zen Buddhism; he taught me how. In my first semester at college, I took a course called Emptiness.[7] In Buddhist philosophy, the concept of emptiness is fundamental; it means that much of what we believe about the world—and about ourselves—is merely an "empty" construct of our own mind and limits us unnecessarily. When you see the world only as perilous, you're correct, but you're only seeing half of the picture. The world is also safe and nurturing. To see it either way alone is incomplete—it is both. When you see yourself only as infallible, you are more likely to miss a blue kidney. When you see yourself only as fallible, you can feel paralyzed. Jon Kabat-Zinn, who popularized mindfulness training in the West, said that being unaware of the labels we place on ourselves is like being in a "straightjacket of unconsciousness."[8] You have no place to move, no place to grow. Emptiness, on the other hand, is being able to see yourself as fallible and infallible at the same time.[9] You are self-assured and confident, but equally aware that you could make an error at any moment. This vision frees you to be whom you need to be—and to do what you need to do—in each moment. Yet freedom takes work—the hard work of being still and cultivating an inner life.

I got a glimpse of that freedom and I wanted more. I left college to spend a few months at the San Francisco Zen Center. Doing sitting meditation for several hours every day was both easy and difficult. I learned that when I had strong feelings—restlessness, impatience, avoidance, self-criticism, loneliness, or fear—I could just *be with* those feelings without having to alter them in any way. I felt centered and resilient, with a sense of dynamic stability. I learned that meditation is not about bliss. Meditation is about a sense of presence, balance, and connection with what is most fundamentally important in your life. It is not about leading a cloistered life; in fact, my time at the Zen Center led me to engage more fully with the world.

Eventually I wanted to translate what I had learned about the inner life so that I could make a difference in the world, and I reconnected with a childhood desire to be a doctor. Yet I was ill prepared for the culture of medical school. I had spent much of my youth in seminars, music studios, and Zen meditation halls. Med school was an environment of extremes. Altogether, I saw too much harshness, mindlessness, and inhumanity. Medical school was dominated by facts, pathways, and mechanisms; residency was about learning to diagnose, treat, and do procedures, framed by a pit-of-the-stomach dread that you might kill someone by missing something or not knowing enough. Given the life-and-death stakes, I found it jarring that, with few exceptions, medical training did not emphasize deep listening—to oneself or to others. While extolling the virtues of reflection and compassion, medical training largely ignores the development of these capacities—and an inner life in general. I felt disappointed and alone and didn't see a path forward.

Then, Reich sent me a groundbreaking article by George Engel about a "biopsychosocial" approach to care.[10] Engel was a prominent internist and psychoanalyst who practiced and taught at the University of Rochester. I wrote to him, and eventually he became a mentor. Engel showed, through exploring patients' illness experience, how patients' psychological makeup and social relationships were as important to illness and health as the biological, genetic, and molecular aspects of disease. His vision was humanistic; using dazzling illustrations, Engel demonstrated that what the patient reported about his illness and how it affected him was as important as any lab test or X-ray. Engel emphasized that physicians are human too—that their emotional responses to uncertainty, tragedy, grief, and loss would affect the care they provide.[11] This resonated with me. Doctoring was a relationship between two people, each of whom had an inner life. I moved to Rochester and worked with Engel and several of his protégés. Engel was fascinated with human experience, but, in my view, was too much of the cold scientist to offer a method for knowing one's inner life more intimately. Several of his protégés filled that role for me. Trained by Engel, they took his work one step further and offered opportunities for reflection, self-awareness, and mindfulness (so-called Balint groups,[12] family-of-origin groups,[13] personal awareness groups,[14] and clinical supervision[15]) that were available in few other settings at the time.

Over time I became more comfortable with my level of knowledge and skill as a clinician, yet I still knew that each day, with each patient, sometimes I was the physician I aspired to be and other times I fell short. Falling short had little to do with knowledge and technique, but rather it had to do with my state of mind, what I noticed and attended to. Sometimes I practiced with clarity and compassion, and other times impatience, distraction, unexamined emotions, and defensiveness got in the way.

Lacking a guidebook, I had to look inside myself. Then I'd match up my states of mind with what I had been learning about the sciences of mind—psychology, philosophy, education, and neuroscience. Wading through a profusion of educational and psychological jargon,[16] I came to three conclusions—good doctors need to be self-aware to practice at their best; self-awareness needs to be in the moment, not just Monday-morning quarterbacking; and no one had a road map.[17]

Ten years after I finished my residency, the connections between my prior training in meditation and music and my medical practice finally crystallized. My dean tasked me with developing a new method for assessing the competence of students that would reflect the biopsychosocial values that Rochester had become known for—no small undertaking. I could find few guideposts, not even a coherent definition of professional competence.[18] I wanted to capture the habits of master clinicians, those to whom doctors might refer a friend or relative, as opposed to those who were merely competent—those who merely aced the test.[19] I started writing about "mindful practice"; I drafted a personal manifesto about excellence in clinical practice and proposed that mindful self-awareness, self-monitoring, and self-regulation were at the root of good judgment, compassion, and attentive care. I had not seen a similar vision articulated before, and I had no idea how it would be received.

The manuscript went back and forth to the *Journal of the American Medical Association* seven times, and each time Charlene Breedlove, my insightful and patient editor, asked me to clarify, hone, and condense before "Mindful Practice" finally went to press in 1999.[20] The article struck a chord. I discovered that I was not alone. I received hundreds of letters and e-mails from other physicians. These practitioners, many of whom had found some form of contemplative practice on their own, felt isolated and in need of a community that would support their efforts to become more mindful, resilient, self-aware, and effective. I was deeply gratified, yet the next steps—to see if mindfulness makes a difference in patient care and how to help clinicians be more mindful—were daunting.

IN THE CLINIC

My colleague Dr. Mary Catherine Beach, at Johns Hopkins, helped to provide an answer. She studied interactions between patients and doctors in AIDS clinics around the United States.[21] People with HIV/AIDS often feel stigmatized and misunderstood, and not surprisingly, many are distrustful of the health care system. Beach and her team audio-recorded visits between doctors and patients and surveyed them afterward, including assessments of mindfulness. Physicians who were more mindful did better at developing rapport, following up on patients' concerns, and addressing psychosocial issues; their patients felt better understood, more connected, and emotionally supported. Mindful physicians won their patients' trust, no trivial matter. A patient's trust in her physician is the best predictor of whether she will take her medications, a crucial factor if you're HIV infected. Missing even a few doses could allow the virus to replicate and become drug resistant. Connection, understanding, and trust are essential.

Still, Beach's study did not answer whether practicing physicians could be *trained* to be more mindful and, if so, whether they would provide better care. For years it had been known that mindfulness training could help patients with a variety of mental and physical disorders. Yet the idea of mindfulness for physicians to enhance their *own* work was new. I found like-minded colleagues—Mick Krasner, Tim Quill, Tony Suchman, Howard Beckman, and others at the University of Rochester—and together we designed a year-long program in mindful practice for experienced primary care physicians.[22] The sessions included different kinds of meditation practice and exercises to promote mindful communication, emphasizing how to bring mindfulness into clinicians' everyday work to help them be attentive and aware. Each session touched on a particular issue—responding to errors, witnessing suffering, facing uncertainty, grieving the loss of a patient, developing compassion, feeling attracted to patients, and others. We also addressed clinician burnout directly, knowing that burned-out physicians provide lower-quality care and are more likely to quit practice altogether. We drew a simple model of what we were trying to do—the technical quality of care, the qualities of caring, and clinicians' resilience and well-being—showing how these three domains were linked and how practicing mindfully could affect all three. We started out with a group of seventy physicians, nearly all of whom scored high on a burnout questionnaire. We didn't know if they'd have the energy and commitment to finish the program or if it would show any positive effects at all.

The results far exceeded our expectations.[23] Physicians' well-being improved and their burnout decreased. They became more empathic and oriented toward their patients' psychosocial needs. We were astonished that they scored higher on conscientiousness and emotional stability, key features of personality that aren't sup-

posed to change in people in their forties and fifties (more about this in chapter 10).[24] They became more attentive and focused, less likely to be derailed by crises, and better able to rely on their inner resources to remain resilient. We interviewed some of the doctors a year later. They continued to affirm that cultivating a practice of mindfulness, creating a community of supportive colleagues, and giving themselves permission to focus on their own growth made them better physicians. They reconnected with the reasons they went into medicine in the first place: to provide effective and humanistic care, and to have meaningful relationships with their patients.[25] They set limits and had a more balanced work life.

A MINDFUL VISION

Medicine is in crisis. Physicians and patients are disillusioned, frustrated by the fragmentation of the health care system. Patients cannot help but notice that I spend more and more time looking at computer screens and less time face-to-face.[26] They experience the consequences of the commodification of medicine that has forced clinicians' focus from the healing of patients to the mechanics of health care—productivity pressures, insurance regulations, actuarial tasks, and demoralizing metrics that measure what can be counted and not what really counts, sometimes ironically in the name of evidence-based and patient-centered care.[27]

I have seen that it is possible to do better, and that is the reason I'm writing this book. Amid this crisis in health care, some physicians are making choices to reacquaint themselves with the heart of medical practice. By looking inward, they are expanding their capacity to provide high-quality care. They are seeing how they, as doctors, have the power to transform and humanize the practice of medicine and how patients can be better consumers of health care, build stronger relationships with their physicians, and identify those who can provide the care they need.

Mindful practice in medicine is more than meditation and personal growth.[28] Being mindful is when I know to stop briefly, look a patient in the eye, and ask, "Have I got it all, or is there more?"—and a patient, whose previously well-controlled diabetes is now uncontrolled, then tells me he hasn't been taking care of himself since his wife died six months ago. It's when I inject an inflamed shoulder joint—with focused attention, visualizing the bones, tendons, and muscles—and the needle slides in easily and painlessly. I'm being mindful when I notice that a patient doesn't look quite right, not her usual self, and then I notice the fatigued expression and the faint rash that are clues to her new diagnosis of lupus. Attending to each patient means that I remember that, although the last patient I saw has only days to live, the next patient—with a stubbed toe—needs the same focused attention.

Medicine and *meditation*, etymologically, come from the same root: to consider, advise, reflect, to take appropriate measures. But while I can try to describe what being mindful is like, words carry just so far; ultimately, mindfulness is an experience—something that we have all encountered at some moment. Perhaps, as you are reading, you might periodically stop for a moment and become aware of your own body and your thoughts, emotions, and expectations; be aware of how present, curious, engaged, and attentive you are feeling. Over time, you will know yourself better. For starters, let this be an invitation to know the lens through which you view the world.

2

Attending

You can observe a lot by just watching.
— Yogi Berra[1]

Emil Laszlo, a sixty-six-year-old Hungarian-American engineer, had been a patient of mine for several years. An avid tennis player, he had had few medical problems other than a bout of rotator-cuff tendinitis of his right shoulder two years prior. Upon my return from a trip, I was surprised to discover an urgent voice mail from his wife. Emil was in the hospital. I called her back and she explained that the doctors suspected that he had cancer. But she was confused because they had seen three different clinicians in my absence, and after each visit to our clinic they had left with the idea that his right shoulder pain was nothing more than a recurrent rotator-cuff problem.

I investigated his chart for clues. On his first visit he saw one of my practice partners. The chart noted that Emil had pain in his right shoulder and it felt as if "there was a swelling there." The physical exam confirmed tenderness and pain on motion, but there was no description of the "swelling." Unlike two years before, though, he did not have some of the typical signs of rotator-cuff tendinitis—such as decreased range of motion or muscle weakness. It wasn't unreasonable to think that this might be a recurrence of his tendinitis; weakness and restriction of motion might not be present early in the clinical course. He was sent home with typical advice for rotator-cuff injuries: a prescription for a nonsteroidal anti-inflammatory medication and physical-therapy exercises. Yet the chart also mentioned that Emil felt feverish and had had a few night sweats. Perhaps because it was flu season, I presume, his doctors had a convenient explanation.

At Emil's second visit to our office, the physician noted a "prominence" near the shoulder. Again, full range of motion. She attributed the "history of night sweats" to a "viral syndrome." Emil also came with several additional concerns: mild prostate-related symptoms, fatigue, and a low vitamin D level. She encouraged him to continue with physical therapy and anti-inflammatory medications, and I can only assume that she thought that the prominence was related to his rotator-cuff problem. Notably, she did not call it a "lump" or a "mass" or anything that might connote something more serious.

On the third visit, he reported worsening fatigue, more than you would expect from the flu. His pain was worsening despite medications and exercise. Yet, the chart still didn't mention a mass. The nurse-practitioner homed in on his disabling fatigue and ordered some blood tests. The results showed an extremely low white blood count. She called Emil at home and sent him to the emergency room. Only then, after the blood test suggested something serious might be going on, was the ten-centimeter tumor extending from his armpit to his shoulder finally "seen." In hindsight it all made sense—pain, a mass, and fatigue are typical for lymphoma—but all three clinicians were stunned by the news and were at a loss to explain how they could have missed something so obvious.[2]

Every day, clinicians fail to attend to something that seems obvious in hindsight. Emil's situation got me wondering why. Clinical care is fast paced. Amid a deluge of patients with potentially preventable acute problems, poorly controlled chronic diseases, and intractable mental health issues, and whose uncooperative insurance companies won't pay for medicines they need, Emil arrives. To his physician's relief, Emil seems to have a problem that is straightforward and easy to solve. I wondered if his clinicians' (mis)diagnoses had to do with misperception (Did they not even look or did they look and not really see the tumor?), misinterpretation (Did they see it yet misjudge its significance?), misprioritization (Because it didn't "make sense" was it relegated to secondary status?), or closed-mindedness (Having arrived at one explanation, did the clinician lose interest in seeking out alternative explanations?). All of these factors can contribute to what psychologists call *inattentional blindness*.

We all experience inattentional blindness in everyday life. Often it is of little consequence; you find your keys in the place where you just looked. Other times it is more serious. A friend of mine had a rear-end collision on a sunny fall morning; he was talking on his hands-free mobile phone and didn't see the car right in front of him. Or take this well-known example: In a video that has gone viral, players dressed in black outfits and white outfits toss a basketball, and the viewer is instructed to count the number of passes between the players in white. The majority of viewers are oblivious of someone in a black gorilla suit moonwalking across the set—until it is pointed out to them.[3] It had been filtered out. Filtering is a neurologic necessity to keep us from being overwhelmed by all the stimuli from the environment; below our awareness, our brains make choices, usually the right ones, but sometimes the wrong ones—especially when the stimulus is unexpected.

Even those who are exquisitely trained to look for visual details miss the unexpected. In one study, a researcher asked radiologists to view a chest CT scan on a computer screen. A small gorilla figure was strategically placed in one of the images. More than three-quarters of the radiologists didn't notice the gorilla. Unbeknownst to the radiologists, the computer had sophisticated visual-tracking technology that confirmed that their eyes had looked directly at it.[4] Their inattentional blindness had little to do with knowledge and years of experience.

Inattentional deafness works the same way: it's an auditory glitch in which we don't hear things that are clearly said to us. More than once I've had a worried parent bring a child to my office for a hearing test, hoping for an explanation for why the child doesn't respond when spoken to, only to find that the hearing is perfect.

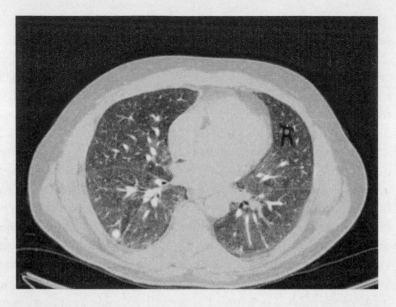

(This happens with married couples too!) As a clinician, I can so easily not hear the unexpected and the unwanted. Like inattentional blindness, it can be benign or life-threatening; in the operating room, it could be fatal.[5]

How can this happen? Research shows how focusing intensely on a visual task—in the operating room or looking at a computer screen—interferes with our ability to listen.[6] The reverse is likely true too; that is why talking on cell phones while driving—even with hands-free devices—leads to accidents. We can't pay attention to everything all the time. Like computers, our brains have a limited capacity for *working memory*—that which we can hold in our awareness at any given moment—and our brains are constantly making choices. More accurately, we prioritize that which is personally meaningful and ignore sensory input that we consider to be of low value—information that is inconsistent with our expectations or information that comes from a presumably unreliable source (such as a third-year medical student). The problem is that these "choices" are usually below our levels of awareness, and thus we don't routinely assess the rational or irrational factors that go into making them.

NOT SEEING, NOT KNOWING

The great physician-teacher William Osler once said, "We miss more by not seeing than by not knowing." It may sound trivial, but simply paying attention is one of the most difficult tasks for clinicians. It's no secret that much of what physicians do is routine. Reading an electrocardiogram or prescribing medications for hypothyroidism or heart failure is often done by protocol, and to save working memory, our brains make most of those tasks automatic, or nearly so. We use what psychologist Daniel Kahneman calls Type 1 processing, or fast thinking.[7] Anyone, even without a medical background, could easily learn the symptoms and treatments for urinary tract infections and get it right about 80 percent of the time. But in 20 percent of the situations, something atypical appears and requires that doctors switch out of autopilot and apply a more conscious, focused attention, what Kahneman calls Type 2 or slow thinking. Medical training is long and arduous largely to help doctors deal with the 20 percent, the unexpected and complex situations that require more than just knowledge, technical skills, and years of experience.[8] Yet doctors aren't trained to notice and make the switch from automatic thinking to a slower—more deliberative—mode. It's easy not to notice the unexpected, especially once we've committed ourselves to a provisional idea about what might be going on.

For twenty-five years I've studied communication in health care settings. As a communications researcher, I notice how physicians systematically pay attention to some kinds of information more than others. It is particularly alarming how often physicians are oblivious to patients' emotional distress, despite their providing clues that they are afraid, distrustful, confused, or depressed. Patients will say, "I'm tired," "Just shoot me," "My sister's cancer is progressing," and get little acknowledgment.[9] In one study of thoracic surgeons seeing patients with lung cancer, over 90 percent of the emotional content of conversations went unacknowledged.[10] Admittedly, some physicians intentionally ignore emotional content, feeling that is not their job (I disagree).[11] Yet, when reviewing audio-recordings of their consultations, physicians are often surprised at how many of those concerns went unheard.

A few years ago, I set out to understand how this kind of inattention happens in primary care. I trained actors to pose as patients with chest pain who made appointments to see primary care physicians in the Rochester area. The doctors had previously consented to participate in the research, but had no idea when the actors would come and what symptoms they might present. The roles were constructed so that the actors were likely to escape detection. Generally it worked. The vast majority of the time physicians thought that they were real patients. In an intentional effort to simulate the ambiguities of primary care practice, the actors portrayed chest pain that was not typical of heart disease, heartburn (gastroesophageal reflux, or GERD), or musculoskeletal pain; sometimes it would be worse with movement or after eating or at night, with no pattern to the symptoms. We also trained the actors to ask the doctors a key question: "Could this be something serious?"

We were intentionally trying to increase physicians' cognitive load, to force them to choose among competing explanations for the patient's symptoms. One doctor said to the patient, "Maybe this is heartburn, let's get an EKG." While an EKG might provide useful information about the heart, it would certainly not help diagnose heartburn. The physicians were befuddled.

Furthermore, when patients asked the "something serious" question, few received any empathy or even acknowledgment of their worry.[12] Rather, physicians tended to ask further questions about physical symptoms, provide bland reassurance or more medical information, or change the topic. If these had been real patients, their fears might have been compounded, or they might have felt sheepish that they had brought up a trivial concern. This might affect their future decisions about when to seek health care and from whom.

I met with a focus group of physicians after the study. None said that they thought their patient's emotional distress was trivial. Rather, they said that they just didn't register the emotional content, that diagnosis and medications were more on their radar.

A gift for you

Hi Afton! I've really enjoyed reading this book and thought you'd find it moving and nourishing also. I hope you enjoy it! Love, Zo From Chiazotam

Cognitive load drove them to distraction. Clearly, talking about serious illness is difficult for both clinicians and patients, and some physicians consciously avoid such discussions. But if these physicians had a moment-to-moment awareness of their own attentional choices, most would have prefaced their response with "I can see how concerned you are about this."

There is some good news, though. Given the opportunity, physicians can be keen detectors of their own blind spots—they can raise that which is just below the level of awareness into consciousness. In a study from the 1990s, I asked physicians to watch video-recordings of their consultations with their patients who were at high risk for AIDS.[13] These patients were often terrified; at that time the treatments for AIDS were not effective. Patients not only feared the disease; they also feared stigmatization. When patients expressed distress, physicians often missed it.

When the doctors reviewed their video-recordings, they were shocked—just as people watching the basketball video a second time couldn't believe that they missed the gorilla. One doctor was mortified when he viewed himself asking questions about intimate sexual behavior (a good thing) as he was performing a testicular exam (not exactly the way to make a young male patient feel less vulnerable). While missing the gorilla in an online video generates amusement and wonder, missing emotions or causing humiliation in the examining room has real and important consequences—the physician may have missed an opportunity to detect and treat the HIV infection before it progressed to AIDS. Patients who feel unheard are less likely to disclose important information and less likely to follow their doctors' recommendations.[14]

I CAN'T HEAR YOU WHILE I'M LISTENING

You might think that if you were in a quiet, controlled setting, such as an exam room, it would be relatively effortless to pay attention. While lack of distraction helps, it's not enough. In a brilliant article from the 1980s, primary care internist Richard Baron wrote about a time when he was listening to a patient's heart with a stethoscope. The patient started talking (uncanny how often they do), and Baron said, "Quiet . . . I can't hear you while I'm listening."[15] While technically true that it is hard to hear speech through a stethoscope and virtually impossible to hear subtle breath sounds and heart murmurs when a patient is talking, it points to the realities of medical practice: that our moment-to-moment choices reside just below our level of conscious awareness, somewhat like our awareness of what's in our peripheral vision.[16] Stimuli compete for clinicians' attention in a time-pressured, psychologically demanding, and unforgiving environment. Clinicians need the ability to focus their attention on the task at hand, while also having access to their subsidiary awareness—perceptions that are just below the surface of awareness.

Learning how attention works is important to both doctors and patients. I know, for example, that long-winded rambles and repetitive descriptions of symptoms by patients tire me, yet buried in their ramblings might be clues to something serious. With practice, I might be able to avert missing something important by increasing my awareness of my attentional habits and blind spots and switch more adeptly between autopilot and focused attention; like a "mental muscle," the capacity for attention can be grown and developed.

Patients can help too. As a patient, when you don't get the information or understanding that you need, you can say, "I just want to make sure I've been clear about _____." Or "I'm particularly worried about _____." Or "I'm not sure I understand what that means." This can help you and your doctor focus on what's most important. Just as doctors need practice to communicate effectively, patients also need practice in assertive communication. It pays off in two ways: you're more likely to reorient your physician's attention toward your needs and you are more likely to get an answer that makes sense. Knowing about inattentional deafness means that you can appreciate that a lack of response from a physician may mean that you've simply not been heard, and not that your concern is unimportant (especially when your doctor has the stethoscope in her ears or is typing on a computer). Fortunately, in conversation, with more flexible parsing of our attention, we can recalibrate and go back to clarify something that has been missed or misunderstood.

The fast pace of clinical practice—accelerated by electronic records—requires juggling multiple tasks seemingly simultaneously. Although commonly thought of as multitasking, multitasking is a misnomer—we actually alternate among tasks. Each time we switch tasks we need time to recover and, during the recovery period, we are less effective. Psychologists call this interruption recovery failure, which sounds a bit like those computer error messages we all dread. We increasingly feel as if we are victims of distractions rather than in control of them.[17]

In addition to information that comes from the outside world, we are constantly processing information that comes from the "sixth sense"—the mind itself. While focusing on a task (for a physician it might be examining a patient's abdomen or suturing a wound), we all have spontaneously arising thoughts, emotions, and visceral sensations that may or may not relate directly to the situation at hand. If you have any doubt about the constant flow of these mental events, take a couple of minutes, close your eyes, and simply watch the flow of sensations, feelings, thoughts, and emotions, without trying to alter them in any way. We doubt ourselves, remind ourselves about other tasks, feel anxious or sad, and notice grumblings in our stomach or tension in our shoulders.

The brain strives for efficiency. Under high cognitive load—when assaulted with difficult problems, too much information, and emotional stress—the brain tends to simplify. It privileges familiar and expected information and relatively ignores that which is novel, unpleasant, or unexpected.[18] In clinical practice, I find that I tend to pay closer attention to the first thing—or the last thing—that the patient says. When Emil Laszlo mentioned his vitamin D level and prostate symptoms in addition to his shoulder pain, he was unknowingly adding to his physician's cognitive load just by virtue of presenting more concerns. In medicine, the imperative to simplify often leads to premature closure—after reaching a certain information threshold, the brain admits no more information, comes to a conclusion, and treats that conclusion as fact. At that point, we tend to consider only that which confirms our initial impression (shoulder pain and a history of tendinitis), and to ignore the rest (fever, sweats, and a lump). Overconfidence and hurry make matters worse. While inattention is the starting point for many failures of clinical reasoning and empathy, the lack of awareness can undermine effective and humanistic care in many other ways.

TOP-DOWN

During the surgery described at the beginning of this book, Dr. Gunderson, the resident, and the nurse were all focused on the right kidney, and with good reason. They wanted to bring their visual awareness, motor skills, and judgment to a delicate task. They knew that with one false move, things could go sour. Their minds were processing vast quantities and varieties of complex sensory information. They needed to anticipate the likely challenges and come up with a game plan. The surgeon might have had an inner dialogue: "Need to be careful not to injure the ureter, so I'll focus exclusively on that part of the anatomy for now."

Goal-directed attention is also known as top-down attention, or orienting attention. It is about anticipating something that is known and expected with heightened vigilance. Although we like to think that we're in control of our minds, most of our thought process occurs outside our everyday awareness.[19] While top-down attention can go awry, as we've seen, it usually serves us well. To take an everyday example, on my short commute to work there is a stop sign at the corner of Hemingway Drive and Elmwood Avenue. As I approach Elmwood, my mind is primed to see that stop sign and to respond accordingly—even though I'm not aware of thinking about it. In clinical practice, when I see a child with a fever, my eyes automatically and effortlessly direct themselves toward her skin (are there spots?), her neck (is she moving it?), and her breathing (fast? slow? shallow?) even before her mother finishes describing the child's symptoms. When in top-down mode,

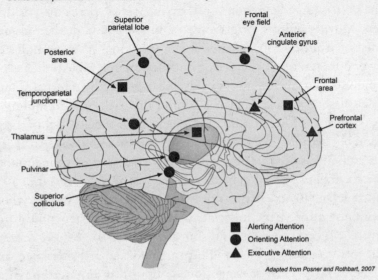

Some Components of the Three Attention Pathways

Adapted from Posner and Rothbart, 2007

I decide what's important (making sure she doesn't have measles or meningitis or pneumonia), and I look and listen for it.[20] Neuroscientists have identified what seems to be the major top-down attention pathway in the brain, known as the dorsal frontoparietal network, which interprets information and guides decision making.

CIRCUIT BREAKERS

While top-down attention is initiated by our expectations and goals, "bottom-up" attention is stimulus driven. It is otherwise known as alerting attention because it maintains vigilance for the *unexpected.* You are driving to work along your usual route, and before you get to that familiar stop sign, a deer suddenly leaps into the road. Your foot reaches the brake before you even realize you're seeing a deer, and not a gorilla or a pedestrian. A surgeon notices red blood in the surgical field and slows down so that her attention can be directed to the bleeder; then she cauterizes it before proceeding.

Some bottom-up stimuli are universal and innate—they capture one's attention whether one grew up in Boston, Barcelona, or Borneo. Moving objects, bright objects, blood, bared teeth, and loud noises activate bottom-up attention in everyone—these stimuli steal away our attention, whether or not they are relevant to the task at hand. Bottom-up attention can also be triggered by internal stimuli from the body itself, such as a pain in the back or a grumbling in the stomach. Other stimuli are "salience dependent"—things that stand out because they are meaningful to us in some way. An everyday example is how we perk up when we hear our name mentioned at a cocktail party. Or, in medicine, the words *chest pressure*.

I saw Jane Rostro in the office—a woman in her seventies whom I've known for years. Like many older patients, she would bring several concerns to each visit, some trivial and some more serious. On this visit her list included hemorrhoids, an arthritic knee, and an itchy rash. Then she mentioned, almost as an afterthought, a funny sensation "right here" while climbing stairs, motioning with a broad gesture encompassing most of her chest and abdomen. It had been worsening over the past several days. A pressure, but not a pain. My attention was diverted by the words *pressure* and *climbing stairs* because of their salience—they might be indicators of angina, a potentially life-threatening situation. Not quite aware I was doing so, I suddenly demoted the itchy rash discourse and put myself on a new set of tracks in a different direction. Once I had made a bottom-up shift in focus, I switched back into top-down mode, now going through a sequence of questions asking about indicators of heart disease—short of breath? puffy legs? family history?—having completely abandoned the itchy rash.

When I told the emergency department about her impending arrival, I mentioned Mrs. Rostro's "chest pain," even though she had called it "pressure" and never used the word *chest*. Unwittingly, I filled in the blanks. I described her symptom to the nurse differently from the way Mrs. Rostro experienced and described it, perhaps because in medical school I learned a category of symptoms called *chest pain* and not *this funny sensation kinda around here*. And I know that *chest pain* tends to capture the attention of the emergency room staff and that the patient will be seen more quickly. If my bottom-up attention had been malfunctioning completely, had I persisted with her itchy rash and hemorrhoids and ignored her vague feeling that something was amiss, the outcome might not have been as good. She was found to have a blockage in her right coronary artery, which was stented, resulting in relief of her symptoms, perhaps saving her life.

Bottom-up attention activates several neural networks. One of those networks resides on the right side of the brain, the side most often associated with intuition, novelty, creativity, hunches, and artistic expression.[21] This makes sense because bottom-up attention is more impressionistic and intuitive. Bottom-up attention also involves the limbic system, which regulates emotions such as fear. Perhaps this is why people often struggle to explain why their attention gets redirected; I find myself saying, "Well, she just *looked* sick," and only later do I put together the pieces of what might have contributed to that impression (pale skin, shallow breathing, lying still). The *just looked sick* intuition, for me and other clinicians, is not innate; it is a product of experience and my ability to assimilate patterns over time. If you're not observant and have trouble educating your intuition, you'll become what educators Carl Bereiter and Marlene Scardamalia call an "experienced non-expert"—someone you wouldn't want to have as your doctor.[22]

By the time doctors finish medical school, certain signs and symptoms become incorporated as salient. They reliably elicit bottom-up responses—for example, if the patient mentions chest pain or has slurred speech, most doctors drop what they're doing and shift gears. Bottom-up attention tends to act like an "involuntary circuit breaker," quickly turning off a top-down process and diverting attention to something more immediate. Other equally important signs and symptoms *don't* trigger physicians' circuit breakers as consistently. Recently, a capable resident took me to see a patient, in his mid-fifties, who was receiving treatment for kidney cancer. The cancer was potentially curable. He was in the hospital because the chemotherapy was making him sick. He seemed a bit flat, perhaps despondent. This is not unusual for patients in the hospital—no one likes being there and no one sleeps well. But then he said that he was thinking of taking early retirement.

I completely missed the salience of that patient's statement; in fact, when I discussed the case with the resident, I couldn't recall having heard it at all, nor did I register the patient's mood. I was totally focused on prescribing medications for pain and nausea. But for the resident, it sounded an alarm. The resident felt a sinking feeling, a sadness. He wondered whether this feeling was triggered by the patient—whether the patient might be depressed or even suicidal—which then tripped his internal circuit breaker and captured his attention. In fact, the patient *was* depressed. We referred him for psychotherapy and he responded well. The resident's ability to pick up on this signal was a direct result of his awareness of his own emotions—the heaviness he felt only grew stronger the more he talked with the patient. This particular resident had good teachers and role models who helped him learn how to be more sensitive to patients' depression. He used his own emotions to inform his care of the patient. But he was exceptional; not all clinicians would have picked up on these clues.[23]

THE INNER MANAGER

Bottom-up attention is capricious. *Any* fast-moving object or loud noise can act as a circuit breaker, even when it is a distraction. Think of what happens when an ambulance goes by while you're trying to have a conversation at a café—you lose your train of thought even though the ambulance's trajectory doesn't intersect yours. And some things should be circuit breakers but aren't. Bottom-up attention tends to fail when things change gradually—a kidney gradually turning blue, a slowly expanding mass, gradual weight loss, deepening depression.[24] Here, only clinicians who are exquisitely attuned to salient cues (such as Mr. Laszlo's night sweats) can see what is really there.

For doctors, electronic health records are one of the most potent circuit breakers. Nearly every time I prescribe a medication, for example, warnings about drug toxicity or drug interactions flash on the computer screen in lurid eye-catching colors, whether the potential for trouble is trivial or life threatening. I lose my train of thought and my gaze is now captured by the computer screen, and the patient is left waiting.[25] It's impossible to investigate all of the warnings in detail; trying to do so would keep the average doctor up past midnight. Barraged with these warnings, it is understandable why clinicians ignore many of them and how they can set the stage for other errors due to fatigue and distraction. Designers of these programs, adept at computer operating systems, clearly were not taking into account the limits of clinicians' inner operating systems.

Executive attention is our "inner manager," which helps us to prioritize one source of information over another. Consider what happens when Mrs. Rostro returns to talking about her itchy rash. My attention is divided between the signs and symptoms of heart disease and the signs and symptoms of eczema, far less serious. If it's a normal day in the office, my visit with Mrs. Rostro might be interrupted by a knock on the door from my nurse, who informs me that the last prescription I wrote for a different patient is not covered by his insurance. I look at my mobile phone to find the phone number for the cardiologist to call regarding Mrs. Rostro, and I note a calendar alert to bring the car in for an oil change. When I hear the distant sound of a car alarm, which I'd usually ignore, I realize that I'd forgotten to bring the car in for the oil change. I sniffle, then become aware that I'm still fatigued, just having gotten over a cold. Executive attention triages stimuli and in the best of circumstances helps me pay attention to what matters — Mrs. Rostro's concerns — and to ignore the rest.

TWENTY MINUTES OF RED

When I was in college in the 1970s, I took a course with Ken Maue, a visionary avant-garde musician. Ken wanted his musicians to experience beauty and harmony by inviting them to see the world differently, in unexpected and surprising ways. He composed a performance piece that was originally intended to last three days—hence the original title, *Three Days of Red.*[26]

The instructions are simple: "For three days record in writing everything red that you see." I actually did it once, back in 1973. Although the act of "seeing red" for three consecutive days for me was life changing (I could never again see the world in the same way), even a few minutes can be instructive (and far more pragmatic). You're instructed to spend twenty minutes (or as long as an hour or as short as seven minutes) walking in the environment (often a hospital or conference center) in silence. I also ask you to notice what's going on in your own mind during the exercise. This exercise directs your top-down, goal-directed attention to things red. While you're observing your reactions, the exercise helps you be more aware of your inner experience, such as bottom-up impressions, emotions, and thoughts that enter your awareness. You might want to stop here and try it.

TWENTY MINUTES OF RED

For the next twenty minutes,
record in writing the name
of everything red that you see.

The red exercise leads participants to realize that there is no "immaculate perception"—we don't see things as they are as much as we see things as conditioned by our expectations and goals.[27] People doing the exercise are frequently surprised at how many red things they now notice that had previously escaped their attention—even in a familiar environment. They ask themselves, "How red does something need to be to be called red?" They discern finer gradations of red, purple, orange, and pink. Some get competitive and try to list more red things, and more unusual red things, than their colleagues. Some get bored, some get excited, some get annoyed, and some worry if they're doing the exercise correctly—all of these thoughts and feelings bubble up unbidden from their bottom-up attention.

One of the reasons people find the red exercise so compelling is that they learn how their minds work; nearly all of them note that anything that is not red tends to be discounted. They literally see the world differently, and they see how inputs from the senses are filtered by their brains before they are apprehended as conscious perceptions. The red objects were always there, but now we notice them and notice how we notice them. It lays mental processes— normally in the background—in plain sight. These mental processes not only filter information that happens to come our way, they also drive our own information-seeking behaviors—we look, seek out, and even redefine objects as red.

The red exercise has its counterparts in medicine. It's common for medical students taking a dermatology rotation to begin to notice every freckle on each passerby. They might be more aware of the different brands of sunscreen on display when they go to the supermarket. During flu season, I see dozens of patients with influenza. I begin to divide the world of patients with respiratory symptoms into "flu" and "not flu." I wonder how "flu-like" the patient's symptoms need to be to consider it a case of flu—and not another respiratory virus or a bacterial pneumonia that would require antibiotics.

But clinical medicine is more complex than simple pattern recognition; we not only see patterns, we enact *scripts*.[28] In the emergency room, when an overweight middle-aged woman describes severe pain in the right upper quadrant of the abdomen, a physician's "gallbladder script" is activated. The physician's top-down attention is directed to listen for symptoms of pain and nausea after eating fatty foods, to consider whether a radiologist is available to interpret an ultrasound of the gallbladder, and to prepare to order intravenous fluids and pain relievers. This all happens in an instant.

But scripts aren't always reliable. For most physicians, the gallbladder script would be triggered by someone who has recently eaten a fatty meal and reinforced if the patient is "fair, fat, fertile, female over forty"—the five F's mnemonic that medical students use to recall features of typical patients with biliary colic, the pain that occurs when a gallstone gets stuck, blocking the exit of bile.

While this script would readily identify the "typical" patient, the majority of patients with biliary colic do not have all of these clinical features; if they've not eaten a fatty meal or if they are black, male, young, or thin, the physician typically takes longer to consider gallbladder disease. Or, conversely, patients with the five F's might not have a gallbladder problem at all—they may have had too much to drink or have heartburn. By assuming that upper abdominal pain is due to gallbladder disease, the physician might not think to ask about other symptoms, such as shortness of breath, that might suggest something far more ominous (a heart attack). The same mental scripts that are helpful and efficient in straightforward situations can prevent us from seeing what is actually there in more complex ones.[29]

The red exercise also has its counterpart in human relationships. If a doctor (or anyone else) has a preconceived idea about others—for example, their intelligence, the legitimacy of their symptoms, or their truthfulness—he will tend to discount evidence to the contrary. The effects of these expectations are even more powerful if the physician harbors unexamined negative emotions such as dislike, fear, guilt, anger, disgust, or annoyance.[30]

Those expectations sometimes affect clinical care. I had a close call several years ago. Patricia Scarpa, a middle-aged woman whom I knew well, did not come to the clinic often, but when she came, it always took a long time. She usually had a litany of aches and pains for which no cause could be found. She was not particularly distressed or depressed; this was just the way she was. Her voice was whiny, and she would elaborate in great detail about each item in her list of symptoms. As much as I tried to be attentive, after a while I couldn't focus. I'd get impatient and annoyed.

On this particular visit, she mentioned worsening vague belly pain and bloating, not severe but noticeable. Finding nothing on her physical exam, I relegated this symptom to another one of her uncomfortable but nonserious concerns for which I could only hope to offer some empathy, reassurance, and symptom relief—and did. Later that evening, when I was completing my notes, my eye darted to the vital-signs portion of her chart. She hadn't mentioned it, but she had lost nearly fifteen pounds since her last visit. The next day I called her and asked how she was doing. No better. I suggested that she come back in a few days. That time, I did a more careful physical exam, worried that she might have cancer. Although it was subtle, I thought I could feel fluid in her belly, not a normal thing. I hadn't scheduled the time for a gynecologic exam, but I took the time to do it—and found a hard mass that proved to be ovarian cancer. Had I not called her in, or if I'd felt rushed or inattentive, the opportunity for a cure might have been lost.[31]

WHAT MINDFUL ATTENTION LOOKS LIKE

A colleague, a seasoned neurologist, greets a new patient. Watching the patient extend his hand for a handshake, something attracts the neurologist's attention, something subtle in the patient's movement—something that would not be noticed by a layperson. She cannot name that "something," yet it triggers the thought "Watch out, be attentive, something is amiss." The patient, previously thought to have Parkinson's disease, just doesn't have the type of hesitancy and difficulty initiating movements that would be expected if he did have Parkinson's. Ultimately the patient is diagnosed with a small stroke, which prompts a different approach to treatment; the neurologist stops the potentially toxic medications for Parkinson's and starts blood thinners to prevent another stroke.

My hunch is that this neurologist—like other master clinicians—uses her whole mind to a greater degree than her less skilled counterparts. Master clinicians attend to the person in front of them while attending to their own mental processes. They don't take for granted their initial impressions, or anyone else's. They attend to that which they can explicitly describe, as well as the vague impressions that influence their judgment. They use their analytic minds—knowledge, evidence, and technical skills—as well as their intuitive and imaginative minds, the sensibilities that we typically associate with the humanities.[32]

What does focused attention feel like? For an experienced cyclist, focused attention means maintaining balance while going around a sharp curve. For a musician, it is making exquisite each brief silence between two notes. For a surgeon, it is applying just the right amount of tension to a suture. For a neurologist, it is knowing when to let a first impression guide your thinking and when those impressions lead you astray. Attending in this way is the result of more than just experience. It takes practice to bring perceptions to awareness when needed, and to allow them to fade below the threshold of awareness at other times to avoid overloading the mental circuits,[33] employing all three kinds of attention to perceive and respond to that which might otherwise have been missed.

Applying focused attention is a *moral* choice, not just a skill. We pay attention to that which we consider important, and by virtue of paying attention to something, we make it important. All physicians take a vow to do their best to relieve suffering and not do harm. But unknowingly, sometimes we attend to some kinds of suffering—and some people who suffer—more than others. Attending to each patient's concerns means more than just becoming more perceptive and attentive; it means being prepared to greet whatever concerns patients bring with curiosity and resolve.

3

Curiosity

The sixty-year-old man lay motionless, and the whooshing sound of the ventilator was the only thing that broke the late-night stillness. He had had a large stroke and his condition hadn't changed during the five days he had been in the hospital. His family was distraught; each day they came in and talked to him, rubbed his hand, wiped his face, desperately trying to establish contact, to see if he could respond in any way. Nothing. Then came their tears. On day number four, I was told, one family member thought that she saw him blink one eye in response to a question; otherwise he was flickerless. He had electrodes on his head for continuous EEG monitoring. The brain waves were normal, meaning that most likely he was "locked in" — able to think, but not able to move or respond in any way, a terrifying prospect. That morning, we rounded quickly. Still no change, no communication, zero. The intern wrote in the chart, "Unresponsive; prognosis poor."

I was still at the hospital late at night and I had just finished my notes. I peered into the patient's darkened room and was surprised to see Dr. Fisher. I was a medical student, fortunate to have been assigned to a renowned senior neurologist, C. Miller Fisher, for a month-long rotation. Fisher was an observant and thoughtful man, but I saw him doing things in the room that struck me as, well, odd. Flashlight in hand, he illuminated parts of the room, then shone it on his own face while talking to the patient, gesticulating wildly and making grotesque facial expressions — sneers, grins, frowns — almost clownlike. Then he'd stop and check the EEG machine for any spike in the visual cortex or the auditory cortex when he was talking and gesticulating—hoping to see what was still working in the patient's brain and to connect in some way with the patient as a person. Fisher assumed that the patient had an inner life and wanted to see if he was capable of a two-way connection with the world. He assumed that "unresponsive" merely meant that he had not found the correct channels for communication. Fisher didn't know what he would find. Ultimately, he noted a flicker of movement around the patient's eyes, just like what the family had described. Fisher noted a simultaneous EEG spike in the visual cortex—confirming the family's impressions that the message was getting through. The patient, otherwise barely showing signs of life, was responding. We communicated this news to the family the next day. Even though we will never know what impact that human gesture had on the patient—his ability to communicate never improved—the family found solace knowing that their messages of love and caring were getting through.

Fisher's curiosity was palpable. Like the late Oliver Sacks, he had perfected the art and joy of observation. Like others who are curious, his gratification was intrinsic; when being curious, we explore new things for their own sake with no extrinsic reward.[1] Inevitably, this kind of exploration yields unexpected surprises.

Curiosity is a fundamental human quality and is essential for survival; during a famine, those who seek out novel sources of food and shelter are likely to fare better (Who would imagine that the inside of a prickly thistle could be a delicacy or that cold slippery ice could be made into a warm cozy igloo?). Curiosity is "wonderment,"[2] a realization that there is always more; personality researchers consider curiosity a manifestation of a psychological trait, "openness to experience."[3] In medicine, curiosity means seeking to know what makes each person tick. An attraction to the unknown, the unusual, and the unexpected is also what makes great physician-scientists. Whereas most scientists were throwing away moldy petri dishes, Alexander Fleming, an inquisitive but otherwise undistinguished scientist, discovered the mold that would be synthesized into penicillin.

Attending

Throughout medical school, residency, and clinical practice, doctors are socialized to be authoritative, knowledgeable, and self-confident. Saying "I don't know" is not an option. Perhaps curiosity is seen as immature or even dangerous. Students' probing questions—a sign of curiosity—are not always well received by supervising physicians.

Curiosity is sidelined by what Jerome Kassirer, former editor of the *New England Journal of Medicine*, called a "stubborn quest for certainty." Being too certain—never being in doubt—paradoxically results in lower-quality care through overtesting, premature conclusions, and tunnel vision.[4] Psychologically, when doctors (or anyone else) are barraged with information and in a hurry, we find it harder to be curious, to explore outside the box, to entertain doubt. The pressure to solve problems quickly leads doctors to rely on rules and mental shortcuts rather than to consider each situation afresh. In their more mindless moments, doctors do tests "just to be sure," then abandon their curiosity when a test confirms their initial impressions. Content with a solution that is expedient and not necessarily optimal, they don't explore a full range of options. They tacitly assume that being open or curious takes too much time and energy, not recognizing that putting on blinders will cost them time later. In a word, they *satisfice*.

Faith Fitzgerald's 1999 essay on curiosity should be required reading for all health professionals.[5] An internist, Fitzgerald was dean of students at the University of California, Davis, School of Medicine. Typically, on rounds, senior physicians ask trainees to present the most interesting patients admitted overnight. *Interesting*—in medical discourse—is code for rare diseases (usually incurable) or atypical manifestations of more common ones, things that are easy to miss. Or, sometimes, a "classic" presentation of a serious disease—the loud murmur signaling a ruptured heart valve or bruises on the abdomen signaling severe pancreatitis. *Interesting* is in contrast to the typical day, which for most clinicians is filled with things that, on the surface, seem quite ordinary; for cardiologists it's chest pain, for neurologists it's headache, for dermatologists it's acne. Fitzgerald, in a brilliant educational exercise, would turn the

37

question on its head; she would ask residents to present their most *boring* patient. Her goal was to promote curiosity by demonstrating that every patient's story was unique, interesting, and vital to her care.

One morning, the residents picked an elderly woman who was admitted for "social" reasons: she had been evicted from her apartment, had nowhere to go, and showed up at the hospital emergency room, destitute and confused, with little in the way of medical illness. Her answers to questions were monosyllabic. Her medical history was sparse, her family was gone, and she seemed to have no interests. Fitzgerald wasn't getting anywhere. Finally she asked the patient if she had ever been hospitalized.

"Yes, I broke my arm," she said.

"How did that happen?"

"A steamer trunk fell on it."

Fitzgerald persisted; answers slowly unfolded. The patient was emigrating from Ireland to the United States. The boat lurched. It had hit an iceberg. The name of the boat—you guessed it.[6] In the same essay, Fitzgerald told another story about a resident who noted a scar in a patient's groin. The patient said that he had been bitten by a snake there. "How did that happen?" Fitzgerald asked. The resident said he didn't know. As Fitzgerald noted, the imagination can run riot with possibilities.

While Fitzgerald's stories relate to knowing the patient as a person, curiosity is also essential to the technical aspects of care. Several years ago, on my first day of a much-needed vacation, I was trying to unstick the quick-release lever on a bicycle seat post. The lever snapped and the rusty broken end impaled the muscle at the base of my left thumb. It was a deep wound. After stitches and a week for the swelling to go down, I still had numbness on the outside (radial side) of the thumb. The hand surgeon explained to his resident (and me) that nerve injury on the radial side of the thumb was less important than on the ulnar side of the thumb because the ulnar side was needed for a pincer grasp—turning screws and handling instruments. Thus, they would not plan any further tests or interventions. They didn't think to ask what I actually do with my hands. For me, doing physical examinations, typing on a computer, and playing the harpsichord are everyday activities that require sensation on the radial side of the thumb. I rarely use a pen, a screwdriver, or a scalpel. As an assertive patient, I objected. They changed their plan and, fortunately, the numbness resolved.

In medicine, feeling not-too-certain leads good clinicians to dig further, to explore the archaeology of each person's illness. Social psychologist Ellen Langer recommends that we consider "facts" as merely provisional or contextual—what's true today in Rochester, New York, might not be true tomorrow—or elsewhere. Facts come to us from our primary senses ("I saw it with my own eyes," etc.) and also through spoken or written language. Any trial lawyer or astute clinician knows better than to accept these primary data as irrevocably true.

Faith Fitzgerald, in her article on curiosity, tells a story of a medical student who presents a patient on rounds as having "BKA times two." In medical jargon, BKA stands for "below-the-knee amputation." Fitzgerald saw the patient and noted two feet sticking out from under the sheets—warm, pink, hairy. Even seeing the patient with Dr. Fitzgerald, the student failed to notice that the patient had feet until she pointed it out. The student was flummoxed, rendered speechless. He said that he reported BKA because it said so in the chart. Apparently, a transcriptionist made an error on a discharge summary. Instead of typing DKA (diabetic ketoacidosis), she typed BKA. The error was carried through several hospital admissions. Once a patient is assigned a diagnosis, whether it be a disease (asthma, for example) or a personal characteristic (e.g., "difficult," "noncompliant"), that diagnosis tends to stick, and it takes what seems like an act of Congress to remove it from the patient's profile.[7] It shuts down consideration of alternatives.

In medicine, curiosity about people is not merely a nicety. A spirit of inquiry, interest, and wonder is good for patients—and fundamental to excellent care—because clinicians then see them in all of their richness and complexity. Adopting an attitude of being not quite certain can release clinicians from the tyranny of categories, or at least soften their edges. They see patients as humans, not merely case studies. Curiosity can help clinicians choose the right treatment; asking someone how he spends his day can help me know whether taking a pill three times a day is realistic or if a once-daily dosing (at slightly higher cost) is better. A deep interest in people is the basis for empathy and understanding. Curiosity, like attention, has a moral dimension: it inspires care that respects and engages with patients' needs, wants, preferences, and values.[8]

FUZZY TRACES

In primary care practice, patients typically present with early and subtle signs of illness, making a diagnosis more difficult. Appendicitis in its early stages can seem just like an ordinary stomachache. Pneumonia and heart failure may be hard to distinguish from one another. An allergic reaction and a staph skin infection may look alike. Some diseases have early signs and symptoms that are just too subtle to detect, but are obvious in retrospect. Sometimes it doesn't matter if the diagnosis is delayed, but at other times an early diagnosis is critical.

As a family physician, I see many children in my office with cold symptoms, often the victims of some virus. However, every once in a while, a child with symptoms similar to those of a virus has something more serious—pneumonia, meningitis, even leukemia. In those situations, often something doesn't feel quite right to me. I feel a sense of unease. My brain is on high alert, yet the accompanying feelings are visceral and hard to describe—I just don't feel comfortable inside. Sometimes I wake up in the middle of the night, worried. Perhaps I told a mother to bring her child back in a week; now that seems too long. These visceral feelings draw upon and also inform what philosopher Michael Polanyi calls "tacit knowledge"[9] (that which we know but find difficult to describe) and what psychologist Valerie Reyna calls "fuzzy traces" (memories that carry the gist of a situation but are often fuzzy about details).[10]

What happens next is particularly important; it would be so easy to ignore the feeling and move along to the next task. But I'm curious when a patient "looks sick." I can explore it, unpack it, and examine it more closely. Perhaps the child is a bit pale or is clinging to his mother more than I'd expect. Perhaps I know that his mother doesn't schedule office visits unless something is really wrong—and she's usually on the mark.

When being curious, this sense of unease piques my interest in the patient. I am attuned in a way that invites further exploration, often before I can characterize why—perhaps in the same way that a sommelier can first identify a great wine and only later finds the adjectives to describe it. Clearly, these impressions are informed by my clinical expertise; I would not have been able to make fine distinctions between "sick" and "really sick" prior to having gone to medical school, just as a sommelier needs to have learned a vocabulary to distinguish different types of grapes and styles of winemaking. From discernment comes curiosity, and then greater discernment. Curiosity is more than mere experience; it links heightened attention ("Something's not quite right") with self-awareness ("I'm feeling uncomfortable"), knowledge ("This situation could be dangerous"), and exploration ("I wonder what's going on").[11]

A BAD DAY

Curiosity suffers when we feel befuddled and besieged. Alexis Brown and I had met just once before, not quite three weeks earlier, shortly after she had been hospitalized with a myocardial infarction—a heart attack. Alexis was only forty-two years old and had considered herself healthy and fit. Today she was scheduled for a complete physical.

The visit started with an initial greeting and a general inquiry about her concerns.

"Things are okay."

"How do you feel you've been recovering since the heart attack?" I asked.

"I didn't have a heart attack."

I was taken aback. "I don't understand. I thought we'd gone over that."

"They did the first test and it was normal, then a few hours later they told me it was abnormal. Then they told me there was no blockage."

Suddenly, doubting my memory, I paused. "Could I check the note your cardiologist wrote?" I wanted to be certain, beyond doubt.

I found the note from the cardiologist. Sure enough, the EKG tracing showed ST-wave changes characteristic of a myocardial infarction. The blood troponin levels were initially normal, then elevated four hours later, indicating heart damage. So far, pretty typical for a heart attack. Her cardiac catheterization didn't reveal fixed blockages in any of her coronary arteries. This was unusual, surprising. However, the right coronary artery went into spasm during the test, transiently blocking blood flow—a characteristic of Prinzmetal's syndrome, an uncommon condition and even more rarely a cause of a heart attack. My notes indicated that I had discussed all of this with Ms. Brown the last time and she had seemed to understand. I was sure I was right. But now, it was as if the prior discussion hadn't occurred.

I asked about exercise.

"I'm not exercising."

"Why is that?"

"They never told me what I could do to prevent this from happening again."

"And medication? I see that they prescribed lisinopril and metoprolol to prevent future heart damage."

"I read the side effects and I'm not taking them."

I was growing annoyed, frustrated. We reviewed her lab tests. Cholesterol good. Stopped smoking in the hospital, none since. Doesn't drink. I tried to plow through.

"So, maybe we should do the physical exam. Here's a gown; I'll be back in about two minutes."

"I don't think I want a physical today."

"Okay, we can wait if you like. I was reviewing your chart and noticed that you don't have a flu shot on record. Can I offer you one?"

A hesitation. "No, I don't think I want it."

"Can I ask why?"

"I don't think I will get the flu."

The more she protested, the more I pushed, offering things, services and recommendations. I had no interest in why she might be acting the way she was.

"I just don't want it," she said.

Now I felt under attack. I thought, "Why the hell is she coming in today, anyway? To torment me?" I was running late already and had no patience for what I perceived as stonewalling.

Perhaps you see this situation more clearly than I did at the time. I didn't welcome her perspective. I was impatient with her lack of cooperation, not seeing that my impatience was the flip side of my need to be an authority, in charge. I just wanted to push ahead with my agenda and get this increasingly unpleasant visit over with. She had seemed so reasonable during our first visit, and now this. To reassert control I started on a quiet rampage, "I thought that we agreed that you'd come in for complete—" Not being able to finish my own sentence, I stopped abruptly. An awkward silence.

Then, I smiled at myself. I realized that *she* was not making me annoyed, that *my own mind* was creating this sense of annoyance because I desired something (a docile, agreeable patient) that was not in the offing. Call this a mindful moment. I realized, with a calm equanimity, that I was trying to push her into compliance and that I was serving my own need to have the visit follow a particular protocol. My breathing had become shallow and I had an almost insatiable desire to sigh. I had been tensing my legs as if preparing to bolt. I wanted to get out of there. I hadn't been curious about how Alexis Brown saw the situation nor about what she felt she needed. I had had no interest in examining my contribution to— and her experience of—our breakdown in communication.

Here, the sense of unease finally roused my curiosity. I inquired, not having any idea how she might respond, "Can I ask you, how are we doing here? I'm not sure what you were hoping for today."

"We're doing okay."

There was another silence, this time less awkward and more expectant.

"I'm the one who's in control here. I know my body and I don't need a physical."

"That's really important. You want to be in control. I understand that to mean you want to know what's going on so that you can be in charge of your health. Is that right?"

"Yes." We had arrived somewhere. She had a few questions, all germane to her illness and its treatment. I still felt uncomfortable.

"So how should we leave things? Normally I'd see someone back a couple of times in the first few weeks after a hospitalization, but it's up to you. You could come back in a week, a month . . ." I expected her to say that she'd call when she needed to and that I'd never see her again.

"How about two weeks."

I was stunned.

"You're the first doctor who explained things."

"I'll try, but you let me know when we go off course." I meant it; I did need her help.

"Okay, see you then."

The next week a note from the cardiologist indicated that she was doing well and was content taking her medications.

TRAVELING IN PACKS AND PRACTICING ALONE

While curiosity is often spontaneous, sometimes it takes effort, especially when things aren't going well. As communication was breaking down with Ms. Brown, I didn't *want* to be curious; I just wanted to get out of there. Physiologically, the stress of conflict activated my three-way fight-or-flight-or-freeze switch—not my curiosity switch. I wanted to place the responsibility and blame for malfunctioning communication on her. How easy it would be to say that she was "in denial" or "noncompliant," leaving a fractured relationship unaddressed and a serious disease untreated. I needed a way of bringing myself back to the present, to engage with her in a more productive way. This took an additional minute or two of time and some additional mental effort, but likely saved me hours down the road.

I tried to dissect what had happened. As I became aware that my breathing was shallow and that I had been tensing my legs, I had a "fuzzy trace" moment—something was amiss but I couldn't put my finger on it. I then noticed the associated emotions—feelings of restlessness and frustration. At first I tried to push those sensations and emotions away, then realized that they were a useful signal. What I was doing wasn't working, and the clue came from feelings in my body. I listened to the signals coming from within and used those signals as triggers to become *more* curious, to slow down and inquire further, even though I was feeling annoyed. While it could have happened sooner (I became curious after having tried several other options!), this subtle transition was instrumental in achieving a positive outcome.

Achieving a transition like that—transforming discomfort into curiosity—takes practice, both in the clinic and outside. One exercise that can be particularly useful is the "body scan," popularized by Jon Kabat-Zinn in his Mindfulness-Based Stress Reduction programs. The body scan is not a relaxation exercise; rather, it's an awareness exercise.[12] Participants are guided through awareness of each part of the body, noting its position in space, tension, relaxation, or other pleasant or unpleasant sensations. When "scanning" the abdomen and chest, the attention is drawn to movement—of the breath, the viscera, and the heart. Sometimes I'll experience a strange sense of unfamiliarity and novelty—for example, when I first noticed that I habitually hold my left shoulder more hunched than the right. Simply noticing and exploring bodily sensations— without trying to change them—lets you observe more fully. Paradoxically, practiced inaction can lead to action. In the clinic that day, a brief taste of that practiced awareness was essential in switching from frustration to inquiry.

Well-functioning clinical teams can also promote curiosity. A palliative care nurse-practitioner colleague routinely explains to patients when we arrive with a group, all in white coats, "We travel in packs for protection."[13] While it's an attempt to make humor out of a potentially threatening situation, there is some truth in it. Several sets of eyes and ears, in a well-functioning team, extend the senses and sensibilities of any one individual. A team member might say, "Did you notice she's looking a bit yellow?" or "She seems to be more confused today than yesterday," or "I don't think that we're all on the same page." A new observation then leads to doubt, reconsideration, and revision of our impressions. Observant teams stimulate an infectious curiosity.

However, as clinicians, we often practice alone. Even in the hospital, after rounds, I visit patients by myself. In my family medicine office, a patient arrives and the door is shut. It's just me and the patient—and possibly a family member or two. No one is watching. Almost no one has directly observed my practice in thirty years—except the occasional medical student. In those situations, curiosity has to start with me. If I'm being mindful, I am curious about the patient and I am curious about my own experience. In a way that is informative and not self-indulgent, I notice what captures my attention as I go about my work, whether I find it pleasant or unpleasant, interesting or annoying. I am "preparing to be unprepared"; I practice what Ellen Langer calls "soft vigilance," an open, receptive awareness, actively looking for something that is new, unexpected, or interesting.[14] Soft vigilance is a relaxed awareness. It is different from hypervigilance—trying to focus on every detail at every moment. Soft vigilance is energizing, whereas hypervigilance can be exhausting. Soft vigilance informs and prepares me to pay attention in a different, more open way.

PURSUING DOUBT

If curiosity is its own reward, one would expect that people—including doctors—would display it more often. Yet being curious also takes people outside their comfort zones because it has to do with *increasing*—not removing—uncertainty. It goes counter to the human tendency to oblige reality to fit our preconceived notions. Being curious involves being aware that the situation is not as tidy as it might seem. This sense of doubt is unsettling for many doctors and patients, especially when the stakes are high.[15] Patients undergoing surgery for cancer want to hear—and surgeons want to say—"I got it all." Patients and doctors want a diagnosis to be definitive, beyond doubt, and a treatment to be the best available. Sometimes we have that degree of certainty, but more often that certainty is elusive—provisional, incomplete, or evolving. While a biopsy can prove that you have cancer, it cannot tell you exactly how long you will live or if you will be the one who will benefit from treatment or the one who won't. Being mindful means *feeling* uncertainty, *not turning away from* that feeling of uncertainty and *not clinging to* the negative emotions that arise.[16]

Curiosity not only draws attention to the outside world, but also draws attention to one's inner experience: "Am I tired? Am I too sure of myself? Am I in a hurry? What's new here?" Even the way clinicians interact with patients can help them be curious: "I'm wondering—have I addressed what's really important to you? Am I missing something? Is there something more that you want to tell me?" I make a habit of asking myself "What's interesting about this patient?" and "What's still unknown?" as a habitual (but not foolproof) way of avoiding self-deception and premature closure.

Curiosity is not only good for patient care; it is also good for health professionals. By enriching their connections with their patients and feeling more effective—on their game—they feel more vitality in their work.[17] Recent research suggests that there's a feedback loop between curiosity on the one hand, and anxiety, defensiveness, and rigidity on the other. For years, psychologists have known (mostly from research in educational settings) that when we're less anxious, defensive, and rigid, curiosity flourishes. New research suggests that it also works the other way; the more curious you are, the less anxious, defensive, and rigid you'll be when under psychological stress. Psychologist Todd Kashdan conducted an interesting set of experiments in which participants were asked to think about their death, imagining what a terminal illness and dying might be like. As predicted by "terror management theory" (and common sense), subjects became defensive; they tried to push away death-related thoughts and tended to cling to familiar beliefs, people, and surroundings. The researchers also measured attentiveness and curiosity, both elements of mindfulness. People who were attentive and curious were less anxious and defensive than those who were equally attentive but had a less curious disposition.[18]

Some people have personalities that seek novelty; they tend to be adventurous and less risk-averse. They see new challenges as exciting rather than terrifying. These tendencies manifest early in childhood, leading to speculation that brain chemistry, genetics, and social environment might all contribute.[19] Curiosity is associated with release of the neurotransmitter dopamine, activating intrinsic reward circuits in the brain.[20] These dopaminergic systems are triggered by novel experiences, especially sensory experiences, and magnified if the experiences are surprising and associated with some risk (Think about adolescents here!). Because dopamine release makes one feel good, curiosity persists even in the absence of tangible external rewards. People who score high on psychological markers of curiosity—in particular, those who have high "openness"—are biochemically different from their peers. Their dopamine receptors are more numerous and their genetic controlling mechanisms are different.[21] The propensity to be curious is, to some degree, encoded on our genes.[22]

Curiosity is not merely genetic; it grows in nurturing social environments. Children's "exploration behaviors"—analogous to the more critical and nuanced curiosity of adults—are expressed to a greater degree among children whose emotional attachment to their parents and other adults is secure. Children raised in a supportive environment feel safer taking small risks and exploring the unknown than children who have experienced less nurturance. For them, curiosity leads to a sense of vividness—children feel that their world "comes alive" and provides a sense of fulfillment and happiness.[23] They want to explore further, widening their reach. In contrast, those raised in abusive or neglectful environments tend to adopt a more fearful, anxious, or avoidant attachment style and cling to the familiar.[24] They don't explore or examine the world around them. They're afraid of rejection and failure. When they become adults, the same factors hold true. Like children, adults are more curious in supportive environments—ones that promote inquiry and in which they can safely share their doubts, discoveries, and mishaps.[25] Yet, clinicians tend to rate their work environments as not particularly supportive. They often rely on the relationships that they develop outside the workplace for support.[26]

While in the past the social/cognitive environment and genetics were seen as opposing explanations for human behavior, the relatively new—and exciting—fields of behavioral and social epigenetics have made clear that the social environment affects the ways in which one's genetic predispositions are actually expressed.[27] If the social environment is safe and supportive, the genes that encode dopamine receptors are turned on. With more receptors, the sense of intrinsic reward from discovery and curiosity is greater. Conversely, if the environment is abusive or inconsistent, the same genes will be turned off. Put simply, genes affect psychological states and social interactions, and also the reverse—these same genes are regulated by the internal psychological environment as well as the social milieu. Even those who might have a low "natural" tendency toward curiosity become more curious if placed in a supportive environment with strong healthy relationships and encouragement to reflect and be self-aware.

Curiosity is part of the social capital of medicine. Just like young children, medical practitioners who are more curious feel a greater sense of vividness and vitality. They are more satisfied with their work, more engaged with their patients, and do a better job of treating illnesses. Entertain, for a moment, the radical thought that health care institutions could actually support healthy learning environments. Clinicians would be more motivated; they'd inquire more deeply about patients' illnesses and distress, form more meaningful relationships, and have a greater sense of self-confidence—all of which would promote greater quality of care.

4

Beginner's Mind

The Zen of Doctoring

When I was nineteen, I spent three months at the San Francisco Zen Center. I had read a book, *Zen Mind, Beginner's Mind*, written by Shunryu Suzuki Roshi, the founding abbot of the center. Shortly thereafter I applied to be a "guest student." In the book, Suzuki Roshi describes in simple language the core principles of mindful living and meditation practice.[1] It's one of my "stranded on a desert island" books—each time I pick up the small volume, I find new wisdom. Suzuki Roshi said, "In the beginner's mind the possibilities are many, in the expert's they are few." By this he meant that expertise can lead you to deep insights, but can also lead your mind away from its true nature—curious, open, creative.[2] At that time I was a beginner, so I found this reassuring. But beginner's mind is even more important for those with some claim to expertise.

During one of my medical school rotations, a classmate was assigned a patient with hairy-cell leukemia, a disease that was fascinating to the physicians caring for her because the genetic basis of the disease had recently been discovered. (It's called "hairy" because of the appearance of the cells under the microscope.) She was considered a "great case." Despite our exquisite understanding of her illness, the treatments available provided no guarantees of a cure. On rounds with my classmate and our supervising residents, I saw a frail woman, bedridden, without family or get-well cards in her room. No one seemed to be addressing either her pain or her iso-

51

lation. It didn't take much—my classmate took a moment to mention to the clinical team that the patient seemed uncomfortable and alone. Once alerted, the team provided a different kind of attention, focused on comfort and dignity; they ordered pain medications and arranged for a chaplain to come to the bedside. My classmate's supervisor, clearly more expert than he, saw her as a "great case"; it took a beginner's eyes to see her as a "suffering person."

Now that I am the senior member of clinical teams, I value medical students' input more than ever. Often the medical student on the team is the one who asks the key question—something as simple as "Why are you doing *that*?" The naïve (and sometimes annoying!) questions of a bright medical student can profoundly alter an experienced clinician's point of view. Recently a medical student asked me whether our social worker could help with transportation for an elderly patient with diabetes. Until he asked, I hadn't considered *why* the patient had missed so many appointments; turns out she had no reliable way of getting to the office, and that's why her diabetes was out of control. In retrospect it seems so obvious.

When Suzuki Roshi talked about beginner's mind, he was talking to (or about) beginners, but his message was even more important for experts. Experts tenaciously hold on to their expertise. They conflate their competence and experience with mastery. After all, we have worked hard to become the experts that we are, and suggesting that this hard-earned expertise should be set aside is a radical notion. But experts don't always see how their expertise can limit their understanding. In the view of the Dreyfus brothers, professors at the University of California, Berkeley, who developed a model of expertise, experts know the answers, but only masters know the important questions. Experts revel in what they know, and masters revel in what they don't.[3]

Expertise can lead doctors to assume that they know things that they cannot. For example, doctors often feel that they are able to assess patients' pain accurately. Patients' accounts (backed up by research) suggest otherwise, that we don't really know much about our patients' distress unless we ask. Physicians' estimates about their patients' level of pain are often no better than chance, meaning that we often provide inadequate (or unnecessarily excessive) pain medication. Psychologist Cleve Shields studies communication between patients and physicians. He read transcripts of audio-recorded patient-physician office visits in which there was some discussion of pain. Physicians who used more "certainty words"—words that connoted that they were sure of themselves, beyond doubt—asked patients fewer questions about their pain: what it was like, what helped and what didn't. The doctors' presumptuousness got in the way of good care.[4] Doctors, as they go through training, often get worse at understanding patients' subjective experience of illness; the doctors' expertise blinds them to patients' experience of suffering and their empathy declines.[5] They give privilege to objective information *about* patients over subjective information *from* patients. They are more likely to treat patients as diagnoses, as objects. Neuroimaging studies suggest that physicians are less emotionally reactive to seeing patients in pain than the general population—a good thing because it keeps them from becoming overwhelmed, a bad thing because sometimes they objectify patients and distance themselves too much.[6]

Beginner's mind uncouples expertise from one's present experience. It is a cultivated naïveté, an intentional setting aside of the knowledge and preconceived notions that one has gained from books, journals, teachers, and past experiences to see the situation with new eyes. I think of it as putting my "expert self" on an imaginary shelf for a moment, easily within reach and readily available, but enough out of the way so that it doesn't become an encumbrance to a more intuitive and holistic way of being. I think, "What does this patient need most today?" Then I seek the evidence to justify or refute my initial impressions. Simply setting my expert self aside helps me to consider new possibilities.

Johann Sebastian Bach is reported to have said, "The problem is not finding [melodies], it's—when getting up in the morning and out of bed—not stepping on them."[7] Bach was a consummate expert, perhaps the greatest composer who ever lived, and was continually creative and inventive within a tradition that had strict rules of composition. However, to be creative, he had to set aside some of his preconceived notions of what music could be to produce something new, fresh, and not formulaic. The same was true of other great composers who created new musical languages: Monteverdi, Beethoven, Wagner, Schönberg, and Cage. Similarly, in medicine, beginner's mind liberates intuition; intuition can then inform my understanding, taking into account my prior ideas, successes, and failures yet remaining unfettered by them. Relying on expertise alone might produce a Dittersdorf,[8] but hardly a Bach; in medicine, it might produce someone who seems to have all the answers but doesn't ask the right questions.

A FLAG IN THE WIND

Gary, a friend of mine, was diagnosed with bladder cancer several years ago—the slow-growing curable kind, fortunately. He had cystoscopic surgery and was sent home with a catheter. After a few days, the catheter was removed, but he got into trouble—he had intense pain when he tried to urinate and developed urinary retention. The catheter was reinserted for a few days and then removed again—on a Thursday afternoon. On Friday, he started having abdominal pain that grew in intensity during the day. His urologist's office was closed, so he went to the busy emergency room of a well-respected California hospital. The physician noted that Gary had little urine output, so he started an IV, perhaps assuming that Gary was dehydrated. He signed out to another physician, who noted that Gary was still not urinating much, so he increased the rate of the IV. They continued the IV drip overnight. In distress, Gary's wife called me early the next morning. Gary was in agonizing pain. I spoke to the nurse on his unit, and I insisted that he be seen by the urology resident. Before the resident arrived, though, the nurse checked Gary's abdomen and said, "Oh my God, your bladder is about to burst." She placed a new catheter, draining two liters of urine from Gary's bladder. He eventually did get well, but he spent two additional days in the hospital before going home because he developed a fever due to a (preventable) kidney infection.

In one sense, this case defies the imagination—how could well-qualified doctors and nurses persist on an erroneous path when an alternative and logical explanation—recurrent urinary retention—would be perfectly obvious to someone with no medical training? It's a striking example of cognitive rigidity—the resistance to changing one's thinking or beliefs, a tenacious adherence to one view of reality. Every clinician can think of a time when he or she fell into a trap like this. In medicine, manifestations of illness are polysemous—they can be interpreted in many ways—creating a field of cognitive traps into which clinicians routinely fall. When harried, clinicians are more likely to stop thinking when they find the first, and not necessarily the best, of multiple interpretations of a situation. Cognitive scientists call this "search satisfaction."[9] Their interpretation then becomes ossified into a rigidly brittle—yet flimsy—"truth."

Novelist F. Scott Fitzgerald once said that "the test of a first-rate intelligence is the ability to hold two opposed ideas in mind at the same time and still retain the ability to function."[10] With the same contexts, scenes, and characters, one could write two completely different plays. Here, the doctors caring for Gary didn't consider the possibility of two different story lines—the dehydration story and urinary retention story. They settled on one of the two and considered it fact, even though the dehydration story was a poor fit. Having once committed to a viewpoint, clinicians can be extraordinarily unwilling to consider another, even if it is a better fit; changing one's mind is a source of shame, rather than a source of wonder. Gary's situation is even more remarkable because all indications suggested that the treatment was not producing the desired effect, even from the beginning—it would be odd for someone who was dehydrated not to urinate after two liters of extra fluid had been pumped into his system. The cognitive rigidity of one clinician was contagious, practically becoming a shared delusion among several health professionals. One definition of insanity is doing the same thing over and over and expecting different results.[11]

Part of the problem is the fast-paced environment of clinical medicine. Clinicians feel under pressure to come to a diagnosis and treatment plan and move on to the next patient. Part of that pressure is internal, though—something about the quick thinking is exciting for physicians. Clinicians need some way of alerting themselves to the possibility that their understanding is provisional and incomplete, that their expertise can lead them astray. They need a trigger to help them slow down when they should.

The fast pace of medicine is only part of the problem. It takes effort to hold two opposed ideas—to consider that a patient can be *both* a great case *and* a suffering person, to see the relevance of both the patient's experience and your own diagnostic formulations. The ability to tolerate—and even embrace—ambiguity is central to being a good diagnostician. Master clinicians see that seemingly contradictory perspectives might offer explanations for an evolving situation; they have the cognitive flexibility to let go of ideas when those ideas are no longer useful. They can see how an illness is caused by a virus *and* by the failure of the body's immune system—and thus allow a wider range of treatment options. They can see that a patient who doesn't take his diabetes medicine regularly is both "noncompliant" and also "struggling to do the best he can"—and that way the clinicians can mobilize support while also encouraging the patient to do a better job. Mindful clinicians can feel confident while retaining some doubt. Just the other day I had to ask a colleague a simple question about a newborn (I don't have many in my practice anymore). It was almost embarrassing, something any intern would know and I knew but needed to make sure I had it right. It takes humility to recruit additional expertise.

A Zen story goes:

> Two monks were watching a flag flapping in the wind. One said to the other, "The flag is moving."
> The other replied, "The wind is moving."
> Huineng, their teacher, overheard this. He said, "Not the flag, not the wind; mind is moving."[12]

Seeing a situation from two perspectives simultaneously can reveal an even more profound truth. Of course the flag is moving and the wind is moving. What we don't always appreciate is how our minds move between two or more views of the world. The ability to hold contradictory perspectives is not only a marker of a great clinician, it also characterizes great scientists. Physicist Niels Bohr is reported to have said "the opposite of a fact is falsehood, but the opposite of one profound truth might very well be another profound truth." For him it was not intuitive to consider that light is both a wave and a particle—a paradox that boggles the imagination—yet the scientific evidence allowed no other explanation.

HOLDING EXPERTISE LIGHTLY

The failure of Gary's clinical team to adopt more than one perspective may have had its roots in an inability to adopt a stance of "not-knowing." Their expertise—or, better yet, the misapplication of their expertise—led to overcertainty, an arrogance in considering their provisional formulation to be an immutable fact. I can only speculate about what was going on in the minds of the clinical team at that time; haste and cognitive overload were likely at play, but there may have been more.

Not-knowing is not the same as laziness. In Suzuki Roshi's words, "Not-knowing doesn't mean that you don't know." Not-knowing means not letting what you know get in the way. It means "to hold what you know lightly, so that you're ready for it to be different."[13] In this way, knowing and not-knowing are not incompatible; they are two sides of the same coin.

Living each moment recognizing that our understanding is incomplete—maintaining a sense of "unfinishedness" in the fast-paced, information-overloaded world of clinical medicine—is not easy. Once I make a diagnosis, I notice that I tend to see information in a different way; anything that conflicts with that sense of "truth" makes me uncomfortable, even more so if I've made a commitment by having declared that truth to someone else. It's dangerous when you feel that it's better to appear certain even if you're wrong than to appear in doubt.

The discomfort that happens when you are confronted by new information that conflicts with your existing beliefs, ideas, values, or behavior—"cognitive dissonance"—is amplified when your sense of certainty is disrupted.[14] Faced with cognitive dissonance, we tend to seek consistency to lessen that sense of disruption. Traditionally, psychologists have identified two primary ways we relieve cognitive dissonance—by changing our ideas, values, beliefs, or behavior to accommodate the new information, or by plowing ahead, favoring information that confirms the old ideas and ignoring or rationalizing that which does not.[15] Too often, we shape the facts to conform to our beliefs. In medicine, patients' accounts of their illnesses are rich with inconsistencies, while chart notes are filled with seemingly coherent stories that confirm a diagnostic impression. Master clinicians find a third route, neither changing their viewpoint nor engaging in delusion. They practice living with the paradox. They accept that there might be two equally legitimate ways of viewing a situation, at least for the moment. Sometimes this paradox can be resolved as the situation evolves and new information becomes available. Other times, clinicians need to learn to live with uncertainties that might never be resolved.

In medicine, up to a third of the symptoms that patients bring to their doctors defy our attempts at diagnosis, and despite doing all the right exams and tests, we aren't able to provide a coherent explanation for the patient's distress.[16] Primary care physicians see scores of patients with leg swelling, which can sometimes be a sign of a life-threatening condition—a blood clot or heart failure—but most often is harmless. More than a third of patients whom cardiologists see with chest pain are found not to have heart disease. Neurologists' offices are filled with patients who are dizzy, but extensive testing reveals no clear diagnosis. In those cases, good clinicians hold on to a sense of unfinishedness for months or years. They know that the next time the same patient reports a symptom, it may prove serious. Clinicians, however, are prone to divide patients into those with serious disease and those with "functional" distress. Some illnesses defy Western medical diagnostic categories and appear to be mind-body illnesses. However, classifying those forms of distress as "functional" can also be a trap; clinicians can miss seemingly similar symptoms that represent something more serious. For example, a patient of mine had chronic unexplained abdominal pain for years. She had undergone extensive diagnostic testing, and no treatments helped. Her pain worsened when she was depressed. I saw her on a Friday and reassured her that it was likely the same pain that she had had for years, even though she protested that the pain was different that day. Three days later she saw one of my partners, who sent her for an ultrasound. She had gallstones. I had completely missed the boat. After surgery, *that* pain resolved. But she still had the same unexplained chronic pain. She had pain that was both unexplained and explainable. This paradox—a patient with two similar symptoms—is common. After a heart attack, patients commonly have aftershocks—chest pains that prove innocuous. Patients with rheumatoid arthritis often have fibromyalgia, too—muscular aches and pains that are not associated with any joint destruction.

DARING TO COME UP EMPTY

Zen is rich with stories that contain evocative pearls of wisdom. One of those pearls is about emptiness. As Suzuki Roshi explains, "If your mind is empty, it is ready for anything." The idea of emptiness is a radical, and somewhat disturbing, notion. One popular Zen story tells of a professor who once visited a Japanese Zen master to inquire about Zen.

> The master served tea while the professor expounded about philosophy. When the visitor's cup was full, the master kept pouring. Tea spilled out of the cup and all over the table.
> "The cup is overflowing!" said the professor. "No more will go in!"
> "Like this cup," said the master, "you are full of your own opinions and speculations. How can I show you Zen unless you first empty your cup?"[17]

On one level, this Zen story—and the concept of emptiness—is about making space so that we are ready for new ideas and can use our limited cognitive capacity more effectively.[18] The educator and philosopher John Dewey captured this spirit in the early twentieth century. Dewey called for emptying the mind as "a kind of intellectual disrobing." He said, "We cannot permanently divest ourselves of [our] intellectual habits. . . . But intelligent furthering of culture demands that we take some of them off, that we inspect them critically to see what they are made of and what wearing them does to us. We cannot achieve recovery of primitive naïveté. But there is attainable a cultivated naïveté of eye, ear and thought."[19]

As recently as thirty years ago, some psychologists believed that the message in this Zen story was nonsense. They believed that we had no risk of the cup's overflowing because we only used a small part of our brains in everyday life and that the capacity of the brain was nearly limitless. This idea—that we only use 10 percent of our brains—has achieved urban-legend status and continues to be stated as fact in the media and pop-psychology publications. Despite its appeal, the 10 percent idea has been proved wrong; research has repeatedly demonstrated that we use all parts of the brain, and that the brain has limited capacity for attention, memory, and problem solving. Doctors, like other high-functioning professionals, need all of their cognitive capabilities—and then some—to deal with the complexity of patient care.

The brain is prepared for overload, however. Your brain is always employing mental shortcuts; you categorize, summarize, see similarities, and aggregate information. That way, you achieve mental economy and process more information more quickly. But mental efficiency comes at a price; by characterizing a patient with a certain set of symptoms as an "example of X," doctors can miss a patient's unique features. As I'll discuss further in the chapter on decision making, efficiency can result in superficial solutions to complex problems.

Emptiness is more profound than simply making space in an overcrowded brain. Emptiness is a way of understanding the world. While objects in the world are real, emptiness means that the theories, categories, and labels that we apply to them are constructions of the mind (or collectives of minds) and therefore lack substance. This idea comes from the Buddhist philosophy of emptiness (as I mentioned in chapter 1) and was also articulated by William James, the father of American psychology and a self-described "pragmatist."[20] James held that mental categories—such as diagnoses—can seem so real, but are fundamentally fragile. They have explanatory power but must be set aside in favor of other ways of seeing the world when their usefulness is tenuous and unproven. Expertise means knowing when to dare to come up empty.

By now it should be clear that assigning a diagnosis can both illuminate and obscure clinicians' thinking. A patient of mine was first considered a "classic" case of temporal lobe epilepsy, then, of borderline personality disorder, bipolar II disorder, post-traumatic stress disorder, and somatization disorder. Ironically, each of these explained her distress, but each was fundamentally unsatisfactory—the patient was all of these and none of them. This flux is true in all areas of medicine. Despite years of evidence that the underlying cause of stomach ulcer is a bacterial infection, doctors were reluctant to give up their notion that stomach ulcers were due to poor nutrition, stress, or excess acid production. Similarly, doctors took years to follow evidence-based guidelines to use beta-blockers to treat heart failure. Until the 1990s, we were all taught the lore that beta-blockers would weaken the heart, not strengthen it. It took over a decade for the medical profession to fully assimilate a new worldview.

Doctors are trained to cling to categories. In medical school one of my professors said that there were 10,000 diseases. That was in 1984. In 2015, the *International Classification of Diseases (ICD-10)* listed over 170,000 different diagnosis codes. In medical school, students learn about "cases" of a particular illness before learning how to care for people who are ill. We learned to call diseases "diagnostic entities," as if diagnoses were "things" that exist in the world, like a table or a kidney. You confuse the living, breathing human being in front of you with the diagnosis codes in a chart.

TWO KINDS OF INTELLIGENCE

There are two kinds of intelligence: one acquired,
as a child in school memorizes facts and concepts

from books and from what the teacher says,
collecting information from the traditional sciences
as well as from the new sciences.

With such intelligence you rise in the world.
You get ranked ahead or behind others
in regard to your competence in retaining
information. You stroll with this intelligence
in and out of fields of knowledge, getting always more
marks on your preserving tablets.

There is another kind of tablet,
one already completed and preserved inside you.
A spring overflowing its springbox. A freshness
in the center of the chest. This other intelligence
does not turn yellow or stagnate. It's fluid,
and it doesn't move from outside to inside
through the conduits of plumbing-learning.

This second knowing is a fountainhead
from within you, moving out.
                    —Jellaludin Rumi (1207–1273)
                    translated by Coleman Barks

The poet Rumi provides a compelling description of beginner's mind. Rumi lived in thirteenth-century Persia, and his writings have enjoyed a well-deserved renaissance in the past few decades; his words are often amazingly timely. In an often-quoted poem,[21] Rumi describes the familiar analytic kind and another kind of intelligence—a "fluid" intelligence and a "freshness" that comes from within. This other intelligence is first-person knowing, the kind of knowledge that emerges from stories rather than textbooks, from reflection rather than analysis, from immediacy rather than categorizing. The "freshness" that Rumi summons is beginner's mind—avoiding being blinded by theories, facts, and concepts, and living a truth, not just describing it. Only eight hundred years later has cognitive science caught up with Rumi's prescience, and now medical educators and psychologists affirm that these two approaches are necessary for good clinical judgment, being complementary and not incompatible.[22]

Prior to the twentieth century, doctors commonly talked about diagnosing the *person*; only later did doctors talk about diagnosing *diseases*. In ancient Greece, and in traditional Chinese medicine, disease was seen as an ever-changing dynamic imbalance of humors.[23] I am not advocating abandoning modern medicine in favor of ancient practices (although some of these too may be effective). Rather, we can learn from those older traditions in the way that they recognize that people are dynamic, their symptoms and experiences change, and their illnesses have trajectories—making the case for clinicians to ask themselves, "Is there something new or different with this patient today?"

Unfortunately, diagnosing people in this dynamic way is not reinforced in current clinical practice. The force in medicine that drives billing is the codable diagnosis—sadly, a billing category. Until beginner's mind is supported by the structure of health care organizations—and I believe that it can be (more on this later)—it needs to come from within, no small task.

THE WATER JAR TEST

Those who engage in meditation have claimed that in doing so they can promote beginner's mind. The trick is in how to prove it. Psychologists had to find a way to observe and measure beginner's mind, or its opposite, the tendency of the mind to be "blinded by experience," known as the Einstellung effect—when rigid thought patterns get in the way of identifying more adaptive and creative solutions to a problem.

A team of Israeli researchers came up with a way to measure the Einstellung effect—the Einstellung water jar test.[24] Typically the water jar test is in two phases. In this experiment, volunteers were trained to solve several problems (dividing water in different ways among several jars of different sizes), each of which required the same complex formula. Then the volunteers were given a new problem, which could be solved using a much simpler approach, and were left to their own devices to figure it out. Those who had prior mindfulness practice figured out the simpler solution more readily. As a researcher, though, I wasn't convinced. For example, the same qualities that led someone to undertake meditation practice might also be the ones that led to better performance on the test.

The researchers then took people who had never done any contemplative practice, meditation, or attention training and divided them randomly into intervention and control groups. An eighteen-hour intervention program over seven weeks introduced five different practices—attention training (focusing on the breath), body scan, open awareness, walking meditation, and compassion meditation—plus various awareness exercises, dialogues, and home practice.[25] Those in the intervention group scored better on the test, less likely to be blinded by experience and more likely to find simpler and creative solutions. They had learned to adopt a beginner's mind.

IN THE CLINIC

Over the years I have developed a habit of pausing momentarily before entering any patient's room. With my hand on the door-knob, I quietly take a breath to help me become more present in preparation for the visit—I mentally set aside everything that has happened with the patient I have just finished seeing and other events of the day so that I can be fresh and available. I let go of expectations. It takes just a second or two and invites the freshness that Rumi describes.

I am not the only one to discover ways of achieving mindfulness-in-action. Julie Connelly, a physician colleague at the University of Virginia, writes eloquently about how poetry can promote beginner's mind.[26] Rumi's poem and other poems that invoke the same openness of mind are now on my computer's screen saver, a reminder to balance my view of each patient, to see through an analytic lens, bringing all of my knowledge, expertise, and experience, and also to cultivate a "freshness" within.

Reflective questions keep me on track and out of trouble. I habitually ask myself, "Is there another way to view this situation? What am I assuming that might not be true? How are prior experiences and expectations affecting how I view the situation? What would a trusted peer say?" These "opening-up" questions help me identify my cognitive rigidity and blind spots, some of which are the consequence of the expertise I worked so hard to develop. Reflective questions are not about factual recall; rather, they are questions that open up one's awareness, raise doubts, and expose uncertainty. Anyone who works in a complex environment (and who doesn't?) will find that questions such as these do lead to greater mindfulness. I use the same questions with students and colleagues. Although I rarely talk about it in this way to students, reflective questions promote what the educator Donald Schön called reflection-in-action;[27] they take little time—a few seconds here and there—and save time in the long run. It's a way of remembering that while I might be good at finding answers, it's more important to know that I'm asking the right questions.

5

Being Present

I delivered babies for many years as part of my family practice. At first, I found it difficult to look directly at the face of women experiencing the intensity of labor. Reflexively, I'd avert my gaze. Witnessing raw and unfiltered expressions of pain made me feel uncomfortable and inadequate. I'd busy myself with a task—check the electronic fetal monitor, talk to the patient's partner, talk to the nurse. When I was doing something—prescribing a medication, actually helping a newborn glide into the world—I felt calm and confident. But I foundered when the situation didn't demand action—or demanded inaction. Perhaps patients noticed, or perhaps they didn't.

I undertook a practice of presence. I began, consciously, taking in each patient's face, recognizing yet resisting the urge to look away. I became aware of my own gaze and my facial expressions, noting when I drew back. I discovered that observing is not necessarily seeing. I could observe a woman's labor without seeing the person. Observing is much like what the philosopher Michel Foucault called the "clinical gaze"—a way of viewing a patient as a disease, a diagnosis, a clinical problem, somewhat less than a person.[1] In contrast, by not merely observing, and instead *seeing*, I could explore what it was like for me to be present.

Gradually I grew more comfortable. Distance—physical distance and emotional distance—seemed to dissolve. I no longer felt that I was going to drown. I could be more helpful, seeing ways in which I could relieve patients' discomfort. It felt genuine, intimate.

At first, presence was an interior experience for me; only later did I realize that it was shared. Patients responded differently when I was present. They looked back, they took my hand. The presence I could bring to a woman in labor seemed like the presence I felt as a performing musician. Being present had an impact on the care I delivered. I discovered what good midwives always knew—that you can "tell" when a woman is progressing in labor; this "telling" depends on presence. I was better able to wait before acting.

THE INEFFABLE

At its most basic, presence is made visible when the clinician makes good eye contact, responds to patients' concerns, and doesn't stand up and leave before the conversation is finished. However, when patients say their doctor is "really there," most patients are referring to a quality of being. Presence is a sense of coherence and imperturbability. Internist Tony Suchman calls it the "connexional" dimension of care, often unspoken.[2] Presence is a quality of listening—without interrupting, interpreting, judging, or minimizing. In case you hadn't noticed, doctors don't do this well. When psychologist Kim Marvel and I analyzed audio-recorded primary care office visits, we saw how doctors would get restless and take control after patients had spoken for an average of only twenty-three seconds.[3]

The philosopher Ralph Harper, in his book *On Presence*,[4] considers presence to be a "bonded resonance" in which two people are in touch and in tune with each other. Presence, according to Harper, is especially important in "boundary situations," times when people feel vulnerable, when life is particularly uncertain and when it's hard to find meaning. In medicine, these are times when patients face serious illness and loss of function, when patients and their loved ones are frightened, when there are unexpected mishaps. Presence is a gift of dignity and respect when patients need it most. Harper also points out that presence is always shared with a real or imagined other; presence requires a witness, even if that witness is another part of oneself—an observing self.[5] In that way I can be present with a patient even when a patient is unable to speak for herself.

I feel a bit daunted in trying to characterize presence, to render the ineffable visible and leave it no less wondrous. Presence has historically been the domain of poets, philosophers, and mystics; however, it is at the core of health care. When clinicians write about presence, they rarely do so using clinical language. They write stories.[6] Surgeons, internists, family physicians, and psychiatrists have described how you cannot force presence into existence, nor does presence reliably happen on its own; you have to make space within which presence can emerge. In that sense, presence depends on emptiness, getting yourself out of the way, setting aside inner chatter—what the Buddha called "monkey mind"—to connect more directly with a person, a task, or a part of yourself. Societally, more than ever we crave presence with ourselves and shared presence with others, patients and clinicians included. With our attention increasingly parsed among tasks that compete for the same set of neural pathways, we are divided into too many fragments—too many to maintain a sense of being whole. Every day our sense of presence is constantly being fractured and repaired—an exhausting prospect. Try having a conversation—a meaningful conversation—while entering data on a computer. At the least, your sentence structure becomes disjointed and you lose your train of thought.

PRESENTNESS OF TIME

Sometimes a simple gesture and a few well-placed words can signal presence. One day on rounds in the hospital, as we walked into the room, Laura Hogan, a nurse-practitioner on our palliative care team, said three words to the patient: "What beautiful flowers." The patient looked at the flowers and smiled. The previous day the patient had had a biopsy that would let her know whether her cancer had progressed; she was still awaiting the results. We all feared that the news would not be good. Laura's comment communicated that even in dire circumstances it is possible to see beauty and to honor those who loved and cared for the patient, that she was not alone. More often, though, presence is communicated nonverbally—a softness of gaze, a quality of touch, a handshake that is felt genuine rather than perfunctory, a gentle examination of a patient's tender abdomen.

Presence is also "presentness" of time. When I feel that I'm being present while caring for patients, time seems to expand or stand still. Several years ago, I went to a jazz concert by Chick Corea's group. During the opening piece, after each of the musicians had had a chance to improvise, the music reached a resting point, a silence that probably only lasted two seconds. Even though the concert was in a three-thousand-seat auditorium, everyone seemed to feel the same sense of intimacy and connection in that silence. That moment had an exquisite spaciousness, as if the outside world had ceased to exist, a spaciousness that resolved only when the musicians simultaneously struck a chord marking a new section of the music. Think of speeches by Martin Luther King Jr. or Mahatma Gandhi. You are captivated, entranced, transported, and time seems to stop or ceases altogether.

When physicians are being present, patients feel that spaciousness. I remember the first time I felt it as a patient. I was in my late teens and had not been feeling well for over a month; I was weak, tired, and feverish, with a sore throat, headaches, and no energy. I would get better for a while, then it would come back. I had recently graduated from my pediatrician to a new "adult" doctor, whom I did not know well. He was thorough and gentle as he examined my ears, throat, neck, chest, and abdomen. I presume that the physical examination was normal and uninformative; it confirmed a diagnosis that he had already made.

Time seemed to stand still. I was worried; he was imperturbably calm. He was much older than I, but that didn't seem to matter; he was warm and his eyes had a softness. I felt that he understood me and my situation, and the distance between us seemed to dissolve. He said that he'd seen this cluster of symptoms, which was probably a lingering virus, and that time would heal. He ordered a blood test just to make sure. That's all I needed.

This was the first time I felt understood and cared for—honored and respected—by a physician. I carried his presence with me after I went home and found his virtual presence quietly reassuring; I was not worrying alone. A couple of weeks later, I began to feel more myself. His image came to me years later as I was contemplating going to medical school and later during the dark moments when I wondered whether memorizing names of bacteria and reciting differential diagnoses was all that it could be about.

Later still, I discovered that I could be present in that way—and share my presence with patients. I had a new patient in my practice—Haqim, sixteen years old, muscular, confident, and robust. He had acne on his back and shoulders. He asked question after question—about hormones and how they affect the skin (and why they make people unattractive), how each medication worked, whether he could try two of them at the same time, and how long it would take for the bumps and cysts to go away.

He was worried—very worried. I listened, without interpreting or reflecting—I just listened. I explained that time would heal, with the help of a few creams and pills. After a few more questions about how the pills actually worked, he relaxed and even smiled. We spent the remaining five minutes of the fifteen-minute visit talking about his family. Since then Haqim has mentioned to me on more than one occasion that he wants to become a doctor.[7]

TIME AND INTIMACY

How can presence happen, though, when office visits are constrained to a mere fifteen to twenty minutes or even shorter? Elapsed time might be out of a doctor's control to some degree, but perceived time can always be created. I teach physicians to sit down while talking with a patient, rather than standing; in a study of surgeons making quick hospital rounds, patients felt that doctors actually spent more time when they sat down, even though the elapsed time was the same as when they stood.[8] A research colleague, Kathy Zoppi, found that parents were more satisfied when they *perceived* that pediatricians spent more time with them—the true elapsed time didn't matter as much.[9] Sometimes time is created through silence. As in music, where silences can have the same exquisite beauty as notes, silence can deepen a relationship between a doctor and a patient. It doesn't take much—a few seconds at most—to reassure a patient that the doctor is there, listening, attending, not rushed.[10] Using silence effectively is even more relevant now that visits—in the hospital and in office practice—are crammed with more administrative imperatives.

Musicians know about presence and its absence. When you're caught up in your thoughts and just going through the motions, your professional colleagues will say you're "just phoning it in." And you'll think, "I played a good concert. Wish I had been there." It's the same in medicine. When you're being present (or when you're phoning it in), patients know and you know. My mentor George Engel would say that patients want to know and understand and to feel known and understood. There's a difference between merely knowing *about* a patient and *knowing* the patient as a person. *Knowing* is much more personal and intimate. During training, supervisors and colleagues warned me of the dangers of becoming too involved with patients. Patients die, and they are ravaged by unspeakable tragedy, depredation, and abuse. Getting too close to the edge of this vortex feels dangerous. You fear that you'll lose perspective and degenerate into a mass of emotional jelly. Clearly, though, boundary situations require a *greater* sense of presence—not less. Only with a radically tenacious shared presence can a clinician maintain the sense of intimacy necessary to truly be there with a suffering patient.[11] In medicine, trainees hear little about how to do this. Staying coldly objective seems safer. It also has its perils. While doctors sometimes have to distance themselves emotionally as a survival strategy, making detachment a habit sterilizes clinical care of its richness and meaning. For me, being present means aiming for the sweet spot in which I am emotionally accessible to myself and others in a way that clarifies my vision of the patient, his clinical situation, and our relationship.

Dirk is a seventy-year-old man with paranoid schizophrenia

whom I have had in my primary care practice for over twenty years. Dirk has spent nearly all of his adult life in mental hospitals and group homes. He'd usually be laconic during our visits: I'd ask questions and he'd answer in a word or two. Over the past year, Dirk has had several episodes of passing out or nearly passing out. His blood pressure was low, likely a side effect of his psychiatric medications. While none of his injuries were serious, I was worried. That day, Dirk was his usual emotionally flat self; I couldn't tell what he was thinking. He recounted having fallen in a stairwell with the same monotone he'd use if he were reading a list of telephone numbers.

Then I said, "I'm worried," and waited. To my surprise, Dirk became more talkative. He said that he was worried too. We talked about the risks and benefits of lowering his medication doses—which might help with the episodes of passing out, but might risk worsening his psychiatric condition. He then talked about how it felt to be different, the stigma of his mental illness. I was speechless; I had completely underestimated his insight.

This brief exchange opened up a new chapter in our long relationship. In the past, I didn't feel that we had achieved any kind of connection. It took twenty years for that moment to emerge, and I now see him as more of a whole person. It's reciprocal—I get the sense that now he sees me as a person, not just "the doctor." Periodically I wonder if I had never given him a chance, that by doing the habitual doctorly things—asking questions, poking, prodding, giving advice—I had inadvertently silenced him. Now we, together, had the opportunity to make a better decision—to lower his medications. I am better able to advocate for him and to address his housing and medication needs and the social activities that give his otherwise impoverished life meaning. Dirk has slowly become more disclosing, sharing more of himself. I have a better understanding of what he fears, what he needs, what he enjoys—and who he is.

STORMY SEAS

Laura Kerner was seventy years old and enjoying her retirement until she had a heart attack followed by pneumonia, septicemia (infection in her bloodstream), and a blood clot to her lungs. During her four weeks in the hospital, despite intensive treatment, she was declining; her heart did not have sufficient reserve; she was suffocating for lack of oxygen; her liver and kidneys were failing; she was dying. She had previously said that she would not want life support if she was not expected to survive.

As the days passed, Laura had fewer and fewer lucid moments and was increasingly agitated and delirious. Suctioning her oral secretions would provoke coughing spells. Drawing blood required multiple attempts. Even moving her in bed made her short of breath and she had to be restrained to keep her from pulling out her IVs. Distressingly, the ICU team had to withhold painkillers and sedatives because they tended to lower her blood pressure. As her chances of a meaningful recovery diminished, her physicians and nurses grew increasingly distressed.

As a palliative care consultant, my job was to help Laura, her family, and the ICU team make important decisions about her care, but no one could agree on anything. Some family members thought Laura would want hospice care, whereas others demanded that "everything" be done, "no matter what." Each day the family divisions grew more acrimonious. Her son would say, "You doctors are trying to kill my mother," "You're just giving up," "She's always been a fighter and you're taking that away from her."

Doing things—explaining, offering opinions, directing—had already backfired; I certainly was *not* going to tell them what to do. All I could do was be attentive and present. I found it easy enough to be aware of my feelings of irritation and anger and my judgments about her family's motives (Are they uncaring?), capacity (Are they paranoid? Do they really understand?), and morals (Are they irresponsible?). It was another thing to set those feelings aside and welcome their questions and take in each of their views. I'd have to consider the possibility that I misperceived their motives and see my own contributions to this mess—perhaps by having taken sides when I shouldn't have. I had to cultivate a sense of hospitality.

THE GUEST HOUSE

This being human is a guest house.
Every morning a new arrival.

A joy, a depression, a meanness,
some momentary awareness comes
as an unexpected visitor.

Welcome and entertain them all!
Even if they are a crowd of sorrows,
who violently sweep your house
empty of its furniture,
still, treat each guest honorably.
He may be clearing you out
for some new delight.

The dark thought, the shame, the malice,
meet them at the door laughing and invite them in.

Be grateful for whatever comes,
because each has been sent
as a guide from beyond.
—Jellaludin Rumi
translated by Coleman Barks

The presence I was seeking had been described in a poem, "The Guest House,"[12] in which the poet Rumi commands you to welcome into awareness the dark thoughts and feelings of chaos, disruption, and powerlessness, and to respond deliberately—by being available, open, receptive, and—yes—cheerful. Easier said than done, I thought. I tried slowing down. I would take a breath and wait before responding—to make sure that I was not reacting out of anger or impatience and was not severing the tenuous connection I had with them. I invited *them* to slow down too. Even with the pressures to rush to a decision, I encouraged them to take a few more minutes to make sure they were comfortable. Eventually, they seemed more present too. They could finally respond thoughtfully to the question "Right now, what are the two or three things you'd most wish for—for Laura and your family?" With the passing days, they allowed us to provide pain medications and attend to Laura's comfort under their close watch, and they could not but notice that she was more peaceful, more comfortable. To my amazement, after she had died a few days later, her family expressed gratitude for our team's care.

MAKING SPACE

Cognitive neuroscientists are now beginning to consider how the interior and personal experience of presence manifests in the brain. As you can imagine, studying presence is one of the hard problems of neuroscience—much harder than studying attention, memory, or perception—because it is so subjective. In exploring the meager research on presence, I was surprised with what I found. My sleuthing led me to research on video games and virtual reality, environments in which people become so fully immersed that they feel that the situations are real, sometimes even more real than real life. Players enter into relationships with humanoid avatars, experiencing a sense of shared presence as if their "companion" were alive. The electronic medium and all of its artificiality seemingly vanish, and people achieve what the Italian neuroscientist Giuseppe Riva calls "embodied immersion";[13] your sense of self dissolves, perhaps like the feeling of presence that musicians, teachers, and doctors feel when they're at the top of their game.

In case you're thinking that video games are mindless and far removed from clinical practice, think again. They aren't. Computer programs now use avatars as virtual doctors and even psychotherapists—quite effectively.[14] Patients become emotionally attached to the computer figure in the same way that they might connect with a psychotherapist. Like Harry Harlow's monkeys, who, in captivity, bonded to an inanimate "mother" made of wire and cloth, humans naturally bond with other people, or what they imagine to be people, even when they know that they're not real. It's because our brains are wired to promote attachment and relationship.[15]

Social presence—or shared presence—is critical for health care. The ability of doctors to see each patient as a complete human being (and vice versa), in my view, is the basis for the trust and understanding that help the patient through the hard times. It is a learned skill, a habit of mind. It reminds me of how I'd prepare for concerts. Performing well in the rehearsal room was only part of it. I'd get the technique down and would let the music speak. Yet, I'd need additional practice to prepare for when I'd be onstage, in relationship with people who I imagined might be approving or critical, being moved or watching my every move. Similarly, clinicians have to prepare for those relationships that place them outside their comfort zone—when there is suffering, conflict, uncertainty, or loss.

It might seem straightforward how humans come to be present with and understand one another. After all, we have language and can communicate what is important to us. Yet shared presence goes beyond language. Philosophers and cognitive scientists have explored how we come to understand the minds and intentions of others, even though it's hard enough to read our own minds, much less those of other people. They emphasize that, as social beings, we *need* to understand others' internal experiences in order to cooperate, collaborate, communicate—and survive. Until recently, human understanding was thought to involve "theory of mind," that we constantly theorize about what might be going on in others' minds—what they're aware of and what they're thinking and feeling. Sometimes we try to verify whether our "theory of mind" is correct; but more often we do not. Those who lacked theory of mind were particularly impaired, such as patients with autism and schizophrenia.

A competing theory about how we understand each other is called embodied simulation, which proposes that we relive in our own bodies and minds the actions and presumed intentions of the other. For example, when I used to do deliveries, I would find myself holding my breath and straining when women were experiencing contractions; I would do this without being aware of it, then it would filter into my consciousness. I entered the raw sensuality of the experience (albeit vicariously). At the same time I could also be aware of my "doctorly" frame of reference; I'd say to myself, "When you're holding your breath and straining, perhaps it's because you know that the patient is entering the second stage of labor."

More recently, social neuroscientists, psychologists, and philosophers have taken another step further. Theory of mind and embodied simulation suggest that we are separate entities, that it is one mind understanding the completely distinct mind of another. This is only partially true. Research suggests that our minds are intertwined, so much so that it seems that our minds are not completely our own. Some part of our cognitive and emotional lives—and our identities—is shared with others.[16] I am not merely an aloof observer of a patient's experience; I am, to some extent, a participant. In that way, presence is intersubjective; it blurs the boundaries between that which is *me* and that which is *you*.[17] Intuitively this makes sense. We engage in shared mental processes all the time; married couples commonly complete each other's sentences, and doctors and patients might both recognize in the same moment that something is wrong.[18] The premise of the field of "team science"—how teams work together—is that teams have shared mental models.[19] Science has only begun to describe how shared mind happens, psychologically and neurobiologically, and the implications are profound.[20] I believe that we are at the cusp of understanding how presence happens—when shared mind is revealed to both parties.[21]

LIKE ME, NOT LIKE ME

Presence—unfortunately—is not naturally democratic. Humans are not only social organisms, we are also tribal—for better and for worse. We connect more easily with people we perceive to be similar to ourselves. "Tribe" can be whatever we define it to be— the tribe of white people, the tribe of those who speak Portuguese, the tribe of the sick, or the tribe of the poor. You might consider yourself a member of several tribes at once. As a result of their— often unconscious—tribal affiliation, people tend to see the world through a particular lens, consciously and unconsciously dividing the world into those whom they perceive as being "like me" and others who are "not like me."

Physicians are tribal too. Perhaps that's why doctors are poorly prepared to be patients when they themselves become ill. When physicians become ill, they really don't like it. Doctors don't only feel more vulnerable because of what they know (. . . and now they're going to do *that* to *me?*), they literally become strangers to themselves.[22] It's as if doctors and patients belong to different tribes, and when doctors become ill, they become involuntary members of both.

While the positive side of tribalism is a sense of belonging and communion, the dark side is bias—a set of unverified and preconceived assumptions about someone, often simply because we think that they belong to a particular group. Everyone harbors biases, whether it be about race, ethnicity, gender, body habitus, sexual behaviors, or something else.[23] Physicians, like everyone else, make different assumptions about people depending on whether they are obese or thin, male or female, black or white, Spanish-speaking or English-speaking, and a myriad of clinically relevant and clinically irrelevant factors. These biases usually are implicit—below the level of awareness.

These biases affect the care that patients receive.[24] When physicians' tribal associations prevail, the seeds of bias are sewn. Witness the early days of the AIDS epidemic, when people who superficially were very much like their treating physicians—well educated, predominantly white, generally healthy males—were "othered"; they were blamed for their illness and sometimes treated as if they were less than human. Staff left hospital food trays at their door, afraid to enter the room. Physicians avoided touching them—even long after everyone knew that HIV was only spread through intimate contact and blood products. They were made into outcasts, in part driven by clinicians' fears—of stigmatization by association, of contagion, of talking about sexual and drug use behavior, and of death.[25] While now—fortunately—the horror stories about clinicians' refusal to care for patients who were HIV infected are well behind us in most communities in the United States, this dynamic persists in large parts of the world.

Tribalism is hardwired in particular parts of the brain—the dorsomedial prefrontal cortex in particular—which respond differently if we feel that the other person is a member of our tribe. Tribalism is expressed through our hormones. Oxytocin, the hormone that promotes labor and milk production, also promotes love and nurturance within one's tribe. However, for those outside one's tribe, oxytocin has the opposite effect—it promotes aggression (think of why it's not a good idea to get between a mother bear and her cub).[26] In case you were wondering, men have oxytocin too, with the same psychological effects. Our tribal tendencies are to some extent a survival strategy—evolutionarily, we've always needed to be able to assess quickly who was friend and who was foe.[27]

The discovery of mirror neurons in the 1990s revolutionized neuroscience by providing a mechanism for human understanding. Mirror neurons fire when we observe others engaging in goal-directed tasks such as reaching for an object (the early experiments used monkeys witnessing other monkeys reaching for food). These nerve cells are located near our motor cortex—the part of the brain that controls our movements—and when they are activated, our brains simulate what it is like for the other person (or monkey) to engage in that action and thus draw conclusions about the other's intentions and goals. More recently, scientists have speculated that some areas of the brain interpret not only the physical actions of others but also their associated emotions. These emotional resonance systems are thought to be the basis of emotional intelligence and social intelligence. One such area—the anterior cingulate—seems to grow and develop in response to mindfulness training.[28]

Being present with a patient (or anyone for that matter) whom I perceive as "not like me" initially feels less natural than with others with whom I share aspects of my identity. I will admit that— initially—I relate more effortlessly to a fellow professional than to someone who is mentally ill or to a recent refugee from an embattled third-world country. It takes effort and imagination to resonate with the other person's experience. I have to ask, "What's it like?"—and hearing the answer usually connects me with a more basic and shared human experience. My brain needs to shift gears to bridge the gap between my life and his.[29]

A PRACTICE OF STILLNESS

Practicing presence, for me, is practicing becoming available (to myself and others) and practicing quieting the mind. Being available means showing up and letting patients know—through words and gestures—that there is space. Patients can recognize presence when they don't feel that they have to say, "I know you are busy, but . . ." or "Sorry to bother you with . . ." Clinicians are afraid of being too available—myself included. They're afraid that patients will call them at all hours of the day and night and invade their personal lives relentlessly. Even though I know that's a real risk, I have to remind myself that being more available often saves time. At the end of a visit, I'll say that usually I'd schedule a follow-up visit in a month, but that they can come back sooner; they usually say no but appreciate knowing that space is there. Sometimes I give out my home phone number to patients who are worried or are seriously ill. Patients rarely call, and in thirty years of practice, I can count on one hand the patients who called inappropriately. Knowing that they can reach me makes them feel that I'm present. I find that they call the practice less often; they don't feel a need to repeat and amplify their concerns.

Quieting the mind makes space within the clinician; it promotes openness. For those who are drawn to it, sitting practice offers one way to quiet the mind, and the presence that is achieved while alone can translate into presence with others. Among doctors who take the time for stillness, nearly all feel that the time one makes for contemplative practices—meditation, reflection, awareness—is soon recaptured in increased clarity. The goal of presence is not necessarily efficiency, but efficiency often arises from presence.

All contemplative practices offer ways of practicing stillness. Yet these practices do not confer immunity to strong emotion; quite the opposite. Even those who've spent thousands of hours meditating have the same kinds of reactions to stress as anyone else.[30] Their hearts race, they feel anxiety and dread, and they experience moral outrage. Research shows that these immediate emotional reactions are at least as robust in experienced practitioners as in those who've never done any contemplative practice. So why bother? The difference is that in experienced practitioners, those stress reactions abate sooner—they don't keep on reverberating. Rather, experienced practitioners discern more rapidly which emotions and experiences are "theirs," and which belong to other people—in other words, they're good at self-other differentiation.[31] They have the skill to "decenter"—they can feel their own emotions and at the same time observe them as if they were standing outside themselves. They develop a capacity for what psychologists call mentalization—they understand their own mental states rather than being oblivious of or mystified by why they feel the way they do. They have learned to see their mental states as something they can control rather than the other way around; they know that these states are transitory and not enduring, that they ebb and flow. For example, they more readily distinguish between *I am* feeling *angry*—an emotion that they can control—and *I am angry*—a person whose anger is part of their identity. They learn to set aside their immediate reactions so that they can respond more mindfully.[32] All of these skills open up space for presence. Physiologically, meditators learn to regulate the expression of certain genes that affect the number and type of receptors to the stress hormones (such as epinephrine, cortisol) that course through our systems when we're aroused and anxious, as well as the neurotransmitters (such as serotonin, dopamine, neuropeptide Y) that play a role in regulating emotion.[33] It's not that you don't have strong and sometimes-distressing feelings; while feeling their immediacy, you learn how not to be consumed or paralyzed by them.[34]

WHERE ARE MY FEET?

You can practice presence. One way is a practice called "Where are my feet?" At first glance, it seems almost too simple. Ask yourself, "Where are my feet?" Give yourself a moment to feel your feet. Are they flat on the floor? Is your weight equally on both feet? Is there any discomfort? Do you feel them inside your shoes? Do they feel strong and reliable? Pay attention to any sensations you might experience. You can do this while standing or sitting. Once you get the hang of it, see if you can ask "Where are my feet?" in a stressful situation. Use it as a way to stay present. Feet are our foundations, our sources of stability, and our engines of mobility; they maintain balance, allow us to be still, and impel us forward. By assuming a physical attitude of stability, strength, and balance, you simultaneously draw attention to and stabilize your thoughts, feelings, and emotions.[35] Your physical presence stabilizes your presence of mind.[36]

Shared presence is cultivated through deep listening. In workshops, I frequently ask participants to write about meaningful experiences in their work settings, moments of connection and times when things did not go well. Participants pair off, and each is given time to read her story or tell it in her own words. However, this is not a social conversation; it's an exercise in listening deeply, with attention, curiosity, and beginner's mind. While it's okay to ask clarifying questions about what happened and how the other person felt, and also to express understanding or empathy when appropriate, I caution listeners to be aware of their impulses to interpret, criticize, judge, or elaborate upon their colleague's emerging story—and to deliberately set those thoughts aside for the moment so that they can be present. To help them respond more mindfully, I'll suggest that listeners have some way of slowing down. For example, if they feel that they have something brilliant or insightful to say, rather than saying it right away, they might count slowly from one to five, and only then share that insight if it still seems as urgent and relevant after the short wait. Deep listening can be remarkably difficult. It feels awkward. We're so used to thinking about our responses before the other person has finished speaking—we feel we have to be doing something and not just be there. With practice, though, most people feel gratified when listening deeply, knowing that the other person feels heard and understood in a space of shared presence.

Yet another way of practicing shared presence was described by Chade-Meng Tan, who created the Search Inside Yourself "mindfulness for engineers" program at Google. In a deceptively simple exercise that he calls Just Like Me,[37] you visualize somebody in your mind and then consider—and even gently speak to yourself—phrases such as "This person has a body and a mind, just like me. This person has feelings, emotions, and thoughts, just like me. This person has, at some point in his or her life, been sad, disappointed, angry, hurt, or confused, just like me. This person has, in his or her life, experienced physical and emotional pain and suffering, just like me. This person wishes to be free from pain and suffering, just like me. This person wishes to be happy, just like me," and so on. You can easily carry this contemplative practice with you into the workplace with colleagues; it's particularly useful with people with whom you don't see eye to eye.

With this and other practices of presence, you open the door to dialogue and understanding, and you build the mental muscles to prepare for the moments when you feel the least prepared. Practicing presence helps clinicians slow down, listen more deeply, think more deliberately, shift from doing to being and from activity to stillness. Practicing presence, even for a moment, can be long enough to avoid a potential error, long enough for a patient to feel acknowledged, heard, and known.

6

Navigating Without a Map

Richard Grayson was a retired professor of epidemiology. He had been a patient of mine for the previous ten years, and I was one of his sole supports during a messy divorce. He was a lover of good food and wine and now had no appetite and couldn't tolerate alcohol. He looked gaunt and tired. He had lost twenty pounds, his skin color was a pasty white, and his eyes were slightly jaundiced. I ordered a CT scan of his abdomen, knowing that the news would not be good. He had a stage IV cancer in his liver—which likely originated in his bile ducts—aggressive and incurable.

Richard wanted to know the facts. The cancer surgeon advised him that surgery would be risky and unlikely to improve survival or quality of life. Richard said that he would never consider chemotherapy, but I encouraged him to see an oncologist, just to find out. This muddied the waters. Richard learned that chemotherapy offered a 20 percent chance of extending his life by an average of a few months while possibly improving his energy and appetite. No one could know whether he would be one of the lucky ones whose cancer would respond—or one of the 80 percent who just had side effects with no benefits at all. He consulted another oncologist, searched the Internet, and wrote to friends and colleagues, including some of the most highly regarded oncologists in the world. The options were dizzying, including a "promising" experimental treatment. Richard knew well that only 5 to 10 percent of experimental cancer drugs prove effective, and no one knew what the side effects might be.

During his entire career Richard had taught students how to design and interpret the results of clinical trials and assess the risks and benefits of treatments. He understood the statistics of his own situation well and knew how his situation was different: the average patients in those research studies were younger and their cancers were less advanced. You couldn't imagine a patient who was better informed. However, the more information and statistics that Richard acquired, the more anxious and bewildered he became. His knowledge of medicine, statistics, research methodology, and probabilities carried him just so far. Despite being well-informed, he felt lost.

Now the decision—which had seemed easy before he started his journey—was harder. He kept changing his mind. He was frightened. A rationalist, he felt that his logical, analytical brain was being hijacked by emotions. Like most patients facing a serious and complex situation, Richard was experiencing cognitive overload; the stakes were high and emotions were raw, medical evidence was unclear, and the risks and the benefits weren't completely known. He came back to see me to help sort this out. He asked, "What would you do if you were me?"

Before I move on to what happened, sit with me for a minute. Imagine you're the physician in the exam room and this question was lobbed into your court. I knew that nothing was going to save Richard's life, that having to make decisions was adding to his burden, and that he was frightened and his fear made it hard for him to think clearly. Whoever made the decision, Richard would have to live with the consequences.

Physicians dread when patients ask, "What would you do if you were me?" As a physician, you're *not* the patient, but the patient wants you to be there, with him, helping him decide. In oncology, physicians have seen countless patients refuse chemo, then with the terror of death looming, change their minds. Thus it's understandable how a doctor might say, "I've not been in that situation"— technically true, but emotionally harsh. When the question comes from a patient who has a terminal illness, it's even more difficult because it brings the physician closer to contemplating her own death. Physicians too get anxious as their patients get sicker; doctors tend to avoid direct discussions of death in favor of focusing on scans, tests, and treatments.[1]

In a previous era when physicians comfortably assumed a paternalist role, the doctor's job was to assemble the facts and provide a plan: "We should start chemotherapy this Friday. My assistant can set it up for you." The patient's voice was secondary. Now things are a bit different, but things haven't changed *that* much. Patients are commonly offered a role in decision making, but doctors often make an offer that is hard to refuse, a choiceless choice. They might say, "Research suggests that for metastatic bile-duct cancer, chemotherapy with gemcitabine plus cisplatin offers the best chance of longer survival; it can give you more time—and in most cases it's high-quality time. And if that doesn't work for you, we have other options. Does that sound reasonable? If so, we can start this Friday." Some physicians will try to build the patient's confidence: "I've had two patients recently who did well on gemcitabine plus cisplatin in similar circumstances." Some offer numerous options and provide exquisite detail about the clinical research upon which their recommendations are based. Giving a nod to patient autonomy, a physician might say, "Go home and discuss the options with your family and let me know what you'd like to do," and if pressed, might even say, "I can't really tell you what to do. Everybody's different. The choice is up to you." But the patient hears, "Chemo or die."

Richard didn't need to know more about risks and benefits for people in general; he needed wisdom in *his* unique set of circumstances. He felt adrift at sea without a compass, navigating without a map. Few people want to make such decisions alone, if for no other reason than it's difficult to think through an issue logically and analytically when faced with our own mortality. Richard needed his physician not only to advise but also to help him understand his values and feelings, cope with uncertainty, sort out his options, and navigate his way.

I sometimes hear physicians say, "It's up to you." This allows them to remain aloof and displaces fear and uncertainty to the patient, leaving the clinician with a false sense of having been patient centered. Rather than promoting the intimate discussions that patients deserve in such circumstances, it disempowers patients by depriving them of the support that they need. They're abandoned to their rights.[2] No one wants a physician who is going to fall apart when facing the possibility of the death of one of his patients, nor do they want a physician who is Teflon coated, unmoved by suffering. Shared decision making is not only providing information; it is facing uncertainty together. That's why it can be emotionally wrenching for physicians too. They have to work with the anxiety that they feel when facing uncertainty, enter into the unknown *with* the patient. Eric Larson calls it "emotional labor"—the emotional work that is part of the job.[3]

In these circumstances, patients want to have their voices heard; however, they exercise their voices less commonly than you might think. I can imagine several reasons why. Having greater choice means assuming a greater burden of responsibility. They're overwhelmed by the sheer quantity of information. They may want to please the physician. Even well-informed, highly educated patients fear that by questioning their physician, they will get lower-quality care.[4]

These factors were weighing on me as I examined Richard's abdomen. I needed time to think. I did a careful exam, not expecting to find anything new, but the exam served two other purposes. I knew that touch, in these circumstances, communicates solidarity. It also allowed me time to regroup, to think about what I could say next, something that would move him toward a decision that was right for him. I sat for a moment with the "What would you do . . . ?" question. I did not want to diminish his question by merely providing an opinion. I assumed that he was looking for understanding as well as clarity and wisdom, not just information.

I said, "Let's walk through this." I started with larger questions, hoping that within them lay the answer to the more specific question about treatment choices: "What's the hardest part? How will you know that the choice is the right one? What in your life, right now, brings you joy? Where do you want to be living, and with whom? When will you know you've done enough? Is there anything about this decision for which you'd not be able to forgive yourself?"

After each question I was silent. Not trying to direct the conversation, I was just listening. The silences were just a few seconds each, but they had a quality of spaciousness, lending a deeper emotional tone to this discussion than the discourse of scans, tests, and drugs that had dominated most of Richard's prior visits with his physicians. Some of the questions went unanswered. It was hard to be silent; it would have been easier to dispense information, recommendations, reassurances. But, by choosing to live with the questions rather than fill the space with mere answers, something else happened. Those five minutes led us to a greater sense of shared understanding. My just listening exposed me to his angst, not just his dilemma. I understood him better and he understood himself better.

"I'm willing to take the chance with the high-dose chemo," he said. "But, I first need to ask whether I can switch to the low dose if it's too much for me." This decision was not "my" decision nor was it Richard's; it was shared, having emerged through conversation, through being together; the decision was navigation more than negotiation. I was surprised; I had misjudged him. Somehow I thought he—as a scientist—would have decided otherwise, given the actuarial odds. He wanted the moon shot and was willing to tolerate the pain.

While this may have been the right choice for *him*, others would have chosen differently. He had enough information and advice, so I asked and didn't recommend. Richard had few side effects from the chemo and enjoyed a reasonable quality of life until six months later, when the tumor again started to grow. He was soon in hospice; he felt that he had made the best choices under the circumstances; he had no regrets.

IT DEPENDS

Health planners Sholom Glouberman and Brenda Zimmerman describe decisions as simple, complicated, or complex.[5] Richard's decision was hardly simple, but Mary Ann's was. A twenty-five-year-old software engineer with all of the typical symptoms of a urinary tract infection, she saw me the same day as Richard. She'd had a similar episode the previous year that resolved after a day of antibiotics. It didn't take much to come to a diagnosis and prescribe an appropriate treatment. The choice among two or three potentially effective antibiotics was based on cost and convenience. I simply followed a recipe, something that barely requires medical training.

But what if Mary Ann also had a high fever and back pain that suggested it was more than a bladder infection? Let's say she had diabetes or kidney stones. Or she was pregnant. This is more serious. The stakes are higher. The decision about which tests to order and which antibiotics to use and whether she needs to be hospitalized also depends on a myriad of social factors such as whether she has someone at home who could watch out for her and whether she has insurance coverage. This is now a complicated problem.

Glouberman and Zimmerman describe complicated problems as a bit like sending a rocket to the moon—you need more than a recipe. You need knowledge and formulas and the expertise to know how to consider a myriad of factors, from ambient temperature to wind speed to availability of personnel to guide the process. Still, the goal is clear and unwavering. There might be several possible trajectories, but all use the same principles of physics. Having sent a rocket to the moon once makes you more confident that you can do it again.

A typical complicated decision is the choice between lumpectomy (removing part of the breast) plus radiation, or a total mastectomy, for breast cancer. Although the treatments offer an equal chance for long-term survival, patients have to live with the trade-offs: convenience, quality of life, body image, and risks of recurrence. Each patient has to figure out what *she* wants, not what anybody else might want.[6] Doctors can help patients choose, recognizing that the patient's choice may differ from what they might want for themselves.[7]

Richard's problem was beyond complicated—it was complex. In

the words of economist Charles Lindblom, in the face of complexity people "muddle through."[8] They set an initial goal, then reorient and redirect their efforts based on evolving information. This is not necessarily a bad thing. Complexity means unpredictability and competing imperatives, and the goal may not be clear until having embarked on a path. At the outset of his illness Richard might have said—like most people—that he wanted to live longer, enjoy a good quality of life, maintain his dignity, and be with family and at home. Sometimes all goals are possible to achieve, but for people with serious illnesses, often they are not, and decisions—such as the decision to embark on chemotherapy—are provisional and conditional. If Richard had had a bad reaction to his first round of chemotherapy, it's likely that he'd have changed course.

Complex decisions have always been part of medical practice. But, in the past twenty-five years, complexity has skyrocketed. In 1990 there was one medication to treat AIDS; now there are more than twenty-five that can be combined in many ways. Ditto for cancer. For nearly every disease I treat as a family physician, including diabetes, heart failure, and high blood pressure, the options have expanded exponentially, and the guidelines that purport to simplify them are ever changing.

In the face of complexity, the mind strives for efficiency. Too often—to paraphrase H. L. Mencken—we find an answer that is "clear, simple, and wrong."[9] Being mindful, in contrast, means taking in the full catastrophe and being reluctant to oversimplify;[10] you use protocols and guidelines but aren't constrained by them; you don't indulge in an illusion of certainty when ambiguity prevails. You assign a diagnosis and continue to maintain an open mind. You know when to break rules and by how much. You know when to seek patient input that can lead to even better choices.

Part of what I love about my work—in family medicine and in palliative care—is that there is a map, but like the areas on navigational charts from the early explorers that blur into the background, it just doesn't have enough detail. In a cookbook that I picked up in India, one of the recipes instructs to add "asafetida to taste" and "cook until nice," not particularly helpful instructions if you've never cooked Indian food before. It feels that way in clinical practice sometimes. Even for common conditions, the answer often is "It depends . . ."[11] Working with complexity requires what William James called "a large acquaintance with particulars"—details of patients and their lives—"that often makes us wiser than the possession of abstract formulas, however deep."[12] The particulars I deal with every day have to do with knowing each patient as a person, his genetics and habits, how he responds to illness, whom he lives with and whom he cannot live without, and how his wishes and aspirations affect his decisions. Finding out what makes patients tick is detective work, the kind of work that anthropologists and investigative reporters do, a human science, recognizing that every patient is, to some degree, an "n-of-1 study," without a control group, and that you have to rely on intuitions and gut feelings. You need know how the patient's world and your own world intersect.

PRACTICAL WISDOM

In medicine, knowledge of diseases, diagnoses, guidelines, and clinical evidence carry you just so far. When you're choosing a doctor, you want one who has something that Aristotle called *phronesis*, loosely translated as "practical wisdom." *Phronesis* is about choosing which actions will serve *this* patient best, right now. William James said, "All human thinking is essentially of two kinds—reasoning on the one hand and narrative, descriptive, contemplative thinking on the other."[13] Good decision makers use both.

Wise decisions in the face of complexity require the whole mind—the thinking mind, the sensing mind, the feeling mind—not just the logical/analytic mind. Just as Richard needed to feel his way through a complex situation, I needed to feel my way too; logic was not enough and the decision was not merely an actuarial task. Nor was it discovery in the usual sense; we did not add to the facts of the case. The decision was relational. We collectively made sense of a bewildering set of information and, to do so, invited multiple perspectives—mine, his oncologists', his family's, his own; we asked questions, built stories about how different choices might devolve, and created partnerships that enabled Richard to clarify his values, goals, and preferences—to exercise his autonomy. This was an intimate project, not merely tolerating ambiguity but embracing it.[14]

SHARED MIND

In my visits with Richard we moved—sometimes haltingly, sometimes directly—toward something I've come to call shared mind.[15] Talking about a "mind" that was shared between us and yet is owned by neither of us is no longer the province of science fiction; as I described in chapter 5, shared mind is at the cutting edge of social neuroscience research. Social neuroscientists are now able to describe how two minds collaborate, how thoughts, emotions, and sensations are constantly shaped by the social relationships that surround us, so much so that thought is shared. "Hyperscanning" research—in which two individuals' brains are scanned while they consider a shared task and communicate with each other—shows how the same areas of the brain are activated in both people to an astounding degree.[16]

I find the neuroimaging research provocative because it sets the stage for interpersonal mindfulness. Just as *intra*personal mindfulness is about knowing one's own mind—one's intentions, aspirations, goals, and foibles—*inter*personal mindfulness is about knowing others'. In all human interactions, we read one another's minds—our intentions, emotions, and thoughts. Doctors do it and so do patients. Mind reading is tricky, though. We make inferences about others' thinking based not only on what we consciously see and hear, but also from information that is outside of everyday awareness; even the beginnings of a smile, a tone of voice, or a brief glance away can build or undermine a relationship (if you're in doubt, read Austen or Proust). People also "read" and respond to each other's pheromones—those smells that we give off that provide subliminal signals about attraction, anxiety, and anger.[17] Our olfactory neural pathways go directly from the nose to the emotion-sensing parts of our brains, in particular the amygdala, which likely also affects our moods and the decisions we make. In this soup of neurotransmitters, deciding together in the face of complexity and strong emotions requires more than one mind. Richard needed to recruit additional help to come to a decision. In this case, two minds were better than one.

A STIFF NECK

I was an intern working in the pediatric emergency department when a young child came in with a high fever in the middle of a frigid January night, brought by understandably worried parents. A respiratory virus was going around. I was hoping that was all it was. I examined the child—irritable, crying. I had been taught that "irritable and inconsolable" equals a hospital admission, and I was relieved when his mother consoled him after a few minutes.[18]

The child was warm to the touch and had a fever of 39.5°C (about 103°F). Protocol in these situations called for a careful physical examination focusing on finding an explanation for the fever, and if no explanation could be found, to do a lumbar puncture—a spinal tap. His eardrums were a bit red, likely from crying and not from infection, and he had a cough but no signs of pneumonia. The examination was otherwise unrevealing.

Then I examined the child's neck to assess if it was stiff or supple. He did not like being taken from his mother's arms, and as I flexed his neck gently, he cried and reached for her. I tried it again, with him in his mother's lap, and it went a bit better. His neck didn't feel stiff—or at least not stiff enough to be called "stiff." But it wasn't really supple either. I flexed his neck again, noting that he didn't flex his hips; if he had, that would have been a classic sign of meningitis. I was a bit relieved, but not completely so; still I needed to convince myself that the child would be okay. I drew some blood and sent it off to the lab. A few minutes later the results came back; the white count was normal, and that tipped the balance. I could now justify not obtaining spinal fluid. I sent the child home and told his parents to bring him back to the clinic in the morning, just a few hours hence.

I went back to the on-call room, but I didn't sleep well, a telling sign that something still felt unresolved. In retrospect I knew that I had convinced myself that things were more "all right" than they might have been. That this all happened at four in the morning changed everything. To do a lumbar puncture, I'd have needed to wake my supervising resident. He was somewhat disagreeable. He'd say that he didn't "mind" being woken at night, but I and others knew otherwise. So I didn't wake him. Had it been at four in the afternoon rather than four in the morning, I would likely have done the lumbar puncture. Fortunately, within a few hours the child had improved. But not doing the lumbar puncture simply because I didn't want to face the possibility of humiliation was still the wrong choice. This time I was lucky, and so was the child; another child with the exact same symptoms and lab tests could have had meningitis. A near miss. Next time I might not be so lucky.

To put all of this into perspective, I'm not alone. A recent article by oncologist Ranjana Srivastava chronicled how she didn't speak up about the safety of planned surgery for a lung tumor;[19] her gut told her to contact the surgeon, but she didn't because she assumed that the surgeon—who was well-known and well-respected—knew what he was doing. She was right and the surgeon was wrong; the patient died. Three other physicians later voiced that they had had doubts, but were afraid that they might have been wrong and so didn't speak up. The surgeon was horrified that others perceived him to be so intimidating.

It is not just in the emergency room, in cancer surgery, or in terminal illness that complex decisions arise. In primary care, I often have to assess which patients with uncontrolled type 2 diabetes should start insulin injections rather than continue with their oral medications. On the surface this might seem a simple problem—there *are* clinical practice guidelines about this issue. However, the real wisdom of clinical practice is to know when to break the rules. In the past couple of years I've broken the diabetes rule several times—with an obese man who was successfully losing weight and whose diabetes would likely improve if he continued, with a woman with progressing metastatic breast cancer, with a homeless young man with a history of suicide attempts who had panic attacks at the thought of a needle, with a frail eighty-year-old woman who wouldn't live long enough to suffer the long-term consequences of diabetes, with a woman who lived alone in a remote location making it harder to get help if she had an insulin reaction. Each of these situations required *phronesis* based on an appreciation of the particulars; amassing more facts and calculating probabilities would amount to what internist Faith Fitzgerald called "the punctilious quantification of the amorphous,"[20] trying to divide a raw egg by slicing it with a sharp knife. No matter how sharp the knife, you end up with a runny mess. The knife is a good tool, just not the right one.

Nonetheless, physicians are now judged by that punctilious quantification. If I don't prescribe insulin and the patient's blood sugar becomes slightly out of control, my care will be considered inadequate even if tighter control might actually have made the patient's health worse;[21] the patient is now considered to have "uncontrolled diabetes," the medical assistants in my office flag the chart for special attention, and insurers consider it a blemish that justifies denying financial bonuses based on "quality."

Glouberman and Zimmerman point out that addressing complex problems is like raising a child. The goal is a healthy outcome, not necessarily a predictable or identical one. If you have more than one child, each turns out differently, even if you've provided the same love, nurturance, guidance, caring, and patience. If you're fortunate, each child will live a fulfilling life, but in different and unpredictable ways. Parenting books and advice are helpful but only up to a point. Then you have to muddle through. As soon as you feel a sense of mastery, though, a new phase arises for which you are again unprepared. There is no clear path and sometimes no map at all.

DECISION SCIENCE

In medicine, sometime in the 1960s decision making was elevated from the realm of intuition and experience to what is now called decision science. By the 1970s, experts proposed that medical decisions be made based on clinical evidence.[22] Clinical questions would be translated quantitatively, such as "Consider a hundred patients with atrial fibrillation [an abnormal heart rhythm that can lead to blood clots and strokes]. Assuming that their risk of stroke is about 5 percent per year, how many patients would you have to treat with blood thinners to reduce the risk of stroke to 2 percent?" No one wants to have a stroke, but blood thinners have their downsides too—not only hemorrhage, but also the annoyance of getting blood tests every week or two to adjust the dose of the medication. It's a balance. To address the balance, researchers developed the concept of "utilities" to quantify the degree to which a life with a small stroke would be worth living, and the degree to which taking a blood thinner, going for frequent blood draws, and the possibility of a hemorrhage would diminish quality of life. This approach often displayed decision trees with multiple branches, each branch ultimately leading to the "right" decision in a specific circumstance, depending on the individual's level of risk.

Proponents of decision algorithms were puzzled when the algorithms were infrequently adopted. They learned that clinicians and patients just didn't think that way, nor did they *want* to. The idea that every patient would have the same "utilities" seemed particularly presumptuous; individual patients might have different values and preferences than the group as a whole,[23] and modeling the sometimes-unstable preferences of individuals faced with complex decisions quickly becomes a statistical nightmare. These models tended to assume that humans are rational decision makers, a proposition that is both attractive and ludicrous—attractive because it improves the likelihood that decisions reflect our underlying values, and ludicrous because so many nonrational factors influence the choices that we make. Psychologists Daniel Kahneman and Amos

Tversky, for example, described how decisions framed as avoiding a loss result in different choices when framed as opportunities for gain.[24] Their experiments explored how humans are not entirely rational even when they seem to be acting logically, and that the biases and heuristics that drive decisions are often below the level of awareness. If a close friend had a complication from a particular medication, wouldn't you feel a bit more reluctant to take it—even if you knew that complication was a one-in-a-million event? And if you were that friend's physician, wouldn't you also be more reluctant to prescribe it even knowing that the chance of the same event happening twice is vanishingly small? Recognizing that patients and physicians are just as vulnerable to unconscious biases as anyone else, decision scientists embraced models of "bounded rationality."[25] But if we're not entirely rational and biases are below the level of awareness, how do we monitor them? Here's where metacognition comes in—literally thinking about your own thinking (and feelings too), regulating your inner operating system, or, in emergency-room physician Patrick Croskerry's words, regulating your own "mindware."[26]

As Croskerry points out, good decisions require a kind of education that most clinicians don't yet receive—an education about how their own minds work so that they can more readily assess their biases and engage strategies to correct them. This "education" is more than reading a book about neuropsychology. He adds that de-biasing involves uncoupling one's observations from expectations, interpretations, and premature judgments. Good decisions also require mental stability, affect regulation, and clarity of purpose—in a word, mindfulness.

Research now demonstrates how attention training and compassion training can increase awareness of our own biases and thus reduce their influence on decision making.[27] Through training, implicit mental processes—including biases—are more accessible to awareness. You hesitate for a moment before reacting; you become more discerning and you uncouple expectations (what you think you'll see) from observations (what you do see). You reconsider.

INTUITION

In medical school we were taught a protocol for diagnosing skin conditions. We'd describe the location of the lesions, their color, whether their margins were distinct or fuzzy, whether their surface was smooth or scaly, and whether they were raised or flat. Based on those features we were taught to propose a list of possible diagnoses, rank them in order of likelihood, and select the most likely. This seems simple enough, but it's not the way that experienced dermatologists actually diagnose skin lesions. When experienced dermatologists try to follow the medical student protocol, they fall down; instead they rely on first impressions.[28] Similarly, experienced doctors know when a patient's story just doesn't "add up" or something doesn't quite "look right."

At first, decision scientists tried to debunk intuition. This is understandable. They were trying to correct the excesses of a prior generation of physicians who, in their arrogance, believed that the care they delivered was better than their colleagues' and relied only on anecdotes to support their views. In their zeal, though, decision scientists were blind to the opposite problem, that when decision making is totally dominated by analytic thinking, doctors get into a different kind of trouble. The challenge is to cultivate an informed intuition that can guide but not completely dominate the decision-making process.

Intuition is murky, visceral, impressionistic, and irrational, making it difficult to describe and study. However, intuition is vital for making sense of complex situations. The current generation of decision scientists take intuition seriously, but still have difficulty describing what it is and how it works. That is because, in part, intuition isn't just one thing, and it goes by different names—gut feelings, fast thinking, fuzzy traces, Type 1 processing—each of which is slightly different in its emphasis on thoughts, emotions, visceral sensations, and memories.[29] Some types of intuition may be employed when encountering familiar problems, such as the dermatologists' pattern recognition, whereas other types of intuition act as a guide to novel situations by helping the decision maker see similarity or analogy to prior situations, or they involve emotional or social intelligence—how to know and interact with others.

In the last decades of the twentieth century, groundbreaking work by neurologist Antonio Damasio suggested that the ability to make wise choices depends on awareness of one's own emotions and those of others—a view that had previously been considered radical by research psychologists and cognitive scientists. In his book, *Descartes' Error*, Damasio discusses the case of Phineas Gage, an unfortunate man who, in 1848, sustained a severe brain injury that impaired one of his frontal cortices, the part of the brain that confers awareness and regulates emotions. Mr. Gage survived the injury, and the rest of his brain was remarkably intact. His memory and abstract logic were good and he could carry on normal conversations. He was able to hold a job, at least for a while. Yet, according to his physician at the time, Gage's personality changed; he was "manifesting but little deference for his fellows, impatient of restraint or advice when it conflicts with his desires, at times pertinaciously obstinate, yet capricious and vacillating, devising many plans of future operations, which are no sooner arranged than they are abandoned in turn for others appearing more feasible."[30] With the loss of his prefrontal cortex, he had lost the ability to recognize and regulate his emotions, anticipate the consequences of his actions, or learn from his mistakes; as a result many of his personal decisions were disastrous.

It makes sense that emotions and intuitions would be important in making life choices. Imagine if this weren't so. Few people would choose a life partner by starting with a list of attributes, then going down a checklist with each potential candidate until the one with the most points wins. Most of us would consider the potential partner's list of attributes while also listening with the heart and the gut—messages from the body that only later can we frame as part of the story of falling in love. This may be as true with complex medical decisions; clinical evidence can only take us so far, and the heart and the gut must also speak.[31]

If emotions, social cognition, and intuition are essential to decision making, how can they be cultivated? The clinician who is willing to engage in the inner work that it requires has two main tasks: moving from fragmented mind to whole mind, and from individual mind to shared mind. Evidence suggests that the potential for whole mind and shared mind is innate. But physicians' professional training undernourishes these capacities.

SAYING NO

A colleague, Stu Farber, died of acute myelogenous leukemia at age sixty-seven. Stu was a palliative care physician and was dealt a difficult and rare diagnosis, one from which only a quarter of patients live for five years and even fewer are cured. In an article written shortly before his death,[32] Stu recounts that he was hospitalized with pneumonia. The chemotherapy had predictably suppressed his immune system. The infectious disease consultant explained that while Stu's pneumonia was likely due to a virus and would likely resolve on its own, it might be a more lethal infection, Pneumocystis, the agent responsible for most of the early deaths from AIDS. To tell the difference between a virus and Pneumocystis would require an invasive lung biopsy under sedation, but given how ill Stu was, there was a greater risk of complications from the procedure, and at best it would take him a few days to recover.

Stu knew that he was dying, but if this was Pneumocystis his life might be prolonged with treatment. His doctors implied that not to do the procedure would be unthinkable, but the pulmonologist still asked, "What do you want to do?" Stu was caught between two worlds—his familiar world as a clinician and the new, and strange, world of being a patient. Fortunately, Stu had the presence of mind to say that he was now comfortable and didn't want to rock the boat; he didn't want the biopsy and would take his chances. To his surprise, the physician then said, "That's the same choice that I would make."

What is stunning about this story and many others like it is that physicians can make very different choices when it comes to their own care than what they might recommend to their patients.[33] Physicians tend to recommend the most aggressive care for their patients, even when that care is likely to cause further discomfort and disability. Yet, when physicians themselves (reluctantly) join the "tribe of the sick," they may want fewer aggressive life-prolonging measures, instead focusing to a greater degree on their comfort and dignity.

How could this be? Even in his final weeks of life, Stu was astute, seeing that while his physicians couldn't easily place themselves in his shoes, they might be able to move beyond protocol and cold logic and appreciate the patient's perspective. But it took prompting by a particularly clear-sighted and knowledgeable patient. Here, Stu's physician, like many others, breathed a sigh of relief when Stu chose to forgo aggressive treatment and to focus on comfort—it unburdened the physician from having to make the decision. But few patients have the knowledge and the clarity to question physicians' recommendations and would benefit from physicians' efforts to apply a beginner's mind to decisions that initially seem self-evident.

BEING A DOCTOR BEING A PATIENT

As I was recovering from an attack of kidney stones, my primary care physician ordered an ultrasound of my kidneys to determine if there were any residual stones. I had had stones before, and a number of ultrasounds and CT scan reports were in my medical records. The ultrasonographer was friendly and chatty, and I enjoyed being able to make out a few anatomical structures on the screen as she scanned my left kidney (where the stone had been), then my right. She seemed to be taking a particularly long time on the right side and taking a lot of snapshots on the computer. Then she went quiet. I noticed that she was lingering quite a bit north of kidneys, ureters, and bladder; we were in liver territory. Perhaps she had found a gallstone, I thought.

I asked what was going on. Generally, technicians are not supposed to reveal findings until they are confirmed by the attending radiologist, but she knew that I was a doctor and had also been looking at the screen. She was reticent at first, then said, "There's something interesting I need to check out with the radiologist." In medicalese, *interesting* is never good. The radiologist explained, "Not only had the ultrasonographer looked at the urinary tract, she also noticed something going on in the liver." She had found an incidentaloma—a baseball-size something-or-other that apparently no one had seen before. I had no interest in having it be *my* incidentaloma; it was an unwelcome guest.

Over the past twenty years I have become personally acquainted with several incidentalomas. In medical slang, an incidentaloma is a surprise, a mass or lesion unexpectedly identified during a routine examination or imaging procedure—X-ray, scan, or ultrasound—or during surgery. Originally referring to benign tumors of the adrenal glands that were completely harmless, the term is now applied to any mass that you're not looking for. Incidentalomas make simple situations complex. While an incidentaloma is usually of no clinical significance, it isn't always. Occasionally, it might be cancer.

The radiologist was diligent. He went back to a CT scan from seven years before, also done after a kidney stone. There it was. No one had noticed it because they weren't looking for it; they had no reason to look for a liver mass. Even with my untrained eye, I could see a subtle shadow there. The radiologist estimated that in the seven years since the CT scan, it had grown in diameter by one millimeter. He was sure that it had grown; the scans are quite accurate. He thought it looked like benign nodular hyperplasia, a harmless nondisease that had gone undetected until scanners got more sophisticated and ultrasonographers more proficient. I did some quick calculations. One millimeter does not sound like a lot, but it might be a 10 percent increase in volume or even more depending on whether it was round or irregularly shaped. That's still pretty slow. I was fifty-two at the time, and I calculated that at that rate of doubling, I'd still have at least some of my liver uninvaded at age ninety. This did not provide much solace, though.

The options were to do nothing and take my chances, do a biopsy to get a definitive diagnosis and risk bleeding or infection, or do a series of MRI scans to see if it was growing at a detectable rate. But, at one millimeter every seven years, you'd have to do a lot of scans over a long time—expensive, unpleasant, and anxiety provoking.

A large part of my professional life consists of helping people make difficult decisions, and I thought of myself as quite capable of making difficult decisions in general. Or so I thought until I found myself asking the same question of my primary care physician that Richard Grayson had asked me only a few months previously: "What would you do?" Now I understood what it felt like to have all of the facts yet to be unable to decide—and how different it was to be on the other side of the stethoscope. My rational mind and emotional mind were at war. Rationally, I knew that one-third of the population has some kind of incidentaloma if you look hard enough, and that over 90 percent of these are benign—and that mine had all of the characteristics of a benign tumor. But it didn't help to hear about other people's incidentalomas because mine was *mine*. I was living with uncertainty—and it was different from anyone else's.

Having a good imagination was a curse. I was convinced that I had the worst kind of liver cancer. I just wanted it cut out, whatever it might be. I thought about whether I'd prefer to have a liver transplant in Rochester, or in Pittsburgh or in Cleveland, where they had more experience. Then I thought about canceling my appointment with my primary care physician, just wanting to forget about it entirely.

Fortunately, my doctor was a good listener. He didn't challenge my fears; he listened patiently. He was quiet for a while, then asked me what I was thinking. I said that I wanted to forget about it. He said he was anxious too and had consulted a couple of his colleagues, who also doubted that forgetting about it would be the wisest choice. That was not what I wanted to hear. I didn't like the idea of getting a biopsy. Nor did he. We chose a middle way—getting a scan every four months for a year. I didn't like that option either; it would prolong uncertainty for months, and even though I knew that the likelihood of finding something serious was small, I would be anxious prior to each test. Yet, I found solace in the knowing that the decision—and the anxiety—was shared. Just like Richard Grayson, I sought shared mind, not just advice or facts.

That I'm sitting here writing about my incidentaloma eight years later means that it is unlikely to be a cancer. But that doesn't mean zero. I chuckled when a few weeks later the MRI scan report identified yet another incidentaloma in my liver, most likely a small tangle of blood vessels, as well as a not-completely-simple cyst (as it was once described to me) in my right kidney that had been seen on a previous set of scans. The next two scans showed no growth of the liver mass nor of any of its "friends." My uninvited guests had become permanent cohabitants, ones with whom I had to make peace.

7

Responding to Suffering

The word *suffering* is strikingly absent in conversations among physicians and patients.[1] Physicians commonly talk about pain, disability, stress, coping, and quality of life. In the research world I inhabit, my scientist colleagues talk about diminished "health-related quality of life" and fewer "quality-adjusted life years." But none of these terms have quite the same meaning as *suffering*, which implies a more personal and pervasive distress, one that affects someone's identity — the ability to be oneself and to be in the world. Suffering is more than symptom checklists and "rate your pain from one to ten."

It's not that doctors don't know what it means to suffer; many people decide to go into medicine as a result of their own suffering or that of a close family member or friend. That suffering might not be dramatic or life threatening, but it usually does raise the specter of impermanence. For me it was childhood asthma. I wanted to understand what was happening to me, why I couldn't run more than a few yards without getting short of breath, why I was different from other kids, and what the future might hold. If I had been born a few decades later, I'd have explored everything about asthma I could find on the Internet. Instead, I turned to our home encyclopedia and learned all I could about asthma and, later, the human body and the illnesses that could afflict it.

But not until two years after college did I decide to change my life course from aspiring musician to physician. I was living in Amsterdam, studying music, and had taken a month off to visit a good friend who was on a Fulbright grant in Varanasi, the spiritual capital of Hinduism, on the banks of the Ganges. Here suffering was made visible. Amid the heat, noise, squalor, and wandering cows, I saw beggars with missing limbs, old men blinded by trachoma with spines deformed by tuberculosis, children with unrepaired cleft palates, and families that had never known anything but hunger. Occasionally, a black sedan with tinted windows would dodge the human and animal masses, carrying the materially content from one island of tranquility to another.

After a few days in Varanasi, I borrowed a bicycle and rode eight miles to the deer park in Sarnath, where the Buddha delivered his first discourse on suffering. By the end of the ride I was hot, dusty, and thirsty. And there, at the entrance to the deer park was an orange-juice vendor, squeezing oranges. The juice was delicious—so cold and sweet.

By the next morning I had developed a fever and abdominal pain. I felt bloated and weak and didn't want to move. I *saw* the vendor squeezing the juice, just juice, no water. Or so I thought. I later learned that orange-juice vendors were notorious for surreptitiously cutting the juice with (presumably contaminated) water. Typhoid was endemic.

I had to get tested. A bicycle rickshaw transported me to the clinic a mile away. There, in the waiting areas, I saw hundreds of people crowded into oppressively hot small spaces, spilling over into the street, wailing in misery and grief, with open fractures. Smells of blood, urine, and vomit. I was overwhelmed by it all and petrified about my own situation—I knew that people could die from typhoid.

A nurse quickly ushered me into a small room. The doctor was dressed in an immaculate starched white tunic. He took my symptoms seriously and examined me carefully. He said that I did not need to be hospitalized, but that I should have blood tests and return the next morning. The test for typhoid was negative, and over the next few days I recovered. But the images of suffering remained indelible. Only later did the irony of the situation—a visit to Sarnath and a lesson in suffering—dawn on me.

A few weeks later, back in Amsterdam, I was awakened before dawn by a viselike pain on the right side of my abdomen, extending to my flank and back. I suspected that it might be a kidney stone; I'd had a friend who'd had one and described it as the worst pain imaginable. His description was no exaggeration; no matter which way I moved, I couldn't get comfortable. Even more than in India, I felt desperate. I needed the pain to stop. Immediately. Again, I was scared.

Luckily, my roommate had a car. She drove me to the university hospital. The emergency room was quiet. I don't recall seeing other patients, even in the waiting room. Soon I was on a gurney, being wheeled down empty corridors, all painted stark white, no windows. The doctor too was all in white—white jacket, white pants. He told me that I'd need an X-ray. Then everyone disappeared and I was left alone in that sterile landscape, without a person in sight, squirming, writhing in pain, not sure what would happen next. One of the nurses came out from behind a closed door and told me to stop moving and not to moan. Then *she* disappeared. Minutes passed. Everything took on a surreal quality. Eventually, someone started an IV and someone else did an X-ray to look for the stone. With some IV pain medications I was pain-free within an hour or two. I went home and was even well enough to go to a concert that evening. In that respect, the care I'd received was excellent. One could say that my health situation had resolved itself.

Except it hadn't. I still felt shaken and vulnerable. And since the X-ray hadn't identified a stone, I was also left with uncertainty. With no definitive diagnosis, I went back for three follow-up visits. Each time, I was asked to produce a small specimen of urine, then interrupt the flow so the doctor could perform a vigorous rectal examination (the technical term, *prostatic massage*, doesn't fully capture the experience), then I'd produce a second specimen, again interrupting the flow, then I'd produce a third. I had two more appointments during which these urinary acrobatics were repeated, and I finally got up the courage to ask, "Why are you doing this?" The doctor explained matter-of-factly that because I had recently been in India, and because they had not identified a stone, they needed to test for other things, including tuberculosis. One clue, he said, could come from a culture of prostatic fluid. The prospect of TB did not sound good. If he had explained this in the first place, it would have left me feeling less embarrassed and also less anxious about what was going on. The TB tests were negative, and we all assumed that this was indeed a kidney stone. I was discharged from the clinic; the doctor's parting words were that I didn't need to come back and that I should drink lots of water. Since then I've had several more episodes. Now, I dread ending up in an emergency room where I might be mistaken for a "drug seeker" and denied pain relievers. Interestingly, no physician has ever thought to ask how having had kidney stones has affected me.

These illness experiences tipped the balance and pushed my decision to go into medicine. I resolved never to let any patient of mine feel abandoned in this way. I learned, in a visceral way, that doctors could reduce or worsen a patient's suffering not only through treatments but also by how they behaved and how they chose to share information—or not. I envisioned my job as not merely to prescribe treatments, but also to heal through sharing information, being present, and being kind. I had no idea how difficult that could be.

INCONVENIENT TRUTHS ABOUT SUFFERING

There are several inconvenient truths about suffering. The first is that even when diseases are considered "cured," suffering can persist. Recently, I cared for a young man who had worked as a skilled machinist. He had been cured of his leukemia with a bone marrow transplant. While this was clearly reason for celebration, he now lived in chronic pain from graft-versus-host disease, a condition in which the transplanted white blood cells—his body's new immune system—rejected the host cells from his own intestinal tract and skin. He could barely eat due to abdominal pain and nausea, and his skin was raw and prone to infection. At age thirty-five, he was facing amputation of both legs due to chronic, untreatable skin infections that had spread to the bone. He spent more than half of his time in hospitals and the rest recuperating at home, socially isolated and impoverished due to his illness. He could barely get out of bed, and his pain required high doses of narcotics. This situation was deeply poignant for his family and the clinical team; he was considered a "survivor," yet each medical "success" only seemed to increase his suffering. I noticed that clinical staff didn't relish entering his room—he was a living reminder of our failures.

Diseases that have no symptoms at all can also cause suffering. Recently I had a patient—also a physician—who was diagnosed with high blood pressure, commonly described as a "silent killer." At first he tried to convince himself—and me—that what he had was "white-coat hypertension"—when patients have normal blood pressure except when in the presence of a doctor. To make sure, I had him wear a blood-pressure monitor for twenty-four hours. I discussed the report with him a few days later, and even though there were only a few normal readings (mostly while he was asleep), he said to me, "I'm not really hypertensive; it's just that my blood pressure is high at times." I was surprised, because he—as a physician—would routinely prescribe antihypertensive medications to patients every day.

This physician-patient offered insight into why some people avoid coming to the doctor, and why others take their medications only when they feel "tense," or not at all. People feel differently about themselves when they are given a diagnosis; they go from being an ordinary citizen to being a reluctant patient. Sometimes they feel less well, or simply flawed, fragile, or not quite whole; sometimes, as studies show, they end up missing more days of work, even though the disease is asymptomatic.[2] I asked him why he was so reluctant to take medications. He said it made him feel like a failure. Having lived a life of healthy eating, meditation, and exercise, he thought that he could somehow manage to avoid high blood pressure despite a genetic predisposition, as if virtue could trump DNA. I said, "Genetics is powerful, isn't it?" We both wished that things might have been otherwise. The pills, which he ultimately was willing to take, might lower his blood pressure but not his sense of failure. About the latter, I wouldn't have known had I not asked.

Sociologist Arthur Frank recounts how he experienced intense health-related suffering even in the absence of pain, illness, or disease. A "suspicious spot" was found on an X-ray several years after a presumed cure of his testicular cancer.[3] He knew all too well that when testicular cancer recurs, often it cannot be cured. Contemplating harsh chemotherapy and an uncertain future, his anxiety was disabling. Ultimately, further testing proved negative—he was and is cancer-free—but he was struck by how his suffering during that waiting period went unnoticed and published an account as a reminder to physicians that "routine" diagnostic tests are rarely routine for the patient.

Even though doctors experience that same kind of anxiety as Frank when they themselves become patients, when in the physician role they find themselves glibly ordering diagnostic tests even for incurable illnesses such as HIV, lupus, or cancer. When executing the series of mouse clicks to order a test, I can forget that, at the same time, a patient might be contemplating his demise. Patients rarely speak up about this kind of suffering, perhaps assuming that it's not part of normal medical discourse. It takes just a moment to notice and acknowledge, "It's going to be a few days before we get the results, and I'll call when I know. How are you doing with all of this?"

THAT WHICH WE CANNOT NAME

The discourse on suffering went into hibernation during the years of impressive technological advances in medicine starting in the 1960s. I suspect that the heady optimism that accompanied the advances in our understanding of the mechanisms of disease and the promise of new treatments obscured the reality that these advances alone would not make suffering vanish. In fact, until the early 2000s, the tagline of the National Cancer Institute was an overly optimistic "to eliminate all death and suffering due to cancer by 2015."

Not until the 1980s was serious discussion about the nature of suffering and goals of medicine rekindled, by Eric Cassell, a New York City internist. Cassell was devoted to understanding communication between patients and physicians—when it worked and when it went awry. He remains a key figure in a countercurrent in medicine concerned with the human experience of illness.

Cassell first described suffering as a holistic experience where there is "severe distress associated with events that threaten the intactness of the person." This definition was radical. By looking at his own practice, as well as listening to and analyzing audio-recordings of consultations between patients and physicians, he realized that doctors often missed the point—they did not see patients' suffering. In a seminal article in the *New England Journal of Medicine* in 1982,[4] he reminded the medical community that the central obligation of healers is to address suffering—not just cure disease or relieve pain. He showed how suffering is only loosely associated with pain; that suffering itself has meaning, and that meaning can affect the severity and quality of a person's distress and the sense he makes of it. After all, the pain of childbirth can be more intense than that of a heart attack, but the overall experience is different—a joyous outcome rather than terror about the future.

Cassell showed how suffering is more than merely having a diseased part—a lung, a kidney, a brain; he said that suffering is experienced by whole persons. Other domains of suffering—psychological, existential, spiritual, financial, social—are often more devastating than physical symptoms. I've heard many chronically ill and dying patients say that the worst part of their situation is not the illness itself but the way the illness has impoverished or otherwise burdened their families. Cassell knew too that contact with the health care system can make a patient's suffering worse—"If we're not a part of the solution, we are a part of the problem."[5]

In the thirty years since Cassell's article, nursing researchers, medical ethicists, and those in hospice and palliative care have brought suffering out of the closet, especially for patients at the end of life. Still, it is remarkable how infrequently physicians ask about suffering. "How are we feeling today?" just doesn't get there.

Ronald Epstein, M.D.

Too often, doctors assume that they understand what is making a particular patient suffer most. The reality is that we usually do not.

In fact, physicians are cautioned *not* to use the word *suffering* for fear that it casts patients as victims, denying them agency and personhood. However, this can go too far. I once prepared a monograph for the National Cancer Institute on enhancing patient-physician communication. The subtitle was "Promoting Healing and Reducing Suffering." Though many of the scientists and clinicians around the table who were reviewing the monograph were supportive of the title and the approach, others were puzzled. They knew how to measure physical and mental health: physical, emotional, social, and existential quality of life; pain and other symptoms; and stress and coping. Nonetheless, healing and suffering were unfamiliar locations on their cancer map, even though most intuitively realized that suffering is not merely the presence of measurable pain or distress, just as health is not merely the absence of disease.

I recently reviewed the mission statements of thirty health care institutions around the country, many of which were impressively long and detailed. Not one mentioned suffering. Instead, they contained phrases such as "exceeding customer expectations," "eliminating cancer," "the highest order," "the best provider," and "trusted partner." One hospital's mission statement even suggested that physicians "treat the body," leaving the care of the hearts and minds of patients to others.

Next, I checked to see if the word *suffering* appeared in any of the 170,000 *International Classification of Diseases* (*ICD-10*) diagnosis codes that are used as the basis for billing, quality metrics, and health statistics. Not even once. Over the past months, I've systematically searched the medical literature for articles that explore how physicians can and should respond to suffering. I found a mere six research studies. Quite a number of thoughtful reflective essays provided compelling *descriptions* of suffering as well as physicians' and nurses' *attitudes* toward suffering; most addressed suffering in end-of-life care only; few touched on other contexts in which suffering occurs, and even fewer proposed ways of responding to it. Perhaps this is because suffering, being a holistic experience, doesn't

114

neatly fit into the way that doctors and researchers tend to think. It is difficult to see—and address—that which we cannot name.[6]

SUFFERING BY ANY OTHER NAME

Karen Volk was in her late thirties when I first met her; she is now fifty-three. Karen was trained as a social worker and has two children. She had left an abusive relationship and was recently remarried. For years, she had been chronically fatigued, yet all her blood tests, including those for Lyme disease, anemia, lupus, thyroid disease, and a host of others, were normal. She complained of migrating joint pains and swelling, but a physical exam showed little of note. She had multiple tender points in her shoulders and back and did not sleep well, all characteristic of fibromyalgia—a poorly understood condition that is a minor annoyance for some and debilitating for others. She had also been diagnosed with interstitial cystitis, a painful bladder condition of unknown cause. For clinicians this is a familiar picture: chronic pain in multiple sites, fatigue, depression, and abuse tend to go together.[7] Her mood was like a roller coaster, but her symptoms didn't necessarily fluctuate with her state of mind or level of stress. A few years before, she had become dependent on narcotics for chronic pain; after having weaned herself off them, she didn't want to risk dependence in the future.

Every few weeks, Karen would land in my office, in pain. I prescribed medications for pain, depression, inflammation, and insomnia. Some were helpful, yet overall Karen declined, until three years later she could barely walk and could no longer work. The less mobile she became, the more weight she gained, putting on fifty pounds. And the pain persisted. At first, we tried to avoid narcotics, but nonnarcotic pain medications just didn't work for her. She had a high tolerance for narcotics and, despite the substantial doses that I prescribed, still had severe pain. The only option was to up her doses, which worried us both.

Before I met Karen, her chart had grown thick with consultations from infectious disease specialists, orthopedic surgeons, neurologists, sleep specialists, rheumatologists, dermatologists, urogyne-cologists, podiatrists, and mental health professionals. Rather than accept and work with uncertainty, some of her specialists created an illusion of knowing and control, proposing "functional" diagnoses—fibromyalgia, migraines, myofascial pain syndrome, somatization, and sleep-onset disorder—all of which only describe symptoms and not their cause. No one could put the picture together into a coherent whole.[8] Karen felt she was not being taken seriously and that no one was in control. When doctors would tell her that her symptoms were due to "stress," she felt even more helpless and felt blamed for her own suffering.[9] Meanwhile, doctors groaned when they saw her name on their schedules; some distanced themselves ("Call me in six months"), and others questioned the legitimacy of her complaints.

Then one day an X-ray of Karen's left ankle looked different from the previous ones. Her ankle joint showed signs of inflammation and destruction of the cartilage, just as one would see in rheumatoid arthritis. Now Karen had a disease that could be seen, with pathological changes. Well, sort of. Her blood tests remained normal; she didn't have evidence of any of the known rheumatologic conditions that could explain her joint destruction. She was again left in limbo. She tried increasingly potent (and potentially toxic) medications.[10] While she improved, she also had severe side effects. Once, she developed an infected ulcer on her right ankle that was resistant to antibiotics and continued to fester. Eventually she had prosthetic joints in her knees and right hip and surgery on her wrists, elbow, and shoulder. Still, she walked with a limp and couldn't lift anything heavier than ten pounds. Narcotics, physical therapy, acupuncture, herbal medicines and nutritional supplements, meditation, and psychotherapy were all somewhat helpful, but overall, her trajectory was worsening. She became despondent and hopeless. Her marriage crumbled. I once took a biopsy of her ankle ulcer and on her way home she started to bleed from the biopsy site. She returned to my office, in tears, saying, "I can't take this anymore." I applied pressure, elevated her leg, put in another stitch, and the bleeding stopped. That was the easy part; fixing the wound didn't even begin to touch her suffering.

Patients such as Karen are humbling to clinicians. She had no definite diagnosis. For reasons no one understood, she seemed to get every possible complication from her treatments and didn't heal as well as other patients. No one could untangle the degree to which the causes of her disability and suffering were physical, psychological, or social. The only clear thing was that her suffering was intense. With each downturn, Karen's illness affected me personally. The more ill and depressed she became, the more helpless I felt. I began to dread our visits.

BEYOND HELPLESSNESS

Then, things changed for me in ways that I am still trying to reconstruct. I realized that it wasn't Karen herself who made me feel helpless. Rather, my feeling of helplessness was rooted in an expectation I had of myself—that I could somehow fix something that would then make her suffering abate. When I couldn't fix things, I felt adrift, uncomfortable. The mindful moment was when I simply allowed myself to *feel* helpless and not push that particularly unpleasant feeling away.

Trying to build a wall between myself and her misery would do no good, nor would blaming myself or anyone else. I realized that *feeling* helpless was okay as long as it alerted me to the need to take a fresh look, to adopt a beginner's mind. So I started asking myself questions: Is there something I'm not seeing? Can I take another perspective? Can I be more present with her without being consumed by her despair? At times, the thing to "do" was to do nothing, not reassure, not fix. By temporarily setting aside my need to fix, I could witness her suffering and share her uncertainty, her ambivalence, her hope. The physical exams I performed at each visit became gestures of solidarity as well as a search for pathology.

Doctors are most comfortable fixing things, and I am no exception. We are trained to first identify something gone awry—a symptom such as pain, anxiety, or even existential distress, or a symptomless disease such as hypertension—then to try to restore the patient to a prior state of health using medications, surgery, or behavioral means. Some of Karen's issues were simply unfixable. Surgery would never restore her joints to their pre-arthritis state of twenty years before. Other treatments had backfired, the side effects outweighing any benefit.

It's understandable that doctors pay more attention to health concerns that they feel they can treat effectively. But when the physician's only tool is a diagnose-and-treat approach, he is at risk of being blind to the full range of a patient's suffering. Instead of looking at the patient as a whole person, physicians often view a patient as the sum of the problems that they can recognize, diagnose, and fix.

Months later, Karen began to improve. Her skin infections resolved, her ulcers healed, and she lost much of the weight she had gained; she had a relatively uncomplicated left-hip replacement surgery and could walk without a limp for the first time in years. After a two-month hiatus, she came into the office, beaming and radiant, and the dark look of despair was gone. She was dressed with simple elegance, wearing her own handmade jewelry. I was thunderstruck. I had never, in all the years I had cared for her, seen her so energized and hopeful.

She announced that she had stopped nearly all of her medicines for pain, depression, and insomnia. She decided to leave her (second) husband and felt stronger for having done so. She had taken charge of her life and had found meaning in her existence. "What's changed?" I asked. I was intrigued when she attributed her transition in large part to the support she'd received from me and my colleagues. I was puzzled, so I asked her again, and she said that more important than any particular treatment was that she had felt seen and accompanied—by me and others on her clinical team. She felt that she was never alone. Rather than take this as flattery, I tried to understand why. I pressed her to articulate her experience. In part, her recovery had to do with my recognizing her intentions and goals and supporting her as she tried to refocus her energies and reclaim those parts of her life that were still available to her— even when her symptoms were at their worst. Her words *refocusing* and *reclaiming* stayed with me.[11] "I also like that you are realistic," she said. "You tell me the truth about my illness, but still give me a reason to hope." She appreciated that whenever she voiced opinions about her care, I'd consider them seriously. But perhaps most surprising to me was when she told me how she felt both frightened *and* reassured when I said, "I don't know." "At least," she said, "I knew you were being honest."

A SHORT, SLOW WALK

Tony Back is an oncologist and palliative care physician in Seattle.[12] Together we've been looking at how doctors can better respond to suffering. Recently, Tony has explored what happens when physicians feel helpless. Helplessness is the dark side of the diagnose-and-treat approach—your heart sinks, you feel like a failure.

Tony points out that helplessness is angst provoking, but can also be instructive.[13] The feeling of wanting to turn away and ignore that which one cannot fix can also be a warning sign: "Stop. Wait a minute. This situation demands another approach. Turn toward suffering, not away. Listen deeply so that you can know and accompany the patient and help the patient feel understood."[14] The novelist Henry James calls it placing an "empty cup of attention" between yourself and the patient.[15] The physician-poet Jack Coulehan calls it "compassionate solidarity."[16] In practice, it means saying, "I want to know how you're doing." The point is to check in. The message for physicians is that your negative feelings—despair, confusion, fear, and angst—are an invitation to explore what irks you, to investigate what you'd rather avoid. No one likes feeling helpless. But by turning toward such uncomfortable feelings, rather than shutting them down, I become more effective as a doctor and feel more alive as a human being.

Patients value feeling supported in this way, knowing that I'm willing and able to turn toward them when they are suffering and treat them as whole persons, even under the direst circumstances, whether or not treatments have been effective. This doesn't always require much on my part. For patients who have trouble walking or who are in pain, for instance, I make a point of walking with them the ten yards from the examination room to the reception desk. I accompany them. Granted, it takes a few extra seconds, time that I could spend doing a physical exam, ordering tests. Tacitly, I am sending a message of understanding, nonabandonment, and patience. People want to know that their doctors will accompany them in this way, even if they are only able to walk slowly. For me, that short, slow walk is a contemplative practice, not unlike the Zen practice of slow-walking meditation that punctuates periods of sitting. I become an empathic witness to patients' suffering.

Turning toward suffering means seeing each patient as a person. I come to know what is unique about her, what strengths she has, why she goes on fighting the illness, what underlies her tendency to become dependent on narcotics. Turning toward suffering is "looking into the patient's eyes"[17] rather than just at the diseased body part or a computer screen, entering the landscape of her suffering rather than being a detached observer. Practically speaking, I ask patients about their day, what they can and cannot do, and what their kids need to help them with. These questions don't take long and give me a glimpse of what life is like and what matters most; they often provide clues to the diagnosis and how I can help.

As physicians, we expect patients to tell us when they are suffering and what it's like. But many don't. Instead, patients assume that if something is important, the doctor will ask, or that we don't want to hear, or that we'll think they're complaining or being too demanding. Mindful of patients' reticence, my Rochester colleague and mentor Tim Quill teaches clinicians to ask patients routinely, "What's the worst part of all this?" Rather than presumptuously assuming that he understands, he might say, "I can only begin to imagine . . . ," then he'll ask for more details. Sometimes, at the right moment, he stays silent, letting the patient know that some things cannot be spoken but can nevertheless be shared.[18] Tim is matter-of-fact, open, curious. His willingness to ask indicates that he has something to learn about the patient's suffering from the patient herself, and that he will be able to tolerate what he hears.

Clinicians get little training in how to step out of the comfortable role of diagnostician and accompany patients in this way. Accompanying is particularly important with the patients I don't understand and those who, on the surface, I don't particularly like—those who yell at me, don't tell the truth, or complain then reject the help I offer. Like anyone else, I can feel angry and frustrated, but trying to understand patients in a deeper way—truly seeing them—usually makes caring for them less difficult. When being mindful, I recognize that my irritation is, in part, a signal that I don't understand them—or myself—well enough. My capacity to respond to the suffering of any patient depends on how well I can recognize that my imaginative projection of what the patient is experiencing is just that and no more.

I first learned about this kind of projection during my residency when I was caring for a nineteen-year-old who was on a ventilator in the ICU. He had been diagnosed with meningitis and had complications that included pneumonia and respiratory failure, a scenario with about a 50 percent mortality rate. Gradually, he recovered. He became more alert well before he could be taken off the ventilator and began writing notes. He seemed to tolerate frequent blood draws, suctioning, and invasions of his privacy. He was engaging and had a sweet smile that won the hearts of the medical and nursing staff. He won my heart too. Every day that he was doing well, I felt energized; with each setback, disheartened. I would dream about him at night—anxiety dreams (*Oh, no, I forgot to check his potassium. . . .*) as well as redemption dreams (imagining him playing soccer, free from any signs of disease).

When the tube came out, he could talk again. He still had that same sweet smile, but he was not the person I had imagined. He was immature, demanding, and ungrateful, treating his parents and the staff poorly. He demanded more and more narcotics, perhaps enjoying the brief high they produced. He complained incessantly about the food (here, I did have some sympathy). I was disillusioned. He didn't seem to be following the script—he wasn't the kind, grateful, thoughtful kid I had imagined him to be.

Then I realized to my dismay that I had fabricated an identity for him, an image that hardly any nineteen-year-old could live up to. I was overinvolved. I began to wonder why, then realized that my fabrication obscured a deep fear I had. He was not that far from my own age, and his near-death experience reminded me of the tenuousness of life, the fragility of health. I created a story so that I didn't need to see his vulnerability, or my own.

REFOCUSING AND RECLAIMING

People who are ill seek to make sense of their experience. At the end of life, people who have been disconnected from family often wish to reconnect. Pride, money, and achievements often matter less. People often construct illness stories that give value and honor to the experience of having been ill.[19]

With illnesses that are chronic, debilitating, or difficult to explain, some—but not all—patients seek meaning and coherence. Amid the terror of decline, these patients are uninterested in merely coping; they seek to thrive despite the brutality and unpredictability of their disease. While I believe that few people truly feel grateful for having contracted a serious illness, some feel grateful for the lessons and courage that illness has given them. They feel that they've grown. Witnessing these realizations brings tears to my eyes; I feel a sense of privilege when I see patients refocusing and reclaiming their lives.

Not every patient is interested in refocusing and reclaiming. But I've seen it enough to know that I need to recognize it and nudge it along when I can. Healing becomes a shared project. Patients who wish to approach their illnesses in this way are extraordinary; you cannot force it. Too often, I have heard clinicians and family members exhort patients to "fight" their illnesses, as if they were engaging in a crusade against evil, or to see illness as bringing them closer to God. Sometimes people urge patients to "accept" their illness, as if that final stage in Elisabeth Kübler-Ross's five stages of dying is a value universally shared.[20] It isn't. While some patients may reach an inflection point where they comfortably shift from curative treatments to comfort and palliation, others derive meaning from raging "against the dying of the light."[21] Expectations that patients should somehow transcend their illnesses can burden them with a sense of moral failure that compounds the insults of the disease.

LEARNING TO LISTEN

A family physician colleague, Lucy Candib, has worked for her entire career with indigent and working-class populations in Worcester, Massachusetts, many of whom have experienced abuse, violence, and deprivation. She hears about horrific experiences, examines scarred bodies, and documents what she hears and sees in the hope that it won't happen again to this person, or to anybody else. She is a passionate advocate for those who lack a voice in society, especially for people who seek health care in the aftermath of a life trauma. Candib believes that clinicians should "treat patients' experience as testimony,"[22] verifying and legitimating the personal (if not absolute) truth of each patient's story. Suffering is personal; we all experience it differently. There is no test, no meter, no scale. Treating patients' experience as testimony means respecting a patient's wish to be heard—on her own terms, not anyone else's. This resonates with me, in part because it sets the conditions from which compassion can emerge.

8

The Shaky State
of Compassion

Early in my third year of medical school, I learned of the writings of George Engel. As I mentioned in chapter 1, Engel was the prominent internist and psychoanalyst who formulated a "biopsychosocial model" of care.[1] I wrote to him about my frustrations as a medical student. He shared with me his view that medical institutions, overly preoccupied with technological advances, had forced the human dimensions of medicine to the edges. That was certainly my experience. Engel suggested that I come to Rochester, where the institutional climate was different. In my training in family medicine and subsequent fellowships with him and several of his protégés, I saw a way to achieve what Engel called "being scientific in the human domain."[2]

Engel had an extraordinary capacity to connect with and know other human beings. Patients would meet him for the first time and reveal themselves in ways that provided clues to their medical diagnoses while also creating a human bond. Engel would *look* curious, with a quizzical gaze. He'd ask, "What happened next?" and "What were you thinking when you did that?" and "You mentioned your daughter. What did she suggest? Did it help?" and "What were they doing when your symptoms started?" He'd keep asking until he got a full visual picture of the patient's home, her family, her habits, and her ideas about what was going on. He'd say, "I wonder . . . ," and you'd *feel* a sense of wonder. Patients felt understood.

Engel's approach was radically different from how most of us typically have a social conversation. Maybe you describe an event or a feeling ("When I threw my back out, it was the worst pain of my life"), and your friend responds with a comment, an interpretation, or a question, or she might mention a personal situation that she considers similar to yours ("Yeah, I was in the hospital with a gallbladder attack last year—that was the worst"). This kind of back-and-forth can instill a sense of shared experience: "Wow, she knows what pain is like too." But it can also flop. The other person's story can make you clam up if it doesn't resonate, if you don't feel understood: "What's a slipped disk compared to a gallbladder attack?" you think, irritated.

Engel liked to say that what patients want most is to know and understand what is happening to them and to feel known and understood. Known, not judged. Deep listening is the first step toward compassion. But deep listening is also important for another reason: it is essential to avoiding miscommunications and errors in clinical care. Sometimes when I find myself in a puzzling or challenging situation, I can almost hear Engel's voice in my head, guiding me to listen more deeply, to adopt his inquiring, curious smile.

Deep listening is a form of contemplative practice; it can be taught and learned. In workshops, for example, I'll ask physicians to write and share stories. First, I ask them to select an important event from their professional lives—it could be a moment of connection or it could be a time when things went wrong. Then they take a few minutes to write about it—what happened, who was there, what made it memorable, and whether they were able to make a difference in a positive way. Participants pair off and tell (or read) their story to a partner, who has been instructed to be an attentive listener, and to be aware of—but avoid acting on—an impulse to offer interpretations, advice, or judgments, or to talk about their own experiences. Rather, the listener should contribute only to encourage the storyteller to elaborate, ask clarifying and reflective questions, and explore the storyteller's experience.

While this kind of listening sounds simple, it isn't, especially for physicians, who have been socialized to assume a dominant role in clinical conversations (physicians account for 60 to 80 percent of the talking during an office visit).[3] It takes practice. But, for most people, the feeling of having been listened to—deeply and without judgment—is validating.

SUFFERING WITH

While compassion—"suffering with"—has always been considered a virtue for clinicians (or anyone else), little has been written for physicians about how to cultivate it. Some think of compassion as innate; you either have it or you don't. But we have all seen people who are compassionate under some circumstances but not under others.[4] I've also seen, in students and colleagues, how compassion can grow or wither during one's career.

Compassion is in short supply. Beth Lown, an internist at Harvard's Mount Auburn Hospital and medical director of the Schwartz Center for Compassionate Healthcare, surveyed 800 recently hospitalized patients and 510 physicians in 2011. While 85 percent of patients and 76 percent of physicians said that compassion is "very important" to successful medical treatment, only 53 percent of patients and 58 percent of physicians said that the health care system generally provides compassionate care.[5] And compassion, like presence, is not doled out equitably. Doctors, like most people, tend to be more compassionate toward those whose illnesses they consider legitimate, and less so for those perceived to be at fault for their situation—those who smoke, are obese, or engage in risky sexual behaviors. When physicians lack compassion—or the ability to express it—they inadvertently add to the burden of patients' suffering.

In his landmark experiments about obedience to authority,[6] psychologist Stanley Milgram demonstrated how fragile compassion can be. In one experiment, an authority figure instructed research participants to give electric shocks of increasing strength to a "student" as part of an "experiment on learning." Unbeknownst to the participants, these were mock electric shocks and the "students" were trained actors. Milgram found that the participants were obedient, even though they experienced obvious distress at delivering the shocks. Many gave shocks in the "lethal" range when instructed to do so and continued even when the "student" repeatedly asked that the experiment be stopped. The participants were debriefed after the study and were clearly troubled by their actions.[7] It took so little for them to leave their compassion in the parking lot.

Even those who have the highest aspirations to act compassionately do so only under certain conditions. In the now-famous 1973 Darley and Batson "Jerusalem to Jericho" study, divinity students were instructed to prepare a talk about the biblical parable of the Good Samaritan, a virtuous man who chose to assist a stranger who had been beaten and left for dead on the side of a road.[8] The experimenters placed a shabbily dressed person—obviously in need—slumped by the path that the students took to get to the lecture hall across campus. Half were told they had ample time; the other half were told to hurry or they'd be late. Those in a hurry were much less likely to stop to assist the man in need.

Medical journals frequently publish stories about how physicians—who, like the divinity students in the Good Samaritan study, think of themselves as compassionate—have acted in uncaring ways they later found disturbing. They inflicted pain, did not take the extra moment with a distressed family member, or were rude with a difficult patient. Recently I read a brutally honest story in a medical journal in which an otherwise conscientious physician found himself cutting patients short during an afternoon clinic session so that he could finish on time. Later, he realized that he was doing so because he wanted to arrive refreshed and relaxed for a prestigious lecture he was about to give.[9] The author, a rheumatologist, is a passionate advocate for effective communication in medicine and does research on quality of care. Ironically, I have found myself in exactly the same situation—for example, prior to a dinner with a visiting professor promoting humanism in health care.

CULTIVATING COMPASSION

Up until now, it hasn't been clear what it might take to change this shaky state of compassion. Exhortations to be more compassionate don't work. Compassion isn't a "muscle" that is reliably developed as a result of caring for the sick; some physicians become more cynical and unkind.

Roshi Joan Halifax, anthropologist and Zen Buddhist teacher, has worked with the dying, with prison populations, and with others at the extremes of life. She writes about how compassion is both "contingent and emergent."[10] By contingent, she means that compassion appears in individuals under certain conditions; none of us is intrinsically compassionate all the time. For compassion to emerge, we have to create the right conditions. These conditions have to do with our inner landscape—our own emotional life, attitudes, and self-awareness—and the outer environment, the institutions in which we work. She points out that compassion is cultivated; it isn't a product that can be manufactured. A good gardener cannot make plants grow; she can only coax them to grow and flourish by cultivating the soil and providing nutrients and water. Similarly, compassion doesn't spring from the earth unbidden and it doesn't easily submit to checklists and industrial models of health care. Compassion is also emergent in that it may manifest in surprising and unpredictable ways—through words, small gestures, advocacy, even silence. The challenge is to create those conditions in which compassion is *most likely* to arise, but not necessarily to expect it to manifest the same way each time.

INGREDIENTS OF COMPASSION

Compassion is the triad of *noticing another's suffering, resonating with their suffering in some way,* and then *acting* on behalf of another person. Research suggests that awareness of our inner states can help us recognize the inner states of others.[11] Some of the same neural circuits are activated when we witness pain as when we experience our own.[12] When we are distressed, we feel it first in the body; we do the same when taking in the distress of others, mapping their experiences onto our own, and feeling pain in response to theirs.[13]

Yet the feelings and sensations that patients elicit in me are not the same ones that patients experience; I resonate with their pain, but it's not the same. This resonance is the second ingredient of compassion—the "suffering with" part. A boundary gets blurred and you hurt too. But if I assume that what I am feeling is exactly what the patient is feeling, I would be wrong much of the time. I've made the mistake of mentioning to patients who've had kidney stones that I've had them too. Some patients take this as an empathic gesture, which leads to a sense of shared experience, but more often my self-disclosure falls flat; patients want me to understand *their* unique experience. They're interested in *their* kidney stones and aren't particularly interested in mine. Although I might think I understand their pain, their bland responses to my revelation confirm that I'm off the mark. My time is better spent asking about what it was like for them.[14]

The third ingredient of compassion is *action* to reduce another's suffering. Like most people, particularly those in helping professions, physicians often experience meaning and purpose when they do things to benefit others; compassion nourishes the healer. Engaging in compassionate action, we release endogenous opioids, which attenuate our own pain; dopamine, which promotes a sense of reward; and oxytocin, which generates feelings of caring, affiliation, and belonging.[15] I suspect this reward response may be part of the reason clinicians work long hours throughout their careers and continue to work into their seventies and eighties, long after people in other professions have retired.

But if compassion is its own reward—if it fills clinicians with a deep sense of purpose and well-being—then why is it in such short supply in health care? The answer has to do with the second of the three ingredients: resonating. When I resonate emotionally with another person's suffering, I experience distress, a discomfort within. If I feel that I can do something to relieve the patient's distress quickly, my own distress also dissipates. But if it's not possible—if I lack the skills or if it's going to take a long time—there's a natural human tendency to withdraw, to pull away in self-protection. Mindfulness, here, is observing, understanding, and regulating my own emotional reactions so I can reliably sustain presence in the face of a patient's distress—and my own.

THE PARADOX OF EMPATHY

Every medical school in North America now has a communication skills course. Typically students are tested on their empathy through exercises with actors trained to portray patients in distress. But these efforts don't seem to have had enough of an effect on the seemingly inevitable decline in empathy during medical training.[16]

Empathy, like compassion, has many definitions, but at its basis is a bodily, emotional, and cognitive insight into another person's emotional life.[17] This insight can be experienced and communicated in a cool and detached way ("If I understand correctly, this has been very difficult for you"), a welling up of emotion ("This is just awful"), or a bodily sensation, such as feeling your heart sinking or a lump in your throat. In medical education, students are taught to recognize and name another's distress as an emotion without experiencing that state themselves—"I can see that you're feeling afraid" or "You're telling me that you were furious with him" or even "Very unsettling, all this uncertainty." This kind of empathy is accurate, but can be chilly.

This cool cognitive empathy is not always what patients want. They want a sense of emotional connection and caring; they want the physician to be warm and attuned to what they are feeling. However, it is a delicate balance for physicians. Sharing their personal feelings with patients is not always helpful and sometimes diverts the conversation away from what concerns the patient.[18] Mindful clinicians are present, attuned, and empathic without appropriating the focus of attention from their patients to themselves.

Juggling three "balls"—being empathically attuned to another person's emotions, being attuned to your own emotions, and acting on the other person's behalf—has been the focus of research by psychologists Carl Batson and Nancy Eisenberg for the past forty years.[19] Using a variety of laboratory experiments, they have found that when we understand and assimilate another person's emotions, we all reach a proverbial fork in the road. One path leads to self-protection: You say and do things to lower your own anxiety. You rationalize your actions. What you do may or may not help the other person. In short, you are focused on yourself and your own feelings. The other path leads to "pro-social" behavior, acts that relieve the patient's distress through words, medications, surgery, or just by being present. It can be an expression of heartfelt connection with the patient—what physician Michael Kearney calls "exquisite empathy"[20]—or compassionate action that directly relieves the patient's suffering.

In a series of experiments, Olga Klimecki at the University of Geneva and her colleagues set out to explore whether she could train people to be more compassionate.[21] She based her training on Batson and Eisenberg's model. First, she trained a group of participants to recognize and resonate with the emotions of others. While in a functional MRI scanner, the participants then watched videos that depicted human suffering and later completed surveys that measured empathy and personal distress. Then, in a second session, she led them in "kindness" meditation practices to evoke feelings of benevolence, kindness, and caring toward themselves and others (friends, "neutral" persons, and "difficult" persons), a practice designed to evoke compassion.[22] Again, the participants were scanned and completed surveys. The results confirmed Batson and Eisenberg's predictions: those trained only to resonate with others—and without skills to translate that resonance into compassion—felt more emotionally distressed; their brain scans showed greater activation in areas of the brain known to be associated with distress and vicarious pain.[23] After receiving just one day of compassion training, these same people had a different neural "signature." They felt energized and had a more positive sense of self. The scans of those who received compassion training showed that their "reward pathways"[24] were activated and the "distress pathways" were no longer active.

These are experiments in a laboratory and present crude models of how the brain—and the mind—works in the real world. But they are revealing in terms of how we train doctors.[25] I finally understood why training physicians to be more sensitive and to resonate with patients' emotional distress—a good thing—can lead to emotional exhaustion and burnout. In fact, when I've surveyed students and residents, some of those who score highest on empathy are sometimes the most burned out. They experience secondary— or vicarious—trauma from having assimilated the suffering of others. For years, I had been training medical students, residents, and practicing physicians to name and acknowledge the patient's feelings, by saying things like "Now I have a better understanding of how much pain you're in." Was this approach all wrong? Could it be that too much empathy was toxic? We had been training our students to share emotions and take the patient's perspective, but had failed to help them be aware of and manage their own strong feelings. Feeling traumatized, they disconnected, assumed a stance of cool objectivity, avoided getting involved. Which is to say that training in empathy is a good thing, but it goes only so far. It's now clear that we also need to train physicians to be compassionate, not only for the sake of their patients, but because compassionate action seems to relieve the emotional tension that is inevitable when we try to imagine the experience of another. It's an antidote to burnout.

We know now that it is possible to train clinicians to be more compassionate, an idea that would have been considered radical just a few years ago. Yet, the emotional "climate" of the health care institutions within which doctors work is typically unsupportive, hardly providing a model of compassion that clinicians can emulate with their patients. To provide compassionate care, we have to address institutional climate and values. Consider the alternative. Empathy—and compassion—are doomed to decline if we continue to neglect the emotional lives of physicians, if we fail to provide the conditions under which they can learn to regulate their emotions, develop mental stability, and have the right kind of equanimity—an engaged equanimity in which clinicians are present with—but not consumed by—patients' emotional needs. And it's not just physicians; "compassion fatigue" is as much of a problem among nurses and other health professionals.

TRAINING IN COMPASSION

But how?

When I learned about metta meditation—sometimes called loving-kindness meditation or compassion practice—it initially struck me as insufferably New Age. I couldn't imagine how dreamy voices, pictures of lotuses, and invitations to a "revolutionary art of happiness"[26] could possibly appeal to hard-edged physicians.

Metta is a Pali word that translates as "friendship" and "kindness," a sincere wish for the welfare and genuine happiness of others. Metta is an attitude that the practitioner aspires to bring to all beings, without exception—so-called nonreferential or unconditional compassion—akin to Aristotle's concept of *philia*, or "brotherly love."[27] If you take the view that humans have the capacity for compassion but are hindered by a distorted view of the world, then it is possible to remove those hindrances through practice.

The first time I experienced it, I was at a workshop. During the guided meditation, the teacher instructed us to imagine ourselves and our positive attributes, then to extend kindness to ourselves, then a "benefactor," a friend, a "neutral person," a "difficult person," and finally "all beings." We were asked to enact silently, in our minds, a series of phrases, first directed toward ourselves: "May I be free from danger, may I be happy, may I be healthy, may I live with ease." Then, to others, in turn: "May they be free from danger, may they be happy, may they be healthy, may they live with ease." And so on.

I took some solace when I learned that compassion practice has been part of meditation traditions for over twenty-five hundred years. But could you really train people to be kind, to befriend, to *care*? Or was this exercise an indulgence, helping well-educated, privileged healthy people feel good about themselves? Somewhat skeptical, I went along with the exercise, trying to keep an open mind. I noticed that it was more difficult to wish myself well than to direct kindness toward a friend. This certainly was revealing in how difficult it is for clinicians to care for themselves. I wondered what a "benefactor" meant to me, and how I had expressed my gratitude for my benefactors' selfless actions. It helped me appreciate how many people had helped me to get where I am. When I was asked to imagine standing beside a "difficult person" and wishing him well, I became more curious about my interactions with people whom I regarded as difficult and began to recognize that their presence was teaching me something helpful too. I found myself feeling deeply grateful—to others and to myself. Being in a room with others, all of whom were working on cultivating something positive, was powerful—it created a sense of community and shared purpose. What had seemed to be a rather odd and forced exercise began to make sense.[28]

Since then, at least one research study has distinguished the neural fingerprint of compassion practice from other forms of contemplative practice. Studying a group of novice meditators for nine months, psychologist Tania Singer's research group at the Max Planck Institute found that compassion practice led to activation of the inferior parietal cortex, the dorsolateral prefrontal cortex, and the nucleus accumbens—demonstrating links between the "reward circuit" in the brain and the parts of the brain that have to do with understanding and resonating with the feelings of others, and the ability to regulate our own emotions (what is commonly called emotional intelligence).[29] While you don't need a functional MRI scan to "prove" that bestowing kindness on yourself and other human beings is a good thing, this line of research[30] is tantalizing now that evidence suggests that through practice people can act more altruistically and expand their emotional compass.

9

When Bad Things Happen

Angela Bradowski had over three hundred pounds on her five-foot-three-inch frame. For the first two years after I diagnosed her with diabetes, she controlled her disease with oral medications. Then her blood sugars started climbing from the 100s to the 200s, then the 300s. I didn't see her for a few months, and when she came back, her blood sugar was nearly 500. When it gets above 600 or so, people are at risk for coma and even death.

Angela had all of the classic signs of poorly controlled diabetes—insatiable thirst, frequent and copious urination, weakness, and blurry vision. I started her on a long-acting insulin (glargine), otherwise known as Lantus. Normally insulin doses range between thirty and eighty units per day, and patients with insulin resistance may need doses in excess of one hundred units. But Angela didn't seem to respond, and with each visit I increased her insulin even further.

I started to feel out of my element when her Lantus dose exceeded one hundred units twice daily. I consulted the medical literature and called a diabetologist. He had had a couple of patients who had needed doses of over four hundred units a day, and some cases in the literature documented patients receiving close to a thousand units. Emboldened, I kept increasing the dose, and eventually Angela was giving herself four hundred units twice a day, and still her sugar was out of control.

I asked Angela about her diet, medications, and physical activity—the usual questions—yet I was baffled. Nothing seemed to explain the situation. She didn't eat all that much. She didn't exercise, but that wouldn't explain her extraordinary resistance to insulin. The most common explanation—not taking her insulin—didn't seem to apply. She had the skin marks to prove it, and she had been refilling her vials of insulin on schedule.

Occasionally people are more sensitive to one formulation of insulin than another. With that in mind and on the advice of the diabetologist, I switched her insulin from long-acting to intermediate-acting (NPH) insulin. Not knowing what would happen, I started her on eighty units twice a day, one-fifth of her previous dose. I was hoping that the more rapid onset might control her blood sugar more effectively. It seemed to be worth a try.

The next day she was hospitalized with a stroke. She was found unconscious at home and her blood sugar was zero when the ambulance arrived. By the time I got to the hospital, she was beginning to wake up; she was drowsy, but couldn't move her left side. In the emergency room, George, her husband, was waiting for news about Angela's condition. He told me that he had been worrying about her because, unbeknownst to me, she had been slaking her unquenchable thirst with three two-liter bottles of sweetened iced tea every day. My heart sank. Now it all made sense. I did a quick calculation—at least two thousand calories in addition to whatever else she was eating.

When diabetes is out of control, glucose doesn't get into the cells and stays in the blood, making people urinate copiously and frequently to try to get rid of the sugar. As a result, they get dehydrated and thirsty. Insulin also makes you hungry and gain weight. Angela's craving for liquids and sweets was insatiable—the more she took in, the worse it got. I had asked what she ate every day, and I had asked about soft drinks, but I hadn't thought to ask about iced tea—and she didn't volunteer it. Because Lantus acts slowly, she could take in enough sugar to keep up with the insulin, and then some. In essence, I was prescribing what for most of us would be a lethal dose of insulin, and she was rescuing herself from hypoglycemia with her own form of resuscitation, which then would send her blood sugar skyrocketing. But, with the switch to NPH insu-

138

lin, this could no longer work. NPH has a more rapid onset and she couldn't keep up, no matter how fast she might drink—even though the dose was lower. She almost died—at least in part from following my instructions.

I vacillated between being furious with her for not telling me an important piece of information and being furious at myself for not having done a more thorough nutritional assessment. She certainly had the opportunity to tell me, but perhaps she felt she needed to hide it, or perhaps it never occurred to her. While I didn't bear sole responsibility for the situation, neither did she. It was somewhere in the middle. She had seen other physicians and the nurse-practitioner on our primary care team. None of them asked either. In that sense, our health care team failed her. One could even say that the larger health care system failed her. She had many life stressors and a long list of physical and psychological conditions, and the fifteen-minute visits that were allotted to her didn't allow enough time to address them all—or even come close. Her insurance covered only a one-time visit to a dietitian, and she had used that up. Perhaps with more time for each visit, or a more sustained relationship with a nutritionist, her iced tea consumption might have been disclosed.

Angela was fortunate. Over the next two days she improved, with seemingly little residual damage. It's remarkable that she survived at all. She went home a few days later on low doses of NPH insulin—and no iced tea. She was scared and never wanted to have something like that happen again. She controlled her diabetes effectively from that point on. She lost weight. I told her that I felt bad about having prescribed a dose of insulin that resulted in a major scare. It's remarkable how forgiving some patients can be. She was grateful to be alive.

After the dust settled, I mentioned the event to a trusted colleague. In an attempt to be supportive, he was all too eager to absolve me of any responsibility before having assimilated the details of the situation, saying that I had done nothing wrong and that the responsibility was the patient's. Strikingly, for him it didn't even register as an error, yet I felt traumatized. In fact, if you ask most physicians whether they have made a significant error during their medical careers, they will more likely than not say no, they haven't. Yet over one hundred thousand patients die each year as a result of medical errors, mostly preventable, and hundreds of thousands more experience nonfatal errors and near misses.[1] Experts on medical errors would define Angela's as a "potentially preventable" error—a near miss.

FATAL MISTAKES

Other errors don't have such positive outcomes. Most dramatic are medication errors and surgical errors. Several years ago I discharged Kathryn Wolk from the hospital with a prescription for methotrexate—a powerful immunosuppressive medication to help control her symptoms of lupus. She was transferred from the hospital to a nursing home under the care of the nursing home physician. Somewhere in the transition to the nursing home, someone—it's not clear who—wrote that Kathryn should be receiving three pills daily. The correct dose—the dose she was receiving in the hospital—was three pills once a week. The incorrect prescription wasn't noticed for months until I received a report from the nursing home. I was furious and incredulous. How could this happen? By that time she had developed pulmonary fibrosis, irreversible scarring of the lungs caused by methotrexate toxicity. She died several weeks later.

Kathryn's daughter was also a patient of mine. I had to explain. "Everyone feels very badly that this happened, myself included. Kathryn clearly got the wrong dose. It was a terrible miscommunication." This explanation didn't sit well with Kathryn's daughter. "Why didn't anyone notice?" she inquired. I was honest: "I scoured the records—at least the ones I have access to—and I can't figure it out. The discharge medication list said three pills weekly rather than three pills daily." She asked, "You mean to tell me that she might have lived longer—maybe a couple of years? Do you think that I should talk to a lawyer?" If there's anything to make a doctor feel on the defensive, to feel judged and inadequate, it is the threat of litigation.

Here, a grief-stricken family member is trying to make sense of a complex series of events. She was puzzled, not only by how the events could have occurred, but also by my response. I felt devastated, but I had been counseled not to say anything that might implicate myself or anyone else. Kathryn's daughter, like most people in these kinds of situations, wanted to know the answers to several simple questions: Did I or didn't I personally make a mistake? Am I really sorry? Shouldn't I apologize? Will this kind of mistake happen again?[2] Even though I knew that I had written the correct order on Kathryn's discharge paperwork, I was questioning myself—did I *really* communicate clearly? Was I really at fault? I was so preoccupied with my own conflicted sense of responsibility that I couldn't be fully present with Kathryn's daughter. I just wanted to hide.

In 2000 the Institute of Medicine published a game-changing report on medical error in which they suggested that most errors in hospitals were problems of institutions, not of individuals.[3] The revelation for most clinicians was that institutions were set up in such a way that errors were inevitable. This radical shift in consciousness impelled health care institutions to enact procedures to reduce errors—especially medication errors and surgical mishaps—through checklists, handoff protocols when patients were transferred to a new unit, team training, and time-outs prior to surgical procedures to assure that important details weren't missed.

The methotrexate disaster occurred a number of years ago, and perhaps tragedies like this are less likely now. But they still happen, and in some cases the solutions designed to prevent future errors, such as electronic health records, create the conditions for a whole new set of errors—for example, those that result from patients being transferred among institutions that have incompatible electronic record systems. Here, the error was a systems failure. It was a demonstration of the "Swiss cheese" model of medical error in which bad things happen when all the holes in the system happen to line up.[4] My intention, though, is not to assign blame or guilt or to propose how these situations could have been avoided or changed. I've already explored how errors happen through inattention, not seeing, not being curious, not having an open mind, not being present—and how the solutions, often unique to each situation, depend on local factors. Here, I am exploring how physicians might approach bad outcomes more mindfully, regardless of their own responsibility.

Physicians generally endorse the approach I took when meeting with Kathryn's family—a measured disclosure and an expression of regret, without falling to pieces emotionally or assuming guilt. Yet when patients sense a lack of heartfelt regret, it only fans the flames of their anger and feelings of abandonment.

Physicians don't apologize because they feel afraid. Lawsuits are just the tip of the iceberg. "Morbidity and mortality" rounds in surgical specialties can be a sadistic ritual in which the guilty party is thrown to the lions; there's no sympathy or support. Even when lawsuits aren't an issue, doctors are afraid to confront their fallibility. When we're afraid, we clam up, which only makes matters worse because patients interpret lack of communication as lack of caring. Most malpractice suits start with a real or perceived error but are carried forward only if patients feel abandoned, if they feel that the doctor hasn't listened or hasn't expressed regret.[5] Research by psychologists, physicians, and attorneys consistently shows that patients want an apology—it improves communication and diffuses anger.[6] One research study even created mock trials; settlements were lower when physicians apologized.[7] By trying to protect themselves, physicians may paradoxically increase their risk of being sued.

With that in mind, most states have enacted "apology laws." These laws, which offer some degree of protection to physicians if they are more fully disclosing about medical errors, have been associated with fewer and smaller malpractice settlements.[8] Yet, physicians still hide, and apologies still don't happen as often and in the way that they should.

THE SECOND VICTIM

With all of the current attention to errors, no one seemed to be paying attention to the inner lives of physicians when things go wrong—the emotional and interpersonal fallout of a bad outcome. In 2007, Amy Waterman, a researcher at Washington University in St. Louis, surveyed 3,171 physicians in the United States and Canada about the aftermath of medical errors and near misses. Of those who reported that they had made errors, most felt traumatized; 61 percent reported that they were more anxious about future errors, and over 40 percent reported loss of confidence, sleeping difficulties, and lower job satisfaction. Even near misses increased stress. I was not surprised that only 10 percent of the physicians surveyed said that their health care organizations were supportive after they or a colleague had made an error; I doubt it's much better now.[9] The emotional climate remains hostile; in general, physicians don't want to hear about one another's errors, and only now are health care institutions recognizing clinicians' psychological trauma.

In a prescient essay in 2000, internist Albert Wu described how physicians can be "second victims" when medical errors happen:

> Virtually every practitioner knows the sickening feeling of making a bad mistake. You feel singled out and exposed—seized by the instinct to see if anyone has noticed. You agonize about what to do, whether to tell anyone, what to say. Later, the event replays itself over and over in your mind. You question your competence but fear being discovered. You know you should confess, but dread the prospect of potential punishment and of the patient's anger.[10]

Wu described the hospital team's reaction to a resident who had misread an electrocardiogram a few hours previously. The patient had pericardial tamponade, a life-threatening situation in which the pericardium—the sac that contains the heart—fills with fluid. The patient was rushed to the operating room in the middle of the night in extremis, a situation that could have been avoided had the

EKG been interpreted correctly. On rounds, the resident's colleagues were stunned and silent, perhaps because they were secretly
afraid that they might have made the same mistake in similar circumstances; they were unable to respond with compassion to their
classmate's shame.

When I was doing one of my medical school rotations, I was
paired with a student who was struggling. He had grown up in
a culture where the interpersonal norms were radically different
from the environment on the wards of a Boston teaching hospital.
When being grilled on rounds, he spoke slowly and modestly—a
virtue in his culture—which only invoked the impatience of his
superiors. I tried to be supportive, but didn't know how. I had a
sense that his experience invoked feelings of shame, but I wasn't
sure even about that. He withdrew further. No wonder doctors
become emotionally unavailable to their patients—they are beaten
into not even being available for themselves.

Even aviation does better. Aviation is not known for being a
warm and fuzzy industry; yet after near misses crew members are
debriefed, counseled, and given time off. They aren't returned to
the workplace until everyone is assured that they've recovered suf-
ficiently.[11] Yet, after being present at a stillbirth, we doctors are
expected to go straightaway into the next room to deliver a healthy
full-term child. An anesthesiologist, after the death of a patient on
the operating table, typically will move on to the next case with
barely five minutes to regroup. Medicine has learned a lot from
aviation in terms of checklists, teamwork, and error prevention,[12]
but much less about managing the emotional impact of disasters
and near misses. Given the imprecision of clinical practice, it's
remarkable that doctors should think of themselves as more infallible than pilots. While feedback and debriefing are now more common, support is often brief and superficial. Without tools to deepen
self-awareness and without exploring thinking processes and emotions in greater depth, the wounds fester and no one learns. Unexamined exposure to repeated trauma cannot but cause trauma itself.

The consequences of secondary traumatization—being the
second victim—weren't talked about much until recently. It has

become clear that when things don't go well and doctors don't get the support that they (or anyone) need, they often go down with the ship. They are at greater risk for depression and burnout. They feel badly about themselves and, as a consequence, are distracted and less emotionally available to their patients; they become less empathic. They lose their self-confidence and are more likely to make errors in the future.[13] They fear future humiliations. Too often, despite experiencing strong emotions, they bury their feelings and instead just focus on survival strategies; awareness and mindful responsiveness take a backseat.

REMEMBERING

Physicians remember their mistakes and are haunted by them. They hold them in silence for years, sometimes decades. Their stories reveal their psychological vulnerabilities—unrelenting perfectionism, unforgiving intolerance of error, unease in the face of ambiguity, a desperate need for certainty. While many physicians will acknowledge these vulnerabilities if asked, during everyday practice they usually lurk just outside awareness.

During one workshop, Mark, a psychiatrist, told of a patient who committed suicide with the medications that Mark had prescribed for him the day before. Mark had never told anyone for fear of being chastised for having given the patient a month's supply of pills. Mark had been living with a discomfiting sense of ambiguity about his own role in the tragedy, still having intrusive dreams, waking up in a sweat. Should he have done a more thorough assessment of the patient's suicidality? Should he have prescribed only a week's worth of medication at a time? He lost his self-confidence. One afternoon at the workshop was devoted to errors in medicine—how we respond when things go wrong. Mark put on paper his recollection of what had happened, what he felt in his body at the time, and the accompanying thoughts, feelings, and emotions. Then he spent twenty minutes sharing his narrative with a partner who had been instructed to listen deeply—to suspend judgment and to try to understand and be curious about the situation and Mark's reactions. As difficult as it was to listen with openness without trying to console or offer advice, Mark's partner was able to be present and not avoid or turn away from the painful moments; this invited Mark to do the same. A burden of fear and apprehension was lifted; he was reenergized, more attentive, less afraid of the difficult moments in his practice. He was able to move on. It seemed simple enough, but in the four years since his patient's suicide, there had been no natural place for Mark to disclose and examine his reactions.

I could relate to Mark's story. I also had a patient who committed suicide with medications that I had prescribed that day. My colleagues tried to assuage my guilt without really listening to the impact that event had on me. Everyone just assumed that was part of being a doctor. Get over it. Move on. I later learned that I'm not alone. It is the norm in medicine for colleagues to offer brief words of consolation, then shut down feelings. Yet the wounds fester and never heal; clinicians remain troubled and act in ways that make patients feel that they're not all there. Some physicians—family doctors, surgeons, psychiatrists—have committed suicide in the aftermath of an error. But when doctors are given the chance to address the impact of a bad outcome, they feel a sense of relief. It's no longer a secret. Addressing errors means accepting their imperfections, paving the way for kindness and compassion toward themselves, which can then enable physicians to do their jobs better, less encumbered.

CONFESSIONS

One of my colleagues in Rochester, Suzie Karan, a senior anesthesiologist, is well aware of how rarely errors and near misses are disclosed and discussed. Anesthesiologists administer powerful medications as a matter of course; without ventilators, IVs, and monitors, these medication doses would be lethal. The work of anesthesiologists in the OR is 90 percent routine and 10 percent terror. When things go sour, there is no tolerance for error or delay. Yet errors do happen and until recently there were few opportunities to debrief.

A few years ago, Karan started the "confessions" project, now implemented in residency programs at several medical centers. The project has been remarkably effective in bringing errors to the collective consciousness of the house staff and faculty—not only with an eye to identify the causes and prevent future errors, but also to address the psychological and educational needs of the clinicians involved. The mandatory sessions occur weekly for beginning residents, then several times a year for the more senior residents and staff. Each resident brings an account of an event, printed on an eight-and-a-half-by-eleven page in 12-point Times New Roman font to ensure that the reports are anonymous. They record their recollections and impressions, what happened, who was there, what they did, and how they felt, then fold the page and place it into the "confessions" pile.

Even though the tone of the word *confessions* implies something gone terribly wrong, the residents do sometimes confess something positive, a disaster averted. At the meetings, the confessions, one from each person, are distributed randomly, and the residents, one by one, read them aloud, not knowing who the writer might be. The residents discuss the event and what they can do going forward. Sometimes the discussions are emotional. Whether the disclosure is about a major catastrophe or a near miss or an everyday mishap, the goal is to help the residents grow their ability to self-regulate while building support and camaraderie.

One story was written by a doctor who accidentally spilled an anesthetic medication on the floor. Foolishly, he tried to clean it up himself, and even though he kept as close to the floor as possible to avoid breathing the highly volatile gases, within a minute he became woozy, nearly unconscious. No one discovered him. He got his bearings after several minutes, left the room, and never told anyone. Another resident accidentally gave ten times the dose of an intravenous anesthetic, and while the patient (fortunately) did fine, he never told anyone for fear of being reprimanded. The discussion inspired a collective sense of mindful vigilance and important safety initiatives, all born out of greater self-awareness. I believe that the real power of Karan's project is in changing the culture of medicine from a culture of secrecy to a culture of inquiry, of curiosity, in which clinicians are vigilant not only of their patients but also of themselves. Karan's approach emphasizes collaborative problem solving, forgiveness, and learning—all in one gesture—to help the residents to direct their attention to what matters right now, learning from the past rather than replaying the events over and over; the residents could see the events more clearly without the distractions of self-blame or self-justification.[14]

GRIEF AND LOSS

I admitted Ruth Miller to the palliative care unit. She had been diagnosed just a few weeks before with an unusually aggressive lung cancer, which had already spread to her ribs, spine, and brain. She had started radiation treatments, but things only got worse; she was confused, disoriented, and in considerable pain. I informed Ruth's family—already in shock from the diagnosis—that she likely had only a few weeks, perhaps as long as three months, to live. Her cancer was not of a type that would respond to one of the new targeted chemotherapies, nor to anything else. Family members from different parts of the country were making plans to fly in to visit.

With medications we controlled Ruth's pain and cleared her confusion enough so that she could talk and interact with her family over the next few days. She was in her best spirits in weeks. Her family left for the evening. Two hours later, David, her nurse, made a routine check, and Ruth wasn't breathing. One of the brain metastases had likely hemorrhaged, sending Ruth into an instant coma followed by respiratory arrest. Nothing could have been done to prevent it even if she had had the most aggressive care possible; hers was a quick and painless demise. David was stunned; he and Ruth's family all thought they had at least a few more days to prepare.

David was grieving but fearless. He had grown close to the family and wanted to be the one to call them. I overheard the conversation. He gave the news. Briefly. Then he waited and listened. He expressed his own sense of sorrow and surprise in a way that I later learned had made the family feel understood. He asked how their last visit with Ruth had been. He explained what would happen next. David's grief was palpable to me; his response, though, was present, attentive, and generous at a time when he himself was in shock. He and I spoke for a few minutes afterward to debrief. His grief triggered compassion rather than self-absorption; he was strong enough to acknowledge and be with his own emotions, yet could set them aside to be present with Ruth's family.

FALLING SHORT AND FALLING APART

Doctors tend to take death, errors, and other bad outcomes as personal setbacks. Perhaps a few Zen masters can consistently approach these kinds of ego-crushing experiences as fodder for growth, but the rest of us need help achieving the fearlessness that is required to look our failures in the eye. It means recognizing the fault lines, allowing ourselves to fall apart just a little bit to feel the pain of failure, but not so much that we become ineffective or overwhelmed. Attention training and other contemplative practices are powerful in part because they help you practice letting go of the need to cement things together.

Grief can be even more intense when clinicians have known patients for months or years. Mitch Porter had seen me for his diabetes for over twenty years. A successful businessman, at age fifty-four he was at the peak of his career. In the past year, he had sold a small business, received a community service award from the local chamber of commerce, and bought a vacation house in Costa Rica. He came to see me because he was having worsening right-flank pain and blood in his urine. I ordered an ultrasound of his kidneys and bladder, expecting to see evidence of a kidney stone. Instead, the ultrasonographer saw a small mass in his kidney and enlarged lymph nodes nearby. Mitch and his partner were terrified and I was filled with dread. I ordered more scans and blood tests to see just how far the cancer had metastasized. The bone scans showed cancer in his spine and nearly every large bone in his body, from his feet to his skull. His lungs were filled with hundreds of metastases, and there was spread to his brain. I started grieving even before he and his family could begin to feel the devastation. I was about to lose someone who had entrusted his well-being to me, and now we were talking weeks.

As the lab and scan results crossed my desk, one by one painting an increasingly lethal picture, I found myself wondering if I could have done something sooner. While trying to be in the present moment, again and again my mind would go in the same circles of self-doubt and self-reassurance. I felt stupid engaging in the seemingly useless exercise of trying to undo the past. I then asked myself, "Is this cycle useful in some way? Where is it directing my attention?" I watched the thoughts rather than labeling them as useless or obsessive, not grasping on to them, not pushing them away. Then the thoughts of self-blame gave way to a deep sadness. Letting go of self-blame didn't mean giving up. Quite the opposite. It energized me to do what needed to be done now, rather than trying to undo the past. I contacted his oncologist and his radiation oncologist to discuss a treatment plan. Having entered into uncertainty and instability with my eyes open, I could clarify what I could and couldn't control.

A SMOKELIKE QUALITY

Leeat Granek is a psychologist in Toronto whose mother died after a twenty-year bout with breast cancer. Granek felt a deep sense of connection with her mother's care team and came to wonder how health professionals deal with their grief when their patients die. So she asked. She interviewed twenty oncologists at different stages in their careers. Although half of their patients will die of their cancer, oncology is a culture in which cure is seen as the goal despite sometimes great odds. Oncologists see their patients frequently. A bond forms. Even when patients have cancers that cannot be cured, many have a reasonable quality of life—for a while.

Then things go sour. Patients lose weight. The chemotherapy stops working. The side effects become more burdensome, outweighing any benefit. Patients get weaker. Oncologists described how they'd drag themselves into patients' rooms, consumed by a sense of failure. They would cry in the car on the way home. Some would excoriate themselves, wondering whether they could have done something differently. Some shut down emotionally. One oncologist said, "It is a very bad thing to become emotionally attached to your patients because *you're* going to suffer." Unexamined grief led some oncologists to offer more aggressive chemotherapy to subsequent patients than they might otherwise have, treatments that lead to more suffering with a negligible chance of improving either quality or quantity of life. Granek was moved by the interviews. She said that the doctors' grief had a "smoke-like quality . . . intangible and invisible . . . pervasive, sticking to the physicians' clothes when they went home after work and slipping under the doors between patient rooms,"[15] a feeling that they couldn't set aside or wash away.

Not all oncologists responded in dysfunctional ways, though. Some were more like David, Ruth's nurse. They described how patients' deaths molded and humbled them, helping them to be more present. Confronting loss made them more careful, more respectful, and less willing merely to accept the status quo. They became activists on their patients' behalf, whether this meant getting approval for a medication that an insurance company didn't want to pay for or spending time talking with a family about how to care for their loved one during his final days. The doctors derived a sense of fulfillment from caring for the dying.

Rachel Rodenbach wanted to find out how and why some oncologists had this capacity for equanimity, advocacy, and activism in the face of death, whereas others didn't.[16] Rachel was a medical student at the time, and now is a resident planning to go into oncology. She sought me as her supervisor for a year-long project, proposing to interview oncology clinicians—doctors, nurse-practitioners, and physician assistants—about their views on their own deaths and how their attitudes influenced their care of patients who were at the end of life. At first I had my doubts. Given how personal these interviews would be, I didn't know how many clinicians would sign up. But Rachel's project struck a chord with them, and the majority of those whom she asked ultimately *did* participate. Despite their impossibly busy schedules, they took the time to talk and reflect. Frequently, the interviews ran over the allotted time; they had a lot to say and found talking to be cathartic.

Rachel first asked the oncologists whether they could accept the idea of their own deaths. Some said that they were completely at peace with their own deaths, and others indicated that they were terrified, but the majority said yes—sort of: "But I've not really had to face it, so I really don't know how I'd feel." They were being self-aware and honest with themselves.

Some reflected on how their sense of peace (or lack thereof) affected their interactions with patients—for example, whether they tended to talk about death directly with patients or whether they tended to use euphemisms or beat around the bush. Some would only discuss death and dying with the patient's family members, sensing their own and the patient's discomfort. Many said that when they were able to be more self-aware, they could bring more of themselves to the patients they were caring for.

Leeat Granek's oncologists, similar to those interviewed by Rachel Rodenbach, saw a need for change in the culture of cancer care; currently, it glorifies the cure and conquest of cancer, treats death as failure, and regards expressions of emotion as a sign of weakness. Yet, oncologists said that they valued training, information, support, and validation to help them deal more effectively with their own grief; they could see that trying to push away painful feelings wasn't an effective way of dealing with them.[17] At Rochester, my colleagues Tim Quill and Michelle Shayne have developed a program to promote reflection and mindfulness for oncologists in training and clinical staff.[18] Six times a year the trainees and clinical staff meet with a senior oncologist, a palliative care specialist, and a clergyman to enhance their awareness of and address the impact of grief and loss on their personal and professional lives. They share stories about patients for whom they cared. They laugh, they cry. Part of the time is set aside for self-care, including meditation. At the end of each session, they hold a moment of silence in remembrance of patients who have died. If so moved, they speak the name of one patient to remember and honor him. It sets a tone that would have been considered radical until recently; it hones clinicians' ability to care for themselves in the service of being more present for patients. It brings awareness of shared humanity and intimacy as well as the relationship between clinicians' vulnerabilities and those of their patients. They realize that feeling and sharing emotions is not self-indulgent, self-pitying, or a sign of weakness; rather, like Karan's confessions project, it makes it more possible to attend to what's really important.

SELF-COMPASSION

Self-compassion—active cultivation of kindness toward oneself[19]—is one antidote to the unforgiving, harsh, and isolating culture of medicine that becomes manifest in the face of bad outcomes. Practicing self-compassion means neither avoiding negative thoughts nor overidentifying with them. You don't try to confront, overcome, or push through emotional pain, nor do you succumb to it. Rather, you inquire deeply and respond with kindness, clarity, and resolve rather than blame, shame, or despair.

As sensible as self-compassion sounds, doctors have a hard time with the idea. It sounds like self-pity or self-indulgence. But it's none of these—self-compassion means not getting carried away with one's own emotional drama; you don't try to buoy a deflated ego or inflate your self-esteem. Rather, it is a movement toward a healthy balance. People who are able to be more self-compassionate—by either virtue of their prior life experiences or specific training in self-compassion—report feeling better able to own up to their failures and shortcomings without being consumed and paralyzed by negative emotions.[20] They accept their own role in negative events;

they experience a sense of loss and tragedy, yet they don't ruminate obsessively. Self-compassion is ultimately altruistic; it frees you to attend to patients and set aside your own distress. While this is a good lesson for life in general, it's especially important for physicians, who tend to be particularly demanding and unforgiving of themselves.

Marc Lesser is a Zen priest, business consultant, and developer of mindfulness training programs for Fortune 500 companies. Marc would say that self-compassion means knowing yourself and forgetting yourself.[21] Knowing yourself seems self-evident; it helps you find your way in the world. But in a quintessentially paradoxical way, Zen also instructs you to forget yourself. By that, Marc means letting go of rigid assumptions about who you are and recognizing that the assemblage of ideas, habits, and perspectives that you call "me" is more evanescent than you think. Forgetting oneself means abandoning the kinds of self-torture that clinicians habitually engage in when things go wrong. For clinicians—and for anyone else—simultaneously knowing yourself and forgetting yourself helps you respond to error, grief, and loss in a healthier and kinder way.

THINKING BIGGER

Secondary trauma is not unique to anesthesiologists or oncologists or family physicians—all clinicians, regardless of specialty, can be "second victims." The health care system has been slow to respond to this form of clinician distress; few clinicians can honestly say that they work within a culture of awareness, listening, compassion, and support.

But some institutions show signs of hope. The University of Missouri Medical Center has a Second Victim Rapid Response Team, which can be called by clinicians who are feeling distressed. The team offers brief peer and collegial support (Level 1), one-on-one counseling and mentoring by trained peer counselors (Level 2), and referral to mental health professionals for those who are more severely distressed (Level 3).[22] Harvard's Brigham and Women's Hospital offers a peer coaching and support program for distressed physicians. The director, Jo Shapiro, is a surgeon who has trained peer coaches—fellow physicians—to attend to their colleagues in distress.[23] Physicians either refer themselves or refer colleagues who they feel might benefit from one-on-one counseling and coaching. There are few data, making it hard to know how well these efforts work. Yet they represent small steps in the direction toward a culture of caring and support, recognizing that clinician well-being is a sign of health of the health care system overall.

San Francisco is mounting one of the largest efforts to address secondary trauma. San Francisco has enormous social and economic disparities. Their public health clinics care for the most challenging patients—those whose lives are an essay in tragedy, loss, and abandonment and who have repeatedly been failed by the social programs that were intended to help them. The emotional toll on health care workers is large, and attrition and burnout are real problems. Recognizing this, the San Francisco County Health Department instituted a mandatory program in trauma awareness to promote changes in the culture of the health care system as a whole. It's a culture change toward mindful awareness, not just a Band-Aid. Eventually all of San Francisco's nine thousand workers will be trained, and two-thirds of those who have participated so far are working toward concrete changes in their work settings.[24] This kind of coordinated, multilevel intervention is rare in health care organizations and has great promise for sustained change. I'll discuss more about individual and organizational efforts to address burnout and trauma in chapters 10 and 12.

10

Healing the Healer

These are the duties of a physician: First . . . to heal his
mind and to give help to himself before giving it to anyone else.
— Epitaph of an Athenian doctor, AD 2[1]

Diane, a midcareer primary care physician, came to our year-long
program in mindful practice. She was passionate about clinical care
and knew that clinical practice could be deeply fulfilling. However,
she was burned out, as she said, "running on empty." Something
had to change.

By all accounts, Diane was an exemplary family physician and
had excellent clinical judgment. She was a good listener, warm, and
empathic, and she won the trust of her patients. Diane would go
the extra mile, making home visits for patients who were terminally ill; she'd even drive an elderly patient home at the end of the
day to avoid having the patient wait outside in the cold for a city
bus. She took care of more than her share of challenging patients
and wouldn't turn anyone away. But her dedication took a toll. She
was always behind and couldn't spend the time she wanted to with
patients.

Meanwhile the landscape of clinical care was changing. More
and more, she had to fight with insurance companies so that her
patients could get the care that they needed. She had to keep up
with eight different prescribing formularies — one for each insur-

ance company—and the rules changed frequently, resulting in prescriptions being denied, and each denial prompted phone calls and paperwork, which cut into face-to-face time with patients. It was, as she put it, sucking her dry.

Then a large health care system bought her practice. Although the health system talked about "quality metrics," in reality these nods to quality amounted to little more than completing meaningless check-boxes[2] and were paled by the pressure to see more patients in less time. "Productivity," not better care. The new electronic health record system provided easy access to patient information, yet because the system was designed primarily to maximize billing, entering clinically relevant data was clumsy and time-consuming. Diane spent more time looking at the computer screen, so much so that on one occasion she didn't notice when a patient left to go to the bathroom and she started talking as if the patient were there. Electronic documentation added an hour to her day, and the promise of increased efficiency was never realized.

This only increased her resolve to work harder to maintain what quality she could. She achieved her productivity goals and quality metrics, but the effort came at a huge cost. At the end of the day, she was beyond tired. She was also increasingly isolated. Like most of her primary care colleagues, Diane had given up hospital privileges because the productivity demands of outpatient practice made it impossible to continue. She barely had time to exchange words with her practice partners during the workday and no longer knew the specialists to whom she referred patients.

The last straw was an encounter with her practice administrator. She saw a patient with worsening depression, and when the "billing specialist" reviewed her documentation of the visit, she suggested that Diane "correct" her diagnosis. Diane had documented the diagnosis as "depression." The administrator suggested that she might write "fatigue" instead. The reason? Money. Reimbursement for mental health diagnoses was just half of that for physical symptoms. While fatigue is part of depression, it's not as accurate a diagnosis. Diane complied. Then she felt nauseous. She realized that her decision was not morally neutral; her limited attention had migrated from the patient's best interest to the financial bottom line.[3]

For the first time in her fifteen-year career as a physician, Diane began to think of her day in terms of quotas and numbers and realized that she was paying less attention to the details of her patients' lives. The bloodless language of health economists had infected her communication patterns and eventually her medical decisions. She felt out of control—of the pace of clinical practice, over hiring employees, or even the design of the office, down to the art on the walls. She began to wonder if medicine was really for her.

Diane took a two-week vacation with her family and felt refreshed, back to her warm and vibrant self. On returning, her symptoms of burnout recurred within days. She couldn't seem to get enough sleep. She had little energy for family and friends. Her staff noticed that she was more irritable, as did her family. Even her patients asked the nurses—or Diane herself—if something was wrong. They knew something had changed, and it wasn't for the better. Diane considered moving to a different practice, but nearly all of the primary care practices in town had already been bought by large health care systems, and her children were in school so a move to a different city would be disruptive. She felt stuck. She thought about quitting practice altogether.

"AN EROSION OF THE SOUL"

Diane's story is, unfortunately, common. It strikes close to home for many doctors. She was a casualty of a national epidemic of physician burnout. After twenty years of research documenting the epidemic, finally in 2016 Dr. Vivek Murthy, the United States surgeon general, announced that physician burnout would be one of two urgent health care problems that the nation needed to address. The reason was obvious—burned-out physicians cannot possibly provide the best care.

The statistics are daunting. Fifty-four percent of physicians nationally reported burnout in 2014, up from 45 percent in 2011.

Those most affected were on the front lines of clinical care—primary care, emergency medicine, and general surgery.[4] Nurses and other health professionals, medical assistants, and secretaries are feeling it too.[5] Although anyone in a high-stress job can experience burnout, in medicine it is particularly nefarious, and patients have reason to worry. Burned-out physicians are more likely to take shortcuts, make diagnostic errors, and prescribe recklessly.[6] They order too many tests and refer more, just because it takes too much effort to think through problems themselves.[7] They don't communicate well, with their patients[8] or their colleagues, and are more likely to abuse alcohol and drugs and engage in unprofessional behaviors— shady billing practices, providing narcotics to addicts, inappropriate use of social media, and violating patient confidentiality. Some physicians are jumping ship. Of primary care internal-medicine physicians starting practice, a quarter of them will quit within five years,[9] and others are taking early retirement. Replacing them is costly—over $300,000 per physician.[10]

Not everyone catches burnout in time. The majority of burned-out physicians will still be burned out a year later. A colleague, an excellent family physician whom I'd mentored when she was a resident, recently took an early retirement. The new medical records system—the four thousand clicks a day and completing charts at midnight—did her in.[11] My own primary care doctor retired last year after I had been a patient of his for only two years. When he left, the practice sent a terse and impersonal letter that said that he was closing his practice after thirty years to "teach and mentor." When I started with him after my previous primary care doctor left practice, he said that he would be good for another five to ten years. It's not difficult to guess what was behind his decision. I called his office to get a personal recommendation for a new physician. I was directed to a list of three hundred local primary care doctors, only eight of whom were taking new patients, all of whom had just finished training. I felt abandoned. Clearly, something had changed.

Dr. Christina Maslach, a psychologist who has devoted her career to studying burnout, describes it as "an erosion of the soul."[12]

Across all human services professions, Maslach found that burnout consisted of three factors: emotional exhaustion, depersonalization (treating people as objects), and a feeling of low personal accomplishment. This three-headed monster makes work an intolerable burden rather than a source of purpose and meaning, making physicians either work harder and harder or just give up.

Medical practice has always been intense. To give you a sense of the emotional burden of practice, let me take you through a typical four-hour session in my primary care office. I saw eleven patients. First was a thirty-eight-year-old amputee, blind and on dialysis due to diabetes, who was about to have his other leg amputated. The next patient, recently inherited from a now-retired physician, was addicted to prescription narcotics and fell asleep at the wheel, plowing into the car in front of him, shattering his knee and his shoulder. He had consumed an entire week's worth of oxycodone in two days, and now he wanted more. Later in the morning were the struggling parents bringing their violent and hyperactive child, who was recently returned to them from foster care. Then, a fifty-five-year-old man with AIDS who forgot to get his blood tests and didn't go for the X-ray to evaluate his pneumonia; I realized that he had the beginnings of AIDS dementia and had no family to care for him. The day ended with the repeated denials of a brilliant psychotherapist whose liver was being consumed by alcoholic cirrhosis. Without the inner scaffolding of presence and mental stability and the outer scaffolding of collegial and institutional support, no one can be expected to respond humanely to all this tragedy.

But now, in the age of the corporatization and widgetization of medicine, there is a new kind of burnout, a slow, relentless "deterioration of values, dignity, spirit and will"[13] that comes from the structure of health care itself. Patients become "covered lives," and the intimacy of a clinical encounter is reduced to RVUs—relative value units—the productivity metrics that determine how much doctors are paid. The more that doctors' work is tied to computer screens and the more "functionalities" that are added to the electronic health record, the worse burnout becomes. Casualties of efficiency, doctors turn off their emotions. They can't wait until the end of the day, the weekend, retirement. They back their cars into their parking spaces so they can make a quick exit at the end of the day. Patients wonder if their doctors care at all.

Burned-out physicians are not only alienated from patients; they are also alienated from themselves. They feel as if they are on an assembly line, and the opportunity for the rich and rewarding human interactions they imagined when they chose to be doctors is reduced to a mere transaction of information. Recently I reviewed an emergency room chart for a six-month-old patient of mine who had had a fever. Apparently, the electronic health record required that the physician fill in templates about smoking, alcohol consumption, and sexual risk behaviors. The amazing thing is that the physician actually wasted his time by checking the boxes. With enough of these occurrences, feeling battered by systems they cannot change, some doctors capitulate and go numb and only later come to a crushing realization that they have abandoned their values. Others feel that their impact is nil, become depressed, and think only about escape. In one study, 17 percent of those reporting burnout considered suicide in the previous year.[14] This is frightening, given that doctors kill themselves at a rate higher than those in any other profession. I've personally known several.

The problem is not only overwork; it's crisis of meaning, resilience, and community. The toxic combination of high responsibility, low sense of control, and isolation sets the stage for a sense of exhaustion, powerlessness, and helplessness.[15] The stresses due to a dysfunctional health care system and the culture of medicine are real, and the health care community has an obligation to fix them. Putting clinicians in morally compromising situations, installing electronic health record systems that are sculpted around billing rather than good patient care, and placing increasing pressure on clinicians to see more patients without regard to quality are practices that need to change.

THE INNER ENVIRONMENT

But changing the health care system won't solve it all. It is important to recognize that burnout has affected clinicians for centuries, and important causes of burnout reside within clinicians themselves. For the first time in memory, perhaps precipitated by the perfect storm of the heavy burden of suffering in the clinic and the increasing dysfunction of the health care system, some doctors are finally paying attention to their inner environment in a systematic way and finding ways to bring greater presence and resilience to the practice of medicine.

Imagine you're choosing a doctor or that you're hiring a physician to join a practice. What qualities would you want the doctor to have? When I ask this question of the general public or groups of clinicians—no matter what their profession or specialty—the answers are always the same. They want someone who is altruistic and hardworking, has excellent technical skills, is knowledgeable, has good judgment, is empathic and caring, and has equanimity in the face of tragedy and loss.

Yet, even these very *desirable* personality characteristics make doctors psychologically vulnerable.[16] Those who are detail oriented can become compulsive, subjecting patients to too many tests and procedures "just to be sure" and waking at night because they think that they may have forgotten something.[17] Altruistic, service-oriented doctors tend to overcommit and then get exhausted trying to follow through. Truly skilled doctors might believe that they can do it all—feeling omniscient, omnipotent, and unable to admit mistakes—a dangerous combination in medicine. Or they feel insecure. When physicians are asked if they ever feel like an impostor, a remarkable percentage (up to 43 percent) say yes.[18] Of all personality factors, the most closely associated with burnout is rigidity. When unaware of his rigidity, a doctor might insist that his is the single best approach for each problem, and blame his frustration and ineffectiveness on other people (including patients) rather than looking inside himself.[19] Even being empathic takes its toll when doctors don't recognize their secondary trauma and negative emotions.[20] Disturbingly, some clinicians wear stress and burnout as badges of honor, part of the macho culture of medicine that further compounds the anguish and isolation of distressed clinicians.[21] Too often, self-awareness is lacking.

WHY SOME PEOPLE DON'T BURN OUT

Things don't have to be this way. Some clinicians, albeit stressed, fare better than others. They not only cope and adapt, they grow in response to challenges so that the next challenge becomes more tractable. In fact, the right kinds and the right amounts of stress can make us stronger—"stress inoculation." Bones and muscles and brains and hearts grow stronger—more resilient—when you exercise and stress them in the right ways. Bearing weight strengthens bones; without stress, they weaken and crumble. Muscles, too, need exercise or else they atrophy. We thrive on mental challenges, and without them we become dull. Resilience is, in Nicholas Taleb's words, becoming "antifragile."[22] We develop resilience best when we are at our growing edge—just a hair beyond our capacities.

We often think about resilience as the capacity to get through a hard time. However, in high-stress professions, the pressures are ongoing and crises are unpredictable; real resilience is being prepared to be unprepared. Only in the past thirty years have psychologists focused on understanding resilience as a positive attribute and not merely a reaction to trauma. However, much of what we know about resilience is from studies of animals in laboratory environments and people who have endured interpersonal violence, a debilitating injury, war, torture, or natural disasters, not those who have voluntarily chosen a lifetime of work that they knew would be emotionally demanding.

Psychiatrists Steve Southwick and Dennis Charney interviewed former POWs, Special Forces instructors, and civilians who had experienced severe psychological traumas such as rape, sexual abuse, the loss of a limb, or cancer.[23] They found that in spite of these extreme events, remarkably few developed depression or post-traumatic stress disorder.[24] Southwick and Charney identified ten "resilience factors" that would make sense to most of us: realistic optimism, facing fear, moral compass, religion and spirituality, social support, role models, physical fitness, brain fitness, cognitive and emotional flexibility, and a sense of meaning and purpose. Personality is important too. Just as some personality factors are associated with greater risks of burnout, others confer greater resilience. Psychologists Richard Ryan and Edward Deci point to three qualities: the ability to form warm and caring relationships with others—so-called secure attachment—a sense of personal autonomy, and perceiving oneself as competent and up to the task.[25]

Resilience is mirrored in our biochemical and genetic makeup. Those who thrive despite severe trauma are biochemically different from their less resilient peers. They have lower levels of stress hormones and neuropeptide Y, the "anxiety" neurotransmitter. They have higher levels of serotonin, which is associated with positive mood, and higher levels of dopamine in the reward centers of their brains. They have higher levels of "brain-derived neurotropic factor," which directs the brain to grow new neural pathways.[26] Because resilience seems to be affected by caring and trusting human relationships, most likely oxytocin—the hormone associated with love and affiliation—is also involved. It appears that not only do resilient people trigger the release of higher levels of these neurotransmitters and hormones, but they also have more receptors for them. Signals are more easily transmitted. And sometimes the receptors are of a different subtype altogether to which a neurotransmitter binds more avidly.

We are now just learning what might lead the body to produce more of these substances and to place more—and more avid—receptors on nerve cells. Just as I discussed in chapter 3, it's epigenetic regulation; social epigenetics to be more precise. Genes that encode for neurotransmitters and receptors turn on when you're in a supportive and safe environment and turn off when you feel vulnerable and traumatized. Those experiencing secondary trauma, isolation, and lack of support are literally—on a biochemical level—less able to muster the resilience they need. This means that doctors who aren't allowed time to debrief after a patient death or who submit to meaningless bureaucratic tasks are likely to become less and less resilient. Admittedly, resilience (and gene regulation) is to some extent influenced by past events which cannot be changed, such as prenatal influences and early childhood traumas. But it is tantalizing to consider recent research by psychologist Douglas Johnson at the Naval Health Research Center in San Diego; his research group demonstrated the mindfulness programs for military recruits promoted self-awareness and resilience and, in doing so, enhanced their "healthy" gene expression.[27]

TIPPY AND UNFLIPPABLE

How do people become more resilient? Part of the answer has to do with mental stability. I am not an expert kayaker, but I do enjoy it. A few years ago, I bought a kayak. In the store, the salesperson talked about primary instability and secondary instability. At first, I was confused. Why would I want to buy a kayak that was unstable? He explained. Kayaks with primary instability are more maneuverable, and it takes less effort to guide them around rocks, sharp bends, and standing waves in a river, but they also feel tippier. Secondary instability refers to how easily the kayak will capsize. Because I wanted a boat that was responsive and I had no interest in getting wet when I least expected it, I chose a kayak that had quite a bit of primary instability and a fair degree of secondary stability.

Once I had it in the water, it took some getting used to. It felt really tippy. It took me a while to distinguish primary from secondary instability and to have the confidence that the kayak wouldn't flip over. With time, I came to tolerate feeling "unbalanced" and I could maneuver the kayak more effortlessly, and I realized that fighting the primary instability put me at greater risk than using it to my advantage. I even came to relish the tippiness. I realized that

I had made progress when one day, kayaking across a lake with a strong crosswind, I leaned into the wind, so much so that I was at a thirty-degree angle, water coming way up one side of the kayak. I was moving in a straight line and the kayak didn't flip.

Mental stability works the same way. It's a dynamic equilibrium. You're never completely in balance. Just as I enjoy the tippiness of my kayak, I've come to enjoy the unpredictable and chaotic corners of medicine; the next patient could be a day old or one hundred years old, and the patient's issues could be trivial or life threatening. There's a certain off-balance thrill to navigating unexpected twists with aplomb.

REMINDERS

In difficult times, I keep coming back to three important "reminders" about resilience. The first is that *resilience is a capacity that can be grown.*[28] With training, you can gain more control over your behavior and well-being, relate to stress in healthier ways, and feel differently about yourself. Resilience doesn't mean hardening the heart; quite the opposite, resilience is about adopting lightness, a sense of humor, and flexibility. You change your personality, just a bit, becoming more focused, more tippable, and less flippable. Participants in our year-long mindful practice program did just that. Over time, they scored higher on two of the Big Five personality factors that relate to focused attention and mental stability—and the changes endured.[29] While the party line in personality psychology had been that personality was immutable after age thirty, more recently researchers have studied people whose personalities *had* changed throughout their lifetimes. Those who changed had three qualities: they were adept at observing themselves, observing others, and listening attentively.[30] In short, they were mindful.

The second reminder is that *well-being is about engagement, not withdrawal.* This is not intuitive. If a situation is pleasant, it makes sense to stick around and want more. But what if a situation is unpleasant? It's only natural to want to get away and avoid people you find difficult. While these survival strategies might help in the short run, the same old problems and their maladaptive solutions are still there. Preventing burnout and developing resilience have more to do with presence than escape.

The third reminder is that *mindfulness is a community activity*. When I was in Bhutan a few years ago, I walked past hermitages scattered high above tiny Himalayan villages in some of the most isolated spots in the world, in caves and steep ravines, beside glaciers and atop three-thousand-foot cliffs. The monks doing three-year-long solitary retreats might not even see the villagers who would bring them food each week, yet they could do what they were doing *because* of the knowledge that the villagers were supporting their efforts and that other monks in other hermitages were engaged in a similar effort. Even in isolation they felt—and were—part of a community.

The same is true for the rest of us; we need a sense of community to sustain a mindful vision. Yet, over the past few years, hospital doctors' lounges have closed, personal relationships among clinicians have eroded, and in the outpatient setting clinicians know each other only as faceless characters sharing an electronic chart. Creating community requires visionary leadership, yet this vision and the leaders to promote it are lacking in the current health care environment.

WHAT IS WELL-BEING, ANYWAY?

I bristle when people say that the key to well-being is achieving "work-life balance." Those who see "life" as everything outside work, necessitating "balance," implicitly assume that when you're at work, you're not fully alive, a sad state of affairs for those of us who are in a profession that is capable of providing such deep rewards (and that takes up so much of our waking existence).[31] It reflects a deeper problem, though. By placing the blame for your unhappiness exclusively on things external to yourself (the work environment), you're assuming that by containing work—by compartmentalizing, pushing it away, or making it "not-me"—you might be happier. This is a trap.

Marc Lesser recounts a famous Zen dialogue:[32]

The monk arrives at the monastery and says to the teacher, "I've arrived. Please give me your teaching."

The teacher says, "Have you eaten your breakfast?"

The monk responds, "Yes, I have."

The teacher says, "Wash your bowl."

The monk understood. What could be more obvious?

Marc explains that this indirect and somewhat bizarre answer is intended to free the mind from habitual and monocular views of a situation and instead invite you to look at your current experience, right here, right now. Marc comments, "If you were to ask, 'How can I find work-life balance?,' I might be inclined to ask if you have eaten your breakfast. . . . And, assuming you have, I suggest you wash your bowl."

Marc continues:

Attempting to achieve work-life balance, as though something is missing or something is wrong (either with you or with your situation), is a set-up for failure, for stress, and for anything but balance. Instead, experiment by bringing your attention to the activities that make up your work. Notice the activities and notice your inner dialogue, the stories you weave, as well as your feelings. Just this act of paying attention can produce positive change—a bit of slowing down, a little more space—opening up the possibility of change, of more calm, even of more appreciation.

Marc's answer invites a deeper and more important question: What is well-being, anyway? We know that when people have a deep sense of meaning and fulfillment, the more superficial trappings—what you have in terms of achievement or pleasure—are less important and may even get you off track. We can tolerate long hours and even welcome stress if work intrinsically brings a sense of purpose, satisfaction, joy, and meaning. That deeper kind of well-being, one that's worth achieving, is what Aristotle called *eudaimonia*. *Eudaimonia* is true human flourishing; it *results from* and *leads to* being more fully engaged with one's work in a healthy and positive way[33] while recognizing that the world is messy, chaotic, imperfect, and not always pleasant. Pushing away only makes matters worse.

THE 20 PERCENT RULE

My wife, Deborah, tells a story about Mary Pedersen, her extraordinary and somewhat eccentric seventh-grade teacher. Deb was thirteen years old and living in Denmark for a year. Mary asked Deb, "Honeylamb"—she really did say this!—"honeylamb, what do *you* like? What do you *like*?" Deb was thunderstruck. No one had ever asked her that question. It got her thinking and led her first to writing, then to Renaissance history, then to seventeenth-century music. Fifteen years later, we visited Mary in Denmark (and she called me "honeylamb" too) in her cottage so overgrown with vines and rosebushes that the patio was reduced to an area just large enough for three small chairs. We learned that she had been a Shakespearean actor; in her youth, she left a secure academic path in England to join a theater troupe. While on tour in Denmark, she fell in love and found a job there at an English-speaking school. Although she worked as an artist, an actor, and a teacher until she was seventy, she felt that she never "worked" a day in her life. We should all be as fortunate as Mary Pedersen. Her capacity for joy was infectious, and Deb caught the bug. She too feels that her career as a musician isn't "work" in the way that most of us think about it, in part because of Mary's influence.

Not many of us have had teachers like Mary who remind us to stop and think, "What, in my work setting, gives me the greatest sense of joy, fulfillment, and meaning?" Think about that question for a moment and then consider—here's the clincher—"In a typical week, how much of my time do I actually spend doing those activities?" It doesn't have to be 100 percent; few people are that fortunate. Research shows that if physicians spend even 20 percent of their work time in the activities that they regard as the most meaningful, they're much less likely to be burned out, meaning that they're more able to tolerate the difficult moments.[34] Makes sense, but most doctors—and others who have some control over their work lives—have never asked themselves these fundamental questions. People shouldn't wait until they are feeling burned out to reflect on what's most nourishing about their work.

THE EARLY SIGNS

Physicians know that it's easier to manage any illness during the early stages rather than waiting until it is full-blown. They know the long list of late signs of distress—insomnia, depression, chronic pain, migraines, GI symptoms, drinking too much, relationship problems, and more. They know that early signs are harder to detect, so it takes vigilance. Yet ironically, doctors are particularly at risk for not seeing these early signs because doctors tend to be stoical. They think that stress is a normal part of the job, are notorious for delaying seeking care, and for self-medicating.

An honest self-appraisal is the first step. During workshops, I'll ask participants to rate their burnout using Maslach's burnout scale,[35] or the simple diagram on the next page. You'll see a list of attributes of burnout and well-being and a scale of 1 to 10. Try it. Are you a 1, a 5, or a 10? As you're doing this, stop, think, and feel the impact of your work environment on your life. Perhaps this might be the moment when you can no longer underestimate your distress.

With training, you can bring these warning signs to your awareness before they get out of hand. Training starts with noticing. Ask yourself, *What are some of my early warning signs of distress in the workplace setting?* Start with the body. *What bodily sensations and behaviors do I notice?* Most of the time, we feel these early warnings as bodily sensations—a tightness in the shoulders, a knot in

Ronald Epstein, M.D.

Burned out / **Resilient**

1 2 3 4 5 6 7 8 9 10

Burned out	Resilient
Withdrawn	Present
Defeated	Bouncing back
Going through the motions	Fully engaged
Brittle, rigid	Bending, not breaking
Cynical, hopeless	Capacity for positivity
Hypercritical	A light touch
Feeling ineffective	Becoming stronger
Treading water	Moving forward
Fearing change	Welcoming change

the stomach, shakiness. *Next, explore any emotions that accompany those warning signs: What are they?* The emotions that often accompany the bodily sensations might be feelings of impatience, fear or anger, and sometimes just a sense of disconnection and blandness. *Now, be aware of thoughts, ideas, interpretations, and judgments that accompany these warning signs.* Sensations and emotions may be accompanied by specific thoughts—such as thinking that you're feeling inadequate in some way. You might notice that your behavior is different—you drive faster, eat less, put off important tasks, clean your desk, or buy things you don't really need—before you consciously register that you are tired, stressed, or annoyed.

One early warning sign for me is when I start making more typos than usual. It's annoying. I go back and correct the error, then compensate by typing faster. Then I pound harder on the keys, as if I could beat them into submission. It only gets worse. I get angry at the computer (*Why is the spell-checker in the medical record so clunky?*), then the clinic (*Why did they have to schedule three extra patients for me today?*), and finally patients themselves (*Why does she always come with forty complaints to deal with in a twenty-minute visit?*).

172

Awareness of these early warning signs can provide a window into our inner state before things get unmanageable. I call them "friends"; they are protectors and reminders. When I notice my typing deteriorating, I can stop for a moment and appreciate that I have a choice, a choice I had not previously acknowledged: I can choose to get annoyed at myself and pound harder, or I can summon a state of curiosity, saying to myself, "Oh, here I am making typos. I wonder what that's about. Am I feeling rushed? Is the task unpleasant? Do I need to feel that way? Is it useful to respond in this way? Can I do anything about it?" It may seem easy to take a new perspective, yet too often all of us just let the pressures mount. Because most of us don't have habits that constantly put us in touch with the early warning signs of stress, we have to develop them. It takes intention, practice, and discipline—qualities that doctors and most high-functioning professionals often bring to other domains of their lives.

When being mindful, I am aware of how my expectations and emotions condition what I see and that I can take a new perspective or readjust the lens through which I see the world. I engage in metacognition: thinking about and appraising my thinking and emotions. It's saying to myself, "I'm feeling pretty stressed. What's that about?" Then asking myself, "Is this situation really altogether negative?" And "Is there something I can learn from it?" I realize that my original view may have been biased or myopic. I recalibrate. Research suggests that those who are able to recalibrate and take a new perspective may grow new neural connections in brain structures associated with emotional intelligence and emotion regulation.[36]

RESILIENCE TRAINING

Some of the most interesting research on resilience training comes from military settings, with soldiers who were about to be deployed into war zones. I initially had trouble with research about people who were being trained to control and kill—and not to empower and heal—until I realized that I was making assumptions that might not be quite true. In many ways, medical settings resemble military settings. In both health care and the military, the physical and emotional stresses are ongoing and extreme, and the training is rigorous and all-consuming. In both settings, the dictum is "first do no harm" (although I wish that doctors and generals would keep that in mind more often) and not be trigger-happy (medications and surgery can kill as well as heal). In both settings, problems are complex. You need mental stability, effective communication, ethical conduct, and wisdom to manage unexpected situations rarely encountered in civilian life. Both settings have hierarchies that often do more harm than good, bringing a huge risk of disconnection between those who are in charge and those who are on the front lines. Both soldiers and doctors experience vicarious trauma frequently—they witness the unbearable suffering, loss, grief, dismemberment, disintegration, and destruction of people who deserve better. Both professions involve huge personal sacrifices, and reflection and self-awareness are not part of either professional culture.

Military mind-fitness programs with a strong emphasis on meditation practice have had positive effects.[37] Participants recovered more rapidly after stressful events. Their heart rates and breathing and stress hormone levels normalized sooner, and they experienced fewer ill effects from subsequent stresses. They made better decisions, had fewer lapses in attention, and were better able to tolerate adversity.

To address the controversy that such programs might just make more attentive—but heartless—killers, the developers of the program have a counterargument: reducing emotional reactivity can reduce the reckless or unethical behaviors that only compound the tragedy of war. They claim that by improving emotional intelligence, soldiers might work as a team and win the hearts and minds of others. I hope that is true. I raise this controversial parallel to medical practice because these studies point to ways in which health professionals and others doing "combat duty" in the public service can become more mindful.

RECAPTURING PURPOSE AND MEANING

Whenever I see a distressed clinician learn to be more resilient, I wonder how she did it. The health care environment has only gotten worse, with more administrative burdens and less social support. The first hurdle is awareness. Diane knew she was distressed, as do most participants in our workshops. They've seen the warning signs. Over the course of a year, Diane started a regular meditation practice, just ten to fifteen minutes each morning, and used an app for her smartphone that would remind her and time her sessions. More important, she prompted herself to incorporate mindful moments into her day—a habit of pausing, opening, relaxing—rather than just plowing through. Even brief moments of self-care were powerful reminders to focus more on what was truly important. She adopted a practice of gratitude, each day intentionally naming one thing for which she was grateful; it helped her to recalibrate. Gradually she saw more clearly which external factors she couldn't change—completing meaningless checklists, wrestling with insurance companies, and dealing with unwieldy electronic record systems—and her attitude changed. She learned that she didn't have to respond to every request made by patients, administrators, and insurance companies, and she mastered a few more shortcuts so that she could work with the electronic health record system more effectively. She started a small insurrection in her office—she put *her* photographs on the walls, and others did the same. She realized that the computer screen could be a barrier, so she had the computer screen remounted and rearranged her office so that she and the patient could look at the screen together—it improved communication and helped her to feel more connected with patients, even when she had to type or look something up. These small changes reflected an incremental change of focus and attitude. She was more honest with herself, listened more deeply to patients and colleagues, and felt a greater sense of community. Despite kayaking in rough waters, she felt that she was no longer about to drown.

11

Becoming Mindful

When you practice being mindful, you reshape your brain. Every year, hundreds of scientific articles explore how this happens and under what conditions. But the very idea that the adult brain could be reshaped was radical until thirty years ago; psychologists and neuroscientists had underestimated the human capacity for neuroplasticity—how our brains continue to grow and develop throughout life. The good news is that you can do more than keep your brain from withering; you can make new connections among neurons and help to grow your brain.

Some of the earliest work on neuroplasticity was done with London taxi drivers. I drove a taxicab in Manhattan while taking my premed courses at Columbia, so I was familiar with the rigors of the job and the creative approaches drivers employ to navigate complex cities. But London is much more complicated than New York, and the training to become a taxi driver is much more rigorous. Potential drivers need to learn the 320 "best routes" connecting thousands of "places of note" along the sixty thousand roads within a six-mile radius of central London—almost none of which go in a straight line and many of which are one-way and change names several times. The exams to become a taxi driver in London (known as Appearances) are notoriously difficult, and people typically spend three to four years acquiring "the Knowledge," a deep familiarity with the particulars of the roads and places of note and how the routes that connect them must be combined and altered, depending on traffic conditions, to get to each destination efficiently.

Eleanor Maguire and Katherine Woollett, neuropsychologists at University College London, were curious. They wanted to see if changes could be noted in the brains of the taxi drivers, particularly in the posterior hippocampus—the area of the brain concerned with spatial memory. They scanned the brains of seventeen taxi drivers and eighteen bus drivers. They found that the posterior hippocampus was larger in taxi drivers, who need to constantly find new routes, compared with bus drivers, who don't.[1] The more the taxi drivers drove, the larger the posterior hippocampus. Then Maguire and Woollett studied seventy-nine taxi trainees and thirty-nine controls. Each driver had psychological testing and MRI scans at the start and end of their training. In those who passed the exam, the posterior hippocampus had grown. It hadn't in the controls or in those who failed.[2] Of note, those who did well spent twice as much time studying as those who didn't.

The ability to assimilate vast quantities of knowledge and construct mental maps would sound familiar to any medical student. Medical students learn thousands of new words during their first two years of medical school, and each word—and the concept that it represents—is linked to other words in complex ways. Just as taxi drivers create mental maps of cities, medical students create mental maps of physiological and pathological pathways that manifest as health and disease. With repeated firing, these neural connections become better "lubricated," so that mental tasks (such as memory and association) that previously took significant effort eventually become automatic. In time, the words are linked to real patients and thereby acquire personal meaning and emotional valence. The brain grows new connections—it rewires and reshapes itself. While behavioral scientist Donald Hebb proposed, as early as 1949, that "neurons that fire together wire together,"[3] until recently you couldn't actually see the rewiring in action. Now with sophisticated neuroimaging, it is possible to see how, with increasing practice, parts of the brain actually grow. The brain grows not only when you practice memory tasks and motor skills, but also when you practice "meta-skills"—skills of being attentive, curious, open-minded, and present. Admittedly, while the psychological and physical benefits of developing attentiveness and other aspects of mindfulness are clear, our knowledge of the actual changes in brain structure, chemistry, and functioning is still rudimentary.

WHAT MAKES A GREAT DOCTOR?

By the time they are a few years out from completing training, master clinicians have shaped their brains in particular ways to enhance specific abilities depending on what their work requires—knowledge, good judgment, emotional responsiveness, compassion, and technical skill. But how do master clinicians get that way? How can we help more clinicians get there?

The answers come from reexamining what we mean by expertise. In psychology, education, and health care, researchers have struggled with the question of expertise. For a long time researchers thought that natural talent accounted for a lot of it; you had a particular aptitude for singing or science, or soccer.

Psychologist Karl Anders Ericsson took another view—that expertise is largely a product of experience. Ericsson observed chess masters, musicians, and athletes and found that true masters don't get that way just because they have natural talent; they engage in what he calls "deliberate practice."[4] Remember that the taxi drivers who passed the test had studied twice as much as those who didn't. In Ericsson's estimation, it takes about ten thousand hours of practice, or ten years, to have expertise in complex skills, whether the skills are chess playing or brain surgery (or taxi driving). However, it has to be high-quality practice, with supervision and feedback.

Ericsson also explored how doctors become experts, noting that expertise is different in medicine than in other pursuits. Chess players, musicians, and athletes typically start acquiring their skills as children, whereas doctors typically begin to acquire their skills when they're in their twenties. Musicians, chess players, and athletes learn how emotions and attitudes affect performance—there's the "inner game" and the "outer game." There is much less talk of emotions in medical training. In chess, music, and sports, it's usually clear that when things go wrong it's due to someone having made an error. In medicine it's not so clear. A patient's outcome is not completely attributable to a doctor's skill; so much depends on the particulars of each patient that are out of a physician's control. Most important, for musicians, training is much more intimate and involves direct observation, critique, and feedback. When I was studying music, I'd be one-on-one with my piano teacher for an hour every week. Over time I'd anticipate and internalize what my teacher might say, and gradually I was able to critique myself. While surgeons benefit from direct supervision in the operating room, in most branches of medicine it is very different. When I was a medical student and a resident, I'd tell my supervising physicians what I had seen and accomplished, but only rarely did they actually observe me with a patient. My mentor George Engel suggested that we imagine what would happen if piano lessons were that way—you'd just report to your teacher what you had done well and where you perceived there were problems.[5] You certainly wouldn't get to Carnegie Hall that way.

Brothers Stuart and Hubert Dreyfus at the University of California, Berkeley, also observed professionals in a variety of fields. They developed a model in which they described a hierarchy from novice, to competent, proficient, and expert, later adding a level for master.[6] For the Dreyfus brothers, expertise involved making automatic what for novices would be deliberate and effortful. The Dreyfuses suggested that experts could then reserve their cognitive resources for more complex tasks. For example, the nurse who took my blood pressure before a recent visit to my doctor was talking to me throughout. An expert, she could easily divide her attention between the automatic task and the (hopefully more interesting) interpersonal interaction, whereas a nursing student would have had to devote her full attention to what she was hearing through the stethoscope. Because these tasks become so automatic, experts, according to the Dreyfus brothers, often have difficulty describing exactly what they do.

Expertise is not merely automatic, though it also includes the ability to alternate—effortlessly—between automatic and effortful cognitive processing.[7] When a nurse in my dentist's office took my blood pressure two days after I saw my doctor, she was chatting just like the previous nurse. Then, suddenly she stopped. She took my pressure again, this time paying closer attention (I was not looking forward to the dental procedure, and my body let us know it). She slowed down. She noted an unusually high blood pressure. She switched gears.

Not every nurse would. While the ten-thousand-hours formula might work for developing basic skills, only if the practice is mindful will people learn to switch from automatic to effortful, to slow down when they should. Mindless practice, in contrast, leads to being an "experienced non-expert," repeating the same mistakes over and over, without the insight to know why. Conversely, "true experts" are mindful and adaptive; they recognize when something's amiss before others do. They observe and respond to context, then switch gears, slowing down and improvising.[8] It's like jazz.[9]

VOLUNTARILY BRINGING BACK A WANDERING ATTENTION

Cultivating and sustaining attention is the sine qua non of good care. Over 120 years ago, William James devoted one of the first chapters of his *Principles of Psychology* to attention. James described—remarkably accurately—how attention works, setting the stage for future research. But he didn't know how to cultivate it. He said, "The faculty of voluntarily bringing back a wandering attention, over and over again, is the very root of judgment, character, and will. . . . An education which should improve this faculty would be the education par excellence. But it is easier to define this ideal than to give practical directions for bringing it about."[10]

Attention training is now common practice. It takes remarkably little to augment your capacity to attend. Even after a week of meditating thirty minutes a day, executive attention improves—if you recall, executive attention helps to reduce and reconcile conflicts between competing demands on your attention (such as someone talking to you when you're trying to add up a column of numbers).[11] After eight weeks of practice you'd likely have better sustained focus (top-down attention) and you'd be less likely to be derailed by the unimportant. With longer practice, some studies suggest that you'd be able to manage your precious cognitive resources more effectively and switch among mental tasks more quickly. You would be better able to remember key information, even when asked to multitask in highly stressful environments.[12] With practice, you'd be more likely to notice and name your emotions, allowing you to respond more intelligently to strong feelings; you'd feel less frustrated when under high cognitive load; and you'd ruminate less about the past and worry less about the future. You'd become more present and more mentally fit.

If you continued practicing, you'd become more aware of how your mind works. You could more readily identify when you are focused or distracted, when you're being curious and when you're more shut down. You'd become a connoisseur of types and qualities of your states of attending and distraction—just as the Inuit become connoisseurs of snow and sommeliers become connoisseurs of wine.[13] Functional brain imaging might show thickening of the gray matter in the brain, deeper folds of the brain (gyrification), and increased connectivity. Studies done by psychologist Al Kaszniak at the University of Arizona suggest that attention training can reverse the natural decline of cognition with age.[14]

BEGINNING

Zen teachers often tell beginners, "Don't meditate, just pay attention." This is because for some people the word *meditation* carries with it expectations and associations.

Meditation practice is skill building,[15] an education of the mind through first-person inquiry.[16] Some people associate meditation with self-absorption, so to make the purpose clear, I call it attention training, awareness training, compassion training, or, simply, practice. I emphasize that the ultimate purpose of meditation is to reduce suffering in the world, not to feel good about yourself. Debate rages about whether meditation is intrinsically "spiritual," but it depends on how you define "spiritual." If you see "spiritual" as anything that lends meaning and coherence to the world, then perhaps meditation is. It certainly does not require any particular religious or philosophical belief system, other than believing that by knowing yourself better you can be more effective at realizing what is most important.[17]

Most practitioners use two or more practices at different points during their training. It's like exercise — you wouldn't only do push-ups if you wanted to get fit. We are only beginning to understand the way in which each meditation practice develops a different part of the brain, and no one can say whether one particular method is "better" than another; they are just different.[18] In the appendix I describe the two most common and widely studied meditation practices, which are known as focused attention practice and open awareness practice. Briefly, focused attention involves focusing the mind on an "object" — the breath or a mantra. Open awareness is a disciplined practice of being aware of whatever is happening right now, in the present moment, but without attention to any particular object. Other practices, such as body scan and compassion training, were described earlier in the book (see chapters 3 and 8).

But what's the threshold? How much (or how little) attention training do we need? It seems that even small doses can make a difference, at least in the short run. A few people even say that their first experience with meditation was transformative — they feel that a door had been opened and would never again be closed. Those who practice daily become more adept than those who don't. And others notice. I was tantalized by a small pilot study by David Schroeder and his colleagues in Portland, Oregon, in which primary care teams who underwent mindfulness training found that their patient ratings were directly proportional to the amount of time they spent practicing.[19] It's not just quantity, though; quality of practice matters too. Just daydreaming won't get you there.[20]

THE BODY

I've wondered why most contemplative practices start with attention to sensory experiences. Only now, though, are neuroscientists, cognitive scientists, and philosophers converging on an understanding that emotions are fundamentally embodied, inextricably linked to our bodily states.[21] We gnash our teeth when working on a difficult problem or grip our seats during a horror movie. Our language is filled with bodily metaphors: *a pain in the neck*, *heartache*, and *shouldering a burden*. We call informative and helpful intuitions *gut feelings*. We describe people in terms of sensory experience: people who are emotionally distant are *cold* and those who seem close are *warm*. We use kinesthetic and spatial expressions: *feeling down in the dumps* or *up to par*; *on top of things* or *under the weather*. We mentally simulate bodily sensations in order to retrieve memories of events, and during exercises such as the body scan (described in chapter 3), by directing awareness to the body we become more aware of thoughts and emotions.

It works the other way too. We can evoke emotions by assuming different bodily postures and expressions. Standing tall imbues dignity; kneeling and bowing evoke submission. My piano lessons always started with posture. In the military, "attention" is a physical stance, which presumably calls up a certain state of mind. Assuming a dignified sitting posture is the first task for beginner meditation students with the goal of preparing them for awareness, mental stability, and humility.

Francesc Borrell-Carrió, an astute colleague, noticed that doctors smile when they greet a patient, even those that they don't particularly like.[22] He wondered why. In those situations, smiling has nothing to do with being happy. It's about preparing oneself to be hospitable, to be present, to understand, and to help. It inspires an attitude of welcoming and good humor and not clinging too tenuously to any preconceived ideas one might have. Even a forced smile can make a difference in terms of how you understand your own and someone else's emotions. In a psychology experiment, psychologist Arthur Glenberg divided participants into two groups; one group held a pencil between the teeth to engage the smile muscles, whereas the other held a pencil between the upper lip and the nose to engage frown muscles. When engaging the smile muscles, participants processed information about pleasant events more readily than about unpleasant events, whereas the reverse was true if they engaged the frown muscles.[23] Psychologist Al Kaszniak has demonstrated greater activation of the zygomatic ("smile") muscles in long-term meditators, perhaps one contribution to their feeling more positive emotions.[24] Science has taken twenty-five hundred years to catch up, providing experimental evidence for what practitioners have always held as obvious.[25]

INTERPERSONAL MINDFULNESS

I asked a recently retired leader at our hospital about his uncanny ability to handle difficult situations. His days were filled with meetings during which he'd often have to tell members of his staff that they had fallen short. After he started the job, his administrative assistant commented to him that whereas physicians leaving his predecessor's office often looked angry and disgruntled, now the same people leaving the same office were smiling. My colleague knew that he had that talent, but couldn't articulate how he did it. His colleagues (including me) could see that he would note the other's distress, acknowledge it, but not give in. If the other person intensified demands, he'd slow down, pause, reflect on what was really important, and then act. He had the presence of mind not to fall into the trap of escalation. His was a clear example of a healthy response to stress; he'd feel that he had done the right thing and he'd sleep well at night.

Not all of us have the natural skill that he did. Some of us need practice. Just as it's possible to practice mindfulness of your own mind, you can also practice mindfulness in relationships—interpersonal mindfulness. Earlier in the book I described how narratives—stories that doctors write about their difficult moments in practice—and deep listening can promote communication, reflection, and presence. Another dyadic contemplative practice is known as Insight Dialogue;[26] participants pair off and have a conversation, usually about a topic that has some personal salience, such as aging or illness or compassion or courage. But it's not an ordinary conversation. Participants are instructed to speak from the heart: first pause, open, and relax, then speak what comes first to mind, trusting that which comes spontaneously, to "listen deeply" and "speak the truth." The goal is to bring the clarity and mindfulness of silent meditation practice directly into conversations with others. Just as meditation helps focus the wandering mind through the practice of awareness of one's interior life, insight dialogues help participants be mindful of their own quality of listening and speaking.

Another interpersonal mindfulness technique is known as Appreciative Inquiry.[27] Here, an interviewer elicits from his or her partner a story of success amid adversity—a time when a positive attribute of the interviewee made a difference. By explicitly focusing on the positive, and having a partner help to maintain that focus, you can bring your strengths to new and unfamiliar situations. Originally conceived as a way of harnessing potential and cohesion in organizations, appreciative interviews start by promoting mindfulness in dialogue. Little is known about how these practices work on a psychological level, much less a neurobiological one. But we do know that people who are in dialogue tend to mirror each other's physiologies, movements, and even patterns of neural firing, likely mediated through mirror neurons. The frontiers of social neuroscience are now being stretched, and new research is exploring our capacity for shared mind, shared presence,[28] and intersubjectivity— and how these human capacities enable us to make deep and healing connections.

EIGHT LEAPS

In this final section of the chapter, I'll share my eight "leaps." Much like Zen koans, I carry these leaps with me in practice because they help me refocus, explore, grow, and begin again with each patient. I invite you, whether or not you're involved in health care, to find your own leaps: What is it that you face every day that is unresolved? What dilemmas and paradoxes do you face? Perhaps you'll see some parallels with your own work situation or your home life.

THE EIGHT LEAPS

From fragmented self to whole self
From othering to engagement
From objectivity to resonance
From detached concern to tenderness and steadiness
From self-protection to self-suspension
From well-being to resilience
From empathy to compassion
From whole mind to shared mind

The first leap I call **"from fragmented self to whole self."** I've become increasingly aware that I bring some positive parts of myself to my clinical work—I'm curious, analytic, and I try to be kind. Other parts of me—my artistic side, perhaps—tend to "reside" at my research office, at vacation spots, and at home. I take these divisions—rarely based on any conscious choice—for granted; sometimes they are appropriate, but sometimes they lead to a sense of fragmentation, of loss. I ask myself each day, "What parts of myself am I engaging in my care of this patient, right now?" And then: "Does it have to be that way?"

The second leap is **"from othering to engagement."** The physician-poet Jack Coulehan proposes two reasons why clinicians detach emotionally from patients—to maintain objectivity, and to avoid being overwhelmed by the patient's suffering.[29] To detach, I use a "doctorly" voice, construct the patient as an "other," "the person in the bed," someone "not like me." The patient inhabits the world of the sick; we, the world of the well. I've even caught myself assuming my doctorly voice with family members, effectively "othering" them, something that wins little affection. While to suggest that I can truly understand someone else's experience would be arrogant, I still can try to "learn from below," letting the patient guide me to an understanding of her experience. This is a process of shared imagination. The philosopher G. C. Spivak calls it a "no-holds-barred self-suspending leap into the other's sea—basically without preparation."[30] When I say, "I can only begin to imagine," to a patient who is seriously ill or distressed, the patient then becomes my teacher; I feel inquisitive and humble. This moral act opens me up to surprises and leads to new ways of understanding. I ask myself, "In what ways is this patient like me?"

The third leap is **"from objectivity to resonance."** In medical school I was trained to be an objective observer. I needed to discern whether a heart murmur is harsh-sounding enough to warrant an echocardiogram, whether a patient's story is coherent or contradictory, or whether I've done enough diagnostic testing for someone with a headache. Objectivity, though, is a stance that I never fully inhabited because it sometimes feels false. Clinical practice is always richer and more satisfying to me and my patients if there is some well-boundaried and heartfelt sharing of emotion.[31] I ask myself, "What would happen if I allowed greater emotional resonance, if I allowed myself to feel just a little bit more?" Here, no particular distance is the "correct" distance; rather, it is the asking of the question that is important.

A related leap is one **"from detached concern to tenderness and steadiness."** Tenderness is a quality of touch—both literal touch or feeling touched through communication. Steadiness is the mental stability to get one's work done—and done well. As Jack Coulehan notes, tenderness and steadiness support each other and don't have to be mutually exclusive.[32] I ask myself, "Can I be both tender and steady even if the seas are turbulent?"

The fifth leap, **"from self-protection to self-suspension,"** has to do with fear. One of my favorite children's books (and my kids' too) is *Doctor De Soto*, about a mouse who is a dentist.[33] His patient is a fox. This is clearly a dangerous relationship. While the fox is imagining eating the mouse, the mouse focuses on the painful tooth. The fox's desire to avoid pain trumps his impulse to eat the mouse. They are able to work together, despite their differences, at least until the pain stops. The mouse, though, doesn't want to take any chances and glues the fox's jaw (temporarily) shut just as he is finishing his work.

Children's books often contain great wisdom. Sometimes our fears as physicians are well justified. A patient of mine who had just completed parole for armed robbery and attempted murder gently requested that I falsify data about his HIV status so that he would be eligible for life insurance. He asked questions about my family; he seemed to know where I lived. I had reason to believe that he had access to a gun. I said no and frankly felt a bit afraid. Even when I'm faced with threats that are illusory, I adopt psychological distance and armor to protect myself.

A few months later I had to give terrible news to this same patient; his headaches and difficulty concentrating were due to progressive multifocal leukoencephalopathy, a rapidly fatal brain disease that is a complication of advanced AIDS. I was bracing for the pain of having to tell him the awfulness of it all; I didn't sleep well, dreaming that he'd hear the news and turn a gun on me, his family, or himself. Yet, the next day, he said that he knew that something was wrong; he was calm and grateful for my candor. I had become aware of how my self-preoccupation had overshadowed my ability to attend to him. I make a habit of asking myself, "Whom am I trying to protect?"

"From well-being to resilience"—the sixth leap—means that trying to achieve "work-life balance" might be misguided. Rather, by focusing on the task at hand I often find joy in the moment, curiosity amid despair, resilience when I feel I'm going to pieces. I let go of distinctions between work and nonwork and instead ask myself, "What do I need to do right now?" "What am I anticipating, looking forward to, prepared for?" "What if something else happens?"

The seventh leap, **"from empathy to compassion,"** is a reminder that even if I have an accurate understanding of a patient's suffering, it doesn't necessarily mean that I'm addressing it adequately. I make a practice of asking myself, "How can I choose to be compassionate in a way that makes a difference?"

The leaps so far have been about me, my mind, and the ways in which I can bring my whole mind to clinical care. The eighth leap takes me **"from whole mind to shared mind."** My clinical life is working with people—patients and their families, clinical teams, health care systems, communities. Shared mind is about being on the same wavelength, adopting a similar frame of reference even when we disagree. This doesn't always happen. I ask myself, "Is this me working alone or is this us working together?" and "Might greater sharing produce better care?"

12

Imagining a Mindful
Health Care System

A cord of three strands is not quickly broken.
—Ecclesiastes 4:12

Imagine that you went to bed tonight and woke tomorrow morning to find that the health care system was transformed. You have a health concern. Perhaps it's something serious or perhaps it's something minor. You call the office. You're amazed that you can contact your doctor and get an appointment the same day. When you arrive, the staff is attentive and courteous and knows you. You're astounded at the care you receive; it's technically proficient, and your clinicians are alert to your concerns. They're interested in who you are—your work, your home life, what's important to you. They help you make decisions, guided not only by the latest research but also by your values and clinical situation. You know that the various doctors, nurses, and other health professionals caring for you are talking to one another, anticipating your needs and making sure that the advice you get is consistent. Safety checks are in place so that you are confident that errors will be extraordinarily rare, and when they do occur, you get a full and complete explanation along with confidence that it won't happen again. Your care is efficient, affordable, and effective.

Imagine that although your doctor is busy, she listens carefully to your concerns. She doesn't interrupt. You feel cared for as a person, not merely as a case or a problem to be solved. She seeks your opinions and encourages you to ask questions and express concerns. She doesn't hide behind her expertise and makes you feel that no question is too simple. She talks with you, not at you. Your health care team provides information and support so that you can participate in decisions regarding your care to the degree that you wish. You have a voice in the aspects of health care that matter most and your time isn't wasted with bureaucratic and administrative hassles. You feel that your health care team provides not only technical expertise but also emotional support when you need it.

Imagine that your doctor feels a sense of meaning in her work. Her work is difficult, stressful, and demanding, but your doctor has the self-awareness, mindfulness, and resilience to stay on top of things. Her meaningful relationships with patients sustain her through the workweek. She has enough control over scheduling and the organization of the office that she feels that she can do a good job. When dealing with the most difficult moments—when losing a patient, when witnessing needless suffering, when considering what might have contributed to a serious error, when making difficult ethical choices—she feels resilient and supported.

This utopian vision of health care is shared by some of those who have the greatest influence in health care today. Don Berwick, M.D., formerly head of Medicare and Medicaid during the Obama administration, coined the "triple aim" of health care—better health care experiences for patients, better health outcomes for the population, and lower cost. Since then, family physicians Tom Bodenheimer and Christine Sinsky have added a fourth aim: improving the work lives of clinicians and staff who provide care. These aims have been embraced, at least in name, by an increasing number of health care organizations nationally.[1]

I am a physician and not an organizational consultant, a CEO, or a manager. I take care of patients, one at a time. It took me a long time to realize that health care organizations have as much influence on my patients' health as I do. Now, with current changes in health care, that reality has become apparent to anyone who has contact with the health care system. But health care organizations aren't all the same. Only some truly embrace a vision of health care in which patients receive care that is effective, efficient, and affordable while sustaining the viability of the health care workforce and make real efforts to achieve those aims.[2] Too often, though, health care institutions think only about productivity and throughput and don't take into account what helps clinicians and staff to be at their best.

Just like people, organizations themselves can be described as attentive, curious, responsive, and present—or not. They have the equivalent of top-down attention based on the goals of the organization as well as bottom-up attention, triggered by unexpected opportunities and challenges. And just like individuals, organizations pay selective attention to some things and ignore others, base decisions on incomplete knowledge, aren't completely rational in their decision making, and muddle through when decisions are complex. Organizations have habits of mind, the collective habits that constitute an organization's culture. Organizations can be described as mindful or less than mindful. In the transformation that I envision, health care organizations would promote mindfulness of individuals, health care teams, and of the organizational culture itself—down to how meetings are conducted, how information is communicated, and what values and behaviors are highlighted. They would create the conditions within which mindfulness could grow. The challenge is how to make this all happen.

COLLECTIVE MIND

The idea of mindfulness in organizations is not new. Karl Weick, at the University of Michigan's Ross School of Business, first described the qualities of so-called high-reliability organizations in the 1990s. He visited aircraft carriers, nuclear power plants, airplane cockpits, and other settings in which a small error spells catastrophe. In the beginning of one of his articles, he asks the reader to imagine life on the flight deck of an aircraft carrier.[3] Planes take off and land on a slippery flight deck at half the intervals that would be allowed at a civilian airport. This is all happening on a ship that is rocking from side to side with its radar turned off to avoid detection—and the whole operation is run by a group of twenty-year-olds. One glitch and the pilot, the airplane, and the ship go up in flames. Yet, errors are rare. It does not take much imagination to see the parallels between flight decks and busy urban trauma centers and operating rooms. However, in medicine we do far worse, with over one hundred thousand deaths per year due to medical error, and not nearly enough improvement in the fifteen years since the publication of a highly publicized report, *To Err Is Human*, by the Institute of Medicine.[4]

Over the next twenty-five years, Weick and his colleagues identified features of what he called "high-reliability organizations" and was curious about how these organizations do their work—what they do, how they think and solve problems, and how they create organizational culture. Mindfulness was the missing link. Along with his colleague Kathleen Sutcliffe, Weick examined how organizations—as if the organizations were organisms—stand to gain by becoming more attentive, responsive, and reliable, and by learning to balance routine with innovation. They showed how freeing the mind from the concepts that constrain our thinking, the importance of beginner's mind, and the concept of emptiness were as fundamental to well-functioning organizations as they were for well-functioning individuals.[5] Weick advanced five basic principles of what he called "collective mind," "organizational mindfulness," and "organizational attention."[6]

First, Weick asserts, you need to be *preoccupied with failure*. There are just too many ways that things can go wrong, each unique and often unpredictable. That's why it's important, in Weick and Sutcliffe's words, to learn how to manage the unexpected—being prepared to be unprepared. This preparation should be part of institutional culture.[7]

Weick and Sutcliffe's second principle is to *be reluctant to simplify*. Just as individuals get derailed by using mental shortcuts, teams and organizations do too. When Mr. Laszlo, the patient I discussed in chapter 2, came in with a painful shoulder, three out of three clinicians sought a simple answer that was logical—and wrong. When my friend Gary went to the emergency room with urinary obstruction (chapter 4), the nurses and doctors caring for him made the same kind of mistake. They picked the most convenient explanation. They didn't question it; their minds were too crowded and there was too much pressure to move on to the next patient. In the ER, there might even have been an underlying organizational culture, one in which having a quick answer—any answer—was rewarded and deeper cognitive processing was not. Those caring for Gary lacked attention and presence, not just individually, but collectively.

Weick and Sutcliffe's third principle is *sensitivity to operations*—management speak for what in medicine is called situation awareness. Here, health care institutions have made progress. In most institutions, clinical teams who work in hospitals—such as in the OR, the ICU, and the labor and delivery floor—undergo team training to help members speak up when they observe a problem. Even when people are not part of a team, they're encouraged to speak up. The person who mops the floors might have better insight into why infections are rampant in an ICU than the director of infection control. Weick suggests that safety be given higher priority than efficiency—not just in word, but in deed. This involves a mindful redirection of attention toward things that might otherwise be ignored.

Commitment to resilience, Weick and Sutcliffe's fourth principle, is more than bouncing back. Like individual resilience, organizational resilience depends on learning and growing from crises, and working outside people's comfort zones. You need teams of *adaptive* experts, people who can learn from the past but also know when to let go of it.

Their last recommendation is the one that surprised me the most, in a pleasant way. Weick and Sutcliffe call for *greater anarchy in organizations*. In healthy organizations, they claim, decisions should be made by the most appropriate member of the hierarchy and shouldn't have to be delayed until they come to the attention of the leadership. Weick and Sutcliffe are not talking about total anarchy here, but about loosening the boundaries just a bit so that more decisions are made by the people closest to the problem. These make routines and structures in the organization a bit more fluid.[8] In my office, medical assistants take patients' pulse, temperature, and blood pressure and ask them what's bothering them when they arrive. The most helpful medical assistants are the ones who note that something is different—the patient's blood pressure is lower or higher than it should be—and interrupt me to bring it to my attention immediately rather than just recording it in the chart. At the other extreme was a medical assistant who recorded the patient's chief concern as "chest pain," entered it into the medical record correctly, then left the patient to wait in a room for a half hour until his physician saw him. The patient was having a heart attack. The medical assistant's failure was not merely an individual's lapse or irresponsibility; it reflected poor training and a culture that didn't reinforce mindfulness.[9]

QUALITY AND SAFETY

Promoting quality in health care should build on a foundation of individual mindfulness and at the same time develop organizational mindfulness. Institutions should be structured so that collective vigilance is the norm, so that it matters less if any one individual suffers a lapse in attention. For example, one difficult problem in health care has been preventing falls among the elderly. Falls are common, and if the patient is injured or in pain, she ends up immobilized. Even after a few days in bed, elderly patients lose strength and require additional rehabilitation, and even still they might not ever get back on their feet. Immobilization leads to infections and blood clots, and mortality can be as high as 50 percent in the ensuing year. Preventing falls takes collective vigilance. Nurses need to be alert to when patients are unstable or are trying to get out of bed when they shouldn't. When a bed alarm goes off, the response has to be quick and coordinated, as it often takes more than one person to get the patient to safety. One factor in reducing falls, according to Timothy Vogus at Vanderbilt University, is collective mindfulness.

He studied ninety-five nursing units to see if scores on a mindfulness survey, assessing the five components defined by Weick and Sutcliffe, would predict on which nursing units patients fell. Those units whose members *collectively* scored higher had fewer falls—and, also of note, fewer medication errors.[10]

Health care organizations should consider the human capacity for attention when designing clinical work spaces, ones free of frequent interruptions and distractions. When I'm working in the emergency room, where the decibel level is high and there's a potential distraction every few seconds, I mentally block out ambient sounds so that I can pay attention to my patient. It's exhausting. When it comes time to write my notes on the computer, I'm faced with a choice—wall myself off with varying degrees of success or go to a quieter space on another unit, a five-minute walk and five flights of stairs away. There has to be a better way. Mindful workspace design can make paying attention possible.

HUMAN CONVERSATIONS

Health care institutions can create the conditions for caring and compassion. Health care consultant and internist Tony Suchman says that part of the answer is in moving from a command-and-control leadership style to one that is more relationship centered.[11] Suchman describes relationship-centered leadership as a style that honors the unique individual contributions of each member while helping them contribute to the overall mission. Mindful leaders enshrine the human side of medicine in hospital culture, provide space for meaningful conversations among members of the organization, and discover employees' untapped strengths. Suchman takes a radical view of organizations—that they are no more than a collection of conversations among people, setting the stage for appreciative inquiry and other methods to enhance motivation and self-awareness, promote effective teamwork, and help individuals sustain a sense of vision, purpose, and meaning.[12]

Leaders should promote inquiry, awareness, and attention to

things that matter and that the organization values. Over the past two years, I spent several days at a large Catholic health care system and was the keynote speaker at a conference of the Catholic Health Association. I was struck with several cultural differences between Catholic health systems and the secular world of university hospitals. First, they had an explicit commitment to caring and compassion. In chapter 7, I described how I checked out hospital mission statements looking for mention of suffering; at the same time I also looked for the word *compassion*. Nearly all of the Catholic health systems mentioned compassion explicitly, whereas almost none of the secular hospital systems did. Perhaps where the word *compassion* is spoken more often, it is enacted more often. But these are interesting times. Catholic hospitals in the United States have traditionally cared for everyone, even those with no means to pay. Historically they were run by nuns. Now they are typically run by lay leadership and are experiencing growing pains as they compete for market share and merge with other hospitals. However, I was intrigued by a role that they still had in their administrative structure and that I had not seen in other hospitals—directors of "formation." These people orient health care workers to consider such questions as "Where do I find meaning each day?" "What grounds this work?" "To what are we called together?" and "How must we respond?" I find these questions important, regardless of one's spiritual orientation. They address the technical as well as the existential, ethical, and social aspects of care. These hospitals' commitment to formation and mission is right on the mark. I found it particularly refreshing after having visited with institutions whose investment in compassion is little more than a sticker on a white lab coat that says I CARE.[13]

Ken Schwartz was a successful Boston attorney who represented health care institutions. He was diagnosed with metastatic cancer at age forty and died ten months later, but not before recognizing what was most important—and sometimes most lacking—in the health care he received. He published his account in the *Boston Globe* and pointed to the small acts of kindness that made "the unbearable bearable." His final wish was to create an organization that would nurture compassion, caregiver-patient relationships, and humane care. Founded in 1995, shortly before Ken Schwartz's death, the Schwartz Center for Compassionate Healthcare[14] has a signature program called Schwartz Rounds, which is currently in place at over five hundred health care institutions in North America and the UK. Schwartz Rounds focus on a patient with complex medical issues that require an interdisciplinary approach. Each session assembles a patient's care team, which may include physicians, nurses, therapists, chaplains, and others who have meaningful contact with the patient and his family. Panelists talk openly about the difficulties they've encountered caring for the patient. Sometimes the patient or a family member is present to add to the discussion.

In a recent Schwartz Rounds at my hospital, a mother reflected on her experiences during a recent hospitalization for her severely disabled son, one of many hospitalizations for seizures, pneumonia, and weight loss. The care team, including a pediatric geneticist, the ICU physician, a nurse, a social worker, and a chaplain, described the child's predicament, how they each were affected by his suffering, knowing that little could be done to reverse his decline. Importantly, the 150 attendees, from a wide variety of disciplines and specialties, as well as the patient's mother, discussed how the health care system could best support the family. Discussions like this, in a well-attended forum, rarely happened in hospitals until the Schwartz Center started supporting them. Now, in our institution and others, Schwartz Rounds occur monthly and are a source of community building for the medical and nursing staff. A few years ago, Beth Lown, an internist and medical director at the Schwartz Center, assessed the impact of Schwartz Rounds.[15] Those who had attended reported deeper insight into the emotional lives of patients and caregivers. They communicated better—verbally and nonverbally—and felt more equipped to respond to patients' needs with compassion. They were more energized about their work. They felt less stressed and isolated and more open to providing and accepting support. They became more mindful by learning to speak from the heart, just as the panelists had done.

The Arnold P. Gold Foundation has a similar mission, and has pioneered the "white coat ceremony," conducted at nearly all of the medical schools in North America, to mark the transition from student to healer. By asking students to develop and commit to a set of professional vows, the ceremony brings students' awareness, at the beginning of their careers, squarely to the values, attitudes, and attributes that they each bring to the profession—a guidepost for more mindful, humane care.

A CORD OF THREE STRANDS

It seems so sensible that quality of care, quality of caring, and clinician resilience would be synergistic. Even in these difficult times in health care, I see more and more health professionals tending to the soil in which their focused attention, curiosity, creativity, compassion, and resilience can grow. Yet, they are doing this in spite of their organizations, which they continue to find unsympathetic and unsupportive. Creating mindful organizations starts with respecting the clinicians who work there. Organizations should provide opportunities during the workday for clinicians to grow professionally and not make those offerings add-ons to an already overcrowded day. At some institutions, self-awareness and mindfulness constitute an essential part of the required curriculum for students and residents,[16] and these institutions frame self-awareness as essential to good patient care. Each of us has a lot at stake. When I teach medical students, I do so knowing that they represent the future of medicine. I assume that each student will become the doctor that I might encounter in the emergency room if I have another kidney stone, in the oncology clinic if I have cancer, or in the hospital if I need surgery. In fact, this has happened; some of my students have been my doctors. And I am hopeful. While some medical school graduates consider medicine as nothing more than a job, when I informally polled several medical school classes recently, the majority had done some kind of contemplative practice and see value in it for themselves as professionals. They see medicine as deeply meaningful work.

Attending—where you focus your precious attentional resources—is a choice, a moral choice. When I started thinking about mindful practice in medicine twenty years ago, I saw it as an individual commitment to be more attentive and curious, have a beginner's mind, and be present. I described the skills necessary to move from being a mere expert to a master, with the associated insight, perspective, and creativity. Now I see the project as much larger. Like the African proverb about raising a child, mindful practice takes a village. Having a community of colleagues, peers, and others who share a vision of mindful practice makes it possible. In clinical care the beneficiaries are our patients, who themselves may bring attention and awareness to their own work, whether they are artists, schoolteachers, bus drivers, or lawyers. Mindfulness is an aspiration of an increasing number of individuals and large educational and corporate institutions that comprise our society. I believe that now it is possible, with the right resolve, to have health care infused with and guided by mindful practice. A cord of three strands—individual, collective, and institutional—is not quickly broken.

Acknowledgments

Attending could never have been realized without the efforts of a few key people. Most notable is Rebecca Gradinger, who through her confidence in me led me to find my voice and sustain the passion and energy for the book. She is an agent extraordinaire, passionate advocate, and tough critic, who never stopped believing in this book even when I was mired in doubt. She answered e-mails at noon and midnight and kept me focused on who I am and what I could give. She and her team at Fletcher & Company, including Jennifer Herrera and Veronica Goldstein, were incredibly supportive. Rebecca introduced me to my editor, Shannon Welch, whose passion for the topic, thoughtful editorial guidance, and commitment helped to make *Attending* the best it could be. Along with her remarkable team at Scribner, including her associate editor, John Glynn, and editor-in-chief, Colin Harrison, she shaped the manuscript so that it spoke with greater clarity and coherence. For their efforts and commitment I'll be forever grateful.

I want to thank Gail Gazelle, Tula Karras, and Paula Derrow, who coached me early on, as I was just conceiving the book. My friend and medical school classmate Dan Siegel and my palliative care colleague Ira Byock gave me important advice about the publishing world, and my friend and college classmate Ron Siegel gave me the real skinny on books and editors and agents. He read, and hated, my first draft of a proposal, advising me that readers want the richness of stories, not merely sterile ideas. As I was drafting the book proposal, Arthur Frank, Jon Kabat-Zinn, Tim Quill, and

203

Acknowledgments

Marc Lesser also offered support, enthusiasm, and helpful critiques through the eyes of those who'd been through it all before. Steven Henry Boldt, Mahala Ruppel, Esther Brown, Maria Milella, Betsy Frarey, and Deborah Fox all read the manuscript in its entirety and provided invaluable editorial suggestions for style, grammar, and sense. Thanks to you all.

I was amazed and grateful when friends and colleagues came out of the woodwork offering to read the manuscript in its entirety and provide specific critiques and impressions, most notably Andy Elliot and Bill Ventres, accomplished writers and busy people. Andy brought a reader's eye to each sentence and reminded me that I was writing to reach out to others as well as to understand myself. Bill provided inspiration, thoughtful critiques, and gentle prods to "get real" when my thinking became too abstract and academic. Saskia Hendriks, a fellow researcher at the Brocher Foundation, provided insightful comments that led to important changes in the first two chapters of the manuscript.

I am a physician and not a neuroscientist, and although I had read hundreds of articles about the neurobiology of attention, resilience, attachment, compassion, and curiosity, I needed help reconciling competing ways of understanding how the brain and the mind work. Al Kaszniak and Jud Brewer read the portions of the manuscript about neuroscience research, correcting my misconceptions and getting me as up-to-date as one can be in a field that is evolving rapidly. Olga Klimecki was kind enough to explain the procedures and limitations of functional-imaging research, including her research on empathy, compassion, and conflict. Conversations with Amishi Jha helped me to understand more deeply the mechanisms of attention, Eric Nestler and Stephen Southwick helped interpret research on resilience, and Jean Decety and Beth Lown helped me to understand better the neurobiology and psychology of empathy and compassion. Anthropologist and Zen teacher Roshi Joan Halifax introduced me to the work of Carl Batson and Nancy Eisenberg, whose theories of empathy, sympathy, and compassion deeply influenced my thinking. Evan Thompson, a philosopher of mind and cognitive scientist, expanded my notion of what minds could do and be, and my Rochester colleague Paul Duberstein introduced me to the idea of collaborative cognition, which informed my ideas about shared mind. Chris Lyddy and Darren Good helped me to develop ideas about organizational mindfulness and sent me literature from the world of business and organizational management that might be applied to medicine. Yishai Mintzker brought to my attention the shared etymologies of *meditation* and *medicine*.

Several chapters represent a shared inspiration. I owe a debt of gratitude to Larry Dyche, who badgered me for months to respond to his offer to cowrite an article on curiosity just as I was beginning to think about writing this book, and the article we wrote together in 2011 influenced chapter 3. Similarly, Tony Back's imprint on chapter 7 and my understanding of suffering is profound, as represented in a 2015 article we coauthored. Jordan Silberman and Dan Siegel helped me develop ideas about self-monitoring, which influenced much of how I frame mindfulness for clinical audiences. The focus on difficult decisions (chapter 6), suffering (chapter 7), compassion (chapter 8), errors and grief (chapter 9), and burnout and resilience (chapter 10) closely parallels the curriculum that Mick Krasner and I developed collaboratively for educational programs for students, residents, and practicing clinicians. I am grateful to all these colleagues for their generosity in sharing their ideas and letting me bring them from the academic realm to the public eye.

I am grateful for the gift of time. My department chair in the Department of Family Medicine at the University of Rochester, Tom Campbell, and Vice-Chair Susan McDaniel, advocated for my 2014 sabbatical—supported by the University of Rochester—during which I monkishly developed the book proposal. I am also grateful for the gift of space. The Brocher Foundation, just outside Geneva, Switzerland, is devoted to the social aspects of medicine, and enthusiastically supported my writing by providing a room and a tranquil study overlooking Lac Léman to complete the first draft of this book in February 2016. Several foundations supported the background work for the book through their funding of my time to develop, implement, and evaluate the educational programs that demonstrated effectiveness of mindful practice training on clinician well-being, resilience, and quality of care they could provide. I am particularly grateful to the Arthur Vining Davis Foundations, the Arnold P. Gold Foundation, the Maria Tussi Kluge and John W. Kluge Foundation, the Mannix Fund, and the Physicians Foundation for Health Systems Excellence.

Several teachers have had an enduring influence. My fifth-grade teacher, Marguerite Britton, ran her classroom as a democratic organization focused on identifying individuals' learning needs and taught me about presence amid chaos, much to my enrichment and the school principal's dismay. In college, my main influences were Randy Huntsberry, who introduced me to emptiness and mindfulness, and how mindfulness and stillness can happen in movement; Ken Maue, music and philosophical visionary; and the late Jon Barlow, who could make connections among anything, including baseball, Charles Ives, and John Ford, and between sixteenth-century English keyboard music and southern-Indian mridangam drumming. They all taught me that the way you see the world is limited only by your expectations and imagination. In medical school, my inspirations were psychiatrists Peter Reich and Les Havens, both humanists bucking the tides of psychoanalytic rigidity and biological reductionism, and later, in Rochester, George Engel, who taught me how to observe and ask. I wish they were still of this world so that I could thank them.

After I finished my medical training, my colleagues became my teachers. The late Ian McWhinney, family physician and philosopher, lived and breathed patient-centered care. My Catalan colleague Francesc Borrell-Carrió has been one of my most treasured intellectual partners and critics. He introduced me to pragmatist philosophers in my own backyard—John Dewey and William James—and has a way of gently questioning and challenging me to be as clear as I can be. David Leach, another Aristotelian, showed me the logic behind breaking rules in the name of wisdom, an idea dear to my anarchist heart, and how organizations themselves could become more mindful in the process. Conversations with Stuart and Hubert Dreyfus, Kevin Eva, Brian Hodges, and Carol-Anne Moulton strongly shaped my concept of expertise in medicine and how to know when you have it. While he was the senior associate dean for medical education at the University of Rochester, Ed Hundert provided the opportunities for me to lay the intellectual groundwork about how we understand and assess competence. Lucy Candib helped me understand the meaning of suffering and oppression and what doctors can do about them. From Susan McDaniel, Dave Seaburn, and Pieter LeRoux I learned a family-systems orientation and family-of-origin awareness that suffuses every moment of my practice, teaching me that there is never just one patient in the room. Peter Franks taught me to adopt healthy skepticism about my own senses and convictions, especially those I hold most strongly. My greatest teachers have often been my patients, who, for confidentiality, must remain unnamed, yet I am grateful for their generosity, tolerance, and patience with me when I was off the mark.

The mindful practice programs that I describe in this book were the collective brainchild of my colleague Mick Krasner and me, with considerable input from Fred Marshall, Tim Quill, Scott McDonald, Stephen Liben, Patricia Lück, Shauna Shapiro, Tony Back, and Heidi Schwarz. Mick, the intuitive, spontaneous extrovert, offers the perfect complement to my analytical, conceptual way of seeing the world, and our educational programming is truly an example of shared mind. I am grateful for intellectual leadership, inspiration, and guidance from Jon Kabat-Zinn and Saki Santorelli and their colleagues at the Center for Mindfulness in Medicine, Health Care, and Society at the University of Massachusetts; from Rita Charon and Tom Inui, who helped me develop the narrative medicine components of the mindful practice programs; and from Penny Williamson, who shared her wisdom about appreciative inquiry. I thank Michael Zimler, Ed Brown, Reb Anderson, Richard Baker, Joseph Goldstein, and Christopher Titmuss for their generosity in helping me develop a meditation practice. I have been deeply influenced by many other conversations with teachers, mentors, friends, and colleagues over the past forty years, and to name them all would be impossible. Sometimes I may have forgotten the source of an idea, but that makes me no less grateful.

Acknowledgments

By far my deepest thanks go to my wife, Deborah. Her clarity about what is important, her insistence that I speak from the heart— my heart and no one else's—her frank critiques, her bullshit detector, her ability to size up people, her willingness to drop everything to help me think of just the right word, and her ability to channel me even when we are continents apart are extraordinary. She is my best editor and most loving critic. She tolerated my grouchiness, brought me tea and ripe pears, and even took over cooking dinner, normally my task, so I could write uninterrupted. My children, Eli and Malka, have helped me see the world through new eyes, and I am moved to tears by their emulation of those parts of me that give me joy, and by their tolerance of those parts that I'm not always proud of. And my parents, Joan and the late Jules Epstein, were totally mystified when my first-semester college transcript listed a course called Emptiness, but kept paying the tuition, trusting that I was doing something valuable even if they couldn't understand it, and didn't flinch when I announced I'd be a harpsichordist, then a Zen student, then a musicologist, then a chef, then an acupuncturist, and then a doctor. Their confidence in me was unwavering, and they knew it would all work out somehow.

Appendix: Attention Practice

In the beginning, meditation—like any new habit—takes practice. First, the effort is in just doing it—making time and being consistent. Frequently, the next challenge is stabilizing one's attention, learning how to be in the present moment and how not to drift into mind-wandering or rumination. After sustained practice, meditation becomes effortless. The hard-won focus and awareness feel natural and simple. For me (and although I've practiced for decades, I make no claim to being an advanced practitioner), meditation is a habit, like brushing my teeth, so much so that the day would feel incomplete without it.

The instructions for both focused attention practice and open awareness practice start with posture; it should be comfortable and "dignified." If sitting in a chair, you should be upright with feet on the floor; if on a cushion, you can be cross-legged or kneeling. Training need not be done sitting; practices can be done while walking, standing, or even lying down (a bit trickier because of the tendency to fall asleep!).

In Zen training, focused attention practice comes first, whereas in Vipassana training (otherwise called mindfulness meditation), both focused attention and open awareness are introduced early on. Focused attention starts with an awareness of the breath. In the Zen tradition, trainees are taught to count breaths—one, two, three, and up to ten, restarting at one and continuing to ten, then back to one, and so forth. In the Vipassana tradition, the focus is on awareness of the breath, and counting is not emphasized; instead attention is directed toward watching its rhythm, depth, and speed. You don't try to control the breath in any way, but rather just notice how it is deep or shallow, fast or slow, regular or irregular.

For open awareness practice, the instructions are a bit different. You don't necessarily focus on the breath, a mantra, or anything else. Rather, you assume an open, receptive, nonjudgmental awareness of all physical sensations, thoughts, and feelings that may be transpiring—whether they arise from within the body or from the external world—without any attempt to alter them in any way. It's like watching a movie and being the main character at the same time—it's observing the observer observing the observed.[1] Open awareness involves naming those sensations: "Oh, I'm feeling my foot itch" or "Oh, there was just a loud noise." Similarly, one can name emotions as they arise: "I'm noticing that I'm feeling angry"—or sad or frustrated. Naming emotions helps us engage in first-person inquiry, be curious, and respond to emotions intelligently, even if our first reactions are avoidance or annoyance.

If you're starting on your own, choose one practice and stick with it. Get any of the dozens of audio-recordings, apps, or books, or go to a workshop.[2] Your choice of practice may depend on whether you can find a partner or a group with whom you can practice—just as with exercise or any other lifestyle change. You may want to dive right in with twenty to forty minutes a day or start more slowly and increase as you can; even five minutes in the morning can make a difference. Importantly, be gentle with yourself—if you're counting breaths and you can never get beyond three or find yourself at 142, gently bring yourself back to the task. A kind smile always helps.

You may remember two other practices mentioned earlier in the book—the body scan (chapter 3) and metta meditation (chapter 8). For these practices a guide can be helpful—either in person, or via one of the innumerable guided meditations available on the Web.

Notes

1. BEING MINDFUL

1 Even if one kidney had sustained permanent damage, given Jake's young age, the other kidney would be highly likely to assume greater functioning over time and his kidney function would normalize—just as it does in people who donate a kidney for transplantation.

2 For descriptions of cognitive traps, see articles by emergency-room physician and decision scientist Patrick Croskerry: P. Croskerry, "The Importance of Cognitive Errors in Diagnosis and Strategies to Minimize Them," *Academic Medicine* 78(8) (2003): 775–80; P. Croskerry and G. Norman, "Overconfidence in Clinical Decision Making," *American Journal of Medicine* 121(5) (2008): S24–S29; P. Croskerry, "A Universal Model of Diagnostic Reasoning," *Academic Medicine* 84(8) (2009): 1022–28; P. Croskerry, "Context Is Everything or How Could I Have Been That Stupid?," *Healthcare Quarterly* 12 (2009): e171–e176; P. Croskerry, "From Mindless to Mindful Practice—Cognitive Bias and Clinical Decision Making," *New England Journal of Medicine* 368(26) (2013): 2445–48; and descriptions of Croskerry's practice in J. E. Groopman, *How Doctors Think* (New York: Houghton Mifflin, 2007).

3 For a detailed discussion of the holistic and multifaceted nature of professional competence of clinicians, see R. M. Epstein and E. M. Hundert, "Defining and Assessing Professional Competence," *JAMA* 287(2) (2002): 226–35; and R. M. Epstein, "Mindful Practice," *JAMA* 282(9) (1999): 833–39.

4 Philosopher Michael Polanyi calls this subsidiary awareness, that which is just beneath the surface, accessible to consciousness, but which is kept tacit so that we do not stumble. A pianist, for example, if asked to constantly be aware of each finger movement, would stumble more than if those movements were maintained outside awareness. See M. Polanyi, *Personal Knowledge: Towards a Post-critical Philosophy* (Chicago: University of Chicago Press, 1974); and M. Polanyi, *The Tacit Dimension* (Gloucester, MA: Peter Smith, 1983). A related construct is pre-attentive processing, in which the brain "selects" which of many sources to attend to. See J. H. Austin, *Zen and the Brain: Toward an Understanding of Meditation and Consciousness* (Cambridge, MA: MIT Press, 1998). Another related construct is process knowledge, knowing

how to do things, often tacit when it involves learned behaviors such as tying knots for a surgeon, riding a bicycle, playing scales for a pianist, etc., a useful construct in education. See M. Eraut, *Developing Professional Knowledge and Competence* (London: Falmer Press, 1994).

5 C.-A. Moulton and R. M. Epstein, "Self-Monitoring in Surgical Practice: Slowing Down When You Should," in *Surgical Education: Theorising an Emerging Domain*, ed. H. Fry and R. Kneebone (New York: Springer, 2011), chap. 10, 169–82; and C.-A. Moulton et al., "Slowing Down When You Should: A New Model of Expert Judgment," *Academic Medicine RIME: Proceedings of the Forty-Sixth Annual Conference* 82(10) (2007): S109–S116.

6 In all fairness, I don't know whether Mehta was curious or not. Perhaps he was, in which case it was an internal experience that he didn't share. Reich's curiosity was visible.

7 I am grateful to Randy Huntsberry, PhD, the professor for this course and others I took while at Wesleyan University. He had a strongly positive transformative effect on me and others.

8 J. Kabat-Zinn, *Wherever You Go, There You Are: Mindfulness Meditation in Everyday Life* (New York: Hyperion, 1994).

9 More accurately, Nagarjuna, the second-century Buddhist philosopher, would propose a fourfold paradox—to see yourself as fallible, to see yourself as infallible, to see yourself as both fallible and infallible, and finally to see yourself as neither fallible nor infallible. See F. J. Streng, *Emptiness: A Study in Religious Meaning* (Nashville, TN: Abingdon Press, 1967).

10 G. L. Engel, "The Need for a New Medical Model: A Challenge for Biomedicine," *Science* 196(4286) (1977): 129–36.

11 G. L. Engel, "The Clinical Application of the Biopsychosocial Model," *American Journal of Psychiatry* 137(5) (1980): 535–44; and G. L. Engel, "From Biomedical to Biopsychosocial: Being Scientific in the Human Domain," *Psychosomatics* 38(6) (1997): 521–28.

12 In the 1950s, British psychiatrist Michael Balint pioneered a group format in which general practitioners would discuss difficult cases. Through deep inquiry, Balint would help the GPs uncover otherwise hidden emotional reactions to patients that could affect the care they provided their patients—positively and negatively. He firmly believed that the person of the physician was as important a therapeutic agent as the drugs physicians could prescribe. See M. Balint, *The Doctor, His Patient, and the Illness* (New York: International Universities Press, 1957); I. R. McWhinney, "Fifty Years On: The Legacy of Michael Balint," *British Journal of General Practice* 49 (1999): 418–19; and L. Scheingold, "Balint Work in England: Lessons for American Family Medicine," *Journal of Family Practice* 26(3) (1988): 315–20.

13 Family-of-origin groups explore the influences of one's own family—history, values, beliefs, use of language, degree of cohesion, etc.—on one's clinical work. See S. H. McDaniel, T. L. Campbell, and D. B. Seaburn, *Family-Oriented Primary Care: A Manual for Medical Providers* (New York: Springer-Verlag, 1990); R. M. Epstein, "Physician Know Thy Family: Looking at One's Family of Origin as a Method of Physician Self-Awareness," *Medical Encounter* 8(1) (1991): 9; S. H. McDaniel and J. Landau-Stanton, "Family-of-Origin Work

and Family Therapy Skills Training: Both-And," *Family Process* 30(4) (1991): 459–71; and M. Mengel, "Physician Ineffectiveness due to Family-of-Origin Issues," *Family Systems Medicine* 5(2) (1987): 176–90.

14 Personal-awareness groups, developed by the American Academy on Communication in Health Care, are a group format for physicians to explore their inner lives and relationships, based on the work of psychologist Carl Rogers. D. H. Novack et al., "Calibrating the Physician: Personal Awareness and Effective Patient Care," *JAMA* 278(6) (1997): 502–9; T. E. Quill and P. R. Williamson, "Healthy Approaches to Physician Stress," *Archives of Internal Medicine* 150(9) (1990): 1857–61; and R. C. Smith et al., "Efficacy of a One-Month Training Block in Psychosocial Medicine for Residents: A Controlled Study," *Journal of General Internal Medicine* 6(6) (1991): 535–43.

15 I am grateful to David Sperber, who led a personal-awareness group for family medicine residents for thirty years, and to David Seaburn, Susan McDaniel, Pieter LeRoux, and others, who led family-of-origin reflection groups during my fellowship training.

16 Concepts that I explored included personal knowledge, procedural knowledge, process knowledge, tacit knowledge, self-reflection, reflective practitioner, reflection-on-action, reflection-in-action, knowledge-in-action, intersubjectivity, enaction, and more, all cited in Epstein, "Mindful Practice."

17 Publications in the late 1990s began to focus on the interior lives of physicians and the impact of self-awareness on clinical practice. See S. L. Shapiro, G. E. Schwartz, and G. Bonner, "Effects of Mindfulness-Based Stress Reduction on Medical and Premedical Students," *Journal of Behavioral Medicine* 21(6) (1998): 581–99; S. L. Shapiro and G. E. Schwartz, "Mindfulness in Medical Education: Fostering the Health of Physicians and Medical Practice," *Integrative Medicine* 1(3) (1998): 93–94; R. C. Smith et al., "Teaching Self-Awareness Enhances Learning about Patient-Centered Interviewing," *Academic Medicine* 74(11) (1999): 1242–48; D. H. Novack, R. M. Epstein, and R. H. Paulsen, "Toward Creating Physician-Healers: Fostering Medical Students' Self-Awareness, Personal Growth, and Well-Being," *Academic Medicine* 74(5) (1999): 516–20; D. H. Novack et al., "Personal Awareness and Professional Growth: A Proposed Curriculum," *Medical Encounter* 13(3) (1997): 2–7; and Novack et al., "Calibrating the Physician."

18 Epstein and Hundert, "Defining and Assessing Professional Competence."

19 The Comprehensive Assessment program for medical students emphasizes the skills of diagnosis and treatment but also the capacity of students to reflect and be self-aware. Students continue to say that it is one of most formative parts of their medical school career, and it gives me hope that students are hungry to know themselves more deeply. See R. M. Epstein et al., "Comprehensive Assessment of Professional Competence: The Rochester Experiment," *Teaching and Learning in Medicine* 16(2) (2004): 186–96.

20 Epstein, "Mindful Practice."

21 M. C. Beach et al., "A Multicenter Study of Physician Mindfulness and Health Care Quality," *Annals of Family Medicine* 11(5) (2013): 421–28. Beach assessed physicians' (lack of) mindfulness using a standard mindfulness survey that included items such as "I tend to walk quickly to where I am going with-

out paying attention to what I experience along the way" or "I find myself listening to someone with one ear, doing something else at the same time" or "I frequently forget a person's name shortly after we meet." Although it is odd to think that one could self-rate one's own mindfulness, the surveys do predict what most would consider to be mindful behaviors and correlate with more experience with meditation. P. Grossman, "On Measuring Mindfulness in Psychosomatic and Psychological Research," *Journal of Psychosomatic Research* 64(4) (2008): 405–8.

22 I discovered a like-minded colleague in Rochester, Dr. Mick Krasner, and the two of us spearheaded workshops and seminars in mindful practice for physicians, residents, students, and medical educators in Rochester. These have blossomed into programs on six continents. Several foundations funded us to help make those ideas a reality. The 1999 *JAMA* "Mindful Practice" article has been cited in the medical literature over a thousand times.

23 We published the results in *JAMA* in 2009 and a follow-up study in *Academic Medicine* in 2012. See H. B. Beckman et al., "The Impact of a Program in Mindful Communication on Primary Care Physicians," *Academic Medicine* 87(6) (2012): 1–5; and M. S. Krasner et al., "Association of an Educational Program in Mindful Communication with Burnout, Empathy, and Attitudes among Primary Care Physicians," *JAMA* 302(12) (2009): 1284–93.

24 We assessed their personalities using the NEO five-factor scale, the most widely used assessment of personality. See P. T. Costa and R. R. McCrae, "NEO PI-R: Professional Manual, Revised Neo Personality Inventory (NEO PI-R), and Neo Five-Factor Inventory (NEO-FFI)" (Odessa, FL: Psychological Assessment Resources, 1992); R. R. McCrae and P. T. Costa Jr., "Personality Trait Structure as a Human Universal," *American Psychologist* 52(5) (1997): 509–16.

25 A 2014 study at the University of Pennsylvania reaffirms that physicians find their relationships with patients to be the most meaningful and rewarding aspects of their work. The researchers asked students and residents to identify physicians who exemplified humanistic patient care. These physicians reported attitudes, such as humility, and habits, such as self-reflection and mindfulness practices, that contributed to their effectiveness as healers and a reduction in burnout. See C. M. Chou, K. Kellom, and J. A. Shea, "Attitudes and Habits of Highly Humanistic Physicians," *Academic Medicine* 89(9) (2014): 1252–58.

26 See A. Verghese, "Culture Shock—Patient as Icon, Icon as Patient," *New England Journal of Medicine* 359(26) (2008): 2748–51.

27 Initially, the concepts of population health and evidence-based medicine ignored individual patients' perspectives and needs or developed quantitative models to incorporate "values" into algorithms that would guide treatment. The limitations have fortunately been addressed in the more recent conceptualizations of evidence-based medicine, which now incorporate elements of patient-centeredness. See D. Bassler et al., "Evidence-Based Medicine Targets the Individual Patient. Part 2: Guides and Tools for Individual Decision-Making," *ACP Journal Club* 149(1) (2008): 2; V. M. Montori and G. H. Guyatt, "Progress in Evidence-Based Medicine," *JAMA* 300(15) (2008):

Notes

1814–16; and G. Guyatt et al., "Patients at the Center: In Our Practice, and in Our Use of Language," *ACP Journal Club* 140(1) (2004): A11–A12.

28 My personal experience has been with the Zen and the Vipassana meditation traditions. These and other contemplative practices have in common a moment-to-moment attention to one's experience, cultivation of focus, and/or receptiveness and a nonjudgmental attitude. For some, martial arts or running or playing music serve similar ends. The important features are dedication, consistency, perseverance, and a sense of community. See chapter 11 and the appendix for more details.

2. ATTENDING

1 This quote is attributed to the late (and great) American baseball hero and philosopher Yogi Berra.

2 Sadly, Emil did not do well. His oncologist assured us, though, that the outcome would have been the same even if he had been diagnosed a month earlier.

3 This observation is now the title of a bestselling book, *The Invisible Gorilla*, which explores the phenomenon in all of its depth. C. Chabris and D. Simons, *The Invisible Gorilla: How Our Intuitions Deceive Us* (New York: Crown, 2011). For one version of this video, see http://www.youtube.com/watch?v=47LCLoidJh4.

4 The gorilla is in the upper-right portion of the (black) lung fields. See T. Drew, M. L. Vo, and J. M. Wolfe, "The Invisible Gorilla Strikes Again: Sustained Inattentional Blindness in Expert Observers," *Psychological Science* 24(9) (2013): 1848–53.

5 I am not sure why others did not speak up. Perhaps they too did not notice, or were afraid of the surgeon's reactions.

6 J. S. Macdonald and N. Lavie, "Visual Perceptual Load Induces Inattentional Deafness," *Attention, Perception, and Psychophysics* 73(6) (2011): 1780–89.

7 D. Kahneman, *Thinking, Fast and Slow* (New York: Farrar, Straus and Giroux, 2013).

8 I thank David Leach, formerly the head of the Accreditation Council for Graduate Medical Education, for introducing me to this Aristotelian concept in the context of medical practice and the literature that supports it. To understand better how expertise is more than just being experienced, see C. Bereiter and M. Scardamalia, *Surpassing Ourselves: An Inquiry into the Nature and Implications of Expertise* (Chicago: Open Court, 1993).

9 W. Levinson, R. Gorawara-Bhat, and J. Lamb, "A Study of Patient Clues and Physician Responses in Primary Care and Surgical Settings," *JAMA* 284(8) (2000): 1021–27; and A. L. Suchman et al., "A Model of Empathic Communication in the Medical Interview," *JAMA* 277(8) (1997): 678–82.

10 D. S. Morse, E. A. Edwardsen, and H. S. Gordon, "Missed Opportunities for Interval Empathy in Lung Cancer Communication," *Archives of Internal Medicine* 168(17) (2008): 1853–58.

11 More about this later in the discussion about the contribution of emotions to decision making in chapter 6.

12 Physicians provided informed consent to participate in the study and agreed to see two "unannounced standardized patients" during the subsequent year. See R. M. Epstein et al., "'Could This Be Something Serious?' Reassurance, Uncertainty, and Empathy in Response to Patients' Expressions of Worry," *Journal of General Internal Medicine* 22(12) (2007): 1731–39; and D. B. Seaburn et al., "Physician Responses to Ambiguous Patient Symptoms," *Journal of General Internal Medicine* 20(6) (2005): 525–30.

13 R. M. Epstein et al., "Awkward Moments in Patient-Physician Communication about HIV Risk," *Annals of Internal Medicine* 128(6) (1998): 435–42.

14 One recent review of the influence of patient-clinician communication and relationships in clinical care is J. M. Kelley et al., "The Influence of the Patient-Clinician Relationship on Healthcare Outcomes: A Systematic Review and Meta-analysis of Randomized Controlled Trials," *PLoS ONE* 9(4) (2014).

15 R. J. Baron, "An Introduction to Medical Phenomenology: I Can't Hear You While I'm Listening," *Annals of Internal Medicine* 103(4) (1985): 606–11.

16 Philosopher Michael Polanyi coined the term *subsidiary awareness*, a prerequisite for the capacity to slow down when you should; and *attention in automaticity* was described by surgeon Carol-Anne Moulton and physician Annie Leung. See M. Polanyi, *The Tacit Dimension* (Gloucester, MA: Peter Smith, 1983); and A. S. O. Leung, R. M. Epstein, and C.-A. Moulton, "The Competent Mind: Beyond Cognition," in *The Question of Competence*, eds. B. D. Hodges and L. Lingard (Ithaca and London: Cornell University Press, 2012), chap. 7, 155–76.

17 D. D. Salvucci, N. A. Taatgen, and J. P. Borst, "Toward a Unified Theory of the Multitasking Continuum: From Concurrent Performance to Task Switching, Interruption, and Resumption," *Proceedings of ACM CHI 2009 Conference on Human Factors in Computing Systems—Understanding UI 2* (2009): 1819–28.

18 There is a large literature in education and psychology on the effects of manipulating extraneous cognitive load (that which is not related to the problem at hand) and germane cognitive load (that which is related) on problem-solving capacity. See J. Sweller, "Cognitive Load During Problem Solving: Effects on Learning," *Cognitive Science* 12(2) (1988): 257–85; N. W. Mulligan, "The Role of Attention during Encoding in Implicit and Explicit Memory," *Journal of Experimental Psychology: Learning, Memory, & Cognition* 21(1) (1998): 27–47; and C. Stangor and D. McMillan, "Memory for Expectancy-Congruent and Expectancy-Incongruent Information," *Psychological Bulletin* 111(1) (1992): 42–61. For a more nuanced understanding of how attitude and motivation can "undo" this effect and promote recognition of inconsistent data, see J. W. Sherman, F. R. Conrey, and C. J. Groom, "Encoding Flexibility Revisited: Evidence for Enhanced Encoding of Stereotype-Inconsistent Information under Cognitive Load," *Social Cognition* 22(2) (2004): 214–32.

19 For a more detailed exploration of top-down and bottom-up attention, see M. Corbetta and G. L. Shulman, "Control of Goal-Directed and Stimulus-Driven Attention in the Brain," *Nature Reviews Neuroscience* 3(3) (2002): 201–15.

20 Rashes are common in innocuous viral illnesses, but some kinds can signal something more serious—measles, meningitis, or severe medication reactions.

Notes

21 For a discussion of the structure and function of the right frontoparietal network, and the importance of the right-sided lateralization, see Corbetta and Shulman, "Control of Goal-Directed." The right-left hemispheric differences are oversimplifications often promoted by popularized neuroscience. Current research suggests there are more similarities in function than differences, yet clearly some dysfunction is localized. For example, depression is associated with overactivity of the right prefrontal cortex compared to the left; those who have had right-sided strokes tend to be oblivious of their deficits, etc.

22 See Bereiter and Scardamalia, *Surpassing Ourselves*.

23 Attending to everything important is not always possible or desirable at any given moment, especially in emergency situations.

24 Psychologists describe "change blindness," in which gradual or unexpected changes in an image go unrecognized. For examples of gradual change blindness, see http://www.youtube.com/watch?v=1nL5ulsWMYc.

25 Drug warnings occur an average of sixty-three times—one every eight to ten minutes—during a typical physician's workday. See A. L. Russ et al., "Prescribers' Interactions with Medication Alerts at the Point of Prescribing: A Multi-method, In Situ Investigation of the Human-Computer Interaction," *International Journal of Medical Informatics* 81(4) (2012): 232–43.

26 The original source is K. Maue, *Water in the Lake: Real Events for the Imagination* (New York: Harper & Row, 1979). Ken Maue taught at Wesleyan University in the 1970s, and his brilliant ways of bringing awareness to the ordinary were stunning. A musician by training, his avant-garde "pieces" became gradually less concerned with sound and more about how we can experience any environment as "music." His pieces reveal our inner lives in ways similar to those of formal contemplative practice—they sculpt our capacity for awareness.

27 The idea of immaculate perception is hardly original. The concept had its origins in both Western and Buddhist philosophy, later to be confirmed with empirical studies. Buddhist philosophy emphasizes both the emptiness of all things including perceptions, and that through meditation one can strip away meaning, judgment, and bias, permitting us to see the world as it is. See F. J. Streng, *Emptiness: A Study in Religious Meaning* (Nashville, TN: Abingdon Press, 1967). Francis Bacon (1605) asserted that immaculate perception was necessary to see the world as it is, "keeping the eye steadily fixed upon the facts of nature and so receiving the images simply as they are." Nietzsche, in *Thus Spake Zarathustra*, refuted that this would be possible, given that we have desires and wishes that will color our perceptions. Author Anaïs Nin reflected this sentiment in her oft-quoted passage on how we "do not see things as they are, we see them as we are." See A. Nin, *The Diary of Anaïs Nin, 1939–1944* (New York: Harcourt, Brace & World, 1969). The lack of immaculate perception has repeatedly been established in social psychology using studies of implicit (unconscious) bias and stereotyping, as noted in T. D. Wilson, *Strangers to Ourselves: Discovering the Adaptive Unconscious* (Cambridge, MA: Belknap Press of Harvard Universtiy Press, 2002). In medicine, these biases have been shown to influence clinical decisions. See A. R. Green et al., "Implicit Bias among Physicians and Its Prediction

of Thrombolysis Decisions for Black and White Patients," *Journal of General Internal Medicine* 22(9) (2007): 1231–38. A TEDx Talk by Jerry Kang exhibits this principle clearly: http://thesituationist.wordpress.com/2014/02/01/immaculate-perception. In this book, I propose that it is possible, through self-awareness, to access some of these processes that are normally below the level of awareness.

28 Scripts are internalized mental stories based on prototypical clinical scenarios—often learned during training. See B. Charlin et al., "Scripts and Clinical Reasoning," *Medical Education* 41(12) (2007): 1178–84.

29 Patrick Croskerry, a Canadian emergency-medicine physician, describes "cognitive dispositions to respond," intrinsic biases that affect clinical decision making. They are described well in J. E. Groopman, *How Doctors Think* (New York: Houghton Mifflin, 2007). Croskerry outlines dozens of sources of bias, stereotyping, and misapplied heuristics in a series of articles over the past fifteen years, from misplaced attribution, overconfidence, and premature closure. Most of these processes are below the level of awareness. For further reading, see P. Croskerry and G. Norman, "Overconfidence in Clinical Decision Making," *American Journal of Medicine* 121(5) (2008): S24–S29; P. Croskerry and G. R. Nimmo, "Better Clinical Decision Making and Reducing Diagnostic Error," *Journal of the Royal College of Physicians of Edinburgh* 41(2) (2011): 155–62; P. Croskerry, A. A. Abbass, and A. W. Wu, "How Doctors Feel: Affective Issues in Patients' Safety," *Lancet* 372(9645) (2008): 1205–6; P. Croskerry, "The Importance of Cognitive Errors in Diagnosis and Strategies to Minimize Them," *Academic Medicine* 78(8) (2003): 775–80; P. Croskerry, "Clinical Cognition and Diagnostic Error: Applications of a Dual Process Model of Reasoning," *Advances in Health Sciences Education* 14(1) (2009): 27–35; and P. Croskerry, "From Mindless to Mindful Practice—Cognitive Bias and Clinical Decision Making," *New England Journal of Medicine* 368(26) (2013): 2445–48.

30 A series of laboratory experiments confirming these observations were done by Mohanty's lab. See A. Mohanty et al., "Search for a Threatening Target Triggers Limbic Guidance of Spatial Attention," *Journal of Neuorscience* 29(34) (2009): 10563–72; and A. Mohanty and T. J. Sussman, "Top-Down Modulation of Attention by Emotion," *Frontiers in Human Neuroscience* 7 (2013): 102.

31 Stereotyping in medicine clearly goes beyond individual patient behaviors and includes race, ethnicity, gender, sexual orientation, habits, obesity, lifestyle choices, and diseases, which I'll discuss in greater detail later in the book.

32 The dermatologist Neil Prose describes a similar situation, in which a patient's psychological distress was only apparent after he looked deeper than her skin. See N. Prose, "Paying Attention," *JAMA* 283(21) (2000): 2763.

33 Carol-Anne Moulton calls this quality "attention in automaticity." See C.-A. Moulton et al., "Slowing Down When You Should: A New Model of Expert Judgment," *Academic Medicine RIME: Proceedings of the Forty-Sixth Annual Conference* 82(10) (2007): S109–S116.

3. CURIOSITY

1 Some of the content of this chapter is drawn from an article I wrote with Larry Dyche: L. Dyche and R. M. Epstein, "Curiosity and Medical Education," *Medical Education* 45(7) (2011): 663–68. Also see D. E. Berlyne, "Novelty and Curiosity as Determinants of Exploratory Behaviour," *British Journal of Psychiatry* 41(1–2) (1950): 68–80.

2 From Erich Leowy, quoted in F. T. Fitzgerald, "Curiosity," *Annals of Internal Medicine* 130(1) (1999): 70–72.

3 Here I'm referring to the five-factor model of personality. See R. R. McCrae et al., "Nature over Nurture: Temperament, Personality, and Life Span Development," *Journal of Personality and Social Psychology* 78(1) (2000): 173–86.

4 Uncertainty in medicine and physicians' reactions to uncertainty have been explored in depth since Renee Fox's seminal 1959 book. Here is a selection of perspectives, but space does not allow inclusion of a comprehensive set of references: R. Fox, *Experiment Perilous: Physicians and Patients Facing the Unknown* (Glencoe, IL: Free Press, 1959); J. P. Kassirer, "Our Stubborn Quest for Diagnostic Certainty: A Cause of Excessive Testing," *New England Journal of Medicine* 320(22) (1989): 1489–91; F. Borrell-Carrió and R. M. Epstein, "Preventing Errors in Clinical Practice: A Call for Self-Awareness," *Annals of Family Medicine* 2(4) (2004): 310–16; G. Gillett, "Clinical Medicine and the Quest for Certainty," *Social Science & Medicine* 58(4) (2004): 727–38; K. G. Volz and G. Gigerenzer, "Cognitive Processes in Decisions under Risk Are Not the Same as in Decisions under Uncertainty," *Frontiers in Decision Neuroscience* 6(105) (2012): 1–6; R. M. Epstein, B. S. Alper, and T. E. Quill, "Communicating Evidence for Participatory Decision Making," *JAMA* 291(19) (2004): 2359–66; R. M. Epstein et al., "'Could This Be Something Serious?' Reassurance, Uncertainty, and Empathy in Response to Patients' Expressions of Worry," *Journal of General Internal Medicine* 22(12) (2007): 1731–39; M. S. Gerrity, R. F. DeVellis, and J. A. Earp, "Physicians' Reactions to Uncertainty in Patient Care: A New Measure and New Insights," *Medical Care* 28(8) (1990): 724–36; G. H. Gordon, S. K. Joos, and J. Byrne, "Physician Expressions of Uncertainty during Patient Encounters," *Patient Education & Counseling* 40(1) (2000): 59–65; C. G. Johnson et al., "Does Physician Uncertainty Affect Patient Satisfaction?," *Journal of General Internal Medicine* 3(2) (1988): 144–49; and J. Ogden et al., "Doctors' Expressions of Uncertainty and Patient Confidence," *Patient Education & Counseling* 48(2) (2002): 171–76.

5 Fitzgerald, "Curiosity."

6 In 1912 the *Titanic* hit an iceberg on its maiden voyage, killing the majority of those on board.

7 Just out of curiosity, I checked my own medical chart. There were thirty problems listed, most of which had resolved decades ago. Only two were actually relevant to my current health.

8 E. Baumgarten, "Curiosity as a Moral Virtue," *International Journal of Applied Philosophy* 15(2) (2001): 23–42; J. Halpern, *From Detached Concern to Empathy: Humanizing Medical Practice* (Oxford: Oxford Univer-

sity Press, 2001); Institute of Medicine, *Crossing the Quality Chasm: A New Health System for the 21st Century* (Washington, DC: National Academies Press, 2001); R. M. Epstein et al., "Measuring Patient-Centered Communication in Patient-Physician Consultations: Theoretical and Practical Issues," *Social Science & Medicine* 61(7) (2005): 1516–28; and C. M. Chou, K. Kellom, and J. A. Shea, "Attitudes and Habits of Highly Humanistic Physicians," *Academic Medicine* 89(9) (2014): 1252–58.

9 See M. Polanyi, "Knowing and Being, the Logic of Tacit Inference," in *Knowing and Being: Essays by Michael Polanyi*, ed. M. Grene (Chicago: University of Chicago Press, 1969), chaps. 9 and 10, 123–58; and M. Polanyi, *Personal Knowledge: Towards a Post-critical Philosophy* (Chicago: University of Chicago Press, 1974).

10 V. F. Reyna, "A Theory of Medical Decision Making and Health: Fuzzy Trace Theory," *Medical Decision Making* 28(6) (2008): 850–65.

11 For interesting discussions about informed intuition in expert practice, see M. C. Price, "Intuitive Decisions on the Fringes of Consciousness: Are They Conscious and Does It Matter?," *Judgment and Decision Making* 3(1) (2008): 28–41; V. F. Reyna and F. J. Lloyd, "Physician Decision Making and Cardiac Risk: Effects of Knowledge, Risk Perception, Risk Tolerance, and Fuzzy Processing," *Journal of Experimental Psychology: Applied* 12(3) (2006): 179; and D. Kahneman and G. Klein, "Conditions for Intuitive Expertise: A Failure to Disagree," *American Psychologist* 64(6) (2009): 515–26.

12 The body scan can be done lying down or sitting, or even standing. The instructions are simple, and guided body scans are readily available on the Web if you want to try it yourself. An audio-recorded guided body scan can be accessed at http://www.urmc.rochester.edu/family-medicine/mindful-practice/curricula-materials/audios.aspx.

13 Thanks to Laura Hogan for this story.

14 E. J. Langer, *The Power of Mindful Learning* (Reading, MA: Perseus Books, 1997); and G. C. Spivak, L. E. Lyons, and C. G. Franklin, "'On the Cusp of the Personal and the Impersonal': An Interview with Gayatri Chakravorty Spivak," *Biography* 27(1) (2004): 203–21.

15 More about doubt and uncertainty in chapters 4 and 6.

16 J. Greenberg and N. Meiran, "Is Mindfulness Meditation Associated with 'Feeling Less'?," *Mindfulness* 5(5) (2014): 471–76.

17 C. R. Horowitz et al., "What Do Doctors Find Meaningful about Their Work?," *Annals of Internal Medicine* 138(9) (2003): 772–75.

18 See T. B. Kashdan et al., "Curiosity Enhances the Role of Mindfulness in Reducing Defensive Responses to Existential Threat," *Personality and Individual Differences* 50(8) (2011): 1227–32; and C. P. Niemiec et al., "Being Present in the Face of Existential Threat: The Role of Trait Mindfulness in Reducing Defensive Responses to Mortality Salience," *Journal of Personality and Social Psychology* 99(2) (2010): 344–65.

19 C. Kidd and B. Y. Hayden, "The Psychology and Neuroscience of Curiosity," *Neuron* 88(3) (2015): 449–60.

20 J. Gottlieb et al., "Information-Seeking, Curiosity, and Attention: Computational and Neural Mechanisms," *Trends in Cognitive Sciences* 17(11) (2013): 585–93.

21 Dopamine drives exploration behaviors in humans and animals and also affects memory and intelligence. In the prefrontal cortex, which processes executive decision making, impulse control, and other cognitive processes, one particular dopamine receptor is strongly expressed, the D4 receptor. Catechol-O-methyltransferase is an enzyme that breaks down dopamine and other neurotransmitters and is also active in the prefrontal cortex. Thus, the current model is that both genes for dopamine D4 receptor and COMT may affect curiosity. R. P. Ebstein et al., "Dopamine D4 Receptor (D4DR) Exon III Polymorphism Associated with the Human Personality Trait of Novelty Seeking," *Nature Genetics* 12(1) (1996): 78–80; and C. G. DeYoung et al., "Sources of Cognitive Exploration: Genetic Variation in the Prefrontal Dopamine System Predicts Openness/Intellect," *Journal of Research in Personality* 45(4) (2011): 364–71.

22 Here, and everywhere in this book, I apologize for the oversimplifications of complex multidimensional biological processes with complex control mechanisms that have been coalesced into pathways for heuristic value, but diminish the marvel of their interconnections. In particular, social epigenetics is in its infancy as an area of scientific pursuit, and while the basic principles—that the social environment affects gene expression—will prove enduring, the details of how this happens will undoubtedly undergo radical revisions.

23 Dyche and Epstein, "Curiosity and Medical Education"; and L. K. Michaelson, A. B. Knight, and D. Flink, *Team-Based Learning: A Transformative Use of Small Groups* (New York: Praeger Publishing, 2002).

24 P. Fonagy et al., *Affect Regulation, Mentalization, and the Development of Self* (New York: Other Press, 2002); and D. W. Winnicott, *The Maturational Processes and the Facilitating Environment* (Madison, CT: International Universities Press, 1965).

25 E. J. Langer, *Mindfulness* (Reading, MA: Addison-Wesley, 1989); Langer, *Power of Mindful Learning*; D. A. Schon, *The Reflective Practitioner* (New York: Basic Books, 1983); N. H. Leonard and M. Harvey, "Curiosity, Mindfulness and Learning Style in the Acquisition of Knowledge by Individuals/Organisations," *International Journal of Learning and Intellectual Capital* 4(3) (2007): 294–314; J. P. Fry, "Interactive Relationship between Inquisitiveness and Student Control of Instruction," *Journal of Educational Psychology* 68(5) (1972): 459–65; and B. Roman and J. Kay, "Fostering Curiosity: Using the Educator-Learner Relationship to Promote a Facilitative Learning Environment," *Psychiatry: Interpersonal and Biological Processes* 70(3) (2007): 205–8.

26 Strong attachment to friends and family during adulthood influences curiosity and exploration in the work environment. Those whose work environments are unsupportive, though, are forced to derive support exclusively from their relationships with family and friends. However, family and friends quickly tire of medical talk and the difficult situations that doctors face. See A. J. Elliot and H. T. Reis, "Attachment and Exploration in Adulthood," *Journal of Personality and Social Psychology* 85(2) (2003): 317–31.

27 E. R. Kandel, "A New Intellectual Framework for Psychiatry," *American Journal of Psychiatry* 155(4) (1998): 457–69.

Notes

4. BEGINNER'S MIND

1 S. Suzuki, *Zen Mind, Beginner's Mind* (New York: Weatherhill, 1980).
2 Suzuki Roshi died three years before I arrived in San Francisco, yet his teachings about beginner's mind were and remain guideposts of practice at the center.
3 Stewart and Hubert Dreyfus observed chess players and professionals in a variety of fields to understand how experts get that way. They developed a model of a hierarchy from novice, advanced beginner, competent, proficient, and expert, only later adding a level for master. See H. L. Dreyfus, *On the Internet (Thinking in Action)* (New York: Routledge, 2001).
4 C. G. Shields et al., "Pain Assessment: The Roles of Physician Certainty and Curiosity," *Health Communication* 28(7) (2013): 740–46.
5 M. Hojat et al., "The Devil Is in the Third Year: A Longitudinal Study of Erosion of Empathy in Medical School," *Academic Medicine* 84(9) (2009): 1182–91.
6 A series of neuroimaging studies conducted by a research group in Taiwan provides some clues as to how this happens. The researchers prepared a set of brief videos in which one set of actors was touched by Q-tips and another set underwent acupuncture. They showed the videos to doctors who practice acupuncture. The control group was nonclinicians, matched for age and educational level. The brain activity of both doctors and nonclinicians was monitored using a variety of functional neuroimaging techniques (initially MRI scanning, with follow-up studies using magnetoencephalography and electroencephalography) to demonstrate how doctors' expertise modulates how they perceive the pain of others. Among nonexperts, witnessing a patient undergoing acupuncture (as compared to being touched by a Q-tip) produced responses in the sensory and emotion-processing parts of the brain, reflecting some degree of emotional resonance and empathy. However, among physician-acupuncturists, those areas were deactivated, and instead, other areas of the brain were activated—particularly those involved in regulating emotions and a cognitive understanding of (but not emotional resonance with) the patient's experience (so-called theory of mind); their growing expertise leads them to see the world differently. This ability—to regulate emotions and categorize illness into disease categories—is fundamental to good care. Yet, there is an unnecessary imbalance, and it doesn't have to be that way—we can have both technical expertise and human understanding. See J. Decety, C. Y. Yang, and Y. Cheng, "Physicians Down-Regulate Their Pain Empathy Response: An Event-Related Brain Potential Study," *NeuroImage* 50(4) (2010): 1676–82; and Y. Cheng et al., "The Perception of Pain in Others Suppresses Somatosensory Oscillations: A Magnetoencephalography Study," *NeuroImage* 40(4) (2008): 1833–40.
7 P. Goldberg, *The Intuitive Edge: Understanding and Developing Intuition* (Los Angeles: J. P. Tarcher, 1983).
8 Karl Ditters von Dittersdorf was a well-respected eighteenth-century composer, whose music is faultless but clearly without the inspiration of Haydn, Mozart, or Bach.

9 P. Croskerry, "From Mindless to Mindful Practice—Cognitive Bias and Clinical Decision Making," *New England Journal of Medicine* 368(26) (2013): 2445–48.

10 The source is F. S. Fitzgerald, "The Crack Up," in *The Crack Up*, ed. E. Wilson (New York: New Directions, 1945). However, the idea is not new. The poet John Keats considered creativity to spring from the rejection of constraining philosophies and absolute truths and the seeking of mystery and doubt. Keats influenced pragmatist philosophers such as John Dewey, and perhaps also Fitzgerald.

11 While this quote has been attributed to Einstein, the source has never been found and many others have made similar observations.

12 This Zen story is quoted in many sources, originally from a Zen classic now in translation as K. Yamada, *The Gateless Gate: The Classic Book of Zen Koans* (New York: Simon & Schuster, 2005).

13 From a talk by G. Fronsdal, "Not-Knowing," http://www.insightmeditation center.org/books-articles/articles/not-knowing.

14 L. Festinger, "Cognitive Dissonance," *Scientific American* 207(4) (1962): 93–107.

15 The many ways in which physicians can deceive themselves during diagnoses is explored in J. E. Groopman, *How Doctors Think* (New York: Houghton Mifflin, 2007).

16 G. E. Simon and O. Gureje, "Stability of Somatization Disorder and Somatization Symptoms among Primary Care Patients," *Archives of General Psychiatry* 56(1) (1999): 90–95.

17 This story has multiple sources, including P. Reps and N. Senzaki, *Zen Flesh, Zen Bones: A Collection of Zen and Pre-Zen Writings* (Clarendon, VT: Tuttle Publishing, 1998).

18 D. J. Levitin, *The Organized Mind: Thinking Straight in the Age of Information Overload* (New York: Dutton Adult, 2014); Croskerry, "From Mindless to Mindful Practice"; P. Croskerry and G. Norman, "Overconfidence in Clinical Decision Making," *American Journal of Medicine* 121(5) (2008): S24–S29; and P. Croskerry, "The Importance of Cognitive Errors in Diagnosis and Strategies to Minimize Them," *Academic Medicine* 78(8) (2003): 775–80.

19 J. Dewey, *Experience and Nature* (New York: Dover, 1958).

20 For an eloquent discussion of fragile categories and their philosophical and pragmatic implications, see W. James, *Pragmatism* (Cambridge, MA: Harvard University Press, 1975). For a Buddhist perspective on the emptiness of categories, see F. J. Streng, *Emptiness: A Study in Religious Meaning* (Nashville, TN: Abingdon Press, 1967).

21 C. Barks, *The Essential Rumi* (London: Castle Books, 1997).

22 G. Norman, M. Young, and L. Brooks, "Non-analytical Models of Clinical Reasoning: The Role of Experience," *Medical Education* 41(12) (2007): 1140–45.

23 See T. J. Kaptchuk, *The Web That Has No Weaver: Understanding Chinese Medicine* (New York: Congdon & Weed, 1983).

24 See J. Greenberg, K. Reiner, and N. Meiran, "'Mind the Trap': Mindfulness Practice Reduces Cognitive Rigidity," *PLoS ONE* 7(5) (2012): e36206.

25 This intervention had many of the same elements as our physician training programs.
26 See J. Connelly, "Being in the Present Moment: Developing the Capacity for Mindfulness in Medicine," *Academic Medicine* 74(4) (1999): 420–24.
27 D. A. Schön, *Educating the Reflective Practitioner* (San Francisco: Jossey-Bass, 1987).

5. BEING PRESENT

1 Philosopher Michel Foucault described how a "clinical gaze," in contrast to usual social interactions, objectifies and disempowers patients, especially in hospital settings. See M. Foucault, *The Birth of the Clinic: An Archaeology of Medical Perception* (New York: Random House, 1994). Philosopher Emmanuel Levinas describes how ethical behavior starts with apprehending another's face, more so than principles, words, and ideas. For further discussion of Levinas's ethical mandate of immediacy in health care contexts, see R. Naef, "Bearing Witness: A Moral Way of Engaging in the Nurse-Person Relationship," *Nursing Philosophy* 7(3) (2006): 146–56; P. Komesaroff, "The Many Faces of the Clinic: A Levinasian View," in *Handbook of Phenomenology and Medicine*, ed. S. K. Toombs (Dordrecht, Netherlands: Kluwer Academic Publishers, 2001), 317–30; and J. V. Welie, "Towards an Ethics of Immediacy: A Defense of a Noncontractual Foundation of the Care Giver–Patient Relationship," *Medicine, Health Care, and Philosophy* 2(1) (1999): 11–19.
2 A. L. Suchman and D. A. Matthews, "What Makes the Patient-Doctor Relationship Therapeutic? Exploring the Connexional Dimension of Medical Care," *Annals of Internal Medicine* 108(1) (1988): 125–30.
3 M. K. Marvel et al., "Soliciting the Patient's Agenda: Have We Improved?," *JAMA* 281(3) (1999): 283–87.
4 I am grateful to Steve McPhee, M.D., who generously shared with me his thoughts on presence and his inspiration by the works of Harper and Marcel. See R. Harper, *On Presence: Variations and Reflections* (Philadelphia: Trinity Press International, 1991).
5 The idea of an observing self has been approached from educational, psychoanalytic, philosophical, and, more recently, neuroscientific perspectives. Here are some entry points into a rich literature: M. Epstein, *Thoughts without a Thinker: Psychotherapy from a Buddhist Perspective* (New York: Basic Books, 1995); R. M. Epstein, D. J. Siegel, and J. Silberman, "Self-Monitoring in Clinical Practice: A Challenge for Medical Educators," *Journal of Continuing Education in the Health Professions* 28(1) (2008): 5–13; and B. J. Baars, T. Z. Ramsoy, and S. Laureys, "Brain, Conscious Experience and the Observing Self," *Trends in Neurosciences* 26(12) (2003): 671–75.
6 J. E. Connelly, "Narrative Possibilities: Using Mindfulness in Clinical Practice," *Perspectives in Biology and Medicine* 48(1) (2005): 84–94; J. Coulehan, "Compassionate Solidarity: Suffering, Poetry, and Medicine," *Perspectives in Biology and Medicine* 52(4) (2009): 585–603; J. L. Coulehan, "Tenderness and Steadiness: Emotions in Medical Practice," *Literature and Medicine* 14(2)

(1995): 222–36; and R. Charon, "Narrative Medicine: Form, Function, and Ethics," *Annals of Internal Medicine* 134(1) (2001): 83–87.

7 This story is discussed in an article and cited with permission in R. M. Epstein, "Making the Ineffable Visible," *Families, Systems, & Health* 33(3) (2015): 280–82.

8 K. J. Swayden et al., "Effect of Sitting vs. Standing on Perception of Provider Time at Bedside: A Pilot Study," *Patient Education & Counseling* 86(2) (2012): 166–71.

9 K. Zoppi, "Communication about Concerns in Well-Child Visits" (Ann Arbor: University of Michigan, 1994).

10 A. L. Back et al., "Compassionate Silence in the Patient-Clinician Encounter: A Contemplative Approach," *Journal of Palliative Medicine* 12(12) (2009): 1113–17; and J. Bartels et al., "Eloquent Silences: A Musical and Lexical Analysis of Conversation between Oncologists and Their Patients," *Patient Education & Counseling* (forthcoming, 2016).

11 C. Lamm, C. D. Batson, and J. Decety, "The Neural Substrate of Human Empathy: Effects of Perspective-Taking and Cognitive Appraisal," *Journal of Cognitive Neuroscience* 19(1) (2007): 42–58.

12 C. Barks, *The Essential Rumi* (London: Castle Books, 1997); and J. E. Connelly, "The Guest House (Commentary)," *Academic Medicine* 83(6) (2008): 588–89.

13 G. Riva et al., "From Intention to Action: The Role of Presence," *New Ideas in Psychology* 29(1) (2011): 24–37.

14 J. Leff et al., "Computer-Assisted Therapy for Medication-Resistant Auditory Hallucinations: Proof-of-Concept Study," *British Journal of Psychiatry* 202(6) (2013): 428–33.

15 This understanding—that the mind is relational—is a radical departure from earlier notions of how the mind works. Giuseppe Riva and philosopher Evan Thompson and neuroscientist Antonio Damasio all suggest—from very different philosophical points of view—that "mind" emerges as a property of the relationship among a brain, a body, and the world, and from that embodied extended mind a sense of self and a sense of presence emerge.

16 See E. Thompson and M. Stapleton, "Making Sense of Sense-Making: Reflections on Enactive and Extended Mind Theories," *Topoi* 28(1) (2009): 23–30.

17 To understand more about intersubjectivity, I'd suggest starting with M. Buber, *I and Thou* (New York: Scribner, 1970); and N. Pembroke, "Human Dimension in Medical Care: Insights from Buber and Marcel," *Southern Medical Journal* 103(12) (2010): 1210–13.

18 As I've mentioned before, this skill "works" only if one has the ability to maintain enough differentiation between oneself and the other person to understand which experiences are yours and which are the other's—otherwise it disintegrates into shared delusion.

19 D. B. Baker, R. Day, and E. Salas, "Teamwork as an Essential Component of High-Reliability Organizations," *Health Services Research* 41(4, pt. 2) (2006): 1576–98.

20 J. Chatel-Goldman et al., "Non-local Mind from the Perspective of Social Cognition," *Frontiers in Human Neuroscience* 7 (2013): 107; and J. Zlatev et

al., "Intersubjectivity: What Makes Us Human?," in *The Shared Mind: Perspectives on Intersubjectivity*, eds. J. Zlatev, T. P. Racine, C. Sinha, and E. Itkonen (Amsterdam and Philadelphia: John Benjamins, 2008), chap. 1, 1–14.

21 W. B. Ventres and R. M. Frankel, "Shared Presence in Physician-Patient Communication: A Graphic Representation," *Families, Systems, & Health* 33(3) (2015): 270–79.

22 See R. Klitzman, *When Doctors Become Patients* (New York: Oxford University Press, 2008).

23 Dozens of studies document implicit bias in health care. Here are a few: D. J. Burgess, "Are Providers More Likely to Contribute to Healthcare Disparities under High Levels of Cognitive Load? How Features of the Healthcare Setting May Lead to Biases in Medical Decision Making," *Medical Decision Making* 30(2) (2010): 246–57; J. A. Sabin, F. P. Rivara, and A. G. Greenwald, "Physician Implicit Attitudes and Stereotypes about Race and Quality of Medical Care," *Medical Care* 46(7) (2008): 678–85; D. J. Burgess, S. S. Fu, and M. van Ryn, "Why Do Providers Contribute to Disparities and What Can Be Done About It?," *Journal of General Internal Medicine* 19(11) (2004): 1154–59; M. van Ryn, "Research on the Provider Contribution to Race/Ethnicity Disparities in Medical Care," *MedCare* 40(1) (2002): I140–I151; and J. Sabin et al., "Physicians' Implicit and Explicit Attitudes about Race by MD Race, Ethnicity, and Gender," *Journal of Health Care for the Poor and Underserved* 20(3) (2009): 896–913.

24 W. J. Hall et al., "Implicit Racial/Ethnic Bias among Health Care Professionals and Its Influence on Health Care Outcomes: A Systematic Review," *American Journal of Public Health* 105(12) (2015): e60–e76.

25 R. M. Epstein et al., "Understanding Fear of Contagion among Physicians Who Care for HIV Patients," *Family Medicine* 25(4) (1993): 264–68; and J. Shapiro, "Walking a Mile in Their Patients' Shoes: Empathy and Othering in Medical Students' Education," *Philosophy, Ethics, and Humanities in Medicine* 3(1) (2008): 1.

26 J. A. Bartz et al., "Oxytocin Selectively Improves Empathic Accuracy," *Psychological Science* 21(10) (2010): 1426–28; and C. K. De Dreu, "Oxytocin Modulates Cooperation within and Competition between Groups: An Integrative Review and Research Agenda," *Hormones and Behavior* 61(3) (2012): 419–28.

27 For an interesting discussion of tribalism in modern culture, see J. Greene, *Moral Tribes: Emotion, Reason, and the Gap between Us and Them* (New York: Penguin Press, 2013).

28 With training, people can experience greater emotional resonance. As tribal beings, though, we squelch the resonance if we label the other person as "not like me." To make matters worse, the tendency to stereotype—and therefore distance—worsens when people are under high cognitive load, such as in the emergency room. T. J. Allen et al., "Stereotype Strength and Attentional Bias: Preference for Confirming versus Disconfirming Information Depends on Processing Capacity," *Journal of Experimental Social Psychology* 45(5) (2009): 1081–87; Burgess, "Are Providers More Likely to Contribute?"; and Burgess, Fu, and van Ryn, "Why Do Providers Contribute to Disparities?" An often-

quoted study by Knox Todd examined prescriptions for pain medications in a busy Los Angeles emergency room prescribed for Latinos and non-Latinos with long-bone fractures of equivalent severity. Latinos received far fewer prescriptions and for lower doses, and twice as many Latinos as Anglos received no pain medication at all: K. H. Todd, N. Samaroo, and J. R. Hoffman, "Ethnicity as a Risk Factor for Inadequate Emergency Department Analgesia," *JAMA* 269(12) (1993): 1537–39. Perhaps the physicians unconsciously viewed Latino patients as more stoic or that they were more likely to abuse medications. I'm not sure why and the study didn't ask. Cognitive load and unexamined bias surely had something to do with it. Bias is not restricted to ethnicity. Physicians use fewer tests for heart disease in women and blacks compared to white males with equivalent risk factors—K. A. Schulman et al., "The Effect of Race and Sex on Physicians' Recommendations for Cardiac Catheterization," *New England Journal of Medicine* 340(8) (1999): 618–26—and provide less adequate breast cancer treatments to black women as compared to white women with the same disease characteristics: V. L. Shavers and M. L. Brown, "Racial and Ethnic Disparities in the Receipt of Cancer Treatment," *Journal of the National Cancer Institute* 94(5) (2002): 334–57. Similar biases exist for patients who are overweight and of low educational level.

Bias is not acceptable for doctors and other professionals; our mandate is to serve everyone, including patients whose life experiences are vastly different from our own. Because people generally disavow bias, the first, and challenging, step is awareness. A somewhat controversial and fascinating test for measuring implicit biases—biases that are below the level of awareness—was developed using computer technology that measures how long you take to respond to questions associating race, for example, with positive and negative words. Called the implicit-association test, the scores correlate with our judgments about people's character, abilities, and potential. A free version can be found at https://implicit.harvard.edu/implicit/takeatest.html. For a good read about the test and its implications, see M. Banaji and A. Greenwald, *Blindspot: Hidden Biases of Good People* (New York: Delacorte Press, 2013). Also see J. F. Dovidio et al., "On the Nature of Prejudice: Automatic and Controlled Processes," *Journal of Experimental Social Psychology* 33(5) (1997): 510–40; and A. G. Greenwald, D. E. McGhee, and J. L. K. Schwartz, "Measuring Individual Differences in Implicit Cognition: The Implicit Association Test," *Journal of Personality and Social Psychology* 74(6) (1998): 1464–80. For example, a well-meaning and otherwise excellent doctor might believe that he treats men's and women's pain similarly, but the way he associates pain with gender during the test may reveal biases of which he is unaware and that influence his prescribing practices. People's reactions to the IAT range from bland acceptance to vehement denial; those who deny their biases, not surprisingly, have fewer means for accommodating and diminishing the effects of bias.

29 Specifically the areas of the brain that involve self-other differentiation and cognitive appraisal (i.e., the dorsomedial prefrontal cortex and right inferior frontal cortex). Social neuroscientists Claus Lamm and Jean Decety have demonstrated changes on functional MRI scans when people make the effort to appreciate the pain of those who are not like them. See C. Lamm, A. N.

Meltzoff, and J. Decety, "How Do We Empathize with Someone Who Is Not Like Us? A Functional Magnetic Resonance Imaging Study," *Journal of Cognitive Neuroscience* 22(2) (2010): 362–76.

30 J. Decety, C. Yang, and Y. Cheng, "Physicians Down-Regulate Their Pain Empathy Response: An Event-Related Brain Potential Study," *NeuroImage* 50(4) (2010): 1676–82.

31 R. L. Reniers et al., "Empathy, ToM, and Self-Other Differentiation: An fMRI Study of Internal States," *Social Neuroscience* 9(1) (2014): 50–62; and Lamm, Batson, Decety, "Neural Substrate of Human Empathy."

32 P. Fonagy et al., *Affect Regulation, Mentalization, and the Development of Self* (New York: Other Press, 2002).

33 See the discussion of social epigenetics in chapter 3, "Curiosity."

34 A. Lutz et al., "Bold Signal in Insula Is Differentially Related to Cardiac Function during Compassion Meditation in Experts vs. Novices," *NeuroImage* 47(3) (2009): 1038–46.

35 Evan Thompson and other cognitive scientists and philosophers have called this embodied cognition, or embodied mind. F. J. Varela, E. Thompson, and E. Rosch, *The Embodied Mind: Cognitive Science and Human Experience* (Cambridge, MA: MIT Press, 1991).

36 Cognitive science has finally caught up with millennia of experience with contemplative practices, helping us to understand, from a scientific standpoint, the connection between awareness of our physical selves and awareness of our thoughts and emotions—that first we experience the smile, then identify the emotion of happiness. A. R. Damasio. *The Feeling of What Happens: Body and Emotion in the Making of Consciousness* (New York: Harcourt Brace, 1999).

37 C.-M. Tan, *Search Inside Yourself* (New York: HarperCollins, 2012). Reprinted from https://siyli.org/two-siyli-ways-to-change-your-mind-2.

6. NAVIGATING WITHOUT A MAP

1 R. A. Rodenbach et al., "Relationships between Personal Attitudes about Death and Communication with Terminally Ill Patients: How Oncology Clinicians Grapple with Mortality," *Patient Education & Counseling* 99(3) (2015): 356–63.

2 The idea that people left to decide for themselves is not always autonomy-supportive and can actually undermine a sense of self-determination was proposed in S. Sherwin, *No Longer Patient: Feminist Ethics and Health Care* (Philadelphia: Temple University Press, 1992).

3 E. B. Larson and X. Yao, "Clinical Empathy as Emotional Labor in the Patient-Physician Relationship," *JAMA* 293(9) (2005): 1100–1106.

4 See J. R. Adams et al., "Communicating with Physicians about Medical Decisions: A Reluctance to Disagree," *Archives of Internal Medicine* 172(15) (2012): 1184–86.

5 S. Glouberman and B. Zimmerman, "Complicated and Complex Systems: What Would Successful Reform of Medicare Look Like?," in *Romanow*

Papers: Changing Health Care in Canada, eds. P.-G. Forest, G. P. Marchildon, and T. McIntosh (Toronto: University of Toronto Press, 2002).

6 Here decision aids for patients that include values checklists, informational videos, and patient testimonials can be helpful. See G. Elwyn et al., "Developing a Quality Criteria Framework for Patient Decision Aids: Online International Delphi Consensus Process," *BMJ* 333(7565) (2006): 417.

7 See T. E. Quill and H. Brody, "Physician Recommendations and Patient Autonomy: Finding a Balance between Physician Power and Patient Choice," *Annals of Internal Medicine* 125(9) (1996): 763–69. Also, for reasons I explored in chapter 4, physicians sometimes recommend treatments that they would not choose for themselves. See D. Gorenstein, "How Doctors Die: Showing Others the Way," *New York Times*, November 19, 2013, http://www.nytimes.com/2013/11/20/your-money/how-doctors-die.html?_r=2.

8 C. E. Lindblom, "The Science of 'Muddling Through,'" *Public Administration Review* 19(2) (1959): 79–88.

9 See https://en.wikiquote.org/w/index.php?title=H._L._Mencken&oldid=2093748.

10 K. M. Weick and K. M. Sutcliffe, *Managing the Unexpected: Assuring High Performance in an Age of Complexity* (San Francisco: Jossey-Bass, 2001).

11 S. Weiner and A. Schwartz, "Contextual Errors in Medical Decision Making: Overlooked and Understudied," *Academic Medicine: Journal of the Association of American Medical Colleges* 91(5) (2015).

12 This quote appears in the preface to W. James, *The Varieties of Religious Experience: A Study in Human Nature* (New York: W. W. Norton, 1902: repr., 1961).

13 I thank Kathryn Montgomery Hunter for this quote and the associated discussion in this paragraph from her blog exploring the nature of clinical practice, including decision making. See K. Montgomery, "Thinking about Thinking: Implications for Patient Safety," *Healthcare Quarterly* (Toronto, Canada) 12 (2008): e191–e194. The William James quote can be found in W. James, *William James: The Essential Writings* (Albany: State University of New York Press, 1986); W. M. James, "Brute and Human Intellect," *Journal of Speculative Philosophy* 12(3) (1878): 236–76; and W. James, "Brute and Human Intellect," in *William James: Writings, 1878–1899* (New York: Library of America, 1992), 11.

14 In that context, here are some other dilemmas that I faced in one day in the office. Do I suggest that a patient agree to take another round of potentially toxic chemotherapy knowing that it only has a 10 percent chance of helping? How frequent or "typical" does chest pain need to be to warrant an invasive procedure to determine whether serious heart disease is present? When do I prescribe narcotics for patients with intractable low-back pain, knowing that a small percentage of patients will become addicted? When do I assume that I should choose the treatment I used the last time I saw a patient similar to the current one, and when does that represent availability bias or some other form of self-deception?

15 Shared mind is when ideas, intuitions, and decisions emerge not only from individuals but from the interactions among them—an intersubjective experience.

R. M. Epstein and R. L. Street Jr., "Shared Mind: Communication, Decision Making, and Autonomy in Serious Illness," *Annals of Family Medicine* 9(5) (2011): 454–61; R. M. Epstein and R. E. Gramling, "What Is Shared in Shared Decision Making? Complex Decisions When the Evidence Is Unclear," *Medical Care Research and Review* 70(1S) (2012): 94–112; R. M. Epstein, "Whole Mind and Shared Mind in Clinical Decision-Making," *Patient Education & Counseling* 90(2) (2013): 200–206; and J. Zlatev et al., *The Shared Mind: Perspectives on Intersubjectivity* (Amsterdam and Philadelphia: John Benjamins, 2008.)

16 A provocative study using hyperscanning (two people in MRI scanners communicating with one another) showed that people whose brain activity is coordinated also are socially more connected. E. Bilek et al., "Information Flow between Interacting Human Brains: Identification, Validation, and Relationship to Social Expertise," *Proceedings of the National Academy of Sciences* 112(16) (2015): 5207–12.

17 L. R. Mujica-Parodi et al., "Chemosensory Cues to Conspecific Emotional Stress Activate Amygdala in Humans," *PLoS ONE* 4(7) (2009): e6415.

18 This vignette was adapted from F. Borrell-Carrió and R. M. Epstein, "Preventing Errors in Clinical Practice: A Call for Self-Awareness," *Annals of Family Medicine* 2(4) (2004): 310–16.

19 R. Srivastava, "Speaking Up—When Doctors Navigate Medical Hierarchy," *New England Journal of Medicine* 368(4) (2013): 302–5.

20 This quote, attributed to Dr. Faith Fitzgerald, appeared in A. K. Smith, D. B. White, and R. M. Arnold, "Uncertainty—the Other Side of Prognosis," *New England Journal of Medicine* 368(26) (2013): 2448–50.

21 F. Ismail-Beigi et al., "Individualizing Glycemic Targets in Type 2 Diabetes Mellitus: Implications of Recent Clinical Trials," *Annals of Internal Medicine* 154(8) (2011): 554–59.

22 D. L. Sackett et al., *Clinical Epidemiology: A Basic Science for Clinical Medicine*, 2nd ed. (Boston: Little, Brown, 1991).

23 G. Guyatt et al., "Patients at the Center: In Our Practice, and in Our Use of Language," *ACP Journal Club* 140(1) (2004): A11–A12. The presence of multiple conditions also affects patients' choices. See M. E. Tinetti, T. R. Fried, and C. M. Boyd, "Designing Health Care for the Most Common Chronic Condition—Multimorbidity," *JAMA* 307(23) (2012): 2493–94.

24 A. Tversky and D. Kahneman, "The Framing of Decisions and the Psychology of Choice," *Science* 211(4481) (1981): 453–58.

25 D. Kahneman, "A Perspective on Judgment and Choice: Mapping Bounded Rationality," *American Psychologist* 58(9) (2003): 697–720.

26 Croskerry suggests that enhancing metacognition would be a good thing for clinicians. If we could only understand our own biases during decision making, then we could have some hope of engaging in what Croskerry calls "de-biasing strategies" to make sounder and better-informed decisions by not only considering information and knowledge that we have, but how we select and use that knowledge and information. For Croskerry, who directs the Critical Thinking Program at Dalhousie University in Nova Scotia, de-biasing often involves switching from autopilot to "mindfulness of one's own thinking." See

P. Croskerry, "From Mindless to Mindful Practice—Cognitive Bias and Clinical Decision Making," *New England Journal of Medicine* 368(26) (2013): 2445–48.

27 Few interventions have shown promise in reducing implicit bias, and reduction in implicit bias has implications far beyond medicine. See Y. Kang, J. R. Gray, and J. F. Dovidio, "The Nondiscriminating Heart: Lovingkindness Meditation Training Decreases Implicit Intergroup Bias," *Journal of Experimental Psychology: General* 143(3) (2014): 1306; Y. Kang, J. Gruber, and J. R. Gray, "Mindfulness and De-automatization," *Emotion Review* 5(2) (2013): 192–201; A. Lueke and B. Gibson, "Mindfulness Meditation Reduces Implicit Age and Race Bias: The Role of Reduced Automaticity of Responding," *Social Psychology and Personality Science* (2014): 1–8; and A. C. Hafenbrack, Z. Kinias, and S. G. Barsade, "Debiasing the Mind through Meditation Mindfulness and the Sunk-Cost Bias," *Psychological Science* 25(2) (2014): 369–76.

28 G. Norman, M. Young, and L. Brooks, "Non-analytical Models of Clinical Reasoning: The Role of Experience," *Medical Education* 41(12) (2007): 1140–45.

29 See P. Croskerry, "A Universal Model of Diagnostic Reasoning," *Academic Medicine* 84(8) (2009): 1022–28.

30 J. M. Harlow, "Recovery after Severe Injury to the Head," *History of Psychiatry* (1993): 274–81 (originally published 1868 in the *Bulletin of the Massachusetts Medical Society*).

31 Epstein and Gramling, "What Is Shared in Shared Decision Making?"

32 S. Farber, "Living Every Minute," *Journal of Pain and Symptom Management* 49(4) (2015): 796–800.

33 K. Murray, "How Doctors Die—It's Not Like the Rest of Us, but It Should Be," *Zócalo Public Square*, November 30, 2011, 1775–77.

7. RESPONDING TO SUFFERING

1 The ideas in this chapter germinated with and expand on an article I coauthored with Tony Back, whom I acknowledge with gratitude, as part of a larger project on suffering and compassion in health care. See R. M. Epstein and A. L. Back, "Responding to Suffering," *JAMA* 314(24) (2015): 2623–24.

2 R. B. Haynes et al., "Increased Absenteeism from Work after Detection and Labeling of Hypertensive Patients," *New England Journal of Medicine* 299(14) (1978): 741–44; and J. E. Dimsdale, "Reflections on the Impact of Antihypertensive Medications on Mood, Sedation, and Neuropsychologic Functioning," *Archives of Internal Medicine* 152(1) (1992): 35–39.

3 A. W. Frank, "Can We Research Suffering?," *Qualitative Health Research* 11(3) (2001): 353–62.

4 E. J. Cassell, "The Nature of Suffering and the Goals of Medicine," *New England Journal of Medicine* 306(11) (1982): 639–45; E. J. Cassell, "Diagnosing Suffering: A Perspective," *Annals of Internal Medicine* 131(7) (1999): 531–34; and E. J. Cassell, "The Phenomenon of Suffering and Its Relationship to Pain," in *Handbook of Phenomenology and Medicine*, ed. S. K. Toombs (Dordrecht, Netherlands: Kluewer Academic Publishers, 2001), 371–90.

5 A slight misquote of Eldridge Cleaver, who said, "There is no more neutrality

in the world. You either have to be part of the solution, or you're going to be part of the problem." But he was not the first or the last to say this.

6 For further elaboration of this theme, see T. H. Lee, "The Word That Shall Not Be Spoken," *New England Journal of Medicine* 369(19) (2013): 1777–79.

7 There is a rich literature on the relationships among unexplained somatic symptoms, traumatic life events, mental illness, and functioning. See P. Salmon, "Patients Who Present Physical Symptoms in the Absence of Physical Pathology: A Challenge to Existing Models of Doctor-Patient Interaction," *Patient Education & Counseling* 39(1) (2000): 105–13; and W. Katon, M. Sullivan, and E. Walker, "Medical Symptoms without Identified Pathology: Relationship to Psychiatric Disorders, Childhood and Adult Trauma, and Personality Traits," *Annals of Internal Medicine* 134(9, pt. 2) (2001): 917–25. For a reference about how physicians respond to such patients, see E. A. Walker et al., "Predictors of Physician Frustration in the Care of Patients with Rheumatological Complaints," *General Hospital Psychiatry* 19(5) (1997): 315–23.

8 Clinicians reading this case report undoubtedly each have a theory of what else could have been done, an additional blood test or scan that would reveal the body's secrets and provide a clear path. Some may assert that the diagnosis is not recognized by mainstream medicine—due to an infectious agent, an environmental toxin, or a psychological process—nor is a humoral diagnosis according to traditional Chinese or ayurvedic medicine. Karen did explore many of these options. The point here is that the possibilities are endless, but investigating further always has a cost. Sometimes that cost is a side effect of a medication; other times it is in energy (seeing lots of doctors can be exhausting) or in finances or is existential (seeing oneself as diminished and fragmented rather than complete and whole).

9 Here are a few sources about the perils of labeling people "somatizers": R. M. Epstein, T. E. Quill, and I. R. McWhinney, "Somatization Reconsidered: Incorporating the Patient's Experience of Illness," *Archives of Internal Medicine* 159(3) (1999): 215–22; I. R. McWhinney, R. M. Epstein, and T. R. Freeman, "Rethinking Somatization," *Advances in Mind-Body Medicine* 17(4) (2001): 232–39; R. M. Epstein et al., "Physicians' Responses to Patients' Medically Unexplained Symptoms," *Psychosomatic Medicine* 68(2) (2006): 269–76; P. Salmon et al., "Doctors' Responses to Patients with Medically Unexplained Symptoms Who Seek Emotional Support: Criticism or Confrontation?," *General Hospital Psychiatry* 29(5) (2007): 454–60; and H. Waitzkin and H. Magana, "The Black Box in Somatization: Unexplained Physical Symptoms, Culture, and Narratives of Trauma," *Social Science & Medicine* 45(6) (1997): 811–25.

10 In her case, methotrexate, several TNF inhibitors, and a selective T-cell costimulation blocker.

11 I am grateful to Tony Back, who picked those words out when I was first recounting Karen's situation as part of an article we've coauthored for *JAMA*. See Epstein and Back, "Responding to Suffering."

12 Tony is also the founder of a new venture called VitalTalk, which offers training to physicians to help improve communication with patients during the most difficult moments.

13 A. L. Back et al., "'Why Are We Doing This?': Clinician Helplessness in the Face of Suffering," *Journal of Palliative Medicine* 18(1) (2015): 26–30.

14 S. E. Thorne et al., "'Being Known': Patients' Perspectives of the Dynamics of Human Connection in Cancer Care," *Psycho-Oncology* 14(10) (2005): 887–98.

15 Reference to Henry James noted in R. Charon, *Narrative Medicine: Honoring the Stories of Illness* (London: Oxford University Press, 2006).

16 J. Coulehan, "Compassionate Solidarity: Suffering, Poetry, and Medicine," *Perspectives in Biology and Medicine* 52(4) (2009): 585–603.

17 M. L. Johansen et al., "'I Deal with the Small Things': The Doctor-Patient Relationship and Professional Identity in GPs' Stories of Cancer Care," *Health* 16(6) (2012): 569–84.

18 A. L. Back et al., "Compassionate Silence in the Patient-Clinician Encounter: A Contemplative Approach," *Journal of Palliative Medicine* 12(12) (2009): 1113–17.

19 A. M. Kleinman, *The Illness Narratives: Suffering, Healing, and the Human Condition* (New York: Basic Books, 1988).

20 Kübler-Ross's five stages of dying—denial, anger, bargaining, depression, acceptance—are described in E. Kübler-Ross, S. Wessler, and L. V. Avioli, "On Death and Dying," *JAMA* 221(1972): 174–79.

21 From "Do Not Go Gentle into the Night," in *The Poems of Dylan Thomas* (New York: New Directions, 1938).

22 L. M. Candib, "Working with Suffering," *Patient Education & Counseling* 48(1) (2002): 43–50.

8. THE SHAKY STATE OF COMPASSION

1 G. L. Engel, "The Need for a New Medical Model: A Challenge for Biomedicine," *Science* 196(4286) (1977): 129–36.

2 G. L. Engel, "From Biomedical to Biopsychosocial: Being Scientific in the Human Domain," *Psychosomatics* 38(6) (1997): 521–28.

3 D. L. Berry et al., "Clinicians Communicating with Patients Experiencing Cancer Pain," *Cancer Investigation* 21(3) (2003): 374–81.

4 G. E. Pence, "Can Compassion Be Taught?," *Journal of Medical Ethics* 9(4) (1983): 189–91.

5 B. A. Lown, J. Rosen, and J. Marttila, "An Agenda for Improving Compassionate Care: A Survey Shows About Half of Patients Say Such Care Is Missing," *Health Affairs* 30(9) (2011): 1772–78.

6 The Milgram experiments were conducted in the early 1960s, shortly after the trial of Nazi war criminal Adolf Eichmann, with the intention of proving that most citizens were vulnerable to ethical compromise. See S. Milgram, "Behavioral Study of Obedience," *Journal of Abnormal Psychology* (1963): 67371–78.

7 It remains controversial whether long-term psychological harm was inflicted on some of the participants and whether the research protocol violated ethical norms at the time. Yet, this study prompted strict rules about informed consent for and the ethical review of all behavioral research.

8 J. M. Darley and C. D. Batson, "'From Jerusalem to Jericho': A Study of Situ-

ation and Dispositional Variables in Helping Behavior," *Journal of Personality and Social Psychology* 27(1) (1973): 100–108.

9 For one recent example, see A. Schattner, "My Most Informative Error," *JAMA Internal Medicine* 175(5) (2015): 681.

10 J. Halifax, "A Heuristic Model of Enactive Compassion," *Current Opinion in Supportive and Palliative Care* 6(2) (2012): 228–35. Also, see her book *Being with Dying* (Boulder, CO: Shambhala Publications, 2008). For an understanding of how one can empathize with someone whom we perceive as different, see C. Lamm, A. N. Meltzoff, and J. Decety, "How Do We Empathize with Someone Who Is Not Like Us? A Functional Magnetic Resonance Imaging Study," *Journal of Cognitive Neuroscience* 22(2) (2010): 362–76.

11 H. Fukushima, Y. Terasawa, and S. Umeda, "Association between Interoception and Empathy: Evidence from Heartbeat-Evoked Brain Potential," *International Journal of Psychophysiology* 79(2) (2011): 259–65; and T. Singer, H. D. Critchley, and K. Preuschoff, "A Common Role of Insula in Feelings, Empathy and Uncertainty," *Trends in Cognitive Sciences* 13(8) (2009): 334–40.

12 C. Lamm, C. D. Batson, and J. Decety, "The Neural Substrate of Human Empathy: Effects of Perspective-Taking and Cognitive Appraisal," *Journal of Cognitive Neuroscience* 19(1) (2007): 42–58.

13 H. De Jaegher and E. Di Paolo, "Participatory Sense-Making: An Enactive Approach to Social Cognition," *Phenomenology and the Cognitive Sciences* 6(4) (2007): 485–507.

14 For some illustrative examples of physician self-disclosure gone awry, see S. H. McDaniel et al., "'Enough about Me, Let's Get Back to You': Physician Self-Disclosure during Primary Care Encounters," *Annals of Internal Medicine* 149(11) (2008): 835–37.

15 A concise summary of these pathways linking the ventral striatum and the medial orbitofrontal cortex can be found in O. M. Klimecki et al., "Differential Pattern of Functional Brain Plasticity after Compassion and Empathy Training," *Social Cognitive and Affective Neuroscience* 9(6) (2014): 873–79.

16 See M. Hojat et al., "The Devil Is in the Third Year: A Longitudinal Study of Erosion of Empathy in Medical School," *Academic Medicine* 84(9) (2009): 1182–91.

17 D. C. Batson, "These Things Called Empathy: Eight Related but Distinct Phenomena," in *The Social Neuroscience of Empathy*, eds. J. Decety and W. Ickes (Denver, CO: Bradford, 2009), chap. 1, 13–15; Lamm, Batson, and Decety, "Neural Substrate of Human Empathy"; and N. Eisenberg and N. D. Eggum, "Empathic Responding: Sympathy and Personal Distress," in *Social Neuroscience of Empathy*, eds. Decety and Ickes, chap. 6, 71–83.

18 For recommendations on how clinicians can use self-disclosure more effectively, see McDaniel et al., "'Enough about Me.'"

19 J. Halpern, "What Is Clinical Empathy?," *Journal of General Internal Medicine* 18(8) (2003): 670–74.

20 M. K. Kearney et al., "Self-Care of Physicians Caring for Patients at the End of Life: 'Being Connected . . . a Key to My Survival,'" *JAMA* 301(11) (2009): 1155–64.

21 J. Decety and C. Lamm, "Empathy versus Personal Distress: Recent Evidence from Social Neuroscience," in *Social Neuroscience of Empathy*, eds. Decety and Ickes, chap. 15, 199–213.

22 S. Salzberg, *Lovingkindness: The Revolutionary Art of Happiness* (Boston: Shambhala, 1997).

23 These areas would be the anterior insula and anterior midcingulate cortex.

24 The dopamine, opioid, and oxytocin centers.

25 F. de Vignemont and T. Singer, "The Empathic Brain: How, When and Why?," *Trends in Cognitive Sciences* 10(10) (2006): 435–41.

26 Salzberg, *Lovingkindness*.

27 Aristotle, *The Nicomachean Ethics*, trans. David Ross, revised with an introduction and notes by Lesley Brown (New York: Oxford University Press, 2009); and T. J. Oord, *Defining Love: A Philosophical, Scientific, and Theological Engagement* (Grand Rapids, MI: Brazos Press, 2010).

28 Here, the work of psychologist Tania Singer at the Max Planck Institute in Leipzig, Germany, is particularly relevant. Singer reported results of an experiment in which people who had never done any kind of meditation agreed to participate in a nine-month program. For three months they practiced focused attention training, alone at home and in group sessions. Then for another three months they practiced a form of dyadic attention training—"attentive listening" to others through structured dialogues conducted in person or by phone. For the final three months they engaged in traditional compassion practice. Singer and her team found that the effects of each contemplative practice built a particular set of skills. Focused attention training enhanced attentional networks and reduced distractibility. Compassion practice had greater effects on pro-social attitudes such as caring and concern for others and desire to ameliorate others' suffering. Singer's study was done with ordinary people from a variety of walks of life, yet could easily apply to those who work in medical settings. See T. Singer and M. Bolz, *Compassion: Bridging Practice and Science* (Munich, Germany: Max Planck Society, 2013).

29 For further information, see H. G. Engen and T. Singer, "Compassion-Based Emotion Regulation Up-Regulates Experienced Positive Affect and Associated Neural Networks," *Social Cognitive and Affective Neuroscience* 10(9) (2015): 1291–301.

30 H. Y. Weng et al., "Compassion Training Alters Altruism and Neural Responses to Suffering," *Psychological Science* 24(7) (2013): 1171–80.

9. WHEN BAD THINGS HAPPEN

1 L. T. Kohn, J. M. Corrigan, and M. S. Donaldson, *To Err Is Human: Building a Safer Health System* (Washington, DC: National Academy Press, 2000).

2 T. H. Gallagher et al., "Patients' and Physicians' Attitudes regarding the Disclosure of Medical Errors," *JAMA* 289(8) (2003): 1001–7.

3 Kohn, Corrigan, and Donaldson, *To Err Is Human*.

4 In this chapter most of the examples about errors that I have chosen are ambiguous. This was intentional. Dramatic errors due to gross incompetence or

neglect—such as amputating the wrong leg or giving a lethal dose of a medication—are uncommon, and the brute force of the litigation system can override mindful attempts to restore balance and connection. In fact, though, much of the total burden to patients and clinicians from bad outcomes results from a combination of small lapses in attention, unfortunate coincidences, miscommunicated intentions, and team and systems failures.

5 H. B. Beckman et al., "The Doctor-Patient Relationship and Malpractice: Lessons from Plaintiff Depositions," *Archives of Internal Medicine* 154(12) (1994): 1365–70.

6 B. Ho and E. Liu, "Does Sorry Work? The Impact of Apology Laws on Medical Malpractice," *Journal of Risk and Uncertainty* 43(2) (2011): 141–67.

7 N. M. Saitta and S. D. Hodge, "Is It Unrealistic to Expect a Doctor to Apologize for an Unforeseen Medical Complication?—a Primer on Apologies Laws," *Pennsylvania Bar Association Quarterly* (2011): 93–110.

8 N. M. Saitta and S. Hodge, "Physician Apologies," *Practical Lawyer*, December 2011, 35–43; and N. Saitta and S. D. Hodge, "Efficacy of a Physician's Words of Empathy: An Overview of State Apology Laws," *Journal of the American Osteopathic Association* 112(5) (2012): 302–6.

9 A. D. Waterman et al., "The Emotional Impact of Medical Errors on Practicing Physicians in the United States and Canada," *Joint Commission Journal on Quality and Patient Safety* 33(8) (2007): 467–76.

10 A. W. Wu, "Medical Error: The Second Victim. The Doctor Who Makes the Mistake Needs Help Too," *Western Journal of Medicine* 172(6) (2000): 358.

11 M. P. Stiegler, "A Piece of My Mind. What I Learned about Adverse Events from Captain Sully: It's Not What You Think," *JAMA* 313(4) (2015): 361–62.

12 S. K. Howard et al., "Anesthesia Crisis Resource Management Training: Teaching Anesthesiologists to Handle Critical Incidents," *Aviation, Space, and Environmental Medicine* 63(9) (1992): 763–70.

13 C. P. West et al., "Association of Perceived Medical Errors with Resident Distress and Empathy: A Prospective Longitudinal Study," *JAMA* 296(9) (2006): 1071–78.

14 In her thoughtful article about the program, Karan reported that a resident drew up medications into two syringes then forgot to mark which drug was in which syringe; another resident administered an entire syringe of a powerful stimulant thinking it was saline solution; another noted that blood-pressure cuffs in the operating room had "questionable" stains on them, likely another patient's blood; and so forth. See S. B. Karan, J. S. Berger, and M. Wajda, "Confessions of Physicians: What Systemic Reporting Does Not Uncover," *Journal of Graduate Medical Education* 7(4) (2015): 528–30.

15 L. Granek, "When Doctors Grieve," *New York Times*, May 27, 2012; and L. Granek et al., "Nature and Impact of Grief over Patient Loss on Oncologists' Personal and Professional Lives," *Archives of Internal Medicine* 172(12) (2012): 964–66.

16 R. A. Rodenbach et al., "Relationships between Personal Attitudes about Death and Communication with Terminally Ill Patients: How Oncology Clinicians Grapple with Mortality," *Patient Education & Counseling* 99(3) (2015): 356–63.

17 L. Granek et al., "What Do Oncologists Want?," *Supportive Care in Cancer* 20(10) (2012): 2627–32.

18 M. Shayne and T. E. Quill, "Oncologists Responding to Grief," *Archives of Internal Medicine* 172(12) (2012): 966–67.

19 C. K. Germer, *The Mindful Path to Self-Compassion: Freeing Yourself from Destructive Thoughts and Emotions* (New York: Guilford Press, 2009); and K. D. Neff and C. K. Germer, "A Pilot Study and Randomized Controlled Trial of the Mindful Self-Compassion Program," *Journal of Clinical Pscyhology* 69(1) (2013): 28–44.

20 K. D. Neff, Y.-P. Hsieh, and K. Dejitterat, "Self-Compassion, Achievement Goals, and Coping with Academic Failure," *Self and Identity* 4(3) (2005): 263–87; Neff and Germer, "Pilot Study and Randomized Controlled Trial"; and M. R. Leary et al., "Self-Compassion and Reactions to Unpleasant Self-Relevant Events: The Implications of Treating Oneself Kindly," *Journal of Personality and Social Psychology* 92(5) (2007): 887.

21 M. Lesser, *Know Yourself, Forget Yourself: Five Truths to Transform Your Work, Relationships, and Everyday Life* (Novato, CA: New World Library, 2013).

22 S. D. Scott et al., "The Natural History of Recovery for the Healthcare Provider 'Second Victim' after Adverse Patient Events," *Quality and Safety in Health Care* 18(5) (2009): 325–30.

23 See http://www.brighamandwomens.org/medical_professionals/career/cpps /default.aspx.

24 The San Francisco Department of Public Health has developed a Trauma Informed Systems (TIS) framework, intended to help improve organizational functioning, increase resilience, and improve workforce experience. This includes mandatory foundational training to all nine thousand public health employees to create a shared language and understanding of trauma, a Champions Learning Community (CLC), a train-the-trainer program, intentional efforts to align TIS with all workforce and policy initiatives, and leadership engagement and outreach to support integration of TIS principles into day-to-day operations as well as promote system change at the program and policy level.

10. HEALING THE HEALER

1 This was quoted in *JAMA* 189 (1964): 97.

2 To give just one of many examples, care for patients with diabetes in primary care is typically measured according to the frequency of testing for hemoglobin A1c, a marker for long-term control of diabetes. Some clinics actually use the test results (normal vs. high vs. very high) as the quality metric. However, frequency of testing does not reliably predict control of diabetes, and long-term outcomes for many people over age sixty-five with type 2 diabetes is minimally affected by whether the A1c level is below 7 (considered optimal) or if it's closer to 8 (considered poor care), and in some cases higher levels are desirable if there is risk of *low* blood sugar. The factors that go into control

of blood sugar go well beyond the prescription pad and are usually unreimbursed (e.g., exercise programs, nutritional counseling, social support). Conversely, the quality of physician empathy is a powerful factor in blood sugar control in patients with diabetes, yet goes unmeasured and unreimbursed. See M. Hojat et al., "Physicians' Empathy and Clinical Outcomes for Diabetic Patients," *Academic Medicine* 86(3) (2011): 359–64.

3 Moral distress—when people are put in situations in which they're kept from doing what they know is right or are forced to do things that conflict with their values—can be blatant, such as being told to deny a patient needed pain medication, or more insidious. See A. Catlin et al., "Conscientious Objection: A Potential Neonatal Nursing Response to Care Orders That Cause Suffering at the End of Life? Study of a Concept," *Neonatal Network—Journal of Neonatal Nursing* 27(2) (2008): 101–8; L. H. Pololi et al., "Why Are a Quarter of Faculty Considering Leaving Academic Medicine? A Study of Their Perceptions of Institutional Culture and Intentions to Leave at 26 Representative US Medical Schools," *Academic Medicine* 87(7) (2012): 859–69; C. H. Rushton, A. W. Kaszniak, and J. S. Halifax, "Addressing Moral Distress: Application of a Framework to Palliative Care Practice," *Journal of Palliative Medicine* 16(9) (2013): 1080–88; C. H. Rushton, A. W. Kaszniak, and J. S. Halifax, "A Framework for Understanding Moral Distress among Palliative Care Clinicians," *Journal of Palliative Medicine* 16(9) (2013): 1074–79; and C. Varcoe et al., "Nurses' Perceptions of and Responses to Morally Distressing Situations," *Nursing Ethics* 19(4) (2012): 488–500.

4 Burnout gets worse toward midcareer, as clinical and administrative responsibilities increase while other aspects of life become more complex. Some surveys suggest that women are more burned out than men, which is understandable given their more complex social roles and responsibilities—and other surveys suggest that they are also more resilient. See T. D. Shanafelt et al., "Changes in Burnout and Satisfaction with Work-Life Balance in Physicians and the General US Working Population between 2011 and 2014," *Mayo Clinic Proceedings* 90(12) (2015): 1600–1613; and http://www.medscape.com/features/slideshow/lifestyle/2016/public/overview#page=1 for 2016 statistics on physician burnout, overall and by physician specialty. Also see M. W. C. Friedberg, PG, K. R. VanBusum, F. M. Aunon, C. Pham, J. P. Caloyeras, S. Mattke, E. Pitchforth, D. D. Quigley, and R. H. Brook, "Factors Affecting Physician Professional Satisfaction and Their Implications for Patient Care, Health Systems, and Health Policy," 2013, http://www.rand.org/content/dam/rand/pubs/research_reports/RR400/RR439/RAND_RR439.pdf; "Physician Wellness Services and Cejka Search: 2011 Physician Stress and Burnout Survey," 2011, http://www.cejkasearch.com/wp-content/uploads/physician-stress-burnout-survey.pdf; and Physicians Foundation, "A Survey of America's Physicians: Practice Patterns and Perspectives, an Examination of the Professional Morale, Practice Patterns, Career Plans, and Healthcare Perspectives of Today's Physicians, Aggregated by Age, Gender, Primary Care/Specialists, and Practice Owners/Employees," 2012, http://www.physiciansfoundation.org/uploads/default/Physicians_Foundation_2012_Biennial_Survey.pdf. An article in the November 2014 *Atlantic* cites five current books

in the popular press documenting the devastating consequences of physician burnout. See M. O'Rourke, "Doctors Tell All—and It's Bad," *Atlantic*, November 2014, http://www.theatlantic.com/magazine/archive/2014/11/doctors-tell-all-and-its-bad/380785/; and D. Ofri, "The Epidemic of Disillusioned Doctors," *Time*, published electronically July 2, 2013, http://ideas.time.com/2013/07/02/the-epidemic-of-disillusioned-doctors.

5 M. D. McHugh et al., "Nurses' Widespread Job Dissatisfaction, Burnout, and Frustration with Health Benefits Signal Problems for Patient Care," *Health Affairs* 30(2) (2011): 202–10; and C. A. J. Dixon et al., "Abusive Behaviour Experienced by Primary Care Receptionists: A Cross-Sectional Survey," *Family Practice* 21(2) (2004): 137–39.

6 Most of the work on physician burnout has been done by a research group at the Mayo Clinic in Minnesota and the Physicians Worklife Study, with some important studies done by other groups. See L. N. Dyrbye et al., "Relationship between Burnout and Professional Conduct and Attitudes among US Medical Students," *JAMA* 304(11) (2010): 1173–80; L. N. Dyrbye et al., "Burnout and Suicidal Ideation among US Medical Students," *Annals of Internal Medicine* 149(5) (2008): 334–41; L. N. Dyrbye et al., "Physician Satisfaction and Burnout at Different Career Stages," *Mayo Clinic Proceedings* 88(12) (2013): 1358–67; A. M. Fahrenkopf et al., "Rates of Medication Errors among Depressed and Burnt Out Residents: Prospective Cohort Study," *BMJ* 1(7642) (2008): 488–91; S. Gabel, "Demoralization: A Precursor to Physician Burnout?," *American Family Physician* 86(9) (2012): 861–62; L. N. Dyrbye et al., "Burnout among US Medical Students, Residents, and Early Career Physicians Relative to the General US Population," *Academic Medicine* 89(3) (2014): 443–51; T. D. Shanafelt et al., "Career Fit and Burnout among Academic Faculty," *Archives of Internal Medicine* 169(10) (2009): 990–95; C. P. West et al., "Association of Resident Fatigue and Distress with Perceived Medical Errors," *JAMA* 302(12) (2009): 1294–300; M. Linzer et al., "Predicting and Preventing Physician Burnout: Results from the United States and the Netherlands," *American Journal of Medicine* 111(2) (2001): 170–75; J. E. McMurray et al., "The Work Lives of Women Physicians: Results from the Physician Work Life Study. The SGIM Career Satisfaction Study Group," *Journal of General Internal Medicine* 15(6) (2000): 372–80; E. Williams et al., "The Relationship of Organizational Culture, Stress, Satisfaction, and Burnout with Physician-Reported Error and Suboptimal Patient Care: Results from the Memo Study," *Health Care Management Review* 32(3) (2007): 203–12; and E. S. Williams et al., "Understanding Physicians' Intentions to Withdraw from Practice: The Role of Job Satisfaction, Job Stress, Mental and Physical Health," *Health Care Management Review* 26(1) (2001): 7–19.

7 T. Kushnir et al., "Is Burnout Associated with Referral Rates among Primary Care Physicians in Community Clinics?," *Family Practice* 31(1) (2014): 44–50; K. H. Bachman and D. K. Freeborn, "HMO Physicians' Use of Referrals," *Social Science & Medicine* 48(4) (1999): 547–57; and B. E. Sirovich, S. Woloshin, and L. M. Schwartz, "Too Little? Too Much? Primary Care Physicians' Views on US Health Care: A Brief Report," *Archives of Internal Medicine* 171(17) (2011): 1582–85.

8 See J. S. Haas et al., "Is the Professional Satisfaction of General Internists Associated with Patient Satisfaction?," *Journal of General Internal Medicine* 15(2) (2000): 122–28.

9 Most of these will continue to practice medicine but not primary care. Many choose urgent care and hospital medicine. Some take on administrative roles.

10 R. L. Lichtenstein, "Review Article: The Job Satisfaction and Retention of Physicians in Organized Settings: A Literature Review," *Medical Care Research and Review* 41(3) (1984): 139–79; J. E. Berger and R. L. Boyle Jr., "How to Avoid the High Costs of Physician Turnover," *Medical Group Management Journal* 39(6) (1991): 80–82; S. B. Buchbinder et al., "Estimates of Costs of Primary Care Physician Turnover," *American Journal of Managed Care* 5(11) (1999): 1431–38; and J. D. Waldman et al., "The Shocking Cost of Turnover in Health Care," *Health Care Management Review* 29(1) (2004): 2–7.

11 R. G. Hill Jr., L. M. Sears, and S. W. Melanson, "4,000 Clicks: A Productivity Analysis of Electronic Medical Records in a Community Hospital ED," *American Journal of Emergency Medicine* 31(11) (2013): 1591–94; and S. Babbott et al., "Electronic Medical Records and Physician Stress in Primary Care: Results from the Memo Study," *Journal of the American Medical Informatics Association* 21(e1) (2014): e100–e106.

12 C. Maslach, "Job Burnout," *Current Directions in Psychological Science* 12(5) (2003): 189–92.

13 A. Spickard Jr., S. G. Gabbe, and J. F. Christensen, "Mid-Career Burnout in Generalist and Specialist Physicians," *JAMA* 288(12) (2002): 1447–50.

14 Dyrbye et al., "Burnout and Suicidal Ideation."

15 L. Y. Abramson, M. E. Seligman, and J. D. Teasdale, "Learned Helplessness in Humans: Critique and Reformulation," *Journal of Abnormal Psychology* 87(1) (1978): 49–74.

16 For a discussion of physicians' psychological vulnerabilities, see A. Nedrow, N. A. Steckler, and J. Hardman, "Physician Resilience and Burnout: Can You Make the Switch?," *Family Practice Management* 20(1) (2013): 25–30; and G. E. Vaillant, N. C. Sobowale, and C. McArthur, "Some Psychologic Vulnerabilities of Physicians," *New England Journal of Medicine* 287 (1972): 372–75.

17 Physicians' overtesting is not entirely driven by fear of malpractice lawsuits. This behavior is also common among doctors in countries with low rates of malpractice litigation. See G. O. Gabbard, "The Role of Compulsiveness in the Normal Physician," *JAMA* 254(20) (1985): 2926–29.

18 See J. Legassie, E. M. Zibrowski, and M. A. Goldszmidt, "Measuring Resident Well-Being: Impostorism and Burnout Syndrome in Residency," *Journal of General Internal Medicine* 23(7) (2008): 1090–94; and P. R. Clance, *The Impostor Phenomenon: When Success Makes You Feel Like a Fake* (New York: Bantam Books, 1986).

19 For further discussion, see A. D. Mancini and G. A. Bonanno, "Predictors and Parameters of Resilience to Loss: Toward an Individual Differences Model," *Journal of Personality* 77(6) (2009): 1805–32.

20 J. Halifax, "A Heuristic Model of Enactive Compassion," *Current Opinion in Supportive and Palliative Care* 6(2) (2012): 228–35.

21 See the "A Piece of My Mind" sections of *JAMA* and "On Being a Doctor" sections of the *Annals of Internal Medicine*.

22 N. N. Taleb, *Antifragile: Things That Gain from Disorder* (New York: Random House, 2014).

23 S. M. Southwick and D. S. Charney, *Resilience: The Science of Mastering Life's Greatest Challenges* (Cambridge: Cambridge University Press, 2012).

24 S. J. Russo et al., "Neurobiology of Resilience," *Nature Neuroscience* 15(11) (2012): 1475–84.

25 Self-determination theory, a psychological model developed at the University of Rochester, suggests that a sense of autonomy (rather than a sense of feeling controlled), a sense that you're competent and have the skills to reach your goals, and strong caring relationships with others would be associated with greater resilience. See E. L. Deci and R. M. Ryan, *Intrinsic Motivation and Self-Determination in Human Behavior* (New York: Plenum Press, 1985).

26 D. Cicchetti and F. A. Rogosch, "Gene × Environment Interaction and Resilience: Effects of Child Maltreatment and Serotonin, Corticotropin Releasing Hormone, Dopamine, and Oxytocin Genes," *Development and Psychopathology* 24(02) (2012): 411–27; A. Feder, E. J. Nestler, and D. S. Charney, "Psychobiology and Molecular Genetics of Resilience," *Nature Reviews Neuroscience* 10(6) (2009): 446–57; and Russo et al., "Neurobiology of Resilience."

27 D. C. Johnson et al., "Modifying Resilience Mechanisms in At-Risk Individuals: A Controlled Study of Mindfulness Training in Marines Preparing for Deployment," *American Journal of Psychiatry* 171(8) (2014): 844–53; G. Wu et al., "Understanding Resilience," *Frontiers in Behavioral Neuroscience* 7(10) (2013); and Russo et al., "Neurobiology of Resilience."

28 K. Olson, K. J. Kemper, and J. D. Mahan, "What Factors Promote Resilience and Protect against Burnout in First-Year Pediatric and Medicine-Pediatric Residents?," *Journal of Evidence-Based Complementary and Alternative Medicine* 20(3) (2015): 192–98; K. J. Kemper and M. Khirallah, "Acute Effects of Online Mind-Body Skills Training on Resilience, Mindfulness, and Empathy," *Journal of Evidence-Based Complementary and Alternative Medicine* 20(4) (2015): 247–53; J. T. Thomas, "Intrapsychic Predictors of Professional Quality of Life: Mindfulness, Empathy, and Emotional Separation" (Lexington: University of Kentucky, 2011); and Johnson et al., "Modifying Resilience Mechanisms."

29 H. B. Beckman et al., "The Impact of a Program in Mindful Communciation on Primary Care Physicians," *Academic Medicine* 87(6) (2012): 1–5; and M. S. Krasner et al., "Association of an Educational Program in Mindful Communication with Burnout, Empathy, and Attitudes among Primary Care Physicians," *JAMA* 302(12) (2009): 1284–93. The Big Five personality factors are neuroticism, extraversion, openness to experience, agreeableness, and conscientiousness. Focused attention is one facet of conscientiousness and mental stability is one facet of (lack of) neuroticism.

30 A. Caspi and B. W. Roberts, "Personality Development across the Life Course: The Argument for Change and Continuity," *Psychological Inquiry* 12(2) (2001): 49–66.

31 The opposite—workaholics who get fulfillment only at work and see home life as dull—are equally deprived of the richness that life can offer.

Notes

32 See http://www.marclesser.net/tag/work-life-balance. I mentioned Marc Lesser in chapter 9. Marc is a Zen priest who runs mindfulness programs for Fortune 500 companies.

33 K. W. Brown and R. M. Ryan, "The Benefits of Being Present: Mindfulness and Its Role in Psychological Well-Being," *Journal of Personality and Social Psychology* 84(4) (2003): 822–48; and N. Weinstein and R. M. Ryan, "When Helping Helps: Autonomous Motivation for Prosocial Behavior and Its Influence on Well-Being for the Helper and Recipient," *Journal of Personality and Social Psychology* 98(2) (2010): 222–44.

34 Shanafelt et al., "Career Fit and Burnout."

35 For a copy, see C. Maslach, S. Jackson, and M. Leiter, "Maslach Burnout Inventory: Third Edition," in *Evaluating Stress: A Book of Resources*, eds. C. P. Zalaquett and R. J. Wood (Lanham, MD: Scarecrow Press, 1998), 191–218; and C. Maslach, W. B. Schaufeli, and M. P. Leiter, "Job Burnout," *Annual Review of Psychology* (2001): 52397–422.

36 Our understanding of what these structures do and how they interact is still rudimentary, and we are a long way from knowing, for example, whether the activation of some of these structures is the cause or the effect of particular mental states. And, while neuroimaging is merely a *marker* for changes in the brain—you cannot actually "see" a thought or an emotion—the results of these experiments are nonetheless compelling. See B. K. Hölzel et al., "How Does Mindfulness Meditation Work? Proposing Mechanisms of Action from a Conceptual and Neural Perspective," *Perspectives on Psychological Science* 6(6) (2011): 537–59; D. Vago and D. Silbersweig, "Self-Awareness, Self-Regulation, and Self-Transcendence (S-Art): A Framework for Understanding the Neurobiological Mechanisms of Mindfulness," *Frontiers in Human Neuroscience* 6(296) (2012): 1–6; and R. J. Davidson et al., "Alterations in Brain and Immune Function Produced by Mindfulness Meditation," *Psychosomatic Medicine* 65(4) (2003): 564–70; Y.-Y. Tang, B. K. Hölzel, and M. I. Posner, "The Neuroscience of Mindfulness Meditation," *Nature Reviews Neuroscience* 16(4) (2015): 213–25; and A. Brewer and K. Garrison, "The Posterior Cingulate Cortex as a Plausible Mechanistic Target of Meditation: Findings from Neuroimaging," *Annals of the New York Academy of Sciences* 1307(1) (2014): 19–27.

37 See D. C. Johnson et al., "Modifying Resilience Mechanisms"; E. A. Stanley et al., "Mindfulness-Based Mind Fitness Training: A Case Study of a High Stress Pre-deployment Military Cohort," *Cognitive and Behavioral Practice* 18(4) (2011): 566–76; E. A. Stanley, "Mindfulness-Based Mind Fitness Training (MMFT): An Approach for Enhancing Performance and Building Resilience in High Stress Contexts," in *The Wiley Blackwell Handbook of Mindfulness*, eds. A. Ie, C. T. Ngnoumen, and E. J. Langer (Hoboken, NJ: Wiley, 2014), 964–85; A. P. Jha et al., "Examining the Protective Effects of Mindfulness Training on Working Memory Capacity and Affective Experience," *Emotion* 10(1) (2010): 54–64; and A. P. Jha et al., "Minds 'at Attention': Mindfulness Training Curbs Attentional Lapses in Military Cohorts," *PLoS ONE* 10(2) (2015): e0116889.

Notes

11. BECOMING MINDFUL

1 E. A. Maguire, K. Woollett, and H. J. Spiers, "London Taxi Drivers and Bus Drivers: A Structural MRI and Neuropsychological Analysis," *Hippocampus* 16(12) (2006): 1091–101.

2 K. Woollett and E. A. Maguire, "Acquiring 'the Knowledge' of London's Layout Drives Structural Brain Changes," *Current Biology* 21(24) (2011): 2109–14.

3 This famous postulate of neuroscience is attributed to Carla Shatz at Stanford University (see C. J. Shatz, "The Developing Brain," *Scientific American* 267(3) (1992): 60–67) and is based on a theory of learning proposed by Donald Hebb in 1949. See D. Hebb, *The Organization of Behavior* (New York: Wiley, 1949). "Wiring together" is positive when it promotes acquisition of skills or habits of mind, but problematic when "firing together" reinforces unwanted mental rumination, obsessions, compulsions, anxiety, and depression.

4 K. A. Ericsson, "An Expert-Performance Perspective of Research on Medical Expertise: The Study of Clinical Performance," *Medical Education* 41(12) (2007): 1124–30. Much of the argument in the next few paragraphs is summarized in A. S. O. Leung, C. A. Moulton, and R. M. Epstein, "The Competent Mind: Beyond Cognition," in *The Question of Competence: Reconsidering Medical Education in the Twenty-First Century*, eds. B. D. Hodges and L. Lingard (Ithaca and London: Cornell University Press, 2012), chap. 7, 155–76.

5 G. L. Engel, "What If Music Students Were Taught to Play Their Instruments as Medical Students Are Taught to Interview?," *Pharos of Alpha Omega Alpha Honor Medical Society* (1982): 4512–13.

6 H. L. Dreyfus, *On the Internet (Thinking in Action)* (New York: Routledge, 2001).

7 See Leung, Moulton, and Epstein, "Competent Mind."

8 For a discussion of adaptive expertise, see G. Hatano and K. Inagaki, "Child Development and Education in Japan," in *Two Courses of Expertise*, eds. H. Stevenson, H. Azuma, and K. Hakuta (New York: Freeman, 1986), 262–72. For a richer discussion of context, see S. Weiner and A. Schwartz, "Contextual Errors in Medical Decision Making: Overlooked and Understudied," *Academic Medicine: Journal of the Association of American Medical Colleges* 91(5) (2016): 657–62.

9 The parallels between jazz and clinical practice have been described in two wonderful articles listed below. Importantly, the ability to improvise depends on years of practice and assimilating the rules of harmony and structure of the music. See P. Haidet, "Jazz and the 'Art' of Medicine: Improvisation in the Medical Encounter," *Annals of Family Medicine* 5(2) (2007): 164–69; and A. F. Shaughnessy, D. C. Slawson, and L. Becker, "Clinical Jazz: Harmonizing Clinical Experience and Evidence-Based Medicine," *Journal of Family Practice* 47(6) (1998): 425–28.

10 W. James, *The Principles of Psychology* (Cambridge, MA: Harvard University Press, 1981).

11 Y.-Y. Tang et al., "Short-Term Meditation Training Improves Attention and Self-Regulation," *Proceedings of the National Academy of Sciences* 104(43) (2007): 17152–56; and Y.-Y. Tang et al., "Central and Autonomic Nervous

System Interaction Is Altered by Short-Term Meditation," *Proceedings of the National Academy of Sciences* 106(22) (2009): 8865–70.

12 D. M. Levy et al., "The Effects of Mindfulness Meditation Training on Multitasking in a High-Stress Information Environment," in *Proceedings of Graphics Interface 2012* (Toronto: Canadian Information Processing Society, 2012), 45–52; R. J. Davidson and A. W. Kaszniak, "Conceptual and Methodological Issues in Research on Mindfulness and Meditation," *American Psychologist* 70(7) (2015): 581–92; B. K. Hölzel et al., "How Does Mindfulness Meditation Work? Proposing Mechanisms of Action from a Conceptual and Neural Perspective," *Perspectives on Psychological Science* 6(6) (2011): 537–59; and Y.-Y. Tang, B. K. Hölzel, and M. I. Posner, "The Neuroscience of Mindfulness Meditation," *Nature Reviews Neuroscience* 16(4) (2015): 213–25.

13 A description of ten stages of attention training, practices used to achieve them, and their implications for living one's life can be found in B. A. Wallace, *The Attention Revolution: Unlocking the Power of the Focused Mind* (Somerville, MA: Wisdom Publications, 2006). The ten stages of attention are directed, continuous, resurgent, close, tamed, pacified, fully pacified, and single-pointed attention, then attentional balance and "shamatha."

14 A. W. Kaszniak, "Meditation, Mindfulness, Cognition, and Emotion: Implications for Community-Based Older Adult Programs," in *Enhancing Cognitive Fitness in Adults*, eds. P. E. Hartman-Stein and A. LaRue (New York: Springer, 2011), chap. 5, 85–104.

15 The word *mindfulness* also can be confusing. People commonly use it to describe a relatively fixed personality trait, a state of mind that can be achieved, and also a specific set of practices such as meditation. Any number of everyday activities can become mindful practices—one can play tennis mindfully, run mindfully, cook and eat mindfully, read poetry mindfully, and listen to or make music mindfully. I prefer what is now considered to be the original meaning of the Pali word *sati*—"remembering"—remembering who you are and what is important, every moment of every day.

16 Jon Kabat-Zinn is responsible for having secularized meditation traditions that originated in South and Southeast Asia and made them accessible to the general Western public. See J. Kabat-Zinn, *Full Catastrophe Living: Using the Wisdom of Your Body and Mind to Face Stress, Pain, and Illness* (New York: Bantam Dell, 1990).

17 For two explorations of how one can engage in awareness practice without adhering to an organized belief system, see S. Batchelor, *Buddhism without Beliefs: A Contemporary Guide to Awakening* (New York: Riverhead Books, 1997); and S. Harris, *Waking Up: A Guide to Spirituality without Religion* (New York: Simon & Schuster, 2015).

18 These pathways are not as well elaborated as attentional pathways and represent a cutting edge of neuroscience research. O. M. Klimecki et al., "Differential Pattern of Functional Brain Plasticity after Compassion and Empathy Training," *Social Cognitive and Affective Neuroscience* 9(6) (2014): 873–79.

19 D. A. Schroeder et al., "A Brief Mindfulness-Based Intervention for Primary Care Physicians: A Pilot Randomized Controlled Trial," *American Journal of Lifestyle Medicine* (2016): 1–9.

20 S. B. Goldberg et al., "The Secret Ingredient in Mindfulness Interventions? A Case for Practice Quality over Quantity," *Journal of Counseling Psychology* 61(3) (2014): 491–97.

21 For very readable introductions into this complex realm, see A. R. Damasio, *Descartes' Error: Emotion, Reason, and the Human Brain* (New York: G. P. Putnam's Sons, 1994); and A. R. Damasio, *The Feeling of What Happens: Body and Emotion in the Making of Consciousness* (New York: Harcourt Brace, 1999). While some of the neuroscientific research is now a bit dated, Damasio's everyday-life descriptions are compelling and still accurate. See also E. Thompson, *Mind in Life: Biology, Phenomenology, and the Sciences of Mind* (Cambridge, MA: Belknap Press of Harvard University Press, 2007); and F. J. Varela, E. Thompson, and E. Rosch, *The Embodied Mind: Cognitive Science and Human Experience* (Cambridge, MA: MIT Press, 1991).

22 In his essay "The Depth of a Smile," my Catalan family-physician colleague Francesc Borrell-Carrió described what he called a "smile of accommodation." See F. Borrell-Carrió, "The Depth of a Smile," *Medical Encounter* 15(2) (2000): 13–14.

23 A. M. Glenberg et al., "Grounding Language in Bodily States: The Case for Emotion," in *Grounding Cognition: The Role of Perception and Action in Memory, Language, and Thinking*, eds. D. Pecher and R. A. Zwaan (Cambridge: Cambridge University Press, 2005).

24 L. Nielsen and A. Kaszniak, "Awareness of Subtle Emotional Feelings: A Comparison of Long-term Meditators and Nonmeditators," *Emotion* 6(3) (2006): 392–405.

25 P. M. Niedenthal, "Embodying Emotion," *Science* 316(5827) (2007): 1002–5.

26 G. Kramer, *Insight Dialogue: The Interpersonal Path to Freedom* (Boulder, CO: Shambhala Publications, 2007).

27 D. L. Cooperrider and D. Whitney, *Appreciative Inquiry: A Positive Revolution in Change* (San Francisco: Berrett-Koehler, 2005).

28 R. M. Epstein, "Making the Ineffable Visible," *Families Systems and Health* 33(3) (2015): 280–82; and J. Zlatev et al., *The Shared Mind: Perspectives on Intersubjectivity* (Amsterdam and Philadelphia: John Benjamins, 2008).

29 J. L. Coulehan, "Tenderness and Steadiness: Emotions in Medical Practice," *Literature and Medicine* 14(2) (1995): 222–36.

30 See G. C. Spivak, L. E. Lyons, and C. G. Franklin, "'On the Cusp of the Personal and the Impersonal': An Interview with Gayatri Chakravorty Spivak," *Biography* 27(1) (2004): 203–21; and R. M. Epstein, "Realizing Engel's Biopsychosocial Vision: Resilience, Compassion, and Quality of Care," *International Journal of Psychiatry in Medicine* 47(4) (2014): 275–87.

31 M. K. Kearney et al., "Self-Care of Physicians Caring for Patients at the End of Life: 'Being Connected . . . a Key to My Survival,'" *JAMA* 301(11) (2009): 1155–64.

32 Coulehan, "Tenderness and Steadiness."

33 W. Steig, *Doctor De Soto* (New York: Square Fish, 2010).

12. IMAGINING A MINDFUL HEALTH CARE SYSTEM

1 See Institute of Medicine, *Crossing the Quality Chasm: A New Health System for the 21st Century* (Washington, DC: National Academies Press, 2001); D. M. Berwick, T. W. Nolan, and J. Whittington, "The Triple Aim: Care, Health, and Cost," *Health Affairs* 27(3) (2008): 759–69; and T. Bodenheimer and C. Sinsky, "From Triple to Quadruple Aim: Care of the Patient Requires Care of the Provider," *Annals of Family Medicine* 12(6) (2014): 573–76.

2 For three of the most influential documents, see Institute of Medicine, *Crossing the Quality Chasm*; Berwick, Nolan, and Whittington, "Triple Aim"; and Bodenheimer and Sinsky, "From Triple to Quadruple Aim."

3 See K. E. Weick and K. H. Roberts, "Collective Mind in Organizations—Heedful Interrelating on Flight Decks," *Administrative Science Quarterly* 38(3) (1993): 357–81. The actual reference to this particular story is G. I. Rochlin, T. R. La Porte, and K. H. Roberts, "The Self-Designing High-Reliability Organization: Aircraft Carrier Flight Operations at Sea," *Naval War College Review* 51(3) (1998): 97.

4 L. T. Kohn, J. M. Corrigan, and M. S. Donaldson, *To Err Is Human: Building a Safer Health System* (Washington, DC: National Academy Press, 2000).

5 K. E. Weick and T. Putnam, "Organizing for Mindfulness: Eastern Wisdom and Western Knowledge," *Journal of Management Inquiry* 15(3) (2006): 275–87; and K. E. Weick and K. M. Sutcliffe, "Mindfulness and the Quality of Organizational Attention," *Organization Science* 17(4) (2006): 514–24.

6 See Weick and Sutcliffe, "Mindfulness and the Quality of Organizational Attention"; D. J. Good et al., "Contemplating Mindfulness at Work: An Integrative Review," *Journal of Management* (2015): 1–29; T. J. Vogus and K. M. Sutcliffe, "Organizational Resilience: Towards a Theory and Research Agenda" (paper presented at the 2007 IEEE International Conference on Systems, Man and Cybernetics, Montreal, Quebec, 2007); T. J. Vogus and K. M. Sutcliffe, "Organizational Mindfulness and Mindful Organizing: A Reconciliation and Path Forward," *Academy of Management Learning & Education* 11(4) (2012): 722–35; and K. M. Weick and K. M. Sutcliffe, *Managing the Unexpected: Assuring High Performance in an Age of Complexity* (San Francisco: Jossey-Bass, 2001).

7 T. J. Vogus and K. M. Sutcliffe, "The Safety Organizing Scale: Development and Validation of a Behavioral Measure of Safety Culture in Hospital Nursing Units," *Medical Care* 45(1) (2007): 46–54.

8 This approach was made famous by Toyota in the 1990s. See the *Harvard Business Review* article at https://hbr.org/1999/09/decoding-the-dna-of-the-toyota-production-system.

9 In case you're worried, the patient went immediately to the emergency room and recovered well.

10 T. J. Vogus and K. M. Sutcliffe, "The Impact of Safety Organizing, Trusted Leadership, and Care Pathways on Reported Medication Errors in Hospital Nursing Units," *Medical Care* 45(10) (2007): 997–1002; and Vogus and Sutcliffe, "Safety Organizing Scale."

11 Here are some references to Suchman's work, which clearly has relevance to other enterprises, not just health care: A. L. Suchman, "Organizations as Machines, Organizations as Conversations: Two Core Metaphors and Their Consequences," *Medical Care* 49 (2011): S43–S48; K. Marvel et al., "Relationship-Centered Administration: Transferring Effective Communication Skills from the Exam Room to the Conference Room," *Journal of Healthcare Management/American College of Healthcare Executives* 48(2) (2002): 112–23, and discussion, 23–24; A. L. Suchman, "The Influence of Health Care Organizations on Well-Being," *Western Journal of Medicine* 174(1) (2001): 43; A. L. Suchman, D. J. Sluyter, and P. R. Williamson, *Leading Change in Healthcare: Transforming Organizations Using Complexity, Positive Psychology, and Relationship-Centered Care* (Abingdon, UK: Radcliffe Publishing, 2011); and A. L. Suchman and P. R. Williamson, "Principles and Practices of Relationship-Centered Meetings" (Rochester, NY: Relationship Centered Health Care, 2006.)

12 D. L. Cooperrider and D. Whitney, *Appreciative Inquiry: A Positive Revolution in Change* (San Francisco: Berrett-Koehler, 2005).

13 Other—secular—health systems are increasingly appointing "chief empathy officers," directors of "the patient experience," and others in similar roles to focus on enhancing trust, communication, and healing relationships.

14 See K. B. Schwartz, "A Patient's Story," *Boston Globe Magazine*, 1995, 16; and Schwartz Center for Compassionate Healthcare, http://www.theschwartz center.org, for further information about the foundation.

15 B. A. Lown and C. F. Manning, "The Schwartz Center Rounds: Evaluation of an Interdisciplinary Approach to Enhancing Patient-Centered Communication, Teamwork, and Provider Support," *Academic Medicine* 85(6) (2010): 1073–81.

16 Monash University, the largest medical school in Australia, and the University of Rochester, where I work, have been the pioneers. At Rochester, we offer five required mindful practice workshops in the third year of medical school. We also offer four- and five-day workshops for practicing physicians and educators who wish to develop their skills further. For information about Rochester's mindful practice programs, see www.mindfulpractice.urmc .edu. Here are a few sample websites for programs that promote well-being in clinicians: http://www.medicine.virginia.edu/administration/faculty/fac ulty-dev/copy_of_home-page; http://www.ohsu.edu/xd/education/schools /school-of-medicine/gme-cme/gme/resident-fellow-wellness-program /index.cfm; http://www.tfme.org/regional-conferences/physician-well-be ing-conference; and http://www.mayo.edu/research/centers-programs/phy sician-well-being-program/overview. For general information about mindfulness and medical education, see P. L. Dobkin and T. A. Hutchinson, "Teaching Mindfulness in Medical School: Where Are We Now and Where Are We Going," *Medical Education* 47(8) (2013): 768–79.

Notes

APPENDIX: ATTENTION PRACTICE

1 R. M. Epstein, "Mindful Practice," *JAMA* 282(9) (1999): 833–39.
2 One accessible guide to different meditation practices for psychotherapists is S. M. Pollak, T. Pedulla, and R. D. Siegel, *Sitting Together: Essential Skills for Mindfulness-Based Psychotherapy* (New York: Guilford Press, 2014). For audio files from our programs, please go to https://www.urmc.rochester .edu/family-medicine/mindful-practice/curricula-materials/audios.aspx. On the Web, guided meditations can be found at http://www.mindfulness-solu tion.com/DownloadMeditations.html and https://www.tarabrach.com/guid ed-meditations. For shorter meditations, try http://marc.ucla.edu/body.cfm ?id=22. A popular app for beginning meditators is "Headspace"—compelling and entertaining.

Reference List

Abramson, L. Y., M. E. Seligman, and J. D. Teasdale. "Learned Helplessness in Humans: Critique and Reformulation." *Journal of Abnormal Psychology* 87(1) (1978): 49–74.

Adams, J. R., G. Elwyn, F. Legare, and D. L. Frosch. "Communicating with Physicians about Medical Decisions: A Reluctance to Disagree." *Archives of Internal Medicine* 172(15) (2012): 1184–86.

Allen, T. J., J. W. Sherman, F. R. Conrey, and S. J. Stroessner. "Stereotype Strength and Attentional Bias: Preference for Confirming versus Disconfirming Information Depends on Processing Capacity." *Journal of Experimental Social Psychology* 45(5) (2009): 1081–87.

Aristotle. *The Nicomachean Ethics,* trans. David Ross. Revised with an introduction and notes by Lesley Brown. New York: Oxford University Press, 2009.

Austin, J. H. *Zen and the Brain: Toward an Understanding of Meditation and Consciousness.* Cambridge, MA: MIT Press, 1998.

Baars, B. J., T. Z. Ramsoy, and S. Laureys. "Brain, Conscious Experience and the Observing Self." *Trends in Neurosciences* 26(12) (2003): 671–75.

Babbott, S., L. B. Manwell, R. Brown, E. Montague, E. Williams, M. Schwartz, E. Hess, and M. Linzer. "Electronic Medical Records and Physician Stress in Primary Care: Results from the Memo Study." *Journal of the American Medical Informatics Association* 21(e1) (2014): e100–e106.

Bachman, K. H., and D. K. Freeborn. "HMO Physicians' Use of Referrals." *Social Science & Medicine* 48(4) (1999): 547–57.

Back, A. L., S. M. Bauer-Wu, C. H. Rushton, and J. Halifax. "Compassionate Silence in the Patient-Clinician Encounter: A Contemplative Approach." *Journal of Palliative Medicine* 12(12) (2009): 1113–17.

Back, A. L., C. H. Rushton, A. W. Kaszniak, and J. S. Halifax. "'Why Are We Doing This?': Clinician Helplessness in the Face of Suffering." *Journal of Palliative Medicine* 18(1) (2015): 26–30.

Baker, D. B., R. Day, and E. Salas. "Teamwork as an Essential Component of High-Reliability Organizations." *Health Services Research* 41(4, pt. 2) (2006): 1576–98.

Balint, M. *The Doctor, His Patient, and the Illness.* New York: International Universities Press, 1957.

Banaji, M., and A. Greenwald. *Blindspot: Hidden Biases of Good People*. New York: Delacorte Press, 2013.

Barks, C. *The Essential Rumi*. London: Castle Books, 1997.

Baron, R. J. "An Introduction to Medical Phenomenology: I Can't Hear You While I'm Listening." *Annals of Internal Medicine* 103(4) (1985): 606–11.

Bartels, J. "Eloquent Silences: A Musical and Lexical Analysis of Conversation between Oncologists and Their Patients." *Patient Education & Counseling* (forthcoming, 2016).

Bartz, J. A., J. Zaki, N. Bolger, E. Hollander, N. N. Ludwig, A. Kolevzon, and K. N. Ochsner. "Oxytocin Selectively Improves Empathic Accuracy." *Psychological Science* 21(10) (2010): 1426–28.

Bassler, D., J. W. Busse, P. J. Karanicolas, and G. H. Guyatt. "Evidence-Based Medicine Targets the Individual Patient. Part 2: Guides and Tools for Individual Decision-Making." *ACP Journal Club* 149(1) (2008): 2.

Batchelor, S. *Buddhism without Beliefs: A Contemporary Guide to Awakening*. New York: Riverhead Books, 1997.

Batson, D. C. "These Things Called Empathy: Eight Related but Distinct Phenomena." In *The Social Neuroscience of Empathy*, edited by J. Decety and W. Ickes, chap. 1, 3–15. Denver, CO: Bradford, 2009.

Baumgarten, E. "Curiosity as a Moral Virtue." *International Journal of Applied Philosophy* 15(2) (2001): 23–42.

Beach, M. C., D. Roter, P. T. Korthuis, R. M. Epstein, V. Sharp, N. Ratanawongsa, J. Cohn, et al. "A Multicenter Study of Physician Mindfulness and Health Care Quality." *Annals of Family Medicine* 11(5) (2013): 421–28.

Beckman, H. B., K. M. Markakis, A. L. Suchman, and R. M. Frankel. "The Doctor-Patient Relationship and Malpractice: Lessons from Plaintiff Depositions." *Archives of Internal Medicine* 154(12) (1994): 1365–70.

Beckman, H. B., M. Wendland, C. Mooney, M. S. Krasner, T. E. Quill, A. L. Suchman, and R. M. Epstein. "The Impact of a Program in Mindful Communication Primary Care Physicians." *Academic Medicine* 87(6) (2012): 1–5.

Bereiter, C., and M. Scardamalia. *Surpassing Ourselves: An Inquiry into the Nature and Implications of Expertise*. Chicago: Open Court Publishing, 1993.

Berger, J. E., and R. L. Boyle Jr. "How to Avoid the High Costs of Physician Turnover." *Medical Group Management Journal* 39(6) (1991): 80–82.

Berlyne, D. E. "Novelty and Curiosity as Determinants of Exploratory Behaviour." *British Journal of Psychiatry* 41(1–2) (1950): 68–80.

Berry, D. L., D. J. Wilkie, C. R. J. Thomas, and P. Fortner. "Clinicians Communicating with Patients Experiencing Cancer Pain." *Cancer Investigation* 21(3) (2003): 374–81.

Berwick, D. M., T. W. Nolan, and J. Whittington. "The Triple Aim: Care, Health, and Cost." *Health Affairs* 27(3) (2008): 759–69.

Bilek, E., M. Ruf, A. Schafer, C. Akdeniz, V. D. Calhoun, C. Schmahl, C. Demanuele, et al. "Information Flow between Interacting Human Brains: Identification, Validation, and Relationship to Social Expertise." *Proceedings of the National Academy of Sciences* 112(16) (2015): 5207–12.

Bodenheimer, T., and C. Sinsky. "From Triple to Quadruple Aim: Care of the

Reference List

Patient Requires Care of the Provider." *Annals of Family Medicine* 12(6) (2014): 573–76.

Borrell-Carrió, F. "The Depth of a Smile." *Medical Encounter* 15(2) (2000): 13–14.

Borrell-Carrió, F., and R. M. Epstein. "Preventing Errors in Clinical Practice: A Call for Self-Awareness." *Annals of Family Medicine* 2(4) (2004): 310–16.

Brewer, A., and K. Garrison. "The Posterior Cingulate Cortex as a Plausible Mechanistic Target of Meditation: Findings from Neuroimaging." *Annals of the New York Academy of Sciences* 1307(1) (2014): 19–27.

Brown, K. W., and R. M. Ryan. "The Benefits of Being Present: Mindfulness and Its Role in Psychological Well-Being." *Journal of Personality and Social Psychology* 84(4) (2003): 822–48.

Buber, M. *I and Thou*. New York: Scribner, 1970.

Buchbinder, S. B., M. Wilson, C. F. Melick, and N. R. Powe. "Estimates of Costs of Primary Care Physician Turnover." *American Journal of Managed Care* 5(11) (1999): 1431–38.

Burgess, D. J. "Are Providers More Likely to Contribute to Healthcare Disparities under High Levels of Cognitive Load? How Features of the Healthcare Setting May Lead to Biases in Medical Decision Making." *Medical Decision Making* 30(2) (2010): 246–57.

Burgess, D. J., S. S. Fu, and M. van Ryn. "Why Do Providers Contribute to Disparities and What Can Be Done about It?" *Journal of General Internal Medicine* 19(11) (2004): 1154–59.

Candib, L. M. "Working with Suffering." *Patient Education & Counseling* 48(1) (2002): 43–50.

Caspi, A., and B. W. Roberts. "Personality Development across the Life Course: The Argument for Change and Continuity." *Psychological Inquiry* 12(2) (2001): 49–66.

Cassell, E. J. "Diagnosing Suffering: A Perspective." *Annals of Internal Medicine* 131(7) (1999): 531–34.

———. "The Nature of Suffering and the Goals of Medicine." *New England Journal of Medicine* 306(11) (1982): 639–45.

———. "The Phenomenon of Suffering and Its Relationship to Pain." In *Handbook of Phenomenology and Medicine*, edited by S. K. Toombs, 371–90. Dordrecht, Netherlands: Kluewer Academic Publishers, 2001.

Catlin, A., C. Armigo, D. Volat, E. Vale, M. A. Hadley, W. Gong, R. Bassir, and K. Anderson. "Conscientious Objection: A Potential Neonatal Nursing Response to Care Orders That Cause Suffering at the End of Life? Study of a Concept." *Neonatal Network — Journal of Neonatal Nursing* 27(2) (2008): 101–8.

Chabris, C., and D. Simons. *The Invisible Gorilla: How Our Intuitions Deceive Us*. New York: Crown, 2011.

Charlin, B., H. P. Boshuizen, E. J. Custers, and P. J. Feltovich. "Scripts and Clinical Reasoning." *Medical Education* 41(12) (2007): 1178–84.

Charon, R. "Narrative Medicine: Form, Function, and Ethics." *Annals of Internal Medicine* 134(1) (2001): 83–87.

———. *Narrative Medicine: Honoring the Stories of Illness*. London: Oxford University Press, 2006.

Reference List

Chatel-Goldman J., J. L. Schwartz, C. Jutten, and M. Congedo. "Non-Local Mind from the Perspective of Social Cognition." *Frontiers in Human Neuroscience* 7 (2013): 107.

Cheng, Y., C.-Y. Yang, C.-P. Lin, P.-L. Lee, and J. Decety. "The Perception of Pain in Others Suppresses Somatosensory Oscillations: A Magnetoencephalography Study." *NeuroImage* 40(4) (2008): 1833–40.

Chou, C. M., K. Kellom, and J. A. Shea. "Attitudes and Habits of Highly Humanistic Physicians." *Academic Medicine* 89(9) (2014): 1252–58.

Cicchetti, D., and F. A. Rogosch. "Gene × Environment Interaction and Resilience: Effects of Child Maltreatment and Serotonin, Corticotropin Releasing Hormone, Dopamine, and Oxytocin Genes." *Development and Psychopathology* 24(2) (2012): 411–27.

Clance, P. R. *The Impostor Phenomenon: When Success Makes You Feel Like a Fake*. New York: Bantam Books, 1986.

Connelly, J. "Being in the Present Moment: Developing the Capacity for Mindfulness in Medicine." *Academic Medicine* 74(4) (1999): 420–24.

Connelly, J. E. "The Guest House (Commentary)." *Academic Medicine* 83(6) (2008): 588–89.

———. "Narrative Possibilities: Using Mindfulness in Clinical Practice." *Perspectives in Biology and Medicine* 48(1) (2005): 84–94.

Cooperrider, D. L., and D. Whitney. *Appreciative Inquiry: A Positive Revolution in Change*. San Francisco: Berrett-Koehler, 2005.

Corbetta, M., and G. L. Shulman. "Control of Goal-Directed and Stimulus-Driven Attention in the Brain." *Nature Reviews Neuroscience* 3(3) (2002): 201–15.

Costa, P. T., and R. R. McCrae. "NEO PI-R: Professional Manual, Revised Neo Personality Inventory (NEO PI-R), and Neo Five-Factor Inventory (NEO-FFI)." Odessa, FL: Psychological Assessment Resources, 1992.

Coulehan, J. "Compassionate Solidarity: Suffering, Poetry, and Medicine." *Perspectives in Biology and Medicine* 52(4) (2009): 585–603.

Coulehan, J. L. "Tenderness and Steadiness: Emotions in Medical Practice." *Literature and Medicine* 14(2) (1995): 222–36.

Croskerry, P. "Clinical Cognition and Diagnostic Error: Applications of a Dual Process Model of Reasoning." *Advances in Health Sciences Education* 14(1) (2009): 27–35.

———. "Context Is Everything or How Could I Have Been That Stupid?" *Healthcare Quarterly* 12 (2009): e171–e76.

———. "From Mindless to Mindful Practice—Cognitive Bias and Clinical Decision Making." *New England Journal of Medicine* 368(26) (2013): 2445–48.

———. "The Importance of Cognitive Errors in Diagnosis and Strategies to Minimize Them." *Academic Medicine* 78(8) (2003): 775–80.

———. "A Universal Model of Diagnostic Reasoning." *Academic Medicine* 84(8) (2009): 1022–28.

Croskerry, P., A. A. Abbass, and A. W. Wu. "How Doctors Feel: Affective Issues in Patients' Safety." *Lancet* 372(9645) (2008): 1205–6.

Croskerry, P., and G. R. Nimmo. "Better Clinical Decision Making and Reducing Diagnostic Error." *Journal of the Royal College of Physicians of Edinburgh* 41(2) (2011): 155–62.

Croskerry, P., and G. Norman. "Overconfidence in Clinical Decision Making." *American Journal of Medicine* 121(5) (2008): S24–S29.

Damasio, A. R. *Descartes' Error: Emotion, Reason, and the Human Brain*. New York: G. P. Putnam's Sons, 1994.

———. *The Feeling of What Happens: Body and Emotion in the Making of Consciousness*. New York: Harcourt Brace, 1999.

Darley, J. M., and C. D. Batson. "'From Jerusalem to Jericho': A Study of Situation and Dispositional Variables in Helping Behavior." *Journal of Personality and Social Psychology* 27(1) (1973): 100–108.

Davidson, R. J. "Anterior Cerebral Asymmetry and the Nature of Emotion." *Brain and Cognition* 20(1) (1992): 125–51.

Davidson, R. J., J. Kabat-Zinn, J. Schumacher, M. Rosenkranz, D. Muller, S. F. Santorelli, F. Urbanowski, et al. "Alterations in Brain and Immune Function Produced by Mindfulness Meditation." *Psychosomatic Medicine* 65(4) (2003): 564–70.

Davidson, R. J., and A. W. Kaszniak. "Conceptual and Methodological Issues in Research on Mindfulness and Meditation." *American Psychologist* 70(7) (2015): 581–92.

Decety, J., and C. Lamm. "Empathy Versus Personal Distress: Recent Evidence from Social Neuroscience." In *The Social Neuroscience of Empathy*, edited by J. Decety and W. Ickes, chap. 15, 199–213. Denver, CO: Bradford, 2009.

Decety, J., C. Y. Yang, and Y. Cheng. "Physicians Down-Regulate Their Pain Empathy Response: An Event-Related Brain Potential Study." *NeuroImage* 50(4) (2010): 1676–82.

Deci, E. L., and R. M. Ryan. *Intrinsic Motivation and Self-Determination in Human Behavior*. New York: Plenum Press, 1985.

De Dreu, C. K. "Oxytocin Modulates Cooperation within and Competition between Groups: An Integrative Review and Research Agenda." *Hormones and Behavior* 61(3) (2012): 419–28.

De Jaegher, H., and E. Di Paolo. "Participatory Sense-Making: An Enactive Approach to Social Cognition." *Phenomenology and the Cognitive Sciences* 6(4) (2007): 485–507.

de Vignemont, F., and T. Singer. "The Empathic Brain: How, When and Why?" *Trends in Cognitive Sciences* 10(10) (2006): 435–41.

Dewey, J. *Experience and Nature*. New York: Dover, 1958.

DeYoung, C. G., D. Cicchetti, F. A. Rogosch, J. R. Gray, M. Eastman, and E. L. Grigorenko. "Sources of Cognitive Exploration: Genetic Variation in the Prefrontal Dopamine System Predicts Openness/Intellect." *Journal of Research in Personality* 45(4) (2011): 364–71.

Dimsdale, J. E. "Reflections on the Impact of Antihypertensive Medications on Mood, Sedation, and Neuropsychologic Functioning." *Archives of Internal Medicine* 152(1) (1992): 35–39.

Dixon, C. A. J., C. N. E. Tompkins, V. L. Allgar, and N. M. J. Wright. "Abusive Behaviour Experienced by Primary Care Receptionists: A Cross-Sectional Survey." *Family Practice* 21(2) (2004): 137–39.

Dobkin, P. L., and T. A. Hutchinson. "Teaching Mindfulness in Medical School:

Where Are We Now and Where Are We Going." *Medical Education* 47(8) (2013): 768–79.

Dovidio, J. F., K. Kawakami, C. Johnson, B. Johnson, and A. Howard. "On the Nature of Prejudice: Automatic and Controlled Processes." *Journal of Experimental Social Psychology* 33(5) (1997): 510–40.

Drew, T., M. L. Vo, and J. M. Wolfe. "The Invisible Gorilla Strikes Again: Sustained Inattentional Blindness in Expert Observers." *Psychological Science* 24(9) (2013): 1848–53.

Dreyfus, H. L. *On the Internet (Thinking in Action)*. New York: Routledge, 2001.

Dyche, L., and R. M. Epstein. "Curiosity and Medical Education." *Medical Education* 45(7) (2011): 663–68.

Dyrbye, L. N., F. S. Massie, A. Eacker, W. Harper, D. Power, S. J. Durning, M. R. Thomas, et al. "Relationship between Burnout and Professional Conduct and Attitudes among US Medical Students." *JAMA* 304(11) (2010): 1173–80.

Dyrbye, L. N., M. R. Thomas, F. S. Massie, D. V. Power, A. Eacker, W. Harper, S. Durning, et al. "Burnout and Suicidal Ideation among US Medical Students." *Annals of Internal Medicine* 149(5) (2008): 334–41.

Dyrbye, L. N., P. Varkey, S. L. Boone, D. V. Satele, J. A. Sloan, and T. D. Shanafelt. "Physician Satisfaction and Burnout at Different Career Stages." *Mayo Clinic Proceedings* 88(12) (2013): 1358–67.

Dyrbye, L. N., C. P. West, D. Satele, S. Boone, L. Tan, J. Sloan, and T. D. Shanafelt. "Burnout among US Medical Students, Residents, and Early Career Physicians Relative to the General US Population." *Academic Medicine* 89(3) (2014): 443–51.

Ebstein, R. P., O. Novick, R. Umansky, B. Priel, Y. Osher, D. Blaine, E. R. Bennett, et al. "Dopamine D4 Receptor (D4DR) Exon III Polymorphism Associated with the Human Personality Trait of Novelty Seeking." *Nature Genetics* 12(1) (1996): 78–80.

Eisenberg, N., and N. D. Eggum. "Empathic Responding: Sympathy and Personal Distress." In *The Social Neuroscience of Empathy*, edited by J. Decety and W. Ickes, chap. 6, 71–83. Denver, CO: Bradford, 2009.

Elliot, A. J., and H. T. Reis. "Attachment and Exploration in Adulthood." *Journal of Personality and Social Psychology* 85(2) (2003): 317–31.

Elwyn, G., A. O'Connor, D. Stacey, R. Volk, A. Edwards, A. Coulter, R. Thomson, et al. "Developing a Quality Criteria Framework for Patient Decision Aids: Online International Delphi Consensus Process." *British Medical Journal* 333(7565) (2006): 417.

Engel, G. L. "The Clinical Application of the Biopsychosocial Model." *American Journal of Psychiatry* 137(5) (1980): 535–44.

———. "From Biomedical to Biopsychosocial: Being Scientific in the Human Domain." *Psychosomatics* 38(6) (1997): 521–28.

———. "The Need for a New Medical Model: A Challenge for Biomedicine." *Science* 196(4286) (1977): 129–36.

———. "What If Music Students Were Taught to Play Their Instruments as Medical Students Are Taught to Interview?" *Pharos of Alpha Omega Alpha Honor Medical Society* (1982), 4512–13.

Engen, H. G., and T. Singer. "Compassion-Based Emotion Regulation Up-

Reference List

Regulates Experienced Positive Affect and Associated Neural Networks." *Social Cognitive and Affective Neuroscience* 10(9) (2015): 1291–301.

Epstein, M. *Thoughts without a Thinker: Psychotherapy from a Buddhist Perspective.* New York: Basic Books, 1995.

Epstein, R. M. "Making the Ineffable Visible." *Families Systems and Health* 33(3) (2015): 280–82.

———. "Mindful Practice." *JAMA* 282(9) (1999): 833–39.

———. "Physician Know Thy Family: Looking at One's Family-of-Origin as a Method of Physician Self-Awareness." *Medical Encounter* 8(1) (1991): 9.

———. "Realizing Engel's Biopsychosocial Vision: Resilience, Compassion, and Quality of Care." *International Journal of Psychiatry in Medicine* 47(4) (2014): 275–87.

———. "Whole Mind and Shared Mind in Clinical Decision-Making." *Patient Education & Counseling* 90(2) (2013): 200–206.

Epstein, R. M., B. S. Alper, and T. E. Quill. "Communicating Evidence for Participatory Decision Making." *JAMA* 291(19) (2004): 2359–66.

Epstein, R. M., and A. L. Back. "Responding to Suffering." *JAMA* 314(24) (2015): 2623–24.

Epstein, R. M., M. Christie, R. Frankel, S. Rousseau, C. Shields, and A. L. Suchman. "Understanding Fear of Contagion among Physicians Who Care for HIV Patients." *Family Medicine* 25(4) (1993): 264–68.

Epstein, R. M., E. F. Dannefer, A. C. Nofziger, J. T. Hansen, S. H. Schultz, N. Jospe, L. W. Connard, et al. "Comprehensive Assessment of Professional Competence: The Rochester Experiment." *Teaching and Learning in Medicine* 16(2) (2004): 186–96.

Epstein, R. M., P. Franks, K. Fiscella, C. G. Shields, S. C. Meldrum, R. L. Kravitz, and P. R. Duberstein. "Measuring Patient-Centered Communication in Patient-Physician Consultations: Theoretical and Practical Issues." *Social Science & Medicine* 61(7) (2005): 1516–28.

Epstein, R. M., and R. E. Gramling. "What Is Shared in Shared Decision Making? Complex Decisions When the Evidence Is Unclear." *Medical Care Research and Review* 70(1S) (2012): 94–112.

Epstein, R. M., T. Hadee, J. Carroll, S. C. Meldrum, J. Lardner, and C. G. Shields. "'Could This Be Something Serious?' Reassurance, Uncertainty, and Empathy in Response to Patients' Expressions of Worry." *Journal of General Internal Medicine* 22(12) (2007): 1731–39.

Epstein, R. M., and E. M. Hundert. "Defining and Assessing Professional Competence." *JAMA* 287(2) (2002): 226–35.

Epstein, R. M., D. S. Morse, R. M. Frankel, L. Frarey, K. Anderson, and H. B. Beckman. "Awkward Moments in Patient-Physician Communication about HIV Risk." *Annals of Internal Medicine* 128(6) (1998): 435–42.

Epstein, R. M., T. E. Quill, and I. R. McWhinney. "Somatization Reconsidered: Incorporating the Patient's Experience of Illness." *Archives of Internal Medicine* 159(3) (1999): 215–22.

Epstein, R. M., C. G. Shields, S. C. Meldrum, K. Fiscella, J. Carroll, P. A. Carney, and P. R. Duberstein. "Physicians' Responses to Patients' Medically Unexplained Symptoms." *Psychosomatic Medicine* 68(2) (2006): 269–76.

Epstein, R. M., D. J. Siegel, and J. Silberman. "Self-Monitoring in Clinical Practice: A Challenge for Medical Educators." *Journal of Continuing Education in the Health Professions* 28(1) (2008): 5–13.

Epstein, R. M., and R. L. Street Jr. "Shared Mind: Communication, Decision Making, and Autonomy in Serious Illness." *Annals of Family Medicine* 9(5) (2011): 454–61.

Eraut, M. *Developing Professional Knowledge and Competence.* London: Falmer Press, 1994.

Ericsson, K. A. "An Expert-Performance Perspective of Research on Medical Expertise: The Study of Clinical Performance." *Medical Education* 41(12) (2007): 1124–30.

Fahrenkopf, A. M., T. C. Sectish, L. K. Barger, P. J. Sharek, D. Lewin, V. W. Chiang, S. Edwards, et al. "Rates of Medication Errors among Depressed and Burnt-Out Residents: Prospective Cohort Study." *BMJ* 1(7642) (2008): 488–91.

Farber, S. "Living Every Minute." *Journal of Pain and Symptom Management* 49(4) (2015): 796–800.

Feder, A., E. J. Nestler, and D. S. Charney. "Psychobiology and Molecular Genetics of Resilience." *Nature Reviews Neuroscience* 10(6) (2009): 446–57.

Festinger, L. "Cognitive Dissonance." *Scientific American* 207(4) (1962): 93–107.

Fitzgerald, F. S. "The Crack Up." In *The Crack Up*, edited by E. Wilson. New York: New Directions, 1945.

Fitzgerald, F. T. "Curiosity." *Annals of Internal Medicine* 130(1) (1999): 70–72.

Fonagy, P., G. Gergely, E. Jurist, and M. Target. *Affect Regulation, Mentalization, and the Development of Self.* New York: Other Press, 2002.

Foucault, M. *The Birth of the Clinic: An Archaeology of Medical Perception.* New York: Random House, 1994.

Fox, R. *Experiment Perilous: Physicians and Patients Facing the Unknown.* Glencoe, IL: Free Press, 1959.

Frank, A. W. "Can We Research Suffering?" *Qualitative Health Research* 11(3) (2001): 353–62.

Friedberg, M. W., P. G. Chen, K. R. Van Busum, F. M. Aunon, C. Pham, J. P. Caloyeras, S. Mattke, et al. "Factors Affecting Physician Professional Satisfaction and Their Implications for Patient Care, Health Systems, and Health Policy." 2013. http://www.rand.org/content/dam/rand/pubs/research_reports/RR400/RR439/RAND_RR439.pdf.

Fronsdal, G. "Not-Knowing." http://www.insightmeditationcenter.org/books-articles/articles/not-knowing.

Fry, J. P. "Interactive Relationship between Inquisitiveness and Student Control of Instruction." *Journal of Educational Psychology* 68(5) (1972): 459–65.

Fukushima, H., Y. Terasawa, and S. Umeda. "Association between Interoception and Empathy: Evidence from Heartbeat-Evoked Brain Potential." *International Journal of Psychophysiology* 79(2) (2011): 259–65.

Gabbard, G. O. "The Role of Compulsiveness in the Normal Physician." *JAMA* 254(20) (1985): 2926–29.

Gabel, S. "Demoralization: A Precursor to Physician Burnout?" *American Family Physician* 86(9) (2012): 861–62.

Gallagher, T. H., A. D. Waterman, A. G. Ebers, V. J. Fraser, and W. Levinson. "Patients' and Physicians' Attitudes regarding the Disclosure of Medical Errors." *JAMA* 289(8) (2003): 1001–7.

Germer, C. K. *The Mindful Path to Self-Compassion: Freeing Yourself from Destructive Thoughts and Emotions.* New York: Guilford Press, 2009.

Gerrity, M. S., R. F. DeVellis, and J. A. Earp. "Physicians' Reactions to Uncertainty in Patient Care. A New Measure and New Insights." *Medical Care* 28(8) (1990): 724–36.

Gillett, G. "Clinical Medicine and the Quest for Certainty." *Social Science & Medicine* 58(4) (2004): 727–38.

Glenberg, A. M., D. Havas, R. Becker, and M. Rinck. "Grounding Language in Bodily States: The Case for Emotion." In *Grounding Cognition: The Role of Perception and Action in Memory, Language, and Thinking,* edited by Diane Pecher and Rolf A. Zwaan. Cambridge: Cambridge University Press, 2005.

Glouberman, S., and B. Zimmerman. "Complicated and Complex Systems: What Would Successful Reform of Medicare Look Like?" In *Romanow Papers: Changing Health Care in Canada,* edited by Pierre-Gerlier Forest, Gregory P. Marchildon, and Tom McIntosh. Toronto: University of Toronto Press, 2002.

Goldberg, P. *The Intuitive Edge: Understanding and Developing Intuition.* Los Angeles: J. P. Tarcher, 1983.

Goldberg, S. B., A. C. Del Re, W. T. Hoyt, and J. M. Davis. "The Secret Ingredient in Mindfulness Interventions? A Case for Practice Quality over Quantity." *Journal of Counseling Psychology* 61(3) (2014): 491–97.

Good, D. J., C. J. Lyddy, T. M. Glomb, J. E. Bono, K. W. Brown, M. K. Duffy, R. A. Baer, et al. "Contemplating Mindfulness at Work: An Integrative Review." *Journal of Management* 42(1) (2015): 1–29.

Gordon, G. H., S. K. Joos, and J. Byrne. "Physician Expressions of Uncertainty during Patient Encounters." *Patient Education & Counseling* 40(1) (2000): 59–65.

Gorenstein, D. "How Doctors Die: Showing Others the Way." *New York Times,* November 19, 2013. http://www.nytimes.com/2013/11/20/your-money/how-doctors-die.html?_r=2.

Gottlieb, J., P.-Y. Oudeyer, M. Lopes, and A. Baranes. "Information-Seeking, Curiosity, and Attention: Computational and Neural Mechanisms." *Trends in Cognitive Sciences* 17(11) (2013): 585–93.

Granek, L. "When Doctors Grieve." *New York Times,* May 27, 2012.

Granek, L., P. Mazzotta, R. Tozer, and M. K. Krzyzanowska. "What Do Oncologists Want?" *Supportive Care in Cancer* 20(10) (2012): 2627–32.

Granek, L., R. Tozer, P. Mazzotta, A. Ramjaun, and M. Krzyzanowska. "Nature and Impact of Grief over Patient Loss on Oncologists' Personal and Professional Lives." *Archives of Internal Medicine* 172(12) (2012): 964–66.

Green, A. R., D. R. Carney, D. J. Pallin, L. H. Ngo, K. L. Raymond, L. I. Iezzoni, and M. R. Banaji. "Implicit Bias among Physicians and Its Prediction of Thrombolysis Decisions for Black and White Patients." *Journal of General Internal Medicine* 22(9) (2007): 1231–38.

Reference List

Greenberg, J., and N. Meiran. "Is Mindfulness Meditation Associated with 'Feeling Less'?" *Mindfulness* 5(5) (2014): 471–76.

Greenberg, J., K. Reiner, and N. Meiran. "'Mind the Trap': Mindfulness Practice Reduces Cognitive Rigidity." *PLoS ONE* 7(5) (2012): e36206.

Greene, J. *Moral Tribes: Emotion, Reason, and the Gap between Us and Them.* New York: Penguin Press, 2013.

Greenwald, A. G., D. E. McGhee, and J. L. K. Schwartz. "Measuring Individual Differences in Implicit Cognition: The Implicit Association Test." *Journal of Personality and Social Psychology* 74(6) (1998): 1464–80.

Groopman, J. E. *How Doctors Think.* New York: Houghton Mifflin, 2007.

Grossman, P. "On Measuring Mindfulness in Psychosomatic and Psychological Research." *Journal of Psychosomatic Research* 64(4) (2008): 405–8.

Guyatt, G., V. Montori, P. J. Devereaux, H. Schunemann, and M. Bhandari. "Patients at the Center: In Our Practice, and in Our Use of Language." *ACP Journal Club* 140(1) (2004): A11–A12.

Haas, J. S., E. F. Cook, A. L. Puopolo, H. R. Burstin, P. D. Cleary, and T. A. Brennan. "Is the Professional Satisfaction of General Internists Associated with Patient Satisfaction?" *Journal of General Internal Medicine* 15(2) (2000): 122–28.

Hafenbrack, A. C., Z. Kinias, and S. G. Barsade. "Debiasing the Mind through Meditation Mindfulness and the Sunk-Cost Bias." *Psychological Science* 25(2) (2014): 369–76.

Haidet, P. "Jazz and the 'Art' of Medicine: Improvisation in the Medical Encounter." *Annals of Family Medicine* 5(2) (2007): 164–69.

Halifax, J. *Being with Dying.* Boulder, CO: Shambhala Publications, 2008.

———. "A Heuristic Model of Enactive Compassion." *Current Opinion in Supportive and Palliative Care* 6(2) (2012): 228–35.

Hall, W. J., M. V. Chapman, K. M. Lee, Y. M. Merino, T. W. Thomas, B. K. Payne, E. Eng, et al. "Implicit Racial/Ethnic Bias among Health Care Professionals and Its Influence on Health Care Outcomes: A Systematic Review." *American Journal of Public Health* 105(12) (2015): e60–e76.

Halpern, J. *From Detached Concern to Empathy: Humanizing Medical Practice.* Oxford: Oxford University Press, 2001.

———. "What Is Clinical Empathy?" *Journal of General Internal Medicine* 18(8) (2003): 670–74.

Harlow, J. M. "Recovery after Severe Injury to the Head." *History of Psychiatry* (1993): 274–81. (Originally published 1868 in the *Bulletin of the Massachusetts Medical Society*).

Harper, R. *On Presence: Variations and Reflections.* Philadelphia: Trinity Press International, 1991.

Harris, S. *Waking Up: A Guide to Spirituality without Religion.* New York: Simon & Schuster, 2015.

Hatano, G., and K. Inagaki. "Child Development and Education in Japan." In *Two Courses of Expertise*, edited by H. Stevenson, H. Azuma, and K. Hakuta, 262–72. New York: Freeman, 1986.

Haynes, R. B., D. L. Sackett, D. W. Taylor, E. S. Gibson, and A. L. Johnson. "Increased Absenteeism from Work after Detection and Labeling of

Reference List

Hypertensive Patients." *New England Journal of Medicine* 299(14) (1978): 741–44.

Hebb, D. *The Organization of Behavior*. New York: Wiley, 1949.

Hill, R. G. Jr., L. M. Sears, and S. W. Melanson. "4,000 Clicks: A Productivity Analysis of Electronic Medical Records in a Community Hospital ED." *American Journal of Emergency Medicine* 31(11) (2013): 1591–94.

Ho, B., and E. Liu. "Does Sorry Work? The Impact of Apology Laws on Medical Malpractice." *Journal of Risk and Uncertainty* 43(2) (2011): 141–67.

Hojat, M., D. Z. Louis, F. W. Markham, R. Wender, C. Rabinowitz, and J. S. Gonnella. "Physicians' Empathy and Clinical Outcomes for Diabetic Patients." *Academic Medicine* 86(3) (2011): 359–64.

Hojat, M., M. J. Vergare, K. Maxwell, G. Brainard, S. K. Herrine, G. A. Isenberg, J. Veloski, et al. "The Devil Is in the Third Year: A Longitudinal Study of Erosion of Empathy in Medical School." *Academic Medicine* 84(9) (2009): 1182–91.

Hölzel, B. K., S. W. Lazar, T. Gard, Z. Schuman-Olivier, D. R. Vago, and U. Ott. "How Does Mindfulness Meditation Work? Proposing Mechanisms of Action from a Conceptual and Neural Perspective." *Perspectives on Psychological Science* 6(6) (2011): 537–59.

Horowitz, C. R., A. L. Suchman, W. T. Branch Jr., and R. M. Frankel. "What Do Doctors Find Meaningful about Their Work?" *Annals of Internal Medicine* 138(9) (2003): 772–75.

Howard, S. K., D. M. Gaba, K. J. Fish, G. Yang, and F. H. Sarnquist. "Anesthesia Crisis Resource Management Training: Teaching Anesthesiologists to Handle Critical Incidents." *Aviation, Space, and Environmental Medicine* 63(9) (1992): 763–70.

Institute of Medicine. *Crossing the Quality Chasm: A New Health System for the 21st Century*. Washington, DC: National Academies Press, 2001.

Ismail-Beigi, F., E. Moghissi, M. Tiktin, I. B. Hirsch, S. E. Inzucchi, and S. Genuth. "Individualizing Glycemic Targets in Type 2 Diabetes Mellitus: Implications of Recent Clinical Trials." *Annals of Internal Medicine* 154(8) (2011): 554–59.

James, W. "Brute and Human Intellect." *In William James: Writings 1878–1899*. New York: Library of America, 1992.

———. *Pragmatism*. Cambridge, MA: Harvard University Press, 1975.

———. *The Principles of Psychology*. Cambridge, MA: Harvard University Press, 1981.

———. *The Varieties of Religious Experience: A Study in Human Nature*. New York: W. W. Norton, 1902; repr., 1961.

———. *William James: The Essential Writings*. Albany: State University of New York Press, 1986.

James, W. M. "Brute and Human Intellect." *Journal of Speculative Philosophy* 12(3) (1878): 236–76.

Jha, A. P., A. B. Morrison, J. Dainer-Best, S. Parker, N. Rostrup, and E. A. Stanley. "Minds 'at Attention': Mindfulness Training Curbs Attentional Lapses in Military Cohorts." *PLoS ONE* 10(2) (2015): e0116889.

Jha, A. P., E. A. Stanley, A. Kiyonaga, L. Wong, and L. Gelfand. "Examining the

Protective Effects of Mindfulness Training on Working Memory Capacity and Affective Experience." *Emotion* 10(1) (2010): 54–64.

Johansen, M. L., K. A. Holtedahl, A. S. Davidsen, and C. E. Rudebeck. "'I Deal with the Small Things': The Doctor-Patient Relationship and Professional Identity in GPs' Stories of Cancer Care." *Health* 16(6) (2012): 569–84.

Johnson, C. G., J. C. Levenkron, A. L. Suchman, and R. Manchester. "Does Physician Uncertainty Affect Patient Satisfaction?" *Journal of General Internal Medicine* 3(2) (1988): 144–49.

Johnson, D. C., N. J. Thom, E. A. Stanley, L. Haase, A. N. Simmons, P.-A. B. Shih, W. K. Thompson, et al. "Modifying Resilience Mechanisms in At-Risk Individuals: A Controlled Study of Mindfulness Training in Marines Preparing for Deployment." *American Journal of Psychiatry* 171(8) (2014): 844–53.

Kabat-Zinn, J. *Full Catastrophe Living: Using the Wisdom of Your Body and Mind to Face Stress, Pain, and Illness*. New York: Bantam Dell, 1990.

———. *Wherever You Go, There You Are: Mindfulness Meditation in Everyday Life*. New York: Hyperion, 1994.

Kahneman, D. "A Perspective on Judgment and Choice: Mapping Bounded Rationality." *American Psychologist* 58(9) (2003): 697–720.

———. *Thinking, Fast and Slow*. New York: Farrar, Straus and Giroux, 2013.

Kahneman, D., and G. Klein. "Conditions for Intuitive Expertise: A Failure to Disagree." *American Psychologist* 64(6) (2009): 515–26.

Kandel, E. R. "A New Intellectual Framework for Psychiatry." *American Journal of Psychiatry* 155(4) (1998): 457–69.

Kang, Y., J. R. Gray, and J. F. Dovidio. "The Nondiscriminating Heart: Lovingkindness Meditation Training Decreases Implicit Intergroup Bias." *Journal of Experimental Psychology: General* 143(3) (2014): 1306.

Kang, Y., J. Gruber, and J. R. Gray. "Mindfulness and De-automatization." *Emotion Review* 5(2) (2013): 192–201.

Kaptchuk, T. J. *The Web That Has No Weaver: Understanding Chinese Medicine*. New York: Congdon & Weed, 1983.

Karan, S. B., J. S. Berger, and M. Wajda. "Confessions of Physicians: What Systemic Reporting Does Not Uncover." *Journal of Graduate Medical Education* 7(4) (2015): 528–30.

Kashdan, T. B., A. Afram, K. W. Brown, M. Birnbeck, and M. Drvoshanov. "Curiosity Enhances the Role of Mindfulness in Reducing Defensive Responses to Existential Threat." *Personality and Individual Differences* 50(8) (2011): 1227–32.

Kassirer, J. P. "Our Stubborn Quest for Diagnostic Certainty. A Cause of Excessive Testing." *New England Journal of Medicine* 320(22) (1989): 1489–91.

Kaszniak, A. W. "Meditation, Mindfulness, Cognition, and Emotion: Implications for Community-Based Older Adult Programs." In *Enhancing Cognitive Fitness in Adults*, edited by Paula E. Hartman-Stein and Asenath LaRue, chap. 5, 85–104. New York: Springer, 2011.

Katon, W., M. Sullivan, and E. Walker. "Medical Symptoms without Identified Pathology: Relationship to Psychiatric Disorders, Childhood and Adult Trauma, and Personality Traits." *Annals of Internal Medicine* 134(9, pt. 2) (2001): 917–25.

Kearney, M. K., R. B. Weininger, M. L. Vachon, R. L. Harrison, and B. M. Mount. "Self-Care of Physicians Caring for Patients at the End of Life: 'Being Connected . . . a Key to My Survival.'" *JAMA* 301(11) (2009): 1155–64.

Kelley, J. M., G. Kraft-Todd, L. Schapira, J. Kossowsky, and H. Riess. "The Influence of the Patient-Clinician Relationship on Healthcare Outcomes: A Systematic Review and Meta-analysis of Randomized Controlled Trials." *PLoS ONE* 9(4) (2014).

Kemper, K. J., and M. Khirallah. "Acute Effects of Online Mind-Body Skills Training on Resilience, Mindfulness, and Empathy." *Journal of Evidence-Based Complementary & Alternative Medicine* 20(4) (2015): 247–53.

Kidd, C., and B. Y. Hayden. "The Psychology and Neuroscience of Curiosity." *Neuron* 88(3) (2015): 449–60.

Kleinman, A. M. *The Illness Narratives: Suffering, Healing, and the Human Condition.* New York: Basic Books, 1988.

Klimecki, O. M., S. Leiberg, M. Ricard, and T. Singer. "Differential Pattern of Functional Brain Plasticity after Compassion and Empathy Training." *Social Cognitive and Affective Neuroscience* 9(6) (2014): 873–79.

Klitzman, R. *When Doctors Become Patients.* New York: Oxford University Press, 2008.

Kohn, L. T., J. M. Corrigan, and M. S. Donaldson. *To Err Is Human: Building a Safer Health System.* Washington, DC: National Academy Press, 2000.

Komesaroff, P. "The Many Faces of the Clinic: A Levinasian View." In *Handbook of Phenomenology and Medicine*, edited by S. K. Toombs, 317–30. Dordrecht, Netherlands: Kluwer Academic Publishers, 2001.

Kramer, G. *Insight Dialogue: The Interpersonal Path to Freedom.* Boulder, CO: Shambhala Publications, 2007.

Krasner, M. S., R. M. Epstein, H. Beckman, A. L. Suchman, B. Chapman, C. J. Mooney, and T. E. Quill. "Association of an Educational Program in Mindful Communication with Burnout, Empathy, and Attitudes among Primary Care Physicians." *JAMA* 302(12) (2009): 1284–93.

Kübler-Ross, E., S. Wessler, and L. V. Avioli. "On Death and Dying." *JAMA* 221 (1972): 174–79.

Kushnir, T., D. Greenberg, N. Madjar, I. Hadari, Y. Yermiahu, and Y. G. Bachner. "Is Burnout Associated with Referral Rates among Primary Care Physicians in Community Clinics?" *Family Practice* 31(1) (2014): 44–50.

Lamm, C., C. D. Batson, and J. Decety. "The Neural Substrate of Human Empathy: Effects of Perspective-Taking and Cognitive Appraisal." *Journal of Cognitive Neuroscience* 19(1) (2007): 42–58.

Lamm, C., A. N. Meltzoff, and J. Decety. "How Do We Empathize with Someone Who Is Not Like Us? A Functional Magnetic Resonance Imaging Study." *Journal of Cognitive Neuroscience* 22(2) (2010): 362–76.

Langer, E. J. *Mindfulness.* Reading, MA: Addison-Wesley, 1989.

———. *The Power of Mindful Learning.* Reading, MA: Perseus Books, 1997.

Larson, E. B., and X. Yao. "Clinical Empathy as Emotional Labor in the Patient-Physician Relationship." *JAMA* 293(9) (2005): 1100–106.

Leary, M. R., E. B. Tate, C. E. Adams, A. Batts Allen, and J. Hancock. "Self-Compassion and Reactions to Unpleasant Self-Relevant Events: The Implications of Treating Oneself Kindly." *Journal of Personality and Social Psychology* 92(5) (2007): 887.

Lee, T. H. "The Word That Shall Not Be Spoken." *New England Journal of Medicine* 369(19) (2013): 1777–79.

Leff, J., G. Williams, M. A. Huckvale, M. Arbuthnot, and A. P. Leff. "Computer-Assisted Therapy for Medication-Resistant Auditory Hallucinations: Proof-of-Concept Study." *British Journal of Psychiatry* 202(6) (2013): 428–33.

Legassie, J., E. M. Zibrowski, and M. A. Goldszmidt. "Measuring Resident Well-Being: Impostorism and Burnout Syndrome in Residency." *Journal of General Internal Medicine* 23(7) (2008): 1090–94.

Leonard, N. H., and M. Harvey. "Curiosity, Mindfulness and Learning Style in the Acquisition of Knowledge by Individuals/Organisations. *International Journal of Learning and Intellectual Capital* 4(3) (2007): 294–314.

Lesser, M. *Know Yourself, Forget Yourself: Five Truths to Transform Your Work, Relationships, and Everyday Life*. Novato, CA: New World Library, 2013.

Leung, A. S. O., R. M. Epstein, and C. A. Moulton. "The Competent Mind: Beyond Cognition." In *The Question of Competence: Reconsidering Medical Education in the Twenty-First Century*, edited by B. D. Hodges and L. Lingard, chap. 7, 155–76. Ithaca and London: Cornell University Press, 2012.

Levinson, W., R. Gorawara-Bhat, and J. Lamb. "A Study of Patient Clues and Physician Responses in Primary Care and Surgical Settings." *JAMA* 284(8) (2000): 1021–27.

Levitin, D. J. *The Organized Mind: Thinking Straight in the Age of Information Overload*. New York: Dutton Adult, 2014.

Levy, D. M., J. O. Wobbrock, A. W. Kaszniak, and M. Ostergren. "The Effects of Mindfulness Meditation Training on Multitasking in a High-Stress Information Environment." In *Proceedings of Graphics Interface 2012*, 45–52. Toronto: Canadian Information Processing Society, 2012.

Lichtenstein, R. L. "Review Article: The Job Satisfaction and Retention of Physicians in Organized Settings: A Literature Review." *Medical Care Research and Review* 41(3) (1984): 139–79.

Lindblom, C. E. "The Science of 'Muddling Through.'" *Public Administration Review* 19(2) (1959): 79–88.

Linzer, M., M. R. Visser, F. J. Oort, E. M. Smets, J. E. McMurray, and H. C. de Haes. "Predicting and Preventing Physician Burnout: Results from the United States and the Netherlands." *American Journal of Medicine* 111(2) (2001): 170–75.

Lown, B. A., and C. F. Manning. "The Schwartz Center Rounds: Evaluation of an Interdisciplinary Approach to Enhancing Patient-Centered Communication, Teamwork, and Provider Support." *Academic Medicine* 85(6) (2010): 1073–81.

Lown, B. A., J. Rosen, and J. Marttila. "An Agenda for Improving Compassionate Care: A Survey Shows About Half of Patients Say Such Care Is Missing." *Health Affairs* 30(9) (2011): 1772–78.

Lueke, A., and B. Gibson. "Mindfulness Meditation Reduces Implicit Age and

Race Bias: The Role of Reduced Automaticity of Responding." *Social Psychological and Personality Science* (2014): 1–8.

Lutz, A., L. L. Greischar, D. M. Perlman, and R. J. Davidson. "Bold Signal in Insula Is Differentially Related to Cardiac Function during Compassion Meditation in Experts vs. Novices." *NeuroImage* 47(3) (2009): 1038–46.

Macdonald, J. S., and N. Lavie. "Visual Perceptual Load Induces Inattentional Deafness." *Attention, Perception, and Psychophysics* 73(6) (2011): 1780–89.

Maguire, E. A., K. Woollett, and H. J. Spiers. "London Taxi Drivers and Bus Drivers: A Structural MRI and Neuropsychological Analysis." *Hippocampus* 16(12) (2006): 1091–101.

Mancini, A. D., and G. A. Bonanno. "Predictors and Parameters of Resilience to Loss: Toward an Individual Differences Model." *Journal of Personality* 77(6) (2009): 1805–32.

Marvel, K., A. Bailey, C. Pfaffly, W. Gunn, and H. Beckman. "Relationship-Centered Administration: Transferring Effective Communication Skills from the Exam Room to the Conference Room." *Journal of Healthcare Management/American College of Healthcare Executives* 48(2) (2002): 112–23; discussion, 23–24.

Marvel, M. K., R. M. Epstein, K. Flowers, and H. B. Beckman. "Soliciting the Patient's Agenda: Have We Improved?" *JAMA* 281(3) (1999): 283–87.

Maslach, C. "Job Burnout." *Current Directions in Psychological Science* 12(5) (2003): 189–92.

Maslach, C., S. Jackson, and M. Leiter. "Maslach Burnout Inventory: Third Edition." In *Evaluating Stress: A Book of Resources*, edited by C. P. Zalaquett and R. J. Wood, 191–218. Lanham, MD: Scarecrow Press, 1998.

Maslach, C., W. B. Schaufeli, and M. P. Leiter. "Job Burnout." *Annual Review of Psychology* (2001): 52397–422.

Maue, K. *Water in the Lake: Real Events for the Imagination*. New York: Harper & Row, 1979.

McCrae, R. R., and P. T. Costa Jr. "Personality Trait Structure as a Human Universal." *American Psychologist* 52(5) (1997): 509–16.

McCrae, R. R., P. T. Costa Jr., F. Ostendorf, A. Angleitner, M. Hrebickova, M. D. Avia, J. Sanz, et al. "Nature over Nurture: Temperament, Personality, and Life Span Development." *Journal of Personality and Social Psychology* 78(1) (2000): 173–86.

McDaniel, S. H., H. B. Beckman, D. S. Morse, J. Silberman, D. B. Seaburn, and R. M. Epstein. "'Enough about Me, Let's Get Back to You': Physician Self-Disclosure during Primary Care Encounters." *Annals of Internal Medicine* 149(11) (2008): 835–37.

McDaniel, S. H., T. L. Campbell, and D. B. Seaburn. *Family-Oriented Primary Care: A Manual for Medical Providers*. New York: Springer-Verlag, 1990.

McDaniel, S. H., and J. Landau-Stanton. "Family-of-Origin Work and Family Therapy Skills Training: Both-And." *Family Process* 30(4) (1991): 459–71.

McHugh, M. D., A. Kutney-Lee, J. P. Cimiotti, D. M. Sloane, and L. H. Aiken. "Nurses' Widespread Job Dissatisfaction, Burnout, and Frustration with Health Benefits Signal Problems for Patient Care." *Health Affairs* 30(2) (2011): 202–10.

McMurray, J. E., M. Linzer, T. R. Konrad, J. Douglas, R. Shugerman, and K. Nelson. "The Work Lives of Women Physicians: Results from the Physician Work Life Study. The SGIM Career Satisfaction Study Group." *Journal of General Internal Medicine* 15(6) (2000): 372–80.

McWhinney, I. R. "Fifty Years On: The Legacy of Michael Balint." *British Journal of General Practice* 49 (1999): 418–19.

McWhinney, I. R., R. M. Epstein, and T. R. Freeman. "Rethinking Somatization." *Advances in Mind-Body Medicine* 17(4) (2001): 232–39.

Mengel, M. "Physician Ineffectiveness due to Family-of-Origin Issues." *Family Systems Medicine* 5(2) (1987): 176–90.

Michaelson, L. K., A. B. Knight, and D. Flink. *Team-Based Learning: A Transformative Use of Small Groups.* New York: Praeger, 2002.

Milgram, S. "Behavioral Study of Obedience." *Journal of Abnormal Psychology* (1963): 67371–78.

Mohanty, A., T. Egner, J. M. Monti, and M. M. Mesulam. "Search for a Threatening Target Triggers Limbic Guidance of Spatial Attention." *Journal of Neuroscience* 29(34) (2009): 10563–72.

Mohanty, A., and T. J. Sussman. "Top-Down Modulation of Attention by Emotion." *Frontiers in Human Neuroscience* 7 (2013): 102.

Montgomery, K. "Thinking about Thinking: Implications for Patient Safety." *Healthcare Quarterly* (Toronto, Canada) 12 (2008): e191–e194.

Montori, V. M., and G. H. Guyatt. "Progress in Evidence-Based Medicine." *JAMA* 300(15) (2008): 1814–16.

Morse, D. S., E. A. Edwardsen, and H. S. Gordon. "Missed Opportunities for Interval Empathy in Lung Cancer Communication." *Archives of Internal Medicine* 168(17) (2008): 1853–58.

Moulton, C. A., and R. M. Epstein. "Self-Monitoring in Surgical Practice: Slowing Down When You Should." In *Surgical Education: Theorising an Emerging Domain*, edited by H. Fry and R. Kneebone, chap. 10, 169–82. New York: Springer, 2011.

Moulton, C. A., G. Regehr, M. Mylopoulos, and H. M. MacRae. "Slowing Down When You Should: A New Model of Expert Judgment." *Academic Medicine RIME: Proceedings of the Forty-Sixth Annual Conference* 82(10) (2007): S109–S116.

Mujica-Parodi, L. R., H. H. Strey, B. Frederick, R. Savoy, D. Cox, Y. Botanov, D. Tolkunov, et al. "Chemosensory Cues to Conspecific Emotional Stress Activate Amygdala in Humans." *PLoS ONE* 4(7) (2009): e6415.

Mulligan, N. W. "The Role of Attention during Encoding in Implicit and Explicit Memory." *Journal of Experimental Psychology: Learning, Memory, & Cognition* 21(1) (1998): 27–47.

Murray, K. "How Doctors Die—It's Not Like the Rest of Us, but It Should Be." *Zócalo Public Square*, November 30, 2011, 1775–77.

Naef, R. "Bearing Witness: A Moral Way of Engaging in the Nurse-Person Relationship." *Nursing Philosophy* 7(3) (2006): 146–56.

Nedrow, A., N. A. Steckler, and J. Hardman. "Physician Resilience and Burnout: Can You Make the Switch?" *Family Practice Management* 20(1) (2013): 25–30.

Neff, K. D., and C. K. Germer. "A Pilot Study and Randomized Controlled Trial of the Mindful Self-Compassion Program." *Journal of Clinical Psychology* 69(1) (2013): 28–44.

Neff, K. D., Y.-P. Hsieh, and K. Dejitterat. "Self-Compassion, Achievement Goals, and Coping with Academic Failure." *Self and Identity* 4(3) (2005): 263–87.

Niedenthal, P. M. "Embodying Emotion." *Science* 316(5827) (2007): 1002–5.

Niemiec, C. P., K. W. Brown, T. B. Kashdan, P. J. Cozzolino, W. E. Breen, C. Levesque-Bristol, and R. M. Ryan. "Being Present in the Face of Existential Threat: The Role of Trait Mindfulness in Reducing Defensive Responses to Mortality Salience." *Journal of Personality and Social Psychology* 99(2) (2010): 344–65.

Nin, A. *The Diary of Anaïs Nin, 1939–1944.* New York: Harcourt, Brace & World, 1969.

Norman, G., M. Young, and L. Brooks. "Non-analytical Models of Clinical Reasoning: The Role of Experience." *Medical Education* 41(12) (2007): 1140–45.

Novack, D. H., R. M. Epstein, and R. H. Paulsen. "Toward Creating Physician-Healers: Fostering Medical Students' Self-Awareness, Personal Growth, and Well-Being." *Academic Medicine* 74(5) (1999): 516–20.

Novack, D. H., C. Kaplan, R. M. Epstein, W. Clark, A. L. Suchman, M. O'Brien, E. Najberg, et al. "Personal Awareness and Professional Growth: A Proposed Curriculum." *Medical Encounter* 13(3) (1997): 2–7.

Novack, D. H., A. L. Suchman, W. Clark, R. M. Epstein, E. Najberg, and C. Kaplan. "Calibrating the Physician. Personal Awareness and Effective Patient Care." *JAMA* 278(6) (1997): 502–9.

Ofri, D. "The Epidemic of Disillusioned Doctors." *Time*, 2013. Published electronically July 2, 2013. http://ideas.time.com/2013/07/02/the-epidemic-of-disillusioned-doctors.

Ogden, J., K. Fuks, M. Gardner, S. Johnson, M. McLean, P. Martin, and R. Shah. "Doctors' Expressions of Uncertainty and Patient Confidence." *Patient Education & Counseling* 48(2) (2002): 171–76.

Olson, K., K. J. Kemper, and J. D. Mahan. "What Factors Promote Resilience and Protect against Burnout in First-Year Pediatric and Medicine-Pediatric Residents?" *Journal of Evidence-Based Complementary & Alternative Medicine* 20(3) (2015): 192–98.

Oord, T. J. *Defining Love: A Philosophical, Scientific, and Theological Engagement.* Ada, MI: Brazos Press, 2010.

O'Rourke, M. "Doctors Tell All—and It's Bad." *Atlantic*, November 2014. http://www.theatlantic.com/magazine/archive/2014/11/doctors-tell-all-and-its-bad/380785.

Pembroke, N. "Human Dimension in Medical Care: Insights from Buber and Marcel." *Southern Medical Journal* 103(12) (2010): 1210–13.

Pence, G. E. "Can Compassion Be Taught?" *Journal of Medical Ethics* 9(4) (1983): 189–91.

"Physician Wellness Services and Cejka Search. 2011 Physician Stress and Burnout Survey." 2011. http://www.cejkasearch.com/wp-content/uploads/physician-stress-burnout-survey.pdf.

Physicians Foundation. "A Survey of America's Physicians: Practice Patterns and

Perspectives, an Examination of the Professional Morale, Practice Patterns, Career Plans, and Healthcare Perspectives of Today's Physicians, Aggregated by Age, Gender, Primary Care/Specialists, and Practice Owners/Employees." 2012. http://www.physiciansfoundation.org/uploads/default/Physicians_Foundation_2012_Biennial_Survey.pdf.

Polanyi, M. "Knowing and Being, the Logic of Tacit Inference." In *Knowing and Being: Essays by Michael Polanyi*, edited by M. Grene, chaps. 9 and 10, 123–58. Chicago: University of Chicago Press, 1969.

———. *Personal Knowledge: Towards a Post-critical Philosophy*. Chicago: University of Chicago Press, 1974.

———. *The Tacit Dimension*. Gloucester, MA: Peter Smith, 1983.

Pollak, S. M., T. Pedulla, and R. D. Siegel. *Sitting Together: Essential Skills for Mindfulness-Based Psychotherapy*. New York: Guilford Press, 2014.

Pololi, L. H., E. Krupat, J. T. Civian, A. S. Ash, and R. T. Brennan. "Why Are a Quarter of Faculty Considering Leaving Academic Medicine? A Study of Their Perceptions of Institutional Culture and Intentions to Leave at 26 Representative US Medical Schools." *Academic Medicine* 87(7) (2012): 859–69.

Price, M. C. "Intuitive Decisions on the Fringes of Consciousness: Are They Conscious and Does It Matter?" *Judgment and Decision Making* 3(1) (2008): 28–41.

Prose, N. "Paying Attention." *JAMA* 283(21) (2000): 2763.

Quill, T. E., and H. Brody. "Physician Recommendations and Patient Autonomy: Finding a Balance between Physician Power and Patient Choice." *Annals of Internal Medicine* 125(9) (1996): 763–69.

Quill, T. E., and P. R. Williamson. "Healthy Approaches to Physician Stress." *Archives of Internal Medicine* 150(9) (1990): 1857–61.

Reniers, R. L., B. A. Vollm, R. Elliott, and R. Corcoran. "Empathy, ToM, and Self-Other Differentiation: An fMRI Study of Internal States." *Social Neuroscience* 9(1) (2014): 50–62.

Reps, P., and N. Senzaki. *Zen Flesh, Zen Bones: A Collection of Zen and Pre-Zen Writings*. Clarendon, VT: Tuttle Publishing, 1998.

Reyna, V. F. "A Theory of Medical Decision Making and Health: Fuzzy Trace Theory." *Medical Decision Making* 28(6) (2008): 850–65.

Reyna, V. F., and F. J. Lloyd. "Physician Decision Making and Cardiac Risk: Effects of Knowledge, Risk Perception, Risk Tolerance, and Fuzzy Processing." *Journal of Experimental Psychology: Applied* 12(3) (2006): 179.

Riva, G., J. A. Waterworth, E. L. Waterworth, and F. Mantovani. "From Intention to Action: The Role of Presence." *New Ideas in Psychology* 29(1) (2011): 24–37.

Rochlin, G. I., T. R. La Porte, and K. H. Roberts. "The Self-Designing High-Reliability Organization: Aircraft Carrier Flight Operations at Sea." *Naval War College Review* 51(3) (1998): 97.

Rodenbach, R. A., K. E. Rodenbach, M. A. Tejani, and R. M. Epstein. "Relationships between Personal Attitudes about Death and Communication with Terminally Ill Patients: How Oncology Clinicians Grapple with Mortality." *Patient Education & Counseling* 99(3) (2015): 356–63.

Roman, B., and J. Kay. "Fostering Curiosity: Using the Educator-Learner Relationship to Promote a Facilitative Learning Environment." *Psychiatry: Interpersonal and Biological Processes* 70(3) (2007): 205–8.

Rushton, C. H., A. W. Kaszniak, and J. S. Halifax. "Addressing Moral Distress: Application of a Framework to Palliative Care Practice." *Journal of Palliative Medicine* 16(9) (2013): 1080–88.

———. "A Framework for Understanding Moral Distress among Palliative Care Clinicians." *Journal of Palliative Medicine* 16(9) (2013): 1074–79.

Russ, A. L., A. J. Zillich, M. S. McManus, B. N. Doebbeling, and J. J. Saleem. "Prescribers' Interactions with Medication Alerts at the Point of Prescribing: A Multi-method, In Situ Investigation of the Human-Computer Interaction." *International Journal of Medical Informatics* 81(4) (2012): 232–43.

Russo, S. J., J. W. Murrough, M.-H. Han, D. S. Charney, and E. J. Nestler. "Neurobiology of Resilience." *Nature Neuroscience* 15(11) (2012): 1475–84.

Sabin, J., B. A. Nosek, A. Greenwald, and F. P. Rivara. "Physicians' Implicit and Explicit Attitudes about Race by MD Race, Ethnicity, and Gender." *Journal of Health Care for the Poor and Underserved* 20(3) (2009): 896–913.

Sabin, J. A., F. P. Rivara, and A. G. Greenwald. "Physician Implicit Attitudes and Stereotypes about Race and Quality of Medical Care." *Medical Care* 46(7) (2008): 678–85.

Sackett, D. L., R. B. Haynes, G. H. Guyatt, and P. Tugwell. *Clinical Epidemiology: A Basic Science for Clinical Medicine.* 2nd ed. Boston: Little Brown, 1991.

Saitta, N., and S. D. Hodge. "Efficacy of a Physician's Words of Empathy: An Overview of State Apology Laws." *Journal of the American Osteopathic Association* 112(5) (2012): 302–6.

———. "Physician Apologies." *Practical Lawyer*, December 2011, 35–43.

———. "Is It Unrealistic to Expect a Doctor to Apologize for an Unforeseen Medical Complication?—a Primer on Apologies Laws." *Pennsylvania Bar Association Quarterly*, July 2011, 93–110.

Salmon P. "Patients Who Present Physical Symptoms in the Absence of Physical Pathology: A Challenge to Existing Models of Doctor-Patient Interaction." *Patient Education & Counseling* 39(1) (2000): 105–13.

Salmon P., L. Wissow, J. Carroll, A. Ring, G. M. Humphris, J. C. Davies, and C. F. Dowrick. "Doctors' Responses to Patients with Medically Unexplained Symptoms Who Seek Emotional Support: Criticism or Confrontation?" *General Hospital Psychiatry* 29(5) (2007): 454–60.

Salvucci, D. D., N. A. Taatgen, and J. P. Borst. "Toward a Unified Theory of the Multitasking Continuum: From Concurrent Performance to Task Switching, Interruption, and Resumption." *Proceedings of ACM CHI 2009 Conference on Human Factors in Computing Systems—Understanding UI 2* (2009), 1819–28.

Salzberg, S. *Lovingkindness: The Revolutionary Art of Happiness.* Boston: Shambhala, 1997.

Schattner, A. "My Most Informative Error." *JAMA Internal Medicine* 175(5) (2015): 681.

Reference List

Scheingold, L. "Balint Work in England: Lessons for American Family Medicine." *Journal of Family Practice* 26(3) (1988): 315–20.

Schon, D. A. *Educating the Reflective Practitioner.* San Francisco: Jossey-Bass, 1987.

———. *The Reflective Practitioner.* New York: Basic Books, 1983.

Schroeder, D. A., E. Stephens, D. Colgan, M. Hunsinger, D. Rubin, and M. S. Christopher. "A Brief Mindfulness-Based Intervention for Primary Care Physicians: A Pilot Randomized Controlled Trial." *American Journal of Lifestyle Medicine* (2016): 1–9.

Schulman, K. A., J. A. Berlin, W. Harless, J. F. Kerner, S. Sistrunk, B. J. Gersh, R. Dube, et al. "The Effect of Race and Sex on Physicians' Recommendations for Cardiac Catheterization." *New England Journal of Medicine* 340(8) (1999): 618–26.

Schwartz, K. B. "A Patient's Story." *Boston Globe Magazine,* 1995, 16.

Schwartz Center for Compassionate Healthcare. http://www.theschwartzcenter.org.

Scott, S. D., L. E. Hirschinger, K. R. Cox, M. McCoig, J. Brandt, and L. W. Hall. "The Natural History of Recovery for the Healthcare Provider 'Second Victim' after Adverse Patient Events." *Quality and Safety in Health Care* 18(5) (2009): 325–30.

Seaburn, D. B., D. Morse, S. H. McDaniel, H. Beckman, J. Silberman, and R. M. Epstein. "Physician Responses to Ambiguous Patient Symptoms." *Journal of General Internal Medicine* 20(6) (2005): 525–30.

Shanafelt, T. D., O. Hasan, L. N. Dyrbye, C. Sinsky, D. Satele, J. Sloan, and C. P. West. "Changes in Burnout and Satisfaction with Work-Life Balance in Physicians and the General US Working Population between 2011 and 2014." *Mayo Clinic Proceedings* 90(12) (2015): 1600–13.

Shanafelt, T. D., C. P. West, J. A. Sloan, P. J. Novotny, G. A. Poland, R. Menaker, T. A. Rummans, et al. "Career Fit and Burnout among Academic Faculty." *Archives of Internal Medicine* 169(10) (2009): 990–95.

Shapiro, J. "Walking a Mile in Their Patients' Shoes: Empathy and Othering in Medical Students' Education." *Philosophy, Ethics, and Humanities in Medicine* 3(1) (2008): 1.

Shapiro, S. L., and G. E. Schwartz. "Mindfulness in Medical Education: Fostering the Health of Physicians and Medical Practice." *Integrative Medicine* 1(3) (1998): 93–94.

Shapiro, S. L., G. E. Schwartz, and G. Bonner. "Effects of Mindfulness-Based Stress Reduction on Medical and Premedical Students." *Journal of Behavioral Medicine* 21(6) (1998): 581–99.

Shatz, C. J. "The Developing Brain." *Scientific American* 267(3) (1992): 60–67.

Shaughnessy, A. F., D. C. Slawson, and L. Becker. "Clinical Jazz: Harmonizing Clinical Experience and Evidence-Based Medicine." *Journal of Family Practice* 47(6) (1998): 425–28.

Shavers, V. L., and M. L. Brown. "Racial and Ethnic Disparities in the Receipt of Cancer Treatment." *Journal of the National Cancer Institute* 94(5) (2002): 334–57.

Shayne, M., and T. E. Quill. "Oncologists Responding to Grief." *Archives of Internal Medicine* 172(12) (2012): 966–67.

Sherman, J. W., F. R. Conrey, and C. J. Groom. "Encoding Flexibility Revisited: Evidence for Enhanced Encoding of Stereotype-Inconsistent Information under Cognitive Load." *Social Cognition* 22(2) (2004): 214–32.

Sherwin, S. *No Longer Patient: Feminist Ethics & Health Care*. Philadelphia: Temple University Press, 1992.

Shields, C. G., M. A. Finley, C. M. Elias, C. J. Coker, J. J. Griggs, K. Fiscella, and R. M. Epstein. "Pain Assessment: The Roles of Physician Certainty and Curiosity." *Health Communication* 28(7) (2013): 740–46.

Simon, G. E., and O. Gureje. "Stability of Somatization Disorder and Somatization Symptoms among Primary Care Patients." *Archives of General Psychiatry* 56(1) (1999): 90–95.

Singer, T., and M. Bolz, *Compassion: Bridging Practice and Science*. Munich, Germany: Max Planck Society, 2013.

Singer, T., H. D. Critchley, and K. Preuschoff. "A Common Role of Insula in Feelings, Empathy and Uncertainty." *Trends in Cognitive Sciences* 13(8) (2009): 334–40.

Sirovich, B. E., S. Woloshin, and L. M. Schwartz. "Too Little? Too Much? Primary Care Physicians' Views on US Health Care: A Brief Report." *Archives of Internal Medicine* 171(17) (2011): 1582–85.

Smith, A. K., D. B. White, and R. M. Arnold. "Uncertainty—the Other Side of Prognosis." *New England Journal of Medicine* 368(26) (2013): 2448–50.

Smith, R. C., A. M. Dorsey, J. S. Lyles, and R. M. Frankel. "Teaching Self-Awareness Enhances Learning about Patient-Centered Interviewing." *Academic Medicine* 74(11) (1999): 1242–48.

Smith, R. C., G. Osborn, R. B. Hoppe, J. S. Lyles, L. Van Egeren, R. Henry, D. Sego, et al. "Efficacy of a One-Month Training Block in Psychosocial Medicine for Residents: A Controlled Study." *Journal of General Internal Medicine* 6(6) (1991): 535–43.

Southwick, S. M., and D. S. Charney. *Resilience: The Science of Mastering Life's Greatest Challenges*. Cambridge: Cambridge University Press, 2012.

Spickard, A. Jr., S. G. Gabbe, and J. F. Christensen. "Mid-Career Burnout in Generalist and Specialist Physicians." *JAMA* 288(12) (2002): 1447–50.

Spivak, G. C., L. E. Lyons, and C. G. Franklin. " 'On the Cusp of the Personal and the Impersonal': An Interview with Gayatri Chakravorty Spivak." *Biography* 27(1) (2004): 203–21.

Srivastava, R. "Speaking up—When Doctors Navigate Medical Hierarchy." *New England Journal of Medicine* 368(4) (2013): 302–5.

Stangor, C., and D. McMillan. "Memory for Expectancy-Congruent and Expectancy-Incongruent Information." *Psychological Bulletin* 111(1) (1992): 42–61.

Stanley, E. A. "Mindfulness-Based Mind Fitness Training (MMFT): An Approach for Enhancing Performance and Building Resilience in High Stress Contexts." In *The Wiley Blackwell Handbook of Mindfulness*, edited by A. Ie, C. T. Ngnoumen, and E. J. Langer, 964–85. Hoboken, NJ: Wiley, 2014.

Stanley, E. A., J. M. Schaldach, A. Kiyonaga, and A. P. Jha. "Mindfulness-Based Mind Fitness Training: A Case Study of a High Stress Pre-deployment Military Cohort." *Cognitive and Behavioral Practice* 18(4) (2011): 566–76.

Steig, W. *Doctor De Soto.* New York: Square Fish, 2010.

Stiegler, M. P. "A Piece of My Mind. What I Learned about Adverse Events from Captain Sully: It's Not What You Think." *JAMA* 313(4) (2015): 361–62.

Streng, F. J. *Emptiness: A Study in Religious Meaning.* Nashville, TN: Abingdon Press, 1967.

Suchman, A. L. "The Influence of Health Care Organizations on Well-Being." *Western Journal of Medicine* 174(1) (2001): 43.

———. "Organizations as Machines, Organizations as Conversations: Two Core Metaphors and Their Consequences." *Medical Care* 49 (2011): S43–S48.

Suchman, A. L., K. Markakis, H. B. Beckman, and R. Frankel. "A Model of Empathic Communication in the Medical Interview." *JAMA* 277(8) (1997): 678–82.

Suchman, A. L., and D. A. Matthews. "What Makes the Patient-Doctor Relationship Therapeutic? Exploring the Connexional Dimension of Medical Care." *Annals of Internal Medicine* 108(1) (1988): 125–30.

Suchman, A. L., D. J. Sluyter, and P. R. Williamson. *Leading Change in Healthcare: Transforming Organizations Using Complexity, Positive Psychology, and Relationship-Centered Care.* Abingdon, UK: Radcliffe Publishing, 2011.

Suchman, A. L., and P. R. Williamson. "Principles and Practices of Relationship-Centered Meetings." Rochester, NY: Relationship Centered Health Care, 2006.

Suzuki, S. *Zen Mind, Beginner's Mind.* New York: Weatherhill, 1980.

Swayden, K. J., K. K. Anderson, L. M. Connelly, J. S. Moran, J. K. McMahon, and P. M. Arnold. "Effect of Sitting vs. Standing on Perception of Provider Time at Bedside: A Pilot Study." *Patient Education and Counseling* 86(2) (2012): 166–71.

Sweller, J. "Cognitive Load During Problem Solving: Effects on Learning." *Cognitive Science* 12(2) (1988): 257–85.

Taleb, N. N. *Antifragile: Things That Gain from Disorder.* New York: Random House, 2014.

Tan, C. M. *Search Inside Yourself.* New York: HarperCollins, 2012.

Tang, Y.-Y., B. K. Hölzel, and M. I. Posner. "The Neuroscience of Mindfulness Meditation." *Nature Reviews Neuroscience* 16(4) (2015): 213–25.

Tang, Y.-Y., Y. Ma, Y. Fan, H. Feng, J. Wang, S. Feng, Q. Lu, et al. "Central and Autonomic Nervous System Interaction Is Altered by Short-Term Meditation." *Proceedings of the National Academy of Sciences* 106(22) (2009): 8865–70.

Tang, Y.-Y., Y. Ma, J. Wang, Y. Fan, S. Feng, Q. Lu, Q. Yu, et al. "Short-Term Meditation Training Improves Attention and Self-Regulation." *Proceedings of the National Academy of Sciences* 104(43) (2007): 17152–56.

Thomas, J. T. "Intrapsychic Predictors of Professional Quality of Life: Mindfulness, Empathy, and Emotional Separation." Lexington: University of Kentucky, 2011.

Thompson, E. *Mind in Life: Biology, Phenomenology, and the Sciences of Mind.* Cambridge, MA: Belknap Press of Harvard University Press, 2007.

Thompson, E., and M. Stapleton. "Making Sense of Sense-Making: Reflections on Enactive and Extended Mind Theories." *Topoi* 28(1) (2009): 23–30.

Reference List

Thorne, S. E., M. Kuo, E. A. Armstrong, G. McPherson, S. R. Harris, And T. G. Hislop. "'Being Known': Patients' Perspectives of the Dynamics of Human Connection in Cancer Care." *Psycho-Oncology* 14(10) (2005): 887–98.

Tinetti, M. E., T. R. Fried, and C. M. Boyd. "Designing Health Care for the Most Common Chronic Condition—Multimorbidity." *JAMA* 307(23) (2012): 2493–94.

Todd, K. H., N. Samaroo, and J. R. Hoffman. "Ethnicity as a Risk Factor for Inadequate Emergency Department Analgesia." *JAMA* 269(12) (1993): 1537–39.

Tversky, A., and D. Kahneman. "The Framing of Decisions and the Psychology of Choice." *Science* 211(4481) (1981): 453–58.

Vago, D., and D. Silbersweig. "Self-Awareness, Self-Regulation, and Self-Transcendence (S-Art): A Framework for Understanding the Neurobiological Mechanisms of Mindfulness." *Frontiers in Human Neuroscience* 6(296) (2012): 1–6.

Vaillant, G. E., N. C. Sobowale, and C. McArthur. "Some Psychologic Vulnerabilities of Physicians." *New England Journal of Medicine* 287 (1972): 372–75.

van Ryn, M. "Research on the Provider Contribution to Race/Ethnicity Disparities in Medical Care." *MedCare* 40(1) (2002): I140–I151.

Varcoe, C., B. Pauly, J. Storch, L. Newton, and K. Makaroff. "Nurses' Perceptions of and Responses to Morally Distressing Situations." *Nursing Ethics* 19(4) (2012): 488–500.

Varela, F. J., E. Thompson, and E. Rosch. *The Embodied Mind: Cognitive Science and Human Experience.* Cambridge, MA: MIT Press, 1991.

Ventres, W. B., and R. M. Frankel. "Shared Presence in Physician-Patient Communication: A Graphic Representation." *Families, Systems, & Health* 33(3) (2015): 270–79.

Verghese, A. "Culture Shock—Patient as Icon, Icon as Patient." *New England Journal of Medicine* 359(26) (2008): 2748–51.

Vogus, T. J., and K. M. Sutcliffe. "The Impact of Safety Organizing, Trusted Leadership, and Care Pathways on Reported Medication Errors in Hospital Nursing Units." *Medical Care* 45(10) (2007): 997–1002.

———. "Organizational Mindfulness and Mindful Organizing: A Reconciliation and Path Forward." *Academy of Management Learning & Education* 11(4) (2012): 722–35.

———. "Organizational Resilience: Towards a Theory and Research Agenda." Paper presented at the 2007 IEEE International Conference on Systems, Man, and Cybernetics, Montreal, Quebec, 2007.

———. "The Safety Organizing Scale: Development and Validation of a Behavioral Measure of Safety Culture in Hospital Nursing Units." *Medical Care* 45(1) (2007): 46–54.

Volz, K. G., and G. Gigerenzer. "Cognitive Processes in Decisions under Risk Are Not the Same as in Decisions under Uncertainty." *Frontiers in Decision Neuroscience* 6(105) (2012): 1–6.

Waitzkin, H., and H. Magana. "The Black Box in Somatization: Unexplained Physical Symptoms, Culture, and Narratives of Trauma." *Social Science & Medicine* 45(6) (1997): 811–25.

Waldman, J. D., F. Kelly, S. Aurora, and H. L. Smith. "The Shocking Cost of Turnover in Health Care." *Health Care Management Review* 29(1) (2004): 2–7.

Walker, E. A., W. J. Katon, D. Keegan, G. Gardner, and M. Sullivan. "Predictors of Physician Frustration in the Care of Patients with Rheumatological Complaints." *General Hospital Psychiatry* 19(5) (1997): 315–23.

Wallace, B. A. *The Attention Revolution: Unlocking the Power of the Focused Mind.* Somerville, MA: Wisdom Publications, 2006.

Waterman, A. D., J. Garbutt, E. Hazel, W. C. Dunagan, W. Levinson, V. J. Fraser, and T. H. Gallagher. "The Emotional Impact of Medical Errors on Practicing Physicians in the United States and Canada." *Joint Commission Journal on Quality and Patient Safety* 33(8) (2007): 467–76.

Weick, K. E., and T. Putnam. "Organizing for Mindfulness: Eastern Wisdom and Western Knowledge." *Journal of Management Inquiry* 15(3) (2006): 275–87.

Weick, K. E., and K. H. Roberts. "Collective Mind in Organizations—Heedful Interrelating on Flight Decks." *Administrative Science Quarterly* 38(3) (1993): 357–81.

Weick, K. E., and K. M. Sutcliffe. "Mindfulness and the Quality of Organizational Attention." *Organization Science* 17(4) (2006): 514–24.

———. *Managing the Unexpected: Assuring High Performance in an Age of Complexity.* San Francisco: Jossey-Bass, 2001.

Weiner, S., and A. Schwartz. "Contextual Errors in Medical Decision Making: Overlooked and Understudied." *Academic Medicine: Journal of the Association of American Medical Colleges* 91(5) (2016): 657–62.

Weinstein, N., and R. M. Ryan. "When Helping Helps: Autonomous Motivation for Prosocial Behavior and Its Influence on Well-Being for the Helper and Recipient." *Journal of Personality and Social Psychology* 98(2) (2010): 222–44.

Welie, J. V. "Towards an Ethics of Immediacy. A Defense of a Noncontractual Foundation of the Care Giver–Patient Relationship." *Medicine, Health Care, and Philosophy* 2(1) (1999): 11–19.

Weng, H. Y., A. S. Fox, A. J. Shackman, D. E. Stodola, J. Z. K. Caldwell, M. C. Olson, G. M. Rogers, and R. J. Davidson. "Compassion Training Alters Altruism and Neural Responses to Suffering." *Psychological Science* 24(7) (2013): 1171–80.

West, C. P., M. M. Huschka, P. J. Novotny, J. A. Sloan, J. C. Kolars, and T. M. Habermann. "Association of Perceived Medical Errors with Resident Distress and Empathy: A Prospective Longitudinal Study." *JAMA* 296(9) (2006): 1071–78.

West, C. P., A. D. Tan, T. M. Habermann, J. A. Sloan, and T. D. Shanafelt. "Association of Resident Fatigue and Distress with Perceived Medical Errors." *JAMA* 302(12) (2009): 1294–300.

Williams, E., L. Manwell, T. Konrad, and M. Linzer. "The Relationship of Organizational Culture, Stress, Satisfaction, and Burnout with Physician-Reported Error and Suboptimal Patient Care: Results from the Memo Study." *Health Care Management Review* 32(3) (2007): 203–12.

Williams, E. S., T. R. Konrad, W. E. Scheckler, D. E. Pathman, M. Linzer, J. E. McMurray, M. Gerrity, and M. Schwartz. "Understanding Physicians' Intentions to Withdraw from Practice: The Role of Job Satisfaction, Job Stress, Mental and Physical Health." *Health Care Management Review* 26(1) (2001): 7–19.

Wilson, T. D. "Strangers to Ourselves: Discovering the Adaptive Unconscious." Cambridge, MA: Belknap Press of Harvard University Press, 2002.

Winnicott, D. W. *The Maturational Processes and the Facilitating Environment.* Madison, CT: International Universities Press, 1965.

Woollett, K., and E. A. Maguire. "Acquiring 'the Knowledge' of London's Layout Drives Structural Brain Changes." *Current Biology* 21(24) (2011): 2109–14.

Wu, A. W. "Medical Error: The Second Victim. The Doctor Who Makes the Mistake Needs Help Too." *Western Journal of Medicine* 172(6) (2000): 358.

Wu, G., A. Feder, H. Cohen, J. J. Kim, S. Calderon, D. S. Charney, and A. A. Mathé. "Understanding Resilience." *Frontiers in Behavioral Neuroscience* 7(10) (2013).

Yamada, K. *The Gateless Gate: The Classic Book of Zen Koans.* New York: Simon & Schuster, 2005.

Zlatev, J., T. P. Racine, C. Sinha, and E. Itkonen. "Intersubjectivity: What Makes Us Human?" In *The Shared Mind: Perspectives on Intersubjectivity,* edited by J. Zlatev, T. P. Racine, C. Sinha, and E. Itkonen, chap. 1, 1–14. Amsterdam and Philadelphia: John Benjamins, 2008.

———. *The Shared Mind: Perspectives on Intersubjectivity.* Amsterdam and Philadelphia: John Benjamins, 2008.

Zoppi, K. "Communication about Concerns in Well-Child Visits." Ann Arbor: University of Michigan, 1994.

Index

Index

Index

expertise
  acquiring, 179–80
  automatic tasks and, 180–81
  beginner's mind and, 51, 52, 53
  cognitive processing and, 181
  diagnosis and, 61
  experience and, 179
  "not knowing" and, 57–58
  reflective questions and, 65
  understanding patients and, 52–53, 54, 56
exquisite empathy, 132

failure
  beginner's mind and, 54
  medical errors and, 141–42, 236n4
  organizational mindfulness and, 194
  patients' sense of, 111–12
  physicians' reaction to death as, 149, 151, 152
  self-compassion and, 153
family-of-origin groups, 9, 207, 212n13
Farber, Stu, 101–2
Fisher, C. Miller, 35–36
Fitzgerald, F. Scott, 55
Fitzgerald, Faith, 37–38, 39, 96
Fleming, Alexander, 36
focused attention, 13, 19, 22, 33–34, 167, 183, 200
focused attention practice, 183, 209–10, 235n28, 241n29
Fox, Deborah, 170
Frank, Arthur, 112
"From Jerusalem to Jericho" (Darley and Batson), 128

Gage, Phineas, 100
Gandhi, Mahatma, 70
Gary (patient), 54–55, 57, 195
gender differences
  burnout and, 238n4
  physicians' awareness of patients' pain and, 227n28
genetic factors
  biopsychosocial approach to care and, 8
  curiosity propensity and, 48

resilience and, 165–66
  social environment and expression of, 49, 221n22
  stress hormone expression and, 82
Glenberg, Arthur, 185
Glouberman, Sholom, 89–90, 96
goal-directed attention, 24–25
Gold Foundation, 199–200
Granek, Leeat, 150–51, 152
Grayson, Richard (patient), 85–87, 89–93, 104, 105
Greece, ancient, 63
"Guest House, The" (Rumi), 75
guided meditation, 134, 210, 220n12, 248n2
Gunderson, Mark, 1–3, 24

Hagopian, Lena (patient), 3–4
Halifax, Joan, 129
Haqim (patient), 71
Harlow, Harry, 77
Harper, Ralph, 68
health care
  compassion versus checklists and industrial models of, 129
  physicians' inattention to patients and decisions to seek, 20
  quality in. See quality in health care
  social (shared) presence needed in, 77
health care institutions
  conditions for caring and compassion in, 197–98
  lack of emotional support in, 133
  medical errors in, 139, 141, 143
  mission statements of, 114, 198
  need for sense of community for physicians in, 168
  number of burned-out physicians in, 159–60
  Schwartz Rounds in, 199
  secondary trauma of physicians and, 154, 155
health care system
  clinician well-being related to health of, 155
  commodification of medicine and, 13
  communication in, 19

280

Index

Index

Index

pain
  accuracy of physicians' estimates of, 52–53
  brain reaction to, 132
  clinicians' failure to notice, 15, 16, 20, 23, 24, 51–52, 54, 196
  communication between patients and physicians about, 53
  dilemmas in treating, 229n14
  doctor's illness experiences with, 108, 109, 110
  inability to diagnose long-term, 58, 59
  Just Like Me exercise on, 84
  medical training to recognize symptoms of, 26–27, 31–32, 37, 117, 133, 171, 194–95
  patient's experience of chronic, 115, 116
  physicians' biases in treating, 227n28
  physicians' emotional reaction to, 53, 67, 107, 130, 152, 222n6
  physicians' sense of shared experience with patients of, 126, 130, 133, 227n29
  suffering related to, 107, 113, 114
  walking with patients to communicate understanding of, 120
pain medications
  chronic pain and, 116
  communication between patients and physicians about, 53
  differences in prescribing, 227n28
  dilemmas in prescribing, 229n14, 238n3
  physicians' focus on prescribing, 20, 28, 52, 73
palliative care, 45–46, 69, 74–75, 91, 113, 122, 148–49
paranoid schizophrenia, 72–73
Pedersen, Mary, 170
peer coaching, 155
peer counselors, 154
personal awareness groups, 9, 213n14
philia (Aristotelian concept), 134
phronesis (Aristotelian concept), 92, 96

Porter, Mitch (patient), 149–50
posture, in Vipassana training, 209
practical wisdom, 92–93
pratices. *See also specific practices*
  choosing, 210
presence (being present), 67–84, 110
  addressing patients' needs and, 3
  approaches used in, 67, 68–69, 69–70
  attending and, 201
  attention training and, 182
  bonded resonance in, 68
  boundary situations and, 68
  brain function and, 76–77, 178
  breathing to help, 64
  burnout prevention and, 168
  compassion and, 127
  contemplative practices and, 82
  death and, 151
  deep listening and, 186
  embodied simulation and, 78
  equanimity and, 134
  examples of, 4, 6, 7, 67, 74–76
  feeling helpless and, 117
  grief and, 149, 150, 161
  hospitality and, 75–76
  inner environment of physicians and, 163
  intuitive approach to, 7
  Just Like Me exercise and, 84
  knowing a patient as a person and, 72–73
  medical errors and, 141, 142
  medical training on, 3
  meditation and, 8, 209
  mindfulness and, 4, 6, 7, 131
  "not like me" patients and, 79, 81
  organizations and, 193, 195
  patients' reactions to, 68, 70, 71
  pro-social behavior and, 132
  relational mind and, 225n15
  self-care and, 153
  shared, 69, 72, 76, 77, 83–84, 186
  shared mind and, 78
  smiling and, 184
  social, 77
  stillness practice and, 81–83
  theory of mind and, 78

Index

Index

Being a Mindful Patient

Ronald Epstein, M.D.

Being a patient can be stressful and has never been more complex. It's easy to become overwhelmed by the sheer volume of information you need to process, and it may be difficult to know whom to trust. With the range of choices for health plans and treatments, it often seems that the more information there is, the more dizzying making a decision can become. Sometimes, each doctor visit leads to more visits, more tests, and more referrals. Other times, you may feel that your doctors haven't paid enough attention to your problem.

While there are many guides to managing specific diseases, there are few guides to how to manage *yourself* when seeking medical care. Although it's not your job to manage your doctor, you'll find that your visits are more productive if you provide some guidance for the doctor about your needs and concerns—even if you're not asked to do so. By being attentive and self-aware and by being as mindful as you can be when under the stress of illness, you'll have a better handle on what your own brain and gut are telling you. And you'll make your interactions with your health care team more mindful too. Here are some questions you might want to ask yourself as you prepare for a visit with someone you're hoping will help you with a health-related concern—whether it's with a doctor, a nurse, a therapist, a dentist, or an acupuncturist.

1. What are you hoping for in this visit?
Everyone has different intentions, hopes, and expectations. Are you wanting information? Reassurance? A recommendation? Treatment options? A sympathetic voice? A healing touch? A second opinion? Assurance that you're doing the right thing? Your doctor won't know what you need unless you tell him or her.

2. What are you paying attention to, and what might you be ignoring?
It's only natural to want to feel better. Often, though, we attribute our misery to only some factors and ignore others. Perhaps you believe

that the cholesterol pill isn't working but are ignoring the fact that you're having trouble keeping to your diet. Or, the reverse, perhaps you are blaming yourself for not feeling better when the pill's the culprit and it might be time for you to speak up and say that things aren't working. Also, we tend to avoid talking about things for which we might feel blamed or stigmatized (sexual behavior, alcohol, smoking, weight, etc.).

3. What are you most afraid of?

A good doctor would ask you this question, and it's helpful to ask yourself and tell your doctor whether or not you are asked. Often our fears are not what doctors assume. Many people fear pain more than death, or fear bankrupting their family with medical bills more than their own suffering. A musician might fear nerve damage from chemotherapy whereas a professor might fear "chemo brain." Your fears might unconsciously influence your treatment choices. It is wise to bring them to the surface so you can monitor their effects and make sure they are not leading to a bad decision.

4. What are you assuming that might not be true?

Everyone has ideas about his or her illness and expectations about what might happen. Sometimes your assumptions are right on. But they might not always be. It's difficult to know when your own ideas about your illness might be off base and when you're trying to confirm rather than examine your own beliefs. Are you thinking that there's a pill for every ill? Or that chemotherapy is always bad? Or that the procedure your doctor suggests is dangerous or painful? Or that "natural" is always better? Or that there's only one right answer? While there might be truth in each of these assumptions some of the time, none of these are universal truths. In other words, each situation demands curiosity and a beginner's mind. Both doctors and patients need to examine their assumptions.

5. Does your doctor or therapist seem distracted? Are you?

Increasingly, health professionals' attention is fragmented. Electronic health records in the office, beeps and buzzers on hospital wards, interruptions for administrative issues, and the sheer complexity of clinical practice are the common culprits. Although electronic interruptions may be unavoidable sometimes, good clinicians learn how to manage these interruptions. They turn away from the screen to face you. When the doctor stares at the screen and doesn't make eye contact, his or her attention is divided and may not attend to what's most important to you. And if you're distracted too, communication really suffers. So what do you do? Perhaps say, "When you're finished with that, I have an important question, but I can wait." This and other "signposting" comments can redirect the doctor's attention and help you to have a shared focus. If your doctor remains distracted, it's time to find a new one.

6. Is your doctor really present? Are you?

Some doctors are truly present, and when they find themselves distracted, their efforts to reconnect are palpable. Just as you want to insist on presence from your doctor when the stakes are high, when communication is most crucial, and when you are distressed, you can become more present yourself. Before your doctor visit, try to set aside potential distractions. Turn off your phone. Read neutral material in the waiting room, not something provocative or upsetting. Don't engage your doctor in talk about politics or gossip. Be prepared to use the time well.

7. Is there shared mind?

Shared mind is when two or more people experience a sense of connection and coherence. You and your doctor are on the same wavelength and, even if you disagree, there is a feeling of mutual understanding. Sometimes shared mind comes naturally, but often it takes effort—from both sides. You need to be open to your doctor's gestures toward sharing and involving you in your care to the degree that you are capable and willing. You, in turn, assert what's important to you while expressing your willingness to be involved in your own care, emphasizing mutual respect for each other's views.

8. How can I best manage the limited time with health professionals?

Your health professionals' time may well be limited, but it shouldn't feel rushed. You can do your part too. Come prepared with a list of your concerns and decide which, for you, is the most important. Be prepared to set aside your agenda if your doctor raises an issue that must be dealt with urgently. Try not to go off on tangents, telling stories that might not be relevant to your care. Also—and this is difficult—don't leave the thing you're most afraid of for last. It is all too common for a patient to mention at the end of a visit, "And, oh, by the way . . . I've been having chest pains." It's understandable because thinking about serious illness is scary. But always raise the biggest concern first. Conversely, if your doctor is going off on a tangent (or worse yet, talking about himself or some other unrelated topic), you can gently redirect the conversation, saying, "You know, I've been worried about XYZ, and I was wondering if I can give you some more information about what's going on."

9. What questions should I ask?

Many patients ask questions, but often not the ones that get to the heart of the matter. Again, it's important to prepare. If the doctor proposes a diagnostic test, ask what you will do if the test is positive, what you will do if it's negative, and what you will do if the result is ambiguous, which happens quite often. (Even tests for cancer can lead to more confusion than clarity.) If your doctor proposes a treatment or a choice of treatments, be prepared to ask about potential benefits and risks (they might be larger or smaller than you think), and what might happen if you did nothing (which can sometimes be the wisest choice). If you don't understand something, don't feel that you're stupid asking the doctor to clarify. Communication is a shared responsibility. Make a list of questions and bring it along to the appointment. You can do that if you're in the hospital too. Prompt lists and decision aids to help patients focus on the most important questions are increasingly available on the Internet and in clinics and hospitals. They may contain questions you hadn't thought of or your doctor neglected to ask.

10. Should I bring a family member or a friend?

There is nothing more important than having an advocate—family member or friend—and an extra set of eyes and ears. They can help you remember and understand important information that you might otherwise forget. If no one is available to accompany you in person, ask your doctor if you can audio or video record your visit so that you can review with them later—easy to do with a smartphone.

Doctors are human too and are usually very appreciative if you're an active partner in your care. Tell your doctor that you're motivated to do your part, to be mindfully attentive, curious, open, and present. That will inspire your doctor to be mindful and will lead to a more collaborative relationship and more effective care.